MARCHMONT

MARCHMONT

by CHARLOTTE SMITH

Edited with an Introduction by

LOGAN E. GEE

WHITLOCK PUBLISHING

ALFRED, NY

Marchmont by Charlotte Smith first published in 1796

First Whitlock Publishing edition 2017

Whitlock Publishing
Alfred, New York
www.whitlockpublishing.com

ISBN 978-1-943115-19-8

This book is set in Garamond on 55# acid-free paper that meets ANSI standards for archival quality.

ACKNOWLEDGEMENTS

Thank you to Dr. Allen Grove, without whom this edition would not have been possible.

INTRODUCTION

When Charlotte Smith published *Marchmont* in 1796, she was not only publishing a love story gone gothic, but also a fictional tale that described events of her life. Althea, the heroine of the novel, resembles Smith in both personality and action, and encounters people throughout the story who mirror those in Smith's life. Through its representations of politics, gender issues, and nature, *Marchmont* offered the English reader something new and set itself apart from other Romantic period works.

Early Life

Smith was born Charlotte Turner on May 4, 1749 in London to Nicholas Turner and Anna Towers; she was the oldest of their three children. After the death of her mother, Smith, who was three at the time, and her two siblings, Catherine and Nicholas Jr., were left in the care of their aunt, Lucy Towers, while their father left London to travel abroad where he gambled much of his money away.

Upon taking guardianship of the children, Lucy Towers decided to immerse Smith in knowledge and at the age of six, Smith began her education with private drawing lessons. Then, at the age of eight, when Smith's father returned from abroad and moved the family to London, these lessons were followed by admittance into a highly-esteemed and expensive school at Kensington where Smith explored writing and dance. At Kensington, Smith studied alongside the daughters of several notable persons who chose the school because of its distinction. Four years later, however, Smith left the school to receive a more economical education with tutors at her home.

In her early life, there are many connections between Smith and Althea in *Marchmont*. In the novel, Althea may be an only child, but she walks the same path as Smith. At an early age, Althea also loses her mother and is placed in the care of her aunt, Mrs. Trevyllian, because her father cannot take care of her after the loss of his wife.

While Althea is living with her aunt, Smith's aunt Lucy Towers is emulated in that Mrs. Trevyllian decides that Althea must be raised as a knowledgeable young woman. Althea grows up surrounded by books and, like Smith, receives a well-rounded and fulfilling education. But life changes when Althea is forced to return to her father while her aunt recovers from an illness. Althea's focus in life is no longer allowed to be education, and instead she must set her mind on her status and appearance.

Middle Life

While Smith was expanding her education at home, she also expanded her knowledge of London's social scene by attending events hosted by her father. According to her sister Catherine's memoir, at the age of fourteen, Charlotte conducted herself in such a mature manner that she caught the attention of well-off older gentlemen. It was at this time that Smith's father and aunt began considering husbands for her and, a few years later, decided to introduce her to the son of her father's acquaintance, Benjamin Smith.

Benjamin Smith was a good-looking 23-year-old who had a promising and wealthy future if he worked with his father, Richard Smith, the Director of the East India Company. When Benjamin and Charlotte met, they found each other agreeable, and in 1765, just shy of Smith's 16th birthday, Charlotte and Benjamin Smith were married and lived together happily for a few years.

Around the same time, Charlotte Smith's father, Nicholas, was also considering a new wife. He soon met Miss Henrietta Meriton, who had recently inherited her father's fortune. They married in 1764, just before his daughter's wedding. The relationship that formed between Smith and her step-mother was not a pleasant one, and Charlotte portrays this between Althea and her step-mother, Lady Dacres, throughout *Marchmont*.

After the death of her aunt, Althea returns to her father's home where he now resides with a new wife and his other children. Sir Audley's second wife, Lady Dacres, is described similarly to Miss Henrietta Meriton in that both women received large amounts of money after the deaths of their fathers, both pulled their husbands away from their first children, and both women could not get along with their new step-daughters. Lady Dacres only cares for her money and status, which Smith makes clear throughout the novel.

But unlike Smith who enjoyed becoming acquainted with society, Althea is forced into her father's social scene because she has to keep up appearances for his reputation. Throughout her encounters with her father's social gatherings, Althea meets several people that she considers as fake and cannot find common ground among any of them.

One other key piece of information worth noting is that both Althea and Smith are around the same age when they begin socializing at parties and gatherings. And though both are young, it is at these ages that both are being coerced into relationships that they are not mature enough to fully understand. The difference, though, is that rather than going along with what is expected of her, Althea goes against her father and step-mother's wishes and voices her opinion even though it meant losing her father's affection.

Writing to Eat

In the almost twenty years that followed their marriage, the Smith's had twelve children, many of whom died very young, and experienced a lot of financial difficulty. In 1783, Benjamin Smith was charged with embezzlement of his trust fund and was placed in King's Bench Prison where he stayed for seven months. Because of his imprisonment, Lys Farm, the Smith's home in Hampshire, was sold by creditors to pay his debt. At this time, left with their children and almost no source of income, Smith decided to send her children to live with her brother, Nicholas Jr, in Bignor Park while she stayed with Benjamin in prison.

In the 18th century, debtor prisons maintained large populations of people, generally men, who were placed there by creditors and stayed until they could pay off what they owed. Unlike barred cells in contemporary prisons, debtor prisons were much like large warehouses where men, depending on the prison, were allowed visitors and could even continue their work. But these men were unable to leave until the full debt was repaid, so many were left imprisoned for years. During the time in which these men were being held, it was common for their wives to stay with them to provide food. Because the prisons generally did not provide free meals, these women helped their husbands survive.

While Benjamin was serving his time, Smith began writing more, looking to make some profit from her works to support her family. In

June of 1784, Smith published *Elegiac Sonnets and Other Essays* By Charlotte Smith of Sussex, with the help of James Dodsley, a publisher and book seller. Because she was in such financial distress at the time of publication, Smith agreed to Dodsley's terms which were that she would receive no advance and therefore minimal profit from the book. But with the money that she did receive, Smith realized that her writing could allow her family to survive.

In this same year, just a month after *Elegiac Sonnets* was published, Benjamin was released from prison on the condition that he give up executorship of his father's trust fund. He relocated to Dieppe, Normandy and was not joined by Smith and his children until months later.

Before debtor's prison, Benjamin had been spending significant amounts of money on gambling and was rumored to have had several mistresses while he traveled and worked. But it was not until April of 1787 that Smith decided to leave Benjamin and move to Wyke, Surrey with her children, all of whom chose to live with her. By then, Smith had published two more works and was continuing with her writing. In April of 1788, she published her first novel, *Emmeline, the Orphan of the Castle,* and finally started to make the profit she had been hoping for.

Emmeline received positive reviews from magazines such as *The Monthly Magazine, The European,* and *The Critical Review,* which pushed Smith to write another novel, *Ethelinde, or the Recluse of the Lake,* a work she published just one year later. The novel received similar praise and both novels were republished in new editions. In the following years, Smith continued to write and published more novels including *Celestina* in 1791, *Desmond* in 1792, *The Old Manor House* in1793, and *Marchmont* in 1796.

The Latter Years

While writing and publishing, Smith remained apart from Benjamin, but due to the fact that they were not legally separated, Benjamin had the right to a percentage of the money that Smith brought in.

In her last few years of life, Smith still wrote to support herself but was weak and almost entirely immobilized. On February 22, 1806, Benjamin, who was nearly 64 and residing in debtor prison at Berwick-on-Tweed, died. When his death was announced in *The Gentleman's Magazine* in March of that year, his name was spelled wrong and his obituary focused mostly on his status as the husband of Charlotte

Smith rather than anything that he had accomplished. When Benjamin died, Smith was finally able to collect the money that had been promised to her in Richard Smith's will.

Smith's death came seven months after Benjamin's, and in September of 1806, Charlotte Smith died at Tilford, located near Farnham, Surrey and was buried at Stoke Church. Though there is not a detailed record of her death and the causes, in one of the letters that Smith writes near the time of her death, she describes unusual bleeding and pain. Scholars have conjectured from this evidence that she may have suffered from an illness of her womb.

But even after her death, Smith's final work, *Beachy Head, Fables, and Other Poems,* was published in 1807. The work would have been published while Smith was still alive, but Joseph Johnson, the publisher of *Beachy Head,* never received the expected preface and held the publication after that.

The Feminine Romantic Ideology

In the last decade of the 18th century, the French Minister of Education for the New Constitution Assembly advocated for public education to be limited to men only. In response to this, Mary Wollstencraft published *A Vindication of the Rights of Women* in 1792. Wollstencraft recognized that by being denied an education, women were being denied personhood, a natural and civil right. With this in mind, she continued her argument by stating that women who received an education were better able to reason and develop stronger moral virtues. Wollstencraft also went on to say that educated women better served the home as mothers and wives.

All of this was taking place around the same time that Smith was publishing and four years before the publication of *Marchmont.* Within her works, Smith creates female characters who are stronger than the average women or heroine. In *Marchmont,* the first character that Smith presents is Mrs. Trevyllian, an older single woman who is getting along just fine. Though her prefix is Mrs., which at this time was common and a sign of respect for older women, she is unwed and raising Althea without any male influence.

The other strong female character that Smith presents is of course Althea, the novel's heroine. In the first volume, Althea is pursued by Mohun, an older gentleman who is an acquaintance of her father. Rather than allowing him to take advantage of her, Althea rejects his advances and advocates for herself. But after this rejection, Sir Audley presents Althea with the choice of marrying Mohun or leaving the pleasant lifestyle that he has given her. And though she knows it will upset her father, Althea chooses to leave and remain independent.

Within *Marchmont*, Smith also pushes back against gender norms. Throughout her novels and works, she provides subtle critiques of masculinity and illustrates the flaws of men. This is exemplified by Sir Audley's portrayal and his dependence on his wife, and later daughter, for money and status. Sir Audley is not wealthy because of his own money or work; he is wealthy because of his wife's inheritance. And when it comes to protecting his daughter or moving up in society, he chooses the latter without hesitation.

In *Marchmont*, Smith, also cautions against romantic love and illustrates the dangers of it through her heroines, as if trying to teach a lesson to her young female readers. Althea does develop feelings for Marchmont, but she does not allow these feels to overshadow the task at hand, which is keeping him safe and out of the grasp of her father's hired creditors. Though the characters do love each other, they understand what is important and do not get swept up in romance.

Also, the character Marchmont provides readers with a very different hero. Rather than being portrayed as better or superior to Althea, they are on the same level and see each other as equals working together.

A Touch of Gothic

While Wordsworth and Coleridge were writing poetry, other writers such as Radcliffe and Lewis were producing novels that revolved around dark themes. This new genre became known as gothic and contained gloomy settings and seemingly supernatural occurrences. Imagination and emotion were central to the period's literature, and gothic literature set itself apart with its focus on an atmosphere of mystery and suspense.

Recognized as the first gothic novel, *The Castle of Ontario* by Horace Walpole was published in 1764. But it was not until almost 30 years later that gothic really became widely read. Writers like Ann Radcliffe and Matthew Lewis with novels such as *The Romance of the Forest* and *The Monk* popularized the genre. Also writing at the time of

Radcliffe and Lewis was Smith, who incorporated elements of gothic into *Marchmont*.

Smith created the character of Vampyre, a dark and menacing creditor who lurks in and out of Althea's life while looking for Marchmont. Like the well-known Dracula, Vampyre sucks the life out of those his clients hire him to track down, but instead of draining them of their blood, Vampyre drains them of their money and sends them to prison. In doing this, Smith exemplifies how equally-destructive a human begin can be to a supernatural monster.

Smith also creates a gothic feeling throughout the novel with her setting. After disobeying her father, Althea is sent to one of his estates, a castle that is falling to pieces and contains many dark corridors and unexplored rooms. This setting is, of course, ideal for gothic literature, and with it, Smith even references some supernatural elements such as possible ghosts who walk throughout the estate. These conventions allow Smith to create suspense for the reader as she taps into the most popular genre of her time.

Conclusions

Charlotte Smith's *Marchmont* provides readers with a window into the late 18th-century English world with her representations of politics and gender issues. Her incorporation of strong female characters who fight their own battles, honest portrayals of men obsessed with money and power, and gothic elements that add mystery and suspense, come together to make a unique and rewarding novel.

Logan E. Gee

CHARLOTTE SMITH TIMELINE

1749	4 May- Charlotte Smith is born to Nicholas Turner and Ann Towers
1752	Ann Towers dies giving birth to her third child; Smith is three at the time
1764	Nicholas Turner remarries Miss Meriton and assumes her large fortune while also separating himself from his daughters
1765	23 February- Charlotte Turner, 15, marries Benjamin Smith, 23 and the son of Richard Smith, Director in the East Indian Company
	Months after their wedding, Smith discovers she is pregnant and gives birth to a boy (No name or birth record is found for this child)
1767	30 April- Smith gives birth to her second son who dies the next day
1768	Smith's third child, William Towers, is born (No record of birth has been found)
1769	2 May- Smith's fourth child, Charlotte Mary, is born
1776	April Another daughter of Smith, Lucy Eleanor, is born
1782	Another daughter, Harriet, is born
1783	December- Benjamin is arrested for debt and embezzlement of his Trust fund and is sent to the King's Bench Prison in London
1784	June- *Elegiac Sonnets and Other Essays by Charlotte Smith of Bignor Park, Sussex* is published
1787	*The Romance of Real Life* is published
	15 April- Charlotte and Benjamin separate, all of the children choose to stay with Charlotte
	Charlotte establishes herself in Wyhe and supported herself and children with her writing
1788	Smith's first novel *Emmeline, the Orphan of the Castle* is published

1789   *Ethelinde, the Recluse of the Lake* is published

1791   *Celestina* is published

1792   *Desmond* is published

1793   *The Old Manor House* and *Wanderings of Warwick* are
published

1794   *The Banished Man* is published

1795   *Montalbert* is published

1796   *Marchmont* is published

1798   *The Young Philosopher* is published

1799   *The Solitary Wanderer* is published

1806   22 February- Benjamin dies at 64 while in debtor's
prison at Berwick-on-Tweed

28 October- Smith dies at age 57

1807   February- *Beachy Head* is published three months
after Smith's death

April- Smith's full obituary appears in *The Monthly
Magazine*

BIBLIOGRAPHY

Fletcher, Loraine. *Charlotte Smith: A Critical Biography*, St. Martin's Press, 1998.

Keane, Angela. *Revolutionary Women Writers: Charlotte Smith and Helen Maria Williams*, Writers and their Work, 2013.

Knowles, Claire. *Sensibility and Female Poetic Tradition, 1780-1860: The Legacy of Charlotte Smith*, 2009.

Labbe, Jacqueline M. *Charlotte Smith in British Romanticism*, Routledge, 2016.

Labbe, Jacqueline M. *Charlotte Smith: Romanticism, Poetry, and the Culture of Gender*, Manchester University Press, 2003.

Labbe, Jacqueline M. *Writing Romanticism: Charlotte Smith and William Wordsworth, 1784-1807*, Palgrave Macmillan, 2011.

Mellor, Anne Kostelanetz. *Romanticism and Gender*, Routledge, 1993.

Richter, David H. *The Progress of Romance: Literary Historiography and the Gothic Novel*, Ohio State University Press, 1996.

Smith, Charlotte. *The Works of Charlotte Smith*, Stuart Curran, Pickering & Chatto, 2005.

Wilson, Carol Shiner and Joel Haefner. *Re-visioning Romanticism: British Women Writers, 1776-1873*, University of Pennsylvania Press, 1994.

Charlotte Smith

MARCHMONT

PREFACE

FEW THINGS PERHAPS are more difficult than to write a preface well, and it is perhaps equally true that no part of a book is so little read.

"Why then," enquires a friend, "should you prefix a preface to a work of mere entertainment? Surely it is what novel readers never expect, and are, of all others, the least likely to attend to; and if you intend it as an apology for defects, would it not be better to give the time it will cost you to correct rather than to excuse them?"

I adhere, however, to my preface – not to palliate the errors of a work which I have executed as well as my situation admitted, but because I wish for an occasion to address my readers, or such of them as will take the trouble of perusing a few prefatory pages. *The egotism, of which I have been accused,* though less excusable in the body of a work, may be allowed me here, because no one is compelled to read it to the interruption of the story, and none can complain that, as in another work, with fictitious sorrows I have mingled my own.

In the composition of what are called novels I have been engaged (from necessity, and by no means from choice) for eight years, and my *thirtysecond* volume is now before the Public. To the pecuniary advantages I have derived from them I owe my family's subsistence and my own, while labouring under the heaviest (and now the most irremediable) oppression that was perhaps ever practised or suffered in a country boasting of its laws. But notwithstanding that, by unremitting labour, I have existed, the consequences of the robbery committed on me and my children have been fatal; and after having resisted, for twelve years, difficulties and distresses such as women are seldom called upon to encounter, *one* dreadful evil has overtaken me, and nearly overwhelmed me—that lovely Being who was the greatest blessing of my life, who alone had the power to sooth my wearied spirit and sweeten my hours of toil, has been torn from me for ever; and this last and bitterest calamity I shall ever impute to the conduct of our inhuman oppressors. Yet in the hour of my extreme

1

misery, while I *dreaded,* and after I had suffered this severity, what did I receive from them—from these men who *then held,* who *still hold,* the property of my family? – Refusal of the most necessary assistance, taunts, and insults:—and I owed it to the friendship of one amiable and exalted female character, to a nobleman eminent for his good actions, and to a physician of the first reputation in London (to whom I was wholly a stranger), that at that period of agonising distress I did not entirely sink; while to a physician at Bath I was indebted for every friendly, every skilful exertion which I could not purchase, but which were unremittingly applied to save me from the blow that has indeed crushed me to the earth, and rendered the residue of my days "labour and sorrow."

But the arrow was fled, and my misery without remedy; yet with a heart torn by such anguish as only they who have felt it can imagine, it was absolutely necessary for me to sit down to finish a novel for which I had received money from my present publisher, who would have been injured if I had not forced myself to fulfil my engagement. Could I *then* have written a preface, this apology for the defects of *Montalbert* would have been in its place; but I was at that time quite unable to ask the indulgence which it was impossible a book written in such circumstances should not have occasion for.

Still continuing (from mere inveterate wickedness on the part of these unjust persons) under the necessity of earning by my pen the subsistence of my remaining family, I began some months afterwards the present work; but suffering in health from the incurable wounds of my mind, I was unable to remain in any fixed habitation, and still more so to return to the country, where alone I had the benefit of literary conversation, for there every scene would remind me of my murdered happiness:—these volumes, therefore, have been written under the disadvantage of wanting a friendly critic on those errors of judgement which occur in every long work entirely dependent on the imagination; nor have I had any correcting eye to detect the more trifling faults of style which will sometimes happen, or of orthography, which those who write to live, and consequently write in haste, can seldom escape committing. From my few books also I have been absent, and the libraries of bathing towns rarely contain such as I have had occasion to refer to: the mottoes and quotations I have used have, therefore, been either copied from memory or a common-place book; and as neither the one nor the other always furnished me with the name of the poet or essayist whose words I borrowed, I have omitted the names of all.

I have been gravely told that I have made enemies by personality. In many instances it has certainly been the consciences of the prototypes that have helped the world to the resemblances; but I do not affect to deny that I have occasionally drawn from the life; and I have no hesitation in saying, that in the present work the character most odious (and that only) is drawn *ad vivum*—but as it represents a reptile whose most hideous features are too offensive to be painted in all their enormity, I have softened rather than overcharged the disgusting resemblance.—It has been observed to me, that such an obscure wretch as an attorney, remarkable only for his skill in saving the ears he has so often deserved to lose, is too contemptible for satire. As an individual he is; but as a specimen of a genus extremely poisonous and noxious he becomes an object to be held up to detestation; and I have figured him here as, in drawings to illustrate natural history, I would delineate the scorpion, whose touch is mortal, or give a figure of the upas-tree-perhaps I should rather say of the strychnos (*nux vomica),* or some more familiar poison—for the deadly upas (if it be not a fable) exists singly: but the destructive monster, armed with the power of doing mischief, and of robbing legally—the wretch without feeling or principle, without honesty or pity—is a nuisance widely diffused, and spreading frequent desolation. That there are honest and good men in the profession I believe, for I know *two;* but I have reason to suppose that the majority are so much otherwise, that it would be well for the world if they were restrained by means more adequate to the purpose than those ever practised in *the present order of things.*

The great master of novel—writing, Fielding, has attacked this legal pestilence long before inferior writers ever touched upon it. If *he* failed of having effect, my feeble pen can do nothing but prove that other Murphys and Dowlings exist in the present day; yet some purpose will be answered if the representation should deter any individual, who has a drop of manly or human blood in his heart, from sharpening the fangs of one of these scourges of the earth against the innocent and defenceless: then perhaps some group of promising children, of unprotected orphans, may escape the misery, desolation, and death, that have fallen on mine!

What will be thought of my peculiar ill fortune, when I assert that I have it in my power to produce a counterpart to this demon? The

Great Man who from paltry pique directed, or from bloated indolence slept over, the injuries we have endured, put us, by way of *protection*, into the trust of a worthy cousin of his own. The worthy cousin, instead of driving away the evil spirit whom he found preying on the wreck, began to consider how he might appropriate a share of it to himself—He croaked, and, lo! his fellows, and his partners, and his agents, flocked around, and numberless vultures fed instead of one:— so that our *Great Director* was like the man in the parable, who being infested with a devil, goeth forth and taketh unto him seven devils, not worse (for that was impossible), but almost as bad as the first, and consequently the last state of the wards of the *Great Man* is undoubtedly *worse than the first.*

A few words may be allowed me on the subject of the present work. It is a fault frequently imputed to novels, that they are directed to no purpose of morality, but rather serve to inflame the imaginations, and enfeeble by false notions of refinement the minds of young persons. I know not what share of those faults may be found in the present production, but my purpose has been to enforce the virtue of fortitude: and if my readers could form any idea of the state of my mind while I have been writing, they would allow that I practise the doctrine I preach.

Marchmont.

For she was just, and friend to virtuous lore,
And pass'd much time in truly virtuous deed.

Chapter I.

IN A BEAUTIFUL village, near one of the most populous towns in the west of England, lived the only unmarried sister of an ancient family—Mrs. Trevyllian, (for she had for some years ceased to write herself Miss) was near fifty; she had never been handsome, but there was something in her countenance more interesting than even the remains of beauty—an expression of goodness, sense, and candour, which seemed to mark her as the friend of the unfortunate, and the guide of the innocent—her person was elegant, and her manners remarkably conciliating and attractive. The small house she inhabited was fitted up with so much taste, that she was become a sort of oracle among those who wished to exhibit elegance in their apartments: she had an excellent collection of books, in a room which opened into a small, but very pretty garden, filled with the sweetest shrubs and flowers. Books and plants supplied to her the place of society, which she was rarely mixed in; and to the gratification of these attachments she applied what others in her situation usually bestow on cards and company. Still, however, she had always a purse in reserve for the necessitous; and her active spirit and sound judgement often did more service than mere pecuniary assistance. Extremely beloved by her friends, living in a course of cheerful and rational piety, enjoying tolerable health, and a competent income, Mrs. Trevyllian knew no other uneasiness than that which arose from her reflections on the future fate of a lovely girl, to whom she had been more than a mother, and for whom she felt all a mother's tenderness.

Althea was the child of her favourite sister, of whom, though she had been dead near thirteen years, Mrs. Trevyllian retained the most affectionate remembrance; and as Althea grew nearer to womanhood, she became doubly dear to her aunt, because her features and manners acquired every day a stronger resemblance to that dear sister; and while she read or conversed, this resemblance, and the tones of her voice, brought so strong a recollection of what her mother was at that age, that Mrs. Trevyllian often caught herself gazing at her with tears in her eyes, while the innocent, unconscious Althea wondered at these painful emotions; but when the cause of them was explained, she would mingle her tears with those of her dear aunt; then smiling as she wept, she tried to win the thoughts of her benefactress from the contemplation which caused them.

But the sadness which arose from recollection of the past was light when compared with the fears which frequently assailed the heart of Mrs. Trevyllian as she looked forward to the future. The father of Althea was a younger brother of good family, who being a cornet of horse quartered in a country town, had fallen violently in love with the fourth daughter of Mr. Trevyllian; and, failing in his attempt to persuade her to elope with him, had at length prevailed on his family and hers to consent to their marriage, and to make up a small income till his promotion in the army should enable him better to support the expence of an establishment; but the dependance and restraint in which this arrangement placed Mr. Dacres, who was ambitious, and addicted to expence, must soon have become so irksome to him, that his wife would probably have been made unhappy, had she lived long; but she died before die end of the second year, leaving only the little Althea, then about ten months old, whom her aunt Trevyllian immediately took charge of. Mr. Dacres, who had now sold out of the army, was at liberty to avail himself of a handsome person, and great family interest, to acquire a more affluent wife. Such a one he soon found in the coheiress of a man who had acquired a considerable fortune in trade, which at his death he left between two daughters, the eldest of whom was married to a newly-created Irish peer; and the youngest divided between her passion for a title and her taste for the handsome figure of Mr. Dacres, at length settled the contest between love and ambition, by bargaining that a certain sum of her money should be appropriated to the purchase of a baronet's title; and though she did not rank so high as her sister, she consoled herself by reflecting, that she was elevated above most of her former acquaintance; and while "Lady Dacres" sounded extremely well, she had the gratification of having for a husband not only a man of fashion, but one of the handsomest men of his time.

A few years brought a numerous family; and Sir Audley, embarked in that political career which he thought necessary to enable him to provide for them, left the management of these children entirely to their mother, while the little Althea was almost lost to his recollection. He seldom saw her, and seldom thought of her. Her aunt, however, deeming it unreasonable that he should be wholly exempt from expence, regularly sent in an account for Althea's board, cloathing, and education, though with no other view than to form of the sums she thus received a little fund for her beloved ward, which she put into the stocks every year, as soon as it was paid. This annual payment, however trifling, was frequently delayed beyond the regular period, and by degrees excuses were made for letting it run far in arrears.—Tenants were not punctual—election expences had been unusually high—or some improvement at his country seat—were occasionally pleaded by Sir Audley; but Mrs. Trevyllian, who was cruelly hurt at evasions which she thought were proofs of his want of affection for Althea, failed not after they had been twice or thrice repeated, to signify that she must insist on more regular payments, adding some hints that she should otherwise be under the necessity of sending her charge home, and a little more attention was observed; for Sir Audley had not the least wish to enlarge his family by the return of his eldest daughter, and Lady Dacres had still less inclination to receive her.

As Mrs. Trevyllian resided at a great distance from London, four years had passed since Sir Audley had seen Althea; and these years, between the age of twelve and sixteen, had made a very favourable change in her person, which was always delicate and interesting.— Mrs. Trevyllian, who had promised to spend some months with an old friend in Hertfordshire, lately become a widow, determined as she passed through London to stay a week or ten days, as well to see some of her own family, to whom she had been long a stranger, as to give Althea an opportunity of paying her duty to her father and Lady Dacres, and to renew with her brothers and sisters the friendship which so long an absence had almost obliterated.

The visit was announced in form, and in form the visitants were to be received. Sir Audley met them at the drawing-room door, and saluted Mrs. Trevyllian with his usual politeness—then advancing to embrace his daughter, he started, seemed astonished, and even affect-ed—for he beheld the very image of his once-adored, his once-re-gretted Althea. She seemed, after fourteen years, to be again present to him. He recovered himself, however, before any one but the object who had caused his confusion observed it; and having kissed Althea, whose eyes were streaming with tears, he led her towards Lady Da-cres, who, coldly saluting her, remarked that "Miss Dacres was very much grown indeed."—Then casting a look, which the watchful and observant eye of Mrs. Trevyllian did not fail to translate into a malig-nant remark, she resumed her seat, and entered on indifferent topics, carefully avoiding any subject which might lead to farther recollection of the long time that had elapsed. The daughters of Lady Dacres, who were of course grown in proportion, made their entrance in great formality with their governess; and the eldest son, a rude Westminster boy, now turned of fourteen, who came with a companion older than himself to dine. These lads voted the old lady, Mrs. Trevyllian, a very great quiz, and their new sister a very pretty girl. Young Dacres even venturing to utter across the room in an audible whisper to the eldest of his sisters—"Caroline, Caroline, this is a prettier sister than ever you will be—here is Montford swears it."

Miss Caroline, who had no great satisfaction in resigning even for one day the name of Miss Dacres, was not put into very good hu-mour by this address. Dinner, however, passed, and the wearied Al-thea, who had been comparing the quiet and rationality of her aunt's house with the irksome parade and tedious ceremony of her father's, secretly rejoiced that an engagement for the evening separated the par-ty at an early hour. She felt, however, as she kissed her father's hand at parting, that she was his child; and though he struggled to check sensations in her favour, he was still sensible of the pleasure of having such a daughter. Another dinner party, and two or three morning visits, passed between Althea and her family, before her aunt left London. Though it was now the gayest season, and though Althea had been much amused with seeing plays, the opera, and Ranelagh, yet did she sincerely rejoice when the day came which conveyed her with her aunt into Hertfordshire.

The house they were expected at was about four and thirty miles from London. They arrived there early in the afternoon; the family had one day's notice of their arrival; and at the gate of a small paddock that surrounded the house an old butler, who had lived many years in the family, waited to receive them. The poor man looked very melancholy, which Mrs. Trevyllian imputed to the recent loss of his master; but when the chaise had entered the gate, he beckoned to the postillion to stop, and, advancing to the window, said in a very depressed tone, "I thought it right, Madam, to let you know the state of our house before you entered it—My poor mistress."—"Good God!" exclaimed Mrs. Trevyllian, "what has happened?"—"My poor mistress," continued the man, "is extremely ill. We have reason to fear the fever infectious, as it began with a servant, who is dead, and two others are ill. My good lady, ever attentive and kind, has attended them herself against the advice of the physician, who warned her of her danger. She is now given over." He burst into tears, and could not proceed.

"And who is with her?" enquired Mrs. Trevyllian. "Only the housemaid, and a nurse from the village, for her own maid and the housekeeper have failed since yesterday."—"Good Heaven! what a situation," said Mrs. Trevyllian, "for my poor friend—ever so ready herself to assist her sick friends, yet to be thus deserted. But what can I do? My dear Althea, I cannot risk your health —I will not even suffer you to enter the house; though, for myself, I can as little think of abandoning my friend in her distress.—How can I act?"... She paused a moment or two for consideration; and Althea, who feared only for her aunt, ventured, while this silence lasted, to say, "Dearest Madam, if you determine to go, I entreat you not to spare me? Why should I fear a danger which my dear aunt determines to encounter? If any ill befals her, of what consequence would be the life of her Althea?"

"You are a dear girl," cried Mrs. Trevyllian, kissing her; "and I every day see occasion to love you more and more—but I cannot think of your going with me to my poor friend. You are of an age to take infection much more easily than those farther advanced in life.—But how to dispose of you, my sweet girl, I know not. I am unacquainted with any person in the neighbourhood to whom I could entrust you. ... However, we will return to the inn where we changed horses, and consider what can be done."

The butler was then directed to assure Mrs. Polwarth, her sick friend, that she was hastening to her, and as fearful for her lovely ward as unapprehensive for herself, Mrs. Trevyllian fell into a deep reverie as they returned to the town, which was about three miles distant.

This melancholy silence Althea at length ventured to interrupt, by asking why none of Mrs. Polwarth's own family were with her?— "The question," replied Mrs. Trevyllian, "is very natural, since you have heard that my friend *has* a family; but her daughter is gone to the West Indies with her husband, whose property lies there; her son is a man of business, who thinks of little else than the political matters in which he is engaged; and as to his wife, she is so fine a lady, such a compound of vanity, extravagance, and affectation, that to attend a sick parent would never occur to her as a necessary duty. Thus my poor friend is left totally without the soothing offices of affection. Her three grand-children are boys, and not of an age, were they of a sex, to attend her sick chamber. If you knew her, my dear Althea, you would not wonder that my heart bleeds for her—that I wish to see her—and if it must be so—to receive her last sigh, her dying wishes. We were friends in our early childhood; and, in the happy days of our youth, we passed much of our time together. I had once a severe and tedious illness; it was at a time when the fairest prospects were opening before my friend, then Henrietta Sebright. She was on the point of being married to a man, equally her parents' choice and her own; yet, regardless of every claim but that of friendship, she hazarded a life, which was likely to be thus happy, to attend on me, through many months of languor, and greatly contributed to the restoration of my health." Mrs. Trevyllian paused a moment, as if to recover from some bitter recollections, and then proceeding in a low voice, said, "It is now more than thirty years ago; but is there any period at which a debt of true gratitude may be cancelled?"

Althea had seldom seen her aunt so much affected, and forbore to question her farther. They soon arrived at the inn, where Mrs. Trevyllian, enquiring for the mistress of the house, desired her to prepare a room for her niece, and to take particular care of her accommodation, as she would remain there that night. Then eagerly assuring Althea that there was nothing to fear for her own safety in visiting her friend, and that she should hear from, or probably see her the next morning, she tenderly kissed the weeping girl, and recommending her to the care of her own woman, whom she left at the inn, she departed for the house of Mrs. Polwarth.

Temporary as this separation was likely to be, Althea felt dejected and miserable, a thousand fears for the health of her beloved guardian assailed her; she passed a sleepless night, but was rendered infinitely more unhappy the next morning, by receiving the following note:

"I found my poor friend very ill, yet sensible, and rejoiced to see me. My presence seems to have revived her; and while she bids me leave her, lest I should suffer by staying, I see that she believes my presence necessary to her restoration. I cannot therefore quit her, my Althea—neither can I consent to your coming hither. In this difficulty I have determined to send you back to London under the care of Morris, and recommend you for the short time of our unavoidable separation to the care of Sir Audley and Lady Dacres. Believe me, dearest Althea, my heart bleeds at the necessity of suffering you to be absent from me even for a day; but under the protection of your father there can be nothing to fear for you, and I trust that the undivided attention I shall then be able to give to my poor sick friend will, under Providence, be the means of restoring her, and that we shall meet again, my very dear Althea, in a few days, to rejoice together in her recovery. I send orders to Morris respecting your journey, and I write to Sir Audley and Lady Dacres. Heaven preserve my dearest girl. This is the incessant prayer of her affectionate,

ANNE TREVYLLIAN."

Althea endeavoured to submit to this painful necessity in the way least likely to give uneasiness to her aunt, but with a heavy and foreboding heart she stepped into the chaise with Morris, and arrived in Lower Grosvenor Street just as the family were sitting down to dinner with a large party of friends.

Althea stopped at the door while the letter she had brought was sent in, and the interval was long enough to allow her to feel much pain from doubts she could not help entertaining of a welcome reception. When one of the footmen, with a message from Sir Audley, desired her to walk in, she trembled so as to be hardly able to leave the chaise, and leaning on the arm of her aunt's woman, slowly followed him, not imagining that Lady Dacres would have so little consideration as to suffer her to enter a room full of company: this, however, she found to be the case. Sir Audley got up, and leading her to a chair next himself, said he was sorry for Mrs. Polwarth's illness—supposed she had not dined, and bade her sit down to table; while Lady Dacres slightly bowed to her from the top of it, and said, with cold civility, that she hoped she was well. In a moment every body seemed to have forgotten she was there—and the common conversation that passes on such occasions was renewed.

Poor Althea, whose thoughts were wholly with the aunt at Abbot-shanger, and who found in this munerous circle not one whose heart seemed to sympathise with hers, felt her spirits sink, and her eyes every moment ready to overflow with tears. She sometimes stole a timid look at her father, in hopes of finding his turned towards her with a tender welcome; but after her first entrance he too seemed to consider her only as one of his guests. She withdrew when the other ladies followed Lady Dacres to the drawing-room, most earnestly wishing for permission to retire to her own—but Lady Dacres continued to converse with her friends on the usual topics, without once addressing herself to, or even noticing Althea, who being in a travelling dress, while the lady of the house, as well as the company, were more dressed than usual, she felt her fatigue and vexation every moment increase, yet she could not acquire courage to rise amid so formidable a circle and retire; neither did she know whither to go, for the young ladies, her half sisters, had not appeared, they not being, to use the common phrase, "come out yet," and only allowed to dine with Sir Audley and Lady Dacres when alone, or merely a family party.

At length some of the company rose to go, and much was said as they departed of a future meeting in the evening, by which Althea found that Lady Dacres was going out. Seven or eight persons yet remained, and some of the gentlemen, attended by Sir Audley, came up to tea; he seemed on seeing Althea to be surprised, as if he had forgotten all that had passed, and approaching his wife, whispered something, to which she answered in a way that Althea thought almost peevish, "Well, well. Sir Audley, I must give orders, I must see about it." She then rang the bell, and directing the housekeeper to attend in her dressing-room, she left the room for a moment, and returning, said to Althea, in a very formal manner, "Miss Dacres, if you chuse to retire, my women have orders in regard to your accommodation: you will, perhaps, not find it very convenient, but my house is too small for my family." Althea, glad on any terms to escape from her present comfortless situation, thanked her in words as cold, but rather more civil than her own, and assured her, she should be perfectly satisfied with whatever her Ladyship had directed, and adding, that she was extremely fatigued, begged leave to retire. She was shewn by a very fine lady, who was, she found, Lady Dacres's woman, to an upper room, which was plainly, but neatly furnished. Her trunk was already placed in it; and dejectedly, by the window, sat Morris, who no sooner found herself at liberty, than she said, with a deep sigh, "Ah! dear me—I trust, Miss Dacres, we shall not have to stay long in this house. I am sure I am weary of it already. But I hope Sir Audley and my lady have made *you* welcome?"

Althea, whose heart was full, burst into tears, and threw herself on the bosom of Morris, who had been as a foster mother to her, where she sobbed aloud; yet feeling from her innate sense of propriety that it was wrong to encourage the murmurs of her aunt's woman in the house of her father, she endeavoured, since she could not stifle her concern, to impute it merely to her fears for her aunt, and regret at their sudden separation. "I believe, nay I am sure," said she, as soon as she recovered herself a little, "that my father is glad to see me; but the suddenness of my arrival, and there being so much company"—"Don't tell me," cried Morris, who had been used to speak her mind—"I've no notion on't for my part. I'm sure a perfect stranger would have been gladder to have seen you than Sir Audley was to see his own child; I know that well enough by what I heard those impertinent laced monkies below say; and as for my *Lady,* she is known to begrudge the least matter in the world for you.—Then they've stuffed you up into this room, which is not much better than a garret—and make a mighty favour of it too."—"Oh! my dear Morris," cried Althea, "the room does very well —I hope I shall not long need it; a palace would make me no amends for being absent from my aunt, and uneasy for her health as I am now."

"They'll take care you shan't trouble them long, I believe; for Mrs. Midgeley forsooth took occasion to tell me, when she shewed me up here, that indeed her Lady's eldest son from Westminster School always slept in this room, and that if he was to come home to stay, as he did every now and then, she did not know how her Lady would do—Such a fuss indeed with her Lady, and her Lady—I took care to tell her, that I thought *my* ladies of quite as much consequence as hers, though they had not titles—and I hinted to her, that if there was any such great matter of inconvenience in your staying here, I was sure you had a good house at home, and that *my* Lady would not suffer you to be troublesome to *her* Lady, or to any body else, but would send you home, and that I could take care of you well enough till such time as *my* Lady could come down herself."—

The honest zeal and mortified pride of Morris combined to give the greatest pain to Althea.—Sensible as she was of the former, she knew not how to repress the latter; yet she foresaw that her stay, of whatever duration it might be, would be rendered doubly uneasy by these heartburnings, and that Lady Dacres, while she considered her as a burden, would look upon Morris as a spy.—Probably the little affection her father had for her would be diminished by the complaints this would occasion, and in whatever view she regarded this unlucky visit, it promised only unhappiness. Her greatest consolation was, that it could not be long; for, in the conversation of the evening, Lady Dacres had taken occasion to tell her company, that they proposed going into the country in about a month; and had dwelt much on this circumstance in conversation, as if on purpose to let Althea understand that her stay could not be prolonged beyond that time.

All the poor Althea could now do was to endeavour to appease the irritable spirit of her aunt's woman; for Morris did not easily consent to give up the indignation which some real or imaginary affront had raised—and at last went murmuring away, leaving Althea to indulge reflexions the most painful she had ever felt.

CHAP. II

…….. Loud, vain, presumptuous,
Proud of his power of tongue, the braggart came.

MRS. TREVYLLIAN WAS not easier at Abbotshanger than Althea was in London; yet more accustomed to the vicissitudes and vexations of life, and being of a firm and steady spirit, she would have blamed her niece for indulging anxiety, could she have known it—and still more her woman for yielding to querulous discontent while she was engaged in a scene where the real evils of life were surrounding her. Her unfortunate friend was sick both in body and mind; Mrs. Trevyllian had however the consolation of feeing that her society soothed her spirits, while her care seemed to have snatched her from the grave; for she was already out of danger, but so extremely weak, that her final recovery was very doubtful.—Her son neglected her; and her daughter, whose absence was a continual source of pain, was not only far from her, but subject to the greatest inconvenience and danger, from the situation of the country to which she was gone— and the afflicted mother dared hardly look after news; yet, when she forbore all inquiry, she found her conjectures even more dreadful than the truth.

Mrs. Trevyllian was incessantly employed in the difficult task of calming these apprehensions, which she felt were generally too well grounded. Several days elapsed while strength returned so slowly to the enfeebled frame of Mrs. Polwarth, that she existed, but could hardly be said to live—while Mrs. Trevyllian, without any new cause, felt her own spirits gradually declining—and at the end of about ten days it was too evident to the medical attendants that she was seized with the fever from which her unwearied care had greatly contributed to recover her friend. Suspecting this herself, she pressed them to avow the truth; and when she had with difficulty extorted it from them, she insisted upon their promising to give her notice of the degree of danger she might be in.—"I do not fear death," said she; "and for my few worldly concerns, they have long since been settled—but I have a dear child who is almost entirely dependant on me, and I would use the last hours of my life in making such a provision as I can for her against the inconveniences that must follow my loss; and therefore it is, Gentlemen, that I wish to hear the truth in every stage of the disorder which has seized me."

If this fortitude of mind made the task easier to the Gentlemen with respect to Mrs. Trevyllian, it became extremely difficult to acquit themselves towards Mrs. Polwarth, who could not bear to hear the most remote hint that her friend was in danger, and threw herself into agonies that endangered her own life.—Fortunately the fever was milder than they had at first reason to fear; and in a few days there was little to apprehend but from the extreme debility it left. As the danger had never been imminent, the illness of her aunt had been carefully concealed from Althea, who could not but wonder she did not hear from her as usual, and that short and incoherent notes from Mrs. Polwarth supplied the place of those instructive and affectionate letters which she had received during the first days of their separation.—At length Mrs. Trevyllian exerted herself to conceal her trembling hand, and, under the pretence of head-ach, excused the shortness of her letter, which appeased the cruel alarms Althea had begun to feel—and, by the returning post, she wrote the following answer:

"It is impossible to express to you, my dear, dear aunt, the delight with which your Althea read a letter written with your own hand. It has removed many apprehensions that I was tormented with: for, notwithstanding Mrs. Polwarth's kind letters, I feared you were very ill; and had it not been that I am determined never to disobey you, I should have surprised you at Abbotshanger.—Have you not been ill?—Oh! yes, I still fear that is the truth—but my dear aunt would never deceive me; and as she assures her Althea she is well, and that we shall soon meet, I will believe her, and appease my apprehensions. I cannot however promise to be as happy as you bid me—for if it were possible for me to feel pleasure where you are absent, indeed it could not be here. You bid me relate what passes, and flatter me that it amuses you to hear my simple narrative.—Alas! I am not like Miss Byron—my journal will not contain an account of the fine things that are said to me, and the approbation I meet with, for I am a mere cypher—or what is worse, I seem to be selected by that odious Mr. Mohun as an object of ridicule—it were better to remain in insignificance.

"You have never seen this very disagreeable man, my dear aunt, or you would not, I am sure, however you may dislike any tendency to satire, think I represented him in colours too unpleasing.—I cannot tell why he singles me out as an object of attention, which I am sure is far from being flattering, and I heartily wish my father would not encourage him in addressing himself to me.—Why he should do it I cannot imagine, as he seems at the same time to consider me as a child and a mere country girl, and impertinently affects to be mightily amused with my simplicity. But there is no judging how hateful he is, unless I describe the sort of man.—He is a tall, awkward, rawbone figure—with a countenance it is impossible to look at without disgust, for it has the most disagreeable expression I ever saw:—when he speaks, which is always more than any body in the room, it reminds me of the voice and manner of the man whom I heard plead against those poor creatures who were prisoners at Exeter, the only time you ever took me into a Court of Law, so that I suppose it is the usual manner of lawyers, and that Mr. Mohun cannot divest himself of it in private company. Whatever he says, however, he says as if it were impossible he could be wrong; and indeed nobody ever ventures to dissent from him. If any unfortunate being has temerity enough to attempt it, Mr. Mohun flies at him like an enraged hornet, and will contrive to sting before he has done with him, for there is nothing rude and brutal he will not say, totally regardless of the pain he may inflict. I have once or twice heard him make such very insolent reflections that I have been astonished he has not excited the resentment of the people to whom he addressed himself: but it seems as if other men, who have probably as much spirit as he has, are thunderstruck and amazed at his excessive assurance.—Nor are his manners towards women at all pleasant—Lady Dacres, with whom he appears to be a great favourite, and who is in general remarkably nice and correct, only laughs at him when he tells long stories of pleadings about divorces, and I know not what scandalous stories, which I am sure Lady Dacres would not suffer from any other person. Her partiality to this man is astonishing, but my father's still more so, for it is impossible any two people can be more unlike each other. They are Members of Parliament, it seems, for the same borough, and Sir Audley has some obligations to him—so he told me this morning—and he bade me never again behave rudely to him. You will naturally ask, my dear aunt, if I *did* behave rudely? —I will tell you what passed, and you shall judge for me yourself. This Mr. Mohun, who lives here, I think, had dined with my father as usual, and there was to be a small card party in the evening. The weather is dreadfully hot in this disagreeable London—and I cannot imagine how any human beings can shut themselves up in a room, and sit down to those everlasting cards. I found my own room, which has windows to the West, so very warm, that, though I generally stay there as long as I can, I came down into the withdrawing rooms earlier than usual, and long before the company were assembled, or Lady Dacres herself had appeared.—Three other gentlemen dined with my father, and I concluded they would be long engaged over their wine; I took my work therefore, and placed myself near a window in the great drawing-room. A few coaches passed with people going to Kensington Gardens—I felt my confinement uneasy, without however envying them. —I wished not to join any of these parties—it was with you I longed to be—a thousand uneasy conjectures assailed me, (for I had not then received your dear letter) and I was more disposed to weep than to go on with my work, when the door of the anti-room suddenly opened, and Mr. Mohun, who seemed to be much affected with the wine he had drank, staggered into that where I was sitting, and, approaching me with some of those disagreeable speeches which he often makes, very confidently sat himself down on the same seat; and putting his arm around my waist, he stared at me, and said, I was the most divine little dear he had ever seen.

I sprang from him in an instant, more terrified than I ever was in my life, for never had I been subject to such impertinence before.—

He besought me to stop; but I flew up to my own room, determined not to leave it till Lady Dacres's company were assembled—nor then unless I was sent for.—Alas! my dear aunt, how every incident concurs to increase my regret at our separation, and with what ardent wishes I look forward to our return into Devonshire!—I was in some hopes that, inconsequential as I am, I might have been forgotten, and have been allowed to remain alone for the rest of the evening, as I never take a place at a card table, and of course could not be wanted.—Ah! no —I was not so fortunate. I received an order from my father to attend Lady Dacres, and reluctantly I obeyed.

"When I entered the room every body was at cards but my father and Mr. Mohun, who were in deep conference at one end of it. I went up to the table where Lady Dacres was at play, and said one of the nothings which one is in a habit of saying to Miss Cornwallis, who was of her party: by a side glance I saw that my father and his friend were talking of me, and that Mohun held his opera glass to his eye—an impertinence he is frequently guilty of, as if to survey me the better.—A moment afterwards Sir Audley called me to him; and, what is very unusual with him, began to talk to me with some degree of interest and affection. So little has your poor Althea been accustomed to listen to the voice of tenderness from a parent, that the slenderest mark of my father's regard always affects me.—He saw that I was affected, and seemed pleased; then, as if some one had beckoned to him from the other side of the room, he suddenly left me, standing near Mohun, who, throwing something into his manner which I suppose he thought was softness, took my hand, and, I believe, was beginning an apology: but I flung from him, and, on his following me to a card-table, whither I had fled for refuge, hurried out of the room, determined rather to incur my father's displeasure than suffer for a moment the renewal of such insolent familiarity.

"I found he staid supper, and therefore excused myself from going down. I hoped indeed that I should have heard no more about him—but this morning, when the post came in, I could not forbear going down; and anxiously inquiring of the porter if there was not a letter for me, I saw that hand-writing which gives me the greatest pleasure of any in the world; and, unable to restrain my impatience, had eagerly torn open my letter as I returned up stairs, when my father came out of his study, and ordered me to come to him there. I obeyed—not without trembling, because he spoke so sternly. He shut the door, and said in a tone of voice which did not serve to quiet my beating heart—'Althea, I am much displeased with you; and I must tell you, that, if you stay with me, I expect very different behaviour.'—Unconscious of what I had done, I asked, in a faltering voice, how I had been so unfortunate as to offend him?—He answered—'You behave with rudeness, and in a manner very unbecoming a young woman, circumstanced as you are, to my best friends.—Come, come—you must not affect to misunderstand me, Althea.—You know perfectly well that I mean Mr. Mohun. He condescends to take notice of you—which, I assure you, is an honour half the women of the highest consequence in town would be flattered by, and you give yourself airs of flippancy and contempt. If it were possible that such a man as my friend Mohun, who will undoubtedly be Chancellor, could think seriously of such a girl, be assured, Althea, it would be the most fortunate circumstance of your life.—That, unhappily, is not at all likely. In the mean time I must insist upon your behaving to him, whenever he addresses himself to you, with the respect that is due to his condition, his fortune, and, above all, to your father's friend. You now know my sentiments; I expect to have no occasion to repeat them. Go, Althea, I will hear no reply' —Indeed, my dear aunt, I had no inclination to answer. I was too much amazed at the purport of what my father spoke, and his peremptory manner, which was so much more than the occasion seemed to demand, that I should not have had voice or courage to have replied, had I not been thus forbidden. I hurried to my own room; and, to tell you the truth, my dearest and best friend, though I began my letter with tolerable composure, I have hardly yet recovered from my uneasy astonishment. Yet my father certainly could not mean more than he said—Oh! my dear, dear aunt, let your poor Althea return to you, wherever you are. Ten thousand fevers are not half so dreadful, in my opinion, as this one Mr. Mohun. If he should have taken it into his head ... but, no —I will not torment myself with such useless conjectures, but repeat, most earnestly repeat—let your Althea return to you directly—Oh! send me permission by the return of the post.—Believe me, though her Ladyship is just civil to me, it is with evident effort, and Lady Dacres will be much relieved by my absence—while to embrace my dearest aunt, never again to quit her, is the first wish of her Althea Dacres."

The recovery of Mrs. Trevyllian was not at all promoted by this letter, which gave occasion to many uneasy conjectures.—She knew that Sir

Audley, with high notions of the power of parents over their children, had long since conquered those sentiments which had, in the early part of life, induced him to sacrifice every other consideration to love. He was now quite a convert to the necessity of prudence and discretion, and thought money and power two things which every man of sense should make it the business of his life to obtain. Mrs. Trevyllian foresaw therefore that, if the sacrifice of Althea could be made subservient to these purposes, Sir Audley would not scruple to insist upon it; and that as to herself, though she might assist the resistance of her niece, the rejection of her father's friend would inevitably disoblige him, and render her future life uncomfortable.—These thoughts pressed more painfully on her mind, because she felt her health so much impaired that she thought the time was probably near when she must leave this beloved girl to the protection of her father, or leave her totally unprotected.—What might, in either case, be her destiny, Mrs. Trevyllian could not think of without losing much of that fortitude which no other contemplation on the future had power to shake.

To a young woman, situated as Althea was likely to be in case of her death, nothing could be so desirable as an honourable and affluent marriage—but Mrs. Trevyllian knew her too well to believe that any advantage could engage her to accept such a man as Mr. Mohun; and that her young and ingenuous heart, though without any prepossession in favour of another, would shrink from his arrogant pretensions, and suffer every degree of inconvenience rather than hazard the misery of passing her life with a man she could not love.

Of the wretchedness of such an union Mrs. Trevyllian was too well aware to think for a moment of promoting it; but she foresaw so much pain and uneasiness likely to arise from the instances of Sir Audley, that to remove Althea from the sight of this unwelcome admirer seemed to be immediately necessary—and this she determined to do, though at the risk of her health, which was by no means in a state that enabled her to travel with safety; but to bring Althea to Abbotshanger would have been so imprudent, that she wrote merely to bid her send Morris to accompany her to London, as she purposed being there on the following Friday. She wrote also to Sir Audley, informing him of her intentions, and requested that her niece might be ready to receive her at her lodgings.

Althea received this news with unallayed transport: it confirmed what she had before some doubts about, that her aunt was well; and it removed her from a scene where, amidst an unceasing round of company and apparent gaiety, she had never tasted a moment's content or pleasure. Lady Dacres heard of the immediate departure of her visitor with satisfaction, which she gave herself very little trouble to conceal, and Sir Audley with indifference; for whatever projects were floating in his mind in regard to Mr. Mohun, he thought they would rather be forwarded than retarded by the influence of a woman who knew so much of the world as Mrs. Trevyllian.

Althea having dispatched Morris, who had never received so welcome a commission, began to count the hours till that fixed for her aunt's arrival. Her clothes were packed up and sent away, and she sat down to anticipate the delight she should have in again embracing, after this painful absence, her first and best friend.—As it was now the end of June, she supposed Mrs. Trevyllian would soon return into Devonshire; Althea therefore, who loved and languished for the country, figured to herself the agreeable exchange she should make of the uncomfortable magnificence of Grosvenor Street for the quiet elegance of her aunt's village-house, with its pleasant garden, and the romantic scenery around it.

At length the time fixed for Mrs. Trevyllian's arrival came—Althea went two hours before to the lodgings in Welbeck Street—saw that every thing was in order; that the beds were aired, and the dinner such as her aunt would like. She then sat at the dining-room window, watching every carriage which came by, and in every post-chaise she eagerly hoped to see that which conveyed her friend. At length it stopped at the house—Althea flew down, and was in at the door of the post-chaise before the servant could open it. But, at the first view of her benefactress, all the hopes of happiness she had been cherishing vanished. So changed, so emaciated appeared that face on which Althea had been used to gaze with hope and delight, and so great and sudden was the shock, that Althea, unable to command her emotion, could not assist in carrying her aunt into the parlour, but followed, pale, trembling, and amazed; and, when she saw her seated there, instead of approaching to embrace her, she sat down, and burst into tears.

Mrs. Trevyllian could not at first collect strength enough to speak; but as soon as she became a little restored she held out her hand, with a faint smile, and, in a voice hardly audible, said—"How is this, my dear Althea?—At what are you alarmed?—Come to me, my best love!"— Althea obeyed; but, afraid of farther giving way to the emotion she felt, she only kissed the hand her aunt gave her, while her tears fell in showers upon it.—"You did not know I had not been quite well," continued that admirable woman, summoning all her strength; "and you are therefore surprised to see me so pale and thin. But, my precious Althea, consider that I am now a little fatigued with my journey: a few days of rest, the sight of my beloved girl, and some good advice, which I intend to send for, will soon restore me."

"Ah!" cried Althea, who now first found her voice, "you came sooner than you ought to have done on my account; it was I that made you uneasy with my foolish letter—but whither shall I send for this advice? Oh! do not let a moment be lost; suffer me to write directly to a physician."

"Do you know," said Mrs. Trevyllian, "that all this solicitude, my love, would be very wrong if I were apt to have depressed spirits? Compose yourself; and be assured, my Althea, that I shall take care of my health, if it be only to spare you pain."—She gave her directions to write to Dr. R——, requesting him to see her in the morning, and then desired to be taken up stairs and put to bed, where she wished to be left quiet for the remainder of the day.

Morris was no sooner dismissed than she gave an unrestrained course to those sad apprehensions which had distressed her ever since she saw her mistress, and which even her consideration for the terrified Althea could no longer restrain. "Ah! Miss Dacres," said she, "do not let us flatter ourselves. My Lady, my dear Lady! it is impossible, I am sure it is, that she should ever recover. I see too well what the end of all this will be.—Oh, my poor mistress! would to God we had never made that accursed journey to Hertfordshire. Oh! would she were well, and we were all happy again at home!"—To these expressions of apprehension which Althea felt to be too justly founded, she could only answer with her tears. Alas! the next day confirmed all their fears. Dr. R—— acknowledged to Althea that he thought his patient in a very precarious state; and she fancied that, to spare her, he spoke even more favourably than he thought. He told her that he had recommended it to Mrs. Trevyllian to go, by slow journies, to Bristol Hot Wells, and to set out as soon as possible, for that he *still* had hopes from that air, from perfect quiet, and, added he, smiling as cheerfully as he could, "from the good nursing and sweet attentions which I know my excellent friend will receive from her lovely niece."—Althea, from all that this worthy man intended as comfort, extracted only sorrow, and, unable to answer, hastened to her own room, that she might recover herself sufficiently to appear with cheerfulness before her aunt, who herself continued to make light of an illness of which Althea saw the almost hourly perceptible ravages with terror.

She now no longer thought of Mr. Mohun, but to blame herself for having ever mentioned his name to her aunt.—Lady Dacres and Sir Audley made their separate visits—Mrs. Trevyllian thanked the former for her attention to Althea, as if she had been a stranger without claim upon her kindness. Sir Audley was alone with her for near half an hour; when he left her she appeared to be much affected, and ordered Morris to leave her till she rang her bell. In about a quarter of an hour she gave this summons; and Althea, on entering her room, found her as composed as usual: but nothing was said of what had passed with Sir Audley.

Preparations were now made for the journey, and it was at length undertaken. By very short stages they arrived—Mrs. Trevyllian not visibly worse; yet Althea, who most anxiously watched every turn of her countenance, and listened with an aching heart to every expression, thought she could perceive from both, that this dear woman felt an internal conviction that her recovery was impossible—yet submitted to try every remedy ordered for her, and really wished to live on account of Althea, though not afraid to die on her own.

This was but too true an estimate of what really passed in the mind of Mrs. Trevyllian. Nor could she always command such a share of the admirable fortitude she possessed as to avoid sometimes expressing in her countenance the pain she felt in reflecting on the loss she must be to this child of her heart.—Althea was not indeed an orphan; and when Mrs. Trevyllian saw Sir Audley in town, she had recommended his daughter to him in the strongest terms, and had endeavoured to awaken his tenderness in her favour, by recalling to his memory the fond attachment he once had for the mother of this beloved girl. Time and other connections had not so far obliterated the remembrance of that mother, but that Sir Audley felt the force of what Mrs. Trevyllian said to him, and assured her, with more marks of being really affected than she thought he could have shewn, that, in case of the unhappy circumstance of her death, Althea should be received into his house, and that no difference should be made between her and the daughters of the present Lady Dacres.—"Allow me, however, to observe, my dear Madam," said Sir Audley in this conference—"that the most fortunate thing which could happen to our dear Althea, whose portion must be very small, would be to find the protection, and share the affluence of some man of family and fortune.—There are such, I dare believe, who might be attracted by her personal merit, and wave the consideration of fortune in favour of that merit, and of her highly respectable connections. Should you have any conversation with her on this subject, it might have great weight, were you to press this; and, I am sure, to your prudence and sagacity a hint is enough."

Mrs. Trevyllian thought this an opportunity to inquire, without naming him, what were the pretensions of Mr. Mohun. She therefore asked Sir Audley, if what he said alluded to any particular person?— Either from his doubts of her approbation, or from his really being uncertain of the intentions of his friend, he evaded the question; and having recourse to general terms to escape from speaking plainer, he merely repeated what he had before said, and soon after took his leave. Mrs. Trevyllian therefore did not think herself authorised merely on the information she had received from what Althea had said, to name Mr. Mohun to him; and as he had never made any attempt to see her niece since her return, it seemed probable that whatever impression she might have made was slight, and that when he no longer saw her, he would think of her no more.

Althea, wholly occupied by her anxiety, was almost unconscious of the objects around her: she sometimes tried to believe that the cruel blow she so dreaded would be spared her; but discouraging symptoms continually arose to destroy her hopes. Change of air by no means mitigated these symptoms; and as the impossibility of her recovery was confirmed to Mrs. Trevyllian herself, she thought it time to fortify the mind of Althea against an inevitable evil, and determined to employ her small remains of strength in returning to her own home, that she might not only settle every thing there in the best manner, but save Althea the additional uneasiness of being left among strangers, and the fatigue of a long journey in the first moments of poignant grief. Having once taken this resolution, she suffered no remonstrances to divert her from it. The weak hope of lingering a little longer had no power to detach her from the consideration of that duty which she owed to the only object who was very dear to her on earth; and this generous fortitude did not seem materially to increase her weakness. She not only bore the journey, though above ninety miles, without suffering much fatigue, but after her arrival at her own house continued nearly in the same state for some weeks.

As too sanguine hopes would serve only to embitter the inevitable moment of separation, Mrs. Trevyllian gradually accustomed Althea to hear her talk of what should be done after her death, with as much calmness as if she was only setting out on a long journey.—"Do not, my dear child," said this admirable woman, "do not now give me pain, for the first time in your life, by indulging this immoderate sorrow. Let me leave the world in the persuasion that your sense and firmness of mind will enable you to conduct yourself well through it. Why should you thus give yourself up to extravagant grief?—Did you imagine I was immortal, my Althea? or did you never consider that, according to the course of nature, I must go before you?—Ah! carry your mind to a more improbable, but not impossible circumstance. Imagine what might have been my situation, had I, by surviving you, found myself at an advanced period of life alone, and a stranger in the world—for what have I to attach me to it, unless it be my Althea? The rest of my family are my relations indeed, but they are so far from being my friends, that the greater part of them are hardly my acquaintance. How sad would have been my close of life, had I found myself a burden among them, when the powers of amusing myself might have been lost in the cheerless hours of solitude and sickness, when none would take the trouble to supply them! for you know, my love, that I have nothing with which to repay the assiduity of relations whose kindness is to be purchased by the hopes of legacies, and that this house and my little income revert, at my death, to the possessor of the family estate."

Althea, far from considering all this in the philosophical light in which Mrs. Trevyllian wished to represent it, could answer only by her tears.

"Ah, my dear love!" re-assumed this admirable woman, after a short pause, which her weakness made necessary—"Ah, my Althea! what is there in a continuation of the most fortunate life that a reasonable being should very ardently covet it? After the gay and sanguine hours of youth are passed, and hope no longer gilds the scene—after repeated convictions of their fallacy have taught us to estimate truly the value of every worldly object—how gloomy and how sad do the remaining prospects appear, when we either live on with indifference, or are forced to call in to our aid artificial helps to animate our existence! for I am convinced 'that the sick heart would still refuse, but dares not.'

"I lived some years ago in the circles of the high-born and affluent; and I have seen that half their lives are passed in contrivances to
get rid of the other half, and that it was not amid such societies that
content (for to talk of happiness is a mere abuse of terms) is ever
found. This conviction, my dearest girl, has reconciled me to that humble state, with respect to fortune, in which I must leave you. It is not
indeed adequate to your birth, but if your father intends you should
move in the sphere in which that has placed you, he will provide for
you better than by your mother's little fortune, and what I have been
able to lay by for you: these sums together do not exceed seventeen
hundred pounds. This however, my love, with some addition which
Sir Audley will make for you, and with your habits and temper, will, I
trust, be enough for the comforts of life: and all beyond is unnecessary, if not burdensome. Many are those within my own observation,
whom, though deemed objects of envy and admiration, I have known
to be the most unhappy beings under their splendid roofs. Often I
have known the fineries gazed after with murmuring comparisons by
the multitude as too glaring proofs of the inequality of fortune, cover
aching hearts, and spirits sickening in the dull round of unvaried prosperity. If happiness, Althea, and why should I discourage you from the
pursuit? is *any* where found, it is in that condition of life that 'gives
neither poverty nor riches;'—that encourages a firm reliance on the
goodness of God—a steady performance of moral duties—a regu-
lation of our wishes—and a constant employment of our time. All
this, my precious Althea, will always be in your power, however limited
your fortune, or however unpleasant the surrounding circumstances
of your life."

Althea, overwhelmed with sorrow, which choked her utterance,
tried to express her fears that in her father's family even her time would
not be her own.—"Ah! how different," said she, "is that family from
yours, my dearest, best friend! and how much, if ever that sad hour
comes, that tears you from me, must your poor Althea be sensible of
the difference!"—"To local circumstances we must submit, my child,"
answered her aunt. But I hope and believe you will find them less
unpleasant in the house of Lady Dacres, if you should be settled in
it as an inmate, than from the short experience you had—you have
accustomed yourself to imagine. You were then only a visitor; you
will hereafter be a part of the family"—(The tears and sobs of Althea
redoubled) "Do not thus distress me, Althea," continued her aunt—

"you, who never in your life gave me pain before, will you embitter these my last moments? I am persuaded you will find in your father, in your natural protector, a tender and affectionate friend. I assure myself he will remember his promises, that he will restore you to his affection, if absence has weakened it. Yes, Althea, from all he said to me I have no doubt but that you will be as dear to him as the children of Lady Dacres. The sight of you must continually recall to his recollection your mother, whom he once so passionately loved, and whose image, lovely as it was when consigned to an early grave, you too much resemble, not to have, even from that likeness alone, a strong claim on his heart.—This claim will daily acquire strength —I know it will, from the sweetness, the gentleness, the innumerable merits of my Althea.

CHAP. III

...... How many stand
Around the death-bed of their dearest friend,
And point the parting anguish.

IN THESE MELANCHOLY conferences, which happened very frequently during the last fortnight of Mrs. Trevyllian's life, Althea had only once the courage to mention Mohun —"I reproach myself," said she, "continually do I reproach myself for having ever named that man. It hastened your journey to London; you came before your strength was sufficiently established, and it was my folly that induced you to do it. Perhaps, after all, it was my weakness, my vanity, which imputed to Mr. Mohun projects he never thought of"—"You have nothing on that head to regret, dearest Althea," replied her aunt; "my coming to town was not injurious to me; on the contrary, it was necessary for advice, which, though I believed it to be useless, I was yet willing for your sake to try. As to Mr. Mohun, I know nothing of him but from public fame—that indeed bespeaks him to be a man whom Althea could never approve, and to whom, whatever may be his fortune, I never could wish to see her united. From the account you gave me, and from his general character, I think it very possible that youth and beauty may have strong attractions for him, and that your father might have encouraged his, perhaps, transient expressions of admiration, in the hope of forming an alliance, which, in his eyes, was an advantageous one.

But as in our conversations in London he never named Mr. Mohun, I trust you will not be troubled with his importunity: if, however, I should be mistaken, a calm and steady refusal will disengage you from the necessity of listening to him; and your father never can press you to marry against your inclination."

With such arguments Mrs. Trevyllian endeavoured to sooth the mind of her unhappy niece, and to arm it with fortitude for the future. But poor Althea, though she made every effort to stifle before her aunt the anguish of her heart, yet felt it increase in proportion as the sad moment approached that was to tear from her the guardian of her youth, her more than mother. But it was inevitable.—The awful hour came: and Althea, more dead than alive, was taken from the bed-side of her dying friend.

The violence of the shock, which was not the less severely felt for having been so long expected, deprived Althea, for some hours, of recollection.—Yet she was but too soon awakened to the sense of her irreparable loss. She looked around her. The world appeared a desert, in which she stood alone; for in her aunt she had lost the only friend who took an interest in her. Mrs. Trevyllian had regulated every thing with so much calmness and presence of mind some time before her death, that Morris had only to follow the orders she had given, and Althea was spared every painful task but that of writing to her father, and to her cousin Mr. Trevyllian, who was now become proprietor of the house in which her aunt had resided, and to whom the annuity, on which she had subsisted, reverted also. The next day, therefore, she sat down to this task; but her hand trembled, and the words, as she wrote them, were almost obliterated by her tears. She had hardly finished her letters, when she received the following note from a neighbouring gentleman, whose mother, the most intimate friend in that country of Mrs. Trevyllian, was absent with one of her married daughters.

"In the absence of my mother, dear Miss Dacres, Mrs. Eversley, Linda, and myself, consider ourselves as her representatives; and, being well assured how she would act if she were here, we must entreat of you to leave the sad scene you are in, and come to Valecombe, where you shall remain alone in your own apartment, or where Linda will be gratified in being allowed to attend you; but indeed you must oblige us. My sister now waits for you in the carriage, and will stay your own time, or return again whenever you shall appoint.—Mrs. Eversley unites in entreating you to make Valecombe your home, with, dear Madam, your most obedient servant,

FRANCIS EVERSLEY."

This attention, though coming from a man for whom Althea had a very high esteem, was extremely distressing to her. She could not bear the thoughts of leaving the house while the remains of her lamented friend continued in it.—To hide herself in solitude was now her only wish; she dreaded the sight of every body but Morris, nor could she even speak to her without yielding anew to the violence of sorrow. To repulse coldly the intended kindness of her friends was, however, not in her nature; but unable to see Miss Eversley, who waited for her, she was about to write her apology, when Morris came in and gave her a paper, in which, among many other directions of the same nature, was written, in Mrs. Trevyllian's hand—"I wish my dear Althea to quit the house as soon as she is able after my eyes are closed. Our good Mrs. Eversley will receive her; and some of that friendly family will return with her here, whenever it is necessary, to regulate the removal of those effects which will belong to her, before Mr. Trevyllian takes possession of the house. In the presence of the Eversley family, as the friends of my niece, I would have my will opened. Mr. Trevyllian will either come, or send, and Sir Audley Dacres will of course have notice."

This memorandum decided the weeping Althea. She bade Morris, to whom every thing was of course entrusted, send up a servant to assist in preparing for her departure. It was done in a few moments; and the unhappy mourner slowly, and with faltering steps, descended the stairs. At the door of her aunt's room she stopped. A thousand painful and tender ideas pressed on her heart. The last sounds she had heard there vibrated in her ears; the last look from those eyes which had ever beamed benevolence and fondness on her, was again present to her. She felt, at that moment, a wish to take a final farewel of all that now remained of her best friend; but, as she would have opened the door, the violence of her grief overcame her: she leaned for support on the servant who led her; and Morris, who had been detained above, now following her, took her other arm, and led her down. She suffered them to put her into the chaise where Miss Eversley was seated, who pressed her hand, but said nothing. On their arrival at Valecombe, Althea retired to the room that had been prepared for her, and, at her own request, was left alone.

In this solitude, or only seeing Miss Eversley for a few moments at a time, she remained for two days, when she received from Mr. Trevyllian the following letter:

"Dear Madam,

My attorney sends, according to my orders, a proper person to be present at opening the will of my late aunt, as a matter of form, and at your request; otherwise I apprehend it needless. You are welcome to remain in the house till you can conveniently remove the personals—should be sorry to hurry you. Wishing you health, &c. I am, dear cousin, your obedient humble servant,

W. TREVYLLIAN.

Otterbourne Park
Sept. 17th, 1794."

Though this relation of Althea's lived only twenty-five miles from the place where she had resided with her aunt ever since she was four years old, she had never seen him above once or twice, and he was then a boy at Eton School. He was now about five-and-twenty, and had been some years in possession of his very large estate, which came to him with a considerable sum of ready money saved during a long minority. Left early his own master, Mr. Trevyllian had indulged his prevailing tastes without restraint; which having lain wholly in the kennel and the stable, his ideas and his expences had gradually centred in them—and he had now no notion of any enjoyment beyond those afforded by the one or the other; or a debauch among the connoisseurs and attendants of each. His guardians had attempted to engage him to marry a young woman of fashion, who might have kept up some degree of that family respectability which he seemed so likely to lose: but he soon convinced them that he was not to be dictated to, and coolly declined the proposals they made him; asserting, that women of fashion were good for nothing but to ruin their husbands, and bring him children which perhaps might not belong to him—that he liked living in the country, and never would be dragged to London tied to any fine lady's apron-string—nor would he be put out of his way to become the husband of a duchess. The friends of his father, who had no wish but for his credit and advantage, soon withdrew from all farther remonstrance. His two sisters were taken by their maternal aunt, as soon as they left school, the house of their brother being extremely improper for them; and Mr. Trevyllian had no longer any one to interfere with his plan of life. He had two or three packs of the best hounds in the country; almost as many pointers and spaniels; several stables well filled with himters of all prices, and of all sorts, in which he became a sort of dealer, as he took care of his money.—He had a great deal of low pride, and sought not to associate with his equals or his superiors; but never failed to find companions that suited his taste much better, among livery stable-keepers, dealers in horses, younger brothers who were unfitted by idleness for any profession, bankrupt tradesmen who by their skill in horse-flesh had found their way into the Gazette—or poor curates, who preferred the conveniences of an occasional residence in such a house to the loss of their field sports:—such were the men who felt content to live at his table (which, as he loved eating himself, was always a good one), and be mounted from his stud: and none of them had feeling enough to be hurt at the price they were expected to pay for these indulgences; for they were the butts of his very coarse wit, and often treated with less respect than his upper servants. Notwithstanding his aversion to matrimony, Mr. Trevyllian had entangled himself with a vulgar woman, the sister of one of his retainers, who, though extremely ugly, and at least twenty years older than himself, had acquired such an ascendency over him, that she governed with the most despotic sway, and had so established herself in his house that, from that moment, he ceased to be the master. This is so common a character that it would be hardly worth describing, but to account for the haste he was in, though he did not absolutely express it, for Althea to quit the house, now fallen to him by the death of his father's sister. It happened that, a few months before, he had made an acquaintance with a person who in youth only was superior to his reigning Sultana, but for whom he had taken such a fancy, that he would willingly have put her in the place of that amiable personage, but had not courage to make the attempt. The lady, however, insisted on an establishment: and nothing could be more à-propos than the vacancy which now happened; the house being not only most elegant and convenient for its size, but admirably situated for field sports, and at such a convenient distance, that Trevyllian might easily divide his week between that and his mansion at Otterbourne, while it was too distant to hazard disagreeable rencontres between the Roxana and Statira who shared his heart. But even the little time which, as his note signified, he was willing to allow for the removal of the effects, he gave with reluctance: but Mr. Peters, his attorney, who had often seen Althea, and who had great influence with Trevyllian, assured him, that in decency he could not do otherwise, adding—"And, 'faith, Sir, your cousin is so pretty a girl, that, if she were in a house of mine, I should not have the heart to send her out of it at all."

Mrs. Trevyllian had never willingly named her nephew, or suffered any conversation about him to pass in her presence; and Althea knew nothing more of him than that he was profligate, and addicted to low company: she was not sorry, therefore, that he sent another to hear her aunt's will read; and she hoped that Sir Audley would himself come down to protect and assist her through a scene which her grief and her little knowledge of the world made formidable, though no dispute or difficulty could arise.

In this, however, she was deceived.—Her father, in answer to the letter which announced her loss, replied, that his presence was by no means necessary; that it would be sufficient if Mr. Eversley were present; and that it was impossible for him then to take so long a journey without the greatest inconvenience.—He added in a postscript—*When the affairs are settled, which, however, cannot be for some time, you will come to us; we shall remain at Capelstoke six weeks longer, and will send to meet you half-way. I understand it to be Lady Dacres's wish, and therefore of course it is mine, that you contrive to accommodate yourself with one of the women-servants now in my house, who shall be directed to attend you. Lady Dacres has an objection to the reception of the elderly person who attended you on your last visit."*

Over this letter the unhappy Althea shed many tears. Cold and reluctant as it certainly was, it appeared to her much more so; and the postscript seemed above all to be needlessly cruel.—"No kind mention of satisfaction in receiving me," said she, as she read it for the third time—"None of the affection of a father soothing my sick soul for the loss of my more than mother. No paternal advice how to conduct myself. No assurances of a kind reception at what must now be my home.—Alas! my father need not have repeated Lady Dacres's orders, and have given them force by adding that they were his. *I* have no pretensions to keep a servant at all. If I had, it could not be the elderly person who has given so much offence to her Ladyship; for Morris, who is richer than I am, and retained in service only by her affection to my aunt, will now retire among her relations, where *her* reception will be far other than what I shall meet with. They are people in humble competence, and are not lost to all sense of family affection. Mine are people in high life. Mine—ah! I have only one—only a father, and he is estranged from me!"

By such sad reflections the dejected spirits of Althea were but little prepared for the distressing ceremony of hearing the will of Mrs. Trevyllian read: this was now to be done in presence of Mr. Eversley, who attended at the request of Sir Audley; the agent of Mr. Peters, an attorney of a neighbouring town, on behalf of Mr. Trevyllian; and Mrs. Morris, who had been entrusted with the will. It contained little of which Althea was not before apprized. The furniture, books, some curious plants which Mrs. Trevyllian had cultivated with great delight; the musical instruments, plate, linen, and a few pictures, which formed the principal part of her property, were given to Althea, with a request that she would herself attend to the removal of them, and not part with any of the books, instruments, or pictures. The small savings from her own fortune, added to what she had accumulated from the allowance Sir Audley gave his daughter, together with what she directed to be sold, might, she thought, increase this little fund to something more than one thousand pounds. This Mrs. Trevyllian gave in trust to Sir Audley for his daughter, with directions that it should be paid on her marriage, or on her majority. It might indeed be considered as her all, at least for many years to come; for the thousand pounds which was her mother's small portion, belonged to Sir Audley during his life. The will also contained a request to Mr. Eversley, to consider Althea in some degree as his ward, and to assist her with his advice and support till she should be under the protection of her father. This distressing ceremony over; and the persons who presided at it departed, Althea retired to her own room to calm her agitated spirits, and endeavour to conquer the dread she felt at returning to the house where her happiest days had passed, but the sight of which must now tear her heart to pieces. It was the command of her lamented benefactress; and she determined, whatever it cost her, most punctually to fulfil it. Morris however, who was called to the consultation as soon as she had a little recovered herself, desired her to stay a few days longer at Valecombe; and Althea was not sorry that this severe trial was to be delayed, though she dreaded the restraint which awaited her at the house of Mr. Eversley, where it would now be expected she should appear with the family; as a longer seclusion would certainly be deemed affectation by Mrs. Eversley, who not having the least sensibility herself, knew not how to make allowance for that of others.

This woman could not but be disagreeable to Althea; for she was ignorant, vain, and arrogant—fond of money, and of admiration—of course despising every one who had not the former, and detesting all those who attracted the latter, to which she had herself very slender pretensions; for, with a very short, ill-made, heavy person, she had coarse-dubbed features—a long upper lip, and two great prominent unmeaning eyes, which, as they were very full, she fancied were very fine, and, as they were a dim slate colour, she valued herself upon, as 'azure of heaven's own tint:' —her coarse light hair, which had no small tendency to red, she really fancied was the most beautiful of all the shades of brown, her eye-brows: which had a still stronger propensity to the colour of flame, she had picked till not enough remained to betray the unlucky shade, supplying this deficiency with some delicate strokes of black lead.—Her eye-lashes could not well undergo the same operation; but they were short, and less distinguishable because of a pink-coloured line which encircled her eyes. Her skin was thick and freckled, and her voice hoarse and disagreeable. But she had near fifty thousand pounds; and the father of Mr. Eversley, who was her guardian, had contrived to prevail on his son to marry her while they were both under age—and in consequence of this, poor Eversley, who was a sensible and an amiable man, was now, at eight-and-twenty, very rich, and very miserable.

As Althea was much admired for her beauty, and had precedence as a Baronet's daughter, she excited, in a particular degree, the spleen and indignation of Mrs. Eversley. But, on this occasion, considering the long intimacy of the families, and the trust Mrs. Trevyllian had placed in her husband, she could not well refuse the request he made her. She complied, perhaps, with less reluctance, because she enjoyed the thoughts of seeing Althea humiliated, and descending to a state of dependance for so it was understood she must be, in consequence of the death of her aunt, her father's estrangement from her, and the small fortune she was likely to possess—for, in the opinion of Mrs. Eversley, a young woman who had no more than a thousand or two thousand pounds ought to go to service—an opinion with which she often insulted her husband's sisters, who she well knew had not so much.

This cruel inclination to insult, with affected pity and arrogant superiority, the innocent dejected Althea could not be gratified while she remained in her own apartment. No sooner therefore was her mourn-

ing arrived, and the first week over, than Mrs. Eversley began to talk
to Linda of affectation, and hypocrisy—and to enquire how long Miss
Dacres was to keep her state in all the paraphernalia of sorrow.—Linda, who was one of those common characters which are formed by
a very moderate understanding, cultivated only by such reading as a
country circulating library can supply, or such society as is to be found
in country towns, failed not to repeat to Althea all the sarcasms of her
sister-in-law, whom she hated. Althea, of course, hastened to join the
family at dinner, however unpleasant it was to her—and wrote to Morris to hasten such preparations for the sale, in the melancholy and transient abode to which she must return, as would save her some painful
hours of hopeless regret.—Too many she knew must be passed, in
despite of these precautions.

CHAP. IV.

The venomous clamours of a jealous woman
Poison more deadly than a mad dog's tooth.

IF THE LADY of the house was unfeeling and insolent, the master of
it was all goodness, humanity, and consideration. His softness of
temper, which had been the cause of his consenting to make himself
miserable, now induced him to bear with calmness the humours and
caprices of a woman he could neither love nor esteem, but who,
having given him her fortune, he thought entitled to his gratitude,
and, having put herself into his power, to his complaisance. As the
slightest contradiction produced passionate retort, tears, and reproaches, he seldom contradicted her at all; but when they totally
differed in their ideas, he went quietly his own way, and avoided the
pain of altercation by not consulting her. This method, however, was
not without its inconveniences; for she always suspected that he was
engaged in something which she was not to know, and sometimes
artfully discovered that he had assisted a friend by a loan, or forgiven his rent to a tenant in distress. On these occasions she failed
not to declaim, with great energy, against the cruelty and injustice
of Mr. Eversley, who had, she said, no more honour than honesty to give away hers, and her children's property—for she had two
girls, both amiable copies of their mamma. It happened that one of

these unfortunate discoveries had been made on the day when Althea
was first to appear at the table of her host. Mrs. Eversley, who had
seen her only once before, received her with a scowling countenance,
and hardly spoke to her. She looked indeed very lovely in her deep
mourning; a circumstance which was alone sufficient to excite the
displeasure of Mrs. Eversley, and to this cause her husband imputed
the unusual degree of ill-humour with which she seemed disposed to
entertain him and his guests. He affected, however, to take no notice
of it, but, with his usual easy good-humour, endeavoured to carry on
the common table conversation with a gentleman who chanced to
be present; occasionally addressing himself to Althea, but oftener to
his wife. The lady sometimes answered with a sullen monosyllable,
sometimes not at all; while her anger becoming more ungovernable,
from the sort of necessity to restrain it which she thought her husband had purposely imposed upon her by the presence of another
stranger, she sat swelling, and fanning herself with great violence.
The day was a remarkably warm one, in the beginning of September,
and the stranger, who was but little acquainted with the family history, observed that it was unusually hot; adding, very innocently, "I am
afraid, Ma'am, you find yourself very much incommoded."—"That
I do, indeed. Sir —*I am* incommoded;—and I am astonished how I
bear things as I do—I am sure it is a mercy that I have strength to
go through it."—"My dear Rebecca," said Mr. Eversley mildly, and
affecting to misunderstand her, "I am very sorry you are unwell; but
do not let us trouble our friends with our maladies—I hope you will
soon be better."

"You hope!" repeated the lady superciliously—"You hope!—So
it seems indeed!—No, Sir; if you cared about me, or my family, you
would not take pleasure in stripping us of our own to enrich a parcel
of swindlers and sharpers."—"Good God! Mrs. Eversley," exclaimed
her husband in uneasy amazement—"For Heaven's sake let us not enter on these discussions now."

'*Now* is as well as any other time. Sir," replied the lady—"I mayn't have
another opportunity of speaking; and for my part I wish all the world was
here—I'd not scruple to say that, when we are all ruined, the fault ought
to be laid to the right person.—Hundreds at a time squandered away, and
upon folks that but t'other day held up their heads so high, and were too
proud to return one's visits!—Any body *must* think it very grating to one—
to have one's own children robbed of their just due, and for people —"

"What people?" cried Eversley impatiently—"on *whom* have I squandered hundreds? However unwilling I am to enter into altercation with you, Mrs. Eversley, I beg, since you have said so *much,* that you will say *more;* name the people for whose sake I have injured you, and your family?"

"For the sake of those Marchmonts," replied she. "You know that, though they were deep in your debt before, you lately lent the old man another sum of money; and what good did it do?—He is dead, and every body says insolvent; and that, when his affairs come to be wound up, he won't pay his creditors half a crown in the pound."

The distress of Mr. Eversley appeared to be redoubled.—He tried to assume composure enough to answer without passion; but finding indignation and resentment conquering his natural equality of temper, he said hastily to the friend at his table—"Mr. Marston, I believe we should do well to finish our wine by and by—perhaps you will now oblige me with your opinion of the plantations I was speaking of before dinner?"—Mr. Marston, extremely glad to comply, immediately arose, and they left the room together; while poor Althea, who dared not go, though she trembled at the thoughts of staying with this unhappy and ungovernable woman, endeavoured, but in vain, to appear unconcerned, and to enter into indifferent conversation with Miss Eversley, who, very little at her ease, was afraid even of making an attempt to deprecate the storm, which she knew must burst somewhere.

Though Mrs. Eversley had no longer her husband to torment, she could not help continuing her harangue against his ridiculous whims, and extravagant friendships; and said so many rude things, which Althea thought immediately pointed at her, that she determined to quit the house the next day.—That such a temper as Mrs. Eversley possessed existed, she had before no idea; and now wondered how it was possible for a man of Mr. Eversley's manners and understanding to live with her. Determining never again to subject herself to her ill humours, Althea begged to be excused going down to tea, under pretence of a slight indisposition; but her friend, the sister of Eversley, dared not absent herself. Althea therefore being alone, and believing she should be in no danger of meeting the hateful mistress of the house, who never walked of evening, and that her slight falsehood was in no danger of being detected, went down into a shrubbery, which led from the garden to the edge of a heath, where Eversley was making more extensive plantations. The trees in the shrubbery afforded an agreeable shade against a September sun; and, though no longer in bloom, they whispered refreshingly to her fatigued senses. The uneasy scene she had just witnessed was already forgotten; and her mind reverted, as it ever did the moment she was alone, to her late irreparable loss. She gathered a branch of acacia, that waved its feathery foliage over the walk she was in, and, sighing, remembered how much her aunt used to admire those trees, and how fond she was of two of them, which she had herself planted at the end of the lawn when she first took possession of her cottage. Other tender recollections followed these, and she wandered on, without much attention, to the path she was taking; when, at a sudden turn, she was met by Mr. Eversley, and another person, whom she took for the gentleman who had dined with them, till she observed that he was in deep mourning, and Eversley introduced him by the name of Mr. Marchmont. Althea, apprehending that she might be an intruder, and recollecting what had passed after dinner, became confused; and, hardly venturing to look at the stranger, walked on—but she saw, in the transient glance she had of him, that he was a young man of genteel appearance, with a very dejected countenance. He was unhappy, and she pitied him; while her esteem for Mr. Eversley was increased by her knowledge of his attempts to serve the family of his friend.

She continued her walk round the grounds; but, before she quitted the wood near the house, she again met Eversley, who was now alone. Though he must have come in search of her, he seemed confused when he met her; but, recovering himself immediately, said—"My dear Miss Dacres, will you allow me a few moments the honour of conversing with you? If you are not fatigued, you will, perhaps, be so good as to take another turn round the shady part of the walks?" Althea, signifying her assent, turned back; and Eversley, walking slowly by her side, remained for some time silent, as if uncertain how to begin. At length he said dejectedly, "I am afraid, my dear Miss Dacres, the scene you witnessed today has given you pain. Poor Mrs. Eversley, having been an only child, was spoiled by her father, and is unfortunately too prone to indulge unwarrantable sallies of ill-humour and suspicion. Having been taught to consider money as the first good, she is always apprehensive of its waste, and has never learned the pleasure of befriending the unhappy. I cannot vindicate, though I sincerely pity her; but to you. Miss Dacres, I would, were it possible, at once apologize for her and for myself. I should be sorry to be thought capable of squandering the fortune she brought me on unworthy objects. The unhappy family of whom she spoke I have indeed attempted, vainly attempted, to save from ruin; ruin brought upon them rather by misfortune than fault. The father of that family was the friend of my father, and early in life rendered him some very important services. With the son, though he is younger than I am, I have for many years been in habits of friendship. I never met with any man who united, in so great a degree, the virtues of a warm heart and a clear head. He is indeed a young man whom any one might be proud of serving—but the little that has been in my power, which I assure you I spared from my own fortune, has been indeed inadequate to enable him to resist the torrent of ill fortune which seems rapidly to pursue him. Mrs. Eversley's invectives shall never deter me from executing the offices of friendship, so far as my own moderate means will allow. But you see I was compelled to hold a conference with him in my garden, without telling him why, since he would have been liable to rudeness and insult, had Mrs. Eversley known of his visit; and she contrives to know every thing by the unworthy expedient of bribing my servants."

A deep sigh, that seemed to arise from the sense of incurable unhappiness, here broke the sentence; but, soon recovering himself, he went on:

"I mean not, however, to trouble you. Madam, with useless lamentations; my lot is cast, and I must endure it.—For my friend I may truly say, that a more generous manly spirit never inhabited a human breast; and had he, poor fellow! the least suspicion of the uneasiness I have suffered on his account, nothing would induce him to accept of the very trifling services I can yet do him. My heart bleeds for him, his mother, and his sisters. I feel indeed, on my own account, that the unworthy part I am condemned to act—"

"I entreat you, Mr. Eversley," said Althea, "never to think of the unpleasant scene of today again; at least on my account; be assured I shall never name it—and I most sincerely hope your friend will never know, what cannot fail of being painful to him. To-morrow," added she, sighing, "to-morrow I shall return to my late home, there to execute the last commands of my deceased parent; and afterwards to take leave of it for ever! Allow me to assure you, Sir, that I depart with a lasting sense of the kindness you have shewn me; and that, in bidding a final adieu to this country, Mr. Eversley, his mother, and my dear Linda, are among those whom I shall sincerely regret."

"You go to-morrow then. Miss Dacres?—Ah! I *did* flatter myself that Linda and I might yet have had your company for a day or two longer: but I see it cannot be; I know I ought not to expect it."

Althea now thought he had nothing more to say—and, complaining of fatigue, turned towards the house. Many reflections indeed occurred, which made a longer continuance of this conference uneasy to her. There was something in the manner of Mr. Eversley more solemn and earnest than the subject demanded, and he appeared more affected than his wife's behaviour, however disagreeable, seemed likely to occasion, since such conduct was probably but too usual. There was an appearance of hesitation and confusion; he looked as if he wished to say more, while conscious that he had said enough; and his manner rather than his words conveyed to Althea a notion that it was wrong to prolong their conversation. Esteem for his general character, pity for his unhappiness, and respect for that generosity of mind which he had exerted towards the family of his friend, were mingled with this dread of impropriety, and with some fear lest Mrs. Eversley might see them together, which would increase her ill-humour and suspicion.

Eversley heard Althea's resolution to depart with evident regret, but attempted not to dissuade her. Early the next morning, therefore, the chaise she had ordered was at the door. As Mrs. Eversley was not an early riser, there was but little probability of seeing her before she went; and as the lady had been informed by Linda of her going the preceding evening, she thought little more ceremony was necessary than to leave a card of thanks. But from her unhappy host she could not so easily escape. He came into the parlour where she sat, while her little baggage was placing on the chaise: his countenance betrayed the extreme concern which he felt, but which he appeared desirous of concealing, however vain his attempts: he hesitated, sighed, and at last said—"Though I am unfortunate enough to lose you. Miss Dacres, so soon, I trust you will still allow me to claim the honourable, though transitory right with which our late lamented friend has invested me. You will have much, and I fear some unpleasant business to do before you quit this country. To be of the least use to you will give me so much pleasure!" ...

"You are very good," said Althea, interrupting him—"I hope I shall get through the little I have to arrange, without troubling you:—all such arrangements must be painful; but, as my friends cannot alleviate that uneasiness, why should I distress them with the sight of it? Be assured. however, that should I have occasion to ask your assistance, I shall not hesitate; and now, Sir," added she, rising, "allow me to thank you for your hospitable kindness, and to wish you much happiness till I see you again."

"Happiness!" whispered he, as he led her to the chaise—"Happiness for me!—Ah! Miss Dacres, if I did not know the goodness of your heart, I should think such an expression an insult on my misery."

He was now too near the servants who attended to say more; and Althea, hastening to be released from such painful and useless conversation, stepped quickly into the chaise, and was soon on her way to the place which had so long been her pleasant home, but which she now dreaded to enter. The sad vacancy she should feel—her solitary and mournful situation, forcibly recurred to her, and all that had just passed was forgotten. The nearer she approached to the house, the more cruel became her reflections; and when the chaise stopped at the gate of the small lawn that surrounded it, and she saw Morris waiting there to receive her, she was so overwhelmed with sorrow, that it was with difficulty she got out, and, leaning on the faithful participater of her grief, slowly entered the house.

Althea's removal to Mr. Eversley's, the restraint she was under there, her anxiety to hear from her father, and the coldness of his letter when it arrived, had occasioned a sort of pause in her grief, which now seemed to return more poignantly than ever. She wandered from room to room as if she expected to find her lost friend—but into the dressing-room, where they had usually sat together, or into her aunt's bed chamber, she could not acquire resolution to enter. From the solitary house she sought the deserted garden, where every tree and every flower brought to her memory her who used to be delighted with them, and they now seemed to droop as if conscious that they were regarded no longer. Twelve or fourteen years had passed since the shrubs, which shaded this little domain, had been planted under the direction of Mrs. Trevyllian; with Althea they had grown up, and her eyes streamed with tears as she viewed the lightly interwoven roof of half-faded verdure, which some of the most luxuriant formed above her head; but her spirits were still more affected by the annual flowers which yet lingered in bloom. She had assisted her aunt to sow the seeds of these before their unfortunate journey to London. The scene was present to her; she again fancied she heard the well-known voice to which she had so often listened in these walks—it repeated the name of Althea.—She stopped, and looked tremblingly around her, as if her fancy had really created a sound. It was the hollow wind of evening sobbing among the trees. She shuddered, and returned to the house.—Unable to stay alone, she desired Morris to sit with her. The good woman, distressed to see her so deeply affected, tried to speak cheerfully; but, after a service of almost thirty years, Morris had no ideas that did not belong to her deceased mistress. Of the past therefore she could not talk, without renewing the sorrow she wished to appease; yet of the future what could she say?—To her the house of Sir Audley, where Althea was now to reside, was, of all other places, the most hateful—and so much did she resent the treatment she had received there, that she could hardly prevail upon herself to speak of any part of the family with patience. Her conversation, therefore, was little likely to relieve the oppressed heart of Althea; nor did the necessity of exertion rouse her. People came to make out inventories of the furniture and plants that were to be sold.—The sight of these men was insupportable; and Althea, amidst the distress of mind such preparations for her removal inflicted on her, almost wished herself again at the comfortless abode of Mr. Eversley.

Nothing indeed could have induced her to have undergone these afflicting scenes but the commands of her aunt; nor could she have supported herself by any other reflections than those which arose from the remembrance of the conferences held, during that illness, with her excellent parent, who had laboured to fortify her mind against the inevitable evil that had overtaken her.

"I will endeavour,' said she, "dear shade of the best of women! Your poor Althea will endeavour not to disgrace, by feebleness of mind, the excellent lessons you gave her. But where shall I find courage to live a life so unlike that to which your indulgence accustomed me?—Ah! how different to me will appear the persons with whom I must associate, and how little interest will they take in my fate!".... Her recollection now glanced towards the reception she should meet with at the house of her father. All that had been unpleasant to her, during her short stay there, recurred to her; and the detested idea of Mohun failed not, in despite of reason, to present itself.—"Yet why," considered she, "why should I think of this Mohun?—Have I not real affliction enough without bewildering my thoughts with future possibilities?—My father can never encourage such a man to persecute me—but if he should!—What if he should?"—She dared trust herself no longer with the contemplation of what *might* follow, and she fled to the first occupation that offered itself to escape from forebodings so painful and useless.

Never was a more melancholy hour passed than that which Althea employed in seeing the books her aunt had given her taken from their shelves, and put into boxes, where they were to remain under the care of the elder Mrs. Eversley until she had a home of her own to receive them.—There was hardly one of these volumes which did not awaken some tender recollection, or that did not draw tears from her eyes. She continued, however, her mournful employment, with the help of Morris, and had got about half way through it, when, owing to the ignorance of a country servant, Mr. Eversley, followed by his friend Marchmont, entered the room without any previous notice.

The eyes of Althea, in which the tears still trembled, were red with weeping; and surprised by so unexpected a visit, amidst a room strewn with books, and in which there was hardly a chair unoccupied, she received them with some embarrassment in her manner. Soon, however, regaining her natural ease, she was able to thank Mr. Eversley for the offers of service which he came to make, to enquire after his family, and to enter on such common topics as usually offer in a short morning visit.—But, as if it had been infectious, her slight confusion on their entrance seemed now to be transferred to her visitors. Eversley was evidently perplexed and melancholy: and when she addressed herself to Mr. Marchmont, his answers were by no means such as the intelligence of his countenance promised; for it seemed as if he was only awakened, by the found of her voice speaking to *him*, from the contemplation of some incurable sorrow; and his eyes were so expressive of the distress of his mind, that Althea, whose tears had been with difficulty restrained on their entrance, felt them again ready to stream, as she repeated to herself— "Here, at least, is a being as unhappy as I am!"

Though neither Eversley nor Marchmont was disposed for conversation, neither of them seemed willing to go; they saw indeed that Althea had been busily employed, and Eversley muttered something about his fear of interrupting her, and once asked if they might not be permitted to assist her.—But the hour of dinner was near; and his watch, which he failed not to consult, had twice told him it was time to depart, before he could determine to rise, or to utter what he had long meditated.—"From all these preparations, Miss Dacres, I suppose this neighbourhood is soon to lose you. Your aunt's confidence in me gives me some right to make an enquiry, which might otherwise be impertinent: When do you go from hence?—When are we to lose you?"

"My business here," answered Althea, sighing deeply, "is nearly finished. I must then inform my father that I am ready to obey him, and await his orders for my removal."

"Sir Audley is, I suppose, in the country at this time of the year?" enquired Eversley.

"At Capelstoke, in Dorsetshire."

"Alas, Miss Dacres! you will soon forget your more Western friends; but pray forgive me—(he saw she was much affected)—and tell me, may I be permitted to bring Linda to take leave of a friend she so much loves?"

"I shall always be happy," answered Althea, "to see my dear Linda—but to take leave is very painful—painful in proportion to the love we have for those to whom we are compelled to bid adieu!"

"Ah! I feel that to be but too true," said Eversley, as he left the room.—Marchmont only bowed; but Althea, without knowing why, felt more concern for his dejection than for that of her old acquaintance.—"Poor young man," said she, "I wish I had interest enough to do him any good. Oh! if, like Sir Audley, I could intercede for the destitute and unhappy, with those who have favours to bestow, surely it would be for a family like this!"—A few days were yet to be passed before her departure—at least so she had calculated from the time of her last writing to her father. She hoped Linda would not come—for to what purpose these sad adieus?—Her heart would be heavy enough, and it could hardly bear any addition to the sorrow that would oppress her, when it became necessary to bid farewel for ever to the scene of her early pleasures, to so many memorials of its ever dear inhabitant—to part too from the faithful Morris, with little probability of ever seeing her again! But this painful period arrived even sooner than she had expected.—Early the next morning a letter was delivered to her from Sir Audley. It only said, that as he imagined she had now settled her business, Lady Dacres had been so obliging as to send her own woman to conduct her to Capelstoke, for which place he desired her immediately to begin her journey.—Short as the notice was, Althea determined to obey, and the hurry in which she set out seemed to prevent much of that anguish she had dreaded.—Enough however remained. Speechless and drowned in tears, she could only wring the hand of Morris; and covering her face with her handkerchief, she took a final leave of a place which so many subsequent hours of life gave her reason to remember with regret.

CHAP. V.

Now this is worshipful society!

SILENT AND SAD, Althea proceeded on the way to Capelstoke. Her road lay along the coast of Devonshire and Dorsetshire, and through a country various and rich; but Althea heeded it not. Every object that had once attracted her attention was now passed by unregarded. She saw nothing but the figure of the friend she deplored; she heard nothing but her last accents. If, calling off her mind a moment from this theme of hopeless regret, she carried it forward to the future, the cold and repulsive looks of Lady Dacres, and the constrained kindness of Sir Audley, were before her. In a family where she knew the mistress of it considered her as an unwelcome addition, how little of real affection and of soothing friendship had she to expect!—Her spirits, agitated by these reflections, sunk in proportion as her journey shortened—and when the chaise drove through the new-built Lodge, about half a mile from the house, she was so totally depressed, that, notwithstanding all her endeavours, she was hardly able, when it arrived at the door of the house, to get out, and follow the footman into a parlour.—The man, as if he neither knew her, nor had received any orders for her reception, asked if her baggage was to be taken from the chaise; then ordering the postillion to drive round to the side of the offices, he went away. Mrs. Midgely, Lady Dacres's woman, a person of infinite delicacy, had already left her, on pretence of being greatly fatigued.

Althea, finding herself alone, looked around with dismay; the room in which she was, though large, and magnificently fitted up, had an air of melancholy and silent gloom, which was but ill compensated by the splendour of the furniture. How different was the reception from that she was wont to receive at her former home, where, after the shortest absence, Mrs. Trevyllian used to welcome her with smiles of delight, and fondly press to her heart its first delight!—Now, the only figure that met her eyes was her own, reflected from a very large French glass which reached from the ceiling to the floor.—She start-

ed as she approached it, then turned away and went to one of the
windows. Comparing this strange reception (for it seemed as if none
intended to notice her being in the house) with that she had formerly
met in London, when she was carried into a room where a number
of strangers were assembled. She thought both very unkind; but this,
however humiliating, was the least unpleasant.

As Althea had been two days on the road, it was early evening
when she arrived. Perhaps Sir Audley and Lady Dacres were walking,
or engaged with company whom could not leave to receive her. She
wished the interview over and—but time passed on, and nobody appeared.

After waiting some time, a heavy step was heard. She supposed it
to be her father—her heart beat quick—but when the door opened a
portly gentlewoman appeared at it, whom Althea had never seen before. A round, broad face, and two black bushy eye-brows shading her
goggle eyes; with a snub nose, fortunate counterpart to a treble chin;
and a mouth, the real dimensions of which she seemed to evade discovering rendered her no very amiable figure.—Her dress was in the
most gorgeous style of the second table—and she seemed perfectly
conscious of the respectable appearance she made, when, advancing
in state, she informed Althea, that she had the honour to serve Lady
Dacres as housekeeper at Capelstoke.—"And my lady, Ma'am, and Sir
Audley being *necessitated* to dine and sup out to-day with a large party
of ladies and gentlemen who are now staying at our house, a *partickeller
frind* having given a ball and supper on his daughter's birth-day; my lady
directed me, if in case you, Ma'am, should come, though she didn't
much expect you till to-morrow, that I should see you had every thing
you pleased to order. Would you like some tea, Ma'am, or shall I get
you an early supper?—and would you please to have the cloth laid in
the dining-room, or the small *liberry* where my lady has a fire o' nights
when we haven't company."

Althea replied that being a good deal fatigued, she rather wished
to retire to her room, where she would have some tea, and go to bed as
soon as possible.—"Oh, to be sure, Ma'am," answered Mrs. Grimsby,
"to be sure!—You must be fatigued, no doubt—So, Ma'am, I'll send
the house-maid to shew you your apartment, which is quite ready."

"And I shall be obliged to you to order me a fire," said Althea.
"Though the day has been hot, I find myself chilled this evening."—
She then enquired after the younger part of the family, and heard the

two eldest ladies were gone with their momma to the ball.—"Sweet dreams!" exclaimed this keeper o confections—"they are both vastly fine young ladies!—and they were so happy! As to the gentlemen, they are at school, except Master Frederic and Master Edmund, and them two and Miss Julie are in the nursery." —Having thus received answers to the questions she thought herself obliged to ask, Althea gladly retired to her apartment, under the guidance of Mrs. Hetty, one of the house-maids. It was a room on the second floor, plainly but conveniently furnished, with a large closet adjoining. While Hetty assisted in placing some of her things, Althea enquired the names of the present visitors at Capelstoke, and heard among them, with inconceivable chagrin, that of Mohun.—Some other of the persons who were mentioned Althea recollected to have seen in London, but there was not one she remembered with pleasure; and never did a deserted wretch, who finds himself cut off from all human society, and left in an uninhabited island, feel more desolate or more miserable than did Althea in the splendid house of her father, surrounded by the luxuries of life, and amid every elegance of polished society.

She hastened early to bed, in hopes of losing her regret of the past, and her sad presentiment of the future, in sleep.—Fatigue assisted her to forget herself; but the moment her eyes were unclosed the sense of her sorrows returned, and with it the consciousness that she must disguise them, or hazard becoming doubly unacceptable to those on whom she was to depend. It was yet so early that none of the servants were up. Althea opened the shutters, and looked into the park. Grey mists hung upon the half-faded groups of trees, and lingered yet more heavily over the distant water which divided a part of the park from the adjoining estate.—About eight years ago Althea had visited Capelstoke with her aunt. It no longer seemed the same place.—"Ah!" thought she, "how little was I then conscious of my own felicity! how little aware that the happiest moments of my life were passing!—I felt not my father's coldness—I knew not that Lady Dacres looked upon me with unkindness—but, secure of the approbation of my dear benefactress, I was content with the present, and thought not of the future.—O that I could now look forward with equal indifference, or that the prospect before me were more cheerful!"

She now began to turn her eyes round her apartment, and then to examine the long light closet which served as a sort of dressing-room:—the walls of this latter were covered with pictures, which seemed to have been removed out of other rooms to give place to more modern ornaments. Some of them appeared to be family portraits belonging to the former possessors of the house (which Sir Audley had purchased soon after his second marriage): they were injured by time, and want of care; and it was difficult to distinguish what sort of beings many of them had been intended to represent. Althea sighed, as a reflection arose in her mind on the inefficacy of art to save from oblivion the evanescent forms of beauty or worth. Thus mournfully moralizing, she turned to the other side of the closet, where she was struck with a whole-length figure of a young and beautiful woman, apparently painted at a much later period than the rest. The features and air of her mother, such as she had seen in her picture carefully preserved by Mrs. Trevyllian, immediately occurred to her; and she dissolved into tears as she read at the edge of the canvas—"Althea Dacres, 1773."—It was the year after her marriage, and preceding the birth of Althea.—"Oh, my mother!" cried the weeping girl, "*you*, at least, seem to welcome your unhappy child! —I am obliged to whoever placed here this representation of what you once were. It is the only pleasure I shall perhaps taste in this house: yet when it was put here, my gratification was not, I imagine, thought of.—No—Lady Dacres could allow it no other place. —I wonder indeed it was brought to this house at all.—Alas! how could Sir Audley review those features, and not nourish continual regret?"

Such melancholy contemplations occupied Althea for some time. She was never weary of looking at the picture.—On a farther examination of the closet, she began to flatter herself that her father had thought more of her accommodation than she at first imagined—for there were a few books, in some of which, on opening them, she found her mother's name—and they were placed over a little inlaid cabinet, which formed a commodious writing-desk: this also had belonged to her mother, for her cypher was inlaid in the centre of the desk.—"Here then at least," sighed Althea, "here I shall not be unhappy.—When my full heart is unable to bear the uninteresting and desultory conversation of mixed company, I may retire hither to weep for both my parents—for those beloved sisters who will here seem present to me, and whose benign spirits may perhaps hover over their poor Althea."

A miniature of her aunt, painted when she was in middle life, was her constant companion. On this she now fixed her eyes filled with tears; but the entrance of Hetty, who came to ask whether she chose to have her breakfast in her own room, or to take it below, put an end to her sorrowful soliloquy.—Distressed by the thoughts of the first interview with her father and Lady Dacres, yet wishing it over, she enquired whether all the party who were in the house usually assembled together in the breakfast-room—and whether Sir Audley and Lady Dacres had any rule in regard to their visitors. The maid replied, that some of the ladies had breakfast in their own apartments; that the rest of the party assembled in the breakfast-room; but that Lady Dacres seldom attended, and Sir Audley never.—To enter among a number of strangers, or, what was worse, to appear in a company where the only person she knew was the person in the world the most disagreeable to her, was certainly to be avoided. She desired therefore to remain where she was; and hardly knew whether to be most hurt or pleased, that she appeared likely to be treated with the same civil indifference as the usual visitors at the house. As far as such conduct would leave her more at liberty, she rejoiced at it; but she could not help feeling a cold and comfortless sensation, when she reflected that the person by whom she was thus put on the footing of an ordinary acquaintance was her father—nor could she fail to recollect that she had now been many hours in his house without being enquired after.

In endeavouring to conquer these depressing thoughts, the time passed till an hour at which Althea thought it impossible but that the master and mistress of the house must be visible to their guests; and at length she was informed by a footman that Lady Dacres desired to see her.—Althea now hoped that she should meet her father and Lady Dacres alone; but she was disappointed; she was shewn into the breakfast-room, where a large circle was assembled—some still at their morning repast; some of the gentlemen in shooting dresses, and preparing to go out, and others talking in small parties. Among the last was Sir Audley, who, when Althea appeared at the door, left the persons he was conversing with (one of whom she immediately saw was Mohun), and, taking her hand, led her to his wife.—Lady Dacres half rose from her chair, while with a forced smile, and in a low voice, she bade her welcome to Capelstoke.—Sir Audley then presented the blushing and half-weeping Althea to two ladies who were next Lady Dacres. "Lady Barbara," said he, "give me leave to present to you my daughter Althea."—Lady Barbara made a cold bow, and surveyed her from head to foot without speaking. He then turned to the other—"My dear Mrs. Polwarth, allow me to make known to you my daughter."—Mrs. Polwarth, rising from her feat, said one of the some-things usual on such occasions; and then whispered Sir Audley loud enough to be heard—"Oh! she is divinely handsome."—A frown from Lady Dacres checked the continuance of this audible whisper—but not the impertinent looks with which this strange woman continued to gaze on Althea, whose heart, already oppressed, could not hear the name of Polwarth without being cruelly affected; for it was impossible for her to forget that to Mrs. Trevyllian's friendship for the mother of Mr. Polwarth (who was also present) she owed the loss of that dear and much-regretted friend.—By this time, however, the ceremony of general introduction was over. Two young women of fashion, of the name of Newmarch, whom Althea had met in town, were also of the party; and to them it seemed as if Lady Dacres was willing to consign her, considering them probably under the general class of misses, and not without hopes that their superiority in point of fortune, knowl-edge of the world, and reputed beauty, would sink Althea at once into the insignificance in which she wished to see her.—They were at a window together, when Lady Dacres, calling to them, begged to in-troduce Miss Dacres once more to their acquaintance. Althea gladly quitted Mohun, who was talking to her in a cold and careless manner, which greatly abated the terror she had conceived at meeting him, and began a sort of conversation with the eldest Miss Newmarch; while Mohun, instead of going out to shoot as seemed by his dress to have been his intention, stood in a lounging way, surveying Althea with the sort of look that a sagacious jockey puts on when he is about to pur-chase a horse—and those who had taken the trouble to examine his countenance might have seen his approbation.—The mourning Althea wore, which was as deep as for a parent, particularly became her.—The confusion of her mind had added to her complexion the roses it some-times wanted; and Mohun thought her infinitely handsomer than when he had seen her in London. Sir Audley, who was interested in his opin-ion of her, failed not to remark this with satisfaction; but Lady Dacres, by no means delighted with the general approbation with which every man in the room seemed to consider Althea, broke up the party by say-ing, "Lady Barbara, is your ladyship disposed to adjourn to my dress-ing-room?—Mrs. Polwarth, how do you dispose of yourself?—You ladies, I suppose, will walk;" speaking to the Miss Newmarches, "and Miss Dacres will doubtless attend you."—"I shall be of *their* party, dear

Madam," cried Mrs. Polwarth; "I am not disposed to be sedentary this morning; I feel extremely young."—"Mrs. Polwarth is always young," whispered a young man, whose dress might have served for the representative of the most outré man of the day in the most outré comedy; "Mrs. Polwarth is always young—always delightful—always the envy of her own sex, and the admiration of ours."—"Oh, flattering creature!" cried the lady to whom this was addressed, "you know you think no such thing—Or, if you do, you wicked animal," added she, rising, and in a half whisper, "if you do—Oh Heavens! keep it to yourself, or I shall have poison put into my cup by the misses." She now walked towards Althea and her companions; Mr. Wardour still following, and whispering to her. Althea gazed at and listened to this woman with astonishment soon mingled with disgust—which, however, Mrs. Polwarth was so unconscious of, that she thus addressed her:

"My dear sweet girl, I have been dying to make an acquaintance with you. I dote upon beauty—there is nothing I delight in half so much. Polwarth tells me sometimes that I am vastly impolitic—but he is the best husband in the world—is he not, Wardour?"

"Who could be otherwise to such perfection?" answered Mr. Wardour, with an expression of countenance that gave this answer very much the air of a sneer. "Ah! who could be otherwise to such a woman?—But, alas! there is but one in the universe such as Mrs. Polwarth."—"Now, my dear Jack," replied the lady, "what a common-place compliment is that! Besides, you know it is just the reverse, for there are a thousand women in the little universe of London like me; and a million there would be, if they dared to be as honest as I am, and own, as I do, that they dote upon flirting. I like always to have half a dozen young fellows round me, and care neither for the envy of the misses, nor the malignity of their mammas and maiden aunts. Oh! Wardour, since you are the only tolerable wretch here, do find something new to say to me. Come, I will give you a study—you shall be my gallant round the park." So saying, she took his arm, and marched out of the room, to the wonder of Althea, who looked at Mr. Polwarth to see if such strange behaviour passed unnoticed. He talked of politics with Sir Audley on the opposite side of the room, and was totally regardless of this sally of his wife's. It seemed not new indeed to any of the few who remained. Lady Dacres and her friend were gone; and no one but Miss Newmarch took notice of Mrs. Polwarth, who, as she passed the window, hanging on the arm of Wardour, exclaimed, "What a woman!" Althea then accompanied Miss Newmarch in a walk which her sister declined. A silence of some moments ensued, which Miss Newmarch, whose character was that of haughty indifference, seemed not disposed to break; and Althea, who feared her father's country residence was not likely to be more pleasant to her than that in London, sunk in cold despondence. Her companion at length broke silence. "*You* are not acquainted with Mrs. Polwarth, Miss Dacres?"—"No, Madam, I never saw her before."—"I must own," continued the lady, with a very significant toss of her head, "that I was surprised to find her here; and my aunt Lady Barbara was not less amazed. It will certainly shorten our visit. Mrs. Polwarth is by no means a person with whom *we* shall be suffered to associate."

Althea, who cared nothing about Mrs. Polwarth, had neither spirits nor inclination to enquire into the particulars of her character; but Miss Newmarch could not resist the malignant pleasure of giving her history. And she was in the midst of these scandalous anecdotes, to which Althea could not prevail upon herself to attend, though she appeared to listen, when they met the subject of their conversation with her attendant. As they passed, and slightly spoke, the countenance of Miss Newmarch sufficiently explained the cause of her peculiar inveteracy, which a very few subsequent observations confirmed. Mr. Wardour was one of those very fine men for whom half the fashionable girls in London were just then dying—one of those irresistibles, who are always seen lounging in St. James's Street, or riding in Hyde-park—who shew themselves for a moment at half a dozen different places—affect to have engagements every where, and to attend to none of them—imagine some ridiculous singularity of dress, and enjoy the paltry pleasure of seeing it adopted first by all who are emulous of being in the world of fashion, and then watch its progress descending among the frequenters of the lobbies, the weekly visitors in Kensington Gardens, lawyers' and bankers' clerks, brokers, the second in the firm, and the Philpots of the day. Miss Newmarch, who made a mighty parade of the strictness of the education she had received, and fancied that it gave some singularity to her character, had not however learned to despise this species of coxcomb. She had seen Wardour in London with very partial eyes, and they had told him that neither prudence nor prudery could withstand his attractions. It was by chance they met at Sir Audley's, when Mr. and Mrs. Polwarth were there for a week on their way into the West. Mrs. Polwarth delighting to shew her power, immediately threw out her lure for Wardour; who professing to be worn to death with the insipidity of misses, and to find a great deal of amusement in the extravagant coquetry of the married lady, paid his court openly to Mrs. Polwarth, and affected to forget that he had ever seen Miss Newmarch before.

Lady Dacres either did not or would not see how very much the conduct of her visitor was out of rule, and Lady Barbara sneered and talked at her in vain. This good lady, the unmarried daughter of an Irish Earl, was near sixty—tall, thin, upright, and formal: she seemed as if her shape had been imagined by some joiner no adept in grace, on purpose to serve as a layman for the clothes she wore. Lady Barbara was a sort of oracle among a certain set of ancient maidens of small fortune, or childless widows of moderate jointures, who formed a little society in the streets immediately around the square where she resided in London. Not having many titled acquaintance, these ladies considered Lady Barbara as their head and patroness. Her name was ever solicited first on the list of subscriptions, and to such charities as were made public she had no objection to contribute. She was supposed to have a predilection in favour of Methodism, was an adept in medicine, and had faith in the science of the illuminés. Above all, her strict and unbending prudence was a source of continual eulogium. Yet there were those who gave her no other credit for this extraordinary portion of rigid austerity, than what arose from her never having had in the younger part of her life any temptation to seek that admiration, or mix in that general society, which, though not inconsistent with real purity of character, often gives occasion to doubt it. Plain and disagreeable in her person, she had been neglected by the men; chilling and severe in her manners, she was detested by the women. Her rank alone had rescued her from entire neglect—her relations visited her as a matter of form; and on the death of one of her sisters, the Miss Newmarches, her two daughters, had fallen under her care. But these young women, who had been educated in a very different style of life, could ill brook the formal dulness of Lady Barbara's house and society, and impatiently expected the time when their majority should release them from her control.

Nothing could assort less than Althea and these two young women: Mrs. Polwarth was still more disagreeable to her; and the society of the elder ladies. Lady Barbara and Lady Dacres, was the subject of her dread; for while the latter considered her as the rival of her daughters, the eldest of whom was now just coming out in the world, the other seemed to look upon her as a proper object on which to exercise her satirical sagacity. She criticised, even before her face, her manners, her air, and her figure—discovered faults which Althea had never before heard of; yet, "merely as her friend," advised her to consider how difficult it was in *these times* for young women of very small fortune, and good family, to procure proper establishments—and exhorted her by a most prudent and circumspect behaviour to do honour to "the memory of her dear deceased aunt."

Althea, who had not the least inclination to deviate from prudence, and saw no temptation to do so if she had, was for some days ignorant whither all these lessons tended: at length, however, she discovered that Lady Barbara was engaged to forward the views of her father and Lady Dacres, and to prepare her for what they were endeavouring to bring about, a passive acceptance of those attentions from Mr. Mohun, which had given her so much disquiet in London, and which he now was evidently disposed to renew.

Mrs. Polwarth, her husband who had not three ideas out of the routine of the office in which he was employed, and the envied irresistible Mr. Wardour, departed in a few days; and the party was reduced to Lady Barbara, her two nieces, and Mr. Mohun, with two or three dependants of Sir Audley's, who were frequently at the house. The evenings were become long, and many were the hours, when Althea was condemned to sit in this dull and uninteresting circle, or to walk round a card table, while Mohun, seating himself at whist, sometimes followed her with his eyes, and sometimes attended to his game, and seemed internally to resolve on not taking much trouble about a silly girl, who had so little judgement as not to value the good opinion of a man of talents so superior, and judgement so indisputable.

Hitherto Althea had contrived to avoid ever meeting him alone, and his professions of admiration, which he was too proud to lavish while any could witness how coldly they were received, hardly seemed to have made any impression. But as his inclination for her increased every day, and as he could not believe a final refusal from her possible, he at length determined to open his pretensions in form. There was now no Mrs. Trevyllian to encourage her refusal; he saw that her present home was very uneasy to her, and he was sure Lady Dacres did not want disposition to make it more so. Sir Audley was not only warmly his friend, but protested to him that this marriage was nearer his heart than any other circumstance in the world. Althea was therefore fated to undergo that sort of persecution which has filled so many novels, and either disoblige her only parent and protector, or devote herself for life to a man she detested.

CHAP. VI.

My parks, my walks, my manors that I had,
Even now forsake me, and all of my lands
Is nothing left me!

SIR AUDLEY HAD watched Althea's manners towards his friend, and was at no loss to understand what they meant; but he was so sure she had no other attachment, that he could not help flattering himself the prospects of splendour and affluence which Mohun could offer her, would have their weight; and accordingly prepared to exert all the power of parental authority to conquer any scruples that his daughter might have, and to hasten the conclusion of the marriage before they returned to London for the winter.

The active timidity of Althea baffled for a few days the intentions of Mohun to address her alone. Her father saw she avoided him; and fearful that his excessive pride would be hurt if she positively refused him, he determined to speak to her before the interview took place, and to prevent the probability of such a repulse by his positive commands.

Poor Althea, whose only tolerable hours were those which she passed alone in the early part of the morning, was as usual enjoying her solitary walk in the park, when a footman informed her Sir Audley desired to speak with her in his study.—Trembling and breathless, for she guessed but too well what she was to hear, she followed him to her father's room, where he waited for her.

"Althea," cried Sir Audley, as soon as she was seated, "I have but a few words to say to you; but I expect that you will attend to them, and consider them as decisive. You cannot be really ignorant of my friend Mr. Mohun's partiality for you. It has survived those girlish and ridiculous airs which would have disgusted a less sensible and discerning man; but he sees that you have a good understanding, and he knows how to make allowances for extreme youth, inexperience, and perhaps some romantic and foolish notions which you have picked up in the course of a retired and country education. He still does you the honour to consider you in the most favourable light; a circumstance that gives the truest pleasure to Lady Dacres, and to me. I know you can have no other attachment—such an idea is impossible. Mr. Mohun offers every advantage that can satisfy a reasonable woman; nay, all that can gratify the most ambitious. He will speak to you himself; and I expect, Althea, that you receive him as a man who is my friend, and who is to be your husband."

It was fortunate for Althea that the length of this harangue gave her time to recollect herself: young as she was, and hitherto without having had any occasion to act for herself, her good sense supported her in this trying moment, and gave her courage to act from the impulse of her unadulterated heart.—Free from every preference, and uninfluenced by every motive but native integrity, her soul revolted at the idea of selling herself to any man; and Mohun was in his person, manners, and morals, equally disagreeable to her.—However averse to disoblige her father, she was yet more unwilling to let him for a moment suppose her capable of making such a sacrifice of principle; and it was better to declare her resolution at once, than to encourage expectations she never could fulfil. Collecting all her courage therefore, yet trembling so that she could hardly articulate her words, she declared to her father, that however sorry she was, not to comply with his and Lady Dacres's wish, yet that her dislike to Mr. Mohun was not to be conquered—that she had no ambition, nor any wish to leave his protection, so long as he would afford it her.

Sir Audley could hardly hear her with patience. Unused to have his will opposed, he could not endure to find opposition where he thought he had a right to implicit obedience; and having by this marriage, in imagination, seen an end to all his solicitude, and to the uneasiness which he foresaw between Lady Dacres and Althea, the refusal of his daughter, which counteracted these hopes, seemed the most unpardonable offence that ever was committed against him. He disdained, however, to argue where he thought he had a right to command; and therefore in very angry and peremptory terms declared to her, that though he had at first condescended to speak to her rather as a friend than as her father, she should find that he would be obeyed. "I have received you," said he, "at the risk of my domestic quiet, into my house, because it appeared to be my duty to do so; but do not imagine, Althea, do not imagine that in performing my duty I shall suffer you to forget yours. I declare to you, and my resolutions are not easily shaken, that if you do not receive Mr. Mohun's proposals, as if you finally meant to accept them, I shall no longer consider you as my daughter."

"The alternative is a very dreadful one," replied Althea; "my father will then abandon his child—for indeed, Sir, indeed I cannot marry Mr. Mohun."

"Go, Madam," said Sir Audley sternly; "you know my final determination —I argue no longer."

At this moment a servant entered the room, and told Sir Audley that Mr. Marchmont was in the parlour, and begged to speak to him.

"Mr. Marchmont!" exclaimed Sir Audley, angrily; "and what does he want? Who let him in? Have I not given orders to be denied to him? Why did you say I was at home?"

"It was not I, Sir," said the footman; "it was Robert who met him at the stables. He had been enquiring for Mr. Addingreve; who not being at home, or expected these two days, he desired, Sir, to see you as a matter of great consequence."

"What are his matters of consequence to me?" cried Sir Audley, in a still more angry tone; "those Marchmonts think one has nothing else to do but to attend to them. I never saw more troublesome people.—Go, Miss Dacres," added he, turning to Althea; "and do you, John, let Mr. Marchmont know —." Althea, glad to be dismissed, now left the room, when in the vestibule she met the same young man who had been so oddly, and, as she thought, improperly introduced to her by Mr. Eversley. He stood in a hesitating way, as if anxiously waiting for Sir Audley's orders of admission. He was paler, thinner, and appeared more dejected than when Althea had before seen him. When he saw her he started, but seemed uncertain whether he ought at such a moment to renew the slight acquaintance he had with her. Althea, whose eyes and manner betrayed the agitation she had been in, blushed at once from the recollection of their former meeting, and from the consciousness of her present appearance; and unable to decide whether she ought to speak to him or no, she courtesied and passed on, while Marchmont stepped forward into the library. Althea involuntarily paused, to learn the reception her father gave him: she heard only, "Well, Sir, since I must be thus troubled"— uttered in the same angry tone which had so lately been used to herself. The door was then shut; and with a heart oppressed by her own sorrows, yet feeling for those of this unfortunate stranger, she slowly returned to her own room.

For a moment she relieved herself by shedding tears, which terror had in some measure restrained while in the presence of her exasperated father. Some cruel reflections which he had thrown out against Mrs. Trevyllian, and the prejudices she had imbibed, hurt Althea as much as his menaces in regard to Mohun; and when she began to reflect on the power he possessed, and his apparent determination to use it, all the bitterness of her loss recurred to her with ten-fold force. "If my father persists," said she, "whither shall I go, or what will become of me? I have not a friend in the world; for my mother's relations are all estranged from me: and who will encourage a child in disobedience to a father, in a case too where so many people would think him right in using the authority that nature has given him? But I never will, I never can give myself to that man. Servitude—daily labour would be preferable to the most brilliant situation which I should owe to him." The violence of her sensations occasioned sickness and languor; and she determined, as it was yet early, to take the walk her father's summons had delayed. Yet dreading lest she should meet Mohun, she rang for Betty; and questioning her how the people in the house had disposed of themselves that morning, she heard that Mr. Mohun, with others, was gone out on a shooting party. Assured, therefore, that he could not cross her way, she put on her hat, and hastened to a considerable distance from the house, where a long row of Spanish chesnut trees joined on one side to a coppice, and on the other to a road which led through the park from a neighbouring town to a sea-port at the distance of eleven miles. The trees yet afforded a shade against the morning sun, though their leaves began slowly to fall; and Althea, soothed by the sighing of the autumnal wind among their branches, and by the perfect solitude of the place, seemed as if she was for a moment at liberty to breathe more freely; and leaning against a hunting-gate that opened into the coppice, she began, with that sad disposition to increase mental anguish which so frequently hangs about the unhappy, to carry her memory back to the same season in the preceding year, when she was blessed with the tenderness and protection of her aunt, without a wish ungratified, and to compare it with the cruel reverse which had now fallen upon her! The sound of an approaching passenger interrupted her reverie.

She looked towards the end of the chesnut walk, and saw Mr.
Marchmont on horseback, but riding so slowly that his horse, which
seemed to be a hired hack, hardly put one foot before the other: the
bridle was laid on the neck of the animal, and Marchmont held one
hand to his forehead and eyes, as if suffering pain: the horse, however,
on seeing Althea, stopped, and then went on a more irregular pace; and
his rider, roused from his feverish dream, looked up and saw her. He
pulled off his hat, and, checking the horse, said in a low and dejected
voice, "I believe I have the honour of seeing Miss Dacres: I hope she
is well." Althea would have answered so common an enquiry in its usual indifference, had not her goodness of heart urged her to be more
than usually civil to a man who she knew was unhappy, and who had,
she feared, been harshly used by Sir Audley. She therefore asked when
he last saw Mr. Eversley's family? If he knew whether the elder Mrs.
Eversley was returned? and such other questions as led to a conversation. Thus encouraged, Marchmont seemed for a moment to forget his
despondence, and, dismounting, appeared extremely gratified in being
acknowledged as an acquaintance. He talked of the Eversley family,
and evidently wished to prolong the pleasure he had thus so unexpectedly been indulged in; while Althea, anxious to know the business
which her father had received with so much ill-humour, made an effort
to satisfy what may be called benevolent curiosity; for though she had
no influence with Sir Audley, she thought it not impossible but that
Addingreve, the old steward, might be induced by her solicitations to
grant a small favour, which was all she supposed Mr. Marchmont likely
to solicit. Under this idea she ventured to say, "I fear, Sir, you have
had the trouble of a long journey without meeting Addingreve, with
whom I understand you had business at home? Sir Audley perhaps,
who leaves almost every thing to him, could not equally transact it?"
The expressive countenance of Marchmont, before lighted up with a
transient ray of pleasure, changed at once; he cast a melancholy look
on Althea, and said, "You are very good. Miss Dacres, to bestow a
thought on so luckless a being as I am. I had indeed business with
Mr. Addingreve; and missing him, as the affair was of importance to
my mother, I ventured to solicit an audience of Sir Audley Dacres. I
hoped he might have obliged me, even without the intervention of his
steward; but he has refused me.—Perhaps my intrusion was wrong:
but when my mother and my sisters are in question, I press forward
without regard to consequences; nor is it indeed always in my power

to forget, that the distance was formerly not so great between me and those from whom it is now my abject fortune to solicit favours—and forbearance."

A deep and indignant sigh, which he yet wished to suppress, burst from the heart of Marchmont, as he finished this sentence. At the word *forbearance,* Althea was struck with an idea that the family of Marchmont was somehow indebted to her father—and she was at once shocked and mortified to think he was an inexorable creditor.

After pausing a moment, Althea said in a low voice—"I lament, Sir, a circumstance which seems to give you pain; I lament it the more, because I have not the least influence with my father, and dare not venture to speak to him on business. I should hope, however, if it were known to Lady Dacres, that your request, relating to the accommodation of your mother, might, through her Ladyship's intercession, be listened to."

"Ah! Miss Dacres," replied Marchmont with increased emotion, "that ingenuous countenance is an index to a mind as ingenuous, to a heart which, generously feeling for the unhappy, believes that others are equally tender and considerate.—Lady Dacres, who, as co-heiress of the late Sir Ralph Gunston, became entitled to the mortgages my father had made on his estates in Devonshire, and others, has directed those mortgages to be foreclosed; and her Ladyship's agents have been some time in possession of Eastwoodleigh, a very ancient house of my ancestors, but which indeed the embarrassed state of my poor father's affairs has not allowed us to reside at since his death. Of this proceeding I have no right to complain—it was but just, and I submit without murmuring; but as Lady Dacres's property is for the greater part secure and out of question, I had hoped that Sir Audley would have allowed my mother and my sisters to have remained, during this winter, at the small house which was also mortgaged to Sir Ralph, near Dorking in Surry. This was the request I had to make—the request that I have been refused! —I should not however have made it," continued he, "but that my mother is in a sad state of health; and I fear"—(the tears, in despite of his endeavours to repress them, filled his eyes)—"I fear that the comforts of such an abode as I can now procure for her will be so inadequate to what her present state demands, that the consequence of her removal will be such as I tremble to think of."—"Gracious Heaven!" exclaimed Althea, "and is it possible Sir Audley and Lady Dacres can have the cruelty to deny you so small a favour? What reason can be alleged for refusing what surely it would give any human being pleasure to grant?"

"The reason," answered Marchmont dejectedly, "is, that a friend of Sir Audley's, who lives in that neighbourhood, has offered to take a very long lease of the house, to give a great rent, for it, and to make I know not what alterations and improvements. With this proposal your father has closed; and the intended tenant, who is some man of fortune and high in the law, has already sent down surveyors to examine the house.—As the season is now approaching when nothing can be done, I hoped the indulgence I asked might have been obtained for my poor mother—I now repent that I have made the attempt—But I forget myself strangely—Miss Dacres," continued Marchmont, observing that Althea was extremely affected, "I have no right in the world to intrude upon you, and indeed I hardly know how I have been betrayed into it. I beg your pardon, and will detain you no longer."

"Do not, however, go, Mr. Marchmont," said Althea eagerly; "do not go till I know whether you think there is not some means by which I may be of use to your mother."—The mention of a lawyer from London as the future tenant of the house made her think of Mohun— to whom it was highly probable it was promised; and though his name was hateful to her, she felt at this moment as if she could almost ask a favour even of *him* to relieve Marchmont from the anguish which seemed to oppress his heart. From such an experiment, however, her heart recoiled; but still she could not bear to relinquish wholly the hope of serving a family for whom she felt herself unusually interested.

While Althea silently debated this with herself, Marchmont gazed at her without the power of answering her question. At length he said—"I cannot again solicit —I have been degraded too much by it already; neither can I ask you, Miss Dacres, to undertake for me a task so painful to a generous mind, because it would probably be so fruitless. I am sorry, indeed I am, that my accidentally meeting you here has given to such a mind the pain of hearing of distress it cannot relieve. May guardian angels watch over your happiness, Madam—and may Heaven reward your humane and generous wishes!"—At this moment the park-gate, from which they were not far distant, shut with considerable noise, and the approach of some persons was announced by voices, and whistling to dogs.—Althea hardly knowing why, nor venturing to ask herself, was yet conscious that she would not be seen talking to Marchmont; and Marchmont, equally uneasy, made no effort to detain her; when springing suddenly from him, she opened the hunting-gate, and was in a moment rendered invisible by the thick underwood of the coppice; while Marchmont, leading his horse, slowly continued his way. Near the great gate of the park, Mohun and another gentleman, with their servants and dogs, passed him. The former stared at him, but noticed him not; and the unhappy young man, miserable every way, and feeling his misery increased by the tender admiration which this interview with Althea had created in his breast, reluctant and mournful, took the road to a neighbouring town, from whence he had hired his horse.

Marchmont was the only son of a gentleman who was heir to a very ancient family, and to such parts of their once great property as had not been dissipated or forfeited in the civil war which desolated England in the middle of the last century. Mr. Marchmont, the father, had entered life with a fortune of above three thousand a year, though it was *nominally* five. All the habits of his ancestors, their family ostentation, as well as their old hospitable customs, clung about him, and about his domains; on the principal of which was an old mansion-house that had been twice besieged by Cromwell's army, and rendered the scene of exploits on which hereditary honour or hereditary pride delighted to dwell. Mr. Marchmont could never endure the thought either of selling or letting this house, though he could not afford to repair, or to live in it with any degree of comfortable sufficiency for years before his death.

Could he have had the resolution, when he came to his estates, to have sold half of them to pay off the mortgages on the rest, he would have enjoyed, and have transmitted to his son, a handsome and competent fortune:—but, from the strange prejudices he had imbibed in his youth, he never could be persuaded to think so; and the mortgages (the interest of which his want of œconomy never allowed him regularly to pay) by degrees devoured the estates themselves. Mr. Marchmont married a very lovely woman without any fortune, by whom he had three daughters and an only son—a son who promised to do honour to the line on which the father's pride so anxiously rested. When therefore the opening merits of this beloved boy rendered the father still more anxious not to dismember his estates, he entered into projects to retrieve them, which unhappily failing, served only to precipitate the ruin of his family, and some public events accelerating this, Marchmont died of a broken heart a very short time before Althea had seen his son at Mr. Eversley's.—The younger Marchmont, to save his mother from the pressure of such inconveniences as immediately threatened her, made himself answerable for his father's debts; it was soon discovered that he had died insolvent; and thus, at the age of twenty three, his son found himself, without a profession, stripped of his paternal property, and not only liable to be pursued for debts he had no means of satisfying, but charged with the support of a mother, whose body and mind equally unfitted her to contend with adversity, and three sisters, whose beauty and helpless indigence rendered them the objects of his constant solicitude and anxiety.

The education of this young man had fitted him, in point of knowledge, for active life; yet his heart, unadulterated by his knowledge of the ways of men, was full of candour and generosity.

The same spirit of loyalty which had attached his more remote ancestors to the cause of monarchy under Charles the First, had devoted their successors to the party of his infatuated and unfortunate son James the Second; in consequence of which another considerable portion of their property had been lost; and a brother of Marchmont's grandfather settling in France, his descendants had there become naturalized: yet, continuing to remember his English origin, the Baron de Lavergnac (which was the name now assumed by the head of that branch of the family) had received his great nephew into his house, which was situated near Toulon, when his father, waving all false pride, had sent him to France with a view of placing him in trade. The increasing embarrassment of his father's affairs, and finally the Revolution, which threatened to put an end to all commercial projects, had occasioned his return to England about twelve months before he became acquainted with Althea.

CHAP. VII.

Ha!—Banishment?
It comes not ill—I hate not to be banished!

THIS CONFERENCE WITH Marchmont, though it had for awhile suspended those anxious thoughts with which Althea had begun her walk, now served only to shew her that there were others even more miserable than herself, and that the very persons who threatened to be the causes of her lasting unhappiness, unfeelingly added to the weight of sorrow that oppressed a man who appeared to deserve a better fate. A comparison could hardly fail to be made between this man and the fortunate, arrogant, eloquent Mohun—but how little to the advantage of the latter! Not merely because she thought one was the handsomest, and the other the ugliest of their species (for Althea did not allow herself to believe that personal beauty had any influence whatever on her mind), but, in proportion as the character of Marchmont appeared amiable and excellent, Mohun rose as a fiend destined to persecute her, and to oppress him; and if any thing could have been added to strengthen her resolution of suffering every extremity rather than become his wife, this new acquaintance was exactly calculated for the purpose.

Her fortitude was soon to be put to a severe trial. Sir Audley still feared that the disdainful and positive manner in which he thought Althea would repulse Mohun, might put an end at once to a plan which he had every hour more and more at heart: Lady Dacres participated his fears, and determined at every event to disengage herself from the necessity of taking to town with her a daughter-in-law whom she so much disliked. They determined to speak separately to Althea, before Mohun's audience. The one was to soothe, the other to threaten; and if these methods failed to induce her to give Mohun a patient hearing, they were then jointly to declare that she must either determine to go to London the wife of Mr. Mohun, or remain in the country—not at Capelstoke as the daughter of Sir Audley Dacres, but to board in some cheap retirement, and live on the interest of the small sum her aunt had left her.

It seemed, in the opinion of Lady Dacres, impossible but that, when these two lots were set before her, Althea must choose that which would secure to her affluence and elegance, in preference to obscurity and a bare subsistence. So Lady Dacres would have acted herself, so would have acted all the women of her acquaintance; and it therefore never entered her head, that Althea could make any other election.

Sir Audley, after he had settled this matter with his wife, and was proceeding to the conversation he had agreed to hold with his daughter, felt something very like a qualm of conscience, which reproached him for the part he was acting. He could not entirely stifle the recollection of what he had himself been, when, at a more advanced age than Althea's, he sacrificed every prospect of fortune, and braved every opposition from his friends, to marry her mother. He reasoned, or rather subdued this impertinent sensation by reflecting, first, that Althea had no predilection in favour of any other person—secondly, that she was too young to have any judgement as to what would make her happy—and lastly, that when, in consulting the peace of his family, he included a plan so evidently advantageous, to hesitate about enforcing it would be injurious both to her and to himself.—As to Lady Dacres, she was so little accustomed to trouble herself about the feelings of others, when the gratifying herself was in question, that she never thought about the cruelty of compelling Althea to make herself a wretch for life, when her caprice and ill humour were to be spared having before them an object whose merit she could not but internally acknowledge; although she hated her as the rival of her children, and as one who claimed, on too just grounds, a share of her husband's affection.—The characters of women in general have been said to be nothing—

"Matter too soft a lasting form to bear."

Perhaps very young women have no striking traits of character to distinguish them, till some circumstance in their lives either calls forth their understanding, or decides that they have none.—What appears discriminating, like the colours of cultivated flowers, is often an accidental variety; the shades and tints are different, the species remains the same. It has been said that Shakespeare, the great delineator of human character, has failed in distinguishing his principal women—and that such as he meant to be amiable are all equally gentle and good. How difficult then is it for a novelist to give to one of his heroines any very marked feature which shall not disfigure her! Too much reason and self-command destroy the interest we take in her distresses. It has been even observed, that Clarissa is so equal to every trial as to diminish our pity. Other virtues than gentleness, pity, filial obedience, or faithful attachment, hardly belong to the sex, and are certainly called forth only by unusual occurrences. Such was undoubtedly the lot of Althea, and they formed her character; for in the hard school of adversity she acquired that fortitude and strength of mind which gave energy to an understanding, naturally of the first class.

It now enabled her to resist alike the unjust commands of her father, the artful cajoleries of Lady Dacres, and the long lectures of Lady Barbara. For the first, she would have made any other sacrifice but this—which her reason told her he had no right to ask.

When, after two days, her resolution remained unshaken, another consultation was held, and another expedient devised, which Lady Dacres thought she could successfully manage herself.

Althea therefore was sent for, on the following morning, at an earlier hour than Lady Dacres usually admitted any body into her dressing-room. She was alone, and seemed desirous that Althea should remark that she had been in tears. Althea knew that, among all her mother-in-law's virtues, sincerity was not the most eminent. She had remarked, that when Lady Dacres had any point to carry she could produce tears as easily as remonstrances, and it required all Althea's candour to believe that she could shed unaffected tears over the victim whom she was thus voluntarily endeavouring to sacrifice.

Preparing, however, to hear her with great calmness, Althea sat silent, till, after some deep sighs, and sundry applications of her hand-kerchief to her eyes. Lady Dacres thus began —

"I know not, my dear Miss Dacres, whether, as I fear you are not free from the too common prejudices against mothers-in-law—I know not, I say, whether what I am going to tell you may be well received, but I am sure that I could not feel more concern were one of my own children in question."

Althea, by a slight motion of her head, seemed to signify that she was obliged to her; but remaining silent, Lady Dacres proceeded:

"I have been trying to persuade Sir Audley to recede from his resolution of insisting on your immediate answer as to Mr. Mohun. I have been almost imploring him on my knees to consider that our likings and aversions are not always under the control of our reason—and I have taken upon me to answer for you, Miss Dacres, that if he will give you a little more time, if he will only allow the merits of Mr. Mohun to be more known to you, you will see his proposals in a very different light."

"I am sorry your Ladyship *has* done so," said Althea with more courage than she had ever exerted before, "because I can never release you from the engagement you have thus made in my behalf, being well assured, that the more I know of Mr. Mohun the more my aversion to him will be confirmed."

"Well, Miss Dacres," replied the lady, "since you are so peremptory, all that remains for me is the very disagreeable task of communicating a resolution, from which I heartily wish you may have influence enough to divert Sir Audley—for I, alas! lament that I have tried in vain to do it."

"I am prepared, Madam," said Althea, "for whatever rigour my father chooses to inflict; and howsoever it may be his pleasure to punish me, I shall only be grieved at his anger, and on his account alone deplore his unkindness."

"Since you think of the matter so philosophically, Madam," resumed the lady, visibly piqued, "I may venture to tell you, that my most earnest persuasions cannot prevail on Sir Audley to let you even remain in this house when we quit it; he declares, that your refusal to accept such an offer—an offer so unexceptionable, so proper, so agreeable to him—dissolves, in his opinion, every other duty beyond that of affording you a bare maintenance, and far removed from him—since, were you to inhabit this house, you would still appear to have more of his consideration than, in his opinion, you deserve."

"I believe, Madam, I heard this before. Mere place is to me a matter of perfect indifference. Since death has deprived me of my only friend, and of the comfortable and cheerful home her kindness afforded me, I assure your Ladyship that I have no choice between the house of Capelstoke and the habitation of the humblest labourer on its domain."

"As you please, Miss Dacres; but I do not imagine it is Sir Audley's intention that you should reside on any of the estates to which he occasionally goes."

"I am certainly at my father's disposal, Madam, as to a place of residence."

"He objects, too, to a country town. He thinks you may there be liable to make improper acquaintance."

"I have never yet sought such, Madam: but indeed I have not yet been in the unprotected state into which it is now my father's pleasure to throw me."

"I really think, Miss Dacres, it would be as proper were you not to condemn your father. You disclaim his care—you throw off his protection."

The tender recollection of Mrs. Trevyllian had so nearly overcome the present fortitude of Althea, that she dared not trust her voice with any reply; and Lady Dacres, finding her silent, proceeded with additional solemnity:

"Sir Audley, justly incensed as he is, is yet unwilling to expose you to the acquaintance of the sort of people who live on narrow incomes in petty towns: besides, he knows no town, however obscure and inconsiderable, where you could in any creditable way lodge and board on so very small an income as yours; to which, I am truly concerned to say, he refuses, notwithstanding all my persuasions, to make any addition."

Althea looked incredulous as to her persuasions, and began to wonder whither all this preamble tended, unless it were to terrify her with the idea of an Italian or Spanish convent: those of France and Flanders were no longer open.—This, however, was a menace which brought no terror with it. Without any local attachment, without any friend whom she particularly wished to be near, she had not the least repugnance either to change of place or country, or to renounce the little portion of liberty she could in her present situation enjoy.

She waited therefore, without any visible emotion, for the farther explanation of a plan which, it was very evident, was opened with so much ceremony only to alarm her with the prospect of some mode of life to which it was supposed she would never have courage to submit. Lady Dacres thus proceeded:

"A mortgage my late father Sir Ralph had in Devonshire, near the sea coast, has been some time foreclosed, and, in my right, Sir Audley is become possessed of an old mansion-house belonging to that unfortunate family, the Marchmonts; by whom, after all, we are likely to be great losers."—At the name of Marchmont Althea blushed deeply: yet she knew not why she blushed, nor why she listened with trembling anxiety for what was to follow.

"You remember," continued the lady, "a house-keeper who lived in the family before I became Sir Audley's wife: she married Wansford, the butler, who had been his valet, and was afterwards much in trust with him."

Althea perfectly recollected this person, who had been her mother's maid, and had, with her husband, been dismissed by the present Lady Dacres for no other reason, as was then believed, but because they were too much attached to the memory of their first mistress.

"Sir Audley," added Lady Dacres, "who was really at that time enough to spoil the best servants in the world, had indulged these two people till they were unfit for their stations: he obliged me by dismissing them, but he stocked a farm for them, and they went on for some years well enough. I don't know, however, how they contrived it, they laid up nothing; indeed their family was large, and Wansford lost money by a brother for whom he was bound—and last year, by endeavouring to save some cattle in the marshes, he caught cold, and lost the use of his limbs: so that, as every thing was going to ruin on the farm, Addingreve advised Sir Audley to take it into his own hands; and this house at Eastwoodleigh being just then delivered up to us, Wansford and his wife were sent to look after it. I really believe, from the account I have had of it, that the wisest thing Sir Audley could do would be to pull it down, and sell the materials: but he says that they will not even pay the expence, since in that country nobody would purchase them. However, till he can determine what to do with it, these people live in that part of it which is habitable; but a great deal of it, I am told, is a mere heap of ruins. Sir Audley, I assure you Miss Dacres, has talked very seriously of your going thither to reside, nor have I yet been able to dissuade him from it."

"I thank you for your endeavours, Madam," said Althea coldly, "since I dare say they were kindly meant; but should my father be pleased to renew the conversation, I shall be obliged to your Ladyship to inform him that I have not the least objection to the plan—and will prepare myself to depart whenever he pleases to send me from him."

"Upon my word, Miss Dacres! You have then no dread of being shut up in this remote and gloomy old mansion, and being buried in such an obscure solitude?"

"I never had the least fear of solitude—and I declare to you, Madam, that had my father the power and the will to banish me to Siberia, I would cheerfully go thither, rather than marry Mr. Mohun."

"Young ladies in love," said Lady Dacres, sneeringly, "and great readers of romances, have, I know, these violent flights."

"But I assure your Ladyship," replied Althea, resuming all the courage she had mustered at the beginning of the dialogue, "that I am neither the one nor the other; yet I most willingly accept what my father proposes, and have no favour whatever to ask of him, but that he will allow me, since I have now made my election, to be released for ever from all persecution about Mr. Mohun, and that he will not part with me in anger."

"Indeed I cannot answer for that —I am sure that he will not be pleased." And as she said this, Lady Dacres sufficiently expressed by her countenance how little she was so herself.

"I suppose there is hardly a tolerable apartment in this horrid old place," continued she.—"It will be some expence, I dare say, to keep out the wind and water. The ridiculous vanity of those Marchmonts made them persist in keeping of it, because I don't know what strange things happened there in the civil wars.—But never were such a set of proud beggars! Notwithstanding they had two or three executions, which deprived them of every thing but lumber which was not worth their carrying away, old Marchmont was absurd enough to betake him to one corner of the house, and thought, I suppose, that some of his ancestors, who the country people say still walk there, would be kind enough to discover to this poor descendant some of the money and jewels which they had concealed in their troubles. But the dead were no civiler to him than the living; not a ghost rummaged out a guinea for him—nor any thing else, unless it was an old-fashioned gold watch, that was found at the root of a great walnut-tree that grew in the court-yard—and this circumstance made the foolish people believe more than ever that there was treasure hid about the house. So that, when first our people took possession of it, Sir Audley was forced to huff them out of the folly of passing their time in pulling down the old wainscoting, and digging wherever their silly fancy made them suppose there was any thing hid. But nothing was ever found afterwards—not even a rat or a mouse; for the Marchmonts were latterly so poor, that the very residents of the wainscots had been starved out. Wansford, however, complains bitterly that they have returned now to their old quarters, so that he is half devoured with them; and that they make such intolerable noises in this great old rambling ruin of a house, that his wife and children are sometimes quite scared by them."

Althea felt, with all the contempt it deserved, that this account, though given in a careless way, was yet meant to impress on her mind such an idea of the place as might make her afraid of going to it, and compel her, through terror, to adopt any expedient that might release her from the dread of passing her life in so dreary an abode.—She answered therefore dryly, that as she had no fears herself, she should not be an unwelcome addition to these poor timid people.—"I am glad," added she, "Wansford's children are there—a house is always cheerful where one hears the voices of children—and as I shall have but little else to do, I will assist their poor mother in working for them."

Lady Dacres now found she had entirely missed her aim, at least so far as it was intended to obtain concessions from Althea in favour of Mohun's pretensions. On the other hand, as she was determined at all events to get rid of her, she was rejoiced to find she had now a fair opportunity of sending her with her own consent to a place where her influence over Sir Audley would be no more dreaded. Lady Dacres often fancied he loved her better than he dared avow, and sometimes believed he traced in her features the resemblance of her mother, which she could not think of with patience.—Her business now was to aggravate Sir Audley by her report, and make him persist in the sentence of banishment: and this she prepared to do the same day; while Althea, feeling an unaccountable satisfaction in a plan which was intended to affect her so differently, feared nothing but that her father might be diverted from it; and studied only how to avoid any particular conversation with Mohun, till the day which was to deliver her from his persecution, though the alternative was a residence, perhaps for life, in dreary solitude and perfect seclusion.

CHAP. VIII.

If weak the pleasure that from these can spring,
The fear to want them is as weak a thing.

WHEN RETURNED TO her room, Althea began to reflect on what had just passed. She saw that there was a determined plan, of which Lady Dacres was the principal contriver, to terrify her into an immediate marriage with Mohun; or, if that did not succeed, to make her refusal a pretence for dismissing her from a residence in her father's family, which, though less satisfactory to Sir Audley himself, would be the next most desirable circumstance to Lady Dacres.

Far, however, from shrinking from the dreary prospect which had been held out to her, she considered it till it became in her opinion eligible. The common comforts and necessaries of life she doubted not but that her father would order her to be supplied with; and in renouncing society so little to her taste as that she had hitherto seen, either in London or at Capelstoke, she thought there was nothing to regret. "How," said she, as she recollected the figures which had passed before her like the distorted and tawdry images exhibited by a magic lanthorn, "how is it to be regretted, that I shall no more be insult-ed by the pride and self-consequence of the Miss Newmarches; or that I am relieved from the formal pedantry and prudish malignity of their insufferable aunt? However rustic the manners, or uncultivated the minds, of the people among whom I may be thrown, it is impossible the grossest ignorance can be half so offensive as the insolent misconduct of Mrs. Polwarth, who seems to glory in shewing how far the affluence and political servility of her husband can bear her out, when she ventures to violate all the common rules of behaviour in civil society. How can I help rejoicing at being released from the necessity of hearing perpetual harangues upon county politics, or the minuter squabbles of contending interests in a paltry country village called a borough, where every malignant passion of the human heart is called into activity, and the baseness of the contending characters is not hid by the greatness of the object for which they contend, as it sometimes is in higher ranks of life? At this solitary house, whither I am to be sent, I shall hear no more orations from Mr. Mohun, the great dictator of the party that frequents my father's table in London. No more of his axioms in politics will offend the feelings of common honesty and plain sense—nor his moral decisions set decency and humanity at defiance. If these graver personages will never be thought of but that I may rejoice I shall see them no more, little otherwise shall I feel in remembering the insipid and wearisome sameness of the tables where I used to be placed, with giggling misses enjoying their own little jokes amidst a general eagerness for the pool.—No: there is not one scene in which I was engaged either last winter or since my luckless destiny has brought me to Capelstoke, not one party that I recollect with pleasure, or in which I ever wish to make one again. But if Lady Dacres's house offered, together with all the elegances and luxuries of life, society I enjoyed, and even friends I loved, it would be impossible to lament quitting it, when those advantages are to be purchased only by being continually subjected to the arrogant pretensions of Mohun, who seems thoroughly persuaded that his political consequence, his legal celebrity, and his increasing fortune, give him a right to disregard and insult the feelings of the rest of the world. If then I shall rejoice at quitting the circle that surround my father, and cannot conciliate his favour by remaining in it, I shall surely accommodate my mind to any situation, however lonely, without casting one lingering look back on what I leave, or feeling any dread lest the recollection of them should embitter one of my solitary moments.

"The intent of such an education as my beloved and lamented instructress gave me, was less to qualify me to shine in the world than to teach me to resign it. Wherever I may be, I shall find some place where I may deposit and enjoy the books she left me—where I can once more sit among them, recollect those she most delighted in, and strengthen my failing fortitude by mediating on the passages marked by her hand. There I shall still seem to hear her advice—she will once more seem to superintend my actions —I shall meet her benign spirit in my lonely walks, and I shall at least wander at liberty over a country to which the returning spring will restore many of those objects which she taught me to contemplate with so much pleasure.—A place, which to Lady Dacres would appear desolate and hideous, will probably to me seem beautiful and romantic; for objects certainly offer themselves to her and to me in very different lights. Some degree of pleasure, though of a melancholy kind, I may perhaps derive from tracing, among the ruins of the deserted mansion, memorials of its former possessors; veneration for the unfortunate loyalist of the last century will mingle with the pity I feel for their unhappy descendants; and as the Marchmont family are probably well known where they have resided so long, my abode there may perhaps afford me the means of being useful to the ladies of a family for whom it is impossible to help feeling particular interest." The thought with which this soliloquy of Althea concluded, was one which had often recurred to her since she had heard that the long-deserted mansion of the Marchmonts was to be her abode. Hardly conscious of it herself, the unfortunate heir of that family had made an impression on her mind; though she would have started had she been told that she thought with particular favour of a young man whom she had seen only twice: yet imperceptibly his idea became continually present to her, while she fancied she was trying to reconcile her mind to the situation she was going to.

However uneasy Althea felt at the impossibility of obeying her father, yet now that she had come to a final resolution, and knew the worst that was to happen, she felt her spirits relieved; and believing herself sure of escaping from the persecution of Mohun, she came down, after her conference with Lady Dacres, with a composed if not a cheerful countenance.

Sir Audley appeared unusually gloomy, and it was evident that something had extremely disturbed him. Lady Dacres affected that mild resignation to his will, of which she knew perfectly well how to assume the semblance. Lady Barbara was severe and sententious; and her two nieces, who had long since ceased to trouble themselves about Althea, (whom they considered as a person quite out of their way) were busied in making remarks on their company; which was, however, very little calculated to amuse them, unless as it afforded food for satire. It consisted, besides the usual company in the house, of a miscellaneous group—officers from the neighbouring barracks; attornies from the next borough; esquires of moderate fortune, who were not rich enough to perform an annual visit to London; and what are not improperly termed Squiriferous Parsons, young men in orders, who shoot, hunt, attend races and cricket matches, and *"but on Sunday hear no bells."*

As the military men who this day attended Sir Audley's table happened to be an old adjutant, and two Scottish subalterns who were without fortune or pretensions, there was not any object in the whole assemblage on whom the Miss Newmarches condescended to look with the slightest degree of favour, or whom they deigned even to speak to with civility. The men of law, and the men of the church, they considered and called Hottentots, Vandals, and Caribs: and the awkward attempts at elegant gallantry, which some of them made, were to these ladies sources of merriment, which they took very little trouble to disguise. Althea looked at the circle with very different sentiments—she had never been accustomed to consider every single man according to his fortune, or to ridicule those of inferior description because they had none. But, her mind thus totally disengaged, she listened without restraint to the "infinite deal of nothing" which was talked; she again congratulated herself that she should so soon enjoy her simple repast in the silent solitude of Eastwoodleigh.

Mohun had a rude and insolent manner of staring, which was cruelly distressing to Althea; and she never felt it more so than now, when, as she was placed near her father at the bottom of the table, Mohun had contrived to place himself exactly opposite to her. To escape as much as possible from meeting his eyes, she busied herself in little civilities to the persons near her; and soon by her easy and interesting manners, mingled with so much condescending sweetness, attracted the particular attention of the old soldier, who himself, the father of a family, thought, he might without any indecorum, express the respectful admiration with which Althea inspired him: but while she conversed with him on such topics as the desultory dialogue of a table allowed, her ears were suddenly struck by the name of Marchmont repeatedly uttered with great earnestness between her father and Mohun. Amid the murmurs of a large company, and the rattling of knives, forks, and plates, she could only now and then catch a word of their discourse—but she collected that they agreed in severely blaming young Marchmont for some step he had lately taken, of which they appeared to have received information from a grim-visaged figure sitting between them.—This tiger-looking man, who was, as she soon discovered, an Attorney, had a piercing sharp voice, and a snapping manner of speaking, which conveyed what he said distinctly, though disagreeably, to the ear. The following sentence therefore could not be mistaken:

"Why yes, Sir—Yes!—your remark is perfectly just, Sir—perfectly just indeed.—True, Sir Audley, true!—As you say, Sir Audley, there are people so wrong—headed, and so—so—so—in short, so conceitedly bewitched to their own opinion, that they never do themselves good. Sir Audley; and this young man, to be sure, is one of that sort. Yes, yes, he is to be sure an unhappy obstinate young fellow, Sir Audley. That, none of his friends can pretend for to deny—nor the friends of his family neither."

"As to friends," said Mohun with a malicious laugh, "I never heard he had any; and for those of his father, the old man dispensed them all long before his death, by attempting to borrow money of them which he knew he could never repay."

"And with some," said Sir Audley sternly, "he succeeded but too well.—I am told that Mr. Eversley has found sufficient reason to repent of his imprudent loans to him."

The Attorney, Mr. Lumbard, looked very significantly, and replied—"Why, Sir, as to that—Mr. Eversley, Sir Audley, is no client of mine —I know but little of his affairs. His wife, to be sure, had a capital fortune; but then he has laid out a great deal of money, and made very expensive improvements—and then his lady, it seems, has been in a *deal* of alarm, upon account of this here affair of Mr. Marchmont; for they say that upon the *upshot* it appears. Sir Audley, that he was deeper in for it with old Marchmont than any body thought for. I am sorry for it; for Mr. Eversley has the name of being a good sort of man: and as to any hope of the Marchmonts' affairs being settled and made up so that the creditors may have their own, and the like, why, bless my soul! it is a matter quite out of the question—for where, Sir Audley Dacres, I say, where is it to come from?"

"Where indeed!" answered Sir Audley: "and therefore, Mr. Lumbard, we will unalterably abide by the resolution which I mentioned to you before dinner; and Mr. Marchmont must be positively given to understand, that ..." The conversation was now carried on in a lower tone; and Althea could only distinguish that it was inimical to poor Marchmont, whose poverty, however incurred, seemed in the opinion of all these gentlemen to be a crime, which should throw him at a distance from all human society.—The ladies soon after leaving the eating-room, Althea escaped to her own, where she found herself in a disposition to shed tears for the fate of this unfortunate stranger—tears which her own distresses had not lately drawn from her. His animated countenance and handsome figure undoubtedly added considerably to the interest with which Althea dwelt on the particulars of their last, indeed their only conversation; for when she had seen him with Mr. Eversley she had hardly spoken to him.—The fortitude he seemed to exert in a situation so different from that wherein he had been born, the tenderness with which he spoke of his mother and his sisters, and the noble resolution he shewed in sacrificing, to the hope of being serviceable to them, his own feelings, acute as they certainly were, could hardly fail of recommending him to such a heart as inhabited the bosom of Althea.—Of all the men she had ever been acquainted with, he seemed the most deserving; yet unwilling to acknowledge, even to herself, how frequently she thought of him, she endeavoured to persuade herself that it was his virtues and his misfortunes alone that had awakened these lively emotions in her mind, and that any other person, equally meritorious and equally unhappy, would be as often the subject of her thoughts.

Thus palliating anxiety, for which no apology would have been necessary, had she not suspected her own heart, a day or two passed without her hearing any thing more of her departure, though preparations were making for the return of the family to London. Lady Barbara and her nieces had left Capelstoke, and the departure of Mohun had been named as soon to take place. He made, however, no attempt to speak to her alone—and seemed to see with pride and resentment that she avoided giving him any opportunity to do so.—He now again affected an air of haughty disdain; which Althea rejoiced to see, and began to flatter herself that, by his desisting from his odious pretensions, the hazard of incurring her father's anger would be at an end. But she entirely mistook the motives of his conduct. Reluctant as he knew her to be, and mortified as his pride was to know it, he yet had so great an inclination for her person, that he by no means relinquished the designs which he had begun to form the preceding spring. He had so thorough a contempt for the understandings of women, that he thought her mind not worth conciliating; a girl who could not know her own wishes, or be any judge of his merit, was too insignificant to give him the trouble of an assiduous courtship; and he remained satisfied, as she had no other prepossession, that her father's commands were sufficient to compel her to consent to be his wife; after which he trusted to his own superiority of intellect, and the authority he should then have, to make her all he wished to see her—for he now, contrary to the custom of other lovers, found a thousand faults with her, and continually told Lady Dacres what a pity it was she had received so strange an education, and how much forming she would require when she first entered the world.

To this gothic education, and the romantic and uncouth ideas which he believed she had imbibed under a formal old maiden aunt, he imputed much of her reserved and cold manner; but as he had come to a perfect understanding with Sir Audley, he began to think it time for him to speak more decidedly to the object of what he was pleased to call his love. The moment this happened, Lady Dacres knew an explanation would take place which would destroy every chance of Althea's being disposed of to Mr. Mohun—and Sir Audley, who had the same apprehension, was willing to make use of every art, before he put all his hopes on the issue of a conference between Mohun and Althea. Both Sir Audley and Lady Dacres therefore had assisted her to avoid him, instead of throwing her in his way; but Sir Audley saw with anger and indignation that his scheme of terror had not only totally failed, but that Althea was even more cheerful than before she was acquainted with the species of imprisonment with which he designed to punish her refusal. As Mohun was to go in a few days to attend on the multiplicity of business that awaited him the ensuing term (which was now near its commencement), it was impossible to put off a final eclaircissement much longer, and Sir Audley saw that he must give up the hope of an alliance which he had more reasons for desiring to complete than even Lady Dacres was acquainted with.—Unable to command the rage and vexation which he felt when he reflected on the provoking obstinacy of Althea, he had not spoken to her for many days; but time now pressed—and Mohun desired to have assurances before he departed for London, that soon after the arrival of Sir Audley's family the marriage should be concluded.—Sir Audley was but too well convinced, that not even compulsion of the most violent nature, if it had been in his power to use it, could now bring this about. However, he determined to make one effort more.—He knew the timid temper of Althea when the happiness of any one she loved was in question; and though he could not in his conscience call himself a good father, yet that he was her father, he thought sufficient to give him such influence over her, as should make her yield to his entreaties the concessions she denied to his threats.

CHAP. IX.

Che ingiusto rigore!
Che fiero consiglio!
Scordarsi l'amore
D'una misera figlia
D'una figlia infelice
Che colpa non ha!

THE POOR PERSECUTED Althea therefore was summoned to another formidable conference. Sir Audley endeavoured to smooth his brow, and began rather by persuasion than authority.

He represented to her the smallness of the fortune to which she would be entitled even in case of his death—that she had, at present, only the interest of the small sum left her by her aunt Trevyllian.—"If you wilfully disoblige me, Althea," said he—"if you refuse a match so perfectly unexceptionable—if you fly from happiness, and embrace obscurity and ruin, how can you think that you will obtain any indulgence from me?—Can I suffer so bad an example to the rest of my family to go unpunished?—What should I expect—what should I deserve if I did?—That they too should despise my advice, and defy my authority"—"There is no danger, I hope, of that. Sir," said Althea in a tremulous voice. "The family of Lady Dacres have been accustomed to more splendid scenes of life than I have ever been among—it is fit they should follow such paths as lead to riches and honours; but why should *I* do so?—I, who am accustomed to obscurity and retirement, have no wish for splendour, and desire only of my dear father that he would not, for the sake of what cannot make me happy, compel me to marry a man who would inevitably render me miserable."

Sir Audley bit his lips, and threw down, in evident displeasure, a pen he had held in his hand: but making an effort to command himself, he was silent; and Althea, hoping that this might be her last conversation on so hateful a subject, acquired courage to proceed.

"Lady Dacres, Sir, has communicated to me your resolution as to my future manner of life—if I do not consent (which indeed I never can) to become the wife of Mr. Mohun. Dear Sir! believe your poor Althea, when she assures you, that the only wish she now forms is to be suffered to remain near you, and to shew you, by her attentive duty, how much, in every other instance but this, it is her desire, and it shall be her study, to oblige you."

"Cant not to *me*," cried Sir Audley in a loud and angry manner—"You cannot impose upon me, Althea Dacres, by this shallow hypocrisy. You say you have been apprized by my wife of the resolution I have taken. If you persist in rejecting my friend, I swear, by all that's sacred, that nothing upon earth shall ever make me recede from that resolution; and that, while I retain a father's just power over you, you never shall leave the place whither I have determined to send you, but as the wife of Mr. Mohun."

"Then, Sir," said Althea firmly, "I must prepare myself to die there. As long as my dear father lives, I shall never consider myself as exempted from his authority, even although the laws of my country may give me liberty to act without consulting him. But though I never will offend him by quitting the place he assigns me, wherever that may be, I never will sell myself to a man I abhor —I never will take an oath to love and honour a being I loath and detest."

"Your words are very strong, young lady," cried Sir Audley. "If such is *your* resolution, you know *mine*—but let me never hear the words duty or affection for me profaned by so worthless an hypocrite. Prepare yourself to leave this house in a few days—I have already indeed given directions for the old servant who lives at Eastwoodleigh to come hither for you, as I cannot spare any of mine or Lady Dacres's people. Perhaps she may be here to-morrow; but, be that as it may, you will remember, wretched infatuated girl! that when once you quit this house, I shall consider you no longer as my child."—Althea, now drowned in tears, and finding her courage begin to yield before her father's wrath, only said, with a deep sigh—"Ah! Sir, however cruel you may be to me, I shall still love and respect you.—Alas! if my *father* forsakes and casts me off, what other friend have I upon earth?" Then fancying that by the expression of his features he was a little softened in her favour, she ventured to throw herself upon her knees before him; and, taking his hand, she kissed it, as she sobbing said—"My father!—if I must go —I submit patiently to your disposal of me. Poor and deserted as I shall be, such a remote situation as Lady Dacres has described to me, may best become my desolate fortune. I only ask that my father will not part with me in anger, will not load me with his displeasure!"

The idea was terrible; and, her fortitude failing under it, she could articulate no more. Sir Audley, who was greatly affected, struggled against the emotions of his heart; and flattering himself that the dread of his anger might now operate on the soft mind of his daughter, and produce the change he so ardently wished in her resolution, he affected even greater anger than he felt, and, throwing himself from her, left her kneeling and weeping before the chair he had quitted. But when he reached the door he turned towards her; and sternly repeating his firm resolution that she should never quit the dreary solitude she was going to but as the wife of Mohun, he left the room, and the house—while Althea, absorbed in anguish, yet unshaken in her determination, continued to weep for some moments in the attitude her father had left her in; then recollecting how fruitless her tears were, and not without some apprehensions that Mohun might find her there, she tried to recover herself, and went to her own apartment.—As she passed by the window of the stair-case, she saw that Mohun had joined her father in the garden—and that they were in deep conference.—Her fate was now, she thought, decided; and when she looked at Mohun she could neither repent of her determination, nor of the courage with which she had sustained this last dreadful conflict—but rejoicing that it was over, and trusting to those remains of tenderness which she flattered herself would still prevent her father's driving his child from him in anger, she endeavoured to compose her mind, and prepare her few effects for a journey which she knew Lady Dacres would not suffer to be long delayed, and which she felt no reluctance to begin.

The party below were more affected than she was—for over their spirits those passions had painful influence, to which the innocent and unadulterated mind of Althea was a stranger. As to Mr. Mohun, *his* conscience never gave him much trouble: having been educated to plead as well against as for it, he seemed to think it a monitor which a man of sense might easily bribe to silence, if not entirely divest himself of the weakness of attending to it; though he thought it might be a bugbear very proper to terrify the vulgar, who could not be kept too much in awe. It was long since he had met with contradiction of any kind; for it was long since he had been rich, and accounted infallible. Born with a hard, selfish, and unfeeling heart, all the defects of his character had been aggravated by his professional success; arms have been proverbially said "to make bad men worse." The remark may with much more truth be applied to the law.

Attached to those whom he called his friends, only in proportion as they could serve his views, or promote his interest, he seemed to think he had a right to aggrandize or to gratify himself by every means, and by all means, not even regarding the opinion of the world, because he was certain that his abilities and his influence would always procure him outward respect, and he troubled himself very little to obtain private esteem. He had a sovereign contempt for the bulk of mankind, which might indeed be excused by the facility with which he saw they were imposed upon by custom, and enslaved by precedent. A libertine with regard to women, he thought the young and handsome highly honoured in being allowed to become objects of his notice and favour; and as to those who had (on whatever pretensions) acquired the name of sensible women, he vehemently declared them to be his aversion; and if ever he spoke of or to them, it was with no other design than to express his conviction of the futility of their understandings, and enforce the arrogant superiority of his own.

To such a man Althea's refusal must of course give all that indignant pain which is inflicted by mortified pride. Sir Audley knew, that if once he felt this acrimonious sensation in all its extent, it would be so insupportable, that the passion he now dignified with the name of love would probably be destroyed by it; and her father had so much hope, that the obstinate resistance of Althea would be conquered by a short probation in the melancholy seclusion of Eastwoodleigh, that he determined to try it before he acknowledged to the haughty suitor that his application must be wholly fruitless. Sir Audley, however, was not very dexterous in disguising a fact so obvious as Althea's aversion: in hopes, therefore, of Lady Dacres's managing it better, he left it to her, and betook himself to his own reflections. These were by no means pleasant. All the worldly sophistry he could call to his aid was insufficient to satisfy him that he was justified in treating his daughter so harshly. He endeavoured to persuade himself that, in compelling her to accept of an offer which was in point of fortune so advantageous,

he only consulted the good of his daughter; but his heart and his conscience gave the lie to his politics. Yet too obstinate to acknowledge
himself in the wrong, and so circumstanced in regard to his domestic
arrangements, that it was hardly possible for him to recede, he felt
pangs which he could not appease, and heard internal remonstrances
that he could not stifle. As to his wife, whose intellects, not originally strong, had been weakened by constant indulgence—she had very
few samples about requiring any sacrifice from others when her own
pleasure or convenience was to be consulted. Accustomed by the example of a purse-proud father, and the servile example of dependants,
to value every one according to their property or their rank, she had
insensibly acquired a habit of forgetting that those who had neither
were beings of the same species; while her respect for affluence had
reconciled her to the extravagant conduct of Mrs. Polwarth, though
she was herself a prude, and to the dull prosing harangues, and the
tedious medley of satire and science, which she eternally heard from
Lady Barbara—though she detested such sort of conversation, and
had no taste for any other society than that which was collected round
a card-table.

Every little narrow passion of this selfish woman was engaged
against poor Althea, whose beauty she saw universally admired—which
might render less striking that of her own daughters; and her avarice
still protested more vehemently against the expence which would be
incurred by Althea's appearing as Miss Dacres—an expence which the
slender income at present her own could by no means answer. The respect which the servants seemed disposed to pay her (for on them the
gentleness and reason which always appeared towards them could not
fail of having its influence) was a continual vexation to their proud and
stately mistress, who mistook haughtiness for dignity. But much more
mortifying was the suspicion that Sir Audley himself really loved his
daughter, and was restrained only by his fear of domestic contention
from expressing towards her the affection he felt.

Thus, if Sir Audley spoke to her, Lady Dacres fancied there was
particular tenderness in his voice; and she persuaded herself that she
had often caught him looking at Althea with mingled concern and
fondness, when he believed himself unobserved. To render this notion
still more uneasy, it occurred to her, that as Althea extremely resembled her mother, he was in these intervals of stolen indulgence tracing
in the countenance of her daughter the still regretted remembrance

of Althea Trevyllian; a suspicion which never failed to occasion tears, sullenness, and sometimes remonstrances: so that Sir Audley was harassed with complaints, importunities, and ill-humour; and whatever were his internal yearnings towards Althea, his peace obliged him to suppress them, since he found it impossible for her to live in the same house with his wife, without subjecting himself to the most painful contentions. However different had been the character of Sir Audley Dacres in more early life, he was now become a convert to those maxims, and had thoroughly adopted those measures, which lead to the possession of power and fortune. The portion he originally had of the latter was so small, that, after an indiscreet marriage of love, he owed his present flourishing circumstances entirely to his more prudent choice of a second wife, and on the advantages he derived from it all his prospects of power and place were founded. He possessed two boroughs in right of Lady Dacres: and having thus acquired a nomination of three voices, together with his own, in parliament, he of course became a man of consequence in the political world; and though he had yet no ostensible post, it was believed that he had ample compensation for the expences of the sort of open house he kept, as well in London as at Capelstoke, for the accommodation and resort of that party which adhered to the *existing powers* in administration. This arrangement, whatever it was, had the visible effect of engaging him to receive all sorts of people who could be made useful in the *existing circumstances*. No man's abilities in political wrangling were more highly in repute than those of Mr. Mohun; no point, therefore, was more solicitously pursued by Sir Audley, and his employers, than to attach him firmly to his party. He had, therefore, not only private but political reasons for wishing to unite him to his family, and to relinquish all hopes of effecting this was one of the severest mortifications he ever was exposed to.

Still unwilling however wholly to resign it, he endeavoured to prevent Mohun's being convinced of Althea's decided aversion, flattering himself that a very short abode at Eastwoodleigh would conquer this unfortunate obstinacy, and that she would consent to be restored to the comforts and pleasures of society on whatever conditions.

In the mean time Althea received a note from her father, which told her in very harsh terms that, after all that had passed, she could not be admitted to his presence. She was directed, therefore, to keep her room; where, on the following day, Mrs. Grimsby, the consequential and confidential housekeeper, herself attended with her dinner; when, probably in consequence of directions she had received, the portly gentlewoman (who was compared by Althea to Mrs. Heidelburgh acted by a stroller) thus began;

"Lord, Miss! I'm quite sorry indeed for this here sad affair —I declare it goes to my very heart to see my good lady in such affliction; and for certain nobody can be more *consarned* for *such famully* troubles than I am."

"I thank you for your concern. Madam," said Althea, coldly, "and am sorry to have been the cause of any affliction to your lady; but as I am going from hence immediately, the cause of her ladyship's affliction, and your concern, will fortunately be removed together."—"Why now that is the very thing. Miss," whined the housekeeper: " 'tis your going as 'twere in such a sad way! and to such a place too. —I declare, Miss, that from all I've heard about it, and Thomas Jackson, and Robert the helper, they have both on em been there; I declare, that tho' *misfortins* have obligated me to go to sarvis as a ouskeeper, I voud not go for to live there, no not though Sir Audley voud make me *presunt* of the land and ous, hout and hout; why, I should die with the unketness of the place."

"As I do not know what that is," said Althea, somewhat impatiently, "I trust it is not an evil with which I shall be greatly affected."

"Lord, Miss! why unketness means dull, and solintary, and molloncolly, and such-like. Besides, I've been told by them as knows that country parfitly well, that the famully as it last belong'd too was fairly drived out of the ous."

"They certainly were," said Althea with a sigh, "driven out of the house—but whether fairly, I rather doubt."

"Well, then, Miss—Bless me! only think, after that would you go to such a dismal kind of a place, and to live there, as one may say, all alone? Why, I purtest I'm all of a creep when I thinks of it."

"Do not think of it then, Mrs. Grimsby," said Aldiea, drily.

"Well, Miss, you know best perhaps; but for my share I own I can't but wonder, that such a fine young lady, and one who might have as 'twere all the world at her feet, should think of burying herself alive."

"It is my father's pleasure," said Althea; "and it is my duty to submit."

"Ah! dear, dear!" cried the housekeeper, shaking her curled head, "Sir Audley I'll be bound for it has no pleasure in it; and as for my lady, in all the time I have lived with her ladyship, I have never seen her ladyship so much cast down."

"And did your lady order you, Mrs. Grimsby, to say all this to me?"

"No, indeed. Ma'am; my lady never opened her lips with any such order.—But it is *impossabul* for good upper sarvants in such a *famully* as ours, not to know *summut* of what is going forward; and Mr. Addingreve and I have been athinking for some time what a sad thing it was; but we was in good hope that you would have thought better of it. For to be sure nobody could suppose, when it came to the *upshot,* that you would go for good and all to live among spirits and ghosts, for they say that it swarms with 'em."

"I have never seen any," said Althea with a smile, "nor heard of any body who has; and I like to make new acquaintance."

"Well, for my share," replied Mrs. Grimsby, "if I did make new acquaintance, I am sure it should be among flesh and blood. However, Miss Althea, I hope there is no harm done. Ma'am, in my just speaking; I am sure I could not mean no other than your good; and as the old man's wife that lives in the house came here about an hour ago to fetch you, I thought perhaps it *middent* be too late—though to be sure, as Counsellor Mohun is gone, it is likely that there is entirely an end of the matter."

"*Is* he gone?" said Althea, her eyes sparkling with pleasure; "is he really gone?"

"Lord, yes, Miss; I should hardly say so if he wasn't. I assure you he went away this morning, almost as soon as *brackfutst* was done, and I heard that all talk of your being to be the Counsellor's lady was over. I am sure I am sorry for it; for Mr. Addingreve says, that he is such a clever man, that there's not one of all the great lawyers to be compared to him; and that as sure as can be, those who live long enough will see him Lord High Chancellor of England."

"I wish he may," said Althea, "with all my heart; and I am really obliged to you, Mrs. Grimsby, for informing me that he is gone, and that Mrs. Wansford is come to fetch me. Perhaps you can tell me also what time my father has fixed for my departure from home?"

"Why, as to that. Ma'am, to be sure I did hear say, that the day after to-morrow was the very longest Sir Audley thought proper for your stay; but I was in hopes —"—"There is no occasion," interrupted Althea, "for any delay—My resolution will not change, nor will Sir Audley relent. I am ready, therefore, to set out *to-morrow* morning, if he directs it; for the child who is unworthy of being admitted to the presence of her father, cannot too soon relieve him by seeking the exile he condemns her to."

Althea said this in a way which evidently testified so much impatience, that Mrs. Grimsby, no longer hoping to make any impression, or to execute to any purpose the orders she had received from her lady, withdrew with "Dear, dear, dear! Alas! how sorry I am!" And Althea, who longed to see Mrs. Wansford, who had been so long the servant of her mother, ventured to write a request to Lady Dacres, that she might speak to her; and expressing her extreme concern for having incurred the displeasure of her father, she professed her readiness to obey his orders—only most earnestly entreated that he would not send her from him in anger—but that before she left his house he would see her, and forgive an involuntary fault—the only one he should, through life, have occasion to reproach her with.

The style in which this billet was written probably gave to Sir Audley and Lady Dacres some hope that she might yet be brought to their purpose, from the fear of offending her father beyond all hopes of forgiveness, for it produced the following answer:

"I am extremely sorry, dear Althea, that I cannot prevail on Sir Audley to see you on terms of affection before you go. But he is so irritated, that I dare no farther press it. He allows you to see Mrs. Wansford. Why am I under the very disagreeable necessity of adding, that he wishes you to set out with her to-morrow morning at a very early hour, unless you can determine to remain a member of our family on terms which are advantageous to yourself, and therefore so necessary to the happiness of your father? I am, dear Miss Dacres,

"Most truly yours,
Eliza Dacres."

To this Althea, with very little hesitation, answered:

"Since it will not be permitted me, dear Madam, to have the pleasure of speaking to you, nor the consolation of throwing myself at my father's feet, unless on conditions with which it is impossible for me ever to comply, I can only testify my submission to his will by acceding to the cruel alternative he has put before me. Be assured, Madam, that were the sacrifice of my life only in question, I would make it with pleasure: I would willingly die to oblige my father, but I cannot live miserably; I cannot become the wife of Mr. Mohun.

"I thank your ladyship for allowing me to see Mrs. Wansford; and will prepare for my departure with her to-morrow. Dear Lady Dacres, intercede with my father to send me his blessing and his forgiveness in writing, if he is indeed determined to drive me from him without allowing the consolation of one affectionate word to his unhappy Althea."

In a short time after having sent this billet, some person tapped at her door, and, on being bid to come in, Mrs. Wansford entered.

This old servant was so much changed since Althea had seen her six or seven years before, that she would hardly have known her. The troubles and disappointments which had so long pursued her, had changed her appearance more than time, and the heavy traces of care were deeply indented on her pale features. Althea, who loved her from recollection as the faithful attendant of her mother, now considered her as one who was to be almost her only friend. She received her with tears, which, however, she immediately repressed when she found the poor woman affected even to agony. It was some time before Althea could prevail on her to be more calm, and some time longer before Mrs. Wansford could be prevailed upon to believe that she consented even cheerfully to accompany her to Eastwoodleigh.

CHAP. X.

Strange things, the neighbours say, have happened here.

THE DESCRIPTION WHICH Mrs. Wansford gave Althea of her future abode was not very flattering.—"Ah! my dear young lady," said she with a deep sigh, "You who have always lived in so much comfort, and had all so pretty and genteel about you with your dear aunt, will find it, I am afraid, a sad hardship to live at such a place as Eastwoodleigh is now. To be sure in times past it was a house of great note, and they say that the greatest Lords in all that country did not afford such good house-keeping as there was at it; but, to my thinking, all that makes the dismal state it is now in, a great deal more sad—and indeed, dear Miss Althea, if I and my poor Wansford had not met with such losses in the world as he has done, so that we had no home for ourselves and our children—besides being so dependent on Sir Audley's good favour—we should have been very sorry indeed to have gone to such a place —"

"Oh! be not concerned, my good friend," replied Althea, "on my account, about the place —I suppose there are rooms that keep out

wind and weather—and in the day-time I can always amuse myself. I
intend to be schoolmistress to your little girls, for I am afraid you have
not much time to attend to them—it will serve to divert me, you know,
and will be doing them good."

"That is so like my late dear lady," interrupted the poor woman.—"Ah! Miss Dacres, how times are altered—I was going to say, in
this house!—But, however, it was not here, to be sure—nor yet in so
large nor so fine a place; but I question whether Sir Audley, if he was
to own the honest truth, has ever been so happy since."

"That is exactly," said Althea, willing to turn the discourse upon
her future abode, "exactly, Wansford, what I have been saying, or at
least meaning to say—that happiness does not depend so much upon
where we are, as upon the manner in which we employ ourselves."—
Mrs. Wansford answered only by shaking her head, as if to say, "You
are yet young, my dear lady"—But Althea, in no way discouraged by
the gloomy prospect held out to her, was oppressed only by the cruel
reflection that she should leave her father's house without being allowed to see him, and to express that affection which she really felt
for him.

One attempt more she determined to make, and therefore wrote
again to Lady Dacres, entreating her to intercede with Sir Audley that
he would see her before she went: but either this commission was
more than the lady had power to execute, or she feared that Sir Audley might be too much softened by his daughter's tears and distress;
for Althea received no other answer, than that she already knew her
father's determination, and that, though Lady Dacres was extremely
sorry to announce such unpleasant intelligence, she had found it impossible to prevail upon him to relax, in the smallest degree, from the
positive resolution he had taken.

To Mrs. Wansford it was at the same time signified, that it was Sir
Audley's pleasure she should be ready to depart as soon as it was light
the next morning—and with this cruel and peremptory order, Althea,
with a heart made more wretched by her father's anger than by any
apprehensions as to her future abode, prepared to comply.

Mrs. Wansford assisted in packing up her clothes, which were to
be sent after her; and Althea, looking round her present apartment,
where she had now passed near six weeks without having tasted one
moment's pleasure, found nothing to regret in leaving it, but the picture of her mother (before which she had so often shed tears), and the

little inlaid desk which had belonged to her. She wished that her father would have indulged her with these two memorials of her lost parent; they would have gratified her beyond any gift he could bestow. But she dared not venture to solicit for them; and with the earliest dawn of the morning she took leave of these inanimate objects, as if they had been two friends whom she was to see no more; and stepping, with streaming eyes and a half-broken heart, into the chaise which waited for her, bade a long, perhaps a last adieu to Capelstoke.

It was now the middle of November; and the dark and gloomy morning, heavy with fogs, which seemed to wrap every object in cold obscurity, was well suited to the beginning of such a journey, and to the disposition of mind in which poor Althea undertook it. As the chaise drove round the sweep to get into the high road through the park, it passed within sight of the windows of Sir Audley's apartment.—Althea looked up towards them, flattering herself that he would in some way notice her departure; but the shutters were closed. Her father was probably deep sunk in sleep, and thought not of his banished child. Cold and blank seemed every object to the desolate Althea; but this idea was the most cruel of any—and so severely did she suffer in believing that he thus cast her off, that it would have subdued the dread of any less irremediable misfortune than that of being the wife of Mohun. When, however, she reflected on the miserable fate that must then await her, her spirits became more composed; though still to be thus thrown from her father's arms, and rendered more destitute than an orphan, since he who should protect her became her persecutor, appeared so sad, that her heart sunk in despondence, and her eyes overflowed with tears.

The poor woman, her companion, naturally of a desponding temper, and sunk still more by misfortune and disappointment, sometimes wept with her, and sometimes made a successless attempt to console her.—Their melancholy journey was unmarked by any incident. They remained the first evening at Sidmouth, and the next morning, at an early hour, proceeded by Exeter to the place of their destination.

Between three and four in the evening they had reached an extensive common, which Mrs. Wansford told Althea had once belonged to Eastwoodleigh estate, and was not far from the house. The road, which was rough and much broken, led in an unfrequented track over the steep inequalities of the ground, covered with brown heath and tawny fern, with a few scattered thorns, and faint remains, in other

places, of neglected plantations—and through the gloom of an evening sky in November the sea, though not above a mile and a half
distant, was not to be distinguished.

From this waste they entered an enclosed ground between two
masses of broken wall, which were, Mrs. Wansford said, the remains
of a lodge once serving as an entrance to the park, the fields they were
now crossing being then the park itself.

Mrs. Wansford pointed out to Althea three or four doddered oaks
and pollard ash, venerable in decay.—"There," said she, "are the marks
of several bullets, and one may still see the great nails remaining which
fastened to it a square plate of lead. The shepherd boys have torn it
down to make the things they play with on the turf; but it once contained a sort of epitaph, or account of one of the family of Marchmont, who was killed near this place in the great rebellion—and those
holes in the trees were made by the same balls. They say that while
old Mr. Marchmont lived, he made a great point of the preservation
of those trees; and they were even spared when his necessities compelled him to cut down almost all the fine timber on his grounds. The
country people have a notion," added she, "that the young man who
was killed here appears near the place continually; and it is not an easy
matter to get the men that work about the farm to come by this way
of a night."—Althea, on whose ear the name of Marchmont never
fell unheeded, had attentively listened to this little narrative.—"I suppose," said she, when Mrs. Wansford ceased speaking, "that there are
a hundred stories of the same kind told about the house itself; for
Mrs. Grimsby, Lady Dacres's housekeeper, attempted to impress on
my mind I know not what fears of ghosts and hobgoblins."

"Ah! yes. Madam, there are strange stories enough, to be sure, told
of this place, as indeed there are about all such old lone houses in the
country—and certainly there are not many places more likely to give
such notions than Eastwoodleigh. But you may now judge for yourself.
Miss Dacres; there is the house before us."

"The house!" cried Althea—"Good Heavens! it seems like the ruins of an immense castle."

"Yes," replied Mrs. Wansford—"it is altogether very large still; yet
some parts of it are quite fallen, and others are grown over with grass
and ivy, having never been rebuilt since they were battered down in
the civil wars." Althea now looked earnestly towards the venerable pile
they were approaching; and her companion, suddenly ceasing her nar-

rative, exclaimed eagerly—"Ah! there are Lucy and Nanny: they hear the chaise, and are come out to meet me—and there is my poor Ned leading little Fanny"—The mother's heart thus flown out to meet her children, Althea was for a moment left to her reflections, while the chaise stopping, and the children approaching it, Mrs. Wansford asked them many questions about their father, who was, they said, so ill with the gout, that he could not come to help the lady out of the carriage, but that he had sent down to the farm-yard for one of the men. Althea, however, wanted no help, and entreated Mrs. Wansford not to mind her, but to attend to her children, who came round her, each with its little history of what had happened in her absence.

The good woman, with an apology for taking Althea into what might be called the kitchen end of the house, because what was properly the great door had not been opened for some time, now passed before to shew her the way—which was, except where the little communication of the house had worn a path, over-run with nettles and weeds, the growth of three or four summers, which had elapsed since the Marchmont family were driven from the dwelling.

This path led under a massy gateway, part of which was boarded up, into a court, round which the high and ponderous walls of the most entire part of the building frowned in mournful grandeur. By the uncertain light of evening, the buttresses, with long stone-framed windows between them, presented altogether such an image of a prison, that Althea shuddered as she went on. Through a large and high-vaulted passage, an old worn door let them into the room that served the present inhabitants for every purpose but sleeping. A screen of boards, which were put up to intercept the winds that gathered in these passages, prevented Althea's immediately seeing the poor invalid servant to whom Sir Audley here afforded an asylum.—His wife was already hanging over him with anxious solicitude, hearing how sadly helpless his lameness had made him in her absence, and how well his Nanny and Lucy had acquitted themselves in helping him, when Althea approaching, he tried to rise, and welcome her to Eastwoodleigh; but a sense of his own infirmities, and of the sad contrast between his situation now, as well as that of his young mistress since they last met, struck so forcibly on his mind, that, instead of speaking, he burst into tears. Althea, though her heart sunk heavily, spoke cheerfully to him; forbade him to attempt standing, and said she was glad to see him looking well, though he was so infirm.

"Ah! my dear young lady," said Wansford, "this is a sad place for you to come to: indeed I could never have thought his honour, Sir Audley, would have sent you hither!—But we will do the best we can for you—for both my poor woman and I would lay down our lives to serve you."

"I shall do well enough, my good friend," answered Althea—"be in no concern about me.—Come, I shall take possession of a chair by your fire.—Make no ceremony with me," continued she, perceiving that Wansford felt awkward at sitting before one on whom he had been used to wait; "I am not now your young lady, Wansford, but your lodger." The poor man, unwilling to trust his voice with an answer, remained silent; and Althea, but little disposed for conversation, surveyed the room where he sat.

It had once been a servant's hall, and was so large and high, that its termination and its ceiling were now alike obscure—for the only light in the room was from a fire of wood and peat in the chimney; a cavity of such dimensions, that it seemed able to contain a modern country villa, such as spring up in rows near London.—The great beams of darkened wood that surrounded it were coarsely carved, and in the centre were the arms of Marchmont—of little better workmanship: they had once been painted and gilt; but smoke and time had long since obliterated their lustre.—The stone pavement was broken in various places, and repaired with bricks; a great oak table, supported by legs which might well be called timber, was placed along two sides of the room, and served for depositing the various household utensils of the family.—Althea did not finish her survey without being sensible that, if the rest of the house corresponded with this part of it in dismalness and magnitude, it would require all the reason she possessed, and all the fortitude she had collected, to make up her mind to her destiny.

In a few moments Mrs. Wansford came, and saying that there was now a better room ready to receive her; that there was a good fire, and that her tea was ready; Althea, though she was really more disposed to remain where she was, followed her hostess, who did not, as she feared, lead her far from the general abode of the family; but merely along a passage which led by a carved door into a parlour—not very large in proportion to the hall she had left. One end of it was entirely occupied by an immense window; but there was a curtain of old-fashioned Decca work that drew round the lower part of it: the wainscot was in those little squares which are still not unfrequently seen in old-fashioned houses; and all along the side, opposite the chimney, seemed to be presses, though the wainscot was the same as the rest. An old plan of the estate and house painted on vellum, but almost effaced by time, hung over the fire; and in another part was a genealogical tree of the Marchmont family. Upon the whole, the appearance of this room, though far from being cheerful, was much less dismal than Althea expected. There was a lively fire, and candles on a small table near it. A clean country girl was waiting.—Althea observed that she looked at her as if greatly surprised to see her there.—Being dismissed, Althea desired Mrs. Wansford and her children to partake of her repast; while relieved from the apprehension of having been sent to a place even less comfortless than had been represented, she became easier, and once more looked forward without despondence.

That part of the house, however, which she was to go through to reach her bed-chamber was less flattering—so large was the gallery-like passage that led to the stairs she was to ascend, that she feared to carry her eye to the end of them. This stair-case, which was not the principal one, led to an apartment, which Mrs. Wansford assured her was one of the most comfortable in the house; it was, however, sufficiently large and gloomy, and the little furniture that was in it was a strange mixture of remnants of former magnificence, and the plainest articles in modern use, such as the common labourer would purchase: the gilding and carving in several parts of the room witnessed the expence that had once been lavished on it; but very common paper had now taken the place of the tapestry or damask hangings, and a piece of the former supplied the place of a carpet.

Althea surveyed the room with a look which Mrs. Wansford could not interpret into a look of approbation.—"I am afraid, my dearest Miss," said she, "that you think your accommodations very uncomfortable here: but I assure you it was the best I could do for you; and I have been contriving and contriving ever since I first heard of your coming hither, and whatever there was left about this unfortunate old place I collected together, and took the best of it for this room.—'Tis, to be sure, but poorly furnished still for you; and I am afraid you will find it dismal cold—but, however, your bed is aired, for I've made my two little girls lie upon it, and here has been a fire in the room these three or four days: I heartily wish, however, that things were better."

Althea, sorry to see the good woman thus concerned, endeavoured to appear less so herself—and assured her the room was even better than she expected.—"I have only one wish about it," said Althea; "I hope it is not at a very great distance from that where you and your husband sleep; for though I have in general no fears, it is impossible to tell what foolish fancies may enter one's head of a night in a strange place, and especially such a place as this. In almost every house there are noises either from wind or from vermin, which, when once a person is used to, or can account for, give no alarm—but to a stranger they are unpleasant; and if I should be made uncomfortable by them, I should not be sorry to know where to find some living creature."

Mrs. Wansford assured Althea, that the room where she, her husband and children slept was only the third door down the passage, on the opposite side. Althea desired it might be pointed out to her; and being satisfied that she was not very far removed from them, she returned to her allotted apartment for the night, and in that confidence which innocence always gives she recommended herself to Heaven; and, retiring to her bed, soon forgot the vexations which had lately worn her spirits, and slept undisturbed till morning.

CHAP. XI.

Sunk are thy bowers in shapeless ruin all,
And the long grass o'ertops the mouldering wall;
While trembling, shrinking, from the spoiler's hand,
Far, far away, thy children leave the land.

THE GIRL, WHO was now taken into the house to assist Mrs. Wansford, awakened Althea in the morning by coming in to make her fire.— Roused to a sense of her new situation, she felt content with having passed a tranquil night, and arose in a disposition to see every object around her, however dreary they might be, in the most favourable light.—The satisfaction which her honest host and hostess expressed at seeing her look well and cheerful, and the grateful delight they took in talking to her of those happy days when they lived with her mother, served to strengthen Althea's sanguine disposition.—She looked around the inhabited part of her abode—it was melancholy enough, but the faces of the inhabitants were the faces of friends—of people really interested for her welfare, and such as she had not, for a very long time, been accustomed to see.—The morning was less gloomy than is usual so late in the year—and Althea, looking from the Gothic windows, endeavoured to picture to herself what the landscape before her would be, when its present mournful hue was exchanged for the verdure of spring. The country around indeed would have been singularly beautiful, if the unfeeling rapacity of the creditors had not long since stripped all the land that formerly belonged to the Marchmont family of its ancient woods, and even of the trees in the hedge-rows that were fit for sale.—The iron ploughshare of oppression, in the form of law, seemed every where to have passed over the domain—and Althea coulld not but recollect with a sigh, that the heir to this once rich and extensive property was now an unhappy dependant, without having even the most moderate portion of it left for his support.—From this reflection it was a natural transition to wish she could know what was become of this unfortunate young man—but it was a wish she had no means of satisfying. The people of the house knew the family of Marchmont only by name; they were probably more known in the village about three miles distant, which their hospitality and expenditure had formerly supported, and which, since they had quitted the neighbourhood, was falling to decay. But thither Althea could not well go abruptly to make enquiries; and she knew nobody but the family of Eversley who were acquainted with that of Marchmont.

Whatever injustice and tyranny there had been in Sir Audley's treatment of her, Althea had so proper a pride, as well as so just a sense of the duty she still owed her father, that she had never complained to the very few correspondents she had—nor had she, as most girls so situated would have done, informed Linda Eversley, "journal wise," of her calamities—but had simply told her, that it being neither Lady Dacres's wish nor her own she should accompany the family to London, she was to remain at Eastwoodleigh for some time.—Cabals against her father would, she knew, have been extremely blamed by her dear and ever lamented friend.—She had therefore avoided writing any letters but those of mere civility; and if she murmured, it was in silence, or in an apostrophe to the spirit of that friend.—Many and dreary were the hours to which Althea was to look forward, before the return of fine weather was likely to afford her even such variety as might be obtained by visiting the nearest villages, wandering among the copses, or towards the sea, which she saw at a distance—and though she felt an interest excited by the interior of her antique prison, which could have happened in no other place, she had been two days in it before she could acquire resolution enough to enquire about the uninhabited apartments of the house; to every one of which Mrs. Wansford told her a story belonged.—"Though, for my part, Madam," said she, "you know I am but a stranger in this country, and I cannot say I have had much curiosity even to ask about this old castle-like house, which, till you came, I am sure I thought the dismallest *unket* place that ever I set my foot into; and God knows, nothing but the want of a home, and our fear of disobliging Sir Audley, would have made Wansford and I think of coming to live here. If I had been fearful and timorous as many people are, it would have been a harder matter to have reconciled me to it; but, for my part, I think, that if one has never done any harm, one may sleep quiet in one's bed, let what will be the stories that go about. I believe it is nothing but the nonsensical notions of the people about here; for, excepting the wind, which does make strange howlings and whistling round the buildings (but so it does round all old houses), I declare I never heard any thing I could not very well account for; though I cannot but say, that when I first heard you were to come here, I thought it a strange thing indeed for Sir Audley to send *you*, Madam, to such a forlorn place!—Ah! well-a-day! if my dear lady had lived, how happy we should all have been!"—Althea, who was softened by this expression of regret for her mother, and her spirits depressed by the very means Mrs. Wansford had taken to raise them, had but little courage to continue the conversation: turning it however once more on the history of Eastwoodleigh House, she told her, that the first fine day she would go all over it.

"Indeed, my dear Miss," answered Mrs. Wansford, "it will be no small undertaking, for it is a great deal bigger than it appears to be—and, for my part, I don't know half the ways about it.—There is an old woman who lives in a small cottage on the edge of the common, next the grounds that they call the old park—a cottage that they say was made partly out of one of the lodges, where the family formerly kept her very well out of gratitude for her past services; but since they have been in trouble themselves, the parish officers have talked of obliging her to go into the workhouse, though I never heard she was chargeable to them yet. So she has lately, poor creature! kept very close. But, when first we came here, it was customary for travellers who had curiosity about this house, because of its being a famous place in the civil wars, to have old Mary Mosely shew them about the place; for, having been a servant in the family I don't know how many years, she knew all the old stories that belong to the house."—Althea, who felt more curiosity than she was willing to avow for every anecdote of the Marchmont family, and who thought there would be a melancholy pleasure in conversing with this their humble and ancient historian, desired that Mrs. Wansford would engage this old servant to come up to the house to resume once more her long-neglected narrative, and the next fair day was fixed for this purpose. Althea, however, in making this request, did not think only of the gratification of her curiosity: she hoped that, small as her power was, it might be enough to give some little relief to this poor solitary creature, who, since her former benefactors were no longer able to support her, seemed to be exposed to the complicated miseries of poverty, age, and neglect; or, what was yet worse, to the unfeeling tyranny of parish officers, more grievous to the desolate victims of extreme indigence, than that want which their interference is intended by the law to remedy.

In the mean time Althea, who had sent for the collection of books left her by her aunt, and which had been deposited in their cases in the house of the elder Mrs. Eversley, was busied in contriving how they might be placed, and in making such other arrangements as would make her abode the most cheerful and comfortable.—Wansford, lame as he was, undertook to be the chief manager of all these operations; and while Althea was telling him how she would have the shelves, or giving him any other direction, he would stop in the midst of his proceedings to say, in faltering accents, and with tears rising in his eyes, that in voice, in manner, in look, she was so much the image of his dear lady, her mother, that he sometimes could not help fancying that it was her very self!—The weather, which during the first week of Althea's arrival had been only a succession of storms, now became more tolerable.—Mrs. Mosely, having had previous notice, was summoned to her task—and Wansford was sent round the house to open the doors, some of which had not been unlocked since every piece of furniture that was worth taking had been torn away by the rapacity of those who had judgements against the elder Marchmont, and little but some pieces of antique and useless lumber, and some old pictures and maps on vellum, was left with the dismantled house for the mortgagee.

The appearance of Mrs. Mosely immediately interested Althea in her favour. Poor as she was, she was remarkably neat; her slender figure was bent with age, and, as it seemed, with trouble—and the little hair,

that appeared under her clean plaited cap, was quite white.—The only
remnant of that dress which had been allowed her in the affluent servitude of better days, was a black velvet cloak, still quite fresh.—And
though the rest did not answer to this piece of once expensive apparel,
there was something about her so respectable, that Althea could hardly help fancying she was one of the family, reserved amid the general
wreck as the authentic chronicle of its buried merit.

If her looks thus excited reverence, her manner served to confirm it.—There was nothing about her of the vulgar gossipping old
woman.—Almost every passion seemed to be subdued in her heart,
except affection for the family she had so long served.—Inured to
disappointments and sorrows, she bore what related merely to herself
with the calmest resignation, and was never heard to complain of her
forlorn and comfortless situation. But when the ruin of her master's
house became, as it too often did, the subject of vulgar triumph, and
among the very tenants who had grown rich by his indulgence, but
who now paid their court to Sir Audley Dacres, the poor woman for a
moment forgot her moderation and mildness, and could hardly refrain
from the bitterest reproaches, however prejudicial they were to her,
who was greatly in the power of the renters of the parish, in which she
was reluctantly suffered to linger out the few sad years that remained.

This sort of conduct, and her making always a cleaner and better appearance than her slender means were supposed able to afford,
together with her having very little communication with any one, except when a sick neighbour wanted her assistance, had raised sundry
strange reports and opinions about her in the neighbouring country.
The lower class of peasantry were not without some suspicions of her
being a witch, though whenever they saw her at all it was in the exercise
of charity and kindness.—Some of the farmers, and still more their
wives, had taken up a notion, that among the vicissitudes to which the
house at Eastwoodleigh had been exposed during the civil war, several sums of money had been hidden in it, or buried in the adjoining
grounds; and that Mrs. Mosely was in the secret, and supplied herself
in this manner with comforts, which to keep concealed, she shut herself up from all intercourse with her neighbours, and affected poverty
she was far from really suffering.

Impressed with this idea, some of the honest and sapient leaders
at the vestry had more than once threatened to remove her to the
workhouse, under pretence of their fearing she would become helpless

and burdensome; and though till she actually was so, and solicited relief, they had no legal right to disturb her, yet as she was a solitary and
helpless being, they ventured to harass her with menaces, in hopes that
in her eagerness to remain where she was they might extort the secret
from her: at all events, their malignity was gratified in having the power
to torment and terrify one, who, humbled as she was, and never above
the rank of an upper servant, seemed to consider these thriving men,
their wives and daughters, as inferior people.

Those who have imagined that at a great distance from London
there reigns Arcadian simplicity, and that envy, detraction, and malice,
only inhabit great cities, have been strangely misled by romantic description. Every bad passion of the human heart thrives as luxuriantly
under the roof of the old-fashioned farm-house, two hundred miles
from the metropolis, as in that hot-bed itself; and some are even more
flourishing.—Ignorance is a powerful auxiliary to scandal, and a thousand exaggerations are added by the illiterate to the tale of ill-nature—
abject poverty is no defence. The very wretch who subsists on casual
alms is sometimes the object of hatred and calumny to those who
believe they have a better right to the charity on which he lives; and so
many instances of this depravity occur, that one wishes what the poet
says was strictly and invariably true—

> Heaven's Sovereign saves all beings but himself
> That hideous sight: a naked human heart.
>
> YOUNG.

When an ancient family is gone to decay, and the opulent creditor seizes on the estate, the few servants that remain attached to their
reduced master are usually the avowed though impotent enemies of
those that come into possession of what he has lost. Mrs. Mosely,
on this principle, detested the very names of Sir Audley and Lady
Dacres; and had *they* sent for her to give an account of the antiquities of Eastwoodleigh, she certainly would have refused to have
attended, however she might have wanted the half-crown, which, on
such occasions, was her usual fee: but when she had heard as much
of Althea's history as Mrs. Wansford chose to tell her, and understood that she was sent from her father's house by the cruelty of her
mother-in-law, she hesitated not a moment, but offered her poor and
trifling services with an earnestness and a simplicity that entirely won
the heart of Althea.

So seldom had this poor woman an opportunity of talking over those passages of her past life which dwelt the most forcibly on her memory, that she seemed relieved and gratified by having found, in Althea, one who not only patiently listened, but by many questions relative to the Marchmont family engaged her to continue her narratives.—Mrs. Wansford had left them to go about her domestic concerns; and poor old Mrs. Mosely, already forgetting that she was to shew the house, was telling at length the history of its former possessors.

"A most worthy and brave race of noble gentlemen they were," said she; "and though their loyalty and all the blood they lost, and the great fortune they laid out in the King's service, never got them a tide, I have heard it was because they never would accept of one. —I have thought sometimes. Madam, that this was a great pity, as things have turned out; for I have heard that Lords and great men who have tides, let their family be ever so much reduced and poor, are always taken care of by the King. But there's our poor dear young man—a gentleman. Madam, who, if you were to see him, you would say was second to none of the first noblemen in the land, yet nothing is done for him—though his family have been undone by their attachment to the Royal cause. I am sure, whenever I think of him—when I remember, at the time he was born what rejoicings were made, and how my dear old master, with tears in his eyes, thanked my Lady for the precious present she had made him—how they both doted upon him as he grew up—and how my poor master, even latterly, while he tried in vain to shut his eyes against the ruin that was coming upon him, lamented it chiefly on account of this dear son, and yet was still willing to flatter himself that he was so accomplished, so clever, that he would repair all by his own merit:—ah! Ma'am, when all this comes across me—(and I think of it, God knows, every day of my sad life)—and when I know how different things are with my dear young master—how little his parents thought of his being a poor wanderer, as I may say he is now, without a home, and without friends—my heart aches so, that I am fain to wish I could lay me down and die at once, if it pleased God!— that I might know no more about it, nor hear what cruel cutting things are said of this dear good young man by those who are not worthy even to look at him!"

Sad remembrance, mingled with wounded pride and affection, here overcame that calmness which time and habitual suffering had taught her.

The aged shed not many tears, but her voice failed, and she sobbed aloud. Althea could say nothing likely to mitigate concern so just—and at once pained by the recital, yet desiring to hear more of Marchmont, she continued silent, till Mrs. Mosely, having a little recovered herself, went on:

"Ah, Madam! what strange changes a few years make in families!— When I came, then a young girl, to wait on my dear lady—it is indeed almost five-and-forty years since, before she was married, though it seems but like yesterday—there was not a family within twenty miles of this place that were looked upon like them. My lady too was of a good family in Dorsetshire, but she had no fortune—my master married her for her beauty—and beautiful as the day to be sure she was!—As tall as you are, Ma'am, and much of your size. There were five sisters of them, and they were called the Dorsetshire Angels; but Mrs. Marchmont was allowed to be the handsomest of them all. There were two of those ladies, her sisters, that married noblemen, and their children are now great people. But they take no notice at all of their near relations, because they are poor!—Yet how they can harden their hearts against such a relation as my young master—a man that a king might be proud to own —I have no notion of—And then if they did but look in his face! He is so like his mother. Madam!—Just her mild open countenance, and fine eyes—one would think every body would have a pride to serve him, and to own him as their relation."

Althea could hardly repress a melancholy smile at the ideas this poor woman had formed of the force of kindred among the great; and at the amazement she expressed that none of his affluent relations espoused the interest of a young man whom, as he was poor, they probably did not know even by name!

"But it is not merely, Madam, his fine and noble person," proceeded Mrs. Mosely, "but his being such a young man at all sorts of learning, that he might do any thing, I am very certain, if he had but friends to help him forward at first. And then there never was such a good temper, nor such a generous heart—ah! too much so! Even to the last, Ma'am, he and his dear mother and sisters have sent me what they hardly had enough of themselves; and to this very hour it is to my good young master that..."

She stopped—as if conscious that her gratitude had nearly conquered her prudence, or perhaps betrayed her into a breach of promise.—Althea, however, from what she had said, guessed that the support she had, and which Mrs. Wansford had said occasioned so much wonder, and so many disadvantageous conjectures, really came from the generous pity of Marchmont towards the old servant of his family. There needed not this trait of his character to interest her in his favour. Yet she felt all its force. The loquacity of her new acquaintance, far from being exhausted, seemed to acquire new spirit, although chastised by many cruel recollections, as she led her over the house—once the scene of hospitality—*"Now to the dust gone down."*

CHAP. XII.

Ye towers sublime, deserted now, and drear!
Ye woods deep sighing to the hollow blast!
The musing wanderer loves to linger here
While History points to all your glory past.

ALTHEA FOLLOWED HER conductress into a high and vaulted room, of which the greater part was in ruins, for the coppers and other fixed utensils of ancient hospitality had been torn away and sold; and as the kitchen was no longer used, no care had been taken to replace the bricks, or repair the walls. Beyond it was the buttery—and Mrs. Mosely bade her remark how the hatch was worn—

"There," said she, "I have often, though it was not indeed exactly my business, given away the weekly dole to folks who then wanted it bad enough, but who since have got up in the world, so that it makes one seem dreaming as it were to think of it.—Yes! the very man who has bought all the lower woodland farm, and built that fine staring great house, that you might see as you came along on the hill, a little beyond Shansbrook corner, that very man was a little ragged dirty boy, who has many a time come for his family's dinner to this very wicket. My good master took pity upon him, and sent him to school—when he was big enough, he made him a sort of clerk, and took him into the steward's room to learn to keep accounts, and after that got him sent out to the Indies; and about five years ago he came home worth such a mint of money, that they say he could buy out half the gentry of the country. Well! I have heard, that when things got so bad here, my mistress, though she could not prevail on my master to do it, yet wrote herself to this Sowden, to desire he would let them have a loan of three thousand pounds, which she thought, poor lady! would have put things to rights; but he had the baseness, the ingratitude to send her a rude denial.—He! that little dirty boy, that owed his all to Mr. Marchmont's bounty! and now he has had the impudence to buy part of that estate that was sold by the assignees!"

Young as Althea was, there was nothing new to her in examples of the worthlessness and ingratitude of mankind. Her veteran Ciceroni, who had seen so much more of the world, yet seemed so keenly to feel this instance of it, that Althea, sorry to perceive her emotion, wished to turn her mind from the indulgence of sentiments so bitter; and therefore, complaining that the place they stood in was very cold, she desired her to pass on.

Before they went, however, Mrs. Mosely bade her observe a place in the lofty ceiling, which she said was a sort of trap door, communicating with the private closet that belonged to the apartments of the lady of the house; who, in days when vigilant œconomy superintended the solemn and regulated hospitality of an ancient English kitchen, was accustomed to overlook from thence the proceedings of her domestics. Reflecting on the different usages and manners of the present time, Althea followed her infirm guide through those parts of the house she had been used to, to others which she had never yet visited.

The way was through a long passage, now nearly dark; for the great window at the end of it was boarded, and the door that led from it to the principal part of the house bricked up: this had been done, that the range of uninhabited rooms might be considered as a separate house, and might not be liable to be taxed for the windows; the same prudent precaution, to avoid the window tax, had nearly darkened the part of it inhabited by Wansford. But on the opposite side a door opened to the once-walled court, and from thence they went round to the porch, or great door, which, long unaccustomed to turn on its massy hinges, had been opened by Wansford for their reception. Althea now found herself in an immense hall—"Here," said her conductress, "at these long tables, which though of oak are now so much decayed, were daily assembled, during the great Rebellion, above three hundred armed men; they were disciplined, clothed, and fed by Sir Armyn Marchmont, who was knighted in the field by King Charles the First; and from hence were led the fifty horse, who just before the battle of Braddock Down went out against a party of Cromwell's army that approached the house; and the brave Edward Marchmont, the second son of the family, fell in his father's park. His mother, who doted upon him, died broken-hearted a few months afterwards; and from that time they say Sir Armyn himself never seemed to enjoy life, though he lingered on for three or four years, and continued to the last to defend this place, and keep it as a garrison for the King."

Althea, while she listened to this detail, compared the past with the present state of the place in which she stood. No loyal and busy crowds now wore the stone pavement: it was hidden with moss. The two windows, which at one end reached from the ceiling to within three feet of the floor, were partly boarded up; the same glass yet remained; but through the broken panes the ivy, which luxuriantly mantled the exterior of die building, had made its way, and was advancing to line the broken walls. The chimney, over which there was again a carving in oak of the arms of the Marchmonts, was large, even in proportion to the room. But instead of blazing now with hospitable fires, it was a receptacle for the store of turf and billets which Wansford had provided for the end of winter; and in several other parts of this great room there were piles of peat put there to dry, and of bavins and brush wood. Nothing could give a stronger idea of desolation than this gloomy apartment; with it, however, the adjoining rooms, into which it opened, perfectly corresponded. "The last of these," Mrs. Mosely said, "was once called the council-room; a name," added she, "which it still retained in my late honoured master's time, who used to relate with pride and pleasure, that here were held those deliberations by the success of which the Queen Henrietta Maria escaped from Exeter, and got safely into France. And above is the room where her majesty slept for three nights. This house too had the honour of receiving the Prince of Wales; when, after the battle of Naseby, he was forced to fly to concealment in the Scilly islands, beyond the coast of Cornwall. That flight was planned, in this council-room, by my master's ancestor and some more of his faithful servants."

Nothing now remained in this chamber but a very old heavy worm-eaten oak table; silence and solitude had long possessed it: and as Althea followed Mrs. Mosely up the great staircase, and the loose oak boards seemed to tremble under their feet, the sound ran along these empty apartments, and was returned in dull murmurs by the bare and mouldering walls.

Opposite the top of the staircase appeared a large folding door, with a heavy pediment of wood-work over it. It gave entrance into a room not very inferior in its dimensions to the hall.

"This," said Mrs. Mosely, as she turned towards Althea with something of increased dejection in her countenance, "this was used to be called the banqueting room. I do not indeed know why; for in my time the family never ate in this room; but it was here that they used to receive their company; for once it was very richly furnished, though indeed the furniture was even then very old fashioned."

Althea cast her eyes around this scene of former gaiety and splendour, now dreary and deserted. The ceiling had once been curiously stuccoed in large copartments; but the swallows had at present a colony among the cornices, and great projecting roses. The room was wainscoted, and ornamented with carving and gilding; now much defaced and broken. Around the chimney had been rich and massy festoons, of which enough was left to shew that they had originally been splendid and expensive. Of the furniture little remained: in one corner some heavy picture frames were piled together; and in a single frame which stood against the wall was a damaged picture, representing a lady in the costume of the court of Charles the Second. The countenance was remarkably pleasing, but pensive, and even dejected.

"It is the picture," said Mrs. Mosely, "of the grandmother of my late master, who was a great beauty in her time; and it was done by some famous painter of that day, as I have heard: but my memory is not so good as it was —I have forgotten his name. It was going with the rest of the pictures; but the men who took them down tore it, so that the dealer from London who bought them left it behind. If troubles had not come so fast on the family," added she, "my dear young master meant to have sent the man the value of it, and to have had it mended.—But now!—Ah! no!—there is no likelihood that he should ever have a house large enough to hang up such a picture. He would have been very glad, dear soul! to have purchased the rest of the family pieces, and some others, that every body set a great value upon, particularly two small oval pictures, one of Lord Falkland, and another of Sir Charles Lucas, both famous men, and one of them the bosom friend of Sir Armyn Marchmont: but when my poor young master talked of reserving of them—Oh! Madam, if you had seen the brutality with which that auctioneer man treated him!—But so it is! Such upstart creatures may be rich, but they are never gentlemen—nor know how to behave as such."

To this natural remark Althea very heartily assented; and having gazed a moment on the faded representation of forgotten beauty, she turned to follow her guide through the long suite of unexplored rooms. In the first, a small anti-room, were the broken remains of a large theorbo, which was formerly a fashionable instrument: the other rooms, originally bed-rooms, were entirely destitute of even the re-mains of furniture, save only that a fragment of tapestry yet hung against the walls of one of them, and represented a group of grim and ghastly heads. Mrs. Mosely related, that many of the rooms had been ornamented with curious hangings, woven with history pieces; "and it was," said she, "such old-fashioned stuff, that it was not worth the taking by the vultures that plundered every thing else: but after the family went away, the farmer that took to the farm for Sir Audley Dacres came to live for a while in the house; and *he* chose, forsooth! to pull down all the arras to make horse-cloths of, and to hang against the stable windows."

Althea thought there was less to regret in this than in any other instance of the dilapidations the house had suffered; and as only na-ked walls and dismantled window shutters presented themselves, she thought her examination of this half-ruined edifice nearly finished: but two of the wings were yet to be surveyed.—In one of them, with a sort of mournful pride, Mrs. Mosely pointed out the room which had once afforded a temporary shelter to fugitive royalty: a circumstance that seemed to create great reverence for that apartment in the mind of the old servant, but it had not now even the remains of furniture. The impression the whole survey had made on the mind of Althea was so melancholy, that she wished it over; but her conductress, mov-ing slowly back through the apartments she had already traversed, led the way across the top of the stair-case, towards what might rather be called a narrow gallery than a passage, into which several rooms opened.

"Here," said she, entering one of them, "here languished, and at last died of his wounds, the only brother of Sir Armyn, who was shot through the shoulder at the battle of Stratton. All the range of rooms on this side were inhabited by the family. That at the end has been nailed up for many many years, till it was opened by the bailiffs with their execution. I wonder they were not ashamed of themselves!

But it was all one to them! Down came the bed, the flowered damask hangings, and all, all the furniture—though it could be worth hardly any thing, because the room was so damp from having been so long unopened."

"And why was it locked up?" said Althea.

"Only, Madam, because it had been reckoned unlucky to the family time out of mind almost; and my lady used to say, that there were rooms enough in the house, and she did not like to be the first to open this. This apartment was that belonging to the only daughter of Sir Armyn; one of the finest young ladies that could be seen. Her father, her mother, and her three brothers, almost worshipped the ground she trod upon! She had lovers enough; and if she was like her picture, which was among those that were carried away, she must have been quite an angel. When she was about seventeen, just before the breaking out of the troubles, she was engaged to be married to a young gentleman, one Mr. Estcourt; he was the only son of a rich family, now all gone and dispersed. That house all so new and staring at Hooper's common is built upon a part of their ground, but the old mansion has been pulled down a long while. The young lady and he loved one another very truly; when, alas! the Rebellion broke out, and this gentleman's father, himself, and all his relations took part with the parliament against the king; whereupon Sir Armyn commanded his daughter to think no more of her lover. But, poor soul! that was, as they say, easier said than done. She wrote a letter to him, and entreated him, if he would not break her heart, to quit the party of those wicked men— but he sent her word he would die with pleasure for *her*, but could not consent to lose his honour, or to serve a tyrant; for so he had learned to call his rightful king. This letter, as ill-fortune would have it, fell into the hands of the lady's father, who thereby came to know that his daughter had written to her lover. He was more angry than ever, and declared to the poor girl that he never would forgive her if ever she attempted to send a line to him again. She promised she would not, and kept her word; but from that time she became quite dejected, and seldom spoke to any body, unless it was to her favourite brother Edward, he who was killed in the park. That very morning before he went out, the poor young lady, as if she had foreseen what was to happen, hung about him weeping for many minutes. Indeed the enemy were so near, that there was reason enough to be frightened: but she, unhappy girl! knew that Mr. Estcourt's house was a garrison for the parliament troops, as this was for the king; and that very likely her lover was among the soldiers her brother was going out to meet. Her brother, though he loved her very dearly, would not seem to understand, that, as well as she dared, she begged him to spare Estcourt if he met him: but she was as much afraid of Estcourt's killing her brother as of her brother's killing him. She neither spoke or ate that whole day; but when the dead body of Mr. Edward was brought home, she insisted upon having it carried into her room, where, as it was soon known that he was quite gone (for a bullet had passed through his heart), she sat by him till he was buried, taking no more nourishment than just enough to keep her alive; and then, without a murmur, or a complaint, she took to her bed in the same room, and grew worse and worse, till in about a fortnight she died. They say, that when her father knew that she was in such danger, he repented that he had been so harsh, and offered to send to Mr. Estcourt, who had not it seems been in the attack where Mr. Edward Marchmont was killed; but the poor young creature said it was then too late, and that she would not have the unfortunate youth come only to see her die. After he knew she was dead he became quite distracted; and; seeking to die also, he fell covered with a hundred wounds at the fight of Landsdown. His father, whose only son he was, did not outlive him long, and the whole house and family went to decay. So the servants that lived here, and the country folks, fancied that the spirits of all these unfortunate people used to meet in that room on certain evenings of the year, there to lament themselves; and I have heard some of these notions were caused by the Cavaliers, who, when their party was quite ruined, were hid about in different places till they could make their escape out of the kingdom. However that was, from one thing to another such stories got about, that one would not inhabit the room, and another would not, till at last it was quite deserted and shut up."

Althea, whose heart sunk as this sad narrative was concluded, felt no inclination to violate again this abode of traditionary sorrow, but followed her conductress into another room, which Mrs. Mosely told her had been the bedchamber of the late Mr. Marchmont.

"Here," said she, "I attended him in that long illness, which, though it did not end in his death then, yet he never knew an hour's health afterwards. Ah! how well I remember the look, the voice of his excellent son, who used to remain by him whole hours trying to raise his spirits and comfort him! Then, when the sad prospect was too much for himself, and he could not hide his fears that his father would be dragged away, sick as he was, to prison, he would go, Madam, into this closet to conceal his tears, and bade me to tell his father he was writing to this friend and that friend, who he was sure would assist them; but he was sometimes quite lost and bewildered, as it were, in thinking of all the difficulties and troubles that surrounded his family. He would lay down his pen, and, crossing his arms upon an old walnut-tree writing desk that stood just here, would remain quite like a statue, till he thought his father might want him; then try to recover himself, would go again to the bed-side with a cheerful countenance."

The figure of Marchmont was at this moment so present to the memory of Althea, that she thought she really saw him leaning dejectedly on his desk. The place seemed sanctified by the fortitude and filial piety of its former inhabitant; and not deterred by the dust and cobwebs with which they were covered, she stooped and took up one of the five or six torn and mouldy books that lay in a corner. One was a Greek testament, which from the date and name had evidently served Marchmont at school. Another was part of a dictionary that appeared also to have been of that juvenile party; and the last, a manuscript book, with some translations and sentences from the French, Latin, and Italian, which seemed to be in the same hand-writing as the name written in the book. The rest were only old acts of parliament, and a few leaves of the Eïkon Basilike.

Althea felt an irresistible desire to possess herself of these books, and eagerly enquired whether she might not take them to her apartment.

"Aye, sure!" replied Mrs. Mosely; "but they are sad dusty old things, and good for nothing, I suppose, or they would not be left here: and they are in some foreign tongue. But perhaps, Ma'am, you can understand them."

Althea, without accounting even to herself for the motives which made them appear so desirable an acquisition, collected them in her lap, and expressed a wish to end her view of the house here. Indeed there was nothing more to see, if there had been light for her farther examination; for though the military man and the antiquary might have found in many of the lower rooms subjects for their enquiry, Althea had heard nearly all that most interested her; and the little mournful narrative of the unfortunate Estcourt and his intended wife, simply as it was told, was to her more affecting than any relations of the progress

of a siege, or a plan of defence. Warlike details always exciting something of a terror mingled with disgust; but the name of Marchmont
carried with it particular interest. Every memorial round the house was
a proof of honourable resistance of his ancestors against what they
considered as the usurped power of rebellious demagogues. To these,
therefore, Althea listened with untired attention; though she would
on any other occasion have shrunk from details of hostile operations,
which, however disguised by circumstances or motives, arc still but
details of horror.

During her incomplete survey, however, the attention she had
shewn, and her sweet and easy manners, had quite engaged the affections of her new acquaintance Mrs. Mosely, to whom she gave every
refreshment she would accept and made her a present much above
her expectations. It then became time to take her leave; but the poor
old woman could hardly prevail upon herself to depart. It was long
since she had heard the voice of kindness—it was long since a being
resembling those she had been used to see had listened to her sorrows,
and relieved her wants; and to *her* Althea appeared rather an angel than
a human creature, when with the most humane consideration she assured her, that the next fair day she would visit her solitary cottage; and
that while she was in that neighbourhood it should want none of those
small comforts which, far as she was from being affluent, she had yet
the power to bestow.

END OF THE FIRST VOLUME.

MARCHMONT.

CHAPTER I.

… His poor self,
A dedicated beggar to the air!
Walks, like Contempt, alone.

WHILE HIS DAUGHTER was gradually accustoming herself to the dreary solitude to which he had condemned her, and even learning to take in it an interest that he little suspected could ever arise, Sir Audley Dacres, amidst the busy scenes of political life in which he was now more deeply than ever engaged, had still leisure to feel uneasiness from the consciousness of having acted wrong. His desire of gratifying Lady Dacres, even in a point which certainly did not raise her character in his esteem; his long-established habits of making himself obeyed; and the various advantages which his ambition continually represented as attending on an alliance with Mr. Mohun—advantages that seemed to justify whatever means he had taken to bring it about—all were considerations insufficient to silence entirely those reproaches which his conscience was so impertinent as to make on the subject of Althea.—It was in vain that his wife (who failed not to perceive his uneasiness) endeavoured, by the most artful methods, to persuade him, that almost any other father, under similar circumstances, would have acted more rigorously. Sir Audley, though he affected to acquiesce, and said hardly any thing on the subject, felt his disquiet continually increase; and amidst the drudgery of party cabals, in which he was deeply engaged, and which required the constant vigilance of those who were admitted to them, he began seriously to consider, if, without bringing his eldest daughter into the house of her step-mother, which he knew would embitter his life with continual feuds, he could find no properer situation for her than

111

a deserted mansion on the confines of Devonshire; no society more eligible than that of his own discarded servants.

This, however, on a nearer view, was less easily found than might be imagined. There were houses of reputation in London, where young women are received who have no proper home; but he knew the expence would be a great objection with Lady Dacres, who must besides, in submitting to such a measure, feel it to be a tacit acknowledgement that she would not admit and protect the daughter of her husband.—Of Althea's own family, there was not one who was likely, or proper, to afford her an asylum—nor did he know, among all the women of his acquaintance who might have been glad to have received her as a temporary visitor, any to whom he could be thoroughly satisfied to entrust her.—She had now been more than a month at Eastwoodleigh; and so far from her banishment having effected what he hoped from it, a change of sentiments in favour of Mohun, her last letters had borne a greater appearance of cheerful resignation than the first. If then, during this dead and dreary month, her resolution had resisted the sadness of such perfect seclusion, there was but little probability that it would fail, when the return of spring should give her the liberty of pursuing those innocent pleasures for which he knew she had acquired a taste, from her education and habits of life.—To insist therefore on her continuing there, did not seem likely to answer the end he proposed; but while he wished to relinquish a plan which he could not but consider as cruel and unwarrantable, he did not believe that the removal of his daughter to those scenes where she ought to appear would by any means accelerate his views in regard to Mohun. He knew that wherever she was seen she could hardly fail of exciting general admiration; and he did not think that the preference of others was likely, in the opinion of Althea, to give value to that of Mohun. But Sir Audley, half disposed to relinquish a plan so little likely to be effected, believed that were Althea to appear in public, attended with those advantages which other young women enjoyed, she could not fail of being advantageously married, notwithstanding the smallness of her fortune; and such an event was surely the most desirable both for Lady Dacres and himself.

Some degree of personal indisposition added to the painful regret with which he sometimes thought of his harsh conduct towards Althea. His views, like those of all ambitious men, opening as he ascended, were yet often overclouded and disappointed. The friendships of politicians he found, above all other reliances, fallacious, and he frequently found himself disappointed and supplanted by the creatures he had himself placed in the way of favour.

The base traffic of his conscience and his understanding against the hopes of a larger income, or a more eminent post, had not hitherto paid him as he expected; and some late instances of the imperious and overbearing temper of Mohun had internally disgusted him, though they were apparently more closely united than ever.

But however frequently his mind adverted to the subject of Althea, he could find no place of residence which would be at once eligible for her, and without objection on the part of Lady Dacres.—While he considered and re-considered the matter, time wore away. His sons, who were his greatest objects, came home for the Christmas recess, and, with the eldest, such a report from the master of the public school where he had been placed, that, though it was conveyed in terms the most considerate, Sir Audley was convinced an instant removal from thence was necessary; and his thoughts were immediately engrossed with so important a debate as of course followed, in regard to what was to be done with a boy so difficult to govern, and so conscious of his own consequence.—Sir Audley was inclined to the University; but Lady Dacres remarking that the sons of some of her acquaintance, who had been there, had turned out extremely ill, and that in the diplomatic line, for which Mr. Dacres was designed, an university education was by no means necessary; it was at length, after much hesitation and debate, determined, that this eldest hope of his family should make the tour of Italy and Germany, since that of France could not now be included; and that he should forthwith be provided with a tutor versed in foreign languages, and proceed in about six weeks on his travels.

These deliberations, and some discoveries of his son's disposition, which forced themselves upon his observation, however he wished not to see them, so entirely occupied his mind, that Althea was almost forgotten—and the time he could spare from his political engagements was wholly given to repress the excesses of this young man, and to the discovery of some proper person to whom he could be entrusted when no longer under parental authority.

During the course of this enquiry, it happened, by the means of Lady Barbara Newmarch, to reach the knowledge of one of those women in a certain rank of life, who with some literature, and much pretence, acquire a sort of authority in such matters; ladies, who have *conversations* instead of routs and assemblies, and who, without making too strict a scrutiny into their motives, may often be allowed the praise of doing some good, by their occasional patronage of obscure merit; though doubts have arisen whether they may not occasionally have done harm, in teaching those to fancy themselves people of genius, who had only assurance, and some powers of imitation.

Be that as it may, Mrs. Gisborough, the lady now in question, having heard of Sir Audley's enquiry after a young man well educated as tutor to Mr. Dacres, lost no time in entreating Lady Barbara to endeavour to keep the appointment open till a gentleman could be written to, who, she was sure, would be unexceptionable.—Sir Audley readily promised the delay of a few days—and then the following letters passed between him and Mrs. Gisborough:

"Dear Sir,

Assured of your strong adherence to those principles which have always distinguished *our* families, and which your present highly respectable connections do so much honour to, I am free to believe that the young gentleman whom I have to mention to you cannot fail of being approved, he owing the decline of his family's fortune to the attachment of his ancestors to the Royal cause in the trying period of 1640, &c. and since they have, with less power, always been a very loyal family, though it has happened that their fortune has, from various causes, declined. The young gentleman, on whose behalf I write, is called Marchmont, and is the last of that ancient family. I am assured, and I believe from my own observations, that he is very well qualified for the undertaking, to which I beg leave to recommend him. I am told that his morals are irreproachable. He speaks the French language perfectly, having resided some years in France (where he has respectable connections), and has a competent knowledge of the Italian and German—a good taste in the polite arts; and, in a word, I am taught to believe, that on farther enquiry you would find Mr. Marchmont eminently qualified to attend your son. I shall be happy in being instrumental in procuring him so honourable and fortunate an engagement; and have the honour to be.

With the greatest respect,

Sir,

Your most obedient humble servant,

A. GISBOROUGH.

Wclbcck-Street,
Jan. 17th."

To this Sir Audley returned, with very little hesitation, the following answer:

"Madam,

"You do at once justice to my principles, and to those sentiments which would render it extremely agreeable to me to obey the commands with which you have honoured me. It therefore gives me very great concern, that it is not in my power to engage the gentleman you mention as a tutor to Mr. Dacres. I believe he may be very deserving; but circumstances, which it is not necessary to recapitulate, make his reception into *my* family impracticable. Be assured, Madam, only the most insuperable objections could weigh against the lively inclination I feel to pay deference to your recommendation, which confers a great obligation on us all.—I have the honour to be, with the highest esteem and regard, Madam,

Your most obliged, and
Most faithful humble servant,
AUDLEY DACRES.

Upper Grosvenor Street,
    Jan. 20th."

Thus, without assigning any reason, because he was conscious that he could not give the true one, he put an end to this solicitation on behalf of a young man who had in reality no other fault than that of being poor—though, with Sir Audley, he had undoubtedly another.—It had been surmised, that the father of Lady Dacres, who was one of that race of beings which, were the rich ever called by their true names, would have been denominated an *usurer,* had taken, by means of an attorney who was entrusted to transact his business, some very unfair advantages of the necessities of the elder Marchmont; and that the estates, of which Sir Audley had become possessed in consequence of that transaction were by no means so honestly come by, or so clear in the title by which he held them, as a very scrupulous man might have wished. Young Marchmont, who dreaded the distress of his mother and his sisters, but was indifferent to his own, had never appeared conscious of this unfair dealing, but had, on the contrary, endeavoured to conciliate Sir Audley, that he might leave the family a little longer in possession of their house in Surry; but Sir Audley, notwithstanding he had not himself been the instrument, felt, in enjoying the fruit of iniquity, that he hated the

person injured as much as if he had himself been the aggressor.—
Strange! that the consciousness of having injured, or participated
in an injury, should create, in the human mind, so much malignity
against the sufferer! Yet so it always is.

Sir Audley, however, by no means allowed, even in arguing the
matter with himself, that Marchmont had any cause of complaint—
and he disliked him, not only for this latent reason, which, though he
repelled it, lurked in his mind, but because, though poor, he seemed
to consider himself still in his former rank, and even when asking a
favour, (as he did when he solicited his mother's continuance in the
Surry house) it was less like a dependant than an equal. Sir Audley,
accustomed since he had lived among place-men to a very different
conduct from those who had any thing to ask, could not reconcile
himself to this manly bearing; and between one cause of dislike and
another he hated Marchmont heartily—and never spoke of him but in
terms of contempt and displeasure.

But the consequence of this repulse was much more material to
Marchmont than merely the loss of an appointment, which, had he
known it was with a son of Sir Audley's, he would not have solicited,
or, had it been procured, have accepted; it deprived him of every hope
of success in his pursuit of a tutorship—for Mrs. Gisborough, who,
together with some of her friends, had undertaken to befriend him,
and who were very likely to succeed, no sooner canvassed Sir Audley's letter than they concluded that their zeal was misplaced, and that
something was undoubtedly wrong in the character of this young man
of which Sir Audley was too generous to speak, yet which was undoubtedly of a nature that rendered it impossible for them to hazard
committing themselves by recommending him.—When therefore he
came from an obscure lodging in Surry, where he lived with his mother
and sisters, to know the event of an application which Mrs. Gisborough had informed him she had made, without telling him to whom,
he was met by a very cold letter from that lady, who, without seeing
him, contented herself with that method of letting him know, "That
her application had failed, and that she was sorry to say she believed
it would not be in her power or that of the friends to whom she had
spoken to serve him in the way they had hoped."

Marchmont wanted not discernment to see that this was only a
civil way of the lady's relieving herself from all farther trouble; he returned dejected to his family, to whom, however, he made light of his

disappointment, that he might not inflict new anguish on the half-broken heart of his mother.

But when he sat down seriously to consider his situation, this disappointment, which followed so many others, fell cold and heavy on his spirits. The creditors had threatened to arrest the remains of his father as they were proceeding towards the parish church of Eastwoodleigh; and Marchmont, in the agony of his mind, had entered into personal engagements to ward off so cruel a blow: subsequent discoveries of the condition of his father's affairs had rendered it impossible for him ever to acquit himself of these engagements from the effects that were left. Nothing therefore remained for him but to attempt, by some exertions of his own, to satisfy the inexorable men to whom he was now personally bound; and who, provoked by their losses, declared their resolution to imprison him, unless some prospect opened which might enable him to discharge the debt he had thus taken upon himself.

To leave England therefore, and to escape from their threats and importunities, while he hoped to obtain, as a tutor, a salary which he might divide between them and his family, was his most earnest wish. But even this humble hope was now frustrated; and though he appeared calm and composed before his mother, who watched his countenance with the most anxious solicitude, he almost for the first time felt what it was to look back on the past without having one crime with which to reproach himself, yet forward to the future without a hope, and almost without a friend!

Generous and candid himself, and respecting men only for their worth and their talents, he had never till now been thoroughly convinced that, with the generality of the world, there is no crime so unpardonable as poverty; and that, when an untitled family fall to decay, their pretensions to ancestry, far from giving them a claim to commiseration, become ridiculous in the opinion of the suddenly fortunate.—He, who might truly be said to be

"Of gentle blood, part shed in honour's cause,"
                                        POPE.

was now pursued for the sum of seven hundred pounds, by a man who called himself a gentleman, but was, in fact, a money-lender, the son of a taylor; and harassed by another for a thousand pounds, who had been an auctioneer, but who, having amassed a considerable sum of money, had quitted the hammer, and was become a banker.

These men, while they despised the indigence of poor Marchmont, and thought, like Briggs, "that a pedigree pays no debts," had yet
taken it into their heads, that a young man so well connected would not
be suffered to remain in prison, and that, if they threatened him with
such an exertion of the power they had acquired over him, they should
obtain at least some part of the money for which he had engaged himself.—It was in vain that he assured them, that of his father's house he
was the last—while of the mined fortunes of that house they could
not be ignorant; that as to the relations of his mother, though two of
her sisters had married men of high rank, he was so far from having
any interest with them, that he was not even by sight known to any of
his maternal relations.

Far from softening the hearts of his pursuers by this representation of his circumstances, he found that the more desperate his situation was, the less they seemed inclined to forbearance.—Tormented
every day by some new plan of the one (who, being himself a schemer,
fancied that Marchmont might relieve himself by some project), and
perplexed by the threats of the other, he found that he must conceal
himself from the persecution of both, or that they would inevitably
avail themselves of that most improvident law, which enables a creditor to imprison the debtor who cannot pay him when he is at liberty;—
as if an unhappy man, torn from his friends, deprived of his credit,
depressed in his talents, and probably ruined in his health, could do
more to pay his debts, than when he is at liberty to pursue his interest,
or make the most of his industry—a law which confounds innocence
with guilt, and equally punishes intentional fraud and inevitable misfortune; yet which exists no where in such force as in a country boasting of its enlarged humanity and perfect freedom.

Such was the sad fate of Marchmont, that though guilty of no
crime, and though he had devoted himself to distress from the purest
motives of integrity and filial piety, he now found himself pursued like
a felon, and had the horrors of perpetual confinement before his eyes.

CHAP. II.

The tenant of a night-haunted ruin!

ACCUSTOMED INSENSIBLY TO her solitude, Althea passed her time without murmuring. Her mind compelled thus to exert its strength at so early a period, and her education having been such as had not enfeebled while it ornamented her excellent understanding, she not only became reconciled to a situation which to most young women would have been intolerable, but every day learned to rejoice at the election she had made, and compare the melancholy tranquillity of her present situation with the splendid wretchedness to which an union with Mohun would have condemned her. Believing that, unless she could sell herself to some equally odious connection, the smallness of her fortune and the peculiar circumstances of her situation (held down as she was by the selfish policy of Lady Dacres) would prevent her ever marrying, she thought of passing her life, if not always in as solitary a manner as she now lived, yet certainly in a single state; and when she recollected all her aunt was, she thought of this rather with complacency than regret. Without predilection in favour of any one (for the infant preference she had felt for Marchmont could hardly be called so), she tried to look forward with cheerfulness to the few and simple duties that in such a situation, and with so small a fortune, she had to fulfil. There is no state of life in which objects for such duties may not be found; but none more forcibly attracted her benevolence than the poor old woman Mrs. Mosely, to whose cottage her lonely rambles were the most frequently directed, and who was become her regular pensioner.

This little hut, for it was hardly more, consisting of only two small rooms on the ground, and two of the same size under the thatched roof, was now by the bounty of Althea rendered as comfortable as it would admit of, and the general condition of its inhabitant much ameliorated. Yet while this poor helpless being incessantly blessed the considerate kindness of her young benefactress, Althea observed something in her manner which indicated some pressure of the mind—something that seemed not to belong to fear of *future* poverty, and she was in no immediate want; but, on the contrary, acknowledged herself to be surrounded with many and unexpected comforts. There were however, at times, such symptoms of a pre-occupied mind, or some peculiar interest affecting it, in the deportment of Mrs. Mosely, that Althea was sometimes tempted to doubt whether she was not, as the people of the country believed, privy to some secret. Yet of what nature could it be? That she was acquainted with a concealed treasure buried somewhere in the domains of her ancient master, seemed very improbable; since the Marchmont family could not have been reduced to distress, had they possessed such a resource; and that the indigence of poor Mrs. Mosely herself was but too real, there were proofs enough.—Yet why did she sometimes, when Althea was with her, start at every sound, appear hurried, breathless, and confused; look eagerly from her little window, and with difficulty command herself so as to shew that attention the presence of her benefactress demanded? Althea often attempted to discover the cause of all this, but was obliged to content herself with the excuses Mrs. Mosely made; that it was owing to the terrors and hurries she had gone through during the latter part of her service in Mr. Marchmont's family, and the poverty she had felt and dreaded since.

Besides this solitary pensioner, Althea had soon a little humble circle, to whom the goodness of her heart prompted her to render a thousand kind offices: she had not indeed much money, but for herself she wanted so little, that she could without imprudence clothe the half-naked infants of one poor cottager, relieve by a trifling weekly allowance the helpless superannuated father of another, pay a nurse for attending the wife of a third, and purchase flax or wool for the industrious family of a fourth. For some she worked herself, others she instructed how to work; and she was always ready to listen to the rustic tale of sorrow, and to give (what the poor do not always find) compassion and attention, even when it was not in her power greatly to alleviate the distresses to which she listened.

The children of her host became the peculiar objects of her generous care. One of them was a little boy of about five years old, who attached himself to her with so much simple affection, that he followed her in all her walks, and crept continually into her room when she was alone; where, if he thought she was busy, and would not like to be interrupted, he sat himself silently down in a corner, and remained quiet till she gave him leave to speak to her.

This boy then became of course peculiarly her favourite; and she not unfrequently found in the sound of his innocent voice a relief against the silence of her dreary habitation, when Mrs. Wansford was busied in her domestic concerns at a distance in the house, and her husband absent, or working as he often did when he was able, in that part of the old garden in which he raised a few vegetables for his family.

At these times it not unfrequently happened that the children attended their parents, or that the elder girl was sent on messages; and then there reigned a silence so dreary around the house, that Althea sometimes went out merely to hear a human voice. If any sounds broke this profound repose, they were only such as impressed melancholy ideas. The ancient dove-house, mark of former manorial dignity, had long since fallen to decay; but Wansford had nailed up some boards within the shelter of one of the thick buttresses, and the hoarse cooing of the few pigeons re-echoed round them. The rooks, long since driven from their flourishing colony in a wood of tall elms that *once* shaded the house, now seemed as they slowly sailed over it to regret their abandoned residence. Sometimes a flight of sea-fowl clamoured amid the billowy clouds; and when the wind blew from the south-west, the heavy waves were heard breaking monotonously on the shore, or distinctly in the stillness of night in low and hollow murmurs;—while, within the house, the least breath of air hummed and sung along the passages, and through the crevices of doors fastened up, producing such effects from various currents, and confinement, as, aided by an imagination addicted to superstition, might have been magnified into low sighs and half-stifled complaints.

The sullen vibrations of a dock which belonged to Wansford, and was placed near the door of what they now called the kitchen, was plainly heard in the room where Althea sat; and the melancholy measure of time was not to her the least unpleasant sound that broke the solemn silence of which she felt the dreariness. She seldom, however, gave way to the dejection which most young persons would have yielded to, but drove it away, sometimes by having recourse to her books (for she had now received and arranged them), and sometimes by playing one of those simple airs, in which she particularly excelled, though she was not a very great proficient in music.

Now, however, arrived the very long evenings of December, and beginning of January, when Wansford happened to be confined to his bed by the rheumatism, and his wife attending on him; so that the part of the house where Althea's sitting-room was situated was of an evening quite deserted, except by the servant girl, who remained alone in the kitchen, often trembling when she remembered the stories she had heard, and looking fearfully towards the door every time the wind shook the old loose boards and rusty lock.

On these nights it was that Althea sometimes found all her fortitude and philosophy almost unequal to repel the comfortless sort of feeling that assailed her. It was not fear, for the moment she began to reason with herself she knew that every kind of fear was groundless and ridiculous. From supernatural agents she could have nothing to apprehend, did they really exist; but against their existence it was with her an unanswerable argument, that the Director of the world would never violate a known law of nature to answer no possible end. Of the intrusion of any living being there was almost as little probability; for what temptation could there be for the nocturnal robber in a house where there was very little more than the simple furniture necessary for a peasant's family? Notwithstanding all this reasoning, however, Althea earnestly wished for the return of more cheerful days; and cast many a wistful look towards the sea, which on a clear day was visible from several of the windows of the house; and to which she fancied her walks might be extended.

It was only during the long and gloomy evenings that she felt distressed by the loneliness and seclusion of her situation. In the day-time she had not a moment unoccupied; and when the weather was such as would not allow her to make her village visits—

> For "now the fields were dank, the ways were mire,"
>
> MILTON.

she not unfrequently had recourse to the great banqueting-room up stairs, where, taking her little companion with her, she walked some hours for exercise. Yet it was certainly not such as greatly exhilarated her spirits; for Marchmont, his dispersed and distressed family, his blasted and ruined fortunes, were continually present to her mind; and while little Wansford, mounted on a stick, gamboled backwards and forwards before her, she figured to herself what Mrs. Mosely had formerly described to her, the infancy of that unfortunate young man, when in these then splendid rooms he was the first object of his doting parents, who gazed at him with prophetic fondness, as the future support—as one who was likely even to increase the respectability, of their ancient family. A month or six weeks passed nearly in the same way. It was late in the month of February, when the weather having been stormy for many days, Aldiea found herself languid and unwell; and believing that exercise would relieve her from an oppressive pain in her head, she took the child with her, not being in spirits to encounter the wide solitude of the apartments alone; and with a book resorted to the banqueting-room, which might indeed have been as well called a gallery.

Here she continued to walk for some time, till another heavy wintry storm coming on, it became suddenly so dark, that she was returning hastily to her own room; when glancing her eyes towards the great folding door which led to the stair-case, half of which was open, she fancied that some living creature ran hastily by. It seemed to be a dog—yet there was none about the house but a large white mastiff, usually chained up in the yard: this, whatever it was, was not so large an animal; and Althea, with something like fear mingling with curiosity, went to the door; and looking along the passage (now almost entirely dark) that led to those apartments of which so terrific an idea had been entertained, she thought she saw the same creature run swiftly along, but she immediately lost sight of it—it disappeared down another passage; and Althea had no inclination to trace it farther, though she felt a considerable deal of surprise. She now hastened down the stairs, not without looking involuntarily behind her: she saw nothing, however, and in some agitation reached her own room.

A moment's reflection restored her to composure. Of what was she afraid?—and how was it extraordinary that a stray dog should wander into a house in so ruinous a condition as were almost all the uninhabited parts of this? She endeavoured by such reflections to drive from her mind a circumstance that was certainly of no consequence: but still it returned to her, and she found the recollection of it attended with some kind of regret, for she no longer felt disposed to take her melancholy walks in the gallery: and this added another deprivation to the many she was compelled already to submit to; for, gloomy as these were, they procured a sort of change in bad weather, which it was unpleasant to relinquish. But now a dread hung about her which she could not immediately conquer, though she was ashamed of owning that she felt it even to herself.

This was perhaps increased by Mrs. Wansford's telling her a day or two afterwards, that as she was sitting up with her husband, who after a violent paroxysm of the rheumatism had fallen into a dose, she had either heard, or fancied she heard, amid the profound stillness of the night, the slow light steps of some person walking about the house.

"Once, Ma'am," said she, "to be sure I thought it must be you coming out of your room, the steps seemed so near; and I was afraid you were ill, and I was going to open the door to see—but just at that moment my heart somehow misgave me; I stopped a little to listen, and I could almost swear that I heard whatever it was go softly, softly, and lightly along the back passage, and go to the rooms where my husband puts our malt and hops. Then I was sure it could not be you; and my heart was up in my mouth! I am sure at the time I thought I had never heard such an unaccountable noise since I have been in this house.—But, after all," continued she, pausing, "after all, perhaps, it might be only fancy."

"I dare say it was nothing more," said Althea; "perhaps you were fatigued, and worn with anxiety; and when that is the case, we are apt to give way to fears and fancies that would never at another time be indulged."

"I should not have thought so much, perhaps, of it," resumed Mrs. Wansford, "but that Tiger has been so restless of nights lately, that it has been impossible for me and the girl to make him quiet. He has flown round the house as if he was mad—then back again—and barking ready to tear up the ground. My husband was waked by him once or twice out of a sound sleep; and I told him what a taking the dog was in, and that I was quite frighted at it, and was afraid it would fright you. But Wansford said it was nothing but nonsense; that there was no reason for fear, and that he was sure it was only a fox, or some vermin about the house, that made Tiger rave so. Sometimes, indeed, in hard weather, we have had foxes come quite into the house, as it were, after our poultry; and perhaps it might be the case now."

"It might be a fox that passed the door," thought Althea; "for why into so lonely and deserted a place should not such an animal come for shelter? It may be one of them that traverses these desolate rooms of a night." Althea thought of the verse in Isaiah—

"But the wild beast of the desert shall lie there, and their houses shall be full of doleful creatures."

"Alas!" added she, with a sigh, "what has this unfortunate family of Marchmont done, that their venerable abode, sanctified by the long sufferings of loyalty, should be under this cruel malediction?"

The solution, however, that she had now received of the causes of those slight disturbances which had alarmed her, quieted the disagreeable sensations she had felt, and insensibly the impression they had made wore away. Notwithstanding the advanced season, the weather now became so severe, as to take from her all disposition to return even to the walk in the banqueting-room. From her poor old pensioner she was for some time excluded; for the snow was deep, and to reach her cottage was difficult till the way was beaten—difficulties which Mrs. Mosely could by no means encounter to come to her. Althea, therefore, was obliged to content herself with sending the servant girl with a supply of provisions, and an enquiry after the solitary inhabitant of the cottage, which she continued to repeat for a few days.

When Althea herself asked this girl after Mrs. Mosely, her answers were such as might be expected; but it happened that passing one day into the kitchen to enquire for her return, she heard her say in her Devonshire dialect to Mrs. Wansford, who was busied there in preparing some food for her husband, "I declare I cannot think what iz coom to the ould wewman—she seems always tew much in a fluster to send back any mezzage to Miss, zoomhow."

"But she was very thankful," said Mrs. Wansford, "was she not, for Miss's goodness?"

"Yes, sure!" answered Hannah, "but, Lord! mythinks she is vastly odd az it twere. Then it is az hard to get tew her az if she was a lady herself. She've creeped away out of the rewm wher she used for to be, intew another little beck rewm, and the dewce at all can I make her hear, she's few diff. I said tew her that I had tewk'd down ever so much of our *cloom** with things as she had had, and that yew had sent for it, so she said I might take back what I whewld; she coonet no hew tell one from tother—So—"

"The poor old woman is not well then?" said Althea, as she entered the room.

Hannah, colouring at having been thus overheard, and afraid that Althea might be offended, answered confusedly, "No, Miss; she be'ent sick, but she seems somehow in trouble."

---

* Crockery ware, or glass

"I will go myself to-morrow," said Althea; "I suppose the weather affects her, poor creature!"

She afterwards made some other enquiries, whether she had sufficient firing, and whether the path to the cottage was practicable, and then returned to her employments.

One of these had lately been the study of that period of English history when the Marchmont family had been so distinguished by its sufferings and fidelity; for this point of time had now, from her situation in the scene of many of the events that had occurred, and from her favourable opinion of the unfortunate successor to the virtues, and, alas! to the misfortunes of these loyalists, acquired particular interest in the opinion of Althea.

In the course of her education she had gone through the history usually put into the hands of young people. Her understanding was equally clear and solid, and her memory remarkably retentive; yet a very young person usually reads the succession of monarchs, and the history of battles at a remote period, so much more as a task than a pleasure, that now her ripened reason gave to her present study at least the advantage of novelty. And that it might be every way profitable, she began with the Saxon heptarchy. But uncertain accounts, mingled and debased with monkish legends, accounts of beings who, with almost the single exception of Alfred, were so far from being fit to reign, that they were not fit to live, could not long detain her; nor was her imagination much cheered by the rude attempts at polishing the half savage Anglo-Saxon by the fierce Norman invader. In following their line through, and those of Plantagenet and Tudor, there is but little to soothe the mind. Ambition, the vice of great minds, is so degraded by ferocity, religion so perverted by superstition, the father is so often armed against the son, the child against the parent, the brothers against each other; so few of those "charities" existed among them which alone render human nature respectable; and the people were so continually the victims of the hateful passions of their princes, that the reader rejoices to bring his observations down to later times, and hopes that when the period in which what is called the *art* of government becomes better understood, order, and of course happiness, might be its effects. But from the *glorious* Queen Elizabeth, she who is pronounced by Lord Bacon to be *"admirable among women, and memorable among princes,"* to the wretched and degraded pensioner of Louis the Fourteenth (Charles the Second), there is hardly an interval that can be read with pleasure by one who, instead of having formed ideas from the little abridged histories so early put into the hands of children, dares to think for himself.

It was to this interval that the particular attention of Althea was turned. The first mention of the Marchmont family was in the reign of James the First. But it was in that of his unhappy son that they became remarkable.

Althea had borrowed of Mrs. Mosely a copy of a sort of memoir of the family begun by the grandfather, and continued by the father of Marchmont; of which a servant had been employed to make two or three copies, and one of them had been given to Mrs. Mosely, which she preserved with great care, and which she had put into Althea's possession, with a long exordium on the eminence and consequence of the persons to whom it related.

To trace through the tumult of civil discord, and the bewildering subtleties of mistaken politics, the bravery and persevering loyalty of a single family, was a task suited to the present state of Althea's mind. It seemed like designing the different appearances of a beautiful tree, which, though now shorn of its most flourishing honours, presented a fine and venerable form to the eye of the painter, and still produced some fair and verdant branches, though its trunk was injured by time and accident.

CHAP. III.

His face most foul and filthy was to see,
　　With squinting eyes, contrary ways extended,
And loathly mouth, unmeet a mouth to be,
　　That not but gall and venom comprehended,
　　And wicked words that God and man offended.

A SECOND FALL of snow now rendered the project Althea had formed of enquiring herself after Mrs. Mosely impracticable. In this western county indeed it lay less than in the more eastern, northern, or midland parts of England; but it had drifted so much against the banks and hedges, that the path to the cottage was again for her impassable.— The mild philosophy of the young recluse struggled against the heavy depression which such perfect seclusion, at a season so dreary, could hardly fail to inflict; but her studies were not much calculated to exhilarate her thoughts.—They led her from the detail of public calamity, to its effects on private life; from the misfortunes of the monarch to the consequent miseries of his servants—and the sad consequences of civil war on domestic happiness.

From the then most respectable condition of a private country gentleman, that ancestor of Marchmont, who first quitted it to attend a court, became personally attached to Charles the First, while Prince of Wales; and afterwards, when these unhappy dissensions broke out between Charles and his Parliament, which ended in the destruction of monarchy, Mr. (afterwards Sir Armyn) Marchmont was one of the first men of property in the West who declared for the King.

In the course of those sad years, which deluged the kingdom with blood, the second of his three sons and his only brother fell in the field. He did not survive them long; and his eldest son yielding for a while to a torrent it was fruitless to resist, and residing at Eastwoodleigh, it became an asylum for the wandering and dispersed royalists; while in rendering it such he narrowly escaped sharing their fate—and only by his being personally inactive, and by his popularity in his immediate neighbourhood. But when the son of the deceased monarch made his last effort at Worcester, Mr. Marchmont (for, his father being only a knight, he had no title) attended him thither with a small but chosen party of followers. After the event of that day, he returned, slightly wounded, towards home, and was for some time concealed in his own house. When it became safe to re-appear, he resumed, with some precaution, his former way of living; but by the sad condition to which his friends were reduced, as well as the restraint he was himself compelled to live under, his spirits and health became so much affected, that he gradually sunk into the grave, leaving his inheritance (impaired by fines, and the assistance he had sent the exiled King) to the eldest of the infant sons of his younger brother.

This young man, who at the Revolution was about five-and-twenty, unable to deny or to defend the misconduct of James, yet detesting from the influence of hereditary prejudice what he deemed the usurpation of William, absented himself entirely from public life; while his brother, who had entered early into the army, followed the fortunes of the misguided monarch, to whom he had sworn allegiance, and, marrying in France, became founder of that family with whom young Marchmont had some time resided.

The next heir, the grandfather of Marchmont, would have acted wisely, had he remained a quiet spectator of the attempts that were made in the year 1715 to re-establish the banished family; but his zeal was so unguarded, that a considerable part of his own and his wife's fortune was hardly sufficient to save him from the consequences of his open adherence to the "good old cause."

But not less bigoted to principle, in pursuance of which he could not act but at the risk of his whole fortune, he educated his children in the same ideas he himself entertained; and thirty years afterwards, in 1745, the family was reckoned so decidedly *Jacobite,* that their horses were seized at that period by the neighbouring Deputy-Lieutenant— and the same precaution was used in regard to him as with the Catholic gentlemen in the neighbourhood. Cut off from every advantage which the respectability of his family, or his own talents, might have given him in public life, while his fortune was sapped by the loans of his predecessors to their banished friends, the father of young Marchmont saw himself, towards the middle of his life, surrounded by a family of three daughters and a son, with only a nominal fortune—for his estates were mortgaged for almost as much as they were worth. When once this happens, the very expedients that are employed to ward off the ruin, bring it on more rapidly. The last Marchmont lived only long enough to see the inevitable destruction of his house—to see the son he so passionately loved likely to become a destitute wanderer, and his wife and daughters destined to indigence.—His heart was broken, and his eyes closed on this cruel prospect; while his unhappy son, by hazarding his personal liberty, rescued, with difficulty, his poor remains from the inhuman gripe of the law.

Such was, in brief, the detail collected by Althea from the family memoirs, to which Mrs. Mosely's narrative served as a supplement. To read over the period of history with which the former account was intimately connected, occasioned, in the mind of Althea, wonder and pity. That there were men who adhered from principle, and still more from personal affection, to Charles the First, misled and obstinate as he was, she could easily conceive; but it was more difficult to account for the infatuation of those who sacrificed their families and their country to the degraded *pensioner* of *France* and the unfeeling employer of *Jeffries*. Still there is something so respectable in the enthusiasm of even mistaken fidelity, something so impressive in the disinterested generosity of sacrificing every thing for an exiled and ruined family, that the ancestors of Marchmont became more than before the objects of her veneration; and their unfortunate descendant, of her pity.

In dwelling frequently on this topic, the mind of Althea turned itself to enquire if nothing could be done to alleviate the melancholy fate of a family so worthy of more prosperous fortune.—She was herself, alas! a more isolated being than any of those whose destiny she lamented, and but very little richer. Yet she could not help frequently returning to consider whether there were no means of befriending them; but as often as she did so, difficulties arose that made her for a while relinquish the hope of being able to accomplish it.

How indeed was it possible for her to address her father on behalf of a family to whom she believed he had conceived some dislike, and with any part of which Sir Audley did not know she had the slightest acquaintance? or how could she apply to Mrs. Marchmont herself with offers of service? Still, however, she could not wholly dismiss the idea; and as it would be doing something, she determined to write to Miss Eversley (with whom she still, though rarely, corresponded), and, making such an excuse for her curiosity as her local situation might well furnish her with, ask for some account of the present state of the Marchmont family.

Althea then was set down to this letter, when, as was Mrs. Wansford's custom, she came into Althea's sitting-room to make the enquiries of the morning after her health.—To those Althea made in her turn—the good woman answered—"Ah, dear Ma'am! this weather is very sad for my poor husband—He gets hardly any better, and I am afraid he will be quite confined again.—I think more of it than I should at another time, because I don't know how I should do to get advice for him; for I am sure Mrs. Cookson won't come through such a deep snow to him, if he should be ever so bad—And then—to be sure I am not afraid—but if any thing should happen, my poor Wansford, cripple as he is, would be of no more use than one of the children."

"If any thing should happen?" said Althea.—"Why what can possibly happen, my good friend?"

"I thought," answered Mrs. Wansford, "to have kept it to myself; but I own I am not easy enough, for all my husband laughs at me, to help telling you:—there certainly is somebody who can have no good design, about the house of a night."

"About the house?" cried Althea.

"Yes, my dear Miss: for these three last nights the girl and I have traced the print of feet clear enough in the snow. The track goes round to the old bow window, at the back of the council-room, and there it is not so distinct. I cannot imagine, for my part, what any living mortal can want here. I am sure there is no earthly thing for any body to take."

"It must be some persons who come with a design on your poultry," said Althea.

"I have never lost even a single chick," replied Mrs. Wansford: "besides, in the name of goodness, what should they do round there, if they came after the fowls? There is no track neither round the yard and outhouse.—My husband laughs at it indeed, and says, What should they come for? —I don't know what they come for, but I'm sure they *do* come—and that is the reason why Tyger never ceased raving for some nights. I shut him up on Thursday night in the kitchen; but even there he did nothing but growl all night long."

"Yet if any body had been in the house," said Althea, "he would have done more than growl—he would have run to the place."

"No," replied Mrs. Wansford; "he could not do that, for he could not get into the old part of the house. The doors above are all shut up, you know, and there is no way below. To be sure I have not much notion what any body should do there; but I firmly believe there are *travellers*, or some strange people, that hide about the house—and I own it *does* fright me."

Althea now recollecting the dog, which she had certainly seen, and feeling by no means delighted with the idea of *such* neighbours as her hostess described, could not help betraying some emotion in her countenance; yet unwilling to add to the terror which she saw had taken possession of Mrs. Wansford, she forbore to say all she thought, and only observed, that if such was really her persuasion, it would be better to make some enquiry into the matter, and to take some precaution against the danger that might follow.

"Why, so I have been telling Wansford," answered she.—"But I declare he is quite provoking—he will insist upon it, that 'tis nothing in the world but my fancy—or some accidental thing of no consequence. —I wish, dear Ma'am, you would but speak to him yourself— He won't tell you it is fancy, perhaps.—If you are not afraid of catching cold, do come out yourself, and see if there is not a track of feet as plain as can be."

To make this enquiry, Althea consented; and it was indeed very evident that a person or persons had gone as far as that part of the house described by Mrs. Wansford, but *there* seemed to have disappeared. Yet there was no visible way by which the house could be entered on that side.—Althea now proposed to Mrs. Wansford to make some examination within side the house—but she declared herself afraid of going, unless some man could be found to accompany her—which she said it was not easy to do, as there was no person about the house who could go with her, and her husband, besides that he was disabled by the rheumatism, became impatient whenever she insisted upon there being any occasion of alarm.—Althea, though far from feeling at this moment any extraordinary portion of courage, yet offered herself as an auxiliary: but the poor woman was too seriously frightened to explore the uninhabited rooms with so slender a guard; and Althea felt that on the approach of night she should be extremely uncomfortable, in the idea that there were near her beings of whom it was much more reasonable to be afraid than of the departed family of the Marchmonts, who were the reputed inhabitants of that part of the house.

Night however came, and with it a sudden thaw that obliterated at once all evidence of the fact of which Mrs. Wansford was so solicitous to convince her husband:—but the impression it had made on her mind, and on Althea's, was not so easily effaced; and Althea found it impossible to go to rest without having recourse to an expedient to which she was generally averse—that of the servant girl bringing her bed into the same room. The door was then as well secured as their united contrivances could effect, and Althea lay down without undressing herself.—The hours, however, passed quietly—there was no unusual noise about the house—and towards the middle of the night, though her thoughtless attendant was in a profound sleep, she went softly to the window, and by the light afforded by the moon, almost at full, yet often obscured by wandering clouds, she could see to some distance around. The view was not indeed on the same side of the house as that to which the footsteps had been traced, but it was difficult for any person going from the nearest villages to reach any quarter of the building without passing along some part of the ground she could now survey. She saw, however, neither animal nor human being—and supposed that, with whatever design these intruders had before approached, the lightness of the night had now deterred them.—Again she wearied herself with conjectures, and again desisted; for she found no way of accounting for such an appearance, but by supposing that the design was to rob: yet why should such a risk be incurred, where there was so certainly nothing to take?

Her apprehensions kept her sleepless till the morning broke: she then sunk into forgetfulness; and it was not till some time after her usual hour that she went down into her parlour to breakfast. As she seldom rang the bell that Wansford had contrived to mend for her, she was going herself into the sort of kitchen where he and his family usually sat, to ask for her breakfast; when she was met in the passage by Mrs. Wansford, who, with a look of dismay, said "Dear Ma'am, I was coming to see for you. There are two such strange-looking men along with my husband!—and they are asking such a number of odd questions!—I cannot, for my life, imagine what they want."

Althea, whose imagination was still full of the track that had been seen in the snow, fancied that these might be the persons who clandestinely visited the house; but as their coming now was a direct contradiction to their motives for coming before, she recollected herself, and asked Mrs. Wansford what sort of people they were?

"That is more than I can tell you, I'm sure," replied the good woman,—"For my part, I do not know what to make of them, and I can see Wansford knows as little; however, he keeps civil to them. —I wish you would come in, my dear Miss, as 'twere by chance."

"I'll come, certainly," said Althea, alarmed, though she knew not why.—"But they cannot be people that want me?"

Then, impelled by fear and curiosity, she entered the room, but instantly shrunk back, for the figures of the two men, who sat opposite Wansford, terrified her. Neither of them arose at her entrance, though *her* appearance was certainly such as demanded that mark of respect from persons of theirs.—One of them was a short mean figure between fifty and sixty, wrapped in an old blue great coat with a red cape, and he wore a carroty scratch wig pulled forward over a face which could not, without an affront to the species, be called human. Squalid and despicable as this wretch was, he seemed to be invested with some authority over the other; whose great athletic figure impressed terror, while that of his companion raised abhorrence. This second man had a broad red face, deeply scarred with the small-pox, with a black patch across his forehead; greasy shock hair, and a shabby coarse surtout, which altogether answered so completely to the idea she had formed of a ruffian, that Althea had, at the moment, no other expectation but that one of these men would confine Wansford, while the other robbed the inhabitants of the house.

Such were the alarming figures that, on the appearance of Althea, seemed, with renewed eagerness, to pursue the enquiry, whatever it was, that they were making of Wansford; who, confused and alarmed by interrogations he did not understand, seemed very desirous of getting rid of his unwelcome visitors, yet afraid of offending them.

Althea, unable to sustain for a moment the insolent looks of the man last described, hurried back into her parlour—Mrs. Wansford, in increased dismay, following her:

"Dear Ma'am," said she—"what do you think of these men? what can they be?—and what can they possibly want?"

"I have never seen bailiffs, or their followers," said Althea; "but I should fear, from the description I have heard of such people, that these are some such men."

"Bailiffs!' exclaimed Mrs. Wansford, turning as pale as ashes, "what can bailiffs want with my husband?—Mercy upon me!—He does not, I am sure, owe any body five pounds in the world—and I am *as* sure he has never done any harm in his life.—Oh, my God! what is going to happen to him?" The poor woman, who had eagerly seized on this alarming notion, was now so overcome with it, that she could not stay in the room; but notwithstanding the terror with which the sight of the men affected her, she was hastening back to that where they were with her husband, when in the passage, feeling his way with his cane, for he was half blind, the elder of the horrid-looking wretches met her.—Wansford, with a mixture of fear and indignation in his countenance, followed him, though so lame that he went on crutches.—Shocked and amazed at his approaching her, Althea had no power to move from the place where she stood. The man, stalking slowly up quite close to her, while she shrunk from his approach, in a loud and slow voice, whose sound would alone have conveyed a perfect idea of the hideous monster that uttered it, thus spoke—"I understand. Madam, that... you ... are ... the ... daughter ... of... Sir Audley... Dacres,... Ba-ro-net,—proprietor of this house.— These people then are your servants?"

"And who are you, Sir," said Althea, collecting all her courage, "that, knowing to whom this house belongs, and who *I* am, take the liberty of thus intruding?"

'My business . . ." began the wretch again.

"Your business cannot be with me, nor with Sir Audley's servants—
They do not know you —I beg you will go from hence."—The man,
who found by the trembling of her voice that she was terrified, now
thought that he should prevail by mere dint of fear: striking therefore
his cane against the ground; he said in a still louder tone—"Understand, Madam, that I am *authorised* in what I demand, and ..."

"For God's sake!" cried Althea, speaking to Wansford, "what does
he want?"

"He insists, Miss, upon being allowed to search the house. I
have refused him; for why?—I'm sure by his looks he don't seem an
honester man than they he pretends to search after—and what if he
was?—He has got no right to search here—or if he has, why don't he
shew it me?—why don't he shew his warrant?—But, instead of that,
he won't even tell me who he looks after!—Come, come, Mr. What's-
your-name, come out of my young lady's room, or I'll shew you that,
lame as I am. I'll not let any such fellows fright her."

"I would explain to the lady," said the disgusting wretch, regardless
of this remonstrance—"first, what my demands are—secondly, the
authority with which I am invested—thirdly, the grounds of my proceeding—fourthly, the consequence of resisting."

"I will hear nothing. Sir," exclaimed Althea; I will not hold any
converse with you. I am perfectly convinced that a person of *your* appearance can have no business in this house, and I must insist upon
your leaving it."

"My appearance!" muttered the horrid fiend—"my appearance! I
see, I see how it is; here is collusion. —I say, man," (turning to Wansford) "that I will execute my duty —I will examine the other part of
the house."

"And I say," cried Wansford, seizing him by the collar with one
hand, while he supported himself with the other, "that you shall go
out of that part of it where you are already." So saying, by the application of all his strength he jerked the man into the passage; Mrs.
Wansford, dreading lest his follower should fall upon her husband,
followed trembling and crying; while Althea, who had never suffered
such an alarm in her life before, shut the door of her room, and bolted
it within.

She listened, and heard a scuffle in the kitchen, which increased her
affright; yet she knew not, in the confusion of her thoughts, whether
she feared these people as common robbers, or as ruffians authorised

by law to hunt some unhappy person to destruction. The latter, though
she knew not whom they sought, seemed to her more detestable than
the former. Her present agitation, however, permitted her only to listen in breathless suspense: she heard Wansford loudly insist on their
leaving the house, declaring he would sue them if they dared to stay;
while the old miscreant preached aloud of his authority, and his power;
and his follower, half-ridiculing and half-menacing Wansford, seemed
determined to support his employer. After this had lasted some time,
to the increasing terror of Althea, she heard other voices interpose,
which very plainly, but somewhat roughly, took the part of Wansford,
and, as it seemed; added more forcible arguments than he had himself
been able to bring forward; for the enemy were now expelled, and she
heard the governor of the fortress engage his auxiliaries to celebrate
their victory in some of his best cyder.

When they were set down to do this, Mrs. Wansford appeared at
the door of Althea's room, which was readily opened to her.

"Oh! my dearest Miss," cried she, as she entered—"Sure I never
in all my whole life have been so frighted—and I am sure you too
must have been terrified!—Dear! how pale you look!—Let me get you
something."

"No," said Althea—"I am very well now.—But tell me who these
people are?—and how, at last, you got them out of the house?"

"Ah! as to who they *are*, I know no more than you do, Ma'am,
but I know they wanted no good. Did any mortal ever see such a
frightful-looking wretch as the ruffian that came in here? My poor
Wansford, cripple as he is, would never have got rid of them, if I had
not bethought me of sending Hannah down to the men at plough in
lower park croft; I knew they'd soon clear the house of 'em; and so
they did.—John Hedbury says they're both bailiffs—or one's a lawyer,
and t'other a catchpole, 'tis much one; and he knows they've been
about this country, and some more along with them, for three or four
weeks—creeping about, and asking this man, and asking t'other man,
what strangers there were in these parts? Some of our neighbours were
talking about these bad-looking fellows at the Nag's-Head, John says,
but last Saturday night; some said they were excisemen, and some that
they were spies—but another again said he knew one of them—that
old one; and he is a lawyer at Plymouth; John Hedbury mentioned
his name, but I can't think of it now. Some thought, it seems, that the
person they are hunting for is one that has run away with money from

his master; another guessed that it was a Jacobine, or Jacobite; I don't know, not I, what they call 'em; but Miller Clayfield said he was sure as could be, that it was some man in debt, and that this lawyer fellow had got a writ against him, and t'other was a bum bailiff."

"Still," said Althea, "I do not comprehend why the search of these pursuers should be so particularly directed to this house?"

"Nor I neither, I am sure. I cannot think why they should come here indeed!—As my husband told them, an Englishman's house is his castle, and he should not have thought of their pretending to search this; for though he was only a servant, he had as much right to keep out any such dirty fellows as the first Lord of the land. We are no likelier than other folks to harbour bad people, and I'm sure there are no people here; though, if there were, and it was only a poor man hiding for debt, I'm sure I'd never tell such as them; for to help such a one out of their clutches would be another thing."

"And do you know any body likely," said Althea, "to want such a friendly concealment? Perhaps Wansford does; and, unknown to you, may have taken some unfortunate person, thus pursued, into the house? Recollect, whether the noises you have heard, and the print of feet traced in the snow, which alarmed you so much, might not have something to do with the person that these bailiffs say they would search for?"

"Bless me! so they might, indeed!—And yet I cannot think, neither, that Wansford would do such a thing without telling me. Besides, who does *he* know? Here we live from one month to another, and not a living soul ever comes near us!—Besides, how, if Wansford had done so, how could he carry the person victuals without my knowing it? Indeed, how could he carry it at all? I never missed the value of a bit of bread. Where could such a person, if one *was* hid in the house, where could he sleep? There is no bed, I'm sure, in it—as you must have seen, Miss, when you went over it. Besides, I'm certain my husband would never do such a thing without telling me."

"You remember, however," said Althea, "that your husband laughed off all your fears, and would believe nothing about the noises that you talked of—as if he had some reason for wishing to avoid enquiry."

Struck with this remark, yet unwilling to believe that Wansford could possess a secret he would not communicate to her, his wife now left Althea, determined to find out the mystery, if there was one; while

Althea, who could neither cease her conjectures, nor fix on any that were probable, and whose spirits had been strangely hurried by the people she had seen, with difficulty composed her mind to follow the occupations of the day.

CHAP. IV.

Great enemy to this, and all the rest
    That in the garden of Adonis springs,
Is wicked Time, who with his seythe addrest
    Doth mow the flowering herbs and goodly things,
    And all their glory to the ground down flings.

IN THE COURSE of the day Wansford related to Althea the conversation these men had held with him.

"They began," said he, "by asking me whether I knew this person and that person in the neighbourhood, and *who* lived in the house? and *who* came to the house? and such a number of questions, that I could not tell, not I, what they would be at! Thinks I, you can't have any good reason, my masters, for all this inquisitiveness? You look very like catchpoles; I don't half like you, so you'll not get much out of me! From one thing to another, they began to tell me that they were employed by some very worthy gentleman to discover a person who had done him a very great injury, and was, they had reason to believe, concealed somewhere in this neighbourhood. The old fellow then said, that, if they could find, and secure this man, but what his name was they did not choose to tell, they were to have a very considerable reward; and hinting that if I would help them, I should have a share, they desired I would let them search the house. For my part, I hate all attornies, having suffered enough once by one of them; and as to your bailiffs, and bailiffs' followers, I'd fain have such rascals dragged through the horsepond. So I told them that, whoever the person was that they wanted, I was very sure he could not be at Eastwoodleigh; but that, if he was, I'd see the whole tribe of spies and sheriffs' officers at the devil, before I'd help one of them to take any poor fellow to prison. Upon that, the old swivel-eyed chap began in his prosing way to persuade me, and, when he found that would not do, to threaten me. Then you, Ma'am, came in, and the impudent fellow thought, I suppose, he could frighten you into ordering me to do it. I never saw such a ruffian. I believe, for my part, that it is Jack-Ketch himself: but Hedbury says his name is Vampyre; that he is an attorney, and has been the ruin of a great many families, for that he is the greatest rascal in all the country! If I catch him or the other blackguard about the house again, I'll show them the way through the lower pond—that they may be sure of."

Althea now very seriously enquired of Wansford, whether there were any grounds for believing that the unfortunate man, of whom these satellites of the law were in search, was concealed about the house? Wansford, with every appearance of sincerity, declared that there could be no such circumstance, he believed it impossible, and could not imagine what had given rise to such a notion.

Althea then mentioned to him the tracks of feet that had been seen in the snow.

"Yes," replied he, "my wife frightened herself strangely about it; but, after all, what was it owing to? These very men, depend upon it. Indeed, they as good as owned to me, that they had been about the house once or twice. I promise them, if they venture again, I shall shew them that there is more in the house than they bargain for. I'd no more mind shooting such pests to the world than a couple of mad dogs."

Althea thought that the bravery of Wansford was a little misplaced, and that it would have been better had he shewn more resolution in preventing the elder of the men from the impertinence of addressing himself to her. Concealing however her thoughts, she dismissed her host for the present, and attempted to lose the uneasy impression that this strange circumstance had left: but it still recurred to her mind; nor could she forbear speaking of it, and suggesting such ideas as arose about it, to Mrs. Wansford, who, after another day or two had elapsed, told her, that she had taken every possible means to discover if Wansford was really engaged in concealing any one in the uninhabited parts of the house, and that she was convinced he had not. Another and another day passed, in one of which Althea visited her ancient friend at the cottage. The poor woman told her she had kept her bed, and expressed in the warmest terms her gratitude for all the kindness she had received. Althea observed none of that confusion and singularity in her manner of which the servant girl had spoken. She was low and languid; but, in so melancholy a state of desertion, with only the darkening prospects of age, poverty, and sickness before her, such dejection was but too natural, and too common. Once or twice she seemed to wish to say something to Althea of more import than common complaints; and at length, on being encouraged to do so, she said, that as she was sure she should not outlive the winter, she wished she could see her nephew, the only relation she had, and that Althea would promise her, that, instead of being interred among the parish poor, she should be laid as near as possible, or as would be allowed, to the family burial place of the Marchmonts, and near her dear master, of whom when she now spoke, she seemed more affected than ever—But the old seldom weep!

Whatever was in Althea's power, she promised with that genuine goodness of heart which marked all her actions. She offered too to write to the relation whom Mrs. Mosely thus named with solicitude, but learned that he was at a great distance in the service of a gentleman, who would probably be unwilling to spare him; and that, if he would, the journey would be so expensive, that it would be impossible for him to undertake it. To this unsatisfied wish, therefore, Althea could apply no remedy; but, leaving her pensioner in better spirits than she found her, returned to her solitary home, with that self-content which always follows the consciousness of doing good.

On entering the parlour she found a letter on her table. It was from Linda Eversley; and after some details relative to persons and affairs much less interesting, the family of Marchmont was thus mentioned—

"You enquire after those unfortunate people the Marchmonts. I know but little of them, as my brother is always hurt if they are spoken of; but when I received your letter I shewed it to him. He said, 'Tell Miss Dacres, that if my poor friend knew how generously she expresses an interest in his fate, I am persuaded he would forget half its bitterness—for very greatly did he admire her, as indeed who does not? However, you may tell her too, Linda, that I hope he is somewhat less unfortunate than he has been; for after several unsuccessful applications to become a tutor (one of which was to Sir Audley, offering to undertake the care of Mr. Dacres), he has at length found a situation in Ireland, not as a tutor, but with a nobleman who is improving and planting a considerable estate, which he has engaged Marchmont to superintend. He is gone to Ireland, as I hear from his mother, who, with his sisters, remains where she did in Surry" So for my brother's information goes.—Poor Marchmont! I agree with you, my dear Althea,

that himself and his family are worthy of a better fate; for I am afraid
Mrs. Marchmont and her daughters are in very uneasy circumstances.
You know that my brother has more will than power to serve them, for
his domestic unhappiness is not at all mitigated."

Miss Eversley then went into the history of her sister-in-law's vulgar tyranny. Althea hurried it over, as one of those incurable evils on
which it is painful to dwell, and returned to lament the sad destiny of
Marchmont and his family.

"How could my father," said she, "refuse to accept him for Mr.
Dacres?" Where would he have found a man better qualified? Her concern, that he was rejected, was equalled however by her surprise that
he should apply to her father; and when she reflected on the former
repulse he had met with, her heart bled to think how cruelly severe
that pressure of adversity must be which had reduced his high spirit to
submit again to ask a favour of Sir Audley.

If it had been possible to add to that undiminished and acute regret with which Althea always thought of her lost friend, her more
than mother, it would have been increased by her now reflecting, that
limited as was that excellent woman's power of giving pecuniary assistance, yet that her active humanity would probably have found the
means of alleviating the sufferings of Mrs. Marchmont and her children. Althea, in imagining all the mortifications, deprivations, and sorrows of that extreme indigence in which they were represented to be,
looked from the window where she stood on the pile of building, of
which only a part was seen, but a part magnificent even in ruins; she
cast her eyes over the domain before it, denuded and changed as it was,
and then tried to conceive what must be the virtue of those who bore
with patient fortitude so cruel a reverse.

To these thoughts succeeded that regret, which what are called
the pleasures of life had never the power of exciting in the breast of
Althea—that regret which arose from her inability to relieve the distresses she deplored. Sometimes she almost determined to write to Sir
Audley, and beseech him to be a friend to these unhappy people. Then
she dreaded his stern repulse; and recollected how improbable it was
that he, who would condemn to a kind of imprisonment his own child,
only for refusing to sacrifice herself to prospects of affluence and
ambition, should be prevailed upon, by any intercession, to interest
himself for persons who had no other claim upon him but *that* poverty
which seemed in his opinion to be a crime.

Among the various plans that Althea thus thought of and rejected, in regard to the mother and sisters of Marchmont, it at length
occurred to her, that she might obtain some information at least about
their present situation, if Mrs. Mosely would write to them; and this
she determined to propose, offering to act as her secretary—a means
by which she thought she might introduce herself, without impertinence or impropriety, to their knowledge. This benevolent project she
put into execution the first day that was favourable for her walk: she
found on the part of Mrs. Mosely rather acquiescence, than any expression of pleasure. "It was long," she said, "since she had written
to her dear ladies—she knew not whether her doing so might not be
troublesome." Althea, however, over-ruled every slight objection; the
letter was written; and she returned home, flattering herself that some
means would be found, by which she might become useful to a family
in whose destiny she felt so deep an interest.

While she expected an answer, which could not arrive in less than
a week or ten days, Althea returned to her solitary amusements. The
weather was fine and mild for the season; and her spirits were revived,
even by that distant promise of returning spring, which is given in
sheltered situations so early as the middle of February. In that piece
of ground which had once been a well cultivated garden, Althea had
hitherto been deterred from walking, by its generally melancholy and
ruinous appearance, when the bleak storm of mid-winter, or its chilling snows, added to the gloom which neglect and desolation spread
over the place. But now the faint tinge of fresh green, which the spurg-
es and some other early leaves lent to the spots of uncultivated earth
(though mingled in many places with masses of fallen walls), were
cheering to the sight, and tempted her to enquire if any of the ornaments of the garden had resisted "*Stern ruin's ploughshare,*" which had so
deeply passed over almost all the rest of the place.

As no temptation had urged the spoilers to bear away the fruit-
trees that lined the thick walls, they still existed; and neglected and
grown heavy with wood, as they were, a few red buds, nearly expanded, were here and there visible. The surface of the broad gravel walk
that encompassed the garden was now covered with moss; and the
borders, which were divided from it by box, grown into a low ragged
hedge, produced only weeds, unless in two or three patches where the
warm shelter of the projecting buttresses had induced Wansford to
sow some early vegetables. The espalier trees were almost timber; and

the shrubs which had once been planted in a quarter behind them, as in a sort of nursery, were grown so large as to overshadow them. At the corners of the cross walks stood ancient heads of rosemary and lavender, overgrown with gray moss, and serving as a sort of specimen of the state of gardening in England when such plants were cultivated with almost as much care as is now given to the tenderest exotics.

In the centre of the garden was the carved pedestal of a large sun-dial, but the plate was gone. From thence, a broad straight walk, bordered with evergreens, of which only a few were alive, led to the ruins of a greenhouse, which Althea had been told opened into a pavilion, where, in the days of their prosperous fortune, the family of Marchmont used to entertain their company, or amuse themselves in the fine evenings of summer; for it looked into the pleasantest part of the then park, where a small river, pouring down from a high ridge of woodland, wound away to supply two large ponds within sight of the windows: but the coppices were now cut down, and the inconsiderable stream to the right lost among tangled brush-wood, furze, and broom. The doors that led into this pavilion were now locked: the green-house windows had been taken out and sold; and of the old orange-trees, and other plants so fondly cherished by the late owner of the place, no traces remained, save two or three broken cases producing funguses, and mouldering into touch-wood. The few garden tools that Wansford possessed, and some parcels of garden seeds and dried herbs fastened to the wall, were now all that was to be seen in this spacious place, once the abode of innocent pleasure. Althea, comparing its appearance with that of a magnificent modern conservatory, the property of a great contractor whose house near London she had visited with Lady Dacres, left it with a sigh, and crossed what once lay before the front windows as a parterre. Among the grass and moss that were now spread over it, a few crocuses and hepaticas still forced their way, and in two or three places the snow-drops had spread themselves so thickly as to silver the ground in despite of obstructing weeds. Pensively philosophizing, Athea gathered some of them: they were hardly blown; but one of the little Wansfords, now running up to her, asked her leave to gather a few also, and then to dig some up, and put them in a pot to carry into the house. This childish project Althea, who loved to see any creature happy, rather encouraged. The child called her brother to help her; the garden pots were collected, filled with earth, and not without some labour carried into the house.—Their mother, however,

objecting to this portable garden being placed in rooms where the purposes of her family œconomy were carrying on, the children proposed
to put them up in the banqueting-room, where they had sometimes
been permitted to play. This, after some opposition from their father,
they were allowed to do, and immediately proceeded to arrange their
new green-house, assisted by the maid;—while Althea, for whom the
simplest pleasure had charms, and who was not sorry to take this opportunity of visiting once more a place of which she had sometimes
thought with fears that she was now half ashamed of, went up with
them, and even directed their operations. She now again surveyed the
room, which her imagination had lately filled with beings more terrific
than spectres. It gave her no other idea than that of solitude and ruin.
She observed that the cornices of this room, as well as the ivy that had
crept into the hall beneath, would soon be peopled; for the sparrow
and the robin had already begun to build among them. From hence
she descended with her party, for she was by no means courageous
enough to go alone, to that part of the building where Mrs. Wansford
had shewn her the footsteps in the snow: but within there was no appearance that any person had been there; though Althea thought that
this room, lighted by a window projecting from the thick wall (and
where an old helmet, a halbert, a pair of gauntlets, and a rusty pike
over the great chimney, were the only movables that appeared), was the
most desolate and gloomy part of the whole house. She was now satisfied, however, that all the fears she had entertained in common with
Mrs. Wansford were unfounded; and that the dog she had seen was,
as Wansford had assured her, a brown terrier which belonged to some
of the neighbours, and which he had often seen about the buildings.

"He comes, I suppose," said he, carelessly, when Althea mentioned
the circumstance, "after the vermin, of which there is enough about
this old place besides rats, which make it impossible for me to keep
any thing in any of these rooms, there are stoats or weasels that breed
about the holes in the battered walls. I saw one of them t'other day run
across the passage."

Althea remembering this, and finding not only the appearance
of the animal she had seen accounted for, but the noises also which
alarmed the lurking superstition of Mrs. Wansford, no longer felt any
reluctance to renew her walks in this great room. Here the good woman of the house, on Althea's report, agreed again to hang her clothes
after a great wash.

"It dries," says she, "there, as well as if 'twas out upon the green; and then no wet can trouble us—so that it would be a thousand pities to give up such a convenient place."

From this period the gardening of the children, and the œconomy of their mother's bleaching operations, occasioned the room to be frequently visited. Some days passed without any remarkable occurrence: Althea visited her old friend Mrs. Mosely, and was surprised to find that no letter had been received from Mrs. Marchmont. In conversation with the ancient woman, Althea related the strange circumstance of Vampyre's inquiry at Eastwoodleigh. Mrs. Mosely answered coldly, that she had heard of it; and immediately transferring the discourse, from the oddness of the visit, to the character of the man who had made it, she said, that he was accounted the greatest rogue within three counties—"Aye, Miss, and as I believe in all England —I hope it does not produce his fellow."

With the usual garrulity of her age, Mrs. Mosely then began to tell several stories about him that had happened within her own knowledge; by which it appeared, that certain ruin followed wherever this disgrace to his profession and to human nature once infixed his empoisoned fangs; and that his insidious friendship was not less fatal to his employers, who were always his dupes, than was his enmity to those against whom they engaged him.

"Many," said she, "aye, very many are the poor people whom he has undone—who have died in jail—and whose children have been turned out to beggary, or have gone to the parish. But, alas-a-day! nobody had more reason to know what a cruel villain he was than my late dear master; and sure I am, that Sir Audley Dacres could never know what a hard thing he did when he put any matters against Mr. Marchmont into the management of this man. If it had not been for that, perhaps—but what is the use now of talking? What is to be, is to be; and what God pleases to direct is for the best."

Althea was too much hurt at the idea that her father had accelerated the ruin of Mr. Marchmont's family, to continue the conversation. She bade her solitary friend a good evening, therefore, and walked pensively homeward, reflecting how strange it was, that, in a country celebrated for its equal laws, a set of men should exist, who, when they are dishonest, contrive by means of the abuse of those laws to inflict more miseries on individuals than can otherwise be produced in human life, save only those which follow the absurdity, madness, and wickedness of war.

CHAP. V.

One out of suits with fortune.

THOUGH SPRING NOW visibly advanced, there were still many disagreeable and variable days before it was probable Althea could make those
excursions into the country around, which promised her the only pleasure it was likely to afford her.—The afternoons now grew long, but
there was little temptation to walk—unless in the banqueting-room
or gallery, taking a book with her. Thither she was generally accompanied by the little Wansfords, whose cheerful voices as they ran about
relieved (without disturbing her meditations) that mournful stillness
which would otherwise have reigned in the deserted rooms—stillness,
unbroken but by the evening song of the robin, or, at a distance in the
fields, the first low chant of the thrush, which at this season is heard
almost singly to sing his faint vespers to the yet remote sun.

It happened that Althea had one day received a letter from Linda
Eversley, who, having very unexpectedly been carried to London by a
relation, was intoxicated with the pleasure and dissipation into which,
during her short stay there, she was permitted to enter; and she wrote
to Althea a long detail of all she had seen, with a lively description of
the parties she anticipated.

Far from feeling any thing like envy, Althea rejoiced in the satisfaction of her friend; yet, as she traversed the gallery, she could hardly
help some involuntary comparisons between *her* situation and that of
most other young women. It was true that it was her own choice; but
she could scarce refrain from thinking Sir Audley cruel, in having given
her no other alternative than this dreary seclusion, or a marriage with
a man she detested. Her reflections were not cheerful; the afternoon
was cold with a north-east wind; and she was on the point of returning to her parlour, when the eldest of Wansford's children, a girl between nine and ten years old, who had been hiding about in the empty
rooms with her brother, came running on tiptoe to Althea, and, pale

and trembling, whispered to her, that looking through a window in one of the closets which had a view into the end room, of that side where she thought her brother was seeking for her, she saw a man, who stood leaning near the chimney.—Althea, at once recollecting, or fancying, that this was the room of which so many stories were beheved, turned as white as her little alarmist—"Surely, Nancy," said she, "surely you fancy this?—Where is your brother?—Perhaps you merely saw him, while he staid to surprise you?"

"Oh, no; indeed," cried the child, "it is no fancy. I saw the man as plain as I see you, I am sure I did.—Oh! let us go call somebody"

"I believe indeed," said Althea, "we had better go—but, let us see for your brother first—he must not be left here."

"Oh! perhaps this man will kill him," cried the girl.—"Oh, dear Miss, I am so afraid! Pray call my brother—pray let us go."

Confused and harassed by the wild expressions of fear which the child very naturally uttered, Althea knew not whether to go or stay. She was by no means weakly timid, yet her courage was unequal to the undertaking of verifying whether the apprehensions of the terrified girl were well founded.—She now listened a moment in breathless silence; and then they heard the boy cry. Whoop!—as a signal to his sister, that, wearied with looking for her, he was hid, and that it was her turn to find him.—Nancy now cried out, as loudly as her apprehensions would let her, that she could play no more, and that they were going.—The boy heard her, and came running down the opposite passage to that from which the closet opened where his sister had been; and Althea, bidding them both go down stairs, was following them as fast as her trembling knees would permit, when *she* distinctly heard a door open—and then footsteps follow her towards the head of the stairs.—She hastened on, not daring to look behind her—but was hardly got to the landing-place of the great stair-case (while the two children, for the girl had communicated her alarm to the other, ran swiftly through the hall) before she heard a voice, which said in a half whisper—"Madam! Madam!—Miss Dacres!—hear me but a moment—I beg of you not to be alarmed!"

Althea, holding by the baluster, looked up. She saw, standing on the top of the stairs, a figure, of which, as his back was to the light which came from the open door of the gallery, she could not distinguish the face.—She was now alone in the house (for the children were already out of hearing); and in a state of mind difficult to describe, she hesitated a moment whether she should stop to hear what this man

had to say, or fly. It was evident that he knew her—his voice and manner were such as seemed not to indicate any evil design. Rapidly these
ideas passed through her mind—while the person, perceiving that she
wavered, approached her.—Althea still descending the stairs, though
with less speed—he spoke to her again.—"Miss Dacres," said he, "will
not surely refuse to hear, for one moment, an unhappy man, whose life
is, perhaps, in her power?"

She now saw his face, and became riveted to the place where she
stood; for through some change, which she was in too much confusion
to consider, she recollected the features and voice of Marchmont.

The immediate terror for herself was now suspended—surprise,
and fear of some disaster to him—a thousand sensations, which it
was impossible to investigate, prevented her speaking; but as she no
longer testified any inclination to escape from him, Marchmont descended the rest of the stairs, and, approaching her with the air of
a man still afraid of offending or alarming her, said—"The children,
whose alarm I heard, will probably bring some persons hither before I
can explain myself. My situation is as extraordinary as it is distressing;
nor is it. Miss Dacres, the least painful of many sad reflections, that I
have occasioned to *you*, as I know I have, uneasiness and alarm. You
will, however, I am sure, do me the justice to believe, that I am not
concealed thus like a robber, amidst the ruins of my father's house,
with any ill intentions—but through misfortunes that have driven me
from society."

He was proceeding, when voices were heard without the great entrance.—"I shall be discovered," cried he, "and the evils which for the
sake of others I have suffered so much to avoid must now come upon
me!"

"For God's sake, Sir," cried Althea, "do not hazard it—return, I
implore you, to your concealment —I will endeavour to divert whatever enquiries may be made."

"You are all goodness," said Marchmont.—"I have seen enough to
convince me that your humanity, your excellent heart may be depended
upon. The higher my admiration of so much virtue arises, the more
ardently I wish to vindicate myself from the suspicions to which this
strange concealment may give occasion. I believe it is in my power effectually to escape from any present pursuit, by ways known only to myself;
but I cannot go till you condescend to promise me the honour of five
minutes conversation once again. Tell me—may I hope for it, Madam?"

The voices became louder and nearer, calling Miss Dacres!—Althea, hardly knowing what she said, and dreading to see this unhappy young man liable to the misfortunes that must follow his detection, answered, with a trembling voice, "That she would be in the banqueting-room about the same hour the next day."

Marchmont, thanking her rather by a look than by words, instantly disappeared; and Althea, who imagined, by the voices of the people of the house, that they were afraid of entering the hall, crossed it as swiftly as she could, and near the door met Nancy, who with the maid, and a labourer they had called from the neighbouring barn, were waiting without the effect of repeating her name, for to enter the house was an undertaking they dared not venture upon. Her countenance was evidence enough, even to such observers, of the terror she had been in—but making an effort to assume composure, she enquired what was the matter?

Hannah then explained, that, frightened out of her wits by the report of the children, who said they had seen a man in the house who would certainly kill Miss Dacres, she had called Thomas from the barn, and they had come to see how they could help her.

Althea, who could not help thinking what such assistance would have done for her had there really been danger, now attempted, as the only means to prevent a farther discovery, to persuade the child to believe she had been mistaken.—"You are fanciful, Nancy," said she, "and must learn not to give way to such silly fears. There was *no* man where you supposed. I went myself to see, and I am sorry you have so needlessly called any body."—She then walked quietly into the other wing of the house, observing that Thomas, who remained behind to fasten the great door, trembled as he did it, and hastened after them as quick as possible, looking up to the windows with every mark of fear and consternation. When he overtook Althea, he seemed to survey her with marks of astonishment, as one who had more courage than belonged to her; and he whispered to Hannah, that, whatever Miss might say, he was sure little Nanny had seen something.—"I know well enough," added he, "what my own mother have tould me, of strange things she knewed—when she lived ous-maid with the 'squire."

Althea, still breathless, as well from the effects of fear as from her endeavours to hide her emotion, hastened to her own apartment, and, shutting herself in, recalled, with increasing astonishment, the circumstances of a discovery so extraordinary.

It happened that neither Wansford nor his wife was at home; the former, having some business at the town about five miles off, had gone thither early in the day and on account of his lameness was accompanied by his wife. They were now, however, every moment expected to return; and Althea had to consider how she was to act to conceal from them what she doubted not their daughter's account would engage them to enquire into. Over the simple spirit of such a child she imagined it possible that she might have influence enough, to convince her she was mistaken; but as it was not likely the alarm the child had received, and communicated to others, should not be known to her mother; Althea thought it would be difficult, if not impossible, long to evade her enquiries, or appease those fears to which the good woman was naturally prone.

Leaving this therefore to settle itself, Althea began to reflect on what Marchmont had requested of her, and on the extraordinary circumstances of his concealment and appearance. There was now no doubt but that, in consequence of those debts so unhappily though so piously incurred, Marchmont was reduced to the sad necessity of seeking this dreary asylum against his merciless creditors; and it was equally certain that it was of him, Vampyre and his myrmidons were in pursuit. A thousand fears for his final safety now mingled themselves with detestation of that ruffian who molested him, and pity for the forlorn condition to which he was reduced. Sometimes she doubted the propriety of her keeping the hasty appointment she had made—yet her generous sensibility would not allow her to evade it: she considered, that Marchmont would hardly have asked it if he had not believed she could render him some friendly service, and she remembered how anxiously she had wished for means and opportunity of relieving his unhappy family. As to the latent partiality she had felt for him, she had yet hardly trusted herself to ask what it meant; or, rather, she imputed entirely to pity for his unmerited misfortunes, that complacency with which she had accustomed herself to think of him since their accidental interview at Capelstoke.

She determined then to keep her promise, which she thought it could not be improper to do. It was impossible Marchmont could have any evil design; and whatever might be the imprudence of meeting thus a person almost a stranger to her, she had no satirical remarks from others to fear, and her own heart told her, that she meant only to obey the dictates of humanity and benevolence. It was true, that young women of her age are not, according to the established rules, to trust themselves with persons who may presume upon their condescension:—but Althea considered herself as placed in a singular situation, where mere forms might be dispensed with; and she looked on Marchmont as a young man who could not have any other claims to attention from her, than those which every human creature in distress has on his fellow being.

Having calmed her mind, and taken her resolution, she awaited the return of her host and hostess; who no sooner arrived at home, than their little girl began to tell her mother the terror she had been in—and to relate also, that Miss Dacres seemed sadly frightened at first, but afterwards went herself to look, and said it was nothing—no, nothing in the world but her fancy!

Wansford, who had invariably discouraged such fears, and who had come fatigued and out of humour, scolded first at the girl, and then at the mother, who had, he said, put such a parcel of nonsense in the poor child's head; that she would grow up fit for nothing at all, and never be qualified to earn her bread in the world. He then sternly bade her be silent; and his wife, as well as his children, knowing the necessity of obedience, the story seemed likely to be stifled for the present; but before Mrs. Wansford went to bed, she could not help gliding into Althea's room, to hear what she said to Nancy's story. After she had related what the child had told her, with many exaggerations, Althea quietly answered, that it was very true she had been at first alarmed at the little girl's report; "for I fancied" said she, "that those horrid men, who were here the other day, might have got into the house; but, on going to the place, I was convinced there was nobody —I am persuaded that she saw only her brother.—It was dusk, and some of the stories she had heard were in Nancy's head. You had better not encourage her in any of these fears: in this instance, I assure you, they are groundless, for I examined into the foundation of her apprehensions myself."

Mrs. Wansford shuddered at this exertion of courage, and left her—far from being convinced that Nanny had been mistaken.

CHAP. VI.

Io sol, fra viventi
L'asilo, non ho!

As THE HOUR approached on which Althea had promised to meet
Marchmont, she became so apprehensive and uneasy, that she could
not for a moment remain in the same place, but traversed the inhabited
rooms with such visible inquietude, that, had not Mrs. Wansford been
at that time busied more than usual, she must have observed it. At any
other period some contrivance would have been necessary to shake
off the attendance of the children, who were accustomed to follow
her when she went for her evening walks in the garden or gallery; but
now the impression of fear was so recent on their minds, that, instead
of importuning her for permission to accompany her, they kept close
to their mother, and Althea, with a beating heart, walked slowly and
unobserved towards the great door of the old hall, which was, she
believed, the only entrance to the deserted buildings. On reaching it,
however, she stopped; recollecting, at that moment, that she neither
knew how to open the door, nor probably had strength to do it. She
hesitated; but not long, for footsteps were heard within, and the door
was opened by Marchmont.

Althea stepped hastily in, but she could not speak. Marchmont
closed after her the great heavy door, and the noise of its shutting
re-echoed through the vacant rooms. Amidst the deep dejection that
visibly hung over him, a gleam of pleasure lightened in the eyes of
Marchmont; yet hardly did he venture to express what he felt, before
it seemed lost in sad reflections on his condition, and how different a
reception he was giving to Miss Dacres from what he might have done
under other circumstances. He was in the place where his ancestors
had dwelt in affluence and in honour; but *he* was himself a wretched
wanderer, concealed like a culprit; receiving a visit of charity and compassion from a young woman, in whom, as he plainly saw by her coun-

tenance and manner, commiseration was not unmingled with terror. Sensations so full of pain and mortification he endeavoured to subdue; and in a manner the most respectful, though his voice trembled as he spoke, he thanked her for her goodness and condescension.—"In this wretched scene of desolation," said he, "*where* can I ask Miss Dacres to honour me with her attention?"

Althea, who perceived how much he was affected, answered, with a faint attempt to look cheerful, that place was altogether immaterial: adding—"If you, Sir, have, as I suspect, resided here some time in the present condition of the house, it cannot surely be any great hardship for *me* to remain, at least as long as may suffice for me to hear how I can be fortunate enough to do you any service."

"I will not," replied Marchmont, as he led the way up to the great room where Althea usually walked—"I will not attempt, Madam, to express how deeply I am sensible of your goodness and condescension. The first moment I saw you, I believed all I have since found to be true of your character.—Your charity to the poor old servant who has shared the calamities of my family, made the deepest impression on my mind. With her I found a temporary asylum; and from her I heard, that Miss Dacres had even the humanity to interest herself for my mother, for my sisters; who, in common with myself, have no other recommendation to her than what we have acquired by misfortune!—Do not, however, imagine that my knowledge of this your tenderness of disposition has engaged me to intrude upon it. I know your situation: I honour, I reverence the noble principles on which you have preferred a residence in this now dreary and sequestered spot, to the highest affluence and prosperity. Long, long may that courage, so consistent with female tenderness and female dignity, support you in your honourable resistance!"

The vehemence with which this sentence was spoken, rendered it very unlike what would have been uttered by the calm voice of disinterested friendship. Marchmont seemed himself conscious of it, and, as if he had been betrayed into an indiscretion, paused to recover himself—Althea had nothing to reply—and, after a moment's silence, he proceeded in a lower tone:

"Too well assured, notwithstanding *that* rectitude of mind which will support its possessor under almost every inconvenience, that you could not fail, Madam, to have uneasiness enough, amid deprivations such as you must endure here, and suffering perhaps from Sir Audley's displeasure —I should never, no, believe me, I should never have presumed to attempt relating to you a detail of afflictions, (I believe I may say) unmerited afflictions, of which, since they cannot be relieved, it must distress a mind like yours to hear! But I find that my removal from this wretched asylum is, from some late circumstances, become necessary. I know not what will be my final destiny; but as long, very long imprisonment it will be hardly possible for me to avoid, as I may never again enjoy the honour of speaking to you, I could not determine to throw myself upon my fate, without attempting to appease those alarms which my enforced concealment, added to the legends which always belong to such houses as this, have very naturally contributed to give, even to a mind guarded, as I am sure yours, Madam, is, by reason and reflection. I cannot render this forsaken place worthy of one who would be the loveliest ornament of a palace; but, by explaining what I know must have given you occasional inquietude, I may at least prevent those apprehensions which must lend additional gloom to these forlorn scenes. May I also without presumption add, that, amid the misfortunes which I go to meet, I shall feel a great satisfaction in knowing that my conduct, which I know has been, and will be still more misrepresented, is at least explained to one on whose good opinion I set infinite value? and that, perhaps, while I am condemned by many, unpitied by others, and neglected by all. Miss Dacres will not think that misfortune is guilt, and will remember me with some concern."—His heart seemed now almost too full for utterance; but he recovered himself instantly, and went on:

"It is not to many people I would *appeal* for their pity—it is not from many people I would *accept* it. But *yours*, Miss Dacres, will be most soothing to a heart which is even at this early period of life outraged by a cruel world. And alas, Madam! driven as I am from my family, not allowed even to afford them the protection they want; an exile from society, and compelled either to live as a wretched vagabond, or submit to see my whole life wasted within the walls of a prison—it is long since I have dared to seek the sad consolation of relating my sorrows; long since I have heard one friendly sentence, unless from that helpless solitary old servant whose wants you have with so much humanity supplied. I believe you are acquainted with some of those circumstances which have reduced my family, from affluence as great as is often enjoyed by private gentlemen, to the state we are now in. Since the death of my poor father I have lived in a continual struggle

with adversity. It will, it must at length overwhelm me. But if I could
have saved my mother, my sisters, amidst the wreck, I should not have
devoted myself in vain! Believe me. Miss Dacres, no interest less dear
than theirs, should have compelled me to submit to the disgrace of
thus ignominiously skulking from the pursuit of the harpies, who have
a legal right to take from me—almost all I possess—the privilege of
breathing the air, and seeing the light of Heaven. But I have been
flattered by hopes; I have been lured into this degrading concealment
by the expectation that a little time might appease the malignity of my
pursuers; that they would be prevailed upon, by the interposition of
Mr. Eversley (the only friend who has, as far as was in his power, adhered to me), to give me time to try what I can do for their satisfaction
by my industry. To await the event of his attempts I submitted to hide
myself, though he was not himself acquainted with, or even suspected,
the place of my retreat. But my poor mother, who alone was privy to
it, has very lately acquainted me that the two creditors who pursue me
with so much rancour are now more inveterate than ever. And indeed
I knew I had little to expect from their mercy, when I found that, while
they appeared to listen to the mediation of Mr. Eversley, they let loose
upon me that *fiend* who, in the shape of an attorney, embittered the last
sad moments of my father; and, before his poor remains were conveyed to their place of rest, had taken measures to turn into the world
unsheltered and pennyless his widow and his children—that *miscreant*
(for it debases the species to call him man), who advised them to stop
the cold ashes of my parent in their way to interment; and to accept no
terms but those of my binding myself for the debt, which he believed
my friends would pay rather than that I should be hurried to prison."

"And this wretch," said Althea, taking advantage of a short pause,
"this Vampyre was, I fear, *first* empowered to pursue and oppress you
by my father, by Sir Audley Dacres?"

"Not exactly so," replied Marchmont. "The villain was one of
many of those agents whom the father of the present Lady Dacres
was used to employ in his money transactions, one of which you know
put his heiress, and in her right Sir Audley, into possession of this
house and estate. I do not blame Sir Audley himself, because, had he
from any motives of generosity been disposed to remove the affairs
that concerned us from the happy talons of this venomous reptile, he
might not have had it in his power; for never yet was the wretch known
to relinquish an employment, while he could by chicane and fraud ex-

tort a guinea from his employer. And indeed, had it been otherwise, I had no claim on the forbearance of Sir Audley Dacres. He never gave me encouragement to hope for his favour; he saw me unfortunate, and it requires more time than he probably had to spare to distinguish *imprudence* from *misfortune*. There *are*, to whom poverty always wears the semblance of blame."

Althea sighed deeply, but did not interrupt him.

"I do not however mean to say," continued Marchmont, "that Sir Audley is of that disposition. His being so nearly related to Miss Dacres would for ever make him respectable in my eyes. But pardon me, I wander from my subject—Vampyre, this attorney, was empowered to arrest me; and he must, I believe, have employed under some false pretence, and engaged by the promise of considerable reward, the myrmidons of the police, or he could never have traced me as he did to the cottage of Mrs. Mosely; where I had hardly been concealed a week, before I found it was besieged by that unfeeling species of the satellites of law who live on the miseries of the unhappy debtor. I had no counsel but a sick and feeble old woman, who, when she found that to be safe in her little hovel was impossible, advised me to have recourse to the parts of this house which had been contrived to conceal fugitives of a very different description. I knew them well, and was, perhaps, the only person who *did* know them. Ah! how little I ever thought, in the happy days of my childhood and early youth, that I should ever linger about the passages which I had frequently explored with a sort of melancholy curiosity, as the asylum of the ruined Cavaliers, and even the unhappy exiles of royal blood, whose history I have often considered with pain, mingled with a degree of that hereditary pride which my father had perhaps too much pleasure in encouraging; while I reflected on the share *my* family had in scenes which I do not now see quite in the same light as I was then taught to behold them!

"I dared not then, Madam, I dared not implore *your* assistance, though from your humanity towards poor Mosely I believed I should have found it; but to secure the coincidence of Mr. Wansford was absolutely necessary. He had the character of an honest man —I knew he had been a faithful servant in your family during the life of your mother. Something was to be hazarded; and I was so beset by the followers of Vampyre, that no other escape appeared practicable. I ventured then to entrust to Wansford the truth of my situation. The man heard it with that disposition which belongs to an unadulterated English spirit. He detested the malignant tyranny of the two rich men, who without any possible advantage to themselves pursued me merely to gratify the rage of disappointed avarice. He had himself suffered from some of the lower retainers of the law. He knew enough of Vampyre's character to hold him in that sort of abhorrence which an honest mind feels towards cunning and cruelty; and he saw no prejudice that could happen to himself from affording me the asylum I asked, which was merely permission to bring a mattress and bed-clothes into one of those small recesses (for they can hardly be called rooms), which have been contrived amid the thick walls of this old building. There are three of them, wide of each other, but communicating by passages so narrow as to admit but one person at a time, and in some places by steps so steep that only an active man could pass them. Into the least damp of these I contrived, by the assistance, or rather the connivance, of Wamsford, to convey some straw, a mattress, and such other necessaries as might secure from the effects of great cold and humidity a man brought up to a more delicate manner of life than he has lately been accustomed to. Adversity is an excellent and radical cure for the errors that fond parents often commit in the education of an only son.

"By the same means the faithful servant who was brought up with me from a boy, and on whom I cannot prevail to seek another master, conveyed to me requisite food. He equipped himself in a round frock, cut off his hair, and exchanged his usual clothes for the coarsest of those worn by the peasants; and thus changed in appearance, he passed for the nephew of Mrs. Mosely, and took a lodging in the next village, from whence he used to creep of a night with such food as he could purchase without suspicion, going, or rather pretending to go, during the day, to his labour in a distant parish.

"It is now a month since I embraced this manner of life, rather in compliance with the wishes of my mother than because I preferred it myself to the imprisonment that awaits me. But the visit that about ten days since that blood-hound Vampyre paid to my humane protector Wansford, left hardly any doubt but that I had been traced hither: and though the resolute refusal of Wansford to admit those wretches to search the house has made their success rather more remote and difficult; yet, having once got scent of me, I know it cannot be long before I must either quit my concealment, or be taken in it."

Althea now, in a tremulous voice that marked how much she was affected, enquired whether, since the private passages and retreats in

the house were so secure from the visits of those who were not acquainted with them, he might not still remain undiscovered?

Marchmont replied, "I possibly might, though the existence of
such hiding- places is too well known to make them very secure against
a strict search; but I fear," added he, with a faint attempt at cheerfulness, "that the siege would inevitably be turned to a blockade, and that
the garrison would be starved into a surrender; for my poor purveyor,
Fenchurch, has lately been alarmed with an account, that as he is a
stranger he is believed to be a deserter from Plymouth; and that a man
who is employed in the impress service at a village on the seacoast has
declared it shall soon be seen *what* he is. This must be a manœuvre of
Vampyre's. The poor fellow, though there is no difficulty or danger
that he would not encounter in my service, is terrified at the idea of
being forced away, and detained on board ship—while my supplies
failing in his absence, I must quit my concealment, and yield without
farther resistance to my pursuers."

Althea heard with increasing concern this threatened accumulation of calamity. Marchmont continued to speak.

"Already, perhaps, my unfortunate companion in adverse fortune
may have fallen into the snare; for since the evening before yesterday
he has not appeared."

"Good God!" exclaimed Althea, "you have been, and are then,
perhaps, without necessary sustenance?"

"Not altogether so—I never was so improvident as to be wholly
without; for I foresaw that many accidents might happen to impede
punctual supplies. I have not, it is true, fared very sumptuously: but
why should not I, who am reduced to a condition even below that of
the peasant who labours for his daily bread, but who is free and independent—why should not I learn to live as scantily as he does?"

Though he said this in a cheerful voice, Althea, looking at him as
he spoke, could hardly refrain from tears.

"Will you allow me," said she, "to send you (unless I may invite
you to share it in my parlour) a part of my supper? I beg your pardon
for using the word *send*—I would not for the world hazard any thing
of that sort—but will you suffer me to *bring* you some kind of food,
better than I fear you can now have? Consider me, Sir, as one of your
sisters, and believe that neither of them could be more rejoiced than I
shall be to contribute such relief as can now be found in a situation so
painful, and which you so little merit."

While she spoke thus, Marchmont gazed at her with an expression in his countenance, to which words can do but little justice.

"It seems," said he in a low voice, "it seems as if the heaviest evils of life are mitigated and softened—perhaps that they may be the longer endured. Your generous compassion, Madam, would be a panacea for greater evils than *I* endure: but, when it becomes painful to you, as I think I plainly perceive it is, I dare not ask its continuance. I ought rather to withdraw myself, and to intrude upon you no more ..."

As if unable to go on, he now paused—while Althea, who fancied she heard footsteps below, and trembled lest he should be surprised, besought him eagerly not to think of any thing but his own safety.

"If," said she, "your servant should have been taken, as his long absence makes but too probable, may it not lead to a discovery?—At the very idea of the wretch whom I saw the other day, my soul recoils. Every thing is surely to be endured rather than that you should be in his power. Tell me, Sir, I beg of you, what you propose?—what I can do for you?"

The voice of Althea betrayed her agitation, and Marchmont recovered himself.

"I am ashamed," said he, "of my weakness; and shocked that I have thus disturbed you. You ask me, most amiable Miss Dacres, what is my design? Alas! I would ask counsel of you; for in truth I know not how to act. For my mother's sake, whose heart will be quite broken by my imprisonment, I would avoid it—but, alas! how?—If Fenchurch is taken, as I very much fear, I cannot remain here—and even if he has been detained only by some accident, I believe my concealment is now too much suspected long to avail me. I would quit it, therefore, in the night, and, making my way to the nearest sea-port, endeavour to escape from the inhuman pursuit of men, with whom my surrender can gratify no passion but vengeance.—Yet even to this there are objections. ... Indeed I know not how I could leave England but as a soldier or a sailor; and to my becoming either one or the other, it seems as if my mother had almost as strong objections as against my incurring the horrors of perpetual confinement."

Althea too well understood, however he evaded naming, the reasons that prevented his quitting England otherwise than in some military capacity—that he had neither means of paying for his passage, nor his support, whithersoever he might be driven.

She now ran over in her mind, though in a hurried way, the possibility of her assisting him in this cruel exigence—but again fancying she heard persons walking beneath the windows of the room, and seeing it was already evening, and that it would be impossible for him to determine on any plan that night, she became solicitous for his present security, and that he might not be longer a sufferer, from the absence of his servant, as to the actual necessaries of life. Collecting, therefore, all her courage, she said,

"Allow me, Sir, to propose to you to return for this night to your sad cell—to-morrow morning I will do myself the pleasure of seeing you again, if you will permit me; and in the mean time pray tell me, if you can devise any safe way by which necessary food may immediately be conveyed to you?"

"How very good you are," said Marchmont, "to be my purveyor! and how little do I deserve such kindness from you, to whom I know I have long been a source of fear, and am now likely to be the cause of trouble! Be not alarmed," added he, seeing by her countenance that she apprehended some intrusion, "I believe I am pretty secure for this evening; and since your long absence may perhaps raise some uneasiness in the good woman of the house (from whom, for what reason I know not, her husband seems very anxious to keep the secret of my concealment), I will most thankfully accept your generous proposal of half an hour's conversation to-morrow morning: and now, if you have courage to trust yourself with me, I will shew you a way by which, without going through the hall, or any of the visible passages, this part of the house has a communication with that you inhabit." Althea professing her readiness to follow him, since she thought it less hazardous for him than her being let out at the hall door, he removed the damaged picture, which, as has been mentioned, rested against the wainscot in the banqueting-room; and, pushing aside a pannel of the lower part of it, a dark and narrow passage appeared, just capable of admitting one person at a time. Marchmont descended into it by two deep steps; and Althea, not without some dread, which, however, she was ashamed of, followed him.

He led her along an avenue, equally dark and narrow, into a room which was not among those she had been shewn by Mrs. Mosely, but more gloomy than any of them, and the evening was now closing in. Marchmont felt her hand tremble as he held it, and said—

"How much I am obliged to you for your noble confidence! I fear this way is very unpleasant to you; but, however, it is very short."

So saying, he opened the door of what appeared to be a large old wainscot press; and urging with some force his foot against the side, it gave way, and delivered them into another obscure but short passage, and from thence into the room where Wansford kept his small stores, such as malt, winter roots, and wheat, which he had by various contrivances secured from the vermin that the house was infested with.

"You see," cried Marchmont, "that I am not so destitute of the power of procuring provisions as you imagined; and that here, like a true prodigal, I might feed on husks and on roots."

Althea could not answer his pleasantry, so deeply was she affected by his situation; but she eagerly enquired whether, by this avenue, Wansford could not convey him food?

"I have never yet proposed it," answered he, "because I have never yet been quite destitute; and I knew it was hardly possible for him constantly to supply me, without betraying to his wife a secret which he seemed to dread her knowing."

"But to-night," said Althea, "may I leave here what you have undoubtedly occasion for?"

"I certainly shall not die of repletion," answered he, "if I do not receive your bounty; for my fare has been to-day and yesterday rather harder than usual: but if I go supperless to bed, fate will not deal worse with me than she does continually with those who have toiled all day."

Althea however, finding that she could thus supply him, insisted upon his remaining concealed near the room till she could return, and then with a palpitating heart hastened to her own bedchamber; where taking off her hat and cloak, she affected to go down to her parlour, as if just returned from walking, and, ringing the bell, ordered her supper.

Mrs. Wansford, who immediately attended, expressed some wonder at her staying out so late, and still more that she had not heard her come in. Althea gave slight answers to her questions; and saying that she had been for a long walk, which had given her an unusual appetite, Mrs. Wansford bestirred herself to produce such cold provisions as she had. Althea having concealed as much of them as she could, sent the rest away, and under pretence of fatigue hastened to her room. Then, after a moment's pause, with light but faltering steps, she hurried towards that where Marchmont waited for her; for, knowing that Mrs. Wansford's fears prevented her ever visiting this room, he had not concealed himself. He would have thanked his trembling benefactress;

but she entreated him, in a whisper, not to speak, and glided as swiftly as possible away; fearing lest her hostess, whose bedroom was at the opposite end of the passage, should discover her before she could make good her retreat.

CHAP. VII.

Povera affetti miei!
Se non sanno impetrar dal tuo bel core
Pieta, se non amore!

ALONE IN HER own room, Althea collected her confused and dissipated thoughts. The first surprise she had felt now gave way to the pity, respect, and apprehension for his safety, with which the manner and the narrative of Marchmont had inspired her, mingled with a sense of the impropriety of her own situation; of which she would probably have been less painfully sensible, had she not been conscious that there was something more than compassion in the extreme concern she felt for Marchmont.

Besides the too great probability there was, that the fiend who hung with such unappeasable rancour on the pursuit would soon force him from his concealment, Althea dreaded lest even from that remote spot the whisper of malignity might reach her father and Lady Dacres; and should that happen, it might be of the utmost prejudice to Marchmont, and create in regard to herself suspicions and opinions which it might never afterwards be in her power to obliterate.

A young man of Marchmont's description concealed for a long space of time in a house of which she was the ostensible inhabitant, must give rise to much scandal were it known; and since it was suspected by Vampyre, it was but too probable that he would assert it, and convey the assertion somehow or other to Sir Audley (to whom indeed he was known), in the hope that by the means of his interference Marchmont might be driven from his asylum, and, by the displeasure his seeking it might create, raise another powerful and vindictive enemy in the person of Sir Audley Dacres.

Tormented and perplexed by these thoughts, Althea could not determine what advice she should give to the unfortunate fugitive. It seemed best to propose his quitting England—yet where could he obtain money, and whither should he go?—The latter question it was, perhaps, easier to answer, even in the present confused state of affairs on the continent, than it was to say, where he should find the means of conveying himself thither—since, though he did not confess it, she was convinced by his manner that his pecuniary exigences were such as made his attempting such a journey impossible.

With that timid deference to the opinion of the world, which is an amiable feature in the character of a young woman, Althea had also that strength of mind that enabled her to be decided when her understanding and conscience told her she was right. In considering, therefore, how far she could in this way assist him, she put aside every other reflection but that of the pleasure it would give her to rescue a fellow-creature from so cruel a fate as that which hung over Marchmont. For any deserving person she felt that she would have made the same exertion: yet she did not deny even to herself, that the personal merit of Marchmont, the promise of prosperous fortune so cruelly disappointed, his filial piety, and the fair expectations of his youth unhappily blasted, contributed to produce in his favour a more lively interest than she would have been sensible of for almost any other being.

On examining her stock of money, which since her residence at East Woodleigh she had but little diminished, she found it consisted of twelve guineas, and two Bank notes of twenty pounds each (the remains of fifty pounds, which she had been paid out of Mrs. Trevyllian's property), and twenty-five which Sir Audley had given her for the expences of her journey: since which he had never sent her any supply, supposing (if he thought about it at all) that at Eastwoodleigh she could have no occasion for money; and it was true that, except her little charities, she had neither wish nor opportunities of indulging in any expence.

Of the sum then in her possession Althea could well spare five-and-forty guineas, which she thought might, with some small sum he probably possessed himself, be sufficient to secure the retreat of Marchmont to Holland or France. But she foresaw, that to offer it to him would be a matter of extreme delicacy. She doubted whether any thing could engage him to accept it; and she foresaw that, if he did not, the supposition that remaining where he was, was disagreeable to her, would hasten his quitting Eastwoodleigh at whatever hazard;—an apprehension which acquired new force, as she recollected some of those broken sentences which, half uttering, he seemed suddenly to

repress. They were indeed the effect of that undescribable variety of
sensations which passed through his mind. He knew that, as far as
related to Althea, his situation under the same roof was altogether improper; and to hazard any injury to her, no consideration that had for
its object only his personal safety could have engaged him. Yet having
once yielded to the pleasure of seeing her, and now of conversing
with her; hearing her voice, and reading in her intelligent eyes that she
was even more interested for him than she wished to avow, he had not
courage to tear himself away, though conscious that to stay at all was
improper—to stay long impossible.

While this contest continued in the breast of Marchmont, Althea
was on her part studying how she might induce him to accept what
she was sure he must greatly want; and no other means occurred to
her, but to contrive that Wansford should convey it to him without his
knowing from whence it came. This, however, was an expedient which
she could not think of adopting without reluctance; and so many were
the objections to it which arose, that at length she determined to postpone any arrangement of this matter till she had again seen and conversed with Marchmont.

She hastened, therefore, to this conference with every precaution
that was necessary to mislead the curiosity of Mrs. Wansford, who
believed her going to make one of her charitable visits at the cottage.
Marchmont was impatiently expecting her; and she was let into the hall
unperceived by any of those whose observation she desired to avoid.

The comfortless state in which he had now so long remained, and
anxiety which every hour increased, had occasioned, even since Althea parted with him the preceding night, a great alteration in the appearance of the unfortunate young man.—His eyes were hollow and
sunk, his face pale, and Althea thought he seemed personally to suffer, though he did not complain. He addressed her with a melancholy
solemnity, thanked her for this additional proof of her goodness of
heart, and then said—

"It is not fit. Miss Dacres, that so unfortunate a being as I am
should trespass thus on that goodness. Since I had the honour of seeing you last, I have thoroughly considered my situation; and I have
determined to submit, to the ignominy of it no longer.—If such are
the laws of my country, that from even an unoffending debtor as I am,
nothing will satisfy those laws but that I should terminate my life in
prison, there with be less disgrace surely in yielding to my destiny, than

there is in the misery of thus shifting from place to place—a burden to the few who have humanity to be interested for me—a burden to myself.

"My mother, my dear unhappy mother! will submit with fortitude when she knows the worst, and knows it to be unavoidable. To inevitable evils they say that the human mind most easily accommodates itself; and when I am confined she will learn, that our resistance is vain, and that our projects are at an end. She will be wretched, I know, but uncertainty and solicitude will be no more. I shall yet exist —I may see her and my poor sisters. Perhaps I may find means to subsist in confinement, as hundreds of others are known to subsist; and one chance will yet remain, towards which my family may look with hope. At some period or other, if humanity should touch the hearts of those who have the power, at the instance of that generous* man who is the pride and honour of his country, an act of insolvency may release me—release me," added he with a deep-drawn sigh, "to the privilege of being a beggar in the world at large!"

Althea heard him with the deepest concern, yet was by no means prepared to controvert his reasoning. After a moment's silence, however, she ventured timidly to enquire whether nothing could be thought of to avoid so painful, so sad an experiment, as that of putting himself into the hands of these pitiless men, to answer no possible purpose.

"Surely," said she, "your friend Mr. Eversley might and would assist you." For at that moment it occurred to Althea, that by his means she could convey to Marchmont the pecuniary help she wished to engage him to accept.

"Eversley!" repeated Marchmont, with quickness—"No—that cannot be. Eversley is an excellent man. I owe him a thousand obligations, but they have cost him too dear. I know how much uneasiness I have been the occasion of, and nothing on earth should induce me to repeat it—Besides, there are other reasons.............My friend is affluent indeed, but I do not envy him; Poor fellow! he is rather an object of pity. Destitute as I am, the fate of Eversley excites my compassion. He does not know, for I had many reasons for my concealment, where I now am."

Althea was on the point of betraying herself, by saying that she heard he was in Ireland from Linda Eversley. But recollecting herself, she continued silent. Marchmont renewed the conversation. He even forced a languid smile as he said—

---

* It is hardly necessary to name Lord Moira

"And suppose that the inveterate malignity of these men, who, like Shylock, insist upon their bond, which they know I cannot pay—suppose it urges them to the greatest extremities? I am of a race, of which many members have been imprisoned, though not indeed for quite the same cause. You recollect, perhaps, a beautiful little piece of poetry* written by a Colonel Richard Lovelace, who was imprisoned in the Gate-house at Westminster for adherence to his unhappy master. He was the brother of my father's grandmother. He died in great obscurity, and poverty. My fate and his may probably in many instances be alike."

Althea instantly recollected the lines, and the name of Althea, by which the unfortunate Lovelace celebrates his mistress; a coincidence which struck her with a thousand indescribable sensations; though it was, she thought, possible that it was *not* on account of that coincidence brought forward by Marchmont. She felt, however, her cheeks dyed with blushes; and to conceal her confusion she passed lightly over the answer, and recurred again to Mr. Eversley.

"Since you are so good," said she, "as to allow me to take an interest in a situation which even those who have not the pleasure of knowing you must lament, suffer me to consult with Mr. Eversley. I <u>am no stranger </u>to the restraint he labours under from the unhappy

---

*   In Wood's Athens page 228, Vol. II. may be seen at large the affecting story of this elegant writer, who, having been distinguished for every gallant and polite accomplishment, the pattern of his own sex, and the darling of the ladies, died in the lowest obscurity, wretchedness, and want, in 1658.—Part of the Song follows:

> "When Love with unconfined wings
> Hovers within my gates.
> And my divine Althea brings
> To whisper at my grates:
> When I lie tangled in her hair.
> And fetter'd with her eye.
> The birds that wanton in the air
> Know no such liberty.
>
> Stone walls do not a prison make.
> Nor iron bars a cage;
> Minds innocent and quiet take
> That for an hermitage:
> If I have freedom in my love.
> And in my soul am free,
> Angels alone that soar above
> Enjoy such liberty."

temper and narrow prejudices of his wife; but by means of his sister I am sure we may correspond on the possibility of serving you, without rendering him liable to her ill-humour."

"I cannot express. Miss Dacres," interrupted Marchmont, "how much I feel your goodness; but there are objections—invincible, unconquerable objections. ... It is impossible," added he, "to trouble you with them: but be assured, that if I had any thing to hope from his friendship, without committing my friend, I would not hesitate:—as it is, I must take my resolution, and already I feel that I ought not to have given you the concern I have done. I am conscious that I have acted wrong—and yet, perhaps, if I dared relate at length the circumstances that have led me into this, the narrative might, to such a mind as yours, plead my apology"

"None is necessary. Sir," said Althea in a low voice; "I beg you will not think of me, unless it be how I can render you any service in regard to your present difficulties. I am very much afraid, from the detention of your servant, that they may multiply around you; and I own, my horror of the man they call Vampyre is such, that nothing would give me more pain than that he should make another visit here more successful than the last."

"For that reason," replied Marchmont, "it were on all accounts wiser to meet, rather than to await the evil; and I trust I have, by reflection, so far subdued the rage and indignation that this villanous fellow used to excite, that I shall calmly acquiesce in an inevitable misfortune, without too much considering the infamous agent."

"Surely," said Althea, "it would be better were you to attempt escaping to the continent till some settlement can be brought about. I think I have heard you have relations in France?"

"Yes," answered Marchmont; "a branch of my family are naturalized there. But if you consider, Madam, the ancestors from whom the Baron de Lavergnac is descended, you will immediately conclude, that if he still remains on his estate, of which I have many doubts, it is but little in his power to afford protection to a stranger—and a stranger, whose country alone would now render him liable to imprisonment. And whether I am to pass my life in the Fleet, or the Abbaye— whether I am to exist under the tyranny of Robespierre or a victim to the chicanery of Vampyre, seems to me a matter so immaterial, that it ought not to induce me to cross the water to embrace the one, or escape the other. Indeed I have another objection, which is, that by going to the

Baron de Lavergnac, admitting it were possible to reach him, I should, perhaps, disturb the security which, from his age and retired habits of life, it is possible he may have been able to preserve, notwithstanding his decided abhorrence of the present rulers in France. It is now so many months since I have heard of him, or any part of his family, that perhaps while I speak of them they exist no longer. His son was in Spain when I had the last news of them. His grandson, a young man of two-and-twenty, had, till then, remained at Lavergnac: but notwithstanding all the inducements he had to continue at home, the anxious solicitude of the venerable old Baron, the agonizing fears of a mother who adores him, and probably the fender and seducing affection of a very lovely young woman, to whom he was seven or eight months ago on the point of being united; notwithstanding all these ties, I cannot but believe my younger relation has either joined his father, or found means to get into Italy or Germany. Would I knew where he is! I had rather join him, though our principles do not exactly accord, than wander about without any fixed purpose, or give to the kind-hearted old Baron another cause of anxiety. ... But indeed," continued Marchmont, after a short pause, "to go into the army as he is probably gone is in every man's power; and if my mother could be prevailed upon to hear of it with patience, why should it not be in mine?"

Althea, from a certain uncomfortable feeling about her heart, doubted whether even the risk of long imprisonment was not preferable. The longer this conference lasted, the less prospect there appeared of her being able to execute those friendly projects on which she had meditated before they met: yet, while her hopes of being instrumental in saving him grew fainter, her wishes that she might do so acquired new force; and notwithstanding all there was to fear should his present abode become known to Sir Audley, she could not without extreme pain think of his delivering himself to the merciless men who pursued him. His uncertainty whither to go, if he could for a while escape them; the situation of every part of his own family, who in times more tranquil would have protected him; the unfeeling dereliction of his relations on the side of his mother, who had so much the power to befriend him; even the fortitude to which he endeavoured to give the appearance of calm indifference, while he prepared to meet the destiny which awaited him; all combined to increase the interest Althea took in that destiny. And why should it be concealed that the greatest, perhaps the only error he was guilty of, had no power to weaken this interest?

Marchmont, far from saying it, did not certainly even acknowledge
to himself, that the strangeness of his comfortless situation, as far as
related to his concealment at Eastwoodleigh, was rather sought for on
his part than avoided: and though he knew every circumstance relative
to Althea's fortune, and that nothing was less likely ever to be within
the reach of possibility, than that *he* could be listened to as a lover; yet
so far had the strength of those impressions he had received in their
former interviews got the better of his reason, that he could not forbear availing himself of an opportunity to be near her—and adding to
all the other misfortunes of his life, that of indulging a passion which
he knew ought *not* to be successful.

When he had first consented to hide himself among the secret
passages of his paternal house, he persuaded himself that he had no
purpose in concealment but to escape from his persecutors, and to
contemplate, without her having any idea of his being near her; this
charming girl, in the exercise of all those virtues, of which he had already heard so much even before the grateful loquacity of Mrs. Mosely
had made her the constant subject of panegyric. Marchmont imagined
that it was possible to consider her as some being of a superior order, altogether out of his reach, but whose beneficence and beauty it
was gratifying to contemplate. Consciousness of the impropriety of
his being thus concealed under the same roof, was only an additional
inducement to the strict vigilance he otherwise meant to observe. He
was sure of Wansford as long as he could pay him, nor indeed had
he any reason to doubt his honesty or humanity; and he had almost
exhausted his last resource to inflame, by the most powerful of all arguments, his natural aversion to attorneys, and the particular antipathy
he knew Vampyre must create wherever he appeared. For some time
he had resolution enough to adhere to the conduct he had determined
upon; and for a while, the dreariness of his confinement, amidst the
rigours of winter, was sweetened by a transient view of Althea from a
window, by hearing her voice in the spacious passages, as she came into
the deserted building, or by catching at a distance its sweeter sound, as
she sang to her own playing amid the silence of a still evening. But insensibly he found, that the more he indulged this growing attachment,
the more importunate were its demands; and when, in consequence of
her alarm arising from the sight of his dog, she for some days forbore
to renew her walks in the gallery, his concealment became so intolerable to him, that he was on the point of leaving it; but Althea appeared

again, and again the desolate apartments which he had so much reason
to contemplate with an aching heart, appeared to him to be irradiated
by the presence of an angel.

His faithful terrier, which had only once broke from the command he had over it, was then more strictly kept to his obedience; and
Marchmont finding that Althea resumed her solitary exercise, determined to be so much on his guard, that nothing should betray him,
while he might still be gratified by the pleasure of hearing her speak, or
even by a distant view as she passed the end of the passages into which
he had the means of looking as he lay hid. For this purpose he had on
the day he was discovered taken his station in a room whither he knew
the legends of Mrs. Mosely would prevent her coming. The circumstance of the children's playing in a closet which had a window looking
into it, he could not foresee: the alarm (which he distinctly heard) once
given, numberless reasons, or what appeared to be reasons, concurred
to determine him on appearing. The absence of his servant indeed
made it a matter of self-preservation; but that alone would probably
have influenced him less than the fear of having terrified Althea, and
of seeing her no more; while her kindness in regard to his mother and
sisters, of which Mrs. Mosely had informed him; the generous pity she
had expressed when they met in the park at Capelstoke; her general
character, and, in short, an impulse too strong to be resisted, were
united to conquer all his prudent resolutions, and determined him to
throw himself at her feet.

In the first conversation that followed, the tender compassion
which she seemed to feel for him, and the ingenuous confidence she
placed in him, were but too well calculated to increase a passion, which,
as he never intended to speak of it to its object, he indulged because he
thought it could hurt nobody but himself.

This second interview had nearly overcome his resolution; and
nothing but reflecting on the cruelty and ingratitude of giving pain to
that bosom which already felt so keenly for him as a friend, could have
deterred him from following, with some more positive declaration of
his sentiments, what half involuntarily escaped him about Colonel
Lovelace. While he yet spoke to Althea, or listened to her compas-
sionate proposals, his heart smote him for the concern he had thus
inflicted on her. But it was now too late to recede; yet so uncertain was
he what he ought to do, or indeed could do, that after a conversation
of near two hours they parted, without having come to any determi-

nation, except that Althea should that evening let Wansford know she was acquainted with Marchmont's concealment, concert with him the means of supplying him with necessary food, and consult with him by what means Fenchurch could be traced—for no circumstance was so alarming as his absence. Althea, after some debate, at length believed she had convinced Marchmont that he ought yet to delay any final determination for a few days. They then, with visible reluctance on the side of Marchmont, and with almost equal, though stifled concern on that of Althea, parted for the day—but not till she had engaged to leave for him in the storeroom of their host some books, with which he might beguile the long, long hours of his imprisonment; for every horror that present anguish, or recollection of the past, could accumulate, returned upon him the moment he had closed the door of the hall after Althea.

CHAP. VIII.

Why courage then!—What cannot be avoided,
'Twere childish weakness to lament or fear!

IT REQUIRED SOME contrivance on the part of Althea to obtain a long conference with Wansford without the knowledge of his wife. She effected it, however, and with hesitation and reluctance disclosed to him the knowledge she had gained of Marchmont's concealment.

Althea was, unfortunately perhaps for her, a great reader of countenances—decidedly a disciple of Lavater's; she fancied that, as far as her small knowledge of the world allowed her to judge, his science was by no means so chimerical or illusive as Sir Audley and many other men of the world held it to be; and she believed she had often discovered the thoughts of those with whom she conversed, when they least intended she should have any idea of them. Attentive therefore to the expression of the man's face to whom she was now talking, she imagined, amidst all the respect he expressed for her, that there was a lurking sneer, when he found how well she was acquainted with Marchmonf's history, and how much interest she evidently took in it. This might be, and probably was, fancy; but Althea felt mortified and uneasy. She failed not to recollect how gross are the apprehensions of the lower ranks of people, and that, even with greater precipitance

than influences those but a little above them in station (and often not
at all more refined in understanding), they decide, that it is impossible
two young people of different sexes can converse together otherwise
than as lovers.

To obviate this impression, which she saw, or believed she saw,
that Wansford entertained, Althea spoke with peculiar earnestness on
the necessity of Marchmont's going; to which Wansford heartily assented.—"Aye, my dear young lady!" said he, "you don't know half the
danger. I heard last night that Vampyre was at T——, which is, you
know, but seven miles off, or so—and what can a want there? I don't
know, for my part, what's to be done! The poor young man cannot be
hid much longer, that's for certain; but if he offers for to go—ah! he'll
be taken by some of that old villain's followers, as sure as I am I."

As all this was not more than the fears of Althea had already sug-
gested to her, she did not suffer any new alarm to mislead her from
every enquiry that she thought might give her light as to what was the
best course for her unhappy friend. Wansford had too strongly marked
the common traits in his character. He loved money, and hated tricking
attorneys; for he had owed to the chicane of one of that description
that he had been turned out of his farm. His avarice thus counteracted, the honest feelings of humanity had room for their influence; and
though he might have made money by betraying his unfortunate guest
to his pursuers, he resisted the temptation, and was eagerly anxious for
his safety.

Althea, who had the faculty, uncommon at her age, of reading the
sentiments of those with whom she conversed, saw, with satisfaction,
that Wansford might be depended upon; she therefore entrusted him,
though not without much hesitation and confusion, with her wishes as
to affording to Marchmont such pecuniary assistance as might enable
him to quit his present comfortless abode, and convey himself out of
the reach of his persecutors.

At the mention of this Althea thought she saw all those half-
formed suspicions arise in the mind of Wansford, which she was so
unwilling he should harbour. He found it difficult to imagine, that a
young lady or any other person would give their money without some
particular liking to those on whom it was bestowed. Of that interest
which compassion for his singular stuation, or mere friendship, could
raise in his favour, Wansford was incapable of forming any notion.
Whatever were his ideas, he endeavoured carefully to conceal them,

and told Althea that he thought he could, by means of Mrs. Mosely, convey to Marchmont whatever she desired, without his knowing from whence it came. She directed him to proceed to do so with the utmost circumspection; and having thus done all that was at present possible, she endeavoured to quiet her spirits, and to think of other subjects besides the merits, sufferings, and danger of Marchmont.

But her tranquillity had been too much disturbed, and her imagination too much affected. Secluded so long from all society and every scene of active life, the strange circumstances under which she found herself had doubly the power to affect her, while to the first favourable impression she had received of Marchmont was added all that interest which pity could excite in a generous mind. However earnestly she tried to check such thoughts, she could not help sometimes regretting (what had never given her any concern before) the smallness of her fortune, and reflecting on the happiness it would afford whoever had the power to rescue from his sad destiny a young man of so much merit. To her she knew he never could owe this obligation, yet she felt a comfortless sensation when she endeavoured to wish that he might receive it from another.—Two days now passed, in which she knew nothing but what she guessed from the nods and shrugs of Wansford, who either could not or would not find an opportunity of conversing with her.—He was absent twice during that time, and Althea concluded he was settling something to effect her present purpose with Dame Mosely.

In the afternoon, however, of the third day of her suspense, she saw him under her window, which, on the signs he made, she hastily opened. He gave into her hands a letter.

Althea did not know the hand; but the countenance and manner of the man awakened so much apprehension, that she had hardly courage to read it.—Casting her eyes on the signature at the bottom, she saw the name of Marchmont, and trembled as she ran over the following lines—

"Madam,

"Every hour, since I first dared to intrude myself and my sorrows upon your notice, has increased my respect and admiration, by affording me some new instance of an exalted mind and an excellent heart; but the last proof you have given of your generosity calls upon me for all my gratitude, though I cannot, I dare not accept it. Notwithstanding the contrivances of the poor old woman at the cottage, and my friend

Wansford, I know the offer I have received of pecuniary assistance could come only from you. I will not enter on the reasons that absolutely forbid my accepting it; Miss Dacres is too candid to impute it to ill-placed pride, when I presume to add, that if she can, in any way not prejudicial to herself, befriend my dear unhappy mother, my young and unprotected sisters, she will find that the Marchmonts are not too proud to be grateful.

"Alas! Madam, those victims to misfortune can never more than now want your pity—for I must leave England. The son, the brother whom they fondly wished to retain in the same country (though he has long been deprived of the power of protecting or supporting them), must yield at last to an inevitable evil, and make his election between imprisonment and exile.

"I prefer the latter—for Miss Dacres condescended to give her opinion that it was the most advisable. There is no time to hesitate, for the fiend who pursues me is again animated to my destruction. My faithful servant Fenchurch has escaped by something like a miracle from the toils this wretch laid for him, and, as good is sometimes derived from evil, has, in his flight, discovered a means of my getting from hence by sea—and the opportunity is likely to offer so soon, that I shall quit my *paternal prison* in the middle of the approaching night, and conceal myself in a place on the shore well known to me in happier days; from whence, with the tide at noon, a boat is engaged to carry me on board a vessel bound to Guernsey: from thence I shall cross to France, and endeavour to discover what is become of the Baron de Lavergnac and his family—to whom it is possible I may be useful.

"I would refrain from expressing, because I am conscious that I ought to do it, the pain I feel at the idea of seeing you no more. I am not so weak and vain as to presume on the kindness you have condescended to shew me. I know I owe it only to the tenderness and humanity of your nature; nor am I capable of forgetting the distance to which fortune has thrown me, from all I might once have aspired to. Perhaps you ought not to forgive me the useless weakness of owning, that thus to repress sentiments which under other circumstances it would have been the pride and glory of my life to avow, is among the most severe of those trials to which my destiny condemns me.

"I submit, however—for I have no right to hazard giving a moment's pain to others; I submit—but will not that generosity I am already so greatly obliged to, pardon me for asking, even, though it cannot perhaps grant, the only favour I will now venture to solicit?

"It is, that before I take a *long*, perhaps a *last* leave of my country, I may see the only friend who is within my reach.—(My mother, my sisters are afar off!)—Is it too presumptuous if I name Miss Dacres as that friend? if I entreat her to allow me to attempt expressing by words all that gratitude I owe her—and to recommend to her the dear unhappy family I leave? Believe me, Madam, *I* never will intrude upon you again; but it will mitigate the anguish which I feel when I consider *how* I have left them, if I can assure myself that they have so great an alleviation as your humanity can bestow—and if you will deign to see me before I get into the boat which is to carry me from this now inhospitable shore, my poor mother, oppressed with too many sorrows already, will at least know from you that I departed with fortitude; and to *her* you will appear as a guardian angel, whose presence and whose wishes shall secure the safety of her son.

"The information Fenchurch has brought me, as well as what I have received to-day from Wansford, convinces me that I risk much by remaining another night beneath this roof. If I did, I dare not again solicit an interview here, but to-morrow the tide does not allow me to depart from my wild retreat on the shore till about twelve o'clock;—it is little more than a mile and a half from this place. Wansford tells me his eldest girl knows the road.—Ah! Miss Dacres! I am conscious how little right I have to ask such a favour of you; but if your goodness extends so far as to forgive my presumption and indulge my weakness, be assured I shall esteem such an obligation greater than any of those I already owe you. There may be impropriety in your granting me such a request; but if you knew how many reasons combine to make me ask it, how grateful I shall be, and how much such condescension will soften the severity of my destiny—I dare venture to believe you would not refuse it.—Ah! Madam! Were it possible to convince you of the veneration, the respect I fed for your virtues, you would not suspect that I would ask what would be derogatory to that gentle dignity, which is one among the thousand graces that surround you. Let me not, however, adopt a style which may offend, even from its sincerity. I know not how to conclude, though conscious I have said too much. Allow me to assure you of the gratitude and esteem with which I must ever be,

Madam,

Your most devoted servant,

EDWARD-ARMYN MARCHMONT."

The thoughts of Althea were never so confused as after the hasty perusal of this letter. Indeed she read it in such disorder of spirits, that, when she came to the end, she hardly understood what was its purpose; and it was not before a third perusal that she was enabled to consider, with some degree of calmness, whether she ought, or could comply with the request it contained.

It was impossible to mistake the meaning of those half explanatory sentences; or, if they had admitted of any other interpretation, the former conduct of Marchmont left little doubt of his attachment to her.—On her part she had, from their earliest acquaintance, been conscious of a favourable opinion of him, which, without pretending to combat (because to think well of him was merely justice), she had endeavoured to confine within the bounds of friendship. The objections to any more intimate connection between them were insurmountable; they never appeared otherwise to Althea: and she had been taught so well to regulate her mind, that she was hardly sensible of the preference she gave Marchmont over all the men she had ever seen, before she endeavoured to check the wishes which involuntarily arose, that he had the fortune possessed by this or that fashionable acquaintance of Sir Audley, who neither deserved or knew how to be happy with the great incomes they possessed.

The very effort not to think of him, but as an unfortunate young man of uncommon merit, brought him more frequently to her mind. Then occurred the benevolent hope of being able to promote his interest with her father; and when that hope vanished, she found herself strangely fixed, by her father's orders, in the very spot where the misfortunes of the Marchmont family were continually present to her, and where she met a faithful chronicler of their virtues. The meeting him in this scene, the persecution of which he was the object, the comfortless state he was reduced to, his fortitude and filial tenderness—all combined to complete her predilection, though obstacles to their being ever any other than friends were rather increased than removed.

With all her understanding and command over her reason, Althea was still but a woman; young, and possessed of a degree of sensibility which the attentive friend of her early years had seen with some pain, and invariably endeavoured to correct.

To her it appeared as if Marchmont's having thus taken shelter in his paternal house, of which she was by such odd circumstances become an inmate, was an accident that seemed providentially ordered, to engage her friendship, and promote his relief. Though no one could be less disposed to that daring violation of the common rules of society, which sets at defiance the opinion of the world, yet she saw not why she should so far enslave herself to a narrow prejudice, as to deny that friendship to a worthy object, only because he was a young man. She asked herself, why she should refuse to act otherwise in regard to Marchmont than if he was her brother? Her heart accused her of no ill, nor even any imprudent intention; and he had, on his part, explicitly declared he had no hopes of engaging more than her sisterly friendship. This was probably the last time they should ever meet—and she enquired of herself, what would be her future feelings, if she should hear that this unfortunate young man perished far from his family, without having had an opportunity of speaking to one friend, before his departure, of all that must necessarily lay on his heart in regard to the mother and sisters from whom he was driven? Besides, as he refused the pecuniary assistance which Wansford had awkwardly betrayed to him her intention of offering, she could not be easy without knowing how he had obtained what made that assistance unnecessary. The last question Althea made in this monologue was, how Mrs. Trevyllian would have ordered her to act, could she know of the circumstances she was in?—and recalling to her mind the universal benevolence of her aunt's mind; her disdain of those narrow and gross prejudices which often check the innocent and honest purposes of the heart; and again repeating that Marchmont could never be to her other than a brother, die question was finally decided, and she determined to go.

Nothing then remained but for her to contrive the means of letting him know it immediately. For this purpose she sought Wansford; whom luckily meeting alone, as he either was or pretended to be settling his farm accounts, she wrote a short note to Marchmont, which was soon conveyed to him.—Wansford, returning, was about to tell her at what hour his persecuted guest was to depart in the night, and much other intelligence, which Althea certainly desired to have; but as his wife was heard at that moment to come in from the village, all he had time to say was, that his eldest girl should be ordered to shew her in the morning to the head-land, under which was the concealment of Marchmont.—"You had better, Madam," said he, "tell the child that you can find your way back; and send her away. Indeed, if you come along upon the shore, you will see Malbourne church just upon the brow, a quarter of a mile or so; and if you keep up towards it, you can't miss the path that brings you over the fields on the left, for you presently get a sight of Eastwoodleigh."

Althea, who thought a great deal more of the interview with Marchmont than how she should herself return home from so short a walk, assured Wansford she could easily find her way back, and then left him—trembling at the idea of her having given a promise, yet not wishing to revoke it.

For some hours, sleep absolutely refused to befriend her. The vague intelligence she had received, as well from Marchmont's letter as from the obscure hints of Wansford, impressed her with dread. She imagined that the satellites of the brutal Vampyre lurked round the house, and that, even amidst the darkness of the night, Marchmont would find it difficult to escape. Full of these fears, she listened to every noise—and imagined more than she heard. A low wind sighed along the passages, and shook at intervals the great old sash frames of her window—then sunk entirely away; and, in the still pause that followed, she fancied there were persons passing slowly and lightly beneath, among the weeds and grass which covered what had once been a great courtyard. Startled at this idea, she left her bed, and went to the window: but the night, though without rain, was dark, and she could not discern even the remains of two lions cut in stone, which (having once been placed over the great gates) were left among other masses of stone-work when the iron was sold, and, from their being white, were distinguishable when darker objects were lost in obscurity. Still a fancied noise tormented her—it might, however, be the footsteps of Marchmont himself and his faithful servant.—"Ah!" thought she, "what a comfort it would be to know he was safe! To-morrow I may, perhaps, be satisfied—but how many hours must first pass!"

She now opened the window slowly; but nothing appeared, nor was any sound heard, save the owls, who inhabited, in great numbers, the old barns and ruined offices which were on the other side of the mansion. Attracted by the light in Althea's window, one of them slowly winged its way round the building, and passed very near her.—She shuddered, not from any absolute fear, but from the uneasy sensation that any animal, to which superstition has attached the notion of being *ill-omened*, gives, even to minds the most free from its influence. But Althea, after some reflection, imagining that the sullen whisper of its heavy wings might have been the noise that alarmed her, closed the window, and once more retired to her bed.

The dawn, however, found her watching its approach with an anxious and uneasy mind. Before the usual hour she went down to her breakfast; Mrs. Wansford, who attended with it, said her husband had gone out very early upon business, and had told her that Nancy was to be ready at eight o'clock to shew Miss Dacres the nearest way to Hascombe-Strand.—Althea found that the good woman, who had not been accustomed to see things otherwise than they were represented to her by those about her, made no remark on this unusual walk; and, again half-doubting whether she ought to go, yet impatient to set out, hastened her little conductress, and began her expedition.

She now found herself at a greater distance from Eastwoodleigh than she had ever been on the side next the sea, and on the other side the cottage had hitherto limited her walks. The way was through lanes bounded by elms, which, though not yet in full leaf, were so closely interwoven in the bank with a luxurious growth of holly, that nothing was to be seen beyond them—till on a sudden the road, ascending a steep hollow way, opened to a kind of common field, forming the top of a high promontory, commanding an immense extent of sea, and, for many miles, the indented cliffs of the western coast.—Such was its elevation, that Althea had no notion how it was possible to descend to the water. With anxious eyes she surveyed the expanse of ocean; it was indeed a "shipless sea," neither boat nor any larger vessel was to be seen, and she feared the people Marchmont had expected might have disappointed him.

The child now shewed her a narrow and rugged descent, made by cutting the red clay and stones, of which the cliffs are here composed, into a sort of rude steps. Here Althea dismissed her guide, bidding her return immediately home; and then, with less fear than she might at another time have felt, descended to the margin of the sea.

On reaching it, she found herself under an almost mural range of rocks, composed of dark earth, and broad strata of reddish-coloured stones, horizontally arranged, as if by the hands of man. The place where she had descended seemed the only practicable part; for a little farther on the height became tremendous, and the face of the rock perpendicular towards the top, while beneath it was eaten by the water into deep caverns: from one of these she expected to see Marchmont appear—but, for some time, she looked around her in vain.

Vast masses, fallen from the cliffs, were scattered between them and the water at the tide of ebb. With the tide of flood, these pieces, worn into grotesque and giant shapes, were half-covered by the waves. Already the rising water broke rippling round the most remote craggs—to their rude surface, clams, limpets, and muscles adhered, among the sea-weed that grew streaming about them. All was wild, solitary, and gloomy; the low murmur of the water formed a sort of accompaniment to the cries of the sand-piper, the *puffin-awk;* while the screaming gull, and the hoarse and heavy cormorant, were heard, at intervals, still louder. Althea, as she sat on a fragment of stone, surveying the scene and listening to these noises, could have fancied herself thrown by shipwreck on some desert coast, where she was left to solitude and despair.

The tide rose slowly in so calm a morning, yet it was now so high, that it seemed certain the hour could not be far off when Marchmont expected the boat. Again she feared some disappointment, some accident; and, quitting her rugged seat, went on towards a part where the view along the sands was less impeded by broken rocks. Two persons soon after appeared, one of whom she knew to be Marchmont. As soon as he perceived Althea, he sprang forward to meet her; while the other person, who was, she thought, his servant, retired out of sight.

CHAP. IX.

Ecco quel fiero istante!

IN APPROACHING ALTHEA, the various emotions that agitated the mind of Marchmont were visible on his countenance and manner.—"How very good you are, Miss Dacres, thus to honour me!" said he—"But I must not attempt to express my gratitude; indeed to do so is out of my power: —I am afraid I have made you wait?—I ought to account for such an additional intrusion on your time and humanity—but the boat which is to take me from hence, perhaps for ever, will very soon be here: I have directed it to wait for me behind those projecting rocks."

His hesitation, the confused and uneasy manner in which he uttered these abrupt sentences, and the anguish so unequivocally marked on his countenance, deeply affected Althea. She trembled, and knew not what to reply. Afraid of expressing all she felt, yet equally afraid of appearing cold and repulsive by her silence, she meditated how to avoid either; but Marchmont, after pausing a moment, proceeded:

"I solicited this honour. Madam, that, in taking my last adieu of my native country, I might—Pardon me!—I hardly know what I would say! My fate, however severe it has appeared to me, never till *now* was so insupportable! It is no time for dissimulation; yet I am but too sensible, that when I dissimulate no longer, I risk the forfeiture of the last hope I have on earth. Can you, ought you to forgive the presumption of a man, who dares to avow his admiration, his love? knowing that he *ought not* to expect any return—and that his hazarding to speak, may deservedly subject him to the loss of that generous friendship with which you have honoured him?"

All the courage that Althea had been collecting was insufficient to enable her to articulate an answer.—It was now to be decided, whether she should for ever relinquish an affection which she had insensibly cherished for so many months, and to the indulgence of which nothing could be opposed but mere worldly prudence, or avow those sentiments that were the natural effects of uncommon merit on an ingenuous and generous mind—sentiments which, however she might endeavour to conceal them, were too deeply impressed ever to be effaced. Marchmont was indeed poor—a fugitive, and an exile; but, was he therefore less estimable?—The causes of his poverty and distress rendered him infinitely more respectable—and was it for *her* to drive him from her, merely because he possessed not those pecuniary advantages which she contemned? Could she bid him go with an impression that her heart was mercenary and narrow?—Could she say, "You are unworthy of my regard, because you are poor; your merit, your birth are nothing, for *I* know no real advantages but money?" It was true, that to encourage his passion would be imprudent in the opinion of the world; but, had not her father taught her to renounce the world—while, in sending her from it, and banishing her his house, he had left her without any connection to attach her, any duty to fulfil? All these thoughts passed with rapidity through her mind—they were less overwhelming, because many of them had been canvassed before; but far from yet having the power to express even that part of her sentiments which she had determined not to disguise, she awaited with a palpitating heart for the conclusion of what Marchmont had to say, who, apparently encouraged by her manner, after a short pause, went on—

"I know, loveliest Miss Dacres, all the circumstances of your situation—I know that to avoid a detested marriage you submitted to the melancholy seclusion of Eastwoodleigh—and I am well aware, that Fortune has been as niggardly of her favours to you, as Nature has been bountiful. God forbid that *I* should ask you to share such a destiny as *mine!*—I have already felt too severely, in the persons of those I most love, all the humiliations and inconveniences of indigence, to entertain such a thought as that of *your* becoming a party. If the definition of true love be, that it prefers the real good of its object to every other consideration, I dare assert that I feel its most powerful influence.—Yet, may I not hope to be spared the cruel necessity of relinquishing all prospect of hearing from you?—of being accounted, whatever may be my destiny, among the number of your friends? I will not, however, affect to say, that I never mean to ask more than your friendship. Whatever may hitherto have been my disappointments, a man of my age ought not to despair—happier fortune may yet give him hopes of aspiring to your favour. But I most solemnly assure you, I will never intrude upon your pity till those better prospects shall open to me; and if, before that time arrives, some enviable man, in a situation more worthy of you, should be deemed deserving your favour, the unfortunate Marchmont shall never be heard to interrupt your felicity with his complaints."

Althea now took courage to say, in a low voice—"Alas! Sir, to what can our correspondence tend, but to render us both unhappy?"

"If it will have that effect *on you*," cried Marchmont, eagerly interrupting her, "I renounce my hopes: but for me—Ah! I have, till this moment, had the presumption to flatter myself.........Yes! I *did* believe that the generosity of which I have had so many proofs would have been extended to this last instance of pity and regard. It will soften to me the horrors of that cruel exile which is the only alternative to a prison;—it will give me courage to endure a life that I have been sometimes half-tempted to escape from. To you, dearest Miss Dacres, how can it be injurious?—If the unfortunate object of your compassion is indifferent to you, *your* peace cannot be disturbed by this act of humanity—If he be not... but I dare not hope it."

Althea, in increased distress, knew not what to say: to refuse seemed inhuman—to consent, imprudent.—Marchmont saw she hesitated.—He pursued his argument with all the ardour lent him by the hope of success. He represented that, whenever she found any inconvenience from the receipt of his letters, she might deprive him of the happiness of corresponding with her—that she was accountable to nobody, since Sir Audley gave himself no trouble to direct her.—He then went on to say—

"Of the person, Madam, who presumes to solicit such a favour of you, it is fit you should know what has been the course of his days. Allow me, since I may never again, or not for a very long time, enjoy the happiness I am now admitted to—allow me to relate the short history of my life since I have been a wanderer in the world. To a mind like that which you possess, I am persuaded that to have endured adversity with some degree of resolution will not appear less meritorious, than not to have abused prosperity."

Althea, whose agitation this prelude was calculated to increase, did not trust her voice with an answer; but she seemed willing to give her attention to what he proposed relating—and Marchmont thus proceeded:

"I believe you have heard from my friend Eversley, and perhaps since from the poor old servant, the former circumstances of a family less fortunate than known. I will not dwell on the consequence and fortune it once possessed; for *some* experience and many mortifications have done away what I was once taught to cherish—pride, on account of *the days that are gone.*—The most painful part of a life, of which none has yet been very fortunate, was *that* when I saw my father vainly struggling with the pressure of adversity; and, towards the close of his life, sacrificing his own ease and quiet, which he might in a great measure have possessed, in the hope of preserving for *me* the remaining part of my patrimony, and that great house of which you are now an inhabitant. I saw the hopelessness of the attempt—I knew, that if to save the ruins of our fortune had been possible, they could never have enabled me to live at Eastwoodleigh. But my poor father heard all my remarks on this subject, whenever he suffered it to be discussed, with something like resentment at my want of what *he* thought proper and laudable ambition; and it became a point of duty, that I should remain a silent though wretched spectator of the Sisyphean labour to which his tenderness for me condemned him.—It was under a sort of dissimulation of my real purpose that I obtained permission of him to go, about two years since, to France. When I was there, I thought that a favourable prospect opened for my entering into business at Bourdeaux; but two things were necessary—my father's consent, and some money—neither of which I had much hope of procuring. However the change of ideas, which was then rapidly making progress in France, helped greatly to facilitate my scheme. The Baron de Lavergnac, notwithstanding the principles of his family and the habits of his life, was reasonable enough to listen to my arguments; and he not only offered me his purse and his credit, but undertook to conquer the prejudices of my father. He in a great degree succeeded; I was received into an eminent mercantile house at Bourdeaux. You know how the Revolution in France, which at its beginning wore, I thought, a more auspicious appearance, has overturned in its progress the prosperity of trade, which it affected to enlarge and to protect: the house, into which I had been received as one of the younger partners, and whose commercial interest I thought myself likely to promote by my English connections, was one of the first that was swept away in the increasing tempest. —I returned to England, without any other advantage than that of having acquired such an additional knowledge of a language I was before a tolerable proficient in, that I might perhaps pass as well for a native of France as of England."

"Alas! I came back, disappointed myself, to witness the more bitter disappointments of my poor father—who, during my absence, had been making new efforts, every one of which was eventually injurious not only to his temporary tranquillity, but to the wreck of that property he was so solicitous to keep together. It would only be giving you pain, Miss Dacres, were I to relate all that I then went through. I now reflect on it with sensations so uneasy, that I am glad to avert my thoughts from every recollection, but the only one that gives me any comfort— that every moment of my time was given to smooth for my unhappy parent the downward path of life.—Ah! Miss Dacres, he was driven prematurely thither by distress of mind! by the cruelty of..."

Althea shuddered:—the idea that Sir Audley had by his severity contributed to the sad close of the life of this unhappy father, was more than she could calmly bear. Marchmont saw her emotion—and instantly guessing the cause, repented of what he had said, and hastened to relate other circumstances that might carry her mind from it.

"I lost this venerated and lamented parent—with what anguish of heart I need not say. It was necessary, however, to check my own feelings, or at least to conceal them, that I might not increase the sad sufferings of my mother, who, ill as she thought of the situation of her family, knew not the extent of the evil; my father having always concealed the worst from her, with impolitic affection—which was, however, at least an amiable weakness. He could not bear to see her unhappy; and my mother, in the same view of saving *him* from pain, concealed how far her knowledge of the truth went, or how much she was affected by what she knew.

"It was upon the same principle of concealing, what it would quite have killed her to have known, that I hastily agreed to any proposition made me by the villain Vampyre, to save even a moment's delay, lest the inhuman step he took in stopping the remains of my father on the day of his burial should be known to her. I have since heard that all he did then was entirely illegal. But I was ignorant myself of all the chicanery of the law; I had no friend near me whom I could at that moment consult, for Eversley dared not appear, or assist me, on account of his wife; and when a certain time had passed after these illegal acts, I found all my attempts at redress set aside by certain rules and forms, of which I understand no more than I do of the causes, why the best of all possible laws are often abused, to the very worst of all possible purposes.

"In this case, as indeed too often happens, my intentions were wholly counteracted, and that which was done to save my mother from one distress, brought upon her another—another, which has never ceased to press upon her since—for from the engagement I was then compelled to enter into I have never since been able to disengage myself.—It has driven me first into concealment, and now into exile."

A pause, that seemed to be the effect of the bitter recollections which arose in his mind, now gave an opportunity for Althea to say,

"But your friend Eversley?—Could not he have come forward in so trying a moment?—Ought he not?"

"Ah! Miss Dacres, my friend Eversley had already done but too much for me. The friendly assistance he had afforded my father had almost exhausted the resources that were peculiarly his own, and I knew had embroiled him with that vulgar and violent woman his wife—who, having been unable during their marriage to find any other cause of reproach, had fixed upon his generosity to *my* family as an unfailing subject of remonstrance and rage. To such misery on my account I could not determine to expose a man so sincerely my friend, and to whom I already owed so many obligations.—Yet such was his kindness, that, when I absolutely refused to suffer his pecuniary interference to an amount so considerable as would have released me from the inveterate

malice of Vampyre, he employed the sum he had prepared for that
purpose, or at least all he could raise, in repurchasing for my mother an
annuity of eighty pounds a year, hers and my sister's sole dependance,
which in the last days of my father's life she had sold, as the only
means that offered to prevent those sad days from being embittered
by the intrusion of bailiffs and attorneys into the very chamber where
he lay dying!"

Again the voice of Marchmont failed him, but in a moment he
conquered his emotion, and went on –

"On the noble humanity of such a friend, I determined, whatever
I might suffer, no farther to trespass. Could I indeed have got over my
reluctance to accept, what I knew cost him all the domestic tranquillity
which he had made so many sacrifices to preserve; I could never have
consented to exhaust for my own convenience that friendly assistance,
which might hereafter be necessary to those whose case was infinitely
dearer to me than my own. I was young, and active; my spirit was yet
unbroken by personal disappointment, for I had hardly on my own
account entered the world. I am naturally of a sanguine temper; and
though I had already been enough initiated into the school of adversity, to have discovered that there were villains among mankind, such as
in the happy simplicity of early youth I had not supposed could exist;
yet, I rather believed we had been particularly unfortunate in the persons with whom we had had dealings, than that *many* such were to be
found in the great mass of society.

"With these impressions, and with perhaps a presumptuous reliance on my own powers, I courageously began a career, in which,
though I knew many others had failed, I for a while believed I might
succeed, and by dint of my own efforts rescue my family from pecuniary distress, and myself from the wretchedness of dependence.
You will smile, perhaps, if I tell you that I was so new to the world in
which I was to struggle, and so confident of the buoyant powers of my
own mind, that I believed these important purposes might be effected
by authorship. You have undoubtedly read the life of the unhappy
Chatterton, which, with that of many other luckless projectors in the
same visionary pursuit, ought to have served as a warning against these
presumptuous and airy hopes. But, though conscious that I had less
genius, I thought I could guard against many of the errors young authors have fallen into; and I even flattered myself that the friends of
my family, who would not come forward before, would promote my

interest when they saw my exertion; while others, I supposed, would
esteem me for the motive by which that exertion was induced. In these
speculations I was not wholly disappointed. Some who had interest
in the world of fashion were not unwilling to *chaperon* my first appearance; but among these were not to be reckoned any of my own
family—for, if any thing could have roused the avaricious apathy of
Lady Silchester, and some of the rest of my mother's relations, to give
me either their interest with government, or their pecuniary help, it
would have been their dislike to having an author among their relatives.
However, as they loved money better than even the indulgence of this
ridiculous pride, they first endeavoured to divert me from my purpose
by promising, if I would turn my attention to another line, that they
would try to get me some small place. I had heard, and been thoroughly convinced, of the futility of such promises before: I refused,
therefore, to lose a moment in listening to them. They affected anger
at my doubts of their executing what they promised, and against the
shame of being related to an author, found a ready resource in wholly
neglecting him. Indeed, from the hour when the fortunes of my father
began evidently to decline, the relations of my mother, who never had
shewn her much attention, began to withdraw from any connection
with her or her children; and till I was once more forced upon the
notice of Lady Silchester by one of her acquaintance, she had affected
to lose sight of us for some years. What *she* did not do, the rest of the
family who were one degree farther removed, thought themselves happily exempted from undertaking. I found others, however, who had,
as I believed, more power to forward my views in the line I had adopted. I was considered as a young man of great promise by some of
those persons zealous for literature and the arts, who love to have their
names often appear as protectors of infant genius; but, to the advantage I was to derive from their countenance, I found some conditions
annexed not very consistent with the spirit of independence which
I had determined to preserve—for it was necessary, if I would avail
myself of literary patronage, to sacrifice my own opinion to the judgement and experience of these my protectors; which I was not always
modest and diffident enough to do without reluctance, and it happened unfortunately that no two of them thought alike.—However, as
an experiment how far using their sagacity was preferable to trusting
to my own inexperience, I consented to follow the advice of him who
seemed to me the best judge of literary business, and he undertook to

shew me how I might lengthen a trifling *jeu d'esprit* that had met with some applause, into a long poem. It cost me a good deal of labour; but when it was published, instead of the profits on which I had calculated, I foumd myself considerably indebted to the printer and publisher; and was told, what I was soon convinced was true, that nobody now ever thinks of reading a poem of above twenty lines—that poetry is quite out of fashion—and that the shelves in the booksellers' warehouses are loaded with poetry unread and unknown: that there has not been above one successful poem for the last ten years; and that a party only agreeing to praise his works, or some unaccountable caprice of fashion, gives a poet the least chance of popularity, even if he is lucky enough to escape the blight of criticism, which often withers his poetical laurels before they are even unfolded.

"My good Sir," said the person, who from experience gave me all this information, "my good Sir, this is not a poetical age.—I assure you, that, whatever may be your talents, nothing can be done in that way, and I verily believe the very best poems will not pay for the printing If you have no turn for politics, which indeed is a line now almost over—occupied, turn your thoughts to novel writing—narrative, let it be about what it will, is read, because the mind quietly acquiesces, and it requires no trouble to think about it. On your part it will demand much less care in the composition. Never mind improbabilities—put together a sufficient number of facts—the more unlikely the better. If you are too idle to choose the trouble of inventing, collect eight or nine of the most popular works of that sort; take a piece of one, and a piece of another, and put them together, only a little altered, just to disguise them; never mind whether what the painters call *keeping*, can in this motley assemblage be attended to; nobody thinks about that: sprinkle the whole plentifully with horrors of some sort of other, to stimulate the languid attention, and you will have a certainty of a sale at least among the circulating libraries, which, after all, is the principal sale that can be expected; for who buy novels?—Who indeed buy books at all in these times? unless it be men of science who cannot do without them. However, if you can produce any thing tolerably new in this line, you will do pretty well, and you will find booksellers who will deal with you."

"The prospect thus offered me," continued Marchmont, "was not very flattering; but I had very little choice, and I set about what is sometimes called an epic in prose, and acknowledged to be, when

well managed, a considerable effort of the human mind; and sometimes stigmatised as a species of work calculated only to enervate the
mind, and inflame with false representations the imagination of youth.
I went on (as I believed myself) pretty well at first; but when my hero
was fairly launched into the history, I found myself surrounded with
difficulties, and in danger, as every page proceeded, of going against
some of those rocks which my instructor had taught me to beware of.
Without incident nothing was to be done, but almost every possible
event was already in print; and notwithstanding what my advisers had
said, I was too proud to borrow. Improbable and forced adventures,
events that never yet happened on the habitable globe, and never could
happen by any chance short of an absolute miracle, disgusted *me;* and
prosing conversations, or circumstances but little elevated above the
daily occurrences of life, would, I thought, disgust my readers. As to
characters, I had not yet seen enough of the world to *imagine* them,
from the faint sketches I had made; and I found that, if I represented
such as had come within my observation, I should be accused of personality. If I made my hero an unfortunate wanderer, existing by his
own efforts, I understood that I should be accused of egotism, and of
having represented my own adventures. If I made him too long or too
suddenly prosperous, nobody would care about him at all. If he were
painted with too many perfections, he would be called a poor imitation
of Sir Charles Grandisone—a faultless monster: but if I gave him a
proportion of those errors to which high-spirited youth is particularly
liable, I should then be accused of having pictured an agreeable libertine, whose example, like those of Ranger, Charles Surface, or Tom
Jones, could not fail of being pernicious.

"Nor was the landscape of my piece less difficult to decide upon
than the figures. If my scene lay in other countries, I must give to my
characters the manners of those countries, which of course rendered
them less interesting to the bulk of my intended readers in this: I might
indeed have carried my story to the reigns of our Edwards and Hen-
ries—but besides that this species of writing was already successfully
occupied, I could not represent modern manners as existing in the
persons of our ancestors in their heavy armour, and fierce prowess;
or in their softer moments, in satin doublets and slashed sleeves. I
found too the preservation of the unities a work of some difficulty.
I was told, and indeed I saw from several examples, that neither time
nor place was much minded, and that I might hazard being equally

careless of chronology and geography; but I piqued myself on having studied Aristotle, and scrupulously attended to the probabilities of time and place. I turned my eyes to the scenes that were passing almost before them, and thought, by relating without much addition from fiction some of the many events that were passing in private life in a neighbouring country, that I might unite interest with truth: I was soon, however, turned aside from this experiment, by hearing that novel-writing has in one respect an affinity to the drama—that time and distance are required to soften for use the harsher features that may be exhibited from real life; that it was almost impossible to bring forward *events* without touching on their *causes;* and that any tendency to political discussion, however liberal or applicable, was not to be tolerated in a sort of work which people took up with no other design than to be amused at the least possible expence of thought. In this case I was to be like the courtly preacher, who deemed it altogether shocking to

"—mention *Hell* to ears polite."

"Thus, in a choice of difficulties, I laboured on—with what success, it now matters not. At some other opportunity (if indeed I dare indulge the hope that, at some future time, I may be allowed the happiness I now enjoy) I may trouble you, Madam, with the history of my progress with *the encouragers of literature,* among whom indeed I found it to be true, that the fraternity of Booksellers are, for the most part, to be relied on, and with *them* at least I so successfully made my way, that I was enabled to assist my family (though by no means to the extent of my wishes), and to supply myself I believe indeed I should have done better in time (as on my *foi-disant* friends of *every description* I ceased to depend), but to carry on this business in obscurity was impossible. No sooner was my name known as being in some degree a successful candidate for literary emolument, than my address was procured by Vampyre from my publisher, and I became more than ever the object of that monster's persecution. He himself ventured, sheltered as he believed by the armour of his profession, to present his own hideous libel on the human form in my lodgings—attended, as he almost always is, by a miserable sneaking being of a clerk.—I listened for two or three minutes to his insolence—and then, though I think I am not of a very choleric temper, found myself seized with an impulse to kick him down stairs, so irresistible, that I immediately shewed him that manner of descending with great velocity, and then handed his clerk after him into the street—where the mob, who in a second of time gather in a populous thorough-fare, hearing, from the people where I lodged, that the reptile they saw so suddenly spring out of the door into the middle of the coach-way was a villanous attorney who had ruined a family, determined to add an epilogue to my figure-dance, by no means to the taste of Mr. Solicitor Vampyre; whose zeal for his clients might well have been cooled by the discipline he received under the next pump, had it not been re-animated by resentment for this personal disgrace. He now had added a fresh cause of vengeance to his native diabolical malignity, and to his desire to find new excuses for getting money from his stupid and wicked employers.—From that time he redoubled his persecution, and I was compelled either to submit to imprisonment, or to fly.—Though this scourge to individuals, and disgrace to the species in general, often practises and resides in *the neighbourhood of a great seaport* not far from the place where we now are, it was here—that—on account of Mrs. Mosely ... (Marchmont hesitated, and seemed to be confused) and for other considerations, I determined to conceal myself. Of the sequel I believe it is unnecessary to speak."

Althea, though her countenance bore evidence how much this narrative had affected her, did not immediately find words that answered to her meaning.—Marchmont availed himself of her silence again to plead for permission to write to her: and his eloquence was perhaps aided by the circumstance of the moment; for a signal was suddenly given from behind some high rocks to the left of that where they sat, and the boat, with Fenchurch and two seamen in it, immediately appeared from beyond a promontory. Marchmont, unwilling to expose Althea to the gaze of these men, now tore himself away, having at length obtained the permission he so ardently solicited—and, hurrying from her, made a signal to Fenchurch to bring the boat on shore farther on, where high cliffs ran out into the sea, and shut out all near view of the spot where he was now compelled to take a reluctant leave of Althea.

When he was gone, she sat down breathless, and with a beating heart, on her former seat; hardly daring to recollect what had passed, or to enter on any self-enquiry as to the propriety of her conduct. With eyes fixed on the sea, she waited in an undescribable state of mind for the sight of the boat, and fancied that, amidst the low and almost imperceptible murmurs of the tide, she heard the dashing oars. Nor was she deceived; in a few moments she saw it slowly appear beyond the promontory. Marchmont was standing in it, his looks apparently fixed on the place where he had left her—but the distance was soon too great to allow her to distinguish his features. She saw, however, that he stretched his arms towards her, then clasped his hands together as if offering a prayer to heaven for her safety. The dull haze that had been long gathering over the sea, now thickened so much, that the boat, and the passengers in it, became indistinct; appearing only like a dark shapeless spot amidst the wide expanse of water; and it was soon afterwards hardly to be seen at all. While Althea could trace, or fancy she could trace it through the mist and intervening distance, she remained on the shore, then reluctantly and slowly returned by the rugged steps to the summit of the cliff; and from thence again surveyed the sea, now undistinguishable from the sky, all being alike overclouded. She thought, however, that she still saw the boat move through the distant waves—till the head-land which forms one side of Torbay* seemed to intervene. It was there, as Marchmont had informed her, the vessel lay that was to receive him.—The heart of Althea, recently awakened to new sensations by the certainty that Marchmont loved her, now sunk in sick and languid despondence; for she reflected that it was more than possible she had lost sight of him for ever.

Hardly distinguishing her way, she now looked around her to be certain that she was in the right road back to the house of Eastwoodleigh, which, large as it was, could not be distinguished even from this high ground, because of the numerous tall elms every where lining the lanes of this country, which in many places appeared like a continual wood. Fortunately she had remarked a singular bank of red-coloured earth in her way, which now served her as a guide to the steep lane she had ascended; and afterwards her road lay entirely along it, till she came to the ivy-clad ruins of one of the lodges of the disparked environs of Eastwoodleigh.

When Althea entered the house, she hastened immediately to her own room, fancying, as she passed Wansford and his wife, that they both looked at her as if they knew she returned from meeting Marchmont—so much power has the imagination when the conscience is not calm. In feet, it was in the present case merely conscience that raised this idea; for, though Wansford knew it, he carefully avoided looking at her as she came in—and his wife had no certain knowledge

---

*   Berry Head

that Marchmont had ever been in the house, and was free from every suspicion that related to Althea.

To a young and ingenuous mind there is nothing so painful as the first idea of having committed an error.—Althea, who had always accustomed herself to enquire whether what she did was perfectly consonant to the maxims she had received from Mrs. Trevyllian, thus establishing a sort of second conscience as her guide, now trembled to make this appeal. Yet, when once it was made, many reflections arose which helped to reconcile her to herself. Though she had died unmarried, Mrs. Trevyllian had none of that prudish reserve which often degenerates into ridiculous austerity at a late period of life. She had not indeed taught Althea, that the first purpose of her life was to attract a man of fortune for a husband, but had rather endeavoured to give her such principles as would make her pass a single life in cheerful content, if such (as was very probable) should be her lot, notwithstanding her personal advantages, and the sweetness of her manners; for Mrs. Trevyllian knew, that to considerations merely interested she never would sacrifice herself; while it was very doubtful whether such a man as united the advantages of fortune to those of a cultivated mind, would ever fall in her way. From this manner of thinking during the course of her education, Althea had acquired an ingenuous simplicity of character. She had no design on the hearts of the men she conversed with, and was therefore always easy and unaffected, without familiarity or flippancy. But she had never been taught to believe, that it was right to fly from or avoid any man because he was indigent; and she knew that Mrs. Trevyllian herself had been much attached to a gentleman of very small fortune, whose death alone prevented their marriage. Though unacquainted with the particular circumstances which had thrown a shade of melancholy over the life of her aunt (for she had never courage to speak of them), Althea was assured, from this instance, that, had her aunt been living, she would not have condemned her partality to Marchmont, though she might have thought marriage very imprudent under the present circumstances of both their fortunes. Nor could Althea help reflecting, that the observation Marchmont made was but too just, when he said that she was accountable to nobody; for her father seemed entirely to abandon her, and she had no other relations who had either inclination or right to direct her. Her situation, therefore, was altogether different from that of a young woman directly under the protection of a parent, or of immediate friends. She broke through no duty; and the tender compassion and personal preference with which she thought of Marchmont, and which had induced her to consent to correspond with him, interfered with none of those principles of conduct which her propriety of mind would never have allowed her to violate.

Having thus reconciled herself to the past, she ventured to look forward to the future; but her courage and hope failed when she thought of the situation in which her unhappy lover had left his native country to go he hardly knew whither, but probably to another where danger and distress were likely to meet him. He had evaded all explanation on money matters: but there was every reason to suppose he was but slenderly supplied with the means of existence; and it appeared very uncertain, whether on his reaching France it would be possible to make his way across the whole kingdom to the southern coast, where, not far from Toulon, his relation the Baron de Lavergnac resided. If he did reach that side of France, from all present intelligence there was too much cause to apprehend that Monsieur de Lavergnac was involved in the general ruin that menaced the royal party, to which he decidedly belonged.

With all these apprehensions continually present to her, Althea now tasted no more peace than when she knew Marchmont to be within a hundred paces of her, and to be in momentary danger of being dragged away to end his life in a prison.

Yet distant and uncertain dangers appeared less hideous than the persecution of the *fiend* Vampyre; and when she remembered that another day might have put Marchmont into his hands, the assurance of his escape seemed a gratifying reflection, and the gloomy uncertainty of what was to come appeared less terrible.

A long interval was yet to pass before any intelligence of the poor wanderer could arrive; and Althea was conscious how tedious and forlorn her desolate solitude would appear. Though she had never been accustomed to confidantes of her own age (for Mrs. Trevyllian had always disliked that girlish caballing which frequently corrupts the minds of young people), she now felt the want of some one to whom she could speak of Marchmont without restraint. Her thoughts again turned towards his mother and his sisters. To them alone could she hazard naming him. But they were far from her; and as Marchmont had assured her that his mother intended, as soon as he was in a place of greater safety, to acknowledge all the kindnesses that Althea had intended, or that Marchmont had received; she was compelled to wait for this overture from Mrs. Marchmont, before she could venture to express the ardent desire she felt to love and serve her.

CHAP. X.

"Ah! do not think thou art alone unhappy!"

THE DAY AFTER the departure of Marchmont, the calm stillness of the morning tempted Althea to revisit the shore, which was in some measure a new object to her, and would now, she thought, afford her a melancholy pleasure. From thence she proposed walking to the cottage of Mrs. Mosely, with whom she wished to converse; and having procured such a direction from Wansford as was likely to be a sufficient guide, she set forth about one o'clock, intending to take a cold dinner at her return.

The same spot, where for perhaps the last time Althea had seen the only man she had ever thought of with approbation, and who might be called indeed almost the only person in the world who felt an interest in her fate, or for whom she was herself interested, could hardly fail of inspiring her with mournful reflections; but with them a degree of pleasure mingled itself, and the sort of day was well calculated to encourage the melancholy yet soothing reverie she fell into.

As on the day preceding, a gauzy mist hovered over the unruffled sea, spreading from thence to the land, and softening every object of the rich coast on either side.

The quiet solemnity of the hour and scene was not broken by the gay and lively verdure of May, for the distant landscape was softened by the hazy vapour; yet, as she wandered slowly along the broad margin of sand, which she had been told led to an easier acclivity of the cliff, from whence her walk to the cottage might be considerably shortened, she remarked some of those plants, inhabitants of the borders of the sea, of which her aunt had taught her the names on a former visit to the coast.

The* sea reed grass, covering many of the broad beds of sand, waved its yet feeble spires in the hardly perceptible breeze; within the

_____

* Arundo Arenaria

immediate spray of the waves the sea[*] holly put forth its gray and thorny leaves; and where the more undisturbed surface of the sands allowed them to be clothed with a slight covering of turf, the small yellow stars of the[†] ladies' bed-straw were just opening among it.— The fairy nosegays, which with this and the beautiful convolvulus[‡], peculiar to the western coast, a native also of the arid beach, she used to delight in making, while walking with her dear protectress, came to her remembrance, and, softened as her mind was before, filled her eyes with tears.

But the recollection of Mrs. Trevyllian was always salutary. In recalling those simple pleasures, the admirable lessons with which every enjoyment was accompanied recurred to her. Among these, fortitude was a virtue on which her aunt had constantly dwelt with peculiar energy; as if she had foreseen how much occasion her beloved Althea would one day have to exert it. Instead, therefore, of allowing herself to dwell on ideas which served only to depress and enervate her mind, she turned it towards the means of fulfilling the parting wishes of Marchmont, who had entreated her to allow his mother and his sisters to be known to her, and to transfer to them all that active benevolence of friendship of which he could not avail himself. The poor old servant at the cottage, too, he had warmly recommended to her humanity; and aroused by these recollections she shook off that pleasing but useless pensiveness which was stealing upon her, and quickened her pace towards the cabin of Mrs. Mosely, which she found with less difficulty than she expected; for, though concealed by the rude inequalities of a common, which was at the western extremity of the grounds of East-woodleigh, it was hardly a mile from the sea. She found the solitary tenant of this lone cottage full of trouble. Whatever terrors she had undergone for '*her dear child, her dear young master*' as she called Marchmont, while for the course of several months he had been hunted by the blood-hounds of the law, they were now forgotten in the cruel idea, that he was '*gone beyond sea;*' which amounted, in the opinion of Mrs. Mosely, to a certainty that she should see him no more.

Wild and vague ideas of scenes passing in France, horrible enough, and rendered more strangely hideous by her long-rooted prejudices, had taken possession of Mrs. Mosely's mind—but still the predomi-

---

[*]   Eryngium Maritimum

[†]   Galium Verum

[‡]   Convolvulus Soldanella

nant impression was, the danger of *'going beyond sea.'*

Althea for a moment attempted to stifle all she felt herself, to combat impressions so painful to a mind already enfeebled by time and calamity; and though to all that she could say the poor old woman gave no other answer than a deep sigh, and a motion with her head that expressed hopeless incredulity as to the safety of her *'dear master,'* Althea began to flatter herself that she should reason her into more tranquillity, when a quick step was heard near the cottage door.

Althea started without knowing why; and Mrs. Mosely, accustomed to be always on the watch since Marchmont's personal safety had been in question, moved to the door as quickly as her infirmities permitted, and, looking out, returned to her seat, saying it was only poor Phoebe.

"And who is poor Phoebe?" enquired Althea.

"Poor unhappy girl!" replied Mrs. Mosely, "she is a godchild, Madam, of mine; and never any body met with greater misfortunes for her station. Her poor brain is hurt by all she has gone through; but she is very harmless, and sometimes her senses return again for a time. I am afraid, poor creature! she is in one of her wandering fits now—for she seldom comes at other times. Indeed, I have not seen her before these two months."

Althea had no time to enquire farther as to the object that had already excited her pity, when a young woman of one or two and twenty, pale and thin, her dress clean but coarse, and without a hat, entered the room with a hurried step; and not seeming to observe that Althea was there, she came up to the old woman, and, taking her hand, smiled— but it was a melancholy smile—then looking steadily in her face, said, "I have got to you at last, my dear friend! They would have hindered me again: but I have stole away from them; and you will let me stay with you, will you not?"

"Yes, Phoebe," said Dame Mosely, "if you will stay in the house, and not leave me without telling where you are going to. But there is the young lady that used to send me so much help when you was here last."

"The young lady!" cried the unhappy girl, "I am in the way then —I am sorry I came. Pray forgive me; I did not know the lady was here. Pray be not angry —I will go home again—indeed I will."

"No, no," interrupted Althea, "you shall stay here, Phoebe. I am myself going presently; and till I do, it will distress me if you do not sit down and talk to your old friend just as you used to do."

Phoebe looked at her with an unsteady yet expressive eye; then, turning to Mrs. Mosely, she said in a half whisper,

"She is like the angels I used to dream of once, when I had hopes of going among them away from this bad world; and I thought they had just such voices."

"That lady *is* as much of an angel as ever was in this world," replied Mrs. Mosely aloud.

Phoebe answered only by a deep sigh. Dame Mosely again spoke to her. She heeded her not, but, fixing her eyes on the window, sighed again as if her heart would break. Then, after a moment's pause, she turned quickly, and said,

"You remember! So now, as you are busy, dear godmother, I will go."

"Not down to the sea-side," answered the other.

"Why! I have not been there a long, long time, till to-day, indeed! and I am better, a great deal better for it."

"Well, well, Phoebe, you must not go again—you must not, indeed. Come, if you do not mind me I shall be angry, and will not let you come to see me again."

"Won't you?—Oh! that will be very cruel. And will you, my oldest and last friend, be as cruel as all other people are? Well, if you will, *do* then! make me be shut up again, and make me to be beat and punished by that cruel ..." (another deep sigh burst from her sad heart, but she went on), "by that cruel... Ah! well, it will be the sooner over! If nobody, nobody at all, is left, who has compassion for me—perhaps it may not be so difficult to die, as I find it now!—But I tire you. Pray, Ma'am, excuse me," (turning to Althea, with a half courtesy) "I am a poor miserable creature, without a friend left in the wide world."

Althea was so affected that she could not answer her, otherwise than by turning to Mrs. Mosely, and begging her to sooth the poor girl rather than contradict her.

"Come, Phoebe," said the old woman, "if you have been to the sea-side, you cannot desire, you know, to go again. You shall go and lie down upon my bed; for I am sure your head aches, and that you are tired. Come, be a good girl, and then you shall stay with me a day or two."

It seemed as if the unsettled mind of this unfortunate being was tremblingly alive to the voice of kindness; for without farther opposition she gave her hand to Mrs. Mosely, and suffered her to lead her out.

When she got to the door she turned towards Althea, and, with her head mournfully declined, sighed out, "God bless you, young lady!"

Mrs. Mosely returned in a few minutes.—"I've made her lie down," said she; "and perhaps she may forget herself while I make her a little tea, which is the only thing she will take."

"Let me assist you, my good woman," said Althea; "and do tell me who this poor young creature is, and by what misfortunes she has been driven to this pitiable state."

"Ah! dear Miss, it is a long story, and you know old folks are apt to be tedious—it will tire you, I fear."

"No, no—on the contrary, I shall not be easy without hearing it. Make her tea, and carry it to her. I will have some too, for I am fatigued this morning, and while she remains quiet you shall relate to me all you know of her. Just now there is nothing I would so willingly listen to."

END OF THE SECOND VOLUME

MARCHMONT.

CHAPTER I.

But who is she in garb of misery clad,
Yet of no vulgar mien? — a look so sad
The mourning maniac wears — so wild, yet meek;
A beam of joy now wanders o'er her cheek,
The pale eye visiting — but leaves it soon,
As fade the dewy glances of the moon,
Upon some wandering cloud, while slow the ray,
Retires, and leaves more dark the heaven's wide way!

"THIS POOR YOUNG creature, Madam," said Mrs. Mosely, "is a godchild of mine, as I told you. Her mother was a servant to Mrs. Marchmont, and a great favourite of every body's — She married very well, the son of one of the richest farmers hereabouts, and they lived with the old people, where this poor girl was born. She was well brought up; but unfortunately her father and mother both died, and the grandfather met with heavy losses, and was grown very old, so that he could not carry on his business; and therefore was forced to give it up to another of his sons, who was a hard, selfish kind of man, and did not much care to be burdened with Phoebe, though, while his father lived, he let her stay to take care of him. — He died at a great age about four years ago, and then Phoebe was desired by her uncle to look out for a service. — She was taken to serve two single ladies who lived at Exeter, who, seeing her a sensible girl, used to make her read to them, and to work in the room with them; so that she learned a little more than common servants generally do. These ladies had a brother, who was captain of an India ship; and returning home from a voyage, he came down to see them. He had a servant, a young man who had been three voyages abroad, and saved a little money. — He fell in love with Phoebe; and as it was a very good match for her, the ladies did not oppose their being married, though they were very sorry to part with her. — She went with her husband, Mr. Prior, to London, being then a young creature not eighteen. — I don't understand how such things happen, having known nothing about them when I was young, so that now I cannot make much out of what people tell me; but it somehow or other came to pass that Mr. Prior, who had laid out the best part of his money in some goods from *Indie*, lost them all by the wicked deceitfulness of a friend he had trusted —I heard that, by reason of their being smuggled, they were all seized by the Custom-house officers — and that so poor Prior lost above four hundred pounds. — Well! — to make the best of it, and to begin the world, as it were, again, (his master, the captain, being gone back to sea) he accepted of an offer that was made him to go out to the West Indies to settle there as a sort of steward, or overseer of a gentleman's estate, and he had the liberty of taking his wife with him. So away they went to Jamaica about two years ago. — Poor Phoebe wrote to me just before they went away, and seemed in high spirits, saying that nobody ever was happier in a good husband than she was, and she hoped to come back and see me one day or other, and all friends in England; but that she did not mind leaving it with such a kind and tender friend as her dear Prior was to her. — When they got there, poor young things! they found, to be sure, all matters as good as they had been promised, as to profit and such like; but Phoebe did not know how to use herself to live among the black people. She had no need, however, poor girl! to argue the matter long with herself; for before they had been at their new place six months, her husband got the bad fever that they say so many hundreds have died of in those parts. Poor Prior did not die, though. His wife, though she was very near her time, nursed him night and day, and he was young and strong, so he did just get through it; but he was so weak and bad, that the doctors said he never would be well if he staid in that country — and his wife brought a dead child, and was very ill afterwards, so that they thought it best to come back to England.

"One would have hoped now that their troubles might have been ended, as much as poor folks troubles can end; but it pleased God to order it otherwise. They had a tedious voyage by reason of contrary winds, but they were within sight of English ground; and poor Phoebe, when she has been able to talk about it, has told me that the very sight of the land did her husband good, so that he was getting quite himself again for all their being so long at sea. — Phoebe's few friends living here in the west country, she wished very much to have come to land at Plymouth: but her husband's sister lived in London; and he hoping to get some employment there, she would not say any thing about it — so they went on in the ship that was loaded with sugar and such like for to sell at London.

"But a terrible storm overtook them a little above here; and not far from Sidmouth the ship was drove ashore, and every body in her drowned, but two sailors, a boy, and poor Phoebe, who having been stunned by the falling of one of the masts as her husband was trying to take her out in his arms, was somehow entangled so among the rigging and ropes, that when the waves washed almost all the rest of the people off the deck she was left: so it was supposed, for nobody could tell exacdy how it happened. — The last thing poor unhappy Phoebe remembers, when her disturbed mind allows her to think of any thing, is, that Prior took her in his arms up from the cabin, and tried to cheer and encourage her; and when somebody advised him to save himself by leaping in to the sea, as he could swim very well, he answered, that he had rather perish with his wife than get on shore without her; but that, if she could but have courage, they might both be safe. — 'At that moment,' says, Phoebe, 'a great sea broke over the ship; she struck with more force than ever; but Prior still held me fast, when on a sudden there was a dreadful crash, and a loud shriek followed —I remember no more.' — She has told me though, some-times, when she has had an interval of reason, that the first thing she afterwards recollects was being on the beach of stones, surrounded by men and women, who, though they saw she was not dead, were taking every thing from her, and that she well remembers their cutting off her wedding ring because her fingers were swelled. — The shock this gave her, and a sort of confused idea of what had happened, and that Prior was perhaps alive, roused her to greater sensibility; but that the people continued to tear off her clothes, and one had just taken and run off with her pockets, in which was all the money Prior had received for his wages in Jamaica. She had then, she says, strength to raise herself up, and she saw two of the men and one bad-looking woman whis-pering together, and is sure they were consulting together to kill her — when a young gentleman on horseback came hastily towards them, and asking some questions, leaped down upon the stones all among the people that were round her, and insisted on their giving back the clothes they had taken from her, and affording her assistance to save her life, instead of thinking of robbing her. — The people only asked what business it was of his, and went away to seek after more plunder, leaving her with very little clothes; and they seemed then very unwilling to go. — Phoebe spoke, and desired the young gentleman to tell her where her husband was? — He could not answer her; and it was with great difficulty he prevailed upon some other women, who were by this time come down to see what they could get too, to lead her among them to the nearest house; where they would not take her in till her had given them all the money he had about him; and then he told the poor distracted creature he would go try to find her husband! — Ah! he knew that would be to no purpose; for he was sure he had spoken to the only three people that, besides Phoebe herself, were saved, and they had told him they saw Prior dashed off the deck by the mast, and were sure he was killed. — But the dear, good young man fetched a surgeon to the poor distressed creature, who was a humane kind man, and by degrees they made her life secure; but as she grew well enough to think, she became more and more delirious. — They could not, you know, help her thinking, nor her knowing when she did, that Prior was drowned; so she was raving mad for a good while, and confined down in her bed.

"Ah! my dearest Miss, who do you think the noble-hearted gentleman was that saved this poor wretched girl? — It was no other but my dear young master himself — It was last October — just the first time he came down to this country to get out of the way — and he was overtaken by the storm, and put up for the night at a little public-house on the wayside about two mile from the sea. — The wind was so terribly high that he could not close his eyes; and before daybreak he heard some men call up the landlord, and tell him there was a great ship ashore at a place they named; and thereupon that man, and two or three more that came in, went away as fast as they could to see for plunder. My good young master, on the contrary, got upon his horse, and rode down to see who he could save. — Dear soul! he was always from a boy trying to do good to all the world! —I wonder when any body will think of serving him?

"God knows how ill he could afford the money it cost him to have poor Phoebe taken care of. Finding she was a native of this country, he enquired out her friends, and had her brought to one of them — that uncle of hers that lives in a lone farm about three miles off; and though he was in such sad distress himself, Mr. Marchmont set about trying to recover for her some little matter that Prior had left in his sister's hands when he went beyond sea. But when that dishonest person, this sister of Prior's, found that her brother was drowned, and that his wife had lost her senses with grief, she knew there was nobody that could maintain any demand against her; so nothing could be got from her but mere trifles from time to time — and the uncle was so unwilling to keep Phoebe, that he got her into a mad-house: but they presently after discharged her, saying that she never would be any better for any thing they could do for her. But, poor thing! she hurts nobody, and all her raving is turned into a sort of melancholy wildness that breaks one's heart. If it had not been for her having lost her senses, the ladies that she lived with before she was married would have taken her again, even although she had not been able to do for them as a servant; but one of those ladies has very bad health, and is at times afflicted with low spirits herself, so that it was impossible for them to have such a poor distracted girl in the house. But they were still very charitable and kind to her; and they, and some of their friends, have agreed among them to pay every year as much as satisfies her uncle for letting her stay at his house. But, poor thing! they take no manner of care of her; and as she is quite inoffensive, nobody hinders her wandering about when she becomes restless. But sometimes she shuts herself for ten or twelve days in her room, and never, if she can help it, will see the light or speak to any body. Now, since Spring is coming on, she is, as the doctor said she would be, more affected. — One of the neighbours told me a few days ago, that poor Phoebe had taken to her rambling again. — Her mind runs upon the notion, that if she goes to the sea-side she shall meet Prior — and when that notion takes her, she will sit whole hours upon the rocks talking to herself, and sometimes fancying he answers her: and once she was lost all night, and was found the evening of next day in one of the caverns down there by the shore, half dead with cold and hunger, and nearly insensible. — The cruel people she lives with were mad with her for the trouble she gave them, and used her so ill, that she was much worse for some time afterwards. One of the ladies that I spoke of before came to the farmer's house, however, and, I believe, promised him more money if he would treat this unhappy creature with less inhumanity — and about the same time his daughter, a sad hard-hearted woman, was married, and he took a decent middle-aged person to keep his house — one that has seen trouble herself, and therefore knows a little more how to pity people that are unfortunate. — Still however it goes hard enough with poor Phoebe — for her uncle, who is the most niggardly man in all this country, likes to make all he can of her, and to be at as little cost about her as ever he can. — Poor soul! he was tried once or twice to make her work and help him one way or other in his business; but as for any out-door work, you see, Ma'am, what a slight creature it is; and when she has sat down to needle-work for a day or two, she has soon flown off again, poor thing! and rambled down to the sea, where she sometimes fancies the ships she sees at a distance are coming from Jamaica, and that Prior is in one of them. And when she talks so, it is very sad indeed to all that hear her, who have any feeling for her: but as to the people she is with, they don't mind her, and are so used to hear her talk wildly, that they hardly heed her more than a dog or a cat about the house. — The worst is of a stormy night — it is a difficult thing then to keep her quiet, because the howling of the wind, and the beating of the rain, puts her in mind of the time she was wrecked. — Sometimes she walks about wringing her hands, and crying out to Prior, her dear Prior, to save her! and sometimes she wants to rush out of the house and go down to the beach — and she entreats the people about her to go also, in order to save any poor creatures who may be shipwrecked — as Mr. Marchmont did save her from being killed by the cruel folks that waited upon the shore. — All! good God," continued Mrs. Mosely, her mind reverting at that moment to the first subject of her own concern, "My Marchmont, far from being able to do so charitable an office, may now want somebody to help him in the same sad condition!"

Althea had been too much affected by the preceding narration to be able to bear this close with composure. Her eyes, that had been half obscured with tears for the hopeless distresses of Phoebe Prior, now streamed afresh, and sobs which she could not repress choked her. — Poor Mrs. Mosely was frightened, and offered to administer such remedies as are usual: but Althea, struggling with the useless weakness she had indulged, recovered herself in a few moments, and, desiring Mrs. Mosely to keep poor Phoebe with her for a day or two, and insisting on her taking a guinea to answer any additional expence it might occasion to her, said, that she would walk homeward, as it was already late. — And indeed tea always serving Mrs. Mosely for her dinner, Althea, deeply interested as she was in the story of the poor maniac, had forgotten the course of time, and that she had not dined herself.

The evening was closing as she walked home, and was even far advanced before she was within sight of Eastwoodleigh; for her languor prevented her walking fast, and many melancholy reflections sat heavy on her spirits. — The new proof she had so accidentally received of the active and humane spirit of Marchmont increased at once her esteem and her regret; and Mrs. Mosely's last remark, that *he* might himself so soon want the pity he had shewn to others, had deeply affected her. — The thoughts of Althea, therefore, wandered between the possibility of doing something to relieve the poor distressed victim of complicated misery, whose story she had just heard, and the cruel parting of the preceding day.

Before her deliberate manner of walking brought her to within the two last enclosures towards the house, she had calmed her spirits by reflecting, that for *her* to repine at present evils, which dwindled indeed into mere inconveniences when compared to the fate of Phoebe Prior, was a sort of unthankful arrogance; and that of the future she had no reason to despair, since, if virtue, integrity, and goodness, were the care of Heaven, its protection must surely be extended to Marchmont.

"I will not be so weak then," said she, reasoning with herself, "as to give up my mind to despondence, which, while it will disable me from assisting others, will make me burdensome to myself. — Marchmont, among real and heavy calamities, never lost sight of his benevolence; and shall I sink in solitary and selfish grief, only from the apprehension of those evils which never may arrive? — If every action of his gives me reason to be proud of the preference he avows for me, let me endeavour to become more worthy of that preference, which a feeble-minded woman cannot be. — Let me, who have no personal distresses to contend with that are not merely imaginary alleviate the heavy afflictions of such an unhappy being as this poor girl; and I shall, when engaged in such offices, be able to say, "If Marchmont could know my employment, he would esteem me more.""

CHAP. II

... Far less abhorr'd than these
Vex'd Scylla, bathing in the sea that parts
Calabria from the hoarse Trinacrian shore.

LOST IN REFLECTION, the increasing obscurity of the evening, occasioned by one of those heavy fogs which the peasants call a blight, increased, without Althea's remarking it, till she could hardly discern the path she was in. She quickened her pace, and looked about her with some degree of uneasiness. There was something fearful in the stillness of the evening; for, unless it was the slow tread of the cattle she heard grazing near her, not a sound broke the air, except from a great distance the dull tinkling of a team with bells, necessary in narrow hollow ways, such as are frequent in this part of England — How poor a substitute for the songstress of the night, which is never heard in this western country —

"With liquid notes to close the eye of day!"

Amid this black and sullen stillness, which seemed like a general pause of nature, Althea at length reached the last field but one next the house, which appeared larger, and frowning in more sublime ruin through the half-obscuring mist.

There was now only the last enclosure to pass, which was divided from that part of the disparked ground she was actually in, by the group of old trees remarkable for having shaded the same spot when Edward Marchmont gave up near it the life so honourably passed and so early lost.

There was something very melancholy in the faint effort of incomplete vegetation that appeared on the wild and most-grown branches that had pushed out from their half-hollow trunks — it reminded Althea of the last ineffectual struggles of their former unfortunate possessors to keep up an appearance of affluence when its reality existed no longer. She broke off as she passed a small branch of almost unfolded leaves from the old beech, to the twisted bole of which the gate-post was fixed — (the ashes and oaks had yet only a few weak buds) — and with many melancholy reflections opened the gate, and passed on; when suddenly from behind one of the trees started a sturdy ragged man, who in a sort of yell asked, or rather demanded, her charity.

His unexpected appearance and rude vociferation almost deprived her of all presence of mind. She continued, however, to walk quickly on, at the same time taking a shilling from her pocket, which she gave the beggar, assuring him, in tremulous voice, that it was all the relief she had in her power to afford him. — As this was a greater alms than is usually bestowed, and as she was now within the court leading to Wansford's rooms, she hoped immediately to escape from so alarming a follower; but the ruffian, now pretending to be as importunate with thanks as he had before been with prayers, pursued her closely to the door. Arriving at it, she called to Mrs. Wansford to let her in (for, since the impudent intrusion of Vampyre, all the doors of the house had been kept shut). The door was opened; but her frightful persecutor still pressed close to her; and forcing a large stick between the door and door-post, before Mrs. Wansford could shut it, he halloo'd: his voice echoing like the Indian war-whoop round the ruined walls. Instantly four other figures as terrific as himself, though less ragged, appeared; and they all rushed together into Wansford's room, where stood Althea half dead with terror; while the children hearing their mother shriek, and seeing the fear Althea was in, clung screaming round them both, crying in vain for their father.

Their father was not in the house; and the poor woman seemed to be so petrified with terror, that she had no power to ask the men their business. They did not, however, leave her long in suspense: one of them, taking off his hat, discovered the diabolical countenance and distorted eyes of the villanous attorney, Vampyre.

He approached Althea in his usual insolent manner; and while she shrunk trembling from him, as from the most noxious reptile, he told her in his loud, slow, and impudent manner, that he was now armed with proper authority to search for "the young 'Squire, who had so long been playing at hide and seek with his clients — and that he hoped *she* had now no objection to his examining the house." — Althea hearing this, felt a confused assemblage of satisfaction and indignation. Her courage, however, returned enough to say, "You seem likely to *rob* the house, and of your authority I believe nothing."

Mrs. Wansford, who really supposed from the appearance of the people that they were robbers and murderers, had no power to speak, and turned her affrighted looks towards Althea, as if to entreat her not to irritate the ruffians, who now proceeded to demand of her the keys of all rooms. Keys she assured them she had none — and the attorney, brandishing the stick with which he guided his steps, declared that they could do very well without them for that he should make no scruple to break open the doors. — "And as for your hiding-places," said the wretch, "with which this fine fellow has evaded the justice of the laws of this land, they will not serve him any longer; for there's an honest fellow," pointing to an ill-looking old man who stood near him, "that can give a pretty good account of them same rogues 'scaping-holes. — Yes, yes, I fancy we shall find the noble 'Squire this bout."

So saying, the gang departed together, and the insolence of their principal directed them first into the parlour usually inhabited by Althea — who remained trembling with indignation, not unmingled with terror, though she rejoiced in the certainty that the persecuted object of search was for out of the reach of their malignity.

Neither Althea nor Mrs. Wansford had courage to speak much to each other for some moments. At length the latter recovered her voice enough to attempt pacifying her children, who, though in whispers, still expressed their fear as they hung round her. — "Ah! I wish your father *was* come in," said she; "Im sure I cannot think where he is. But if he was here, what could he do — he's but one, and lame too — against all these fellows, as don't seem to mind how much mischief they do no more than nothing? Perhaps, if he went for to contradict them, why they might do him a hurt, or that filthy old villain might take the law of him. — Hark! don't you hear what a noise they make?" — "What can they be doing?" said Althea. — "I believe they are in our store-room," replied Mrs. Wansford; "we've got no great matters, indeed, but I'm sure they'll take what they can." Althea now recollected the door in that room, which led into the centre of the house, and from whence, if once they found it, they could descend to the place where Marchmont had been so long concealed, and where there was, probably, still evidence enough of his having resided there. — On such a discovery it was impossible for Althea to reflect without apprehensions; for though Marchmont was no longer liable to suffer from their abuse of the laws of the best governed of all possible communities, yet Vampyre would obtain, from what he saw, the certain knowledge that Marchmont had been concealed in a house of which *she* was the inhabitant. Such a circumstance could in no light be seen without her dreading the blame that might be imputed to her, and from which she had no means of clearing herself, since the truth could not in such a case be explained. When to these reflections was added, her recollection of the strange dislike her father had always shewn to Marchmont, and when she remembered that Vampyre was known to Sir Audley, and had been employed by him at least once in his proceedings against the Marchmont family, she could not do otherwise than dread the effect the discovery might have on her future peace, and good understanding with her father.

Yet her generous unadulterated spirit felt against the malignant reptile, Vampyre, such detestation and abhorrence, that evils, even greater than those she foresaw, could not have tempted her to check the symptoms of the indignation his detested character and his present conduct excited; and for the first time in her life, her heart, good and gentle as it was, swelled with anger, mingled with something like regret, that her feeble sex denied her the privilege of chastising, as he deserved, a monster, who, disgracing the name of man, seemed to be some subaltern agent of Mammon and Moloch let loose to blast all on whom his *evil eyes* were turned, and commissioned to poison the happiness and blast the hopes of youth and of honour.

Ah! little did she *then* know the extent to which the laws of this country (by some breach surely in their construction, or some negligence in their administration) permit such wretches to carry the most ruinous injustice, the most fetal oppression!

As the helpless party below remained, almost silent, and anxiously listening, they heard the gang of ruffians walking heavily through the great rooms, where the loose boards and vacant walls reechoed to their steps.

Althea, amid all her inquietude, reflected with exultation on the disappointment of the miscreant, Vampyre, who seemed sure of now gratifying his odious thirst of money and vengeance by dragging Marchmont from his concealment to a prison.

It was between ten and eleven o'clock — Althea, afraid of leaving the little protection Mrs. Wansford afforded, remained with her and her children; that poor woman, to all the dread of having such people in the house, now added apprehensions for the safety of her husband, who had not for some years staid out till so late an hour — she feared she knew not what. These frightful men looked very like assassins. It was the general report of the country, that Vampyre, who was known to have been guilty of almost every other crime, had been the suborner of murderers — why not the immediate director of them, if he could screen himself from the vengeance of the law in *that* instance as he had done in *forgery* and *perjury*? Mrs. Wansford remembered with terror the rough manner in which her husband had treated this noxious animal on his first impudent intrusion into their house; and she trembled lest revenge should have actuated so unprincipled a wretch to do him some mischief.

Nor was Althea, though she did not imagine he could be guilty of such atrocity, at all easier, when she reflected on the extraordinary absence of Wansford — and that, defenceless as they were, they had no means of hastening the departure of the banditti, whose remaining the night there could not be thought of without terror.

The servant girl, who though greatly alarmed, had at this moment the most recollection, reminded her mistress how very strange it was that the men should be wandering about the house so long without light. — Some time after this remark, Althea was willing to flatter herself that these objects of her dread, wearied by their fruitless search, had let themselves out at the front door, and departed; but another moment, by attentively listening, she was convinced they were still in the house. — Hannah had now the courage to go out into the ruinous court that was between Wansford's rooms and the fields. By getting up on a mass of broken stones, she could see many of the projecting windows of the north front of the house and she soon came running in breathless to say that there was a light gliding from window to window. — Althea plainly saw by the girl's manner, that, added to her fears about the men, she recollected the stories that belonged to the house, and supposed she knew not what of imaginary horrors; for she had not the courage to go out again, and looked paler than before she had made this experiment; while Mrs. Wansford, listening with an aching heart for some signal that might announce her husband's return, fancied she heard moanings and complaints — and turned towards Althea looks so full of distress and terror, that her blood ran chill through her veins, and she had never yet experienced sensations of vague dread so complicated and disagreeable.

Another long half hour passed. — The clock struck eleven; and the fears of Mrs. Wansford for her husband's life became more insupportable, while Althea herself began to doubt whether something terrible had not befallen him. — Listening in this cruel suspense, they at length thought they heard the men coming down the stairs that led from the inhabited part above to that division of the house at the termination of a long stone passage, in which on one side was the door to Althea's parlour, and quite at the end that of the room where they were. To the door of this last there was a piece of glass let in to give light to the passage, because the great window on the other extremity; had been boarded up to save the tax. — Hannah took courage to look through this glass. She saw the men at the other end of the passage. One of them had a small lanthorn in his hand; the others stood round him as if in consultation. — When she reported this in a whisper, Althea remarked that they had probably struck a light. — "I fancy," said she, "such people do not usually go on these expeditions without such precautions, and I dare say they have also firearms."

This observation, though Althea was far from meaning to increase her apprehensions, redoubled the agony of the poor woman, whose immediate fears of the ruffians now approaching them could hardly prevent her exclaiming with shrieks and cries that they had murdered her husband. — Althea, who had reasoned herself into more resolution, now exerted herself to appease apprehensions so horrible — and repeated, that they were certainly only bailiffs coming as they did before to search for Mr. Marchmont, and that they could have no design against Wansford. — "Ah, dear Miss, why does not he return then?" cried the half-distracted woman. "He has never once staid out in this manner before," — To this Althea had nothing immediately to reply: nor had she indeed time, for the villanous group now entered the room: — and it was easy to see by their countenances that they had not found the prize they had taken so much trouble to secure.

A stout ill-looking fellow, on a sign from Vampyre, approached the poor woman, and bellowed out — "Mistress! you must take a little walk with us, and shew us a few more of the dog-holes about this d—n'd old place. — Come, come, good woman, you know where 'Squire *Skulk* is hid: we have a little business with him, and we don't go till we've spoke to his honour, d—n him." He then seized her roughly by the arm — and the poor woman and her children uttered a scream of terror; which was so far from making the brute desist, that he was

dragging her away with brutish glee, when Althea, roused by such inhumanity, turned courageously towards Vampyre, and said, "Thou
wretch! who by an illegal act hast brought these people here, at *your peril*
suffer them to do the least injury to any person in this house. Whoever
you seek here (if you are authorised to seek any body, which I do not
believe), you *can* have no right to assault Sir Audley Dacres's servant
in his house — in *my* house." — Like the fiend whom he resembled
in malignity, the Satanic agent of abused law looked askaunce and
somewhat confounded at Althea, who — "severe in youthful beauty"
— thus checked his daring presumption. — His followers, the cowardice of guilt struggling with their accustomed habits of insult and
brutality; looked towards him for instructions whether to proceed or
desist. — The old monster, with his usual action of thumping his stick
against the ground, came nearer to Althea, rightly imagining perhaps
that nothing could be more terrific than a view of a face that was libel
on the human countenance; and in his detestable sonorous voice he
began —

"Madam, I observe you take great interest in the concealment of
this fugitive young fellow. Sir Audley Dacres, Baronet, your worthy
father, who has been a client of mine, I having been recommended to
him by the late Sir Ralph Gunston, Knight and Baronet, my very good
friend and client, who entrusted me with his very important affairs, on
the occasion of my being engaged for him in the celebrated contested
election, at a certain, time, against the Honourable John Anthony —"
He was proceeding thus, when the report of a pistol without, yet very
near the door, put a sudden stop to his eloquence.

Mrs. Wansford now uttered another piercing shriek, having, as she
believed, a dreadful confirmation of all she dreaded in regard to her
husband. Althea was so hurried by the various and fearful apprehensions that assailed her, as to be unable to fix on any. Little time, however, was allowed for conjecture: a violent blow against the outside of
the door almost shook it from its hinges — and in an instant five or six
men, some armed with pitchforks and scythes, one with a pistol, and
another with a rusty hanger, hurried into the room. Two of them supported Wansford, who, unable as he appeared to make any exertion,
hastened to disengage himself from them, and, approaching Vampyre,
took him by the collar, and, twisting him round, gave him a kick, which
sent him hastily to the door; whence a young labourer that stood near
presently sent him, by the same method, with inconceivable velocity,

into the yard; and in half a second his satellites, sturdy as they were, were obliged to obey the same sort of impulse, and found themselves all without side the door, and at liberty to go to supper with *"what appetite they might."*

CHAP. III.

D'où vien le Mal?

THE DOOR WAS now strongly barricaded within side, and Wansford, soon recovering himself, sent his friends to procure for themselves the refreshments his wife was by the terror she had undergone disqualified to fetch for them. He then attended Althea to her room, where he briefly related to her, that, having gone, according to his weekly custom, late in the afternoon to the Three Horse-shoes, a small ale-house and smith's shop, where letters and parcels were left, he had found drinking there a very creditable looking man, a stranger in those parts, who said he was on the road to see a nephew of his, who had married his daughter, and rented a large farm not far from Plymouth, where he was thriving apace. — He was a little tired, he said, with his two days journey; for he had come the day before from beyond Ringwood in Hampshire, and so thought to put up at the Three Horse-shoes for the night. "A seemed a vast plausible man," said Wansford — "and a knew all the goings on in London, and concerning the war, and such like; and me thought he was a sensible *dissarning* sort of a man; and I found a knew abundance of people about Hampshire: and I, you know, Miss, being a Hampshire: man, liked well enough to talk over the people we both knew in that country; for he might be for age, I thought, about my own standing. — At first we had only a pint of cyder a-piece; but he said he would not part with an old countryman so — we would have a tiff of punch — and he must needs treat me. — And so, my dear Madam — But what shall we say? — Every man may be overtaken sometimes. — I'm not more like to be free from that there, you know, than another. — What was the upshot? — Gads my life, if I don't believe though that the cheating fly rascal put *summot* in my drink, for after a little — and yet my head's as strong as my neighbours — after a little, d'ye see, I becomed all of sudden as muzzled! as muzzled! — and then the villain went away and left me — and when I woke, landlady told me what o'clock it was, and as how I had been fast asleep ever so long; but she wa'n't willing, she said, to disturb me. — Gads my life, I began to look sharp — for, thinks I, may be this same fly rogue, with his long story, have stole my watch, and my money — though my money was not no great matters. However, they were both as safe as could be. — Eh! thinks I, bethought me, that may be 'twas some trick of that son of Belzebub himself, Vampyre. — Ah! ha! thinks I, master of mine, be you thereabouts? — You're devilish cunning — but 'twon't do this time. — You must try again, old pettifog. — But I bethought me, Miss, that I'd get two or three honest fellows to come home with me; which they were willing enough to leave their beds for to do, for they're all pretty keen upon the scent of that rascally polecat of a lawyer. — So away we comes — and found the carrion crows sure enough. — I believe they won't come again in a hurry. — Egad, they've had enough on't. — But if they've a mind to try again, why let 'um. — No harm done, you know," continued Wansford, winking significantly at Althea — "no harm at all done — for the bird you know is flown, and I for my part" — (and he reached down an old musket without a lock from the chimney rack) "for my part, if they do come — I'd no more mind shooting that old pillory-faced blood-hound through the head, than I would mad dog — no, nor so much."

Althea now plainly perceived that Wansford had by no means recovered the effects of the stratagem that had been used to disable him from returning home, and that he was in his own phrase pot valiant. He was more likely therefore to increase than to appease her anxiety, occasioned by her desire to know whether Vampyre and his satellites had explored the late concealment of Marchmont; and though she trembled at the thoughts of being alone, she found it necessary to disengage herself from his loquacity, and to endeavour to calm her spirits, too much agitated by the circumstances of the day and night. However her reason endeavoured to combat such an apprehension, she could not help fearing that one of the ruffians might remain lurking in the house; and she now thought herself more than ever unprotected, for Wansford was in no condition to hear or succour her. Unable to contend with the terrors that possessed her, it was wiser to yield to them, and she therefore directed the servant girl to bring her bed and lay it on the floor in her room — where, after every search had been made to assure them that they did not enclose a foe, the door was fastened, and Althea, envying the tranquillity of her companion, who was soon in a profound sleep, endeavoured to obtain some repose.

To sleep, however, was impossible till the morning, when the light that awakens the thoughtless and the happy to renew the labours or the pleasures of the day, broke through the long casement opposite the feet of her bed; and while it seemed to lend her security, her wearied spirits sunk into forgetfulness.

But in a few hours she awoke to the recollection of what had so much troubled her the preceding evening. The dread that Vampyre, having discovered the long inhabited retreat of Marchmont, would relate it to Sir Audley — the terrors of her father's anger appeared insupportable — and they were aggravated by every distressing idea that her imagination could suggest. She was not yet of age, and was therefore wholly in Sir Audley's power. The steps he had already taken to induce her to consent to give herself to Mohun, authorised her fear that he would not scruple to adopt others yet more harsh, to compel her to a measure he had so much at heart, especially if he should once believe that her obstinate refusal was supported by a predilection in favour of Marchmont, the man whom of all others Sir Audley seemed to hate.

To communicate these fears to Wansford, as her reason for wishing to visit the caverns of the house, was extremely disagreeable to her — and to penetrate these melancholy recesses alone was an undertaking to which her courage was not equal; yet to rest in her present state of anxiety seemed to be impossible.

Two days passed. Wansford, whenever he had an opportunity, continued, though he was become sober, to menace the impudent intruders, and at length from threatening them with his own vengeance, he declared his resolution to expose them to that of his master, Sir Audley, who would, he said, certainly sue lawyer Vampyre for a trespass upon his premises. Althea, who had lately seen more of this man's propensity to drink, and to prate when he had drank too much, than she had ever before had an opportunity of observing, shrunk more than ever from giving him her confidence, and not knowing what step to take, she took none; sometimes tormenting herself with the fears of Sir Audley's knowledge of Marchmont's concealment, and at others flattering herself that Vampyre, disappointed of his prey, would turn his attention to some more profitable victims than the unhappy family of Marchmont; and that, as none were likely to pay him for persecuting *her*, she should never hear his detested name again.

Now therefore Althea endeavoured to reason herself into some degree of tranquillity, that she might indulge that quiet melancholy, which, when she parted with Marchmont, she had looked forward to with a sort of sad resignation not unmingled with pleasure.

Spring was now so far advanced that the scene around her received all the advantages returning verdure could give it, but that scene was very far from inspiring her with cheerful ideas. In the uncultivated quarters of the great garden, a few shrubs, the nipped and half-vegetating successors of those that had shaded and adorned it in happier days, faintly flowered, while their stems were grey with moss; and what verdure there was, was rather that of neglect than of culture. The female fern waved its feathery fans among the broken walls, covering then where the knotty and cankered arms of the old fruit-trees were nearly leafless. But these ruined buttresses and sapless trunks afforded a convenient asylum to a great number of birds, who were now building nests which Althea was very earnest to save from the useless and wanton depredations of Wansford's children; insisting at the same time on his forbearing to shoot the birds themselves, as he was, he said, used to do — "for, plague upon them nasty tuoads! they eat up all his peason."

Althea now felt, what she had never before allowed herself to be so much overcome by, that which it had been the principal purpose of her education to guard against, the weariness which such total seclusion could hardly fail of bringing upon any one. During the winter she had contended with it by persuading herself that spring would allow her exercise, and bring cheerfulness, while it enlarged her pursuits; but since the terror she had undergone from the pretended beggar, she had no longer the courage to extend her walks beyond the walls that surrounded her gloomy residence; and within their deserted area seemed to lurk the cruel images of ruin and desolation, threatening to pursue through life the wretched wandering Marchmont, who, thus cut off as Althea was from every other society, took more and more possession of her imagination. Her thoughts were often turned towards his mother and his sisters. He had promised they should write to her, but no intelligence of them came. Not having yet recovered resolution enough to go herself to Dame Mosely, she was compelled to content herself by again sending Hannah with an enquiry after the poor old woman and Phoebe Prior. The former answered by promising to come up to the great house the first day she was able; Phoebe Prior she said was gone, and she was afraid would ramble about again.

The generous heart of Althea throbbed with pity when she thought of this hapless being, whose sorrows she could not even alleviate. Then she returned to reflect on her own uneasinesses, and from thence on what would relieve her from them. Nothing could afford her the least satisfaction but to hear of Marchmont; and when she was likely to do that, she had no means of calculation; for, when he had so earnestly solicited permission to write to her, he had never told her, and she had no courage to ask, from whence he proposed to send his first letter, or how he was likely to secure its conveyance to Mrs. Mosely, who was to deliver it — though, as the old woman had never mentioned or even hinted at it, she doubted whether he had apprized her of his intentions. At all events, it would be yet some time before it was possible that she could know whither his destiny had driven him.

It was now many weeks since Althea had heard of her father, and the last time was by a cold letter from Lady Dacres, merely informing her that Sir Audley had been confined by the gout, which disabled him from writing. Since that, she had written several times, with very earnest enquiries, but had received no answer. However accustomed to endure neglect, it seemed very comfortless to be totally forgotten, even by her father, and absolutely alone in the world, where there was not one being, except Marchmont, now separated from her very probably for ever, that seemed to take the least interest in her existence. Dreadful as was the idea of Sir Audley's discovering Marchmont's strange concealment, and suspecting her partiality towards him, there was something more depressing in suspecting that she was absolutely deserted. She therefore wrote again to her father, who, at this season of the year, was always in London. Time enough passed for her to receive an answer, but none came.

For Althea the world seemed no longer to be progressive. Without one prospect for the future but what was overclouded with doubts, distresses, and difficulties which she was afraid to investigate; for the present buried alive, and cut off not only from general society but from her own family, her spirits sunk, and her mind, strengthened as its natural solidity was by reason and reflection, became heavy and enervated. She still continued, mechanically, the charities and duties she had undertaken, but the pleasure that had at first attended their execution was gone. She did the little good that she was able to do, from humanity and from habit; but that cheerfulness, the result of conscious goodness, which she used to feel, no longer dissipated the heavy gloom that hung over her. Almost the only thing that now afforded her pleasure was to listen to the long, but to her attractive stories, which, when she could see the poor old servant, she encouraged her to tell, of what had formerly passed in the Marehmont family.

Many anecdotes, such as garrulous old age loves to repeat, which would have appeared tedious and uninteresting had they related to any other persons, Althea now sat to hear, not only with patience but with pleasure; for though they all began with the honours of Marchmont's ancestors, much of which was adventitious, they generally ended in simple but affecting proofs of merit and goodness all his own. And stripped as he was of the decorations of fortune, nothing could have demanded such a tribute of praise but a heart like that he possessed.

Althea, in these conversations, frequently attempted to form, from the accounts of Mrs. Mosely, some idea of the characters of his mother and his sisters. They seemed strangely to have shrunk from her advances. Was it the dejection of sorrow or the reserve of mortified pride that had caused them to do so? This question Althea continually asked herself. She had no way of satisfying it, but by putting repeated questions to Mrs. Mosely, who, well as she knew the parties, was but ill qualified to answer her direcdy. She had been so habituated to love her mistress, that she had no idea of the light she appeared in to others — to her, she always seemed the best and most unfortunate of women. The three young ladies, she said, were very handsome — one of them was the very image of her brother. Althea thought that, whenever she made an acquaintance with them, this would be her greatest favourite.

On renewing on this interview with Mrs. Mosely her humane enquiry after Phoebe, the old woman told her, that the unhappy creature had left her. — "Two days after you, Madam, had seen her at my cot," said she, "her uncle sent his dairy-woman to fetch her back; for the ladies who keep her had heard of her being wandering about, and were very angry. Alas a-day! the poor girl was sadly unwilling to go; and when she found she must, she would not speak a word even to me — but looked so strangely with her eyes! —I am afraid, indeed, it will not be long before she breaks out again as had as ever; and I do think that she will come to some untimely end, if she is thwarted and vexed."

"Poor Phoebe!" thought Althea to herself, "for *thy* sorrows there is no cure; there is not even any mitigation! After the loss of such a husband, I hardly know if the loss of reason be a misfortune!"

"How much happier mightest thou have been," continued Althea, still indulging this train of reflection, "how much happier had thy poor Prior been, contented with the humble lot to which he was probably born! — Why did he, in search of a higher fortune, go to those climates where the soil, manured with blood, seems to produce only disease and death?"

Althea, as she thus meditated, was walking homeward, attended by Hannah, for she now never ventured alone. As it was noon and the sun very hot, the girl under took to shew her a way through a lane, which, though it led farther about, afforded more shelter from the heat. A very miserable cabin, half formed of rock and roots to which it clung, in a hollow way, was within fight of her path. Three half-naked, half-starved children ran from it — one bearing in its feeble arms a famished infant. They eagerly implored her charity; and Althea, struck with a spectacle of distress which had never before crossed her, enquired, while she gave them all the small money about her, to whom they belonged? — They were the children of a day labourer — their father had lately *gone for a soldier*; and their mother had been ill and confined to her bed ever since the birth of the youngest of the children; and they lived, if living it might be called, on a parish allowance, that did not afford them even bread! — Althea could not, on hearing this, content herself with transient charity. Though it was already later than the hour she had ventured to remain out since her alarm, she hastened into the cottage, or rather hovel; and the scene she saw there penetrated her heart with sensations so painful, that she had instantly recourse to the means most likely to assist the objects whose condition had excited it.

Having given them such immediate relief as was in her power, she continued her walk, meditating on what she could afterwards do for them, and on the strange inequalities of fortune; her mind the more deeply impressed, perhaps, because, since she had been so much alone, and having for want of novelty been driven to a course of reading which she had not entered upon before, she had been reading Rousseau, and some other authors not usually making part of the studies of young women; and thus, the accidental circumstance of being so long alone in a house like Eastwoodleigh, whither Mrs. Trevyllian's library (where there were more than mere books of amusement) had been brought, had given her thoughts a direction which in the common intercourse of the world they would perhaps never have taken.

"Gone for a soldier in mere despair, and to avoid the sight of his family's misery! — Good heaven!" said Althea as she repeated thus to herself what the poor woman had told her; "and is this the boasted happiness of our country? When I heard the sad story of Phoebe Prior, I lamented that her husband had ever forsaken the laborious though peaceable life to which I imagined him to have been born, for the advantage offered him in another hemisphere, where he must have executed a sort of authority over those human beings that Europeans make slaves, which seemed, to me, repugnant to all the honest principles of such a man. But if scenes like *these* are to be found in the cabin of the industrious labourer, who can wonder that any man should quit his paternal cottage? — or how can it be strange that our peasantry fly to America? —I have heard that all ideas of equality are visionary — that they can never be realized — and I believe it. But surely, though there must be hewers of wood, and drawers of water, they ought to have the absolute necessaries of life. It does not seem as if such a family as I have just now seen can obtain them, even by the most unremitting labour of its principal."

This train of thought was not easily exchanged for any other. Althea could not help reflecting, how much difference to the poor of a neighbourhood the residence of such a family as Marchmont's once was, must make. — "While *they* were here," said she, "I am sure the voice of sorrow, that they could relieve, was never heard. How much of evil the ruin of such a house brings with it! — How sad to think, that the friendly protection the members of this family lent to others, they now want for themselves!" — Nor could other more general reflections escape her. "I have somewhere read," said she, "a calculation, that if only a third or a fourth of the sums yearly raised from the people of one country, to annoy, by war, the people of another, were applied to the mitigation of the sufferings of the aged and infant poor, every labouring man might then labour for the rich, yet possessing himself a certain degree of comfort; the country would become more populous, and of course more powerful to resist all encroachment from nations less wise. Yet other sage persons in *their* works tell me, that the glory of this country is founded on its conquests. A plain understanding, however, naturally enquires why we should desire to conquer other countries when there is so much waste land in our own? And surely a plain understanding cannot help regarding with astonishment the infatuation of mankind, who, from habit and custom (for it never can be the result of reason and choice), enter on a manner of life altogether unnatural, where more perish by sickness than by the sword, as they are often transported, in floating prisons pregnant with infection and death, to another region of the globe, to kill if they can, or be killed by, men whose language they do not understand, whose country they have no desire to possess, and with whom they cannot have the slightest cause of quarrel. Surely, of all the absurdities that have been reduced to system, this is one of the greatest."

Ah! candid and unadulterated mind! you have learned early to reflect; but take care left this habit, hitherto so well applied, should totally unfit you for society. It will strew thorns in your path, while other young women of your age seek only flowers.

By imagining yourself in the place of others, as you now continually do, you will learn to feel for all the unhappy, or even for those who appear so; whereas it might save a great deal of (for the most part useless) pain, if you could contrive to feel only for yourself. Soon, very soon you are to enter into the world, where a young woman, who has refused such an advancing and prosperous man as Mohun, only because she could not love him, to give her affections to a poor undone wanderer, like Marchmont, will be looked upon as one without common understanding, or perhaps as having lost it by the study of romances; and of course you will be pointed out by the old as a warning, and willingly avoided by their daughters, as "a strange young woman that nobody understands."

CHAP. IV.

She heard the doleful tidings of his death,
And never smiled again!

THOUGH FATIGUED MORE than usual by her walk, the spirits of Althea were too much affected to allow her to sleep. She was not even disposed to undress herself at the usual hour, but sat reading a periodical publication, which, after waiting for many days, Wansford had that evening got from the nearest town.

To one so long secluded, most of the articles had the attraction of novelty. Her attention, however, was at length wearied. She put by the pamphlet, and began to unpin her clothes, when she heard the clock blow strike twelve. Every thing was so perfectly silent, that an involuntary shudder came over her as she repeated to herself

"Tis now the very witching time of night
"When church-yards yawn!"

The stories she had learned from Mrs. Mosely, occurred to her; for that day the old woman had told her some she had never heard before. Ashamed; however, of vague fears, from which her good sense revolted, Althea would have shaken them off — and hoping to lose them in sleep, she hastened to undress herself; when, approaching the table on which her glass stood to deposit some part of her dress, she again felt chilled by the profound and dead silence around her; while her single candle, in a high, long, old-fashion room, with a dark blue morine bed at the end of it, threw over her own figure, as she saw it in the glass, a dim obscurity. "I look," said she, hardly trusting her eyes to survey it, "surely I look like a ghost myself!"

Hardly had she said so, when she heard, or fancied she heard, footsteps in the passage: but so softly and so lightly did they seem to fall, that the course of a dead leaf driven by the wind would have been almost as distinct. They died away at the other end of the passage. — Was it fancy? — Surely it could be nothing more. Althea listened, almost fearing to breathe, while the cold dew hung on her temples. The noise came again — a little louder than before — at her door it ceased, and she fancied somebody breathed. Still arguing with herself that it could be nothing but imagination, she almost acquired courage enough to open the door, and be satisfied; but as she stood listening, and reasoning herself up to this resolution, a deepdrawn and broken sigh was very evidently heard. — Althea recoiled, and again waited in trembling expectation. The sigh, or rather half-stifled groan, was twice more repeated, and then the light footsteps, fainter and fainter, seemed to depart from her door, till all was again as silent as death.

Some minutes elapsed before she could move — so entirely had terror overcome her. The weak apprehensions of supernatural agency which she had indulged, now gave way to more substantial terrors; and the idea of Vampyre or some of his satellites was so present to her, that she determined to ring a bell (which had been contrived near her bed to reach to the room where Wansford and his family slept). To this she now applied herself: and it was not long before Wansford, with his wife trembling beside him, appeared at the door; which, on hearing him speak, Althea opened, and: briefly explained the cause of her alarm.

Wansford, who often affected to be very stout-hearted, now turned pale, and trembled. While he knew Marchmont to be in the house, and that his servant used to leave it of a night to procure provisions which were left at Mrs. Mosely's, he had always affected to treat his wife's fears, occasioned by the noises she heard, with great contempt. But now, that he knew that cause existed not, his old notions and prejudices were remembered; and as he was sure that none of Vampyre's people could be about the house, and believed his young lady very unlikely to terrify herself for nothing, all the family of Marchmont seemed, to his frightened imagination, to have left their sepulchres to wander round their old habitation.

When the question followed from Althea of what was to be done, Wansford hesitated, and so plainly betrayed his apprehension, that as she was determined not to go to her bed till she was assured no living being was about the house, she acquired firmness enough to declare she would accompany him on his search, if he would make it. After such a proposal he could not refuse; and they returned altogether to his room, where, arming himself with an old broad sword which seemed to have served in the civil wars, he marched with no very firm step before Althea and his wife, who each held a candle in her hand.

In this order they descended the stairs into the room Wansford inhabited below. There was nothing to be seen but the old favourite cat watching among the wood embers for a few crickets, that had not yet betaken themselves to the fields.

Wansford, though he looked paler and paler at every step he took, proceeded to examine the place that served them for a wash-house; peeped into another in which was a safe; and having done so, he declared there was nothing to be seen. Althea's parlour and a sort of store room in the same passage were next examined. No unusual circumstance appeared; and then, as every part of this small inhabited portion of the house below had been explored, it only remained to search the store room above; and indeed it was there that Althea's fears principally pointed — recollecting the secret avenue by which Marchmont had led her thither from the ruinous and deserted buildings beyond.

Thither therefore they repaired — Althea by no means the most courageous of the party — but every thing remained there just as it had been left the night before. Wansford now assuming a little courage, stepped beyond a heap of malt that was spread near it, and tried the pannel that opened to give a secret passage to the body of the house. It was fast; he had secured it himself some days before with redoubled precaution; and he was convinced that no alteration had since been made in the fastenings.

Nothing therefore resulted from this search, but a persuasion in the minds of those who had made it, that either Althea must have been seized with some groundless panic, or that she had been justly alarmed by a supernatural cause — and this last notion was to the feeble mind of Mrs. Wansford so pregnant with terror, that, forgetting her accustomed prudence, she said, "Ah, well, — this is something more than common; I remember now what Dame Mosely told me only the last time we had any talk together." — "And what has she told you?" enquired Althea with quickness.

"That always, before any of 'Squire Marchmont's family died, or any ill came to them, there was moanings heard about the house, and something seemed to glide from room to room with deep sighs, and as it were warning them by melancholy noises........"

"And was any evil ever avoided by attending to the information of these warning spirits?" interrupted Althea, half peevishly.

"Not as I ever heard," replied the terrified woman. "But hush! hush! my dear young lady, sure I heard it again?"

"No, no," said Althea, "there is nothing — but do awaken Hannah, and let her bring her bed into my room, as she did some nights ago. Though believe it might, after all, be only the wind or rats, or my own fancy, yet my spirits are harassed, and I cannot remain alone."

Hannah, now roused from her sound sleep, was obliged to obey this order; and when the arrangement was settled according to the directions of Althea, she went to her own bed and tried to compose herself to sleep — but to sleep was for her become more impossible than ever. — The superstitious legend in regard to the Marchmont family, which Mrs. Wansford had so simply related, haunted her imagination, and gave her more lasting pain than she had before felt transient terror.

It was in vain that all the arguments reason affords were brought forward against these impressions, which, if they are indulged, aggravate every present evil, but have never yet been found to save any one

from those which they are supposed to predict in future. The noise
Althea was sure she had heard; and if it could not be accounted for by
any probable supposition that it arose from a living being, it was difficult to combat the idea of some supernatural agency.

The morning found her dejected and weary. Want of rest, and
the strange anxiety she felt about Marchmont, gave her the look of a
person that had just left a sick bed. Sometimes she thought of going
of Mrs. Mosely's; yet the dread of conversation that would increase instead of appeasing her apprehensions deterred her. However, as soon
as she could see Wansford, she endeavoured to engage him to search
the uninhabited part of the house. But the man seemed to be struck
with terror, and, though he ridiculed all fear before, seemed to feel it
now to a greater degree than those had done at whom he had laughed
for their absurdity.

At length, however, Althea prevailed upon him to make an enquiry, without which she found it impossible to sleep in the house. But
nothing could induce him to search the subterraneous passages, all of
which he was not sure that he knew, unless he took some other person
with him; and Althea was very unwilling that any other, unless it was
his wife, should be let into the secret, which probably they must discover, of Marchmont's late and long concealment there. Nor was it on
other accounts desirable that any of the neighbouring hinds should be
made acquainted with hidingplaces which in the present state of the
house might be used for many bad purposes. It was determined then
that Wansford and his wife should to together on this exploit; while
Althea, the maid, and Wansford's children, were to remain about the
uninhabited rooms, ready to give the alarm, on the least appearance of
danger, to two labourers whom Wansford engaged, as if on his own
account, to do an hour's work for him in his garden.

This party then set out about seven o'clock in the evening; the sun
was yet above the horizon, and shone bright. — Wansford ascertained
that the two labourers were near at hand; and then, Althea and the
children accompanying them, he and his wife went to a place quite
remote from that which Marchmont had shewn to Althea, and entered
on his secret expedition with a candle in his hand, while she walked
backwards and forwards in the great room, and the children ran about
where they would, the servant girl following them.

Althea, now on the same spot where she had first conversed with
Marchmont, was lost for a moment in the recollection of what he had

then said to her, when the voices of the children having ceased on a sudden, she was seized with the dread of being left alone, and went to the door that opened on the great stair-case to look for them. She called, but they did not answer her; and she was hastily passing across the wide landing place to follow them, when, casting her eyes, not without some degree of undefined fear, towards the long and dark passage that led to the rooms so marked in the Marchmont family by misfortune, she saw, as if coming from thence, a slender female figure that slowly approached, yet without seeming to look at her; while, riveted to the place, she had no power to stir. — The spectre, for such it seemed to be, still came deliberately on, and appeared to be of air, for it was not heard to move. Althea, trembling like an aspen-leaf, stepped back into the banqueting-room. The shape soon appeared at the door, with one finger held to its lips, as if to enjoin silence. It came quite up to her — it was poor Phoebe Prior!

"Gracious Heaven!" exclaimed Althea, relieved from a species of dread she could not long have supported, "how came you here, Phoebe?"

"Softly, softly, my dear young lady," said she in a whisper, "I shall find him yet."

"Find whom?"

"Ah, Madam!" sighed the poor lunatic girl, "don't speak to me as if you too were angry with me. I think I shall find him; for this is the time and the place where he bade me look for him — it is his birth-day — the nineteenth of May! He never deceived me, and so I sat up all night waiting for the time. But if my uncle comes and finds me here!.... You will not send for that hard-hearted man; *will* you, Ma'am? My good friend told me you would not; and see, Madam, what I have bought with the money you sent me. I have wished for it a great while. A boy picked it up at last, just by the sad spot. —I never will part with it — no never."

The unhappy girl then shewed a perforated pebble, such as are often found on the shore, through which she had passed a blue ribband, and tied it upon her bosom. By her manner it seemed as if she fancied it some trinket that belonged to her drowned husband.

Weakened as the spirits of Althea had been before by watching and by terror, the piteous spectacle now before her affected her too much. Instead of being able to speak soothingly to the wretched wanderer, the tears streamed down her checks, and she sobbed audibly.

"Ah!" cried Phoebe — "do you cry? you who are happy — and who have a lover faithful, and kind, and good, who adores the very ground you walk upon! He will come soon, and you will be married to him, and yet you cry! — while you never see *me* shed a tear —I who have lost — Hah! what? — what have I lost?"

Althea, amazed by her strange conjecture, terrified by the wildness of her looks, and imagining she was about to be seized with a raving fit, stepped quickly forward, and called for Wansford; who now emerging from his search, which had not been very long, appeared with his wife, and was of course much surprised by the sight of Phoebe — though her appearance seemed to account for the noises that had occasioned them so much trouble and apprehension.

Althea insisted on their treating her with gentleness; and as soon as she had a little recovered from the extreme fear she had undergone, the poor girl, who so gready excited her pity, became the object of her attention. It was necessary, however, rather to soothe, than to question her as to means by which she got into the house, and concealed herself the preceding evening; for she continued to be so wild and incoherent, still talking of the nineteenth of May, and that she was come to seek for her poor Harry, that nothing certain could be understood from her. Althea directed her to be taken care of till the morning, when she hoped Mrs. Mosely might find the means to reason her into some degree of tranquillity.

Once more retired to her own parlour, Althea endeavoured to collect and compose her spirits; but she had not been seated five minutes before Mrs. Wansford came in, in even greater emotion than when she believed she had to encounter a ghost, and delivered into Althea's hands a letter, which she said was just brought by a man on horseback. The first thing that struck Althea was, that it was from Marchmont; she did not know the hand — and in such confusion that she hardly comprehended them she read these words:

"Bath, May 5th.

"Madam,

I am commanded by Sir Audley to inform you, that he is very ill at Bath; and my Lady not being well enough to accompany him at present, Sir Audley desires that, upon the receipt hereof, you will be pleased to set out, with his servant James Eades to attend you, for Bath. Sir Audley has the gout in his hands, whereby he is prevented

from writing. I am commanded to add, that James has directions for
the journey, and that Mr. Wansford's wife may attend upon you, for
more safety, if you choose. — By Sir Audley's order, from, Madam,

Your most dutiful servant
to command,
NATHANIEL WELSH."

A thousand uneasy and alarming sensations now beset Althea.
The first was, apprehensions for the life of her father, who must be
very ill thus to use another hand, and whose feelings towards her must
be greatly changed. That Lady Dacres should not, on such an occasion,
attend him, seemed unaccountable; and that Sir Audley, if she was too
ill to be with him, should think of his deserted Althea, seemed very
improbable, or at least very remote from all that was likely to happen,
according to the observations she had formerly made. There was, however, very little time for conjectures or hesitation; for Wansford in a
few moments followed his wife to say, that Mr. Eades had desired him
to let Miss Dacres know, that the post-chaise that was ordered from
the town at seven miles distance, and which he had bespoke as he
passed through it, would probably soon be at the house.

"And do you know this James Eades, Wansford?" enquired Althea.

"Lord! Yes, Miss — Why, he is Sir Audley's head-groom, and have
lived there, as near as I can guess, about five years. — Perhaps you
would like to speak to him?"

Althea directing the groom to be sent to her, heard, with concern
that absorbed every consideration for herself, that Sir Audley had been
in what the man called "a poor way" for two or three months before
he was ordered to Bath by his physicians; that he had been very unwilling to go, because Lady Dacres was near lying-in, and in a bad state
of health, and one of the children, the third boy, one that they were
both very fond of, had died of the measles, and the rest had been very
bad — so that sickness and sorrow seemed to have assailed the household of Sir Audley in various forms. Nor was this all. — On making
a few more enquiries, Althea learned that Mr. Dacres, the eldest of
her half-brothers, who being taken from Westminster School by the
desire of the masters, was with so many precautions sent to travel had
been not more than three months in Italy before he quitted his tutor,
and was lost for some time; till his want of money compelling him to
apply to his father indirectly, it was discovered that he had returned

to England, and concealed himself in a very discreditable neighbourhood, where he had sold his watch and some other valuable trinkets,
and from whence Sir Audley, with some difficulty, extricated him: after
which his father was, however, reluctantly forced to consent to his going into the Guards. The battalion to which he belonged was ordered
abroad; and the illness of both his parents seemed to have been in a
great measure owing to the uneasiness his conduct first, and now the
dangers to which he was exposed, had given them.

The *truly* tender and affectionate heart of Althea bled to think
what must have been her father's distress and anguish: — nor did she
fail to feel for Lady Dacres, who seemed to have laid up for herself
a bitter store of repentance, by her foolish indulgence to this unfortunate boy. — "And *this* young man," said Althea, "is the pupil of
modern education! raised in the lap of the most luxurious prosperity!
This young man, who at seventeen appears to have run more than half
way in the career of mature vice! — Ah! it was not thus that Marchmont is described at that age! — But Marchmont has been the child
of adversity!"

From this natural reflection her mind immediately returned to
her father; whom she now as anxiously wished to see as she had ever
dreaded it. Nothing but the affectionate ardour with which she desired to discharge her filial duties could have induced her to set out
at such an hour, and so unprepared; but as the groom had strongly
represented Sir Audley's car nestness to see her, and the danger he
was in, she determined not to lose a moment more than was necessary
to comfort Mrs. Wansford (whose services on the road she declined)
for her departure, by assuring her it was probable she should soon
return. She gave her ten guineas as a present from herself, promising
to take the first opportunity of recommending her and her family to
the favour of Sir Audley, that, if any new arrangements took place in
regard to the old house, they might be preferred to some more comfortable situation. — Then, her few clothes being packed up, she got
into the chaise, and, late as it was, determined to drive round to Mrs.
Mosely's, at once to relieve herself from the anxiety she should have
about Marchmont's letters, and to recommend to her care the unhappy Phoebe Prior; whom, as she was now quite tranquil, and sunk into
almost speechless stupor, Althea admitted into the chaise with her,
that she might be left with the only person that appeared to have much
influence over her disordered mind.

The grief and lamentations of the poor old woman, when she learned that Althea was going, were very distressing to her. And indeed this was the only deprivation which she could now feel: Althea seemed to her like a good angel, sent with the last ray of light that was to fall on the dreary and comfortless close of her latter days. This was now to disappear.

Althea, affected by her sorrow, with difficulty prevailed upon her to listen to what it was so material she should perfectly understand about Marchmont, and it was the most difficult task to her that she could possibly undertake. Her purse was almost emptied into Mrs. Mosely's hands, while, as the only condition annexed to the present, she was enjoined to take care, as far as was possible, of poor Phoebe, and to let her remain at the cottage whenever she was easier there — Althea promising at the same time to provide farther for the comfort of them both.

The moon affording light enough to prevent much danger from the very indifferent roads she was to pass before she reached Exeter, Althea then stepped into the chaise, and between twelve and one o'clock, attended by her father's groom on horseback, proceeded on her journey.

CHAP. V.

Thro' many a sunless day and cheerless night
The unhappy lover, exiled from the light,
Each wild vicissitude of passion proves,
Now sinks in cold despair; now hopes, because he loves.

THE SOLITARY AND agitated traveller, as she journeyed by the light of the moon the first tedious stage, recalled the strange circumstances of the last twelve hours, as if she had been endeavouring to remember and ascertain the confused traces of a severish dream.

Just before Wansford took leave of her he had called her aside, and with a mysterious air had given her several letters, or papers which appeared to be such.

"I found them," said he, "down below in a little drawer under an old table, where our poor young gentlemen used to eat his morsel! — You had better take them. Miss."

Althea received them in silence, and now wished to see what these papers were; but as she did not get out at the two first post-houses, the morning dawned before she had an opportunity of gratifying her curiosity.

They contained detached sentences of Italian and French poetry, expressive of his state of mind, who had thus beguiled the hours of solitude and confinement by exercising his memory; for Althea recollected that Marchmont had told her he had no books, nor the means of getting any.

By his melancholy rush-light it was that he had written these — sometimes to strengthen his resolution, at others to indulge the taste and talents he had received from nature; for some were marked as quotations, while others seemed to be his own.

Althea fancied, as she read them, that she could distinguish the time when they were written; and the earliest appeared to have been recorded as incitements to that patience and fortitude which subsequent events had somewhat lessened the power of exerting. — There were some lines from Metastasio. —

> "Combatti i rigori
> Di sorte inconstante
> In vario sembiante
> L'istessa virtù."

On another paper a sentence from Lord Bacon —

"Certainly virtue bears similitude to some precious odours, which are most fragrant when incens'd or crush'd — for a prosperous fortune discovers men's vices, — but an adverse one their virtues."

And from some French author —

"Mais au moins de mon malheur je sus tirer quelque avantage. J'appris à m'endureir contre l'advetsité."

On another paper, which seemed to be more recently written, there were other quotations from different writers, mingled with comments of his own.

One of these texts was marked as being from Jean Baptiste Rousseau, the Poet —

> "Que n'ai - je pu, de vos plaisirs épris.
> Tendre Amitié, dont je sens tout le prix.
> Dans une joie, et si douce et si pure,
> Vivre oublié toute la nature?"

And Marchmont had written under it —

"But *I* dare not aspire to happiness, lest I should involve others in my calamities. Oh, weakness! to indulge hopes that never must be realized! dreams of future pleasure, which serve but to embitter the sad realities that surround me waking!

"Yet such visionary hopes I have lately suffered to take possession of my mind!

"Hopes of what? Ah! would I, if I *could,* unite the destiny of the woman I love with mine? Ought I? — who may say —

> "... forlorn I rove.
> Without a crime, unjustly banished!*

But surely I might go on too with the stanzas that follow:

> "Safe thy charms with me should rest,
>   Hither did thy pity send thee;
> Pure the love that fills my breast,
>   From itself it would defend thee!
>
> Ah! what ills are mine to bear!
>   Life's fair morn with clouds o'ercasting;
> Doom'd the victim of despair,
>   Youth's gay bloom pale sorrow blasting.
>
> Oh! thou dear hoard of treasur'd love!
>   Tho' these fond arms should ne'er possess thee,
> Still this fond heart shall faithful prove,
>   And its last sighs shall breathe to bless thee."

The paper on which the following lines were written was torn asunder, as if he had meant to destroy it.

"If I linger here, shall I ever conquer this unhappy passion? Do I not feed it by thus lurking within a few paces of its object? Yet whither fly? Amid the stillness of the night when I have left my cavern, and like a guilty wretch, lighter only in conscience and in design, have stolen softly to the door of the chamber where Althea, secure in native innocence, calmly slept — when I have indulged my fancy by believing I heard her breathe — when I have really heard her sigh, and since our interview have dared to hope that the recollection of the unhappy Marchmont might sometimes occasion one of those sighs. — What have I done? — What? but aggravate certain and unavoidable suffer-

* These and the following quatrains are in the poems published by Miss Brooke, from the original Irish, a book not so much known as it deserves to be—Miss Brooke is now dead

ings, by thus seeking food for visionary indulgence; and having yielded
to these mockeries of hope, have I not awakened under ten-fold anguish, when I have allowed reason to shew me *what I am,* and *must be?*

Wayward as my destiny is, and while I see no means of escaping
from it, should I thus suffer my mind to become enervate? But it is
in vain I know what I *ought* to do. One glimpse of her I love, as she
walks slowly and pensively down the garden — as I catch a transient
sight of her among the old laburnums and larches that remain of the
shrubbery — or even the echo of her light steps, as I listen at the door
which opens into the passage near her room; the distant sound of her
enchanting voice, speaking even to give a common order, all have their
charms for me — such charms, that I forget every thing but the pleasure of being near her: and I form, in despite of reason, those dreams
of felicity, from which, when it regains its power, I relapse into more
acute pain.

SONNET.

Where with incumbent night the forests frown,
    The care-worn pilgrim seeks his doubtful way:
Till weary on the grass he throws him down,
    To wait in broken sleep the dawn of day.
Thro' boughs just waving in the silent air.
    With pale capricious light the Summer Moon
Conquers his humid couch; while Fancy there,
    That loves to wanton in the night's deep noon,
Calls, from the mossy roots, and fountain's edge,
    Ideal forms of Nymphs that haunt the shade,
And Naiads rising from the whispering sedge:
    Then, 'mid the beauteous group, his dcar-lov'd maid
Seems beckoning him with smiles to join the train...
    Till, starting from his dream — he feels his woes again.

Such were some of the contents of the pacquet Althea perused.
The effect they had upon her was that of heightening the tenderness,
affection, and regret with which she thought of Marchmont. The
knowledge of his having watched near her room as she slept — of
having anxiously waited for a slight view of her as she passed among
the shrubs in the garden — and the struggles he had evidently made to
tear himself away, that he might not disturb her peace by his unhappy
love, gave her certain conviction of the sincerity and the purity of his

regard of her. But having for a while yielded to these reflections of mingled pain and pleasure, she recollected whither she was going; and trembling lest Sir Audley's knowledge of their attachment should have been one cause of his sending for her, whom he never seemed to wish near him on any former occasion; Althea doubted whether, when with her father, she should be allowed the means of hearing of her wandering and unhappy lover — whether she should ever see him more.

Almost overcome with anxiety and fatigue she arrived at Bath. Welsh, her father's servant, who had been waiting for her arrival, came down to receive her; and informed her that Sir Audley had been so very ill the night before, that his life was thought to be in danger: the man added, that Sir Audley had been very impatient for her arrival, but his spirits were in such a state that it was necessary to let him know she was in the house, some time before she entered his room. Lady Dacres had been delivered of a son that had lived only a few hours; and Sir Audley, between his anxiety on her account, and some new vexation that had arisen from the conduct of Mr. Dacres, had lost all his firmness of mind, and fluctuated between peevishness and despondence, equally injurious to his health.

As soon as he knew Althea was arrived, he desired to see her. She entered the room trembling so much, that it was with difficulty she supported herself. But when she beheld the very great alteration that had happened in the countenance and figure of her father, she had need of all her resolution to conceal how much she was affected. His voice was as much charged as his person; — feeble and tremulous like that of a very old person, it seemed to fail alike from weakness as emotion, as, drawing his daughter gently towards him, he said —

"Althea, my poor girl! are you willing to be my nurse a little while? I may not want your attendance long. They tell me I am better —I hope I am. It will do me good to have you near me."

He appeared to recollect how little he had deserved the tenderness he now solicited from his long-neglected Althea, whose looks and broken accents sufficiently evinced how affectionately her heart answered this return of regard, and with how much sweetness and duty she was disposed to repay it.

When Sir Audley became more composed, he said, "You have heard, Althea, of what had happened? My family afflictions have been heavy. Lady Dacres is hardly now, I fear, out of danger. I wish I were well enough to begin my journey to London — it is dreadful to be absent at such a time!"

Althea now exerted herself to persuade Sir Audley that the best thing he could do would be to compose his spirits, which would more than any thing hasten his recovery. She assured him, that if her unremitting attention could assist in the least degree that desirable end, she should be happier than she had ever been before. Her voice failed her as she would have gone on; and her father, who seemed to understand her sensations, while he tried to repress his own, said, "You are a dear good girl, Althea." — They both seemed to think it was better to put an end to the conversation.

Althea from that evening entered on a new task, attendance in the sick room of her father, where she acquitted herself so much to his satisfaction, that it became to her a source of the most heartfelt satisfaction; while Sir Audley felt like an indigent man who had suddenly discovered a mine of gold on his ground that he never dreamed of possessing: — he was, however, unwilling to express his present sentiments, lest they should seem too strongly to reproach him with his former harshness and neglect.

In being assured, as she soon was, that Sir Audley knew nothing of what had passed in regard to Marchmont, a heavy weight was taken from the mind of his daughter. The greater part of every day was passed either in writing letters for him on business; letters to his wife, with accounts of his health; or in reading political tracts, all on the side of the question to which he was attached — and Sir Audley was thoroughly a courtier. Blind servility, wilful misrepresentation, or the rhodomontade of declamation, of which most of these party pamphlets consisted, made them alike disgusting to her reason and her taste; but she would have executed the task, which often continued through great part of the night, with more cheerfulness, had she not observed, as she waded through these tinsel or fulsome pages with the most patient assiduity, that, ill as Sir Audley was, his mind was still agitated by views that were likely so soon to vanish in that awful futurity, on the brink of which he seemed to be trembling — and that at every interval of ease he returned to the sanguine contemplation of projects which death would probably prevent his ever executing. Then, having wearied and exhausted his spirits, she saw him suddenly sink in mental and bodily anguish; and recollecting the helpless family he had to leave, of whom his eldest son so little promised to be a protector, he felt all the futility of the plans he had been forming for *himself*, and hardly dared think of the reverse that might befall *them*.

In all the conversations he had yet held with Althea, Sir Audley had evaded speaking much or seriously of Mr. Dacres; but she saw that he was almost always the first subject of his thoughts. What she considered still more extraordinary was, that her father had never mentioned Mohun to her, and seemed to have forgotten, or to wish to forget, all that had formerly passed about him. — Althea, who never thought of him without shuddering, considered this silence on the part of her father as the most certain indication of a change in his disposition in her favour; and when he appeared to gain upon his disorder, and there were symptoms of his conquering it, she ventured to encourage hopes that she might be restored to his tenderness, and taken into his paternal protection, without being compelled to sacrifice, for those advantages, all the happiness and quiet of her future life.

But though Mohun seemed to be out of the question, there was no reason to believe that, to Sir Audley, Marchmont could ever become acceptable; and when her thoughts were turned towards him, which always happened the moment she was alone, she was sometimes compelled to divert them from the painful enquiry of what would be the event of an attachment that had now gained an unconquerable power over her heart; and at other times she persuaded herself to believe, that if his merit should procure him a marriage with some woman of fortune, who might relieve him from all his embarrassments, she should herself rejoice at it; though, certain that it was impossible to find a man, in her opinion, of equal merit, she should never marry herself. — If the future, however, looked comfortless, the present was wrapped in more disquieting obscurity; it was now six weeks since Marchmont had taken leave of her. — What was become of him? whither was he gone? — Never, perhaps, might they meet again!

Days and weeks passed on — Sir Audley made but little progress towards his recovery, a fortnight after Althea's arrival, and his physicians seemed to doubt whether he would derive any farther benefit from the Bath waters: they rather recommended his returning to London, because his absence from his family seemed to prey upon his mind. It was settled then that he should undertake the journey: — Althea heard with mingled concern and satisfaction, that he had determined she should accompany him.

Nothing could be more repugnant to her than going to reside with Lady Dacres, whose temper would probably be irritated by sickness and disappointment, and certainly would not be sweetened when she should witness the newly-restored affection of her husband to his eldest daughter. In removing so far from Eastwoodleigh, the probability of hearing of Marchmont would be lessened, and the means of hearing rendered more difficult. If her father died, she should be left, perhaps, wholly in Lady Dacres's power: if he recovered, she might again become a source of uneasiness between them.

But, easily melted by the kindness she had been but little accustomed to, the delight she felt in being useful to her father, in possessing the power to sooth his pains, and to render tolerable the confinement of a sick room, which it was likely he might long be destined to undergo, counterbalanced, in the mind of Althea, all the reasons of her dislike — and she thought, that if she contributed to the re-establishment of a health so necessary to her family, Lady Dacres would not scruple to own her obligations to her, and lose the paltry jealousy she had before shewn, in the pursuit of their common interest in her father's life.

By being in town, Althea thought she might obtain an opportunity of seeing Mrs. Marchmont and her daughters who resided near it; and with this contrariety of sensation, all, however, occasionally absorbed in solicitude for her father, she began her journey.

Sir Audley bearing the fatigue better than they had reason to expect, he desired they might proceed to Newbury, as the nearer he approached to London the greater became his anxiety to get thither. — Althea saw, with satisfaction, that he appeared not likely to suffer from the journey, as she had feared: he insisted on her leaving him for the night at an earlier hour than she had been accustomed to do, and blessed her as he bade her good night.

Althea retired to her bed, and had enjoyed, for two or three hours, undisturbed repose, when she was suddenly startled by a noise at her door. Some person rapped at it violently, but seemed unable to articulate more than — "Madam! Miss Dacres — Oh! for God's sake, get up." — She arose in terror, asking in vain who was there, while she hastily put on her clothes. The voice had ceased, and the person seemed to be gone from thence; but others were heard running about the house. The idea of fire was the first that occurred to Althea, and her first impulse was to run towards he father's room, though she was not sure she could find it. In a moment she was dressed; and taking the candle that was in the room, she hurried, with trembling step, along a sort of open gallery: at the top of the stairs she met Welsh; — he was pale, his lips quivered, and his knees seemed to refuse to support him.

"What is the matter, Welsh?" exclaimed Althea.

"Ah! Madam, my master!"

"What of your master? — is he ill?"

"Indeed, Madam, he is very ill — so ill, that —"

Althea, without speaking, was running towards the room. — Welsh took her arm, and the mistress of the inn, who at that moment came up to them, said — "You had better tell the young lady the truth: — it is in vain to attempt deceiving her."

"The truth?" cried Althea. "Gracious God! — my father is dead then?"

"We are afraid so, Madam," said Welsh.

"Who is with him? — who is with him?" asked she impatiently — "I will see him."

"It is very useless, Sir," said Mrs. ——, "to let the lady have the shock of going into the room —I have left it since you have — Sir Audley is certainly dead. You had better go to his room," added she, speaking to Welsh, "I will take care of Miss Dacres. Come, Madam, let me lead you back to your chamber."

Althea was so stunned by a blow thus unexpected, that she became giddy and sick, and, leaning on the arm of the person who offered her assistance, was led back to the room she had left. She shed no tear, nor uttered a single word. It seemed as if she was arguing with herself as to the reality of what had just passed, and then, as having some hope she might be deceived, suddenly rose, and said she must go to her father's room. She was, however, again prevented; and in a moment afterwards a medical man, who had been sent for to Sir Audley, came to her. He talked very rationally; desired she would go to bed and take something to calm her spirits; and assured her, that to her father she could not now be of use, unless it were in so far commanding herself as to give the necessary orders. — To these, however, Althea, notwith-standing all attempts to collect some degree of fortitude, was wholly unequal. She besought the gentleman to spare her, by taking upon himself the direction of every thing; and then, that she might prevail on the well-meaning but officious people about her to leave her alone, she consented to go to bed.

Mrs. Trevyllian, among the various excellent lessons she had given her beloved Althea, had inculcated none with more frequency and earnestness than the necessity of presence of mind and fortitude. In a moment that brought to her recollection all the anguish she had suffered for the loss of her first and best friend, the maxims she had taught forcibly recurred to her, and there was now occasion for her to practise them. Cold and even unfeeling as had been the conduct of Lady Dacres, the good heart of Althea bled, when she thought of the sorrow that would overwhelm her when she knew that her children had no longer a father — and the state of health in which she was represented to be, added to the poignant concern with which Althea considered the situation of her step-mother. How to mitigate, as much as she could, the violence of the first shock, was now to be considered — and to determine on something was immediately necessary, left the fatal news should reach Lady Dacres without any precaution at all.

Instead therefore of indulging that depression of spirit which would have deprived her of the power of being useful, Althea, after remaining alone about an hour, sent for the mistress of the house; and, as she could not herself see Sir Audley's servant (who she desired would on no account quit the remains of his master), left an order with her that he should put down the names of the friends most intimate in her father's family, and of the physician who usually attended Lady Dacres.

The name of the confidential friend was Mohun. — To him Althea could not resolve to send, but determined, by a letter, to inform Dr. B. of what had happened, and to entreat he would go himself to disclose the melancholy intelligence to Lady Dacres. — This letter was immediately written, and sent off express — and Althea, having so far executed her duty, began to consider, in this great and material change in the family, what was to become of herself.

There was no reason to believe that the heart of Lady Dacres was softened towards her; and she had often had occasion to remark, in late conversations with her father, that he seemed distressed when it was necessary to speak of her future residence with them, as if he were afraid of promising too much as to her reception. Now that her father was no more, it was very uncertain whether her mother-in-law would receive her at all, or whether it was right to put her reluctant complaisance to the trial: yet had Althea no other connection on earth, nor any friend whose protection she could claim. To Eastwoodleigh, indeed, she might still return: yet it was possible that even that melancholy asylum might be after a time denied her, since Lady Dacres had often said, that it was folly in Sir Audley to keep the house in its present state, though it would be a still greater to attempt repairing it; and that the only wise way of getting rid of such an incumbrance would be to pull it down, and sell the materials, since there were farm-houses enough upon the estate.

It was therefore probable that, such being Lady Dacres's sentiments, she would soon dismiss the servants, and raze the house.

Althea, thus compelled to think of her future destiny, foresaw, not without some dismay, that the hour was now at hand, when, totally alone in the world, and slenderly, very slenderly provided for, she should, perhaps, have cause to regret even the lonely seclusion of Eastwoodleigh, and possibly to wonder how she could ever have been unhappy when she enjoyed, however remotely, the protection of a father.

CHAP. VI.

"There is nothing so affecting as the dignified fortitude of a family, who, fallen into indigence, have recourse for independence to virtuous industry."

AT AN EARLIER hour than Althea expected, the physician, to whom she had written, arrived himself; he came post, and said that it was Lady Dacres's request that Miss Dacres would return with him to London, after he had given all the necessary orders for conveying the remains of Sir Audley to Capelstoke. — Althea enquired, with tender earnestness, after Lady Dacres, and was consoled to hear that she was tolerably composed. Eager to do every thing that might contribute to ease the mind of one who had been dear to her father, she hastened to obey the summons thus sent her; and flattered herself that, since all jealously of her favour with Sir Audley must now be at an end, his widow would forget every former prejudice against her, and admit her to share the cares that would attend the education of the younger part of his family, to whose service she proposed, with the truest filial affection towards his memory; to devote herself.

At the end of her melancholy journey, which was soon performed, Althea found herself under the roof so lately her father's, with very different sensations from those with which she had left it to attend on her aunt. Indeed the house was in every respect changed. — The servants, who were then noisy, insolent, and presumptuous, now glided about like spectres; and a mournful silence reigned where lately the continual entrance of company, and sometimes the same sort of bustle that is seen at a statesman's levee, used to disturb the street. Lady Dacres sent her woman, with an excuse to Althea for not seeing her, even on the morning of the third day after her arrival. It was not difficult for her to believe, that their meeting might affect her too much; but she could not help thinking it strange that her sisters had never appeared. — At length, however, these young ladies, after sending a formal notice of their intentions, came to her apartment. The eldest, now about sixteen, *seemed* to wipe her eyes; but her demeanour, which was extremely cold and reserved, gave no encouragement to the sensible heart of Althea to consider her as a sister, or as one deeply interested in their recent loss. The other two were still under the direction of a very formal governess, who entered with them, and sat perpendicular as a statue by them, while Althea endeavoured to make out something like affectionate conversation, which, however, ended only in 'Yes,' or 'No!' on their parts. Then, after remaining under this restraint for a quarter of an hour, the elder sister arose, and took as ceremonious a leave as if it had been of a perfect stranger, and the governess, with her tow bridling pupils, departed in great form at the same time.

This was too much for poor Althea, who, forlorn as her situation at Eastwoodleigh had been, never felt herself so totally alone in the world as at this moment. Her heart sunk in cold and blank despondence when she considered, that it was uncertain whether the universe contained one human being that cared whether she existed or no! To write to Mrs. Marchmont she had not yet resolution, nor was it indeed quite proper so immediately after her father's death. Living alone in her room, she saw none but servants, who seemed hardly to consider her as a part of the family. On the fifth day, however, a stranger desired admittance. It was the attorney employed by Sir Audley in his affairs. This man, who seemed to be very well convinced of his own importance, informed her, after a preface which contained a panegyric on Lady Dacres, that he was directed by her Ladyship to wait on Miss Dacres to read to her the will of the late Sir Audley, her father. Althea, totally ignorant of the forms usually observed in such cases, and who had hardly yet thought of the disposition of her father's effects,

assented to what Mr. Grimworth proposed; who thereupon, in a ridiculous tone, began to read a scroll he held; by which Althea presently
understood that all her expectations, of any increase of fortune from
Sir Audley's paternal affection were at an end.

The two thousand pounds settled upon her on her mother's marriage, and hardly a thousand left her by her aunt, was all she was ever
likely to possess: of the latter she became mistress on attaining the age
of twenty-one; the larger sum was in trust, and the interest only was to
be paid her; the trustees in whose names it stood being directed in the
will to see it settled on her whenever she married; which, in another
passage, it was enjoined her not to do without the consent of Lady
Dacres — to whom was given every power that her husband, Sir Audley, could bestow upon her: and the personals of every kind were hers,
except a diamond cross which had belonged to the mother of Althea,
and which was now directed to be given her, with a ring, and some
articles of inferior value. Lady Dacres and Mr. Mohun were executors.

To all this Althea, whatever she thought, had nothing to say in the
presence of the consequential person who made the communication.
As soon as he took his leave, her present circumstances, and future
prospects, forcibly took possession of her mind: the contemplation
was not flattering, yet she felt no inclination to blame her father. —
The will was made almost immediately after the death of Mrs. Trevyllian, when her father's disposition towards her was certainly much less
affectionate than it had been towards the end of his life. Yet, had he
then made another will, to do much in favour of Althea could not have
been in his power; for the far greater part of it should be alienated.
— From her, if any judgement was to be formed from her present
conduct, Althea had nothing to expect; and the idea of continuing
in the protection of, and in some measure dependent on, a person
who seemed to be little disposed to treat her with that affection which
springs from the heart, was of all the uneasiness she had yet felt, the
most difficult to endure with fortitude.

Lady Dacres, like all those who feel very keenly for their personal convenience, lamented her husband, because much of her consequence, and no inconsiderable part of their income, was lost with him;
but she was incapable of really loving any body but herself, and her
children because they *were* hers.— Yet conscious, perhaps, how little
of real tenderness and regret was in her heart, she observed the most
minute gradations in the *forms* of grief. Althea was, after some days,

admitted to see her in her half-darkened apartment; but a very few
words passed between them, and those few were so coldly delivered,
that Althea relinquished at once every hope that remained of finding a
real friend in the widow of her father.

The truth was, that Lady Dacres, under the first surprise and
concern on the unexpected death of her husband, had consented to
the proposal of Dr. B——, who was, at that moment, her adviser,
and who justly remarked, that decency and affection demanded that
Sir Audley's daughter should, at such a time, find protection with the
rest of his family. But no sooner had the first tumult of her spirits
subsided, than she saw innumerable objections to Althea's residing
with her, the chief of which was the expence, though a consideration
that had *almost* as much weight, was the fear (hardly acknowledged
even to herself) of this step-daughter's eclipsing her own — for, with
all her ridiculous partiality, she was compelled internally to acknowledge the personal loveliness of Althea; though of the mind that animated her face, and gave it its peculiar charms, Lady Dacres was
wholly insensible.

Could this narrow-minded woman have contrived to have placed
the daughter of her husband as the superintendant of her nursery, and
to have kept her in a state of abject dependence, she would willingly
have preferred her to the people she now employed: but the small
independence Althea possessed, and the proper pride which she had
often shewn, precluded every attempt of that sort; and if she staid at
all with her mother-in-law, it could only be as Miss Dacres.

Time, however, slowly moved on; a short conference every day at
dinner and tea with Lady Dacres, or silent airing with the children and
their prim governess, were the only periods at which Althea left the
solitude of her own room. When she was admitted to that where the
afflicted widow shut herself up, their conversation was languid, and,
on the part of Lady Dacres, under visible restraint. — Althea was too
delicate to speak on what was, however, uppermost in her droughts,
nor had she indeed any thing to propose: the observation of every day
strengthened the supposition that she was not a welcome visitor where
she was — yet, whither could she go? — Frequently were her thoughts
turned towards Mrs. Marchmont and her daughters; and she sometimes believed that they might gladly receive her as a boarder, because
what she should pay would probably be of great use to them: but how
could she propose this, or how make farther advances towards the ac-

quaintance of a family who had so strangely appeared to recede from those she had made already?

It was now two months since the departure of Marchmont — and in all that time he would surely have commenced the correspondence he had so earnestly solicited, had not some new calamity put it out of his power. Perhaps he no longer existed: — this dreadful idea sometimes forced itself on the mind of Althea, but she repelled it as resolutely as she could: it was too terrible to be endured.

The gay crowds that so lately in habited that part of the town had now disappeared, and hardly a straggling coach passed through the deserted streets. Nothing could be more oppressive to the spirits than the appearance of every thing around her. The windows of the opposite houses were half shut, and the idle solitary servants stood loitering away their afternoons at the doors. — Here and there were seen a group of unemployed chairmen, whose hoarse voices, and the cries of the fruit-venders, were all the sounds heard amidst the sullen desertion of the hot and dusty streets.

Such was the comfortless situation of Althea, who continually thought of seeking Mrs. Marchmont, without being able to determine on it. — At length she resolved to write to her — and, waving every other consideration, to think of her only as the mother of Marchmont, and one whose misfortunes it might be possible for her to alleviate.

A piece of information she learned the day she had made this resolution quickened its execution.

Lady Dacres sent an excuse for not receiving her as usual — illness was the reason given, as had sometimes happened before. The governess, Mrs. Bentham, and the young ladies, however, assembled as usual; and it happened that the former was somewhat more communicative than usual, and from her Althea learned that Lady Dacres, unable to visit Capelstoke this summer on account of the state of her spirits, had thoughts of going to Margate — and Althea discovered that it was intended she should perceive, by the hints Mrs. Bentham dropped, that the great expence, on account of her having so large a family to remove, had deterred her from yet beginning a journey which was thought to be necessary to her health. It was not difficult to perceive that Lady Dacres wished for an opportunity of shaking her off, and thought this removal offered one. — There was therefore no time to hesitate; and Althea wrote the letter she had meditated to Mrs. Marchmont, who now, as she believed, resided at Fulham. It contained merely a request of leave to wait upon her; and, though with great reluctance, she determined not to speak to Lady Dacres of quitting her till she received Mrs. Marchmont's answer, or even to delay it till she had visited her, and was enabled to judge whether she could hope to find, in the mother of Marchmont, the maternal friendship which was become so necessary in her desolate and unprotected situation. — In the interim, whenever she saw Lady Dacres, the conversation was invariably turned to the subject of œconomy. Sir Audley had possessed a considerable sinecure, and participated *en croupe* a very large share of a place which his interest procured for one of his friends. The loss of these emoluments Lady Dacres failed not to lament, with as many remarks on her extreme ill fortune as if she had nothing left. Althea indeed sometimes thought that, in deploring this diminution of income, she forgot the husband through whose means she had enjoyed it.

Avarice was always the leading feature in the character of Lady Dacres; and it is a fault which always increases with years; but with her it had acquired strength from another circumstance, which Althea now discovered — the excessive extravagance of her eldest son, now Sir Gunston Dacres, whom, during his father's life, she had privately supplied with money, and for whom her ill-judged fondness now urged her to amass it for his future aggrandisement and gratification, even at the expence of her other children.

Althea, convinced of this, saw an additional reason for believing, that she should not long be a guest with whom Lady Dacres would constrain herself to keep up even the forms of kindness.

Uncertain how to act in a situation so distressing, and uncertain whither to go, the three days, during which she expected the answer from Mrs. Marchmont, seemed the longest and most painful she had ever yet passed. At length a letter was brought to her: she opened it trembling: scarce could the writing of Marchmont himself have affected her more than did this, which she believed to be from his mother. — The handwriting was remarkably elegant, yet free, and without any of the formality which is hardly to be avoided in elaborate fine writing. — The letter follows —

"Madam,

You will, I hope, allow me, in the absence of my mother, to thank you for your most obliging letter; yet indeed, dearest Madam, I never found myself so much at a loss. I would fain express all I feel of gratitude for repeated kindness, to which I am sure we must seem to have very little claim; for how strange must our conduct have appeared to you! I dare not trouble you with a long explanation in writing; but, if I am so happy as to see you, I will endeavour to convince you that it has been from the most laudable motives that my poor mother has denied herself the gratification of becoming known to you. — Ah! Madam, we account ourselves *so* unhappy, that we are afraid lest the *infection* of our distress should injure those who have not thrown us off; and, alas! they are *so* few! — Yet to the very small number of benevolent and feeling minds, who are affected by our situation without the power of relieving us, my mother has been afraid of adding Miss Dacres; and this, with some other reasons which I am sure you would not condemn, have together prevented her from availing herself of the generous attempts you have made to give us, what we have heard enough of you to make us highly value, the honour and pleasure of your acquaintance.

"But surely, under our present circumstances, it is no time to deny ourselves the little good that Heaven seems to offer us. I believe, Madam, that if I am so fortunate as to see you, I should find myself utterly unable to speak all I have to say; I hope, therefore, there will be no impropriety in writing. There are, perhaps, forms which ought to be observed, yet I cannot but believe that Miss Dacres will forgive me if I break through them.

"Indeed our struggle, with some remains of pride, is so ineffectual, that we should long since have given it up, had not my mother still lingered in the hope that her own family would render the step unnecessary, which they were too proud to allow her to take as *their* relation. She has a sister, Lady Silchester, who, ever since our fortunes have been so deplorably changed, has endeavoured to escape from the relationship; but, as it is too well known, she has at last declared, that if my mother *does* go into business, she will assist her upon no other terms than her changing her name. While my brother was in England, he positively refused to consent to this; nor could he indeed bear to think that his mother and his sisters should engage in a manner of life, of which the pride of a very ancient family has, perhaps, given him, and all of us, false ideas. His objections, and the languid despondence of my dear mother, have deterred my sisters and myself from the undertaking, rather than the selfish arrogance of Lady Silchester. But as we are convinced she never will effectually befriend us, nor indeed can we well endure to be under obligations to her, (which we should be made to feel more heavily than any other state of dependence) we have at length prevailed on my mother to allow us to try what we can do, to procure for her and for ourselves a subsistence, which surely is not dishonourable. Her tenderness, however, will not permit only us to appear in this, as we were desirous of doing; she thinks we are too young, and that the intention, which ought to command respect, will not always secure us from the malice of the censorious, or the impertinence of the profligate. She therefore sacrifices her own feelings to give us the protection of her appearance in our little shop, and, with my eldest sister, is gone down to Margate to begin on this mode of life. A change of air, and particularly to the sea air, we hope will be of great use to her health, which is often in a state that makes us tremble for her life — and where she is not known, the new task, undertaken on motives so laudable, will, we trust, affect her less. I stay here for about ten days longer with my younger sister, till we can finish some of the articles which are to become part of our stock in trade, and we are then to follow her. — And can you, Madam, will you condescend to visit us? —I hardly dare hope it! — Yet when I reflect on your character, such as it has been represented to me, I cannot but flatter myself you will give me an opportunity of expressing the gratitude which we owe you, and accounting for the apparent insensibility of hearts, which indeed, dearest Madam, are all as conscious of their obligations, as is that of

Your most obedient and

Faithful humble servant,

LUCY MARCHMONT.

"I would do myself the honour of waiting on you, but I cannot leave my youngest sister; and to be ingenuous, the expence, small as it is, would be some object to us just now."

Calm and generally mistress of herself as Althea was, for some moments she was so much affected by this letter, as to be unable to determine what to do — but, as soon as the first painful, yet pleasurable emotions subsided, she determined to hasten to these interesting young women, who more than ever were become objects of her solicitude and regard. Their projects of industry, which were likely to lead them to the very same place where Lady Dacres intended to go, put another difficulty in the way of what Althea had projected, when she thought of offering herself as a boarder in their family; and again she looked around her in uncertainty whither to go, while almost every moment gave occasion to some remark on the conduct of the family where she now was, that added to the uneasiness she felt from the necessity of staying in it.

Her first purpose, however, was to visit Lucy Marchmont, and she determined to do so the next day.

Another difficulty, however, arose. Though Lady Dacres had hitherto appeared perfectly indifferent how she disposed of her time, yet her father's will seemed to put her very much in the power of her mother-in-law; and Althea knew that there is in many minds such a love of authority, that it is often exerted where the governors have no affection for the governed, or interest in the actions they would control. — Lady Dacres was aware that Althea had not one acquaintance in or near London: and should she either borrow one of the carriages, or hire one, to make a visit in the neighborhood of the town, it would probably be enquired to whom it was to be made; and the name of Marchmont was that of all others to which Lady Dacres seemed to inherit from her father, and to have taught to Sir Audley, an aversion, which their misfortunes appeared to have increased.

While Althea was debating with herself how to act, she was surprised by a visit from Mrs. Glaston, formerly Linda Eversley, with whom her correspondence had languished for some months, but who, as Althea had heard since she came to London, was lately married to a man of very large fortune. Her own troubles, and the reluctance with which such sort of letters are usually written, had hitherto prevented her renewing their correspondence by a congratulation in form; and she thought of nothing less than such a visit when Mrs. Glaston was introduced.

Althea stared in astonishment when she saw her, so entirely was she changed! It was no longer the simple, unaffected, good-natured Linda Eversley, who had been the companion of her early youth. She now met a very fine lady, dressed in the extremity of the fashion, with cheeks very red, and a voice very loud — who affected, however, to be extremely glad to see her, and told her so in phrases which were a strange mixture between her former Devonshire dialect and the cant words of the day.

Althea could at any other time have found great amusement in the fantastic attempts of her friend to imitate supreme fashion; but, her mind entirely occupied by the Marchmonts, she seized this opportunity to enquire what was known of their history, by one who was once the friend of the younger part of the family, and who had lived among those by whom, in the days of their prosperity, the Marchmonts had been looked up to as the first people in the neighbourhood.

CHAP. VII.

N'écoutant, n'envisageant, que soi!

THE NEW-MARRIED LADY was much taken up with the idea of her own importance, and in describing to Althea the fineries of which she had become possessed, and the fine people she lived among. — Nothing is more ridiculous than the consequence of a silly creature, who, by some unexpected circumstance, is suddenly placed in a situation greatly above her former rank of life. The unballasted head of Linda Eversley, a girl whom even her own family had been used to consider as of small account, was quite overset by it, and she seemed to have visited Althea less in the intention of renewing their former acquaintance, than for the purpose of exhibiting to her her imaginary importance. Althea, pitying her weakness, heard her for above half an hour with her usual quiet complaisance; and at length took occasion, on her slightly naming some of their former acquaintance, to say — "But pray, among all your Devonshire friends, what have you to tell me of the Marchmont family?"

"The Marchmonts? — Oh! I had lost sight of them so long! — Poor souls! I heard lately, I think, that they were sadly off, and living somewhere about Lonnon; I actually meant tew or three times to have asked about 'em, but somehow it always went out of my head, and Mr. Glaston talks of our leaving Lonnon so sewn, that I shall hardly have time. Its vastly savage in me, though — don't you think so?"

"Yes, indeed I *do*" said Althea; "I am sure your brother, who had so great an affection for some part of that family, would think so too ..."

"My brother!" interrupted the lady. "Lord, do you know that we vote him quite a quiz! He is *so* altered you would not know him — and leads such a miserable life! always mope, mope, mope in the country, talking about gardening and planting, and wearing one really quite to a thread. As to his horrible wife, she's just the same as she was; and I think by degrees, do you know, she'll make my poor brother like her: for my part, she used to *savage* me so, when I was forced to be there, that I shall never go near them any more."

"I cannot blame you," said Althea, "for escaping from the lady; but surely Mr. Eversley's having the misfortune to have so unhappy a tempered woman for his wife, should rather strengthen than lessen the affection of his family towards *him* especially as you know he married her on the most laudable motives."

"Aye, that's very true, and I really love my brother vastly well; but that odious puss of a woman! I'm sure, if I were to see her, I should downright quarrel with her; and, dear! you know one can do him no gued; and what's the use, you know, of making one's self unhappy by seeing one's friends miserable, when, after all, one cannot help them?"

"And is it," said Althea, "upon that principle that you have so entirely given up the Marchmonts?"

"I don't know that I have given them up; but what can one do, you know? — Mr. Glaston has such newmeroos connections, and he expects me to visit them all — then, besides, I really don't know where those poor people live. — But do you know, my dear, that somebody was a-telling me the other day, that young Marchmont was run away for debt, and that his mother and sisters were going to set up a shop?"

"You cannot have forgotten," said Althea, whose cheeks were suffused with crimson when Marchmont was thus named, "the noble and generous motives by which that respectable and worthy young man was actuated, when he incurred the debt for which he has since been so inhumanly persecuted; and surely, if he has been compelled to quit his country that he may escape from those who have so cruelly pursued him, you should not give his evasion so harsh a term as that of having *run away*."

"Well," replied Mrs. Glaston coldly, "call it that you will — in fact, you know it *is* really running away, though."

"But," enquired Althea, interrupting her, "if it be true that Mrs. Marchmont and her daughters have taken the resolution to enter into any way of business, surely they are highly to be respected for it — and would not all their former friends, do you think, endeavour to encourage and assist them?"

"Yes, sure! yes, indeed! — I'm sure, for my part, I'd be very glad to encourage them, poor things! and would recommend them to all my friends. —I dare say they'll meet with success, and I'll take care to go to them as soon as I hear they're set up — but I really don't know whu to enquire of. I can't imagine, my dear, how I shall know when they're set up."

Though Althea was disgusted enough with these insolent airs of protection and patronage, from a person who was so lately raised, as far as money could do it, above those in every other respect so greatly her superiors, she debated a moment with herself whether she should not, by saying what she knew to be the Marchmonts' intentions, secure such good offices as Mrs. Glaston could do them, though at the risk of subjecting them to her childish impertinence; and it occurred to her that, by means of this foolish woman, she might be enabled to make her visit without any disagreeable explanations with Lady Dacres; though, being so accompanied, if indeed Mrs. Glaston would deign to visit people who proposed *keeping a shop*, would, she feared, make her own visit less welcome.

Something, however, it was worth while to risk: she therefore related to Mrs. Glaston what she knew of the present situation of the female part of the Marchmont family.

During this little narration, the cold exclamation of— "Indeed? — Really? — Poor things! — Oh! I think them quite right —" gave to Althea but little hope of having moved the selfish insipidity of her auditor; to whom, however, she at length ventured to disclose her wish of visiting them, and asked if Mrs. Glaston would accompany her.

"What, to Fulham? Lord, my dear, I am afraid I can never go so far tomorrow; for we go out of town in less than a week, and I have ten thousand things to do — but," added she, after a moment's pause, "if *my* carriage will be of any use to you, you shall be vastly welcome to it. We have *tew*, and I can take the coach out to-morrow, if you chuse to have the chariot."

Althea, considering from how many difficulties this offer would deliver her, accepted it, though she was aware that Mrs. Glaston offered it much more from ostentation than friendship.

Mrs. Glaston then assured her it should be at the door at ten o'clock the next morning; and, rising to go away, said — "You will give *my service* to the poor girls, and pray tell them, that though I can't get so far out of town, I shall be vastly glad to see their pretty ingenious works, whenever it *lays in my way;* and that I'll recommend them to a great many of my friends, who are going to Margate this season, if they set up there. Well! good day to you, my dear! I'll try to see you

again before I go out of town. Good morning to you! — You are vastly welcome to the chariot."

To all this, which passed as Mrs. Glaston descended the stairs,
Althea answered very slightly, and, returning to her own room, almost
repented that she had accepted her half-insulting kindness; while her
visitor withdrew mightily satisfied with herself, and with the impression of her elegance and importance, which she nothing doubted having left on the mind of her old acquaintance.

Althea now sent a message to Lady Dacres, to say she was going
to pay a visit the next morning, a few miles from London, in Mrs.
Glaston's carriage, "if her Ladyship had no objection?" — A cold acquiescence was immediately returned.

At an early hour then, the following morning, Althea set out on
her short journey. As she went, a thousand reflections occupied her
mind. She was now, for the first time, to see one of Marchmont's family — she was to learn, what hitherto had appeared mysterious to her,
the character and temper of his mother, which would probably be
discovered by the manner of her daughter. Busied in these conjectures, and in recalling all that had passed with Marchmont himself, the
road was hardly discerned, nor was Althea roused from her reverie till
she found herself at the door of a small lodging-house, a little distant
from the end of the town, whither she had been directed. As Lucy
Marchmont was not apprised of her arrival, she had the precaution to
write a card before she set out—remembering, that hardly any thing is
so uneasy as a first visit, where the parties are unknown to each other.
Having sent in this note, her anxious expectation did not last long; for
Lucy Marchmont, whom she would almost any where have known
from her resemblance to her brother, came down to receive her. In
that sort of breathless agitation, which a desire to please particularly,
and the fear of not pleasing, give to a young and timid mind, she led
her visitor to a small sitting-room on the first floor, and introduced
her to her youngest sister: then, recovering a little from her confusion,
Lucy began to express her gratitude to Althea for coming; but, trying
to speak of her mother and of her brother, her voice failed her, and
she burst into tears.

By the sensible mildness of Althea, had she been in a condition to
have exerted it, her new friend would soon have been re-assured; but
it was so long since she had seen any one whom she was disposed to
love, and with whom she could yield to the tenderness and affection of

her character towards those who interested her, that Althea was unable to help weeping too; and, instead of the first meeting of two strangers, it appeared to be the renewal of some long-cherished friendship that had been interrupted by misfortune.

As there was great good sense on both sides, without any of that affected sensibility which is hardly less unpleasant than cold indifference, they soon recovered their composure; and Althea, though she had never accustomed herself to those violent slights of sudden friendship which sometimes are pretended to be felt at first sight, yet soon discovered that, in Lucy Marchmont, she had found a person capable of awakening her from the lifeless and joyless state in which she had lived ever since the departure of Marchmont himself. And indeed it was so long since the voice of kindness and real affection had met her ear, it was so long since her heart had felt any but unpleasant sensations, that the style of mind and conversation of Lucy appeared to her doubly attractive; and when, in addition to her personal merit, she considered her as the sister of Marchmont, it seemed as if in her was concentred all that could attract and delight her.

It was less the beauty of this charming girl, that was so suddenly seducing, than the mingled simplicity and vivacity of her manner. Her pleasing voice, her expressive countenance, and the soul that seemed to animate her eyes; the tender enthusiasm with which she mentioned her brother, and the more serious affection mingled with something like uneasiness and concern, which Althea remarked, when she spoke of her mother; the good sense and courage that seemed to enter into all her ideas as to their proposed plan of life; and that desire of independence, however humble, in which true and laudable pride really consists; all these traits of character impressed on the mind of Althea the most favourable idea of her young friend: she seemed to have acquired something like a new existence in having found a mind corresponding with her own; and Marchmont from that moment became dearer to her than ever — she loved him for his sister, and for himself.

Before Althea spoke of him, she wished to know how much of what had passed during his residence at Eastwoodleigh he had communicated to his family — while Lucy Marchmont, who really knew more of his attachment to Althea than the rest, dared not even hint at the knowledge she had; for nothing like hope had ever entered into those little sketches of the rise and progress of his passion, with which he had occasionally indulged himself when he talked to Lucy.

Equally ingenuous however, and with minds so well suited, they soon understood each other; and Lucy Marchmont spoke with very little reserve on the affairs of her family, as believing she was speaking to one generously concerned for what related to them.

"Though I have seen," said she, "but little of the world, indeed nothing of that sort of society that is generally called so, I am not ignorant that young women totally destitute of fortune as we are have no chance of marrying. Well! it is very sad, to be sure, to be predestined old maids: but a million of others, with as many pretensions as we could have had, had our poor father been more fortunate, live single; and I am sure there are such who are living happier, and more quietly and comfortably, than many women who have families. But I *must* not, says family pride, go into business, for I am descended from people who were of great consequence two hundred years ago, and of still more in the last century. Ah, dear! my ancestors will *now* do nothing for me. Not a citizen, not even a wealthy tradesman, will take either of us to ennoble his house; for in this country it is very certain money is respected the most, whatever influence rank may have when united to it. What then are we to do? If we could exist without doing something for ourselves, which I am convinced, whatever struggles we may make, is utterly impossible, I declare I think we shall be happier if we have something to employ us. Two or three forlorn ancient spinsters, just creeping through a vegetative sort of life in a cheap country town, has something to my apprehension most woefully gloomy and depressive. Who will care for us? The people among whom we live will no more respect us, though our great grandfathers were cavaliers, than they reverence the royal oak itself: half the world know nothing about Charles, or his martyrdom; and more than half the rest think the English people on the other side were in the right, and the cavaliers only obstinate proud fools.— Whereas, if we exert the few faculties we have, we shall be too busy to think of the neglect of those who were once our equals, or to dread the supercilious scorn of people that know no crime so great as poverty. By degrees our repugnance will wear away. We shall be amply repaid for the sacrifice of our pride, by the delight of obtaining more conveniences and comforts for my mother; of having a cheerful home for our brother, *when* he returns!"

Althea could not stifle a sigh, as her new friend said this; for she seemed to speak doubtfully, and to lay peculiar emphasis on the word *when.* Lucy Marchmont hesitated a moment, and proceeded.

"My eldest sister now seems to be convinced that we cannot do better; and we have together, I hope, conquered the remaining reluctance of my mother herself — though she still doubts whether, on my brother's account (at least till we have his consent to do so), we should exhibit the name of Marchmont on a shop-bill. But indeed, my dear Miss Dacres, this seems to me to be a distinction without a difference; and though I have in general the greatest deference for my mother's opinion, I cannot discover that we should gain any thing by this last indulgence of lingering pride, while we should certainly lose considerable advantages. Besides, I have no notion of humouring the arrogance of that Lady Silchester, who does not choose forsooth that her relations should be shop-women! She affects to say at the same time, that, living only on her jointure, she cannot do any thing for us. For my part, I declare that if she could, I should prefer the humblest independence to the misery of existing on the *bounty*, or, as one may well call it, the *charity*, of that aunt of mine, and so far from thinking this a want of pride, it seems to me to be the truest pride. It is not however surprising, that my sister and I should feel and judge differently. She is, you know, two years older than my brother, and of course was brought up in affluence, and looked forward to a life of prosperity from her first recollection; while *I*, who am almost five years younger, have, since I have been growing up, been witness to the difficulties and distresses of my family, and in consequence have insensibly become more prepared to meet them. It is true, that my poor father, who could not endure that my mother should ever suffer the least anxiety, always tried to hide from her and from us the decaying state of his fortunes. She affected to be deceived, because he wished to deceive her; but she used to weep for hours together as we younger children were at play round her: and when they did not suspect me of attending to their conversation, I have listened to many heart-breaking dialogues between her and Amelia; while, as soon as he thought me old enough to be reasonable, my brother used to confide to me his fears for his father and all of us, for of himself he never seemed to think; and very often, before he went last to France (for it was long before my father would consent to that), he used to form schemes for entering on the world in some business or profession that might assist us, and retrieve his father's affairs. Perhaps you may have remarked a part of the grounds that were once the park at Eastwoodleigh, down beyond where the cascade then was, there was formerly a long row of walnut and chesnut trees, reaching near half a mile. They are cut down now, and only the roots remain! It

was there, that in the fine evenings of the last two summers our dear Armyn were accustomed to walk with me, and that we used, as we traversed
the avenue backwards and forwards, to weary ourselves with hopes and
fears, with conjectures and schemes: and sometimes all my brother's
courage did not prevent him from communicating to me anticipations
of future calamity, which have, alas! been too fatally verified since. As he
remarked the beauty of the view, while the setting-sun illuminating the
sea appeared magnificently through the branches and boles of those fine
trees, how often has he said, that if he could but see his father and his
dear mother happy in a more humble situation, he should relinquish all
the beauties of his native place without a sigh; but that to live in it as we
then lived, and to see the ineffectual struggles of his father undermin-
ing and destroying his constitution, was more than he was able to bear.
Then, perhaps, when evening had stolen upon us unawares, he saw by
the lights in the house, that my father was gone up to his bedroom, and
we hastened in, when usually my brother took a book and read to him till
he went to sleep. — Ah! I well remember the effort Armyn made to appear calm and easy on those occasions. He usually took care to procure
no books of fiction but such as were of a cheerful cast; but once, among
some other works of entertainment that he had sent for, was the novel
of Julia de Roubigné. We had heard it praised, and, as my father was
pretty well that night, he bade us all come into his room; when, after he
was in bed, Armyn sat down to read it. But he had not gone farther than
that pathetic and natural description of the old servant Le Blanc, when
he had seen his master's favourite horse neglected by the owner of the
estate he had lost, than Armyn affected not to like the book. My father,
however, bidding him go on, his voice faltered more and more, till at last
he threw it down, and hastened away. Poor Amelia took it up, and put
it silently on the table. Nobody offered to go on with it — nobody was
able to speak. Ah! how many such scenes recur to my mind as I now sit
of an evening in these poor lodgings, and look over the little bit of garden that belongs to them, and the nursery and kitchen grounds beyond!
All that then passed seems present to me — but such retrospect only
gives me pain, and disables me from looking steadily towards the future,
which after all one must determine to do, if one would not be useless in
one's self, and perhaps burdensome to others."

   More and more pleased with the sensibility and sense of this interesting girl, the good heart of Althea made her endeavour to explain,
that her own situation was neither much superior in point of fortune,

nor at all more enviable in regard to other circumstances, than that she had just heard described. Every moment increased her pleasure in the company of Lucy Marchmont, till she found it difficult to determine on leaving her. Nothing had yet been said of the project she had formed of offering to become a boarder in the house of Mrs. Marchmont, wherever she might be fixed. If Althea had before thought of this as the most desirable plan that could offer itself, the present interview with Lucy redoubled all her anxiety to adopt it. — At length she ventured to speak of it; and was instantly convinced, as the lucid eyes of her young friend sparkled with delight, that by one of the family at least her offer would be joyfully received.

Their mutual confidence was now rapid in its progress; and before they parted, which Althea delayed till the very last moment possible, it was settled that Lucy Marchmont should write to her mother; while Althea on her part was to attempt to discover what were Lady Dacres's intentions; and, should she have reason to believe her Ladyship wished her to choose some other residence — in that case she was to endeavour at obtaining her sanction for making her election with Mrs. Marchmont. The hope that this plan might finally succeed, reconciled them to the painful ceremony of bidding adieu — when Lucy was left happier than she had been for some time, and Althea returned, with increased attachment for the Marchmonts, to her solitude in a fashionable street in a great city.

CHAP. VIII.

... In adversity
The mind grows tough by buffeting the tempest.

THE USUAL ACCOMPANIMENTS of a narrow mind and a selfish heart, cunning and suspicion, were strongly marked in the character of Lady Dacres. Althea, though formerly a sufferer from both, was little upon her guard against either. Artless herself, it never entered her head to imagine that her mother-in-law hardly

"Drank her tea without a stratagem,"

or that she owed even the little forbearance from rudeness she had experienced since her father's death, and the apartment and board that were sullenly afforded her, to a hope entertained by Lady Dacres, that her little fortune, which she notwithstanding affected to treat with so much contempt, might, by Althea's dying unmarried, belong at some future period to her own children. Somebody had besides hinted lately to this genuine descendant of Sir Ralph Gunstone, that Althea, and two female cousins whom she hardly knew, would be coheiresses to the fortune of Mr. Trevyllian, should he, as was not improbable from his manner of life, die without legitimate children. In that case Althea might possess the third of the very considerable landed property, which being entailed on the heirs of his father, he could not alienate; and though she herself scarcely recollected that such a man as this relation of hers existed, Lady Dacres, who had received the hint from Mohun, failed not occasionally to make enquiries after him: and the reports she had lately collected, greatly helped to reconcile her to the present abode of Althea at her house, and even to the idea of her adding another member to the family during their intended abode at Margate — though even this plan had not efficacy enough to take from the manner of Lady Dacres, towards her daughter-in-law, that ungracious and repulsive coldness which always made Althea comfortless and uneasy in her presence; a manner, which now that it was contrasted by the ingenuous simplicity and unaffected warmth of Lucy Marchmont, seemed to become more and more insupportable. In quitting the apartment of her step-mother after the next interview on the evening of the day of visiting Fulham, she had almost determined to leave her house at whatever risk of incurring blame for imprudence, or even of throwing herself, unsolicited, into a family, to the principal of which she was still a stranger.

On cooler reflection, however, the good sense and propriety of mind that Althea in a superior degree possessed, operated to deter her from any proceeding that might call her correctness of character in question, or seem to indicate the slightest failure of respect to the memory of her father. She saw from the late conduct of Lady Dacres, that her fears of additional expence were for some reason or other less prevalent. — She had even named herself her intention of removing her family to Margate, adding a formal proposal for Althea to accompany them; and the governess seemed to have had orders gradually to unsay all she had said before on this subject: yet still there was a style of treating her, which she now found more difficult than ever submit to. After mature deliberation, therefore, Althea determined to practise in this instance what she had been early taught — and to sacrifice to prudence, and to the opinion of the world, her own wishes, which led her to become an inmate with the female part of the Marchmont family, however they might quit the rank of life they had formerly filled.

This sacrifice of inclination to duty had the greater merit, as ever since Althea had seen Lucy Marchmont she had indulged herself in reflecting with pleasure on the power she possessed of assisting in the respectable industry to which Mrs. Marchmont and her daughters had devoted themselves. The habits she had been accustomed to in early life had been such as took from the ideas of confinement, and constant occupation, all their unpleasant circumstances; and her skill as a milliner, little as it had lately been called into practice, was by no means inconsiderable. The passion of Mrs. Trevyllian for plants had taught her niece, without the assistance of a master, to delineate them*: by copying attentively the best botanical plates, and afterwards drawing with minute exactness from nature itself, Althea had in this art acquired unusual perfection. — But during her residence at Eastwoodleigh, having no longer her maternal friend to gratify, as there were no vegetable novelties to copy, and she had already exhausted all the printed collection of her aunt, she had amused herself with another species of drawing, which she imagined might now be applied to ornamental works for sale, and create for her unfortunate friends another branch of their little trade.

On these projects, which seemed to originate almost solely in her friendship for Lucy Marchmont, but which were, perhaps,

"Still but lurking love at last,"

Althea had dwelt till she became so fond of them, that it was only the joint effort of reason and virtue that could induce her even to postpone them, to accompany Lady Dacres to Margate (should she go thither), and act afterwards as the circumstances of her behaviour and the situation of the Marchmonts might determine. It was not, however, without the most painful anxiety that Althea awaited the answer which Lucy expected from her mother. It came — but accompanied by such a packet from Marchmont himself to his sister, as for a while suspended every idea but of him; of the dangers he had incurred, and was still liable to; and the cruel apprehensions it brought with it, that she might never see him more. The following were the contents of his

---

* Any occupation of this kind has lately been called by an Author, whose Dramas are more numerous than his Novels—"libelling Nature!"

letter to Lucy — it was without name or date; and from the different colours of the ink, and the manner of the writing, it had evidently been done by snatches and starts, as the pressure of circumstances allowed.

LETTER.

"So strange, my Lucy, have been the scenes I have passed through, I look back to them with a mind so much bewildered by their rapidity and singularity, as to be almost unable to trace their progress distinctly, even if the situation I am in now would allow me to send you my eventful history. Ah! how much pain has (I hope) been saved to my poor mother by her not knowing whither her exile was gone! for, had my being at Paris been certain, what apprehensions would not the accounts you have seen in the public prints (accounts too well authenticated) have given to her, you my Lucy, and the other dear girls! There, however, I have been; and it is not at a great distance from that scene of phrensy and of horrors that I now write to you: but I am safe, and shall soon be on my way southward.

"A Swiss servant travelling with an Englishman who has with great difficulty procured a protection by which he can safely return, or at least which encourages him to attempt it, has promised to put this into the post-office at the first town he reaches in England."

"'If Englishmen then can obtain passports, why does my brother remain in dangers and horrors?'

"Such is the question my Lucy seems to ask. But (besides that I arrived here at a moment when I was compelled to pass for a man of another nation, and to assign very different causes for my coming, which at the present moment I cannot explain) wherefore should I return to my country? — To be a burden to those I love? — to make their little less? — and to embitter their hours by fears for my personal safety, which at this distance they cannot feel? Even the fear of a prison, in another division of the globe, from which I have escaped, when many others have been confined in it, is infinitely less terrible to my imagination than confinement in my own.

"'In great oppressions,' says Lord Bacon, 'the same things that provoke the patience, also break the courage.'

"I am no complainer, my Lucy; but I own that, in regard to the pains and penalties which wait on poverty in my native land, I am a coward — and whence arises this? Because I was brought up to think so highly of the government under which I was born, that I believed it faultless, incapable of losing its spirit of justice, and impossible to be amended: yet at the age when I am most susceptible of pain and pleasure, when I trust my mind is unadulterated by systems, and my heart untainted by either vice or prejudice —I find myself, by the abuse of those very laws I so highly venerated, condemned to become an exile from my country, or to add, in the very prime of my youth, another unhappy victim to the numbers condemned to linger out their years in the squalid misery of legal confinement.

"I have been suddenly broken in upon, and compelled, though rather on account of others than on my own, to remove; and my Swiss acquaintance has been obliged to disappear. There is no describing the strange and fluctuating state of every thing here — at least till an interval of calm shall suffer the mind to survey the succession of events with more coolness and precision. Let me turn from them now to what yet makes my own country dear to me. Ah! why even there must I implore the assistance of that *sanguine disposition* that ought not to forsake us at three-and-twenty? Why must *I try to* believe that the dear group are well? and that I see in my mind's eye my mother looking less like a fine marble statue than she did when, struggling to argue down her acute sensibility, she gave me, with pale lips and eyes incapable of weeping, her farewell blessing, bidding me for her sake preserve my liberty, and be careful of my life! It is now many months since, and very strange have been the scenes I have witnessed — my heart has been severely torn. Driven by private calamity from England to witness more extended misery here, where I had been used to hear the voice of joy, and to see only the most thoughtless gaiety — continually involved in circumstances the most extraordinary, and living in a course of deception, to which not even self-preservation would *reconcile* me if it were not necessary to secure my safety, that I may live for my family, or if it were injurious to any human being here, I sometimes think myself in the delirium of a fever, and sometimes I feel, as I see every body else do, in that kind of astonishment that has the effect of giving a temporary palsy to the mind.

"We cease, even where it seems safe, to communicate remarks to each other; but every one looks on his neighbour, where he yet happens to have one, silently awaiting what is to happen next.

The beginning of August.

"I renew my letter, which I have kept by me many days. I am now removed farther from the crater of the volcano. However, though I have lost the opportunity that seemed to be offered me, I will continue to write. — One day or other, if not immediately, it may reach you. At least I may now have less to apprehend from *les visites domiciliaires,* which, where I have lately been, were likely to involve those in some unpleasant difficulties, on whom papers were found that could be even construed into meanings of disapprobation.

"You will hear from other quarters of general events, and can perhaps imagine so much of the scenes of anarchy and wildness, that mine shall be all sketches of the individual. My Lucy will allow me to be an egotist to her. In this confidence then I leave both accounts of, or remarks on, those striking events which have harrowed up the heart, while they have baffled the calculation of the coldest politician, to relate some of my *own feelings* rather than the whole of my adventures.

"At a little cabaret, far from any high road, in that part of France that was formerly the Bourbonnois, I am writing to you, my Lucy. It is now near a fortnight since I have left Paris — in less than another I hope to reach the abode of Lavergnac, of whom I have no certain intelligence. I wish I could convey to a picture of the simple scene before me — it forms a strange contrast to that I have left, here all is tranquil, though it is now no longer gay: — my old landlord looks at me inquisitively, as he presents me with the black bread, in which buck-wheat is often intermixed, but which ripe fruit makes sufficiently palatable. He pours out with a trembling hand (for he is in his eighty-fifth year) the weak wine of the country, and asks if I insist on his drinking with me to *Vive la Republique!* —I answer, that I am not a Frenchman, and hold it wrong to concern myself with their politics. — *Comment, Monsieur? Cadidée,* (my old friend is a Gascon) *Monsieu n'est pas Français?* — His grand-children. Jaquette and Louison, and Henri and Phillippe, come in from the village. They relate what they have seen, and deposit the necessaries they have purchased. His old female servant, Monique, is called to put them away, and *Monsieu* escapes to the hill behind the house, where a stream runs through a wild valley — reminding me of the scene in that drama we have so often read together, when we projected how we would act "As You Like It" in the wood which was *once* the scene of our early happiness. Ah! how perpetually before me are those scenes, and still more so others I *have since passed* at Eastwoodleigh! They seize on my imagination as if they were yet present; I forget, for a time, where I am. Then a group of children, from a neighbouring vineyard, pass me at a distance, singing, in their way, patriotic tunes, of the meaning of which they have no idea; or a straggling cow, with a bell round her neck, that has been seeking her food near me, is sought for, by her owner, with all that lively clamour so general among the women of these provinces. I start from my dream, and find myself — ah! how far from happiness, and from *that* country, which, step-mother as surely it has proved to me, I still consider as mine!

"But it is not only in this solitary and remote place, inhabited only by peasants, that I have had leisure to indulge all that gloomy retrospection which a continual course of painful events has for some time rendered habitual to me. I had determined to leave Paris, less on account of the personal danger which menaced the English of every description, than because my very soul was sick of the wild assemblage of ideotism and phrensy which I every day saw; and was eager, at all events, to quit people whose folly called for my contempt, while their ferocity excited my abhorrence.

"The plan of my journey (with the intended arrangement of which it is not necessary to trouble you) I had concerted some days before with a French friend, whom I believed to be a very good judge of the state of the country; and having settled every thing at my lodgings, I left the town on foot, and walked to Versailles, where I was to find a person in the park at night-fall who was to be my companion a part of the way.

"By the time I reached the spot where we had appointed to find each other, it was four o'clock in the evening. A heavy gloom hung over every object, and the excessive heat seemed to have had already the effect of autumnal winds on the trees; for the leaves were in many places faded, and slowly fell on my melancholy path.

"I waited in vain for my friend. It was already past the hour when he assured me he would be ready, and I was sure I had not mistaken the place. Another and another hour wore away — the gloom increased around me — the usual noises of a town, though Versailles is now indeed more than half-deserted, became fainter and fainter. It seemed certain that my friend had been prevented. Perhaps he was arrested and imprisoned. I became so uneasy, that I should have sought him at his abode, about a half-mile from that part of the park where we had agreed to meet; but I considered that, if any thing like what I feared had happened, I should endanger my own safety without being at all enabled to contribute to his. Sometimes I determined to return to Paris; but there I was less likely to know what had been his destiny.

I had now for two hours vainly expected him; and I no longer believed myself safe where I was, yet was uncertain whither to go, and indeed almost indifferent. The despondence that crept upon me half annihilated my faculties; but I thought of all I had dear to me in England, and became ashamed of indulging it. You know, my Lucy, that I have tried very earnestly to acquire a certain degree of fortitude, with less success, perhaps, than would have been mine if I had not been vulnerable on the side of beings for whose sake only I wish to live.

It is but a gloomy kind of resignation that we learn from comparing our lot with the fate of others; and never, I own, did it contribute much to reconcile me to my wayward destiny. — 'Why should you complain?' have some of those sage friends often said to me, who, like Sir Peter Teazle, never in their lives refused me *their advice*. 'Why should you complain? Are not Mr. Such-a-one, and Captain Such-a-one, nay. Sir John, and Lord***, as much under pecuniary difficulties as you are? — Possibly they may, my good Sirs; but those considerations do not enable me at all the better to endure the evils that surround me. I am very sorry for *them*, but quite as sorry for myself, as if I saw *them* enjoying the highest prosperity. — 'But, my dear Sir,' cry my consolers, 'they bear their misfortunes lightly, and even gaily — and yet they brought them all upon themselves.' — There, indeed, have I replied, I have the advantage of them.

"Thus, my dearest Lucy, if I could have found at this moment any consolation in comparison, the poor wandering individual, alone in a foreign and an hostile country, might have found objects of compassion, in reflecting on the fate of the late possessors of the immense pile I saw before me; and I might have said, The exile, once the owner and heir of Eastwoodleigh, is less wretched than the surviving owners of Versailles!

"Instead, however, of long indulging these or any other speculations, it was more to the purpose to consider what was to be done. My resolutions on this head were quickened by the sudden appearance of a man, who asked me, abruptly enough, if I did not wait there for Citoyen D'Albiac, which was the name my friend was known by. I answered, with some hesitation, that I did. The man then put into my hand a short note, which I with difficulty read. He conjured me to hasten to him at Paris; adding only, that he could not then assign his reasons for breaking his appointment, or for the request he made, but that much depended on his seeing me immediately at the place

whither the bearer of his note would conduct me. I agreed to go without hesitation, though I drew no favourable augury from the style of
D'Albiac's note, or the manner of my companion, which was hurried,
incoherent, and confused. Anxiety for my friend was not unmingled
with some suspicions in regard to my own security; but something was
to be risqued, and I followed my conductor into one of those vehicles
for the accommodation of chance passengers which pass at almost all
hours between Paris and Versailles.

"We got out near the Pont Royal; and my guide, who had hardly
spoken on the way, because there were other people in the cabriolet,
now desired me to follow him. There was an unusual bustle in the
streets; and on our reaching the Place Louis Quinze (the scene of so
much calamity under its new name) we saw the people all running
towards the Thuilleries. Of the few I addressed, who would give themselves time to answer any question — of what is the matter? each gave
me a different, and some very absurd and impossible reasons, as the
cause of the crowd they were so eagerly hastening to increase. It was
fortunate for me that none of them seemed to have the least suspicion
of my being an Englishman.

"On advancing farther, the numbers increased, and I lost my conductor. — Les gens d'armes on horseback, and parties of armed cit-
izens, were attempting to disperse the people, and to prevent them
from pressing into the garden of the Thuilleries. Some severe *coups de
sabre* fell among them as I passed, being carried, by the press, across
le Pont Tournant. When I found myself in the gardens, I looked again
around me for the man who was to carry me where D'Albiac expected
me; but I could neither see him, nor indeed distinguish any longer the
faces of the hurrying crowds, who either ran or were driven past me by
the soldiers: but, for whatever reason, the *Terras des Feuillans* seemed to
be their *point de ralliement;* while my only purpose was, to make my way
through the upper gate, and from thence to endeavour to gain some
intelligence of D'Albiac among some of' his former connections.

"But from what I had by this time collected from the flying
crowd, I found that several persons had been imprisoned, and there
was an order to arrest all the English. I could now hardly doubt but
the D'Albiac, whom I believed to have been some time among the
suspected, was one of those who were confined; and I thought that
he had sent for me to give me notice of my danger before his own
was so apparent.

"While, doubting what to do, I concealed myself amidst the darkest shade of the trees, I found the shouts of the people and the menaces of the soldiers suddenly cease. A storm threatening, though it did not fall, had helped the endeavours of the armed parties thus suddenly to clear the gardens. The orator, mounted on a stool, who had been propounding political axioms to the crowd, was gone, with all his audience. But from whatever cause his eloquence had been so peremptorily silenced, it was highly probable that whoever was now found attempting to quit this place would undergo a strict interrogatory; and once more I felt myself guilty of having an English countenance, which disdained always to befriend me as effectually as my tongue. However, I went towards the *Pont Tournant* once more: but the guard was mounted there; and by their quick and fierce *"Qui va là?"* and *"Point d'entrée, Messieurs!"* which I heard, I was soon convinced that for me there was *"point de sortie"* without great hazard. This certainty determined me to remain where I was. I thought I might easily pass unobserved among the first crowds that should enter in the morning, and then gain some intelligence of D'Albiac. My clothes were dark, the trees large, and the gloomy evening sunk so entirely into night, that I was no longer in any apprehension of being observed.

"The murmur of the streets was the only noise I heard — cries of *'La séance du Soir,'* or, *'Des Evénemens nouveaux,'* somewhat louder than the rest: even these, by degrees, died away, and the hum became fainter and fainter, till I heard nothing but the hoarse and sullen voices of the sentinels round the Thuilleries, answered by those at the Louvre, and the word going solemnly round from post to post. If heavy clouds were for a little broken away, I saw a few faint stars, as they appeared from time to time, and were lost among the black and billowy vapours; and added to the hideous gloom of all around me were sensations of uncertainty, more uneasy than actual fear of some visible danger. I left my concealment, and walked up towards the front of the palace. All was desolate, silent, dreary — and the idea of what it *had* been contrasted strongly with what it was!

"I had been reading, a few days before, a pompous account of these gardens, and of the Chateau such as it was in the time of Louis the Fourteenth. One of the avenues was then called L'Allée des Soupirs. I turned to that which I imagined had, at such a period, been the haunt of happy lovers. Alas! it might still be called L'Allée des Soupirs — but from causes how different!

I have written so much, my Lucy, of my reflections, that I must pass lightly over facts, or the little paper I have here will fail me. Imagine me then, in despite of my English visage, escaping unnoticed, with the first influx of people, into the garden of the Thuilleries, and my concern to find that all my fears of the detention of D'Albiac were but too true. Imagine the necessity there was for my immediate departure, weary as I found myself, for I knew I was in the most imminent danger of arrest. The barriers were shut, but I found means to get through them; and with the passport I had procured the day before, in pursuance of my friend's plan, I set forward, and walked about four leagues; when being quite exhausted, and believing myself out of any immediate danger, I took some repose at a small inn, frequented, like this, only by the lower ranks of people. The quiet I found here, and indeed a slight indisposition from the extreme heat, induced me to prolong my stay: and there I met with the Swiss servant, by whom I thought I could have forwarded my letter; but I was soon taught how precarious was any reliance of that sort. My acquaintance suddenly disappeared, without coming for my letter, and I had reason to believe, that it would be prudent to remove to a greater distance from Paris, which I forthwith set about.

"Since that, nothing worth noticing has befallen your itinerant brother; but, with redoubled eagerness, his soul thirsts for news from England. — Ah! my Lucy, besides that dear, dear group, is there a kind, a benevolent heart interested in the destiny of Marchmont? I dare not trust myself on the subject, and now hastily I must bid you adieu! — for an occasion offers of sending my letter without any hazard to myself, or to him who conveys is. — Let it assure you, my ever-loved Lucy, of my safety, and of the tender attachment of

> Your
>
> E—A—M—.

"If I am not greatly deceived, I shall have better opportunities soon of writing to you, and, I hope, news of poor Lavergnac that will be acceptable to you. — Heaven preserve you all!"

In breathless agitation, Althea hurried over this letter. Hardly had she finished it, when Lady Dacres sent to beg she might speak with her; and trembling, as if she believed what she had been reading could be guessed at, she locked it up, and unwillingly went down to the drawing-room.

CHAP. IX.

Envy and avarice counteract each other.

WHEN ALTHEA ENTERED the room where Lady Dacres and her family were assembled in their usual formal circle, she found the lady speaking to her auditors on the future projects for passing all that remained of what is generally called summer. And turning in her cold and solemn way to Althea, she said,

"You will not be surprised, Miss Dacres, at my having changed my mind as to the place I intended going to. In *my* unhappy situation it is difficult to decide. — Alas! I shall carry with me the cause of sadness wherever I go!"

Lady Dacres could not weep, but she did her best to give what she said the same effect as if it had been accompanied by tears. The governess and the young ladies re-echoed back the deep sigh with which the sentence ended. — A dead pause ensued, for Althea had nothing to reply. Lady Dacres slowly proceeded:

"I find myself quite unequal to the sort of bustle which one must be subjected to in a public place — yet I cannot indeed go to Capelstoke. Heaven only knows whether I shall ever prevail on myself to revisit that once favourite spot!"

Another deep sigh and another long silence again intervened, during which Althea had time to guess whither all this prelude tended; and it was not difficult to see that the scheme of getting her away, which for some reason or other had been suspended, was again resumed. Nothing could be more agreeable to her present views, and her heart beat quick left she should be mistaken as to her mother-in-law's meaning. Another sentence, however, served to put her out of suspense.

"Now," continued she, "the thing is this — I have had a letter from my dear friend Mrs. Fordham — an unhappy widow like myself, who about a year before I lost the best of men followed good Mr. Fordham

to the grave! and has never recovered herself since, poor woman! —
for she is of a most tender and affectionate disposition. God knows
how melancholy a visit it will be to me, and how unwilling I am to take
any young persons into a house, which to be sure must be very bad,
and quite depressing to *their* spirits; though, as to my own, it is quite
that sort of place fit for unhappy *me!* My good and kind friend indeed
wished me to take Caroline with me, as her house, though small, could
accommodate us two; and I shall of servants only have Midgely and
Richard; for as to my horses I shall send them to Capelstoke. — Now
the difficulty is..."

Here an uncertainty how she should best word what she had to say
gave Althea an opportunity of interposing:

"If your Ladyship has any difficulty as to how/shall dispose of
myself, I beg leave immediately to remove it. I wish very much to visit
the family of.."

A consciousness of her partiality for Marchmont, and that it was
of his family she was speaking, made her blush and hesitate. Lady Dacres looked at her, but it was merely with earnestness occasioned by
fluctuating avarice: for at that moment, on hearing she had a friend to
whom she wished to go, a debate arose, whether it would not be more
politic to suffer her daughter-in-law to remain, at whatever inconvenience, in her own house. While she deliberated, Althea made two or
three attempts to speak; but she dreaded lest Lady Dacres should enquire with whom she meant to reside, and that, being compelled to
name the Marchmonts, she should receive a prohibition against going
to them. Lady Dacres, however, who could not determine to invite her
heartily to Capelstoke, said,

"Now, as I was going to say, the difficulty is, that to be sure, Miss
Dacres, Capelstoke can in no way be agreeable to you: it is extremely
dull at all times; and now that the former dear master of it is gone,
and my son not in England, to be sure every thing must wear a most
gloomy aspect; and I was thinking how, unless indeed it could be *made*
any ways agreeable to you..."

"I have no apprehension of solitude, Madam," interrupted Althea.
"Indeed," added she, smiling, "after having so long lived at Eastwoodleigh, an inhabited house like Capelstoke, were it not for those recollections your Ladyship speaks of, would be comparatively cheerful."

Lady Dacres made the sort of motion with her lips and eyes,
which those who were accustomed to her knew was a certain symp-

tom of her being displeased. Althea well understood it; and sorry that any thing she had said might be interpreted into a reflection on her step-mother's former conduct, she would have recalled, or palliated her unlucky speech: but it was too late. So great had always been the dislike which lay lurking in the mind of this malignant woman, that a trifle, however unintended or immaterial, was always enough to raise it into something like aversion.

Her naturally unpleasing countenance now scowled upon Althea, with an expression that made her tremble: then, as if checking herself by a painful effort, she screwed her face into something that resembled sullenly stifled revenge; while tossing up her head, and speaking through her nose, she said

"Unhappily, Miss Dacres, Sir Audley found, as indeed has since been but too evident, the case..."

"Dear Lady Dacres," said Althea, dreading whither her sudden ill-humour would carry her, "I beg your pardon, if any thing I have inadvertently said has been improper. I had not the smallest intention of recalling past events —I merely meant to say, that in consequence of my being long, indeed for the greatest part of my life, accustomed to it, I have no dread of seclusion of any kind; and that, whatever may be my own wishes, if my accompanying to Capelstoke the younger part of your Ladyship's family would be of any use..."

She was proceeding, when the governess, who saw by the manner of the lady of the house how far she might go, interrupted Althea.

"Of use, Ma'am? I'm sure my Lady will not do me so little justice as to believe I shall want *any body's* assistance in the care of my sweet young charges, while her Ladyship's distressed state of spirits compels her to be away from them. — No, indeed ... if my Lady thinks, as I am sure I hope she does, that she may rely on..."

Althea now believing this was a concerted plan to quarrel with and get rid of her, and rather rejoicing at than regretting a circumstance which would, she hoped, release her at once to pursue her plan of residing with Mrs. Marchmont; interrupted in her turn the eloquent speaker, and said in a resolute though calm way to Lady Dacres,

"It is not, Madam, difficult for me to understand the meaning of all this. I am afraid I have long been thought a burden to your Ladyship; I am sure I am considered as such now. — It is time, therefore, to relieve you. Be assured. Madam, that in quitting your house I leave it with my best wishes for you and your children ... and shall consider it as one of the happiest circumstances of my life, if at any future time I may be allowed to testify to them my friendship and regard."

Then, fearful that she could trust her voice no longer, Althea hurried to her own room — but when she arrived there the tumult of her mind overcame her, and she burst into tears. The point was now she thought decided, and decided just as she had wished; so far as that she was left at liberty to go unquestioned whithersoever she would. Yet the rude unfeelingness of Lady Dacres, which her imagination already exaggerated, shocked and mortified her. Nor was that alone a source of disquiet; for, when able to think with more calmness, she recollected that she was thus dismissed from present protection, without being sure she should find another, for whether Mrs. Marchmont would receive her was extremely uncertain. Her former coldness, the distance she had kept by withdrawing continually from her advances, and even the *manner* of Lucy Marchmont when she spoke of her mother, all immediately returned to the memory of Althea, serving to torment her with apprehensions that the asylum she so anxiously desired to find would be shut against her.

Determined, however, to remove from the house of Lady Dacres, in which she thought the very dependents commissioned to insult her, she determined, if Mrs. Marchmont should have any reasons for not receiving her, to find some place in the country, where she might board in the entire seclusion, which, if she could not associate with the Marchmont family, was her sole wish.

Of Lady Dacres she did not expect to hear again — and unpleasant as had been many situations of her former life, she thought her present state the most comfortless she had yet experienced; for she fancied that even the trifling services of the domestics were performed with reluctance, and every hour her residence became more uneasy to her. The mistress of it was preparing for her removal — the servants were running about all day on commissions, and scarcely had time to bring into a small dressing-room Althea's breakfast and dinner; for now the message of the morning that used to salute her on the first weeks of her arrival was again resorted to; and every day it was formally announced, with *her Ladyship's compliments, that her Ladyship was too unwell to dine in company.* — To which Althea as constantly answered, that "she was very sorry, and begged leave to dine in the dressing-room."

So passed three or four days, during which she had copied, and returned to Lucy her brother's letter — and waited in great perturbation of mind for that which was to be expected from Margate. On the last of these days she learned from the servants that the journey of Lady Dacres's family to Capelstoke was fixed for the next, and that she herself and her eldest daughter were to remain only another day after them. Something, therefore, must be determined upon immediately on the part of Althea, and the silence of Lucy Marchmont became every moment more distressing.

At length one of the servants announced "a young lady" and Althea saw her beloved Lucy enter the room. Pleasure lightened up her animated countenance, and in the half-breathless agitation of joy she said— "My dear Miss Dacres, I am the happiest creature in the world. We have news of my brother from Toulon, which is, you know, in possession of the English — he is well, and has been of the greatest service to the poor old Baron. Neither of them is in danger any longer. I know not when I have received so cheerful a letter from my mother as that in which she related to me these tidings, and in which Amelia enclosed me part of Armyn's letter — for, it to England by a private hand, and it contained only good news, it was delivered immediately to my mother. — My dearest Miss Dacres, do not imagine that, amidst the very unusual happiness that this intelligence has conferred on us, we are capable of forgetting, for a moment, the kind, the generous, the delightful proposal which you ordered me to make to my mother."

Althea, happy even beyond what she dared to avow, at the safety of Marchmont, waited in eager and breathless expectation for his mother's answer, whose consent to her proposal was now more necessary than ever. Lucy was as much agitated, and was obliged to take time, to sit down and compose herself a moment, before, drawing her mother's letter from her pocket, she read to Althea the part that related to her.

LETTER.

"It would be difficult for me, my Lucy, to express to you how much the generous and unexpected proposal of Miss Dacres delights and distresses me. That you are charmed with her, I can easily believe; for in my mind, (which cannot have been prejudiced by personal beauty, since I never saw her) her character excites a sensation totally unlike what I ever felt for any other person. I cannot, however, describe this impression. You know, where my heart is deeply concerned I do not readily command either my pen or my words.

"Alas! my dear girl, has this admirable young woman well considered what she offers, when she thinks of becoming an inmate of our house, circumstanced as we now are? Has she weighed the difference between the easy affluence in which she has hitherto lived, and the straitened circumstances with which I and my poor girls must struggle? Considering her only as a lodger, ought Miss Dacres to lodge in a shop? As a friend, ought she to associate with those who are about to keep one?

"She has greatness of mind enough to consider us rather as what we were, than as what we are — to believe that by an exertion made necessary by no fault of our own we are not degraded — But, will the world think so? — And at her age, has Miss Dacres, who ought from birth, from accomplishments, from personal perfections, to have that world at her feet, will she be content to brave its opinion? —I know how much so exalted a mind as hers is capable of sacrificing to friendship— but on her friendship what claims have we? — people hardly known to her longer than yesterday, unless it be by name. Why should she descend from, her station for us? I cannot bear that, misled by the enthusiasm of youthful generosity, she should put herself into a situation she may afterwards repent. — Think not because I say this, that I am too proud to receive from such hands an obligation; for an obligation I know she intends it to be, and an obligation I should assuredly consider it. No, my Lucy: amidst all the severe mortifications I have suffered, amidst all my efforts to submit to the sad difference of fortune, of which so many have made me feel all the bitterness, I have never shrunk from the kindness of the truly generous. Why must I add, that my submission in this respect to receive favours has not been put to many proofs? — Ah, my child! those who are, like you, setting out in life, even under the inauspicious influence of family depression, can yet form no idea of the cruel, the accumulated convictions of the selfishness and unfeelingness of the world that *I* have seen, since the hour when your dear father's pecuniary circumstances began to decline. Wonder not, therefore, that the unexampled instance of Miss Dacres's benevolent wishes to become a resident in my family should excite my surprise, as well as my admiration and gratitude.

If, after she has duly reflected on the great difference she must find between such a table, such a manner of living as we have adopted, and that to which she must always have been accustomed; if she can voluntarily descend from the conveniencies of Lady Dacres's establishment,

to two maids, or rather one and a girl — to reside with a family struggling with, I trust, unmerited adversity — oh! greatly indeed will it be in
her power to alleviate the hardships of their fate — less from that pecuniary assistance she so generously offers, useful as it must be, than from
the soothing comfort it will afford me, to think that I am considered as
worthy of a charge so precious; that my Amelia and my Lucy are worthy
of such a friend; and that, in addition to their example, my Millicente will
have before her such an example of all that a young person ought to be.

"Go then, Lucy, to this amiable Miss Dacres — tell her what I say,
and represent our situation exactly as it is; and, if you find her still disposed to make us happy, arrange with her every thing for your immediate journey hither, where I think I shall stay till my son returns to
England. The season is now so far advanced; that I know not whether
our project can be carried into execution with any prospect of success.
My timidity, the repulses I have met with, the superior advantages of
competitors regularly settled in the business, and my renewed doubts of
Marchmont's cheerful acquiescence, have lately concurred to shake my
resolution. I know that the irresolute do nothing well — but how can I
be sanguine? — How indeed can I urge my mind to any steady exertion?
There are times when it sinks into absolute imbecility, when I sit whole
days unoccupied, unfitted for occupation, and, by dwelling too much on
the past, embitter the present, and have no longer any courage to look
steadily towards the future. My poor Amelia partakes but too much of
my languor — we want your animating presence, my Lucy, and the innocent cheerfulness of my little Milly. If, added to these, you can bring to
us the sense and polished sweetness of your incomparable friend, I shall
surely regain some portion of tranquillity; for Armyn is safe. He has, in
prospect, advantages which, though he does not explain them, promise
much, I am sure, for his sanguine manner of speaking of them. Perhaps
the heavy tide of calamity, that has so long run against us, is turning —I
may yet see my children happy, and in peace rejoin their father."

The voice of Lucy Marchmont trembled as she concluded this part
of her mother's letter: yet it contained, in general, nothing but what
gave pleasure to her and to her friend, who was not only delighted and
surprised to find Mrs. Marchmont so different from the idea she had
formed of her, but, as she believed, all her difficulties removed, and
herself secure of being joyfully received as a resident in their house,
by the persons whom she most desired to consider as her friends —

whose ideas and manners seemed most accordant to her own.

Very little time, however, remained for the two young friends to consult on the journey they were equally eager to undertake; for Lucy Marchmont was to return to Fulham, as she had come from thence in a stage. It was the first time in her life that she had never been in such a conveyance alone; and though naturally fearless, and never indulging those ridiculous personal apprehensions which the remarkably plain are much more apt to express than the young and handsome, neither she nor Althea could think without some uneasiness of her returning in a stage at a late hour.

Instead, therefore, of allowing themselves to discuss those future plans, which now seemed so flattering to them both, they hastened to agree on that which was immediately necessary. Althea, who had no doubt but that it was perfectly indifferent to Lady Dacres whither she went provided she did go, concluded to send her Ladyship a note early on the following morning to name her intentions, and request her to pay whatever might become due to her to Mr. Booth, a gentleman in London (whom Lucy Marchmont had named as her mother's friend, for Althea herself knew nobody); and that as her clothes, most of which, on account of her mourning, she had never unpacked, would be soon ready, she would send them off for the Margate packet early, and be herself ready at two o'clock in a post-chaise to fetch the two Miss Marchmonts from the house of Mr. Booth, whither they would go by an early stage; and from thence they were to proceed together on their way to Margate, intending to sleep one night on the road.

This arrangement made, Lucy Marchmont rose to depart: but it was already dusk; and Althea could not bear to think of her walking to alone to Piccadilly, where she was to find the stage. She had so little authority in the house of Lady Dacres, that she could not even direct a footman to follow her — but it occurred to her to order a hackney-coach, for which she sent the maid who usually waited in her room. But still not satisfied for the safety of a lovely girl, whom she thought too young and pretty not to be liable to many unpleasant adventures, she determined to go with her herself. Together then they went out, and fortunately reached the stand a moment before the Fulham stage was to set off. Althea found there were only women in it, and saw her fair friend depart without any fear, and with a gay heart, in expectation of their meeting the next day to part no more.

Althea, happier than she had ever been since the death of her aunt, returned in the hack to Grosvenor-street, and no sooner re-entered her own room, than she sat down to write to Lady Dacres the note she had mediated; a task which was by no means so easy as she had imagined. Doubts now arose, whether, if she named the Marchmont family as that with which she meant to fix her residence, Lady Dacres, whose unaccountable aversion to them she well knew, might so easily acquiesce as she had reason to believe she would, in regard to almost any other persons with whom she might choose to place herself. Yet to give false name, to misrepresent her intention, was what she could not bring herself to do; so remote from her disposition and her principles was every species of deceit.

A middle way, however, seemed to offer itself; and though even to temporise was unpleasant to her, Althea thought that the little consideration shewn to her by Lady Dacres, demanded less candour, on her part, than she ought and was willing to shew towards every being who either really felt, or thought it worth while to testify, any interest in her affairs or any solicitude for her welfare. — In pursuance of this idea, she wrote as follows:

"Madam,

"After the intimation received from your Ladyship, and my knowledge of the preparations that are making for your family's immediate removal, I imagine it will be agreeable to your Ladyship to know, that I shall not intrude upon you in Grosvenor-street, or at any other of your residences, having settled to go to the house of a friend, who is so good as to receive me as the companion of her daughters; but as the circumstances of the family are not such as can authorise my availing myself of their friendship to add to their expence, I trust your Ladyship will have the goodness to arrange the little money matters I have, in such a way as may enable me to pay half-yearly for my board during my stay. I beg leave at the same time to assure you, Madam, that should it at any future period be in my power to render to my brothers and sisters any service, or to your Ladyship any satisfaction, I shall have great pleasure in returning to your house, in every manner to testify how much I desire to convince your Ladyship of the respect and good wishes of,

Madam,

Your most obedient

humble servant,

ALTHEA DACRES.

Grosvenor-Street,
   Sept. 5th."

This letter was given to the house-maid, who waited generally in her chamber, with orders to send it by Lady Dacres's woman as soon as her Lady arose in the morning.

Though this was never very soon, Althea was unable to remain in bed after a very early hour. Her packing served to occupy some part of this tedious interval: the trunks being ready, she directed them, and, ordering a porter, sent them to the packet, writing on them, "To be left at the Warehouse at Margate till called for." — They had not long been dispatched, before the maid brought her the following letter:

"Madam,

"I am, I must own, rather surprised at your note, and could have wished you had informed me of the name of the persons you are a-going to put yourself under the care of. I can't but say I think it might have been more proper if you had thought fit to consult me thereon; but I dare to say it is no intention of yesterday, but intended some time. At the same time I am free to say, I think your conduct in my house might have been more prudently regulated. Indeed it is not very discreet to receive visits from one hardly knows who, and to go in hackney-coaches at a late hour of the evening. — In regard to what you mention farther, I must observe to you, Miss, Althea, that if it is not agreeable to you to remain yourself under my care, the will of my dear Sir Audley has entrusted me with your small fortune, at least till such time as you are of age; wherefore I hold it a point of duty to prevent your placing *that* at least in improper hands. If you have any doubts of my right to do this, you will give me leave to refer you to the other executor, Mr. Mohun, who doubtless will, as a lawyer, satisfy you of the propriety of this. In regard to the little sum of money left you by your aunt, I have nothing to say to that: but, though you have little right to expect advice from me, and I dare to say will not follow it, you will excuse my taking this opportunity to warn you against the artfulness of that family of the Marchmonts that you are going to; for they are entirely beggars, and only intend to make a prey of you. It is a pity but what you could have made your mind up, to remain in the care your good father left you in. However, I have done my duty, and wash my hands of the affair. Certainly nobody can blame me, if you choose to throw yourself away, and let yourself down. I am truly sorry, for the sake of those that you belonged to, and, on their account, sincerely wish you may not repent what you are a-going to do, when it will be too late. — I am so much indisposed, that it is very inconvenient to me to be obliged to write such long letters. — However,

I am, Madam, still
Your well-wisher and servant,
MARY DACRES."

Nothing short of an absolute prohibition to leave the house could have given Althea more concern and astonishment than this letter. That Lady Dacres should know to whom she was going, and judge so hardly of the lovely and innocent Lucy, were equally subjects of wonder. That she should mean, as the letter certainly intimated, to detain the interest of her fortune, save only the part left by her aunt (which did not amount to a thousand pounds), was a source of the acutest concern — for from the interest of that it was impossible for her to make to the family she was going to reside with, such a compensation as would satisfy her own liberal sentiment, or be of that use to them which was, above all other things, her wish.

Struck with this reflection, and extremely distressed and shocked at the reference to Mohun, whose odious name she had hardly heard mentioned before since her father's death, Althea now hesitated as to the immediate execution of the project on which she had set her heart; and endeavoured calmly to consider, whether to resign it, at least for the present, and to condemn herself to endure life at Capelstoke, rather than irritate the malignant and vindictive woman in whose power she must yet remain two years, might not be most conducive to her own ease, and even to the welfare of' the friends for whom she was so anxious. But, on the other hand, she considered that, by yielding thus to the capricious tyranny of her step-mother, who first appeared desirous of dismissing her, and then seemed to wish her stay only to torment her, she was in fact acknowledging her power not only over her fortune but her person. The mention of the hateful Mohun, who had already been the cause of so much uneasiness, alarmed and terrified her. She thought it possible that there was a design to expose her to pecuniary inconveniences, to mortify and oppress her, that the discomforts she underwent might make the affluence and splendour he could offer her more readily embraced. Yet, if such were the plan, it was strange that Mohun had never once appeared, and that his name, unless by accident, had not been mentioned in her hearing ever since her residence with Lady Dacres. The mere idea, however, of being under the necessity of holding any converse with him, of being in some measure in his power, filled her with dread and vexation. This possible aggravation of the uneasiness she might experience in being left in the lone solitude of Capelstoke, during the months of autumn too, which would so forcibly recall the scenes of a preceding year — the formal importance and over-bearing impertinence of Mrs. Bentham the governess — and the uninteresting flippancy of her half sisters, girls of eleven and ten years old, who had been instructed not to love her — the sensation of dependance on Lady Dacres, and of being accounted a stranger and a burden in her father's house — all were, in her mind, placed in formidable array; while the other scheme offered nothing but what was attractive to her imagination, and soothing to her feelings.

As Lady Dacres offered her no plan of future life as an alternative to that she opposed — as she had even confessed her difficulties how to dispose of her daughter-in-law, and now so suddenly discovered that the habitation she had chosen was improper, though she proposed no other — every motive of duty seemed to be out of the question, while every motive of comfort and satisfaction urged her to throw herself into the protection of Marchmont's mother. She read once more the part of her letter which Lucy had left with her; she read over that she had copied of Marchmont's; she reflected on the plea-sure of passing her life with people whom she loved so much as she already loved all she knew of his family; and then endeavoured with sanguine hope to believe, that when Lady Dacres saw her determined, she would not think of detaining so small a sum as her yearly income, and would be glad to be quietly released from any trouble about, or any reflections on her treatment of, a person she did not love. With present money she was well provided, having still a great part of what she had possessed at Eastwoodleigh; and fifty guineas she had received since for mourning, of which she had expended very little. This was a sufficient fund for her present personal expences, and for such a compliment as might be useful to her friends on her becoming an inmate of their house. — The debate ended in her writing a cold but calm letter to Lady Dacres, in which she explained her reasons for leaving her; the principal of which were, that her Ladyship herself had seemed to desire it, and that from the engagements she had made, in consequence of having believed so, it was now impossible for her to recede. She added — "I am persuaded your Ladyship will not think it worth while to detain the small interest of my fortune; and I have only to repeat, that whenever I am recalled with kindness I shall return to your protection with pleasure."

Having done this, and left among the servants some tokens of her generosity, she got into a hackney-coach, and soon found herself at the place where Lucy and Milly Marchmont were impatiently waiting for her. From thence a post-chaise conveyed them rapidly on the Kentish road; and Althea, notwithstanding her habits of reasoning and reflecting on every circumstance of her life, almost forgot all her recent uneasiness in the delight of seeing the happiness she bestowed on her companions.

CHAP. X.

Whither thou goest I will go; and where thou lodgest I will lodge.

IF THE JOURNEY was delightful to Althea from happiness possessed and reflected, its close awakened all her sensibility. The meeting of the mother and the daughters, of the eldest sister and the two who now rejoined her, was a scene that drew tears from Althea; but, like those of the immediate actors, they were tears of pleasure. The reception Mrs. Marchmont gave to her visitor was full of dignified gratitude. And so different were the person and manners of Mrs. Marchmont from those which Althea had imagined, that she could never cease wondering at the false ideas she had formed, nor rejoicing that for once the reality was infinitely more interesting than the imaginary semblance.

Mrs. Marchmont, who had been remarkable for an uncommon share of personal beauty, was still more than a fine ruin. It is the privilege of some faces to gain in expression what they lose in bloom. On that of Mrs. Marchmont sorrow seemed to have laid its blighting hand; but the traces were so softened by resignation and reason, that, had it been necessary to personify mildness and fortitude united in one form, she might have sat for the picture. And this expression her countenance seldom lost, unless when her son was in question. So passionately fond was she of him, and so much had she suffered from continual fears for his safety, that, whenever he was named, her feelings became evidently most acute. She at present believed him in safety; and the apparent tranquillity, which was often a mere effort of resolution, was now the effect of that persuasion.

In a few days Althea found herself perfectly at ease with her; the little arrangements of the family were made — and every day she saw more reason to rejoice in having made this choice; for the taste, the temper and manners of the mother and the daughters so exactly coincided with her own, that, having never since the death of Mrs. Trevyllian passed one hour of satisfaction, she seemed suddenly to have regained faculties that had long been repressed. Her charming talents and her charming temper occasionally regained their early brilliancy. Yet there was still much occasion for fortitude; for many trials were threatened to the latter by Lady Dacres, to whom, within a month after her being settled at Margate, she again wrote very respectfully on the subject of her interest money, which would become due in October. Lady Dacres, as if enraged at Althea's having taken the very measure to which she was conscious she had herself driven her, referred her in a very rude letter to her attorney and Mr. Mohun. "She left," she said, "her part of the business to the solicitor employed by her late dear husband, who advised her against paying any thing for a purpose so contrary to his will;" and then, in her usual hypocritical style, added, "You will excuse me, Miss Dacres, if I desire you will please to refer yourself altogether to him; for, to say the truth, my spirits are so much affected by the indiscreet and improper conduct of a person so nearly related to my dear, ever dear Sir Audley, that care for my own health, not for my own sake indeed, but for that of the precious pledges he had left me, demands of me that I decline a correspondence so distressing to my sensibility."

Althea, though already of some experience, had not yet seen the farce of The World played long enough to read without a sudden emotion of indignation this fulsome cant, adopted to colour purposes so unjust and cruel. From her knowledge of Vampyre, and another wretch of the same description, of whom she had occasionally heard anecdotes, she detested the very name of an attorney, and she could not determine, at least till the last moment, to apply to one; still less to address herself on any account to Mr. Mohun.

Althea, on weighing all these circumstances, thought it more necessary than ever to promote the little plan of industry which had been thought of when first she made overtures for residing with the Marchmonts, but which now seemed to languish, and to be only partially executed.

Mrs. Marchmont, notwithstanding her acquired fortitude, and the resolution she seemed to have wrought herself up to, found her firmness recoil before the mortifications to which even the slight essay she had consented to exposed her. During the very height of the season nobody thought much of the intimations that were occasionally given by two or three ladies, lovers of the minor branches of the fine arts, that the Miss Marchmonts, poor things! had some little elegant articles of their own ingenious works, which their situation made it convenient to dispose of. The raffle of the morning, the public breakfast, the ball, or the play, with the necessary attention to changes of dress, and consultations on the most fantastic way of disguising the human form, engrossed every woman, from those of the wastly genteel famully who hired a glass coach for a month, to elegant leaders of fashion, that look down on *them* with as much scorn as on the importations of the stages and hoys.

But when the concourse began a little to decline, as was the case soon after Althea's arrival, it now and then happened that idleness, or curiosity, under the semblance of benevolence, procured to the little repository visits, which, seldom producing any advantage, gave more sensations of humiliation to Mrs. Marchmont than almost any advantage could have repaid her for.

Amelia Marchmont, naturally of a reserved though gentle temper, who had been brought up with the same ideas that from his family prejudices had influenced the conduct and life of her father, could ill endure the contumely that in her opinion was annexed to that necessity which now induced her family to avail themselves of talents acquired for amusement, to contribute to their support. — She therefore timidly, and yet with feelings half indignant, retired from notice when it was unavoidably attracted, as it sometimes was, by those who, without any feeling for the reduced circumstances of the persons to whom they spoke, treated them as they would the tradespeople they commonly dealt with, or sometimes even with less ceremony; at others, mingling in their manner that sort of half kindness which is affected by little minds towards the objects of their charity.

Amelia Marchmont, therefore, after a trial or two never appeared; but Lucy, who had at an earlier period of life learned the necessity there was for combating the pride of family, so importunately uneasy to the poor, who from the quickness of her observation often saw more to pity than envy in the idle and ignorant children of unenjoyed prosperity, and who felt all the conscious superiority of talents and understanding, sometimes was even amused with the applications from which her sister shrunk with disgust. The name of Marchmont was little known in a part of England so remote from the western county where it had so long flourished: and of its historical honours few were aware, and none appeared to consider them. They were looked upon merely as the widow and daughters of an indigent gentleman compelled to descend from their former station in society to procure a subsistence; and of such so many examples had occurred within a few years, that the attraction of novelty was not added to the claims of compassion.

It soon, however, began to be whispered, that associated with his family, and taking a part in their labours, was a baronet's daughter. This circumstance, first hinted by the servants, who found their pride gratified by divulging it, was soon enlarged into a little history, which accumulating anecdotes from every mouth it passed through, at length gave a grave detail of "a young lady, the daughter of a titled man, who was extremely beautiful, would be possessed of a considerable fortune when she came of age, and was very highly accomplished; who had most unaccountably determined to quit her own respectable family, and live with these Marchmonts." — It followed, that some undue arts must have been used on their part to induce a young woman of fashion to adopt so strange a resolution; and the conduct of Mrs. Marchmont and her daughters began to be canvassed with all the malignant impertinence which ignorance, and a desire to find the unfortunate to blame, generate amidst what is called the *sociable* parties of a place of public resort. That the purity of female friendship should have influenced Althea to take such a step, soon began to be considered as extremely improbable; and, on farther enquiry, it was discovered that Mrs. Marchmont had a son. A day or two afterwards it was known, that this on had absconded for debt. The debts were next asserted to have been contracted by his own extravagance; and, in a short time afterwards, Marchmont was transformed into a gamester, who had broken his father's heart — and Althea into an irregular-minded and ungovernable young woman, who had quitted the matronly protection of her father's widow, to associate herself, on the account of young Marchmont, with the fallen fortunes of his designing mother and insinuating sisters.

These reports, or rather romances, were so far from deterring the amiable inventors and propagators of them from visiting the parties, that they raised great curiosity, and it soon became a sort of fashion to call at the house in the expectation of seeing this indiscreet young woman of fashion; and though the curiosity (which Althea was at first far from suspecting) was seldom or never gratified, much continued to be told of her attractions, and to be invented of her motives for the extraordinary sacrifice she was supposed to make.

At length she was one morning desired to go down into the parlour to speak to a lady, who came, as the maid who delivered the message said, in the *sweetest, most genteelest carridge* that ever she seed, with a pair of dappul grey hosses, with long tails tied up in knots! Althea, who was not much dazzled by this descriptions, desired she favour of the Lady's name. It was Mrs. Glaston — and Althea went to receive her old friend, metamorphosed into a finer lady than she appeared even on their first meeting after her marriage.

When the first common forms were over — "Lord! my dear!" said Mrs. Glaston, "you can't think how I was surprised to hear of you here!"

"Were you?" answered Althea. — "Why so?"

"Dear! Why, because you know it is such an old thing. —I told the people that talked to me about it, that I was sure it must be some mistake; but they insisted upon it, it was you — and then you can't think, my dear friend, what odd things they have got into their heads. Why, do you know? they say you are in love with young Marchmont. A likely story indeed! —I told them, says I, to my certain knowledge, that's *quite* impossible; for, says I, *I* ought to know, who was so well acquainted with Miss Dacres formerly; and I'm sure 'tis no such thing. Lord! I dare say she hardly knows the man, says I; and you've no notion, besides, what a grave, formal, half-alive sort of a man he is. I'm sure, says I, I remember well enough when he was a friend of my brother's; he used to be in our house sometimes for a week together; and as to a smart young man, though he is not ugly, yet somehow he is just as stupid as the picture of his great grandfather walked out of its frame. — I mean the picture my brother bought at the sale there at the old cathedral place, when all went to pieces; that great frightful figure, in a ruff and jack boots, enough to fright one into fits, that my brother, from some strange whim, sets such prodigious store by. But as for being gay and amusing one, and talking pretty sort of small talk, like other men of his age, Marchmont has no more notion of it than the picture itself; and therefore I'm sure Miss Dacres, who I don't believe ever saw him twice in her life, is no more in love with him ... than — than ... she would be with the Pope, or any odd old quiz one can name."

Fortunately for Althea; the loquacious lady was so occupied by herself, and had such pleasure in hearing the sound of her own voice, while she contemplated the graceful play of her feathers, as the saw them in an opposite glass, that she had not either at the beginning or close of this harangue looked in the face of the person she was talking to. Twice the blood had risen to the betraying cheeks of Althea; the last time it had hardly receded back to her palpitating heart, when Mrs. Glaston, having no more to add, turned towards her, and, observing something very unusual in her look, hardly had fixed her eyes attentively upon her before she became of a deadly pale.

"Lord! my dear!" cried the thoughless creature, "I hope I have not been telling lies all this while about you. — Bless me! what is the matter? — Why, you don't know young Marchmont, do you? 'Twa'n't upon his account, was it, that you left Lady Dacres, and came here to keep shop with his mother and sisters?"

"Upon *his* account!" faintly articulated Althea. Then making an effort to recover the calm feelings of conscious rectitude, and to recollect of how little consequence were the idle remarks of people for whose opinions she felt so little respect, she forced a smile, and said — "How can you, dear Mrs. Glaston, listen to or bestow another though on, these legends? For Heaven's sake, what have the people who say all this to do with me, or I with them? I came hither because the manners of this family were agreeable to me; I ask not the approbation of strangers, since strangers cannot judge of my motives; I never interfere in *their* concerns; would they could be prevailed upon to allow me the management of my own!"

"Well, but, my dear," cried Mrs. Glaston, returning to the charge, "you know it is quite impossible to stop people's tongues — and to be sure I can't help thinking it strange, you should like Mrs. Marchmont. Lord! I remember, when I was quite a child, I used to go there to stay sometimes with grandmama, and I hated it so! The misses, instead of playing and romping, used to be shewing me books and pictures, and telling stories about them, especially Miss Marchmont the eldest; a prim thing — and as for their mother ..."

"She is one of the best of women," said Althea, who found she could not hear without impatience any reflections on her friends, even from the insignificant tongue of folly. — "She is one of the best of women, and her understanding is as good as her heart."

"I am sure I remember that she was reckoned very proud though," eagerly interrupted Mrs. Glaston — "and that is not, I suppose, counted a sign of great sense, especially where people are so poor."

"Mrs. Marchmont was, for a great while, extremely unhappy," replied Althea; "and it is not easy for mere visiting acquaintance to distinguish between dejection and haughtiness; but I believe there is little use in our discussing, at this time, the opinions of people six or seven years ago, and at two hundred miles distance from hence."

"Perhaps you don't care, neither, for what the people say here at this present time?" said Mrs. Glaston, half spitefully.

"Why, not much, I must confess. — Those who have sense and good nature will not judge hardly of me — and for others who have neither why should I disturb myself?"

"Well, you know best, Miss Dacres. I'm sure I'd no motive myself but friendship in saying any thing at all about it — though, when I came down here, all the world began open-mouthed upon me. But pray," added she, looking significantly, "pray what is become of young Marchmont?"

"What is *become* of him? — He is abroad."

"Lord'"rejoined Mrs. Glaston, "what a number of lies *was* told about him! My brother insisted upon making us believe that he was gone to Ireland as a steward to some man of fortune; but there was people that knew better."

Althea, who imagined this related to his concealment at East-woodleigh, and who had not courage to enquire how far that circumstance had been known and talked of, now blushed deeper than before; but, desirous of turning the discourse, said drily, "I cannot imagine how it should interest any body, unless indeed those who, like Mr. Eversley your brother, were generous enough to try to do him good."

"Oh! the word will talk, you know, my dear — but, come, tell me how long do you intend to stay here? Do you ever go to the Rooms? It is not true, is it, that you are partner in the Marchmonts' shop? You'll go back to Lady Dacres in the winter, to be sure?"

Of these questions Althea, very weary and impatient, answered only two. — "I never go to the Rooms —I have, at present, no intention of returning to Lady Dacres."

"But, bless me, my dear! — what am I to say to the folks who ask me questions about you? Do you know, I have been quite distressed ever since I came, with one and the other teasing me so about you. Dear! I thought, to be sure, what they said was lies and invention from the beginning to the end. — But then Mrs. Higgenbottom, and her sister Miss Carraway, and Lady Buzzard, and her daughter Miss Marianne, said all of them, that, for their parts, they knew it to be trew; and Lady Buzzard said she knew a lady who had bought a pair of fire-screens here, which they knew were your doing."

"How these worthy people should know that, I cannot imagine, not is it indeed very material. For the rest, you are not now, Mrs. Glaston, to learn, that Mrs. Marchmont and her family, whom you so well knew formerly in a very different situation of life, *have* had recourse to their own work to obtain an increase of income — an effort of virtue which, *I* think, is so far from debasing them, that whoever *does* think so, and should therefore slight and despise them, would sink, in my opinion, into the lowest contempt. — The gossiping remarks of such people I never desire to hear: themselves I never desire to see."

This answer, so unlike the usual gentleness of Althea, seemed equally to surprise and offend the person to whom it was addressed, who, without asking to see any of the Marchmont family, rang for her carriage, at the same moment that another drove up to the door.

The maid, having no orders to the contrary, ushered into the room a lady whose face Althea did not recollect; while Mrs. Glaston, without repeating the usual leave-taking compliments, departed, and, driving to a milliner's, was soon so entirely occupied and enchanted by the fight of some most elegant new articles from London, that, for some time, her spleen against her old friend was forgotten.

Althea, in the mean time, having desired her newly-arrived guest, and the gentlemen who attended her, to sit down, enquired whether she wished to speak to Mrs. Marchmont. While Althea said this, the puppy-looking animal who came with her taking out an opera-glass, looked at her a moment; then, turning on his heel, hummed an Italian air, and went to the window. The lady was not so silent.

"So!" cried she, "you have quite forgot me, I see?"

"I beg your pardon," answered Althea, who now remembered the voice and affected manner — "I believe I speak to Mrs. Polwarth."

"Just so. — Well! I am glad you remember me: you must know I hate vastly to be forgot. Though I should not have pardoned even the suspicion of it, if you had not seen me among *such* a set at that horrible old house of Sir Audley's, where my carissimo sposo used to drag me once a year to mortify with that most irksome of all twaddlers, Lady Dacres. Wardy, don't you remember you were there with me once, and helped me to hoax the whole set? and a precious set they were. 'Tis partly my detestation of them, and knowing how I hated them myself, that, added to my amazing good-nature, and my liberal opinions, that makes me your champion; and I declare every where in the screwed-up faces of a legion of tabbies, that you have done vastly right in pleasing yourself, and that I dote upon your spirit and resolution — for that I have always done as I pleased myself, and always intend it."

Althea not at all guessing to what purpose all this tended, and indeed believing it meant nothing, made no reply.

The slender beau, in his pantaloons reaching to his heels, and something like an old great coat on his shoulders, stood drumming against the window, and lent no assistance to the conversation.

"I suppose," resumed the Lady, "that all the world (that is, all of the world that have any sense) think just as I do, though not half of them have the courage to avow it. Who would stay with such a tedious selfish biddy as Lady Dacres? Oh! I have fought fifty battles about you."

Althea, very sorry to have become the subject of conversation, and not at all ambitious of such an advocate, did not look very grateful.

"But come," cried the Lady, "come! let us look, *ma petite amie* at some of the pretty nick-nacks that I hear you and Co. make for sale. I intend that Wardy shall make me a present of something."

"There is, I believe," answered Althea coldly, "nothing at all worth producing for such a purpose; but if there were, Mrs. Marchmont is not at home, and in her absence I have no authority to dispose of, or even to shew, the work."

"Well! never mind then; I'll make the wretch go with me somewhere else. But à propos, Miss Dacres, I want vastly to hear *your* account of these friends of yours, these Marchmonts, that I have heard so much about. Here is my card — pray call upon me some morning; I shall be very glad to see you — you'll make no ceremony —I am not like any mortal else you know on this earth, and delight in, adore all sort of eccentricity, and to make honest matter-of-fact folks stare! If there was any thing I could possibly devise to cause those stupid boors to open their round owl's eyes wider upon me than they do already, I should certainly sport it."

"As my ambition, Madam," said Althea, still more drily, "is not of the same soaring sort, I merely wish to know what part of my conduct it can possibly be that has given rise to the malignity, against which you have been at so much generous pains to defend me — malignity, which seems to have been indulged by people among whom I am hardly known even by name."

"Oh! my charming girl! never apply to me for such a history — rather go ask the old fadges who, perhaps, invented half of it. I dare say there is not an ancient maiden, either native or foreigner, of this place, not for ten miles round, who would not be delighted to tell it to your face with emendations and additions: but, for myself, I assure you that I am the best-natured creature in the world; therefore I'll tell you nothing of what I hear, only what I see with my own eyes, which is — You are vastly handsomer than you used to be. I don't wonder, indeed, that Lady Prim, your mother-in-law, used you as she did to get rid of you."

"I have nothing to complain of, Madam, in regard to Lady Dacres," said Althea.

"That must be owing to your patience, I am sure, rather than to any good in her — a nasty, ill-natured, spiteful old puss! I wish with all my soul she may marry her butler. — Well, but since you won't tell me how you came to muster resolution enough to act for yourself, I'll go now, and come another day. I'm in a horrible hurry, and that faithless fellow looks as if he longed to leave me to go to my appointment alone. — Come, you animal," added she, rising and taking Wardour (who was still her attendant) by the arm, "let us go."

They then got into the carriage that was waiting, and departed together — to the great relief of Althea, who returned not, however, to the tranquillity she had enjoyed before. The strange and unpleasant circumstance of having become the conversation of a place where she thought herself hardly known, the motives which were imputed to her for her residence with Mrs. Marchmont, the certainty that her attachment to the son of the family was suspected, if not actually known — all served to fill her with grief and vexation: she thought that such reports could have come only from Lady Dacres; and though the consciousness of the purity of her mind, and the innocence and propriety of her conduct, soon gave her self-satisfaction enough to enable her to rise above these vague and idle rumours, yet nothing could be more distressing than the certainty of Lady Dacres's malignity towards her, which could hardly fail of being productive of so many inconveniences both to her fortune and reputation: and these injuries coming from the very hand that ought to have been held forth offering friendship and protection, seemed doubly cruel, and very difficult calmly to endure.

It gave her also great pain to reflect, that when all these reports became known to Mrs. Marchmont, which she knew must soon happen, the comfort and pleasure they had found in being together would be empoisoned, and that she should be the cause of giving uneasiness to the persons she most loved and esteemed.

Alas! there were but too many causes of concern already. Mrs. Marchmont, in a continual struggle between her dread of the future and the uncertainty how she ought to act at present, delayed from time to time the decision which alone could have rendered her proposed plan eligible. This delay she imputed to the necessity of waiting for letters from her son; but it was partly owing to the lingering remains of that reluctant pride which often returned to the charge, even when she thought her fortitude and her reason had conquered it for ever. The question continually recurred to the mother's heart: Ought she, for the sake of a trifling pecuniary advantage, to humble her daughters' prospects in life? Who would marry girls from a shop? — To this Reason constantly replied, that the man who happening to prefer one of them, should on that account reject her, must be a poor-spirited creature, with whom it was unlikely she would be happy.

Her health, however, gradually declined in the contest; and she insensibly to herself, yet visibly to others, lost the advantage she at first seemed to derive from sea air, and from having quitted the neighbourhood of London.

Althea was already disgusted with a plan which exposed her to the repetition of such impertinence as she had lately been teased with; and dreading lest, in the month of October now at hand, Lady Dacres should refuse to pay even the interest of Mrs. Trevyllian's legacy, she sunk in despite of her own resolution, and the buoyant spirits of the happy-tempered Lucy, into frequent fits of despondence; without, however, avowing even to herself, what she felt to be true, that the long silence of Marchmont, the uncertainty of what was the situation of the place where he was supposed to be, and the deep concern that sometimes on his account seemed to bow the spirit of his mother to the earth, had more influence in impressing pain on her heart, than any thing that related to herself or her situation.

To remain with his mother, however, so long as she had the means of making it an object of some advantage, was her steady resolution; and in avoiding every one likely to repeat what she had already heard with so much uneasiness, in soothing and sweetening some of the very bitter hours Mrs. Marchmont passed in silent solicitude, another fortnight passed.

At the end of that time Mrs. Marchmont was one day surprised by a letter, enclosing from a woman of high rank a Bank note of a hundred pounds. Instead of that *graciousness* which often embitters such gifts, the letter explaining from whom it came was couched in terms so delicate, so truly good; that Mrs. Marchmont for once received an obligation without feeling herself humbled by it. The almost immediate consequence was, a resolution, in which her daughters and Althea warmly concurred, to remove from a public place, relinquish their plan for the present, and wait for news from Marchmont in a cottage at a village in Kent, which precisely at that time happened to be vacant. — Thither they immediately were settled, and there passed part of the month of October. The whole of November, and midwinter arrived, without their being sensible of any new uneasiness, save only from the now very long silence of Marchmont. Althea had received her small dividend in due course, and from some unaccountable effort of generosity Lady Dacres had sent an additional thirty pounds — but without saying on what account, or writing a line of any kind in the blank cover in which it was enclosed.

END OF THE THIRD VOLUME.

MARCHMONT.
CHAPTER I.

Me tenet... ægrum Phæacia terris.
Abstineas avidas Mors violenta manus!
Abstineas, Mors atra! precor, non hic mihi Mater:
Quæ legat in mœstos ossa perusta sinus?
Non Soror, Assyrios cineri quæ dedat odores,
Et sleat effusis ante sepulchra comis:
Delia non usquam...

HAD THE SAFETY of Marchmont been certain, had his letters removed, even temporarily, the continual fears that on his account oppressed the hearts of his mother and his sisters, as well as that of Althea, who, though she said nothing, was by no means the least agitated among them, their days would have passed in more tranquillity and comfort than, after all the former had suffered, they could ever expect. But the vague and uncertain reports which continually reached them from that part of the continent where they believed Marchmont still to be, the histories of horror that every day met their eyes in the newspapers, and his not having written since he first found protection with the English at Toulon, formed together so much ground for apprehension on the part of those who loved him, that their days were overclouded by continual anxiety; they all often, without daring to communicate their sentiments to each other, felt that the dread is often more difficult to support than the certainty of an evil, and that it deprived them of every enjoyment of life.

Althea watched, with trembling solicitude, the fading countenance of Mrs. Marchmont, and the eager anxious looks of the animated Lucy; while Amelia, amidst all her efforts to speak comfort, sunk into hopeless despondence; and, while she sought to find arguments against the terrors that preyed on her mother, seemed to feel how well grounded those terrors were, and to want herself the comfort she attempted to bestow.

Sometimes, as if afraid of being together lest the communication of their thoughts should increase their mutual sufferings, Mrs. Marchmont, who was frequently ill, remained alone in her own room, and Amelia shut herself in hers; while Althea, Lucy, and Milly, not daring to speak on the subject nearest their hearts, and yet unable to enter on any other, sat sad and silent at their work, expecting, with almost agonizing apprehensions, the newspaper and the post, and trembling at every knock they heard at the door.

Such was the cruel situation of the family, when one morning, in the middle of January, a gentleman rode up to the door of their cottage: he enquired for Miss Dacres. — Althea, who had only a slight view of him without distinguishing his face as he rode by the window, imagined it was some person on business from Lady Dacres; and however reluctantly, yet supposing it to be necessary, she directed him to be admitted to the parlour, from whence her two young companions went out, to leave her at liberty to speak to the stranger.

What was her surprise, and, after a moment, her alarm, to see Mr. Eversley!

Not even the domestic unhappiness which Althea well knew had so long embittered his life, could account for the expression of his countenance. It was evidently recent and very deep concern that affected him. He tried to make the usual compliments of salutation, but failed. He sat down, fetched a deep and tremulous sigh, and his lips quivered as he faintly uttered —

"How are the ladies? — How is poor Mrs. Marchmont? ... Will Miss Dacres pardon my intruding on her? — Her friendship for this unfortunate family makes me hope it."

"Good God!" exclaimed Althea, "what new misfortune has befallen them? Ah! Mr. Eversley, some great evil has overtaken your friend Marchmont — He is, perhaps, no more!"— Then struck to the heart by so terrible a supposition, she clasped her hands together, and remained silent and breathless.

"I hope," said Mr. Eversley, trying to speak with more firmness, "that he is yet alive: but I cannot conceal the truth. He has been — he still is, I fear, in the most imminent danger: — in the dreadful affair at Toulon he has been a severe sufferer. He did not escape by sea like the rest: his friendship for the Lavergnac family has engaged him in difficulties, from which it is much to be apprehended he will find it hard to extricate himself, even if the bad effect of all he has endured should be resisted by his strength of constitution and his youth."

"He has been ill, then?" articulated Althea faintly. "Ah! Mr. Eversley, to *me* at least, you may disclose the truth, though I fear it will destroy his unfortunate mother — Marchmont is dead?"

"Not that I am assured of," replied Mr. Eversley; "I can only repeat that, from his incoherent letter, his situation appears to me to be so precarious, that I thought it my duty, as almost the only remaining friend of the family, and as that letter was addressed to me, to take some means of preparing the mind of that admirable woman for a blow that may, if it falls suddenly and unexpectedly upon her, quite overwhelm her, and leave the poor girls without the protection either of their mother or their brother."

"Alas!" said Althea, "it will be but killing her by lingering tortures, instead of one death-stroke. Yet your precaution — yet the trouble you have taken is very good — very friendly! What would you advise *me*, Sir, to do? How shall I venture to communicate such intelligence? — If there is yet hope that your friend may escape, would it not be better ...?" Althea found it impossible to proceed —

"I see," said Mr. Eversley in a low voice, "how greatly you are affected. I almost repent of having afflicted you. The painful duty of wounding where I wish only to heal and to console, I would not transfer to you, did I not know how tender a hand it requires; and were I not persuaded that there are few evils which must not be greatly alleviated by sympathy such as yours. — Alas! Miss Dacres, it is I who feel assuredly more than any body, that there are many, many calamities in life, to the endurance of which early death is infinitely preferable. Good God! how much better to die as Marchmont may, so beloved, and so regretted, than to live as ..." He checked himself, and, leaving the sentence incomplete, added, in a halfstifled voice — "Forgive my folly — The wretched are always egotists —I too naturally, though too weakly, recur to myself!"

"Would it not be better," asked Althea, collecting as much firmness as she could — "would it not be better, since poor Marchmonts fate is still uncertain, to conceal the worst we know, and the still worse we apprehend, from his mother, till the final event be assured? If it be fatal, it will then be time enough to open to her the cruel tidings. Should Providence interpose in her favour, and save her son, perhaps we shall, by delay, avoid inflicting a wound that may be followed by the most dreadful consequences."

"I believe you are right, Madam," answered Mr. Eversley. — "Goodness and wisdom are alike conspicuous in every thing you say. But, if my being here is known, how shall I excuse to Mrs. Marchmont my not appearing before her?"

"It need not be known — I believe she has no servants here who lived with her when she used to see you. The younger of her daughters, who had a very slight view of you as you passed the windows, do not at all, I believe, recollect you. They imagine it is some gentleman come to me on the part of Lady Dacres, and the severity of the weather may excuse concealing your face as you go out. May I, Sir," continued Althea, her voice faltering — "may I ask to be entrusted with the letter that informs you of the sufferings and situation of Marchmont? I will endeavour — since from the service of my friends I will not shrink, however painful it may be to myself —I will endeavour to compel myself to act with calmness and deliberation, and to proceed towards giving or withholding from my poor unhappy friend the heart-breaking intelligence, as circumstances seem to demand."

"I have no scruple," said Mr. Eversley, taking the letter from his pocket, and giving it to her, "to entrust you with it — as I would, indeed, with all that is, or ought to be, most precious to myself. — But how, dearest Madam, if I should receive any other communication from our friend, how shall I transmit it to you?"

Althea, who found herself almost unable to support the conversation, informed him, that nothing was more easy than for him to do it by letter; and that all that remained for her was, to assume resolution enough to conceal the shock she might receive, should his information be what they dreaded.

Eversley, without saying so, signified that he was well aware, from her partiality to Marchmont, how very difficult this would be — "But," added he, "there is no elevation of sentiment or conduct to which the superior understanding of Miss Dacres does not render her equal. Oh, Marchmont! in life or in death, it must be my lot to envy you!"

Althea recollecting what had formerly passed, when she fancied, and with great reason, that Eversley was more attached to her than merely the friendship between their families could authorise, answered slightly; and Eversley, as if conscious of the impropriety and uselessness of what he had unguardedly said, seemed tempted to repeat apologies; till, suddenly recollecting that he might only be betrayed into a repetition of the offence, he hastily arose.

"I will wait at the inn at Sittingbourne," said he, "to-night, lest, after having perused our friend's letter, you should have any commands for me. — Should I hear nothing before twelve o'clock to-morrow, I shall depart for London, where, according to this address," giving Althea a card, "I have taken a house for three months — and where I shall be always ready to obey the commands of Miss Dacres, or of her friends."

Mr. Eversley then hastily departed, taking the precautions Althea had hinted at to conceal his face; while she, unable to speak to Lucy Marchmont till she had read the dreadful letter, hurried, hardly knowing what she did, to her own room, and locked the door.

She then, panting for breath, took it from her pocket, and attempted to read it: but the direction was blotted and confused; the seal, the hand-writing were all so many testimonies of the agitated and wretched condition in which the writer had been when it was dispatched.

Althea tried to read it twice before she could command composure enough to succeed; the letters floated before her eyes; their characters were indistinct; she fancied them traced in the blood of the unhappy writer.

At length, having drank a glass of water, and argued herself into what she hoped would be a sufficient degree of resolution to enable her to bear a detail the horrors of which might possibly be aggravated by their obscurity, she read, or rather with difficulty decyphered, as follows:

To W. EVERSLEY, *ESQUIRE.*

"My very dear Friend,

"When you learn that Marchmont, not certainly of a very desponding temper, supposes that this is the last trouble he shall ever give you, you will believe that his situation is such as for himself he should meet, he trusts, with fortitude, were he not dragged back to life by his tenderness, his fears, his regret — did he not think of those who have hardly any support, any comfort, any hope but what is attached to his life. — Oh! my beloved mother, my unprotected sisters — it is for you I would live. — There is yet another tie that would bind me to life, but sacred is the adored name of her that has formed it. She is so much of an angel, that perhaps Heaven has directed it for her preservation from greater evils, when I am dismissed from a world where my misfortunes might have been communicated to her. What can fortify me against the fear of death like such a supposition? Yet indeed, my friend, if the most ardent love, if the tenderest gratitude could have reconciled her to humble fortune, she would not with me have been unhappy!

"It is passed! —I am wounded — they tell me, mortally — and in a prison where I am not considered as a prisoner of war; and from whence, if the surgeons who have visited me should be mistaken, I shall, in all probability, be dismissed, only to perish on a scaffold.

"*Nil desperandum* used to be my motto — not, however, with too much reason; for I think that from the time when, in perfect possession of my reason, I dared to lift the veil which my poor father's affectionate hands endeavoured to spread between me and the dark shadows that hung over the fortunes of our family, every year has brought an accumulation of evil; which, while I was chained down to its endurance, I was, from combined and unconquerable difficulties, precluded from attempting to remove, by such efforts as a man of my age and education, under almost any other circumstances, might and ought to have attempted.

"And is such a persecuted existence as I have sustained worthy of regret? — Ah! yes, my friend — I am not philosopher enough to despise, with all its evils, (and to whose share have greater evils fallen?) an existence which might have been useful to the dear object of my filial and fraternal affection — which might have been endeared by the possession of the woman I adore. — But I waste in declamation the little time that may be allowed me. I exhaust the little strength I have left. — I will briefly relate how I came into my present situation, and what that situation is.

"The same conveyance by which this letter (if I am not deceived as to its being conveyed at all) will reach England, will bring you accounts too numerous, and too true, of the circumstances that have driven the English and their allies from Toulon; with details which, had I time and power to give them, my heart sickens to recollect. To the accounts then that must be made public I refer you for an idea of the magnitude, and, alas! the consequences of this fatal retreat — while I confine myself to the sad story of those individuals, for whom, since Marchmont is one of them, the friendly and generous heart of Eversley will be deeply interested. I am faint after a visit to my wound, and must lay down my pen; not, however, till it has told you that the bad symptoms are rather less threatening, and that this young French surgeon, who is now allowed to attend me, does not seem to think so ill of it as his principal. He appears to want neither skill nor humanity; nor is he so bigoted to republican ideas as the *Maître Chirurgien* who has till yesterday inspected the condition of the prisoners. I never believed the wound absolutely mortal after the ball was extracted. I still think it is not. Yet it is certain that I am very weak. But a constitution hitherto untouched by disease may do much for a man in his twenty-fourth year. — Yet what avails my recovery, if the means fail me, as they almost certainly will, of prevailing on the committee, to whom my case will be referred, to believe me an English subject, and to treat me as a prisoner of war?

"I am not able now to relate the circumstances to which this is ow-ing. If I live, you shall have my short eventful history. If I live! — Ah! how vain to indulge such a hope! I probably now see through the grat-ing of my prison the wintry sun (which still in this climate is bright) of the opening year, the last I shall ever behold.

"My purpose in writing to you, Eversley, is to secure your good offices in conveying to my unhappy family the intelligence which will in all human probability precede my death. To whose friendship but to yours *can* I entrust this painful task? — and should it be executed by unskillful hands, how sad may be the consequences!

"I have been making once more a feeble attempt to discover what chance there is of my being permitted to live, if my wound should be cured: I perceive that money, if immediately applied, might do much, but money I have none — and it is likely that after a few days it would lose its efficacy were I to procure it; for the French commissioner, who is then expected, is a man of brutal manners, sanguinary by his nature, and from national prejudice detesting the very name of an Englishman; so that it is very probable the efforts I have made to ascertain my being a British subject may serve only to expose me to his ferocity. My only ray of hope, and it is very faint, arises from the kindness and humanity of the young surgeon. One of his family was obliged by some family in England during the last war: he remembers it with gratitude, and has naturally a liberal temper and a good heart. But he is a very young man — he is only an assistant surgeon; and any attempt in which he was not absolutely sure of success, would send me immediately to the scaffold, and involve him in my fate. How then can I press him to help me, even if I were enough recovered to meditate my escape?

"It is more worthy of those principles I have through life endeavoured to cultivate, to submit to an inevitable evil with calmness, rather than to involve my friends by attempting to evade it.

"Some pangs, some very severe pangs I certainly feel: they are less for myself, cruel as a violent death is at twenty-four, than for those I must leave.

"Eversley! I consign them perhaps in my last hours (for the commissioner is come) — I consign my family to your unwearied friendship. But remember that, as it never was my wish, while living, that such friendship should embitter your life, you must not suffer it to do so after my death.

"And now, my last, best friend, adieu! I bid you farewell, in all probability for the last time. — Should I yet exist, my first care will be to greet you. My worthy and friendly Deslormes undertakes, and even at some hazard, to put this letter on its way to England.

"God preserve you, my dear Eversley! Let my memory be dear to you. If it should ever be painful, you will think of all your good actions towards me; you will continue such friendly offices as you can towards those I leave, and you will find a pleasure even in your concern. — Once more farewell!

E. A. M."

CHAP. II

Injustice, swift, erect, and unconfin'd,
Sweeps the wide earth, and tramples on mankind,
While prayers to heal her wrongs more slowly move behind.

WORDS CAN BUT inadequately describe the condition of Althea's mind, when, after a second reading, she comprehended the whole purport of the foregoing letter.

Again and again she read it. — Sometimes the hopes Marchmont seemed to hold out made her flatter herself that he might yet be preserved. But the doubts that had been raised of his country — but the dreadfully ferocious commissioner! — As these arose before her, she felt it out of her power reasonably to hope, and terror and despair took possession of her heart.

Nothing, however, was so immediately requisite as to compose herself for meeting Mrs. Marchmont at dinner; for after mature deliberation she determined, if it were possible, to keep to herself all she knew, and not to divulge, till it became inevitable, the fatal secret even to Lucy herself.

This undertaking was terrible to her. Had she considered March-mont only as a common acquaintance, it would have been very difficult to have concealed her concern from the eyes of a mother so trem-blingly anxious about her son. As it was, the most heroic resolution was requisite to stifle the agonies she endured, rather than unnecessari-ly wound a bosom dear to her on account of Marchmont, as well as for itself. Let those who have ever been called upon for such an exertion of friendship imagine how difficult was the part she had to act, and what she must have suffered only for the short time it was incumbent upon her to go through it.

She dreaded the moment of being summoned to dinner, which, however, she could not avoid obeying. Mrs. Marchmont had all the morning confined herself to her room, for the depression of her spir-its was such as she had that day found it impossible to conquer. She felt what she sometimes had described in the words used by a celebrated French author, who in his last illness said he felt no pain, only *"une dif-ficulté de vivre."* This difficulty — this reluctance to drag on a life where so much was to be dreaded for the future fate of those she loved, while little of hope offered itself, Mrs. Marchmont, with the good sense of a reasoning being, and the firmness of a Christian, endeavoured to resist. She looked at her lovely daughters. — It was for them she knew her life, with all its active powers, to be necessary; but when all that might befall them, unportioned and unprotected as they were, became present to her mind; when she remembered how far their brother was from them, and how uncertain it was whether he would ever be able to appear as their guardian and friend; the absence of that dear son, ever the first object of his mother's affections, and the cruel circumstances that had blighted all the fair prospects of his youth, and marred the promise his talents, his temper, and his person had given, seemed to be evils so real and insupportable, that her fortitude gave way before it; and the resolves she had made not to increase, by timid despondence, evils which only active virtue could mitigate, sunk into that cold inert tranquillity which sometimes appears like patience and resignation.

In such a frame of mind, increased by personal indisposition, was Mrs. Marchmont, when it became the cruel task of Althea to put on some degree of cheerfulness, to endeavour to appear as usual, while she knew that this unhappy mother was really more wretched than in her darkest moments of dread and despondence she had ever believed herself.

This, however, she could not so well perform but that the struggle was evident; and that something had given Althea unusual concern appeared through all her attempts to conceal it. It was natural enough for the family, who supposed a gentleman had that morning been with her from Lady Dacres, to impute her evident confusion and distress of mind to something that had passed in regard to her pecuniary affairs.

The innocent yet questioning eyes of Lucy examined those of Althea with particular earnestness. The general idea, however, was hers, that Lady Dacres had sent her some rude or unkind message. Her heart ached for her beloved friend: but she forbore to ask any direct questions, concluding that whatever it was proper for her to know, Althea would tell her; and Mrs. Marchmont and Amelia remained silent from the same motives of delicacy. Their meal was the most melancholy they had ever eaten together: as soon as it was over they separated; for to remain long under such restraint, her heart actually bursting with anguish, Althea found to be impossible.

Lucy, more alarmed than before, ventured to take her hand as she passed her to go up stairs:

"My dear friend!" said she, in a low and trembling voice.

Althea understood the appeal — "Follow me to my room, Lucy," said she; "but pray take no notice of my concern."

They entered the chamber of Althea, who, finding it wholly out of her power to restrain any longer the anguish of her mind, sat down in tears; while Lucy, hanging over her, said, "That cruel Lady Dacres is the occasion of giving you more uneasiness?"

Althea, unused to every species of deceit, and quite incapable of using it to a friend whom she considered as more than a sister, then thought it better to tell her the truth; for she believed the good sense Lucy Marchmont possessed would rather support her in the difficult and arduous task she had undertaken, than weaken the resolution with which she determined to attempt going through it.

Desiring, therefore, in a low voice, that Lucy would shut the door, she first endeavoured to arm her with calmness to endure the evil tidings that it was thus her lot to impart, and then put Marchmony's letter into her hand.

Whatever were the elevated spirit and sanguine temper of Lucy, the dreadful uncertainly (an uncertainty that could hardly terminate favourably) seemed, and perhaps was, more difficult to bear than any certainty would have been at the instant; yet a little reflection, and her observing how deeply Althea was affected, helped to restore her to some apparent composure; and both were soon enabled, by this participation of sorrows, to console and in a certain degree to reassure each other.

They were equally aware that nothing was more dear to the poor exile, whose fate they thus deplored, than the peace and health of his mother; and both had that right sense of what they owed the absent or the dead, to feel that the best way of testifying the tender regard they bore him, was to alleviate, as far as to alleviate was possible, the distress of those their lamented Marchmont loved. Yet sad, heavy, and difficult to be performed was the task; and they so gready dreaded meeting Mrs. Marchmont at their simple supper, and were so afraid, should she talk about her son, that they should betray themselves, that their very fears almost divested them of the caution they tried to observe. Lucy, trembling lest her mother, Amelia or Milly, should begin to speak of her brother, talked on indifferent matters with a vivacity and perseverance that it was easy to see was forced; while Althea, incapable of any actual exertion, sat in almost torpid despondence — sometimes looking at Mrs. Marchmont with eyes filling with tears; then catching herself indulging so useless a weakness, she complained of being unwell, of having a cold in her head, and made that an excuse for retiring more early than usual to her bed.

Mrs. Marchmont, as well as her eldest and youngest daughter, observed that something had vexed her; but the idea of some unkind message from Lady Dacres precluded all farther enquiry.

This artificial and dearly purchased calm could not, as Lucy now recollected, last long; for, not to live entirely without intelligence of what was going on, yet to avoid the expence of a daily paper, Mrs. Marchmont took one in that was weekly published in the county, and carried round every Saturday by an itinerant newsman.

In this paper the events that had so recently happened at Toulon would undoubtedly be detailed, and every distress which by the concealment of Marchmont's letter they hoped to save the mind of his mother, would thus suddenly be inflicted on it. To know, as she did, that her son was at Toulon at the period of such general danger, and not to know whether he escaped with the English, gave hardly less occasion for anguish and terror than what was already known about him. After some consideration, therefore, Lucy determined to receive the paper herself from the man, and to say to her mother that it had missed coming, as had sometimes accidentally happened before. This was not attended with much difficulty, and thus was obtained another week of respite; but it was a week of rather increased misery to Althea and to Lucy, who dreaded lest each person they saw approach the door should prove to be some one who might relate the current news as a matter of entertainment; and as another Saturday drew near, their uncertainty how to act and their dread of the event increased.

On the day, however, preceding that, the post brought a letter to Althea, who saw, with breathless solicitude, that it was directed and sealed by Mr. Eversley. Totally unable to open it, she sat down trembling, and bade Lucy, who was but little more capable of doing it than herself, break the seal. Scarce had she done so, when she exclaimed — "There is a letter from my brother! — Thank God! — he is alive then — he has escaped!"

"For God's sake, look at the date!" said Althea. "Before we rejoice, let us see at what time and from whence he writes."

"It is dated above a fortnight later than the last," exclaimed Lucy: then running over a few words, she added, though almost inarticulate with joy — "Oh! Heaven be praised, dearest, dearest Althea, he has escaped! — he is *not* in danger from his wound! — We shall see him again — Our brother! the best, the dearest, kindest..." — Her voice totally failed; and Althea, having gathered courage from this beginning, collected her agitated spirits to read as follows:

LETTER.

"From the contents of my last letter it is probable my dear Eversley has given me up. I know what his friendly and affectionate heart will feel in hearing I am in a place of present safety; and though it is difficult to say, in the actual state of the continent, when I shall be so fortunate as once more to revisit my native land, my friend will be glad to know I do not despair of it; he will rejoice to have *such* tidings to communicate to my family, who, if he has imparted to them the situation in which (with perhaps a too great tendency to despond) I described myself, will be recalled from the most wretched suspense, if not anguish, to hope and life — for it is but too certain, that the life of my mother depends on that of her son. — Ah! May *his* be dedicated to render the rest of it, if not *happy* (it is a word we have no business with), at least comfortable.

"But let me equally avoid despondence and presumption, and avail myself of this short interval of ease and tranquillity to give you as clear a narrative as I can of the strange things I have seen — of the hairbreadth escape I have had from a violent death.

"If you do not already know the particulars, and have any curiosity to enquire, the little history of myself (till I reached an obscure cabaret in the very centre of the Bourbonnois) is in the hands of my mother. I go on then to relate what happened to me, when, after having remained there unmolested some days, again renewed my journey, sometimes on a hired horse, sometimes taking an occasional assistance from the vehicles of the peasantry, but still oftener on foot, towards the house of my venerable relation de Lavergnac, situated in a mountainous country, about three leagues westward of Toulon — so that I had almost half France to traverse. On my way to that place, I shall have to relate less what I suffered than what I thought. My Eversley is not, I think, of that description of men who measure the consequence of opinions by the situation of those who offer such opinions; nor will he wonder if the vicissitudes of my life, short as it has been, and the knowledge that adversity has given me of mankind, should have taught me a habit of reflecting — a habit which, when once acquired, helps the possessor to divest himself of the prejudices (often destructive to happiness, and never, that I can discover, contributing to it) which are with so much pain inculcated by rote at the beginning of our lives — as if the only use of memory were to assist mankind in getting rid of their reason, and to substitute in its place systems which the cunning have invented for the subjection of the weak.

"Do not imagine, however, my dear friend, that I have any intention to plead in favour of that universal licence, that wild and impracticable scheme of general equality, which has, within a few years, gained ground from the writings of visionary speculatists, and from the propensity of mankind to run into extremes, and to pervert the best general rules to the most unworthy private purposes.

"Surely, my friend, I am *not* a misanthrope — Yet I own that when I see the follies, the wickedness of the beings with whom I am to act, I am unavoidably led to enquire wherefore the great Author of the Universe has peopled this planet with animals so worthless and so wretched; — creatures who, while their reason seems to have been

wholly inadequate to the purpose of procuring for them a moderate
share of content, have misused the other lights lent to them, so as to
make them new sources of persecution and of misery. You will tell me
I have read Swift, Voltaire, and Rousseau, with too much approbation.
— Alas! my dear friend, look at almost every man you know, in the decline of life; see how sad is their existence, and you will be compelled
to acknowledge, that when I say human creatures are foolish, wicked,
and unhappy, my estimate is but too just.

"But in a world thus peopled, a man, as soon as he emerges from
infancy, finds himself without any consent of his own; and, whether
he likes his station or no, he must abide in it. — It seems therefore to
be true wisdom, early to learn to live as easily as we can, though to live
happily is (as I think we soon discover) out of the question. — In *my*
case, for example: so far from being allowed to live in *any way* with ease,
I am almost denied the privilege of *living at all*—, at least, it does not
seem that European earth will permit me to exist on its surface!

"From my own country, which every man, and I think particularly
every Englishman, is taught to love and venerate as soon as he can lisp
its name, from my 'natale solum' I am driven by the persecutions of
a miserable wretch whom they call an attorney; — a fellow stained by
every vice — the disgrace of his species — who lives in the constant
violation of those *laws* which are the boast and glory of Britons — but
which, by some strange *abuse* (by all complained of, nay execrated —
by none attempted to be remedied), are made the shield under which
robberies are committed, rather than the sword by which they are punished. For this glaring defect, occasioning more extended and incalcu-
lable misery than any of the senseless perversions of mankind (except
only the madness of war), there is, it seems, no remedy! — None!
— for nothing must be changed; and though individuals among the
majority of villains who plunder under the masks of attorneys are now
and then punished, no radical cure can be administered to the mass of
this crying evil — for it may be injurious to the sanctity of the laws.
— Oh! never then let such laws be boasted of! — If a physician were
to tell me that the medicine he was going to administer for the cure
of a cold, could only be conveyed through the medium of a poisoned
vehicle, which might subject me to long years of lingering torture, and
destroy me at last, should I not entreat him to dispense with my taking
his prescription? Yet this is precisely what happens, when a luckless
man is advised, as the only means of redress against injuries, to apply

to the laws of his country. 'It is an affair which from the very nature of it can only be settled by Chancery,' says my Counsellor: 'you must apply to that court undoubtedly; yet I own I can hardly advise it, for the costs and time will be immense.'— 'Calculate,' say I, 'the costs, and the time.'— 'Why,' returns my friend, 'as to the costs, it is not easy to say what *they* may amount to among so many parties: and then, as for the *time*, it will be at least *three* terms, but more likely *six*, nine, twelve, or fifteen, before your adversaries will put in their answers; and if they are hostile, why it may be *three or four years;* and then your bill must be amended perhaps: and then, if any of the parties die among the three-and-twenty individuals whom you must make parties (people of all ages, from the old man of seventy-five to an infant born last week), why in that case, you know, you will have all the business to begin over again.' Not knowing, however, what else to do, after every other attempt fails which I have made to accommodate the affair, I venture into this labyrinth, and I engage a man who calls himself *a Solicitor in Chancery*, to draw up my bill; and a learned Chancery Lawyer (a Special Pleader, I believe), *to settle it*. This done, and a heavy charge incurred, I desire in all humility to read it, and find it not only devoid of common sense, but going in no one point to my meaning, or to the truth; while the composition appears to me to be absolutely nonsense. I object very much to this, and say, that where I am to appear before the Chancellor of Great Britain as *his orator*, I don't at all like to prate like a driveller — That it seems to me an insult to talk, before the greatest law officer, stuff that for falsehood and folly would be scouted in a company of haberdashers and toymen. I am answered with great indignation, that all bills in Chancery *are nonsense* — That it is the custom to make them so, and that *they are better understood*. Such a position being incomprehensible, and adding to the repugnance with which I set out, I desire to stay proceedings. My learned Chancery Lawyer allows me to do so, because he begins to suspect that my money and my patience may equally be at an end before I have gone another step in this blessed pilgrimage: but he sends me in his bill, and, to convince me that in Chancery as well as in almost every thing else '*C'est le premier pas qui coûte,*' he presents me with a charge of *only* seventy pounds. It is impossible for me to pay it — and he detains all the papers he had got into his hands on pretence of seeking redress for me — it being, it seems, a rule for lawyers never to restore papers till they are paid, though they have volunteered in the cause, and though the very detention of these documents may be in itself a greater evil than they undertook to cure, and may prevent its ever being cured at all. — Oh! my friend, after even this sketch of a case *which has actually happened to me*, which I know happens to thousands, and is not by many degrees the most injurious trick of these *legal* banditti — where is the Englishman (not himself a lawyer) who can venture to make the proud boast that the law in his country is the palladium of liberty, and the protector of property? War, earthquake, pestilence, famine, tempest, all the calamities of this best of all possible worlds, which we pray against in the liturgy, do not, I am convinced, occasion more anguish to *'the poor creature of the earth*, than these locusts, which we ourselves arm with stings and claws — because it is the custom.

"Don't wonder at this long dissertation — I still smart under the festering scratches of one of these fiends; and even in Switzerland, the loveliest, once the happiest spot of Europe, I saw in the very few days I have this time been in it, a poor family literally destroyed by a procureur. The same obnoxious professional men are accused by the French nobility of having been the cause of, and chief gainers in, the revolution; which in truth I believe, as I think no other set of people could have done so much mischief, brought down such miseries on a great nation, or turned what might have been comforts and blessings into plagues and curses. Of these reptiles, therefore, it may be said, they are like the visitations of Pharaoh; and of our own country especially, quoting a line of a great modern poet, we may say,

'And the land stank, so numerous was the fry.'

"And now I will for the present cease to speak of these authorized scalpers — these disturbers of the living, who prey even upon those that are no more—

'Cruel as death, and hungry as the grave.'

"Ah!" exclaimed Lucy, half sobbing as she read over Althea's shoulder, "how sad were the sensations, how bitter the recollections of my poor brother when he wrote thus!"

"Let us, however," said Althea, from whose mind the most dreadful weight seemed to be removed — "let us, my Lucy, rejoice that he lived to write it; and we will try, my dear girl, thankfully to calm our spirits to follow the rest of a narrative to us so interesting."

CHAP. III.

... La mauvaise fortune avoit déja flétri son cœur; l'adversité et le
mépria avoient abattu son courage; et sa fierté, changée en dépit
amer, ne lui montroit que l'injustice et la dureté des hommes.

ALTHEA AND LUCY proceeded then to read the narrative of Marchmont:

"It was the middle of September when I set forward alone from the
asylum I had for some days found in the Bourbonnois, but which I dared
no longer trust, for three national soldiers from the south suddenly appeared; and though I happened to be wandering in the fields during their
short visit, I found from my host, on my return, that they only preceded
a company of Marseillois who were going to Paris, and I easily conceived
that my stay was no longer safe either for the old man or myself. I left
him not dissatisfied with me; and I knew that, whatever he suspected, it
was not his interest, and did not seem to be in his nature, to betray me.

With my haversack on my back, I set out at eight o'clock of a
warm and mild evening, taking no other precaution than to avoid the
high-roads, by which the persons I desired to escape from directed
their march. Though I knew nothing of the country, it was not difficult
to do this where there are few inclosures, and the villages are thinly
scattered among the mountainous tracks planted with vineyards, or
shadowed with extensive woods of sweet chesnut, affording at once
shelter and food to the formerly contented, though poor inhabitants.

"It was in a deep recess of one of these woods that I slept on the
first night of my pilgrimage; my knapsack forming my pillow, and the
fallen leaves of the preceding year my mattress. — Were I a soldier, how
much worse might I have fared! — I awaked refreshed with the earliest
dawn of the morning, and followed an obscure path leading through
a yet wilder line of country, which seemed to have been made by the
woodcutters, and which I knew must conduct me to some habitation.
After walking about four miles, I found myself near a few scattered

houses; and addressing myself to a vigneron, who was cutting spars at his door, I asked for such refreshment as his cottage afforded; for which I offered to pay.

The man made none of those questions which, in a more populous district, might have compelled me to exert my ingenuity at the expence of my veracity; but bade me walk in, and called his wife to set before me what she had, which was chesnut-bread, figs, and eggs. Did I not fare sumptuously? — My friendly vigneron appeared to be one of those honest simple creatures that walk straight onward in their humble path, and preserve their peace by looking neither to the right nor the left. — I sat eating my vegetable meal on the turf seat at his door, shaded by a great elm older than the cottage, which it almost inclosed in its green arms; and saw him reclining at its foot, shaping, with care, the spars he had been cutting to answer some purpose in his vineyard. I remarked his open unthinking forehead, on which the few scattered locks were mingled with grey, but where care seemed to have nothing to do with the strong sunburnt lines; and I enquired of myself, if such a being was not to be envied? — He, said I, meditates nothing about Revolutions — he hardly understands the term. Under the old government he worked hard; — the new one has made to him (fortunate man!) no sensible change: he still works hard for the daily bread he eats. He has heard that mass is abolished — that the religion of his country is annihilated; but *his* religion consisted merely in one simple and uniform routine of the duties necessary to enable his family to exist from one week to another. It was four leagues from his cabin to the nearest chapel, and it was not of late years worth the while of the rich possessors of the neighbouring benefices to send or to come among the inhabitants of these five small cabins in the extremity of the Bourbonnois, on the very edge of a mountainous tract of the mountainous Auvergne.

'*Is* it good then to be such a being? When I reflect on the vice, the folly of cultivated, of polished life, I am ready to answer, that it but Rosalind's* remark recurs to me. — 'It were then good to be a post!' — I hesitate, and consider whether a human being, no more enlightened, rises as many degrees as he ought to do in the scale of intelligent creatures designed to be

'— only lower than the angels;'

_____
*   Rosalind in 'As You Like It'

and finally, whether I would exchange my sensibility, (I hate the word, it is so prostituted) though you have told me, and I have sometimes thought, I possessed almost a morbid degree of it, for the calm stupor of ignorance, for the stagnating content of an animal who in the human form is, in intellectual rank, hardly superior to the cattle he drives a-field!

"I decide, that I would *not* exchange my sense of existence for his; yet I think there can be no doubt but that his is the happier.

"Are you tired of my speculations? I hope not; for I told you my relation for some time was rather to be of what I thought than of what I suffered.

"I had a small map of France with me, I mean as it was, for the division into eighty-one departments puzzles and perplexes me — I took it out to consider which way I should turn.

"I found, in consequence of the questions I asked, that there were two roads at my option, without pursuing the immediate road to Toulon: one lay eastward through Auvergne, but it was a great circuit for one who was probably to journey almost entirely on foot: the other, which was indeed still farther from the spot where I was, would lead me through a small angle of the ci-devant Burgundy into Dauphine, from whence I might make my way to the shore of the Mediterranean eastward of Toulon. You will not recollect why I was compelled to prefer either of these to the usual route, unless I remind you of the state of Lyons at that period.— Not only that unhappy town, but every *grande route* that lay in a direct communication, it was absolutely necessary for so equivocal a character as I was to avoid.

"Having at length made my election, and determined to pass through Auvergne, I set out once more alone on foot, and, soon buried among the wild mountains and deep defiles of its eastern boundary, I travelled for some days, faring very hardly; for cottages were thinly scattered, and the only two chateaux I saw I forbore to approach. — The weather was now extremely warm, and I found myself too much fatigued to proceed in this way much farther; nor was it desirable to appear entirely like a wandering fugitive. I was therefore glad to meet with a sort of itinerant merchant of almost every commodity, either of necessity or finery, to French peasants, who had just received a cargo of goods, which he was now going to sell, against the close of the vintage, among the lone villages of Auvergne, Guienne, and Provence. His only associate was a boy of nine or ten years old; and I found, on talking to him, that, if he could meet a companion he could depend upon, he should be rather relieved by travelling somewhat better guarded against accidents than he had been the preceding year, when he had been robbed, and narrowly escaped with his life, in a forest of the Limousin. I know not what prejudiced him in my favour; but after I had been two days with him upon sufferance, he proposed to me to continue in his company, and to relieve him and the boy in driving their cart occasionally; while at other times I should take my turn to be conveyed in it.

"Though I foresaw that this must oblige me to go some leagues out of my way, yet the scheme offered so many advantages that I closed with it; telling him, however, that when we came to Lodeve, in Languedoc, I should be compelled to leave him, as I was going to the neighbourhood of Montpellier. My new friend was, as well as my honest Vigneron, one of those useful but unreflecting beings, who, entirely occupied by their own affairs, look no farther. His sole care was, whether the new order of things would, when the government was settled, affect his trade, *et si il sera toujours également bien ses affaires.* — He told me how much money he had gained by his traffic in the space of nine years, and described his little menage, the comforts of which had been greatly interrupted by his eldest son, a youth of seventeen, who till then used to travel with him, having been put in requisition: he was himself, he said, too old for a soldier. He did not much understand what all the *tapage* was about, for, notwithstanding the pains taken to *enlighten* the people of the country, there are parts of it where this illumination makes its way very incompletely. — Alas! the distant *flames* lend but a lurid and glaring light, and only serve to scorch and to destroy!

"Such a man was, however, much better adapted to my purpose, than a more intelligent or more informed fellow-traveller; and I endeavoured to increase the confidence he seemed so suddenly to place in me. I bore my own expences, which were not very heavy in such a mode of travelling; and in a week we had proceeded about thirty leagues, every day more and more content with each other. He had no suspicion that I was an Englishman. Nay, his notion of what an Englishman might be was altogether vague and confused. He only knew that the French and English were often at war together; that he had a brother and two uncles who were either killed by them, or died in the armies serving against them; but where these hostile people lived, or whether they were Turks or Jews, he was not very clear, though he had heard from the priest who had the care of his conscience and his wife's, that they were heretics, and would infallibly go to the Devil. He knew, however, that *ils faisoient bien leurs affaires ici bas,* for he had gained a great deal of money by selling knives, scissors, watch-chains, buckles, and many other such articles, the manufacture of these remote people; and he regretted that *the new order of things* had put an entire stop to his commerce in that line; which, together with his being compelled to take all payments in assignats, that every day became more and more depreciated in their value, gave him a suspicion, that *the new order of things* was less favourable to him than the old. His wife, he said, was furious against the *Patriotes,* and that she had incurred great risk of being denounced to the Municipality of the district; but her son's being forced to the army, and *his* own authority, who had insisted on her stifling her opinions, had hitherto kept them unmolested in their house: '*Et après tout, Monsieur*' said he — '*pourquoi nous perdrons nous pour une différence d'opinion ? — Qu'est-ce que tout cela me fait, pourvu que je fasse toujours bien mes affaires**' — I had seen almost enough to think as I said, when I answered — '*Mon ami, tu as raison†.*'

"If *his* reflections troubled himself or me but little, mine were not so easily subdued. — Alas! how often did they return towards England, and the dear family I had left there! How often did I ask when, or if ever, I should be restored to them, and the liberty, which alone I coveted, *of breathing in peace and security my native air.*

'We had now traversed Auvergne, and, continuing on the eastern boundary of Guienne, Caille (for so was my *ami du voyage* called) had some debts to receive at the town of Severac, that were likely to detain him a day or two; but he was impatient to be *installé* at Pezenas, on a certain day, when there was to be a fair, at which he usually made considerable profit. As he could travel on his little bidet much quicker than with his caravan, and as he had by this time the most assured reliance on my integrity and care, he desired I would go slowly on, accompanied by the boy, with his moveable warehouse; and he would himself overtake us in a day or two.

---

* And, after all, why should we risk being undone for a difference of opinion? What are all of those matters to me, provided I can but continue to prosper in my business?

† My friend, you are right.

"We proceeded, therefore, from Severac to the banks of the Tarn, which I failed not to apostrophise —

'Tarn! how delightful flow thy willow'd waves!'

but I lost the responsive rhyme, in being compelled to change the next line for—

'But, ah! they fructify a land of — Lunatics.'

"At St. Rome, where we rested half a day, I strolled into the Church, an old, gloomy, gothic building, the first I had examined since I left Paris.

"There had been soldiers quartered in it occasionally, as they passed through the town; and almost every part of its furniture as a sacred edifice had been carried away. It had also been made use of as a sort of workshop for the women, who were employed, either voluntarily or by requisition, to make tents and military clothing: but now it was quite deserted and empty; and as by the diminished light of evening I cast my eyes along the arched avenues and dilapidated choir, now vocal no more, I thought I had never before felt a more painful sensation than this half-demolished church impressed on my mind. —I listened to the wind that sighed round the massy pillars, till I could almost have persuaded myself the disturbed spirits of the dead murmured, from the ruined sepulchres on each side, maledictions against the barbarous intruders; and that

'... the gloomy aisles,
Black, plaster'd, and hung round with shreds of 'scutcheons,
And tatter'd coats of arms, sent back the sound
Laden with heavier airs from the low vaults
And mansions of the dead!'

"Nor could I think without a mixture of indignation and regret, how often I had seen suffering humanity relieved by pouring out its sorrows at the foot of those altars which were now levelled with the dust; and how many solitary pilgrims, who now dared not enter the violated walls, I used to observe asking, in these sanctuaries, either the forgiveness, or the blessings of Heaven.

"It may be urged, that many of the persons who were formerly to be seen from morning till night, in the churches of Roman Catholic countries, prostrate before the image of a favourite saint, or sitting or kneeling in some obscure corner, lost to the world and absorbed in penitence and prayer, were guilty of neglecting their families, and of a sinful waste of the time which would have clothed and fed them. — This may be true. But, alas! many of these poor creatures were of those, who on earth had neither relatives nor children to love, nor any social duties to fulfil. — Ah! who that has ever felt or dreaded that cold and dreary vacancy of the heart, can help lamenting, that in these asylums of penitence and piety the solitary mourner, whom the world deserts, finds no longer a relief by pouring out his sorrows before his God, and contemplating the representations given by human art of the sufferings of the Saviour of the World, by whose merits these poor and desolate children of affliction look forward to a future state of retribution! "

Impressed with these melancholy thoughts, I proceeded on my journey. We passed the river Sorgue the next day; and as I walked slowly on a bye road that was not far from the banks of the stream, I saw a chateau which excited my curiosity, because it appeared to be entirely deserted, and because it reminded me of Eastwoodleigh. I had time enough before me, and approached it. The situation, on a rising ground embosomed in trees, and on one side looking towards high and varied mountains, was singularly beautiful; but, when I entered the house, I found that it was, as I had imagined, quite without inhabitants. In many places the croisées had lost their glass, and no furniture remained. The doors were all open — some fallen from their hinges; and no living creature appeared to exist within its walls, save a bat or two (which I had probably disturbed by my intrusion at that early hour of the morning, for it was before sun-rise) flitting through the high vacant apartments. The dead silence of this forsaken mansion was chilling and depressive, the beauty of the site made its desertion seem the more to be regretted; and though I was ignorant even of the names of the former possessors of the place, I felt disposed to lament them as if they had been my friends!

"I wandered into the garden; it had been laid out in the English taste, or what the French consider as such, but so long neglected, that the trees were run into wildness, preferable perhaps in point of beauty to their more regular state. Towards the extremity, the cedars, cypresses, bay and Portugal laurels were grown into an almost impenetrable shade. I made my way among them — till the river broke suddenly upon me, brightening in the sun now just risen above the horizon. — Little were the sensations of my mind respondent to this burst of brilliancy! —I followed a grassy path that led along the river's edge, half hid by weeping willow. Trout were springing from the crystal waves, which were indeed so clear that I could distinguish every pebble at the bottom, and every minnow that wandered among them. The path I was in was terminated by a sort of summer-house of lattice-work, and the *treillage* with which it was covered was the passion flower*, now in luxuriant bloom, spangling with its large and radiant stars the dark palmated leaves that embowered every part of the lattice, and hung in elegant festoons from the windows, which looked immediately down on the water, while the odorous flowers were

'Wasting their sweetness on the desert air.'

"I sat down in this arbour of fragrance, and listened to the rippling of the current. A spot more calculated for the indulgence of the most delicious visions can hardly be imagined, and I, alas! am but too prone to indulge them. For awhile the sad spirit of presentiment yielded to the beauty of the place. Evils, whether real or apprehended, which might well

'Shade every flower, and darken every green,'

were, for a short moment, suspended. I saw myself in *such* a scene with one, who alone of all the world would make me happy in *any*, and who would herself feel and delight in the beauties of a spot so lovely —

'Je la voyois partout, entre les fleurs et la verdure;'

and I was lost in a dream of Elysium, from which I felt it a sort of outrage to be recalled, as I soon was by the voice of the boy, who was alarmed by my stay.

Slowly and reluctantly I rejoined him; and as it was not easy to recall my thoughts from the place, I enquired if he knew to whom it had belonged, and why it was deserted. The boy knew nothing; but at a little cabaret on the edge of a vineyard about a league farther, I heard, on asking the same question, that it had been the property of a ci-devant Duke, but for many years preceding the Revolution had been rented by English families.

"Afterwards, as I journeyed on, I recollected that Sterne, in one of his letters, talks of a house he inhabited on the banks of the Sorgue, where, in a pavilion, they might fish for trout from the windows. This,

* Passiflora Cærulea

perhaps, was the very residence he described. — Alas! how changed, since his animated pen depicted it, are all but the local charms of this country!

"This change had, since I entered Guienne, gradually become more visible; and many forsaken dwellings, as well as that I had left, had brought many sad recollections to my mind.

"There was then a time when an Englishman, driven like me from his own country either by his own improvidence or the wicked persecution of others, might have found here such an asylum as would have left him but little to regret; for who, that was not rooted by the most obstinate prejudices to the soil, would hesitate to prefer this lovely climate, and this lovely country, even though he must quit all the society he has been used to (and indeed society of all sorts), to the summer verdure and boasted freedom of England — when on the other side of the account he may see through the country fogs, bailiffs and attorneys dogging him, and a not very distant view of a prison for life terminating the prospect? Whoever has had, as a distressed man, much to do with the money-getting and money-saving part of the British nation, will not talk in a very elevated strain of its liberal minds and noble spirits in exclusion of all others. That there are many among them who are, though very high in the commercial, as eminent in the moral world, is undoubted; but for the bulk of those who have been brought up over account-books to consider money as the first good, I know not if any country has less to boast of as to their genuine liberality and enlargement of mind than England.

"It can as little be denied, that no where is he who is struggling to rise, or he who has fallen from his rank, kept down with more inveterate malignity, more over-bearing pride, than in England. — There it is, that he who is once able to make a figure, and is esteemed rich, sees all the crimes forgotten by which he became so. There the profligate pensioner, the titled parasite, the plunderer of his own country or of any other, and even the private robber who has address enough to rob within the pale of the law, is not only tolerated but respected. Let every man who is compelled to leave his native land recollect all this, and leave behind him prejudices and local attachments that make a great part of the miseries of life.

"Oh, Eversley! my imagination, to which you have often told me I too much give the reins — my imagination represents to me how happy, how supremely happy I could be in such a place as I have just described, with my family — with ... Ah! dear and cruel remembrance! — It seemed made for the retreat of those who have less taste for the artificial pleasures of the world, than for the simple unwearying delights that nature so bountifully offers in a climate like this. Might not the loveliest and most elegant of minds have here been content, nay happy, in her favourite pursuits; and have found

'... rich amends
For a lost world in solitude and love?'

"But I wander wildly indeed from my narrative, to which it is more than time to recall my pen, though I have very little to say till I reached Lodeve, where I took a reluctant leave of my Marchand de Balle, to whose accommodation I had been obliged for protection and conveyance during near three weeks, and for a journey of above seventy leagues. We parted, well satisfied with each other. I had still a long and hazardous route before me; and, from the hourly observations I made, I found that the risk I had already run was nothing in comparison of that I must probably encounter before I could reach the residence of my venerable relation De Lavergnac, of whose safety every thing I now heard and saw made me entertain a thousand doubts.

"Towards the troubled scene into which, from motives of gratitude and affection, I was determined to throw myself, I looked not with fear, for to me life seemed every day less and less desirable, but with the same kind of reluctance (though heavier) that I used to feel, when I have been compelled to quit the country to attend in London, on business, the wretches who either persecuted my poor father, or pretended, while they were entangling him the more, to deliver him from persecution. I remembered how in my early youth I have waited for hours and days in the dark caverns of iniquity, called lawyers' chambers, where the very air seemed to be infected by the poison of the reptiles who inhabited them, and where the registers of the victims they had devoured, or were devouring, were the only furniture of the walls. I remembered how, while I appeared to listen to their jargon, I often failed to comprehend it; while my mind had fled back to the scenes I had left — scenes which I now indeed possess in idea only; for Sir Ralph Gunstone and his emissaries had touched them, and Robespierre and his agents are not more destructive and more cruel.

"To places where these latter had carried death and desolation, I however bent my course; much doubting, as I approached Lavergnac, whether I was not too late to be of the least use to the poor old Baron, who could hardly, I thought, have remained there unmolested, even if he had submitted (which I did not believe probable) to temporize with the ruffians he could not resist.

"As alone I traversed a mountainous and woody tract, through which the river Gardon wanders to meet the Rhone, I felt the cruel contrast between the delicious quiet and independence I seemed here to enjoy, and the miseries that awaited me where my species, and even my countrymen, were collected in the sad task of defence against violence, or the wretched one of offence towards others: for, from what I had lately learned on my way, I found Toulon was in possession of the English, and I thought highly probable what I afterwards found to be true, that if De Lavergnac yet lived, he had fled thither."

At this moment the friends were interrupted by Amelia Marchmont, who came in excessive agitation to tell them, that the farmer, of whom her mother rented the house, had just been to receive his monthly rent; and sitting down to prose in the sort of half-intelligent way that such men generally talk in, he had told her with strange circumstances, which it was difficult to credit, of the evacuation of Toulon, such as it had been related in a country paper which he had just seen. To this man the scene was remote, and the interest weak; for he considered only how it might, by prolonging the war, prolong or increase the taxes he already grumbled to pay. Of Mrs. Marchmont's sensations he had no conception; nor could he imagine why, having eagerly seized on the first word he had uttered about Toulon, she had listened in breathless silence to the report he made from the newspaper, growing pale and paler as he proceeded, till she fell back lifeless in her chair. The farmer then rang the bell for help; and Mrs. Marchmont was but just restored to life when Lucy, and with her Althea, hurried to relieve and console her.

CHAP. IV.

Quel traits me présentent vos fasles,
Impitoyables conquérans?
Des vœux outrès, des projets vastes,
Des Rois vaincus par des tyrans;
Des murs que la flamme ravage,
Des vainqueurs sumans de carnage.

WHAT HAPPINESS TO Althea, as well as to the sisters of Marchmont, to be enabled to restore his mother to hope, and indeed to life, by shewing her the letter, which assured, beyond a doubt, his safety!

As soon as they had gone through the preceding pages of his letter, and by that means convinced Mrs. Marchmont that he was, when he wrote it, in so much security, as to be able to reflect calmly on, as well as to relate distinctly, the circumstances of his past danger; her own good sense and solicitude to hear the rest, assisted her to compose her spirits, and she listened anxiously, though silently, to the sequel of his letter.

CONTINUATION OF MARCHMONT'S LETTER.

"After some perils, and a great deal of fatigue, I arrived at what was once the Chateau de Lavergnac.

You have heard me say it was never a very large or splendid structure, for it was built by the son of that Marchmont who, preferring his loyalty to his country, was an exile, or, as we should now say, an emigrant with James the Second; and who was infinitely more fortunate than most of the followers of that unhappy prince by marrying an heiress of Languedoc, and being in favour with the French monarch! But though the house, less magnificent than commodious, rather resembled the old-fashioned but comfortable mansion of an English country gentleman of moderate fortune, than the seat of a French nobleman, it was, when I had visited it before, a residence which might have satisfied any man not extremely fastidious; and the bastide that belonged to it, contained every thing that could create plenty and convenience in a country establishment. The vineyards around it produce wine of a remarkably excellent quality; and olives, capers, oranges, and white mulberries, formed the boundaries of the enclosures.

"In some, the great American aloe gave a new and singular feature to the landscape, while it formed an admirable fence; and firs, pines, and chesnuts, shaded and mitigated the glow of the too rich and luxurious scenery.

"Such was the place when I last saw it — What it was now I will leave you to imagine as a proprietor of land, when I tell you it had been seized and sold as a national domain, to one who had formerly been a workman on the estate. The man, probably because he believed his tenure precarious, had turned every thing into present money. The house was without furniture — a part of it only was inhabited by a peasant and his family. The grounds which my venerable and worthy old friend had ornamented and cultivated as much for his pleasure as his profit, were now by their mercenary usurper applied wholly to the latter purpose. The particulars of this cruel devastation I had no means, nor indeed any heart, to enquire. It was not without great precaution, and many difficulties, that I learned the fate of the Baron and his family, which, as I believe you know, consisted of the old Baron, his only son, and his grandson, a young man of two-and-twenty, married in ninety-two to a young Swiss lady.

"I trembled as I at length heard their destiny. Monsieur de Lavergnac had emigrated at the end of 1793. His father, the old Baron, and his son, who was called the Chevalier de Remiremont, remained at Lavergnac. The latter had quitted his regiment, of which a great part had emigrated, and thought he might be allowed to attend on the declining age of his grandfather, who took no part in public affairs from the moment that he saw of how little use he could be, and who was so universally beloved in his neighbourhood, that for the first four years of the convulsions that shook France he had remained respected and unmolested. At his express desire the engagement the Chevalier had made with Mademoiselle —— of Lausanne was completed. It had not long taken place when the fatal intelligence reached the Baron of the death of his son in Germany, and he was in the same week driven from his house. For some time a faithful servant, who had grown rich by his bounty, sheltered him; while the Chevalier and his wife endeavoured,

at his earnest entreaties, to escape into Switzerland, and nothing has
since been heard of them. The Baron, laden with years and sorrow,
lost no part of his fortitude; and he seemed to have been preserved by
the particular intervention of Providence, till the period when Toulon
being in possession of the English, the venerable fugitive took refuge
within its walls; and there he was still supposed to be when one of his
old domestics, to whom I made myself known, gave me this account.

"There I determined to seek him — though I dreaded a meeting,
for what misery had we not reciprocally to relate! But I hoped to be
of use to him; to supply to him the son he had lost, the grandson
whom his tenderness for this last branch of his family had compelled
to consult his own safety. I obtained admittance then into the town,
and made myself known to the Baron. I cannot describe our meeting;
but he seemed still to encourage hope of better days, which I who was
so much younger dared hardly at that juncture entertain. The respect
that the virtues and age of De Lavergnac had commanded, even from
ferocious republicans, followed him. The English shewed him every
attention their circumstances admitted; and as it was soon known who
I was, and what had been my purpose in passing at so great a hazard
through France, I was noticed by the British commanders, and placed
in a commissary's office, where, if honest men *can* rise in such employments, I might perhaps have risen to a more profitable post. It was in
such a hope I wrote to my mother; and while I flattered myself that
I might become useful to her and my family, I had the satisfaction of
soothing the sorrows of the venerable Baron, and returning a part of
those obligations I owed him.

"Alas! this power and these hopes were but of short duration. You
know the fatal catastrophe at Toulon! I will not attempt to describe a
scene, of which language must fail in conveying an adequate idea. My
greatest solicitude was to carry off my poor old friend to the English
ships. In that I succeeded; and having seen him safe, I could not bear
to remain inactive on board, while danger and death surrounded so
many of my countrymen, and still more the wretched inhabitants of
the town that had received them. I went off, therefore, again from the
man of war to the shore with a party of sailors, who were employed in
delivering the unhappy people from the fury of the republicans, and,
what was still worse, of the galley slaves. I had the good fortune to
help in saving, at least from immediate destruction, above twenty of
these luckless victims; and I was with the same set of active seamen

returning a third time to the shore, when our boat was blown out of the water by the explosion of one of the ships. You remember that I was always a good swimmer; I was not wounded, though so stunned, that I think it must have been a minute or two before I recollected myself, and made my way by swimming to the shore, where I almost instantly received a pistol shot, and fell senseless on the beach. The man who fired at me probably believed me dead; a belief to which I undoubtedly owed my preservation; for he in all likelihood went to wreak his vengeance in some other quarter, and I found myself alone and bleeding on the shore. The flames that were raging around, the groans of the dying, the shrieks of the prisoners, and the savage shouts of triumph, recalled me to a consciousness of my situation. I tried to get up, though I knew that to escape was impossible, and that my death was inevitable; but when I would have arisen, I found myself so weak from loss of blood, and my clothes so heavy with the water, that I was quite unable to stand; I therefore crawled towards a broken boat that lay a few yards farther, and, lying down beneath it, prepared, as well as the confused state of my head would let me, for the death that awaited me."

Mrs. Marchmont, as well as her daughters, and Althea who had undertaken to read, all found themselves too much affected at this passage to be able to proceed for some time. The mother could not hear without agony of the danger her son had been in, though certain that he had finally escaped it.

As soon, however, as they had all a little recovered themselves, Lucy undertook to relieve the faltering, trembling Althea, and thus went on:

Marchmont's Letter continued.

"The pain of my wound prevented my losing all sense of my condition, as I think I should otherwise have done from weakness and loss of blood. I saw, amidst horrors which are not to be described, the morning break, which I concluded was the last I should ever see. Soon after my spirits gradually forsook me; I thought with anguish on what my poor mother and my sisters would suffer, when they should know that I was no more.

"One other person, and you, my dear long-tried friend, flitted before my departing senses. I murmured out an eternal adieu, and my last prayer was for the happiness of the *six* beings, who only were very dear to me on earth, and for whose sake alone I regretted that I was now to leave it.

"I was unconscious how long I lay in this state of stupor; but when I was recalled to sense, I found myself in a cart with three other bodies, which they were going to bury. I spoke, or at least attempted it. The soldier who drove the cart lifted me up, and asked who I was? I had not recollection enough to consider what it would be most conducive to my safety to pass for, and answered in a faint voice that I was an Englishman.

"From nine out of ten among the people into whose hands I had fallen, it is certain that this answer, far from serving as a protection, would have brought upon me a stroke of the bayonet, which would have ended my life at once. But it happened that the man to whom I spoke was an old invalid; he had been a prisoner to the English in the American war; had been cured of a wound he received in the action; well treated, and exchanged as soon as he was able to move. To this circumstance I owe my life. The old soldier remembered his own situation, and pitied mine. My accent convinced him I was what I represented; and instead of destroying me he took me into a house, and, having placed me on some straw on the floor, and given me some wine and water, which seemed to revive me so as that I could distinctly speak, he left me to the care of a woman who did not seem so humane as he was, and went to finish his mournful business of burying the dead, promising to return as soon as he could, and to bring or send a surgeon.

"The pain and weakness I endured again became excessive; and again I believed myself dying, and indeed wished to die rather than to linger, as seemed but too probable, in tortures for many days, only to perish at last. The uncommon strength of my constitution still resisted the complicated mischiefs that had fallen upon me. It was not till night that the friendly old soldier returned; he administered all he could with the greatest humanity, and himself extracted the bullet that was lodged between my shoulder and collar bone: but though it had not penetrated very deep, his want of skill put me to inconceivable torture, and the muscles were so torn in the operation, that a great part of the danger I was afterwards in arose from that circumstance.

"If you ever received my former letter, you already know the imminent peril I was in during my imprisonment; for though I was at first considered as an Englishman, one of the peasants who had seen me at Lavergnac when I was in search of the Baron, came into the corps that occasionally guarded the prisoners; and this man deposed, that he knew me to be a relation of the Baron's, and a Frenchman. In consequence of which I should probably have died on the scaffold with a number of other wretched victims, if the young surgeon, of whom I spoke in that letter, had not added to the friendly care by which he saved my life, the inestimable blessing of liberty which he contrived to give me at the utmost risk of perishing in my place. I cannot help remarking, my friend, that while one set of professional men have occasioned to me all the miseries of my life (I mean men of the law), from those of *another* profession I have received the most liberal kindness, the most remarkable proofs of disinterested friendship; and it is to a medical man I owe the existence, which, probably, if ever I reach my native country, the other description of men will contrive still to embitter. Alas! dear Eversley, amidst the horrors of a French prison — among strangers and enemies —I saw nothing so hideous to *my* eyes, so detestable to *my* feelings, as Vampyre and another wretch of the same species: I suffered nothing so painful as what *their* persecution had in England inflicted upon me, and on those whose peace is dearer to me than my own. Released at once from imprisonment, and the fear of death, and furnished by my generous and amiable friend with money enough for my perilous journey, I implicitly followed his directions, and made my way into Switzerland. A journal of my stratagems, and hazards, would make my letter too long, and sometimes I am willing to hope that we may meet in England, and once more enjoy the delight of confidential friendship......... To that time I will refer a regular history of my wanderings; and you will at the present period of my narrative imagine me arrived at Bienne in safety, yet extremely fatigued, and at a season when this country is sometimes passable only in the beaten road. However, to stay at Bienne was impossible — I therefore merely delivered the letters given me by my friend Deslormes, which procured me a passport from the magistrates, and a farther supply of money, and I determined to proceed to Basle.

"I will check the disposition I even now feel to describe the valley of Munster— to tell you how, in passing it, I sometimes forgot the rigors of winter, even all I had suffered, and all I dreaded, and was lost in admiring the wildness and singularity of the scene. I passed a night in one of the deepest excavations of its rocks in such perfect repose, that not a peasant girl came with her little offering, or little orison, to *our lady of the cave,* a rude image held in great veneration by the people of the country, which is placed in a niche cut in the rock at the farther end, over a rustic altar table of the same materials.

"To this night's lodging, however, for it was excessively cold, I owed the pain I felt the next day in my ill-healed wound. It was indeed so acute, that I doubted for some time whether any exertion of resolution would enable me to go on. I would now have been glad to meet any human being who could have informed me of my way, or have assisted my feeble steps to pursue it; yet it was long since I had avoided meeting my own species. — Strange and wretched perversion of the social propensities of our own nature, when the pilgrim is compelled to fly from his fellow man!

"I should now, at any risk, have spoken to whomever I had met, even a republican soldier of France; but I saw no one as I walked, or rather crept along, for about three miles towards the Pierce Pertuis* — then faint with pain, I became unable to continue my route, and with little hope of regaining strength enough to get to any place of shelter that night; in which case it was most likely I should perish with cold before morning. I sat down under one of those rude cliffs that bound the river Birze, as it hastens through the valley among narrow straits formed of incumbent rock. A stupor stole fast over my wearied senses, and blunted the pain which I had felt from the irritation of my wound; and I should probably have sunk wholly from inanition, weakness, and that hopeless languor that is often the effect of bodily pain and fatigue extended beyond the strength of the sufferer, had I not towards evening been roused from this state of half annihilation by a Swiss peasant, who crossing one of those many rustic bridges thrown over the Birze, saw me, and, approaching, spoke to me in the patois of the country. I was unable to answer. He sat down by me, and with humanity and good sense that would have done honour to more polished life, endeavoured to rouse me to exertion. After some time he succeeded; and though he has since told me he believed me to be a French patriot, which at that period was a name dreaded by many of the Swiss, he generously forgot his prejudice or his fear, in consideration of my calamitous situation; and putting me upon a small horse, with which he was conveying some necessaries for his family from Bienne, he walked by its side, encouraging me with the most patient pity to endure the present evil in the assurance of immediate relief. — It was, however,

---

* A rock, through which an arched way is cut to facilitate the communication between Basle and Bienne.

with great difficulty, and at a late hour of the night, that I reached his hospitable cottage, in the village of Lauffen.

Here the repose I enjoyed, and kindness I received from these honest people, rare, but I hope not unique, specimens of ancient Swiss hospitality and humanity, soon restored me — not to ease, for my wound was still extremely painful at times — but to so much strength of mind and body, as enabled me to consider what I could and ought to do: and the recollection of my mother and my sisters, of the cruel suspense they must be in, of the addition their fears for my life and safety must make to their other sorrows, determined me, whatever personal inconvenience might still await me in England, to return thither. My mother had continually, in my half-delirious state from pain and long want of sleep, been present to me. Now more perfectly in possession of my senses, all the scenes I had formerly witnessed in England with her returned to my remembrance. Her hardly-acquired fortitude when the delicacy of her frame ill supported the dignity of her mind; her mild submission to evils, heavy because inflicted by men; her patient descent from the place she had been accustomed to, and had so good a right to fill; and her quiet acquiescence under every oppression but those which threatened to deprive her of her children; and, as these impressions were renewed, the dread of all she might have endured in my absence of pecuniary hardship, became almost insupportable. — Ah, my dear Eversley! I sometimes reproach myself with cowardice in having ever left her, though at her own earnest entreaty —

> 'Oppress'd by a base world, perhaps she bends
> Beneath the weight of other ills than grief;
> And, desolate, implores of Heaven the aid
> Her son should give!'

"Alas! the resolution to return to England was more easily made than executed. To my generous host, however, I owed another kindness in addition to all those he had already shewn me. When he saw how uneasy I was, and (already knowing I was English) heard why I desired to return to my native country, he undertook to conduct me himself to Fribourg, from whence he thought I might reach Hanover, and among Englishmen, whom I should undoubtedly find there, obtain with less difficulty a conveyance to England.

"This plan then, as far as it depended on him, was immediately executed. — After staying a day or two at Fribourg, I found myself

CHARLOTTE SMTIH

well, and strong enough to resume my former method of travelling on foot. I parted with this honest and worthy man with regret, most sincerely anxious for the time when I should be able to repay him for all his kindness, and doubting, as I approached the country, where, since it was belonging to the King of England, I expected to meet many of my countrymen, whether I should find, even among them, more generous minds, more friendly spirits, than I had been so fortunate as to encounter in Deslormes, and this man Andre Vanette. If I had ever felt a disposition to indulge that national arrogance, and national prejudice, with which Englishmen in the middling or lower ranks of life are from their infancy impressed, I should surely have divested myself of it in the observations I had now occasion to make. But thrown by misfortune from the bosom of my country, I early learned to be a Citizen of the World. — In what obscure corner of it, Eversley, shall *I* ever find a quiet asylum?

"That, my dear friend, is an enquiry which it is not now a moment to make. — I hasten to conclude the little I have to relate.

"Imagine me then among Englishmen and Germans, nearly connected with them — myself a soi-disant Englishman, but without recommendation, without acquaintance, without any means of ascertaining what I was, or to whom I belonged. My language indeed might have answered for my country; but as I spoke another equally well, and had evidently been rambling about the world; as I had passed through France at a time when such a *trajet* seemed impossible to a man not well affected towards the then governors; as I called myself a gentleman, yet none of my connections seemed to *countenance* me; the persons to whom I addressed myself (as I hoped, without baseness, and certainly without the shadow of deception) seemed to suspect me as an Avanturier; perhaps an Avanturier of a dangerous description, with whom it would be unsafe for them to have any thing to do. — The repulsive coldness, the constrained half civility I was received with, soon taught me that I had but little to expect from the higher in power among those, on whom *I thought* my being an Englishman, and of decided loyalty, might have given me some sort of claim to what I solicited; which was, to be employed either in a civil or military capacity there, till I could, in some public trust, be sent to England. I had even fancied, that the knowledge I had acquired of the situation of France would have been useful; but I found that even my having been there was a crime, and laid me open to suspicions either felt or *feigned.* I sometimes thought that they were the *latter,* and assumed merely as an excuse for the refusal it was determined I should generally experience. For, when once the persons of *consequence* had repulsed me, I found the same tone assumed by the rest — and I was *bowed out* by the subalterns with even less civility than I had received from their masters. — Among others whom it was my lot to meet with, was a nephew of Lady Silchester's deceased Lord ——I must go back a little to relate the circumstance and its consequence.

"Do not imagine, my dear Eversley, that, when it appeared necessary for me to say *who* I was, I had spoken of my near relationship to that foolish, proud, unfeeling woman, as either a boast or a designation; but, when I named myself, a secretary who sat with the great man I was talking to observed very coldly, that the late Lord Silchester had married a lady, whose other sister was the wife of a Mr. Marchmont. This man, it seems, was a genealogist, and piqued himself upon the knowledge of all the intermarriages of the nobility; so that he might have been a very oracle to those who hardly knew they had a grandfather, if to enquire had been their object, after they had once satisfied themselves by being duly enrolled in the records of those *'gentle historians*, who dip their pen in nothing but the milk of human kindness; who seek no further for merit than the preamble of a patent; or the inscription of a tomb; with whom every man created a Peer, is first an hero ready made; who judge of every man's capacity by the offices he has filled — and the more offices the more ability; with whom every General Officer is a Marlborough; every Statesman a Burleigh; every Judge a Murray, or a Yorke; so that men who alive were laughed at or pitied by all their acquaintance, make as good a figure as the best of them in the pages of Gwillim, Edmondson, and Collins.'*

"To this observation of the Commis, Mr. Platt, relative to Lady Silchester, I answered, without however feeling myself at all honoured by the alliance — 'That it was true. The lady he spoke of was my mother's sister.'

"I saw doubt hang on the countenances of both the great man and his secretary, or it was rather perhaps *fear* that if I could make out any such noble connection, they should feel themselves compelled to do me some kindness. However that might be, my indignant spirit, which I had with difficulty subdued to the meanness of solicitation at all, now

---

*   Vide Burke's Letter to a Nobel Lord.——This is, undoubtedly, an anachronism; for which the author can only apologize by saying, that it was impossible to find any other form of words equally adapted to her meaning.

rose against the degradation of being questioned either by the insolent military man, or his cold-blooded underling. —I arose, and, forbearing with difficulty to express what I thought, quitted the audience, with a resolution to return to it no more.

"I had determined to set out once again either on foot or by the conveyance afforded by rivers, to make my way to Hamburgh, and from thence to England; but some preliminaries, not very easy to settle, were of necessity to be thought of, before I could, even in this cheap and independent manner of travelling, begin another journey.

"While I was deliberating how to act, I was met in the street by the great man's secretary and the nephew of Lady Silchester, together with another young officer. It seemed as if the Commis, who I was sure had regarded me with an evil eye when he had before seen me, was seeking an opportunity to detect me as an impostor; for he immediately addressed himself to Captain Melincourt, and said, slightly touching his hat to me — 'This, Captain Melincourt, is the Mr. Marchmont I mentioned to you.' — The military boy, who at first view appeared to be a great coxcomb, stared at me — 'I have not the honour to know the gentleman,' said he, with a cold drawl. — 'I believe not,' answered I with more spirit than I suppose became my appearance; 'for I do not know that I ever saw you before.' — I was turning away, when the secretary, Mr. Platt, chose to add — 'And yet, Sir, I thought you had given yourself out for a relation by marriage to Captain Melincourt?' — 'I given myself out. Sir? — If you dare to assert *that*, I tell you, you utter a falsehood. — What, Sir! do you imagine that any circumstances could urge me to say the thing that is *not*? or, if I *were* so degraded, that I should descend yet a step lower, in trying to derive any credit from accidental relationship to contemptible and insignificant beings, only because they bear titles?' —I then walked away, leaving the Commis and the Captain to digest this brusquerie as they thought proper. They stood still a moment, as if wondering that a poor man, a wanderer as I was, should dare to resent an insult; while I returned to my obscure lodging, not without feeling the necessity of calling to my assistance all my fortitude, or, rather, all those reflections that teach it. I compared *myself*, the faculties of my own mind, and the power of enduring evil or of rising above it, with the intellectual possessions of the two creatures who looked upon me with contempt; and I asked myself, whether, destitute wanderer and houseless stranger as I was, I would, for a moment, exchange situations with either of these paltry fellows?

My heart proudly disdained the question; and, without bestowing on them another thought, I was calmly renewing such little preparations as I could make for my departure, which I meant to take that evening, when I saw enter the third person who had been in company with the Commis and Captain Melincourt. Though I had no other idea than that he came with a repetition of insult, I received him as a gentleman; for *he* at least had not yet offended me, and there was something in his countenance and figure that prejudiced me in his favour.

"He was a man about my own age, but appeared, by his diffident yet ingenuous manner, to have been but little conversant with the world. He was evidently embarrassed how to begin the conversation, which confirmed me in my idea, that he had some message to deliver that he felt to be rude and brutal; for I did not imagine that the gentlemen who had spoken to me considered me of sufficient consequence to receive a *cartel* from men who fancied themselves of so much.

"After some seconds of hesitation and confusion, my visitor thus explained himself:

"'I do not know, Sir, whether you will accept the apology it is necessary for a stranger to make, who comes without any introduction; but as your countryman, I wait upon you with offers of such service as I can render you. The most fortunate may have occasion for the good offices of a *compatriot* in a strange land. I understand you are far from your friends, and have escaped from France. You may be out of money to facilitate your return to England. Allow me to be your banker. — My power as a younger brother, and a mere soldier of fortune, is not great; but such as it is, I beg you will command it with as little scruple as I trust you would do if we had long been friends.'

"Nothing could be so remote as was this address from what I expected. It would be tedious to relate the whole dialogue that followed. I learned that my new acquaintance was a Captain Forrester, one of the aides-de-camp to a general officer, and the younger son of the Earl of Stanwarden: that he was accidentally walking with Mr. Platt and Captain Melincourt when they met me, and was shocked at their unprovoked insolence: 'I own,' said he, 'I was pleased with the spirit you shewed, and not sorry to see Platt mortified; for he is an arrogant and stupid fellow, presuming on the office he fills, which, though the meanest abilities are adequate to its execution, he fancies gives him great dignity, and is a proof of profound wisdom and uncommon genius. He is a solemn coxcomb. If he does but sign a passport, or an order for forage, he assumes an air of the greatest importance, and talks of the *laborious business* he is engaged in — *the prodigious fatigue* of his office — the *vast weight* of the affairs that lay on his shoulders. Over every thing he does, though it be only writing to his gardener in England, whom he pompously calls his homme d'affaires, he throws a veil of mystery; so that any one who observed without knowing him, would conclude he was engaged in a correspondence with Ministry of the utmost importance to his country — whereas he is probably only giving directions about the management of his cucumber beds for an early crop, or regulating the site of his melon frames; for this fungus is, like most such fort of men, very fond of the table. When he speaks of himself it is always in the plural — 'We of the diplomatique corps — Persons of a certain description like *us*, entrusted by Government — We, the friends of Administration — To us, who are in the secret of all that — To *efficient* men of our department.' Such is the language of this consequential secretary, who is also among those who used to be called Croakers, but who have of late assumed the more tremendous title of Alarmists; insomuch that I have sometimes recommended it to him to recollect the fable of the boy and the wolf. To prove, however, at once, and exercise his sagacity, he is continually discovering plots and conspiracies — French agents, and lurking Jacobins: and it was probably some such character that he intended to fix upon you.

"'When you left us just now, I could not help enquiring who you was? Platt answered, that you pretended your name was Marchmont — that it might be so for aught he knew, but that Captain Melincourt, whose uncle had married a near relation of that family, did not know you; and that even if you were the person you pretended to be, he thought you of a very suspicious character. There was a young fellow of that name in London,' said he, 'a year or two ago. He was a writer for the booksellers; and I was assured (for I have no time to read such trifles myself), that there were sentences in his books (I have no recollection of the name of them) that were to be discouraged. Such necessitous people running about Europe, writing their remarks, and promulgating and propagating their wild and impertinent theories just at this time, under the name of *travels*, or novels, are to be discouraged and repressed. I will have nothing to do with Mr. Marchmont, *or soi-disant tel*; and I have advised my Lord not to give him the smallest countenance.'

"'You believe him an impostor then,' said I, 'and, thus impressed, think yourself justified in withholding from him the protection and assistance which he does not otherwise seem to have forfeited, and which as an Englishman he has an undoubted right to expect?'

"'The secretary,' continued Captain Forrester, 'gave me a look of contempt; told me I was a young man, but for a man of fashion had strange tramontane ideas — That he knew no claims but such as arose from some service to Government — That an Englishman whose principles he was not sure of was to him no more than a Frenchman, or a Dutchman — That, in short, he did not half like you, and thought the sooner you left this place the better. Offended,' added my generous defender, 'with the overbearing impertinence of this official puppy, I determined to see you myself; and from our short conversation I am already persuaded, that you have the most undoubted claims to credit for all you have said as to yourself, and certainly to every friendly office which the natives of the same country owe to each other when they meet at a distance from it.'

"From this moment," said the continuation of Marchmont's letter, "from this moment the most friendly and unreserved intimacy originated between me and Captain Forrester, whom I found to be a man of the most ingenuous mind, the most elegant manners — which his reserve, and even diffidence among strangers, serve to render yet more pleasing to those few whom he esteems. These the goodness of his heart and the sweetness of his temper attach to him most affectionately. Brave even to faulty rashness, yet full of tenderness and humanity, he abhors the cold and cruel policy the views of which he is professionally engaged to promote, and not unfrequently finds his candour and his good nature insufficient to enable him to observe the forms of civility with the men with whom he is often obliged to associate. Bred up, like many other younger sons of the nobility, in the army, he is far from considering war as right and necessary because it is his profession; but, as an individual, his benevolence is continually exerted to mitigate its horrors, and to meliorate the condition of the soldiers under his command. His soldiers of course adore him, and yet there is not a company so well disciplined as his — not one where punishment, or even reprimand, is so little necessary.

"I could write a volume, and yet not exhaust this topic. I reserve it, therefore, to the hour of our meeting, my dear Eversley, and proceed to tell you, that after a few days Captain Forrester, from the confidence that subsisted between us, was perfectly acquainted with my situation, and the difficulties that were in the way of my returning to England:

but he thought with me that I ought to brave those difficulties; and by his assistance, for from such a man I had no scruple to accept it, I am now on my way to Hamburgh. — Yet from the situation of public affairs at this moment I know not when I shall arrive there, or when get from thence. My late experience, dear Eversley, convinces me, that mankind are less under the influence of education and climate than we are generally taught to believe. To pass over the demagogues of France, (men who are intoxicated with sudden power, perverted by false ambition, or awed by terror), I speak only of those farther removed from the concussions of the great volcano. Of the two French surgeons, for example — one of them seemed glad to pronounce me in danger of dying, as if he thought it a general benefit that there should be one Englishman (if I was one), or at least one royalist, less in the world; while the other relieved and liberated me at his own imminent hazard. Yet these two men were both educated in the same profession, and the same principles, under the same animating sun: the one was proud, morose, vindictive, and a bigot to he knew not what chimæras; while the other was liberal-minded, generous, and humane, considering nothing but how he might do good to his fellow-men, whatever might be their country, their religion, or their politics. It is true that the latter of these was young, the other a man near fifty; and I believe, from all I have hitherto observed, that Lord Bacon's observation is but too just —

'Age improves rather in the powers of the understanding, than in the virtues of the will and affections.'

Shall I say nothing of my *illustrious* Swiss peasant, Andre Vanette? who might indeed be termed

'A noble, of Nature's own creation!'

the good Samaritan, who received me sick and a stranger, who poured oil and wine into my wounds when so many others would have

'Against the houseless stranger shut the door!'

Yes! I will assert, that though I trust Nature has scattered here and there such hearts in *all* climates and countries, I never met with one in that rank of life at all to be compared to him in any part of the world.

"Let us, to follow this chain of thought, contemplate the characters of Captain Melincourt and Captain Forrester, two men born with equal personal advantages, both of noble families, both younger sons of nearly equal expectations, and both, after the same course of education, entering at the age of sixteen into the army.

"Melincourt is effeminate, insipid, selfish, and as insolent as his insolence will allow him to be. He loves money, because he can purchase with it pleasures, of which his vacant mind is always in search, though nothing has power to rouse him long from the apathy of satiety. Sick of himself, yet loving nothing else, he lives in perpetual solicitude, less for the actual safety than the want of accommodation for that dear sweet person of his; though so burdensome is it, notwithstanding all the most studied indulgences, that, like the wretched Roman Emperor, he is almost ready to offer a premium to whoever could find something that might give new interest to his mawkish existence.

"What Forrester is, the traits I have given you of his character may help you to imagine. If climate, education, or the government under which they have lived, influenced the characters of men, surely these two could never so radically, so totally differ. I will hope, my friend, to make Forrester known to you in England. — In England! — Alas! how many events may have happened there, to render my return thither the most painful moment of my life! I will not again, however, enter on such disquisitions: they are useless, and would carry me too far.

"My dear and excellent friend, adieu! Wherever he is, your happiness is among the first wishes of

E. A. M."

CHAP. V

Già riede primavera
Col suo fiorita aspetto;
Già il grato zeffiretto
Scherza fra l'erbe, e il fior —
— Tornan le frondi agli alberi,
L'erbette al prato tornano,
Sol non ritorna a me,
La pace del mio cor.

WHEN THE MIND of Mrs. Marchmont was as much composed as the nature of her situation and the remaining uncertainty would admit, some degree of tranquility, however chastised by fear, was restored to every breast but that of Althea. For *her* there was not even the semblance of repose to be found; for, released from the extreme concern she had felt for the life of Marchmont, she now turned her thoughts to her future conduct in regard to him, and asked herself, whether on his return it would be prudent or consistent for her to reside in the house which, whether his persecutors allowed him always to be there, or drove him occasionally into concealment, could not but be considered as his home. Yet how could she propose quitting Mrs. Marchmont, because her son was about to return to her? Althea was to this hour ignorant whether she knew of Marchmont's attachment to her; for she had never once mentioned, or even remotely hinted at it. That Lucy was in possession of her brother's confidence was certain: but even she had never spoken quite plainly to Althea, who, from all the observations she had made on the mother as well as the daughters, thought she saw, that while they should think of Marchmont as most fortunate in becoming the husband of Althea, they considered her prospects, and even her present fortune, as placing her entirely out of his reach; for the latter was not enough to put it in her power to give even a competent share of affluence to the man she should prefer, if he had himself nothing, as was literally the case with Marchmont; and while the style of life she had been used to, and which she preferred, seemed to assimilate their destinies, Mrs. Marchmont could not bear to have it supposed, that she wished to take advantage of Althea's partiality to *her* family, to engage her in an alliance which that of Sir Audley Dacres might deem so unequal on account of the indigence and distress to which Marchmont and his family were reduced; though in point of family antiquity they had the advantage. Such Althea fancied were the sentiments of her female friends; and if her ideas were just, she foresaw that her stay might be painful to the disinterested delicacy of Mrs. Marchmont; while on the other hand her partial tenderness for Marchmont was so far from having suffered any abatement, that all she had thought, all she had heard of him; every little anecdote expressive of his heart and manners in his boyish days, which accidentally fell from his sisters; of late,

'The dangers he had met;'

and, above all, his manner of supporting them — every circumstance contributed to render indelible the impression she had from their earliest acquaintance conceived of his merit: whatever worldly wisdom, or prudence in its most gentle form, could say, Althea was on examination of her heart convinced, that all that the world could offer of adulation, all it could afford of those pleasures which occupy the lives of the rich or noble, would give to her neither content nor gratification; and that with Marchmont, a retirement in which she thought her fortune might suffice for their support, would be in her opinion the only scheme of happiness. How much such a plan coincided with the sentiments of Marchmont himself, his own letters sufficiently testified, for, though he had too much respectful reserve to name her to Eversley, it was easy to see to whom many expressions in his letters alluded.

Many days, and even some weeks, passed, while Althea, occupied in these reflections, and debating what she ought to do, came to no resolution. Uneasiness and doubt again oppressed Mrs. Marchmont; it seemed certain that if her son had, as he intended, directed his course towards England, he must long before now have arrived there. What then could be the reason that they had not now heard of him for more than ten weeks — Where was he? What could have happened to him? If his journey had been impeded, could he not have written? — Every day in its progress increased the painful apprehensions that these reflections brought with them, and with every setting sun that hope grew fainter and fainter, by which alone the languid and ill-confirmed fortitude of Mrs. Marchmont was sustained.

Althea more than participated in the pain this cruel suspense inflicted. She now no longer thought of how she should act when Marchmont arrived. Marchmont came not! perhaps might never more appear — While she had been debating how she should receive him and act towards him, he perhaps was already no more — Some strange mistake, some unforeseen and cruel accident had perhaps destroyed him after all his former escapes; and nothing might now remain of him but a name, and the fond and bitter remembrance of his virtues and his misfortunes in the breasts of those who had loved him.

Overwhelmed with these tormenting fears, which, though they never gave her a moment's respite, she yet commanded herself enough not to communicate to friends made miserable enough by their own, Althea almost forgot a circumstance that would at any other time have given her considerable disquiet. This was, that the time of her receiving her small dividend was passed, and it had not been sent. During the winter she had repeatedly written to Lady Dacres, entreating to have that which arose from her mother's fortune and settlement of two thousand pounds: but she had received no answer from her Ladyship herself, and but once any notice, when an attorney, a sort of deputy to the man she intrusted with her affairs, wrote to Althea to this effect:

MISS ALTHEA DACRES.

"Madam,

This serves to let you know, by order of my Lady, that her Ladyship hath received yours of the 26th ultimo; and that as to contents thereof, she desires you will apply to Mr. Serjeant Mohun on the same; her Ladyship not being thereon able or willing to act alone, as may be known, reference being had to the last will and testament of Sir Audley Dacres, baronet, deceased.

You will please, therefore, on the subject matter abovesaid, to apply accordingly to the learned Serjeant as above-mentioned — Not doubting but he will give you due information and satisfactory opinion thereon. By order of the Dowager Lady Dacres, I remain, for Anthony Skin'em, Esq.

MADAM,

Your humble Servant,

JAMES TYGERFACE.

Holborn-court, Gray's-inn."

As Althea, however she might dread being inconvenienced, could not prevail on her herself to make this enquiry, days, and weeks, and months passed on. Again the dividend became due from the two thousand pounds. There was now upwards of a hundred pounds due to her, but her present applications were as fruitless as the past. How she was to continue to live on so slender a stipend as the interest of eight hundred pounds, Lady Dacres never deigned to enquire. But though Althea was not now as during her short stay at Margate in the way of hearing it, she had reason to believe that Lady Dacres, more than ever detesting her whom she determined to injure, had been busy with her fame; and in fact she had contrived, by means of the idle, silly, and malignant gossips with whom she was now much connected, to spread injurious reports of Althea, where she was only known by name, and by being the daughter of Sir Audley. In one of these circles it was said that her temper was so intolerable, that, had she not been inveigled away by the fawning adulation of the necessitous Marchmonts, it would have been impossible for Lady Dacres long to have endured her. — In another party it was asserted, that she was *so extravagant that a mine would not suffice for her support;* and in a third it was whispered, that "a clandestine and most degrading attachment had put her excellent mother-in-law under the painful necessity of conniving at, and indeed of encouraging, her removal into another family."

There was not one of these insinuations but what gathered something from the malevolence or folly of every one who repeated it; and some of them reached Mr. Eversley during his residence in London, to the inconceivable delight of his wife, whose envy of Althea neither time nor distance had weakened. The poor man, whose health was literally wasting under the hopeless misery inflicted by this domestic plague, never mentioned, still less defended Althea, when his wife, on purpose to torment him, began the conversation. — But convinced himself of her uncommon worth, and her spotless innocence, while of her personal attractions he had long been but too sensible, he contented himself with silently doing her all the service in his power, and felt almost the only consolation of his life in performing acts of friendship towards her and Marchmont. Utterly without hope himself, he tried to reduce his affection for Althea (which had insensibly crept on his heart even before the death of Mrs. Trevyllian) into the bounds of friendship. — Mingled as it was with some degree of pain and regret, it yet afforded him almost the only pleasurable sensation his sick heart was sensible of. The idea of her being one day united to Marchmont had sometimes given him acute uneasiness; but when he had resolution to reason about it, he was compelled to acknowledge that no other man could deserve her — that with no other man was it probable she would be happy; and then, sensible that he could have nothing to hope for himself, he resolved with sincerity to promote by such means as might occur the felicity of his friend.

In the mean time, and during the cruel suspense they were in as to what had befallen Marchmont after his last letter, Eversley, who had a house in town for what is called the education of the two fair copies of their mama's perfections, stole twice into Kent to visit, for a few hours, Althea and the family of his friend: and it was from hints that he dropped in these conversations that the former gathered what she knew of the malignity with which Lady Dacres defamed and traduced her.

To him, on the second of these interviews, Althea communicated her increasing uneasiness at the obstinate silence of Lady Dacres, or the unfeeling reference to Mr. Mohun, which was still more irksome to her. Eversley advised her to conquer her repugnance, and write to Mohun. She could not determine upon it. So great was the dislike she had originally felt towards this man, that, though she supposed his transient inclination for her had long since been at an end; though she now never heard his name mentioned with her own, and indeed hardly at all in the retirement she now lived in; yet her antipathy continued almost in its first force, and she persuaded herself that to write to him would only be to solicit contumely and affront. — Eversley, who knew little of him but from his public character, knew, however, enough to believe the aversion of Althea well-founded; and at the same time to fear, that if he himself applied to such a man on behalf of Althea, it would give fresh food to Lady Dacres's malice, and embroil him anew with his wife, who insisted upon it in private, and often declared in her fits of ill humour, even before company, that he was in love with Althea. These considerations would, notwithstanding, have yielded to his ardent wish of doing her service, but he doubted whether that purpose might not be better answered by the application of a lawyer — and he thought he knew, that rare character, an honest one; to whom, as he was himself little connected with him, he thought he might recommend the business of Althea, without its being known that he interfered in it.

To this proposal Althea consented — not, however, without reluctance, but as the only means that remained untried, to procure for
her what undoubtedly belonged to her; and it was agreed that Mr. Bargrave should write to Mr. Mohun for leave to see the will of Sir Audley
(which Althea had only once heard read in a cursory and confused
manner); that he should afterwards inspect the marriage settlement of
Althea's mother, if it could be had, and then see what was the legality
of the resolution Lady Dacres seemed to have formed to distress her,
by withholding, at least till she was of age, the small income arising
from money undoubtedly her own.

Amidst these uneasy reflections on pecuniary business, and those
still more cruelly painful, that were occasioned by the uncertainty of
Marchmont's fate, time wore heavily away; but spring once more returned — joyless to Althea, joyless to her friends! for it served only
to remind them of the long absence of him to whom they were all
so passionately attached; to convince them that the scene and season,
however lovely, serve only to embitter the anguish of the unhappy.
The months of spring have above all others this effect. The eye weakened by tears supports with pain that brilliant freshness which conveys
to the happy sensations of gaiety and pleasure; and nature in its joyous
progression seems to insult the sick heart in which hope is dead.

Such, however unhappy they were, was not precisely the case with
the, inhabitants of the Kentish cottage. — Mrs. Marchmont, though
her solicitude and impatience hourly increased, still cherished the hope
that her son would return in safety: yet oppressed by fears that he
might not, and by a sort of anxious and even nervous despondence,
the effect of former sorrows and disappointments, she could not bear
the least personal exertion; and while she encouraged and entreated her daughters and Althea to walk, and to enjoy as much as they
could the refreshing beauty of the advancing year, she often remained
alone in her room, trying to acquire fortitude to meet with resignation
and calmness whatever of sorrow might yet be before her: yet often
shrinking from the painful effort, she involuntarily indulged the natural weakness of wishing to escape from the world, rather than to hear
that her greatest blessing had left it.

What had been the situation of the object of her fond solicitude, may be seen by the following account given of himself by
Marchmont to Eversley, who chose that medium to communicate
it to his family.

The comfort that family derived from seeing the date, may be more easily imagined than described.

Dorchester, April 10th.

"Once more from English ground your friend addresses you; on that soil from whence twelve months since he was driven to avoid perpetual imprisonment. It is impossible to describe to you, my dear Eversley, the sensations I have felt in revisiting my native country; and particularly this place and county, which I have so often passed through formerly on my way from London to Eastwoodleigh. All the ideas of those days are again present to me. —I am at the same inn, and sitting in the same room, where I once met Vampyre by appointment; when some arrangement of the affairs was proposed by which we hoped to have escaped the distresses that afterwards overtook us. It was, however, certain, that the proposals were only offered by that execrable wretch to draw us deeper into the snares he had laid for us. Even now I see the old hideous monster before me, prosing and attempting to entrap me; and I start up. Indignation and rage seize me for a moment, till I recollect the scenes I have since gone through. — My dying father surrounded by the inhuman satellites of the law, from whom I could hardly rescue his poor remains — my mother, pale and silent with terror and anguish, seem again before me. I see that countenance to the expression of which it is impossible to do justice; it is turned on me, and seems to forebode all that has since happened. My sisters are once more weeping round me. I see the consternation of the servants: some only anxious for their master and his family — others selfishly, yet naturally enough, drinking of themselves. —

'The Wolf that made this spoil' —

once more seems present; and, like a malignant fiend, enjoying the havock he has made. —I then remember my blasted prospects — my ruined hopes. —I feel, ah! too acutely feel, what I might have been, and what I am. Some deprivations, and many mortifications, I have learned to endure, and, I think, with manly fortitude, where they relate wholly to myself; but there is one loss that must follow, that ought to follow my loss of fortune! — Yes, Eversley, I know that I ought to submit too. — Why should I hesitate to avow a passion that I ought rather to glory in feeling? It was you, my dear friend, that first pointed out to me the beauties of that lovely mind, so admirably assorted to a

person that could not be seen with indifference as the fairest work of
heaven; but which, animated as it is with such a soul, cannot fail of inspiring the most ardent passion. Eversley! I adore this charming woman. I have always adored her from the first moment I saw her. Does she
still bear the same name as when I left England? Can so much beauty
remain unsought in obscurity? Can so much mildness have resisted
parental authority? Ah! no, I cannot, I dare not hope it. Perhaps there
is no longer such a person existing as her of whom I think in her single
state; and I return to England only to be convinced that no place on
this earth can afford to me the shadow of happiness.

"Eversley, will you pardon my weakness? I know it is a weakness,
though I might with a little parade qualify it by the names of precaution and prudence. But I cannot determine to proceed to London till
I know what I am to hear there, and in what situation is my family. I
shall therefore await your answer at the next village, for this place is
too public: I shall go thither presently; and if I find there is time before
the post goes out, I will add to this a detail of all that has befallen me
since my last letter."

At Hinton, a village on the
road near Dorchester.

"I find my letter will not go till tomorrow between two and three
o'clock: let me, therefore, employ the interval in relating how I set
forward under the auspices of my new friend Captain Forrester, and
journeyed in safety some leagues. I was then stopped, notwithstanding
my passport, by a general order which prevented any one passing the
lines — a circumstance that was less painful to me, as I imagined a few
days would end it; as Forrester's name and recommendation procured
me kindness and accommodation every where, and I learned that his
detachment was sent for, and was to join the troops with whom I was.

"There is something infectious, my friend, in that sensation of the
human mind which we call a thirst of glory. I felt it growing upon me,
and often asked myself whether there was not something shabby and
unworthy in my creeping back clandestinely to England, when here I
might hew out an honourable subsistence with my sword, or find an
honourable grave.

'Why should a man whose heart is warm within
Sit like his grandsire on a monument?'

And often, very often I determined, though my soul sickened as I nearly surveyed the miseries of war, to enter a volunteer in any regiment that would receive me. Consideration for my mother, who often had expressed her fears that I should take this resolution, was the only thing that gave me a moment's hesitation. —I found arguments to prove that even she would consent, and conquer her repugnance, when the matter was no longer in debate, and when she could calmly consider the reasons I had to offer. My mind being so far made up, I had written to my mother and to you, and waited for nothing but Forrester's arrival, whose advice was to determine me as to the regiment I should engage in. He was to join the next day. Instead of which, an account came that his party had been met by a detachment of the enemy of three times their number, and after an obstinate resistance, in which many gallant fellows had fallen, Captain Forrester had been dangerously wounded, and taken prisoner. It is impossible to describe to you the general concern felt for this amiable young man; and mine was as deep and as sincere as those who had long known him. One would have imagined that every man who spoke of or came to enquire about him, had themselves lost a brother or some very dear friend. While his fate was uncertain, I could only determine not to leave the place till some intelligence was received of him; and fortunately this came sooner than, from the apprehended ferocity of the enemy, we thought likely. Poor Forrester lay at a little town in possession of the French; his servant was missing, and the principal danger he was in was for want of attendance. Having fallen into the hands of a man of decent manners, and who was not without those generous feelings that soften the horrors of war, he was allowed to write for a surgeon, and for some person to attend him if his old and faithful servant could not be found. It was almost certain that the poor fellow had been killed when his master was taken. To find a substitute for him at such a time, and at such a place, was not easy. I entreated and obtained leave to go as his friend. I was in no military capacity, and the commanding officer, very anxious for the life of Forrester, accepted my offer with pleasure. I found my poor friend in such a state that only the skill of his surgeon, applied at the moment it was, would have carried him through. He recovered but very slowly; and I had the comfort of believing what he warmly acknowledged, that he owed his recovery, indeed he thought his life, to my unwearied attendance on him. At length, after a painful interval of ten weeks, during which time the poor convalescent was compelled to move three times as his captors found it convenient, he was adjudged well enough to be sent to Paris, whither I would have attended him; but this the French would not permit: we were therefore obliged to part. I procured a passport for Ostend, for the English army were now removed, and, proceeding thither, embarked a fort-night since in a small Danish vessel which was on the point of sailing the night of my arrival. Impatient to reach England, I threw myself into it without enquiry, and did not suspect, till we were some leagues at sea in a very tempestuous night, such as frequently precedes or follows the equinox, that there were not hands enough on board to navigate the vessel, and that the few that we had were young in their business, and totally unacquainted with the English coast, on which they had undertaken to land us.

"This intelligence was communicated to me by a passenger who seemed to set a higher value on his life than I did on mine, and who was so very restless and uneasy (and to say the truth, the storm did furiously increase), that I was at length induced to go upon deck; and from the little I knew of the matter I did not think the apprehensions of my fellow-traveller very ill grounded. The wind blew violently from the north-east; and instead of our making Dover or Deal, which indeed soon became almost impossible, I thought we were quite as likely to be driven on shore on the back of the Isle of Wight, or even farther westward. The night was totally dark, and what was at first a heavy gale became soon a hurricane. Of our three men and a boy, one of the former got drunk and went to sleep with the utmost composure; and I know not by what miracle it was, that instead of driving against the rocks of the Isle of Wight we kept down Channel, so that when day broke we were near Portland. What it was our sailors knew not; but I was well acquainted with the coast, having often failed along it from the west. I desired immediately to be put on shore. I had paid my Dane at Ostend, and my baggage consisted only of a small portmanteau. It was indifferent to these men what became of me, and I was glad to have no farther to go with such unskilful conductors. The other passenger, notwithstanding his fears, preferred following his first destination; and the vessel not having received much damage, with a favourable wind (for it had changed at sun-rise to the west) they returned up Channel; while I, with my portmanteau under my arm, desired and found a temporary shelter in one of the two little inns, which any where else would be called alehouses, on this barren and dreary spot.

"I was excessively fatigued, and found some inconvenience from a braise I had received by having been thrown violently down when the vessel had suddenly pitched during the night. I therefore went to bed, and, after having slept some hours, awoke with an odd sensation of wonder, as I said, 'Well! I am once more then on English ground! —I am, where a few hours would convey me to London. — Ha! and what shall I learn there? When I go to the bookseller who usually receives my letters for me, and with whom I desired my family to leave the direction where they might be found — how shall I tremble to ask if they are all well! And even this enquiry I must make by stealth — and I go to hide myself in some obscure corner of the town, and again have recourse to the precarious occupation of an author — for, alas! what other means have I of existence? What! Must I then submit to all the miserable expedients I have already been compelled to practise? And to escape from the fangs of that wretch Vampyre must I undergo all the inconveniences that a felon is subject to?'

"Ah! my dear friend, as former scenes arose to my mind, I almost wished that I had in France met the fate that menaced me; or that the storm of the preceding day had ended my troubles. Accuse me not of weakness, or unmanly repining, Eversley; but think of the course of my life, and own that I have not hitherto ill endured my very severe destiny. Thousands you have sometimes told me are *as* unfortunate, and tens of thousands *more* unfortunate than I am. I am afraid the estimate, sad as it is, is short of the truth; but not one ray of comfort do I derive from so melancholy a reflection.

> 'I feel by proof,
> That fellowship in pain divides nor smart,
> Nor lightens aught each man's particular load.'

"In this disposition of mind I walked out. It was a dull and gloomy evening. The sun had disappeared beneath volumes of heavy clouds in the south-west, and this naturally cheerless and forlorn spot of earth, or rather of stone, never appeared more desolate. It seemed to suit my fortune as well as my disposition. A group of half-naked children followed me, offering to sell shells and pieces of shining stone, the produce of their miserable island. I gave them all the small money I had, to engage them to leave me to my sad meditations: but a boy, and then a young woman, pursued me — one with some canes, another with a piece of linen, which they said had been picked up on the sands, the remains of a wreck that had been driven on shore about a fortnight before. I assured them that I had no occasion for such articles, and, made peevish by their importunity, while I could consider them as little otherwise than plunderers who lived on the spoils of the dead, I went on to that spot of remarkable wildness and horror, where the pile of ruin called Bow-and-Arrow, and sometimes known by the name of Rufus's Castle, hangs on a crag of stone over the remains of the ancient church, of which some considerable detached parts are now standing: many broken tombs are still seen in the rough area that was once the church-yard. —I sat down on one of them; and as I looked around me and saw another equinoctial storm gathering in the south-west, and blunting by accumulated clouds the rays of the sun as it sunk beyond them, tingeing them with a dull purplish red, I thought I had never been in a place so adapted to the residence of desolation and despair.

"You will perhaps think it strange that at such a time, with a body fatigued and a mind ill at ease, I should write or indeed think of poetry; but the faculty of composing it, though never I think to be command-ed, sometimes serves to mitigate by amusing the hours of pain, of languor, and uneasiness: not however when anxiety is very acute. But I was now in a state of uncertainty as to those I most loved, which I knew a few hours might terminate at my own choice, and was just enough present to the scene I was in, which was indeed perfectly in unison with my feelings, to describe it.

"It would be a waste of time to apologise farther for such a trifle, and I know you are rather a partial than a severe critic.

DESCRIPTIVE ODE,

Written among the Ruins of the Old Church, on the West Side of Portland; above which are Ruins called Bow-and-Arrow, or Ru-fus's Castle.

CHAOTIC pile, of barren stone,
That nature's hurrying hand has thrown,
Half-finish'd, from the troubled waves;
On whose rude brow the risted tow'r
Has scowl'd through many a stormy hour,
On this drear site of tempest-beaten graves!

Sure, Desolation loves to shroud
His hideous form within the cloud

That hovers round thy rugged head;
 And, as through broken vaults beneath
 The future storms low-muttering breathe,
He seems to hear the murmurs of the dead.

 Here marks the Fiend, with eager eyes,
 Far out at sea the fogs arise
That dimly hide the beacon'd strand;
 Hence listens the portentous roar
 Of sullen waves, as on the shore
Monotonous they burst, and tell the storm at hand.

 Northward the Demon's eyes are cast,
 O'er yonder bare and sterile waste,
Where, born to hew and heave the block,
 Man, lost in ignorance and toil,
 Becomes associate to the soil,
And his heart hardens like his native rock.

 On the bleak hills, with flint o'erspread,
 No blossoms rear the purple head,
No shrub perfumes the Zephyr's breath;
 But o'er the cold and cheerless down
 Grim Desolation seems to frown,
And blast the ungrateful soil with partial death.

 Here the scath'd trees, with leaves half-drest,
 Shade no soft songster's secret nest,
Whose spring-notes soothe the pensive ear;
 But high the croaking Cormorant flics,
 And Mews, and Awks with clamorous cries,
Tire the lone echoes of these caverns drear.

 Forlorn, among these ruins gray,
 Some widow'd Mourner loves to stray,
Marking the melancholy main;
 Where once afar she could discern
 Through the blue waves *his* sails return,
Who never, never now, returns again!

 Long on these tombs, by storms uptorn,

The hopeless wretch will lingering mourn,
Till, from the Ocean rising red,
    The misty Moon, with lurid ray,
    Lights her reluctant on her way,
To sleep in tears her solitary bed.

    Here the dire Spirit oft surveys
    The ship, that to the western bays,
With favouring gales, pursues its course;
    Then calls the vapour dark that blinds
    The pilot; — calls the felon winds;
That heave the billows with resistless force.

    Commixing with the blotted skies
    High and more high the wild waves rise;
Till, as impetuous torrents urge,
    Driven on yon fatal bank accurst,
    The vessel's massy timbers burst,
And the crew sinks beneath the infuriate surge.

    There find the weak an early grave;
    While youthful strength the whelming wave
Repels; and, labouring for the land,
    With shorten'd breath and upturn'd eyes,
    Sees the rough shore above him rise,
Nor dreams that rapine meets him on the strand.

    And are there then, in human form,
    Monsters more savage than the storm,
Who from the gasping sufferer tear
    The dripping weed? — who dare to reap
    The inhuman harvest of the deep
From half-drown'd victims whom the tempests spare?

    Ah! yes! — By avarice once possest,
    No pity moves the rustic's breast:
Callous he proves — as those who haply wait,
    Till I (a pilgrim weary worn)
    To my own native land return,
With legal toils to drag me to my fate!

You see, my dear Eversley, how naturally the ideas of the poet return *to his own business and bosom*. I shall wait to hear from you before I proceed. You, I know, will not despise me, while I acknowledge myself to be, in all that relates to my family, and to one other person, a coward.

"Farewell, my dear friend — I direct this, as my. former ones, to your friend in London. If it should travel after you into Devonshire, how many days longer must I endure this miserable suspense?

E. A. M."

CHAP. VI.

Se poi ritorno
Presso al mio bene
Torna la speme
Fugge il timor.

AFTER THIS LETTER, which Eversley had thus sent to Mrs. Marchmont without any reserve or alteration, it could be no longer doubted that her son's passion for Althea was perfectly understood. Althea and Lucy had read the letter together. For awhile, anxiety for the vicissitudes he had passed through, and joy that he was in present safety, suspended every other sentiment; but the moment Althea was left to her reflections all those passages in which she was so unreservedly spoken of returned to her recollection, and overwhelmed her with confusion. She now dreaded to meet the eyes of Mrs. Marchmont, mild and dejected as they were; and more than ever it became necessary to determine what she was to do, since Marchmont only waited Eversley's answer, which was already gone to him, to come to his mother and his family. In this uneasy situation Althea shut herself for an hour in her own room to debate the matter with herself; and she had never yet been in a predicament where it was so difficult to decide.

Had she been possessed of her small fortune, and could have been sure that Mrs. Marchmont would have desired as earnestly as she knew her daughters did, that she should give her hand to Marchmont, she found that what is termed worldly prudence would have had no power to prevent her giving herself to the only man for whom she had ever felt the slightest degree of interest. Some men of fortune she would not, though they were to offer themselves, accept: many others would not seek her. — Were such men as Mohun, as Wardour, as the elegant Captain Melincourt described by Marchmont, and fifty others that she had seen — were *these* persons with whom the most splendid pecuniary possessions would induce her to live? — Certainly not. With any one of these, or any that resembled them, she was certain she must be miserable; with Marchmont, in despite of any pecuniary inconveniences, and in any rank of life, as sure that she must be happy.

It would be yet above twelve months before she became of age; and it seemed but too evident that Lady Dacres, influenced either by malice, avarice, or both, was determined to keep possession of her little fortune, both interest and principal, till then. But thinking steadily on what her aunt used to say, when anxiety for her future fate had occasionally turned the conversation on matters relative to her fortune, she thought she had a clear recollection of having heard that this small portion was by her mother's marriage articles so settled, that it was to be paid either on her attaining her majority, *or* day of marriage. If this were so, she had it as she hoped in her power immediately to give it to Marchmont on becoming his wife.

But from the lawyer employed by Mr. Eversley she had yet no answer, and anxiety and doubt were still to cloud the mind of Althea; anxiety and doubt that never were more painfully felt than at the moment she was first to meet Mrs. Marchmont. They neither of them spoke: the sisters were equally silent; but when Althea stole a glance at Mrs. Marchmont, she thought there was affection towards her, mingled with the tenderness and complacency that the certainty of her son's return had thrown into her countenance. — As soon as the dinner was removed, the three girls, as if they had been directed to do so, went out of the room. Althea understood that the moment was arrived when their mother would speak to her in regard to him who was nearest both their hearts; and though hers beat so much that she could hardly breathe, she determined not to evade a conversation which she at once wished for and dreaded.

Mrs. Marchmont, with more resolution, though not with less trembling earnestness than was shewn by Althea herself, entered immediately on the little history of her sentiments since her son's attachment to Althea had been suspected or known; and Althea was convinced that only motives of the most disinterested delicacy had prevented the mother's delighted acquiescence and encouragement. — "Where, my dear Miss Dacres," said she, "where could the most ambitious look for birth, for accomplishments, temper and person, superior to yours? Believe me, I felt all their value; and was sure that there was not a woman on earth so capable of making Marchmont amends for all the misfortunes of his untoward destiny. — But when I thought of the right all these gave you to fill the most elevated rank in society; when I considered the very humble condition to which *we* are reduced, and imagined how much malice would have to say if we seduced you from happier fortune to share, and, as the world would assert, to mitigate our indigence; I could not bear to be accessary to what, while it drew on us the cruelest reflections, might hereafter be to you a source of regret and repentance."

"I am very sure, Madam," said Althea in a tremulous voice, "that I shall never repent of sharing any condition of life with your family." — Then recovering a little more courage, she added — "I will be above disguise, my dear Mrs. Marchmont, on a subject so interesting to us both; I will own to you that, almost from my first acquaintance with your son, he appeared to me a young man of great merit, and nothing ever hurt me more than my father's coldness and dislike towards him, for which I never could account. — When a strange chance drove me to Eastwoodleigh, I heard many anecdotes that confirmed me in my good opinion of him. You know," added she, blushing, "that we met, while the cruel persecution he underwent confined him within the deserted walls of his paternal house: then the partiality I had at an early period entertained for him was confirmed; and, from the moment I avowed that he was not indifferent to me, I have thought of nothing but regulating my mind and my wishes to that situation of life which I determined to share with him, whenever it should be in my power to fulfil the engagement I had made; a tacit engagement indeed, since he was too generous to solicit my promise — but, nevertheless, an engagement which worlds would not tempt me to recede from."

It is unnecessary to relate Mrs. Marchmont's answer to this generous declaration. — From this moment the mother awaited, with redoubled delight, the hourly-expected arrival of her son; while Althea yielded, for the first time, to her extreme affection for him, unchecked by any of those fears with which it had, till then, been chastised. Some apprehensions yet hung over the whole party, which however seemed lighter, since they were now, without scruple, discussed. It was so long since Vampyre had been baffled in his pursuit, that the sanguine spirits

of Lucy persisted in believing it impossible he should think of renewing it; while Mrs. Marchmont, who had a deeper horror of his inveterate infamy, and Amelia, who had a more trembling dread of him from
all she so well remembered of her father's sufferings, hardly dared
encourage the confidence of his safety which Althea and Lucy were
delighted to cherish — the former indeed, less from the hope that the
rancorous villain might abate his malice, than from a secret resolution
she made to sacrifice all the fortune that was in her own power to purchase the safety of Marchmont. While these hopes, fears, and projects
took their turn with his female friends and family, the ever-generous
and faithful Eversley was better contriving for his immediate safety.
Far from being lulled into security by the length of his absence, or the
apparent tranquillity of his enemies, he was sure that malice and avarice keep no holidays; and he knew that Vampyre, like a blood-hound,
would instantly regain the scent, and pursue his unhappy victim even
to death, if he had once the slightest intimation of his being in England. — Instantly, therefore, on receiving Marchmont's first letter,
he wrote to him by the earliest stage, assuring him of the health of
his family, acquainting him with Althea's residence among them, and
entreating him to quit the western road, for him so full of danger, and
without entering London, where he might the next moment meet one
of Vampyre's emissaries, to make the best of his way through Hampshire and Surry, to the neighbourhood of Sitting-bourne.

Marchmont, who waited for information from Eversley before he
left the little inn from whence his last letter was dated, no sooner received this welcome news, than all the gloom that had so lately hung
over his mind was dissipated; his transient misanthropy was forgot,
with the uneasiness that had taught it him; and hope seemed, with redoubled splendour, to enlighten his path to happiness. Althea finding a
home with his mother — Althea added to the dear group that now so
anxiously expected him! was an image so delicious, that he could hardly believe it real. A thousand times he read over that part of Eversley's
letter; and so eager was he to realize the lovely vision it presented to
his eyes, that he would hardly have had prudence to attend implicitly
to the advice given in the subsequent part of it, if he had not found,
on enquiry, and by consulting an old smoky map that hung over the
chimney of the alehouse parlour, that he could make his way rather
sooner with hired horses into Kent, by cross roads, than if he had gone
round by London. — Horses, therefore, he immediately procured; for,

besides what he had left from the money paid him at Ostend which Forrester had given him an order for, Eversley had sent him a bank note. Expence, therefore, being less an object to him at this moment, he took post-horses from town to town, which he thought were less liable to delays than post-chaises, as he could go his own pace.

Very different, as he travelled among the trees of the New Forest, now just putting forth the tender shade of the future summer, were the sensations of Marchmont from those he had long felt. Every wood scent that floated in the air, every tree, whose earlier foliage half-expanded above his head, were, for him, pregnant with delight. He stopped, as evening approached, at another humble cabin, that hung out its rustic sign on the skirts of the forest, to rest himself and the horses, before he went on to Winchester — a plan in which he was sure to have the thorough concurrence of the postillion, who accompanied him to lead them back; and, leaving him to take care of them and of himself for an hour, Marchmont wandered into the wood.

Within its wild recesses a thousand birds were singing their evening hymns to the sun, as his last rays tinged the boles and branches with rosy gold. — Gradually all became silent; but, after a moment's pause, the nightingale rather practised than performed her superior serenade, just trying her long-suspended powers, and then becoming mute for a moment, as if to recollect every link of harmony. This recalled to the memory of Marchmont his reflections and sensations of the preceding year, when, in making his way to Paris he had often lingered among the woods, and particularly at Fontainebleau: — then, from the state of his mind, the same sounds that now soothed him, served only to increase his depression.

The beautiful sonnet of Petrarch he had then repeated, with particular emphasis on the two lines –

> E tuttè notte par che m'accompagne
> E mi rammente la mia dura sorte.

Then too he had read, with feelings too exactly coinciding, from Jean Baptiste Rousseau, this apostrophe to a nightingale —

> Hélas! que mes tristes pensées
> M'offrent des maux bien plus cuisans!
> Vous pleurez des peines passées,
> Je pleure mes ennuis présens:
> Et quand la nature attentive

Cherche à calmer vos deplaisirs,
Il faut même que je me prive
De la douceur de mes soupirs!

But now it seemed as if the face of nature had felt as new and rapid a change, within the few days since Marchmont had left the Isle of
Portland, as he himself had experienced since he had received Eversley's letter; for in believing, as he now did, that Althea would soon be
all his own, he seemed to possess a renovated existence. — While he
yielded to hopes so enchanting, those symptoms of the renovation
of nature which he saw about him soothed his imagination; and the
soliloquy he uttered took almost insensibly the form of verse, which
he wrote down, meaning, if the lines were worth it, to polish them at
some future time when he should be with Althea, to whose fondness
for flowers they had particular reference.

LINES,

Written in the New Forest in early Spring.
As in the woods, where leathery lichen weaves
Its wintry web, among the sallow leaves,
Which (through cold months in whirling eddies blown)
Decay beneath the branches once their own,
From the brown shelter of their foliage fear,
Spring the young blooms that lead the floral year: —
When, wak'd by vernal suns, the Pilewort* dares
Expand her spotted leaves, and shining stars,
And (veins empurpling all her tassels pale)
Bends the soft Wind-flower† in the tepid gale,
Uncultured bells of azure Jacynths‡ blow,
And the breeze-scenting Violet§ lurks below: —
So views the wanderer, with delighted eyes,
Reviving hopes from blank despondence rise,
When, blighted by Adversity's chill breath,
Those hopes had felt a temporary death;
Then with gay heart he looks to future hours,
When Love shall dress for him the summer bowers!

---

*   Pilewort – The Renunculus Ficaria

†   Wind-flower – The wood Anemony – Anemone nemorsa

‡   Jacynthe, Fr. Hyacinth. Non scriptus. V. Hare-Bell

§   Violet – Viola Odorata

> And, as delicious dreams enchant his mind;
> Forgets his sorrows past, and gives them to the wind.

Marchmont now crossed the heaths of Surry; and as from a height he caught a very distant view of St. Paul's, and saw the atmosphere darkly tinctured by the volume of smoke that continually hovers over London, the charming visions with which he was indulging his fancy were for a moment checked, and two lines of Dr. Johnson occurred to him: —

> The ambush there relentless villains lay;
> And there the fell Attorney prowls for prey!

But all unpleasant retrospect was forgotten, when, looking eastward, he figured to himself Althea, his adored Althea, adding her tender congratulations to those of his family, and all ready to receive the returned wanderer with delight!

CHAP. VII.

> L'homme est vraiment déplorable,
> Qui, de la *fortune* amoureux,
> Se rend lui-même misérable
> En travaillant pour être heureux.

DESCRIPTION, HOWEVER LABOURED, would fail to convey an idea of the meeting of Marchmont with his family. Althea declined being present when he arrived; and never yet had she so much occasion to collect that mild fortitude which her early instructress (alarmed for her happiness when she saw her trembling sensibility) had laboured to make part of her character. Between the time when his safety and arrival in England were known and the present moment, the thoughts of Althea had been wholly occupied by the idea of seeing him as an accepted lover; for that he was such could not fail to be understood, nor did she mean affectedly or prudishly to disavow what her heart dictated. Had she been mistress of millions, it was to Marchmont she would have given them. Possessing hardly a gentlewoman's support, and even part of that likely to be disputed or withheld, it was with him she determined to share it; and if this resolution was taken while he was absent, his presence, his ardent affection for her, were certain to confirm it.

On his part, violent as had been the passion he had conceived for Althea, even from their first meeting, and long before it could be encouraged by a ray of hope, it was now so heightened by esteem, by gratitude, and by that tender admiration which such a mind lodged in so lovely a form could not fail to excite, that, when to all this her generous partiality to him was added, it was perhaps impossible that an attachment more ardent, or more tender, could inhabit a human heart.

Eversley, always fearful of the machinations of the fiend Vampyre, whose persecution he thought as inveterate and as much to be dreaded as the pursuit of the secret tribunal in the fifteenth century, had earnestly entreated Marchmont not to expose himself to a renewal of all the mischief this *legal* monster was capable of doing him, by appearing publicly, or exposing himself carelessly to the attempts that might still be made by a wretch, who, to the basest and most sordid cupidity of the lowest of his profession, added the desire of personal vengeance for the expence he had been put to, or rather which he had put his clients to, in a fruitless pursuit, as well as for the buffets he had received. Eversley, therefore, in his letters to Marchmont, had earnestly enforced the necessity of prudence and concealment, till something could be done with the clients of Vampyre to whom he proposed to apply, flattering himself that these two men were already weary of continuing a persecution that promised so little advantage, at such an expence as he knew Vampyre had put them to already: for Eversley had heard from an acquaintance of one of them, that he complained of having already paid Vampyre three hundred pounds for what he had done against Marchmont, whose debt to him was originally but nine hundred. The other creditor was not less discontented; but as they were both of that description of men who love money better than reputation, and had not the least idea of honour or honesty, they had found Vampyre, who hesitated not at perjury, where he could venture it, or even forgery in the same case, a very useful though diabolical instrument in the contrivances which usurers are often obliged to concert with attorneys; and as a great deal of iniquity had gone on among them, they felt themselves so entangled with the infamous instrument of their peculation, that, even when they saw him pursue a course which could do good to nobody but himself, they were afraid of stopping his villanous career.

Eversley, however, flattering himself that they must at length be tired, and that they would be glad to accept a composition which he proposed to offer, especially if they believed Marchmont was still out of their reach, again and again exhorted him to remain concealed. The servants who now lived with his mother did not know him; in the country where she now resided he was totally a stranger. "Surely therefore," said Eversley in his letter to him, "surely it is advisable, my dear friend, to keep yourself as much as possible concealed; you know the devil, they say, never sleeps." To this exhortation Marchmont answered, with more spirit than prudence, in the words of Hotspur: —

'Oh! but I'll shame the devil;
Speak truth, and shame the devil!'

Then continuing more calmly, he added, "If in the short retrospect of my life, my dear Eversley, there is any recollection that brings with it unpleasurable sensations, it is when I think over the stratagems I was, or fancied I was, compelled to use, when I was trying to escape from the toils of that poisonous reptile. I feel myself degraded whenever I represent myself as fearing so contemptible, so base a miscreant, and can feel nothing now but indignation and shame that I ever submitted to them —

'Let pale-faced fear keep with the mean-born man.'

"I cannot endure that it should for the future control one of my actions. Besides, my dear Eversley, consider how little these precautions, if I could consent to take them, would avail me. You say I am not known to my mother's servants. — But for whom can I pass? Is it, do you really think, possible for me to return to, or to be received by, my family under a borrowed name, in a fictitious character? And were it possible, could I in a circumstance so evidently humiliating pretend to the favour of Miss Dacres? She would surely despise me; or if her sweetness, her tenderness of disposition pleaded for me, still I should despise myself, and feel a man who stoops to act like an impostor, unworthy of her good opinion. No; I will take no false name — I will use no means of concealment; but I will certainly not throw myself in the way of Vampyre or his employers, and I think it possible, that, retired as we shall live in Kent, which is a great way from the haunts of this pest of society, I may remain unnoticed."

Eversley was well assured that this hope was ill-founded. However, as he thought himself acquitted towards his friend in having offered his opinion, he urged the matter no farther; but considered by what means his application to the two inexorable creditors could be made with the greatest prospect of success.

In the instant, however, of his setting about this friendly office, and only two days after the arrival of Marchmont at the house of his mother, Mrs. Eversley, as if she had known how earnestly her husband wished to see his friend, took it into her head to follow the advice the physicians had long given her in vain, and to go into Devonshire. This wretched woman, whose temper alone would have worn out the strongest frame, had inherited a diseased frame from her parents, which was one among the many objections Eversley had against marrying her, though it was over-ruled by his father's earnest importunities. And indeed the personal infirmities this had brought upon her, rendered her to the generous mind of Eversley an object of pity, and made him often endure with more patience her insufferable ill-humour and strange fits of caprice, which had the appearance of starts of insanity. Within the last two or three years these had been more frequent, and it was at last evident that they were brought on and aggravated by drinking. This vice inflaming her blood, occasioned her constitutional complaints to recur with redoubled violence; and she now thought herself, as the physicians had long thought her, in danger. Relinquishing, therefore, the plan she had hitherto insisted upon of passing the spring months in London (a plan for which no reason could possibly be given, unless it was that she knew her husband preferred being in the country), she now hastened to their home; and Eversley, who particularly wished to conceal the return of Marchmont from her, was compelled to attend her, flattering himself that, on pretence of finishing some business which he really had in London, he should be able to return within a month. In this, however, he was mistaken. The lady suddenly took it into her head that their house was exposed to the north winds; that it was cold and damp; and having heard in London of some sick person that had recovered by going to Penzance — thither she resolved to go. Her unhappy husband accompanied her, and was thus at a very great distance from Marchmont; without any consolation for such a disappointment, unless it was that he endeavoured very sincerely to rejoice at his friend's prospect of happiness, while he sometimes felt that it was well for his continuance in this frame of mind, that he had not too frequent opportunities of comparing nearly the good fortune of Marchmont, as the husband of Althea, with his own intolerable destiny.

In the mean time Marchmont availed himself, at the earnest instance of Althea, of the steps Mr. Eversley's friend had taken to ascertain her right to her fortune. As this Mr. Bargrave seemed intelligent,
and had a very good character, Marchmont made no scruple to entrust
him with the reason of his enquiry: but after numberless applications,
which were always evaded, Mr. Bargrave had recourse to Doctors'
Commons, where he found that the portion of Althea was, besides
the savings of her aunt, a thousand pounds, payable on the day of her
majority or marriage, the disposition of which he had no power to
change by will; and one thousand more settled upon her, which, had
he lived, he might have retained, but which it did not appear that he
had any right to alienate, as he seemed to have intended, by leaving a
sort of right to Lady Dacres to pay or to withhold it, as Althea might
or might not consult or please her in her choice of a husband. This
information Mr. Bargrave gathered, as well from the marriage articles
of Althea's mother, as from the will of her father. Neither of them
were remarkable for clearness and precision; and the will seemed to
be that of a man who, wishing to do right, was yet impelled to act
contrary to his feelings and his conscience, and failed in his attempt
to reconcile clashing interests. Mr. Bargrave having obtained copies of
these papers, laid them before a Counsellor of eminence, who declared
that the moment Althea was married she would become possessed of
all her fortune, in despite of the clause in her father's will, or any thing
that could be pleaded on any pretence to the contrary.

This then, with what she already possessed, would produce an income of about a hundred-and-forty pounds a year. — Mrs. Marchmont had almost a hundred; and on this sum Althea thought they
could live all together in some cheap part of England, which, at a great
distance from the metropolis, it might yet be possible to find.

Marchmont sometimes seemed, amidst their most interesting conversations, to shrink from the idea of taking advantage of her affection for him, to engage her to share his indigence; and while his love
every day increased, he often appeared to be struggling with his wishes,
and to attempt rather to remain wretched himself, than to risk reduc-
ing Althea below her rank in life. Althea was conscious of all this; but
while it increased her esteem, it also piqued her generosity. The matter
therefore, as to the possession of her fortune on her marriage, being,
as they believed, out of doubt, it remained only to be considered on
the part of Marchmont whether he could be happy on so limited an

income, and whether, resigning every project which his birth and his talents might qualify him to succeed in, he could prefer a remote retirement, and a very small income, which Althea, now well versed in all the history of his former life, thought his knowledge in farming might greatly help to increase?

Now it happened, as was indeed very likely, that this very same project had taken possession of the mind as often recoiled, from the idea of owing every thing to Althea, and of being unable to offer any thing to her, on whom he would have lavished worlds: — when, however, two people are agreed in a general sentiment, it is not long before that agreement becomes known to each other. — Althea, having once made up her mind that this plan of life would make her happy, had no hesitation in proposing it, though not immediately to Marchmont, to Lucy. Of course, it easily found its way to the person most interested; and, in the next conversation they had together, Althea found means to silence the delicate scruples of Marchmont, who, no longer attempting at the stoic virtue of refusing the supreme happiness in his power, thought only of hastening it. When, however, they talked every circumstance over, it became his task to obviate objections, for Althea now thought it would be highly indecorous not to inform Lady Dacres of her intentions; whereas Marchmont, who knew perfectly well her Ladyship's aversion to him, and her reasons for it, dreaded left she should find some means to prevent it. He was sure that her consent was not to be obtained; and had no doubt but Althea's acting against it, if she affected to ask it, would irritate her, and set her upon trying not only to enforce, but to go beyond the power given her by the will of her husband. Besides all this, Marchmont knew that Vampyre, who had been one of the agents of Sir Ralph Gunston, was still occasionally employed by the heiress of his property; and there was some strange juggle about the mortgage given by the elder Marchmont to Sir Ralph, in which Vampyre had a principal concern. Indeed it had always been suspected by Eversley, that the iniquity of that transaction, and the fear, if Marchmont had money or success in the world, that it might be enquired into, were very strong motives for the malignity of all the parties against him, and for their perseverance in harassing and distressing him, to keep him down. Of all other people then, except Vampyre himself, Lady Dacres was the last to whom he wished to have Althea's intentions in his favour communicated: — "And, after all," said he, as they discoursed upon this, "what do you owe this woman?

a creature who not only attempted to estrange from you your father's affections, but dared to propose sacrificing you for life, merely because she could not bear the sight of supreme excellence and loveliness! — Not content with so base an attempt, you see that she has endeavoured to usurp a power over you, by inducing your father to make a will contrary to the sense of a former and irrevocable deed: yet how backward she continued to give you any protection which that power ought to have implied, her conduct towards you, for the three or four months you remained in her house, surely is a sufficient specimen. Can my Althea, who generally sees objects with judgment so true, can she really be so influenced by prejudice as to believe she ought to compliment away even one hour of her repose, to keep up forms of deference and affection where they do not exist?"

"It is less," answered Althea, "to appear to retain deference towards her, than not to violate the rules that the world has prescribed on these occasions, and the respect which seems annexed to one who bears my father's name, and to whose family I am so nearly related."

"And yet," resumed Marchmont, "Lady Dacres has herself been the example of paying very little respect to the memory of your father; for she afforded you neither friendship nor protection, but suffered her malignant envy to counteract every feeling that she ought to have had towards the daughter of her husband. As to the world, let me, most beloved Althea, ask you what it is you understand by the term? — There is, I trust, nobody who is less disposed than I am to argue against that respect for general opinion, which is a very proper and salutary feeling in a certain degree, and is not unfrequently the guardian of virtue and honour when other defences might perhaps fail; but, believe me, the world, in this case, are quite as likely to take your part as that of Lady Dacres, who, certainly, is not generally beloved. Let us, however, investigate what we mean when we talk of the world. I suppose what is generally understood by it, is the great mass of society, or, to use a formerly fashionable term, *les Gens comme il faut*, who have a certain degree of consequence because they have money or resources enough to appear at every fashionable place in London during the winter; have handsome houses in or near some of the squares; and go in the summer to the places of public resort. I take it for granted, that this is the world. — Well! and what do they know of my Althea? She has hardly ever been among them; her beauty has never been shewn where it might excite the admiration of the men, or the envy of the women.

In such a narrow circle as Margate in the declining season, the extraordinary resolution you seemed to have taken, and the impertinent talk of two foolish women who knew you, excited a momentary, and only a momentary, curiosity. But in London, where something new and strange, or what plain people may think so, occurs every two or three days, the remarks that your marriage with a ruined man would make, would be hardly of an hour's duration. Is this, therefore, the world to whom my Althea would make the slightest sacrifice of her own opinion? for whom she would change one of her intentions? — But, as it has been well observed, that all persons are of consequence to themselves, and those who are the most so form an atmosphere of their own around them, and call that the world, let us examine the world of Lady Dacres, to which I have no doubt but that she will make bitter exclamations. You must know, my Althea, that during your father's life she was visited, as fifty other such personages are visited, because she kept a card assembly, gave good dinners, had a title, and was known to possess a great deal of money: but among all the people who left cards at her house, or made money by them within it; among all who talked to her at St. James's when she once a year made her courtesy there, or ate the dinners and courted the interest of Sir Audley, is there one, do you think, who would care a single straw whether or no they ever saw her again? Assuredly not. — *Her* world, therefore, is confined to two or three Dowagers, who, like her, love to save money, and who meet to wrangle and say spiteful things over their card-table, but are otherwise the best friends; that is, they talk about their œconomy, and compare notes; relate the conduct of their servants, and the prices they give for the various articles they have occasion to buy; lament the dearness of provisions, and the expence of a family; and wonder, if they who have such handsome incomes cannot live, how such a one can dress herself and daughters as she does; and cannot imagine how Mr. Such-a-one lives as he does, but suppose there will be a violent end to such dashing doings. Such," continued Marchmont, "are the beings who constitute the world of Lady Dacres; with them I have no doubt but that we shall serve for exclamation and abuse for a fortnight at least: perhaps for three weeks or a month Lady Dacres will complain, and her dear friends will pity — but it seems to me that such will be the very worst that can happen. — And let me ask my adored Athea if it can, if it ought to interfere with our world, which we shall find in our own hearts, in each other, and in our family?"

It may easily be believed that Athea acquiesced in reasoning, which even from a less beloved mouth she might have heard with conviction. Nothing now remained but for Marchmont to obtain Athea's consent to name the day when they should be united. But here a real difficulty occurred — Athea was not of age; Lady Dacres was undoubtedly her nearest relation, and stood, with Mr. Mohun, in place of her father, whose executors they were. To celebrate the marriage therefore was impossible, unless by going to Scotland, or by banns published in the parish church. The former plan was too expensive to be thought of, even if Athea had not declared her decided repugnance to it. The last alone remained; and many were the objections that might be urged against it: with these, however, Marchmont contended as well as he could — still enforcing the idea, that they were so little known in the part of England where they now resided, that it was extremely unlikely the publicity of their intended union should reach the knowledge of the persons from whom they desired to conceal not only the marriage, but the return of Marchmont to England.

Mrs. Marchmont, who at her son's earnest entreaty undertook to assist in conquering the scruples that again assailed Althea, felt their force increased by her apprehensions that the persecutions of Vampyre might be renewed with redoubled vigilance; — apprehensions which none of the fearless arguments of Marchmont had ever appeased, and which she now thought would be too certainly realized. However, as the experiment was of necessity to be made, and as since Marchmont's return no attempt whatever seemed to have been thought of on the part of his persecutors to renew their fruitless and wanton attacks on his personal freedom, his mother, while her heart was still oppressed with anxiety endeavoured to put on the semblance of hope she was far from feeling. Certain that he would be miserable without Althea, and having from some months observation convinced herself that Althea's happiness was equally interested in her union with him, she thought that she had no right, merely from those fears which depression of spirit from long-continued sorrow might perhaps make her weakly and unnecessarily indulge, to raise any obstacles to a marriage evidently advantageous to her son; while she was too fond of him, and too partial to his really uncommon merit, not to think that he deserved any woman, and that with him none could fail of finding happiness in any station of life.

Althea too, when alone, took resolution steadily to consider her situation; and soon convinced herself that the step she was about to

take was dictated by reason as well as by inclination. Alone and unconnected in the world, at a period when other young women are guarded
by the vigilant affection of parents or of brothers, she was destiute
not only of personal protection, but of any defence against the injustice of Lady Dacres. She could not doubt, but that the more forlorn
and unfriended her condition was, the more oppression she should
suffer from the cupidity and malice of her mother-in-law, aided, as it
probably would be, by the professional power of Mohun sharpened by
pique. The spirit, the firmness, and the talents of Marchmont, when
he should be empowered by his marriage to claim her rights, would,
she supposed, awe these two people into doing her tardy justice; and
in the guardianship of the man she loved, she believed no real evil
could overtake her. Humble fortune she did not consider as such; and
was very sure that the most elevated, without Marchmont, would have
been for her only splendid wretchedness.

Having by these arguments, added to the earnest persuasions of
Lucy and the milder expostulations of her mother, conquered the reluctance she had at first felt to the public manner in which her marriage
was to be announced — she consented that it should be so, and five
weeks after his return to England the ceremony was performed in the
village church, that united Althea for ever to the happy Marchmont.

Marchmont, now esteeming himself blest beyond the ordinary lot
of man, was long unwilling to think of any thing that by recalling
him to reflections on the future might embitter his present felicity.
But Mr. Bargrave, the solicitor whom Eversley had employed for him,
reminded him at the end of three weeks that it was highly necessary
he should, as the husband of Althea, make a formal application to
the executors of her father for the payment of her fortune. This he
thought should be done in person; and however unwilling he was to go
to London, yet determined not to shrink from any service in which his
adored Althea was interested, he appointed a time when Mr. Bargrave
was to meet him, and set out on this unpleasant expedition.

Lady Dacres, however, was not in town: but Mohun, who was
attending the courts with his usual assiduity, was to be heard of at his
chambers in the Temple; and there Marchmont, accompanied by Mr.
Bargrave, procured admission to him.

Marchmont could not enter on this conference without feeling a
great degree of curiosity to see how Mohun, whom he only knew by
sight, and by the invidious manner in which he had possessed himself of

the house in Surry (which had belonged to his father, and was inhabited by his family), would receive a man he had treated with rudeness already, and who now was to appear before him as a claimant of property which the sage counsellor seemed indisposed to relinquish, and in the still more obnoxious character of a successful and happy rival.

CHAP. VIII.

In vain our plans of happiness we raise:
Pain is our lot, and patience is our praise.

MOHUN, THOUGH HE was well aware whom it was that he saw, and on what occasion he was come, affected the most complete ignorance. This he did to put Marchmont in the most disagreeable of all circumstances, that of telling his name, and relating his business.

This, however, Marchmont did in a few words, and with that firmness and dignity which a certain degree of conscious merit ought to give every man. Mohun, thrown back in his chair, his eyes half closed, and his lips drawn in, heard him almost to the end; and then, interrupting him with a cold and supercilious air, said, putting out his hand as in the action of silencing a person, "Well, Sir; well! You need not trouble yourself to say any more — You are come then to inform me, that you, a man acknowledging yourself not worth a shilling, without a profession, without any means of subsistence, have contrived to marry the daughter of my late friend Sir Audley Dacres. And what, Sir, do you expect me to say to such information? What should I say, but that I am very sorry for it?"

"It is perfectly indifferent to me," replied Marchmont, "what you say. I came not here to listen to your remarks, but to know when you will appoint a day for meeting me to pay or transfer the money which I am entitled to in right of my wife"

"What money?"

"Her fortune, to which you know her to have become entitled."

"Oh! no doubt you took care to inform yourself of all that; for indeed, however small it is, and under whatever restrictions, it was still an object to *you.* "

"Look'ye, Mr. Mohun," said Marchmont impatiently, "I will not be insulted. What I ask I have a right to know. From you I shall insist upon an answer — and let me assure you, Sir ..."

"*Good* Sir!" interrupted Mohun contemptuously, "don't heat your-self. Be assured I am not to be moved by all that. As far as I am em-powered to act under the will of my late friend, I shall certainly abide by his meaning, whomsoever it may displease. If you think, or any of your wise advisers will tell you, that you have a *remedy* against me — take it, Sir! take it; I have no manner of objection to meeting you on legal ground."

He then called to his clerk, and, bidding him shew the gentlemen out, rose from his seat, and marched into another room. Marchmont warmly expostulated, and might have done something more as he passed, if Mr. Bargrave had not almost by force withheld him till Mo-hun disappeared, and shut the door with the air of a man who held his visitor too cheap to shew him the usual forms of civility.

Indignation and rage possessed Marchmont at being obliged to submit to such treatment without instantly resenting it; and Bargrave, with some difficulty, prevailed upon him to leave the house. His first emotions led him to go into a coffee-house and write to Mohun; but Bargrave entreated him to give himself only one hour's reflection, after which, he said, he would no longer oppose any thing he determined upon. Marchmont now missed the friendship and council of Eversley — He felt himself too much irritated to trust to his own judgment; and of his present adviser he knew but little, and had a prejudice against him on account of his profession. In this turbulent state of mind he walked from the Temple towards Charing Cross, heedless of the sur-rounding objects, and uncertain whither he was going, when he saw a crowd gather round a waggon in the street, where there was a press of coaches, and heard some women exclaiming against the horror of the sight, and what a shame it was that so many poor fellows should suffer so. — Roused by the eagerness of one woman, who was speaking and weeping, Marchmont asked what was the matter.

"The matter!" answered the complainer: "Why it is a wagon-load of wounded soldiers from beyond sea — some without legs, and some without arms: and, for my part, I could tear my flesh to see them; for I've lost my only brother, and a fine lad as ever was seen, in this cursed war!"

"The better was his luck," said a decent but rough-looking man who stood near her; "better to die ten times over than be crippled like those poor fellows. However, 'tis not a tythe, no nor a fiftieth hardly, of only the last cargo; for most of them have been sent on by water that they might not be seen, because the people grumble." The man then passed on with a significant shrug; and Marchmont, casting his eyes towards the waggon, was struck with the uniform of the regiment in which Captain Forrester served, and almost instantly recognized an old serjeant who belonged to his company. Marchmont stepped hastily towards him, and, enquiring after Captain Forrester, learned, with inexpressible satisfaction, that he had been exchanged, and either was arrived or would very soon be in London. — Having given the honest veteran a small present, and promised to enquire after him, Marchmont now hastened on towards Curzon-street, where his elder brother had a house, at which, when he was in town, Forrester usually resided. All this while Bargrave had followed Marchmont, now and then venturing a gentle expostulation, to which, as he had it not in his nature to be rude to any man unprovoked, Marchmont answered as civilly as he could, though without having much attended to the pacific and legal arguments the Solicitor so sedulously offered. — These Bargrave renewed with more warmth and seriousness as they got into quieter streets, where he hoped to be heard to more advantage; but Marchmont, who had now an object towards which his immediate views were directed, walked faster than ever; so that Bargrave, who was a short man, not higher than Marchmont's elbow, and immoderately fat, could by no means keep pace with his enormous strides. The weather was extremely warm; and the poor lawyer, trotting along he knew not whither, yet dreading that his client was going to execute some act of violence, or at least to prepare for one, took off his hat, puffed and blew, and, when he had by great exertion got near enough, seized the arm of his too active companion, saying, "Mr. Marchmont, Sir! — Consider, Sir! — For mercy's sake, Sir!" — The word mercy struck on the ear of Marchmont. "Mercy?" answered he. — "My good friend, what have you lawyers to do with *Mercy?* Your business, you know, is only with *Justice.*"

"Well, but dear Sir, let me speak! — Poh! poh! — Bless me, it is vastly hot! — Do, Sir — give me leave, Sir! — Suppose we walk a little slower. I hope there is no hurry — Allow me just to state to you —"

"State what you will," replied Marchmont, "but prithee make haste, for I shall be obliged to wish you a good morning in a minute —I am going to meet one of my best friends."

This expression, and the vehemence with which Marchmont uttered it, seemed to imply seconds and pistols and, impressed with this idea. Bargrave began once more to plead for peace, or at least only the legal weapons which he was himself able to wield.

"My dear Sir," said he, "I only entreat to be attended to for five minutes — for five minutes only. You are unused to the practice of us lawyers. — You have never, perhaps, attended the Courts — else you would know, that when a great pleader behaves cavalierly, as perhaps Mr. Mohun might do to you to-day, he means nothing in the world, nothing in the whole world, rude to the individual: it is merely, as one may say, a way, a form, a manner — and any body that should go for to resent such a thing would be reckoned vastly absurd. — Lord, Sir, if you were to hear the things the counsel say to each other! Why, while they call one another learned brother and learned friend, they sometimes, aye very often, are so abusive, that you would think, perhaps, they must fight as soon as they come out of court. — Not at all. Sir — no such thing — they are the best friends in the world."

"Very likely," replied Marchmont. "I can have no objection to the gentlemen's amusing themselves in that manner; but you must excuse me if I decline being made the object, out of court or in it either, of Mohun's insolence." — "Why, my dear good Sir," resumed Bargrave, "what can you do?"

"It is not necessary, I believe, Mr. Bargrave, for you to enquire," cried Marchmont a little peevishly. — "Good God! Sir — why, do but consider — why, Sir, you cannot challenge Mr. Mohun?"

"Why not? — Does he not call himself a gentleman? and is it not all a man *can* do when insulted as you saw him insult me, to write as I have written?"

"Well; but, Sir, Mr. Mohun will not fight."

"Very likely not; but if the impudent braggart will not be compelled to behave like a gentleman in *any* way, I will kick him wherever I meet him."

"Kick him!" exclaimed the attorney, "kick him! kick Mr. Mohun? — Why, Sir, he'll have a Chief-Justice's warrant against you — he will upon my soul…"

At that moment Marchmont arrived at the door that, from its number, he knew to belong to the house whither Forrester had directed him. He knocked eagerly at it. A servant presently appeared, who, on his earnest enquiry for Captain Forrester, imagined he knew something of his arrival; and, hearing his name, told him that his master, Lord Rochdale, was at home, and would be glad to see him.

Marchmont, disappointed at not finding his friend arrived, yet anxious to converse with one so nearly related to him, slightly wished Mr. Bargrave a good morning, and walked into the house. While Bargrave returned to his chambers in Lincoln's-Inn, not much delighted with his hot walk, nor with the little attention Marchmont seemed to give to his advice — "Yes, yes," muttered he to himself, "he will have a Chief-Justice's warrant after him — let him reckon upon that."

Marchmont found, in Lord Rochdale, the elder brother of his friend, a young man greatly resembling him in person, yet without that generous warmth and active spirit of benevolence which gave so much interest to the manner, and so much energy to the character, of the younger brother. Lord Rochdale, from the message his servant had delivered, imagined Marchmont to be some officer who came with intelligence of his brother, for whose return and health he seemed warmly interested: and when Marchmont explained who he was, Lord Rochdale expressed himself with all the kindness and civility it was in his nature to shew; desired to see him again; enquired where he could wait upon him; and assured him, that when Lord Stanwarden returned out of the North, he would join with all the Forrester family in testifying how true a sense they had of Mr. Marchmont's generous and serviceable friendship towards a person so dear to them all.

Marchmont, whose ardent spirit and ingenuous temper induced him to speak highly of his friend and openly of himself, related the rise of his acquaintance with Captain Forrester. Lord Rochdale heard him with attention; and when Marchmont took his leave, he was assured, that as soon as Captain Forrester arrived, he should have notice, by letter, according to the direction he left.

The moment Marchmont got into the street after this interview, all that had passed with Mohun recurred to him. The hope of being able to consult Forrester, the satisfaction of seeing him, as he had expected to do, returned well to England after so many perils, had for a while suspended the pain inflicted by the insults of Mohun, and the pecuniary distress to which injustice must expose the lovely being to whom his fate was united. But now it all rushed upon his mind at once. He saw that he had for his adversary a man who, to the natural hardness and arrogance of his temper and his profession, added a personal dislike to him; and he felt himself equally unable to bear his affronts patiently, or to contend against the advantages his law talents gave him to defend the wrong. Vexed to have such a repulse to relate to Althea, and altogether uncertain how to act, he went into a coffee-house, and wrote to Eversley an account of what had happened. He forbore to express any intention of personally resenting the insolence of Mohun, which he thought the prudence of Eversley might oppose; but desired in general his advice, and stated his fears lest chicane and quirk, dreadful weapons in the hands of such a man as Mohun, should deprive Althea, at least for a very long time, of the two thousand pounds, which previous to his marriage he had, by the most binding deed Bargrave could imagine, settled wholly on her.

To a generous and liberal mind there is nothing so impossible to support as the unblushing injustice of men who commit robbery and call it *legal;* and now, that the very means provided by men in society for their mutual protection should be converted into those of oppression, plunder, and ruin, seemed such a defect, such a blot in the history of a great nation, that Marchmont could not endure to think of it. Already suffering from the fatal law entanglements of his father, which had reduced his family from affluence to indigence, he held the whole fraternity in a sort of abhorrence, almost forgetting his natural candour when he thought of them. — Yet there are, undoubtedly, in this profession, men of equal integrity and ability. It is only to be lamented, that even the most eminent should adhere to the maxim of undertaking any cause for which they are engaged, however unjust may be the pretensions of the client, and that

"To make the worse appear the better reason"

is often the purpose for which the most brilliant eloquence is exerted, by men who, in private life, are the models of moral virtue and unshaken integrity.

Perhaps no man in any rank or profession had ever so little claim to these last virtues as he in whose power the little fortune of Althea was placed. — Profligate, proud, violent and consequential, totally regardless of the feelings of others, or rather delighting in his power of inflicting pain, Mohun had, in a thousand instances, deserved the brief character given of the tyrant Henry the Eighth. Unprincipled and savage even in his intercourse with women, he had never been tempted to think of marriage but in the instance of Althea. Her beauty had made an impression on his ferocious heart, which he could not now recollect without feeling the most diabolical hatred against the man who had, under all the disadvantages of poverty, supplanted him. — Disdaining, as he generally did, to look back on any circumstances that had displeased or mortified him, he however remembered that Marchmont (whom he knew by sight) had been at Capelstoke about the time that Althea, resolutely dismissing him, had preferred the dismal seclusion of Eastwoodleigh to the opulence and splendour she might have enjoyed as his wife. — Not doubting, therefore, on putting circumstances together, but that Althea had even then an attachment to this undone wanderer, and that her refusal of *him* had been its consequence; he thought with the most inveterate rancour of the man who had thus been preferred, and dwelt with malignant delight on the power he now possessed to oppress and persecute these unfortunate people: — and it was too certain that he possessed this power to a greater degree than they, much as they dreaded him, were aware of.

To these faculties for hurting them, Marchmont's warmth of temper unhappily added another. While he wrote to Eversley, he recalled, indignantly recalled, every circumstance of the supercilious and insolent treatment he had experienced from Mohun. His blood boiled in his veins, as he dwelt on the scornful, the unworthy manners, towards him, of a man to whom he merely applied as a matter of right, and who, even if he were not disposed to admit his claims, could have no motive, but meaning directly to insult him, for forgetting he was a gentleman. Reason and experience had in a great measure conquered the prejudices which his father (a bigot to family pride, and to what used to be called *Toryism*) had taught him to cherish; yet the sentiments of the old cavaliers, the blood of an ancient and high-minded family, acting on the warm and active spirits of three-and- twenty, were altogether of too inflammable a nature not to silence the voice of prudence, and set at nought the pacific advice of Bargrave, to which indeed he had hardly listened. He could not bear to think of returning to Althea to relate that he had been treated like a slave, and had tamely endured it; endured it too, when her rights and her property were in question. He determined therefore not to say, when he arrived at home, what had passed, and to wait in expectation of some farther explanation from Mohun, which he thought could not fail to be brought on by the following short

LETTER.

"Sir,

When I this morning applied to you, I supposed I was addressing myself to a professional man and a gentleman. In the former character you seem determined not to give me the answer or the satisfaction I have a right to demand —I therefore expect, Sir, if you persist in this resolution, that you will think of replying to me in the latter. —I am to be heard of at this place; and, expecting your early notice,

I am, Sir,

Your humble servant,

E. A. MARCHMONT.

Cecil-Street Coffee-House,
    June 22d."

Having dispatched this by a porter, Marchmont proceeded to the stables where he had left the horse which had brought him out of Kent, and returned to his family.

He found Althea and his three sisters waiting at the gate of the court that surrounded their little habitation. As soon as by the light of the moon they were sure it was he, each expressed her joy at his return; and Althea, taking his arm as they walked into the house, said — "We have been uneasy at your stay, Marchmont; — after what you said yesterday when you left us, we had hopes you would return early in the day, and your mother has so alarmed herself that she is quite ill."

Marchmont adored his mother, and his heart now shrunk from the idea of the pain she would feel did she know the truth; nor was the tender solicitude of Althea less distressing to him. He made therefore an effort entirely to stifle his feelings, and conceal the true state of his mind; and though he somewhat overacted his part, his mother, his wife, and his sisters, were too happy, in seeing him returned, to allow themselves to make any remarks that might disturb their satisfaction.

The next day, however, the task that he had imposed upon himself became more difficult. Unused to dissimulation, and with a countenance that expressed every emotion of his heart, he knew not how to evade either the enquiring looks of Mrs. Marchmont, or the questions naturally asked by Althea as to the event of his application to Mohun. He could only answer in general, that he saw Mohun only for a moment, and that he was to go to town again the following Wednesday; when they were to meet on the business.

Though this account, and the evident wish to escape from the conversation, which Althea remarked, were far from being satisfactory, yet she forbore to tease him with any farther questions, convinced that to his judgment she might implicitly trust the management of their affairs, and that whenever he had any thing pleasant to relate she should certainly know it. She assumed, therefore, an air of cheerfulness, in the hope of dispelling the dejection which, in despite of all her endeavours to conquer it, hung over Mrs. Marchmont, as well as a fort of transient chagrin that occasionally seemed to mark the features of Marchmont himself, and which she thought he made efforts (not always successful) to drive away.

Fenchurch, his faithful servant, who had lived with him from a boy, had at Marchmont's own desire left him, and landed at Plymouth, when he was on his way to France. It was with the utmost difficulty that he had been prevailed upon to do this; but not being able to endure the thoughts of entering into any other service, he had returned to his father, who was a small farmer in the north of Devonshire, where he entreated his master to send to him whenever he should mean to take a servant, in whatever country he might be. Marchmont had a great regard for the man, and held this promise sacred: as soon, therefore, as his marriage was certain, and a servant became necessary to him, he had written to this honest fellow, who instantly hastened to resume the service of a master whom he loved, and he had now been some time established in it.

It was to him, therefore, that Marchmont gave the charge of going to London, the next day after his interview with Mohun and the letter he had written, to see if there were any answer to it left at the coffee-house; charging him, if he found any, not to deliver it on his return in the presence of his mother, or of his wife or sisters. Fenchurch, ever anxious for his master's safety, obeyed, but not without uneasiness. He returned with uncommon expedition. There was no letter from Mohun — Another and another day passed — The people of the coffee-house had then been directed to send any letters to him, but from Mohun none arrived. Fenchurch, therefore, was again dispatched to London, with orders to go with a verbal message to Mr. Mohun at his chambers, saying, that he came from Mr. Marchmont, desiring an answer to a letter left the Saturday before. Fenchurch returned with his usual celerity: he had seen the clerk at Mr. Mohun's chambers, who told him that he knew nothing of any answer — that Mr. Mohun went out of town on Saturday evening, and, as Term was now over, would only return for a few days before he left London for the whole summer.

If any thing could add to the affronting insolence of the reception which Mohun had given to Marchmont, it was this rude and contemptuous manner of declaring that he was beneath any answer at all. All the philosophy that Marchmont thought he had acquired in the school of adversity, was insufficient to save him from suffering the most violent paroxysm of rage and indignation. Dreading the enquiries and even the looks of his family, lest they should discover how much he was disturbed, he walked hastily from the house, though it was late in the evening, as if he hoped to appease the agitation of his mind by action. Not far from the habitation of his mother was the large and well wooded park of a nobleman, in which since his return he had taken many delightful evening walks with Althea and his sisters. Towards it, almost mechanically, he now directed his steps: he crossed a broad green lane that led along under the park paling: the moon, now at full, threw across it the long shadows of the trees in the park that bounded it, and of the thorns and brush-wood that grew in a road so little frequented; when proceeding towards a stile, Marchmont thought he saw a man hastily pass from one to another of these shrubby tufts. Had the man, whoever he was, still continued his way, he would have concluded it to be a labourer, and would hardly have noticed him; but, as it was, there was an evident desire of concealment that indicated some bad intention. To detect such he thought every man's business; and though he had no weapon in his hand, not even a stick, yet being of a fearless disposition, he stepped forward to the place where he believed the man had skulked among the bushes, but saw nobody. He forced himself between them — stopped, listened, went round on the other side — Again he stopped, and, looking forward under the paling, thought he saw at a considerable distance something creeping along in the shade they and the trees above them made. Marchmont, thoughtless of consequences, darted after it. The man, for such he with difficulty distinguished the figure to be, now rose to his natural stature, and ran with speed towards the high road at about a mile distance. Marchmont, swift of foot, kept him still in sight, and gained upon him: but just before he reached the road, he unaccountably disappeared; and Marchmont, after a long search, recollecting how far he had been led from the house by a circumstance which, suspicious as it was, he might never get explained; and being afraid that he should give some uneasiness at home by so late a walk, returned the nearest way he could, still meditating on Mohun. — When he entered the house he found, as they all knew his fondness for walking by moon-light, that they had not been alarmed. Althea and Lucy gently chid him for not making them of the party: he answered them in the same tone, and they all set down to their simple supper.

Lucy, full of animation and spirit, was now engaged in a description of a party who had that day been (to the wonder of the family) to pay a bridal visit to Althea. It consisted of a widow and her three maiden sisters, all ladies between fifty and sixty, who resided on a very handsome income, the greatest part of the year, at a very good family house about four miles off. But having unfortunately nothing to do but to see that their mansion and gardens were kept in order — that their coach-horses looked sleek, and their servants were all orderly — business which, settled as it had been for years in a regular routine, was insufficient to occupy any one of them — they were under the necessity of turning their talents to the inspection of their neighbours' affairs. Even the humble and retired family of Mrs. Marchmont at such a distance could not escape their curiosity. The farmer of whom she rented the house was a tenant of theirs, and she had hardly been settled a fortnight before most of the particulars of her history were known to these four Sybils. Though all that could be heard of Mrs. Marchmont ought to have excited only respect, she was so much reduced in circumstances, drat such rich antiquities would not have thought of cultivating an acquaintance with her, but to gratify their insatiable thirst of knowing every thing that related to every body. However, as they foresaw that they must in the course of this communication send their coach to fetch the family, an operation to which they and their coachman had an equal aversion, they had hesitated and doubted, till Marchmont's return, and Althea's marriage, irritated their desire of information and of remark to such a degree, that, as it was summer, Mrs. Aconite and the three amiable ladies her sisters, the Mrs. Henbanes, had ventured to an afternoon visit. They had known something of Lady Dacres when she was Miss Gunston, and longed to see her daughter-in-law, who had been represented at Margate, where they passed six weeks every year, as such a very eccentric young person.

This first essay had in a great measure been disappointed — for Althea was walking with Marchmont when they arrived; and though she returned to the house before they went, she did not choose to appear. Lucy, therefore, was describing these their unexpected and unwelcome visitors to her brother and Althea.

"They are just such *dry specimens,*" said she, alluding to Althea's botanical collection, "as you described Lady Barbara Newmarch to be. The widow lady is rather less a curiosity than the rest; for she affects great gravity, which becomes her age — though I am sure she is the most malignant and spiteful of them all. But Mrs. Henbane is a politician, fierce as ten furies. She talks of revolutions, till she really looks fit for a straight waistcoat; and no poissarde of Paris ever hunted an aristocrat in a fine coat with more fury than she would fly at any unfortunate wight who should venture to say that any republican might still be possibly a human being. I protest she frightened me, and counteracted her own ends; for she wanted to know of what party *you* were, brother, and how you got through France; for she had heard, I cannot guess how, that you have been there. As to Mama and Amelia, they had no inclination to answer her, nor I neither. However, I was going to say something, when she burst out again like a new eruption of Mount Vesuvius; and if I had said a word she did not like, I'm sure she would have got up and shaken me. So I let her rave on, and said nothing. — The next, Mrs. Lydia Henbane, and the youngest, who is still called Miss Deborah, though I'm sure she is seventy, both began talking at the same time, and therefore luckily there was not much occasion for me to speak. I cannot tell exactly what they said; but I thought Mrs. Lydia praised some publication on the subject of politics, and Mrs. (cry her mercy!) *Miss* Deborah spoke of the last new fashions. I knew no more of one than of the other of these topics; and right glad was I to be released from them all, for I fancied myself surrounded by Madame Hecate, and Mesdemoiselles Alecto, Tysiphone, and Magara, her maids of honour." — Mrs. Marchmont, though she had learned to consider such people with the calmest indifference, herself could not help smiling at the vivacity of her daughter; yet she was about gently to check that spirit of satire which from her gaiety of heart, and acuteness of perception, Lucy sometimes indulged too far, when she was suddenly interrupted by a noise at the front door of the house. It seemed like violent blows given by one person to another, who cried out and remonstrated. Marchmont at the sound of distress leaped up; and though his mother, turning pale and trembling, entreated him not to go out, at least without Fenchurch, for whom she violently rang the bell, he ran in a moment to the door. — His mother, Althea, and his sisters, still endeavouring to detain him, pressed thither also; and Fenchurch, with fear and terror in his countenance, rushed after him. It was too late — The moment he put his foot out of the door, he was roughly seized in the King's name by two ill-looking fellows, while four others surrounded him. He was at no loss to guess who they were. He desired them to suffer him to return into the house; and approaching his mother, who, unless supported by Althea and Lucy, would have sunk on the ground before him, he besought her not to increase his distress by her agonies; then turning to Althea, who though pale and trembling seemed to attempt something like resolution, his voice faltered, and he could only say, "My Althea, my angel!" The men now led him between them into the parlour; the four others followed — and while one of the ruffians desired Fenchurch to go out, which however he refused, the others sat down with great familiarity, and he who seemed to be the principal among them thus began:

"So, 'Squire! we are like to be better acquainted at last. I was afeard we should not have met no more, you and I — but now it's my belief we shall have time to get thorough good friends, hah? Don't be frought, Ma'am," addressing himself to Mrs. Marchmont, to whom her terrifred daughters were administering drops and water; "we won't hurt the young 'Squire. Never you fear neither, young ladies, we'll do un no harm — Nor I never likes, not I, to put ladies, and above all such pretty ladies, in any quondary. — We'll not do his Honour the smallest harm upon yearth — Only it's my believe he must take a small trip with us to Maidstone; unless, perhaps, he can find frinds more nigher to help settle these small matters here."

What are they?" said Marchmont, in a calm tone.

"Why, in the first place I've got two writs against you. I fancy you guesses the names to um — Eh, Master Marchmont! — Old stories, you know — The same as we used to have a few journies about afore you set off on your travels beyond sea. — There, Sir; there's the stuff. You see the names and the sums. Both together are — aye, let me see — *nineteen hundred and ninety-six pounds!* I'm sure I hope your Honour will get bail with all my heart — and then, no doubt, you'll not find it hard to get t'other matter settled — though 'tis rather a toughish job, as one may say, that there."

"What do you mean?" said Marchmont: "to what do you allude?"

"Why, Master, only this — You've a thought proper to send a challenge."

"A challenge!"

"Aye, your Honour — Our gemmen of the law, look ye, are of a peaceful disposition; and so Counsellor Mohun thought it right, you

see, to put you under a little sort of arrest, by order of my Lord Chief
Justice, just till such time as you may cool upon it a bit."

"Cowardly scoundrel!" exclaimed Marchmont, "base poltroon! —
Well, Sir! and what is to be the consequence of this?"

"Oh! nothing — nothing in the world, Sir — but that you must
just be put into custody till you find security to keep the peace — But
that there business indeed is no affair of mine. That worthy gemman
yonder has all that in his dippartumment — Come, Bobby, my man,
speak to his Honour."

Another of the men then approached Marchmont, and said he
had orders to arrest him under the Chief-Justice's warrant, which he
read; and concluded with saying, that he must either go into confinement, or be bound himself in the penalty of three hundred pounds,
and find two sureties in three hundred each, for keeping the peace.

Marchmont now saw immediate imprisonment before him. Far
from the only two friends who would come forward to save him from
it, had it been in their power, either of these arrests was more than sufficient to condemn him to long, if not to perpetual confinement. The
cruelty of loading him with these double and heavy chains, could, he
knew, be owing to nothing but the resolution of his persecutors to put
it out of the reach of any friends he might have to save him, since the
whole of the securities demanded amounted to three thousand pounds.
He was in a neighbourhood where he had not a single acquaintance; and
nothing remained for him but to endeavour to explain with calm resolution the miserable truth to his agonised family, and to soften to them as
much as he could the pain of this dreadful separation.

He turned to Althea, who pale as ashes, but tearless and immove-
able, sat by him during this scene. "Althea, my dearest love," said he,
"now is the moment to shew that presence of mind, that reasonable
fortitude, and truly feminine courage, which I have before had occasion to admire. Do not, my angel, by yielding to this shock, give me
cause to fear that you repent sharing so bitter a lot; and if you love
me, think less of some trifling present inconveniences that I may go
through, than of preserving the dearest part of me — yourself; while
you become the heavenly comforter of my mother."

"Whatever you bid me do," answered Althea, trying in vain to command her faltering voice, "whatever you tell me will give you the least
comfort, that I will do. But, remember, Marchmont, we do not part:
whithersoever you are obliged to go, thither I will accompany you."

"Impossible, my love! To-night I apprehend these honest gentle-men will take me from hence."

"Yes, that's pretty near the right of the thing," said one of the men, roughly; "you must go to Maidstone to-night, that's for sartin.— You may move yourself up to Banco by habbus coppas as soon as you will ater-rard."

"My dear Althea!" resumed Marchmont, "you see how it is — Go! my dear girl, to my mother (Mrs. Marchmont had left the room in an agony not to be described) — try to induce her to bear better this severe blow — nothing will do it so effectually as seeing you calm."

"You will not go then before I return?" said Althea, as she left the room.

"Certainly not. But, gentlemen, you see how my family are dis-tressed — Could you not let me speak a few words to my mother and my wife in another room?"

"God bless you, my Master, how can we do any such a thing? — No, no! that's quite out of character: you may say as much as ever you will to the ladies, one and all, but your Honour must not go out of the sight of some two of us upon no account."

"Well, then," said Marchmont, meeting with all the courage he could this bitter foretaste of imprisonment, "I suppose all I have to do is to prepare, still favoured by your attendance, for my removal. Tell me how this removal is to be made at such an hour, and in a place where a chaise is not to be had in a moment?"

"Why, as to that matter, we should not to be sure much mind staying with your Honour here till to-morrow," cried one of these au-thorised raffians; "that is upon proper considerations, and the like: but then we must make bold to desire you'll sit up with us; for as Muster Trickman there says, who knows all our business as well as ere a man in Englunt, you mid'nt no how be out of our sight. But I warrant you would not have no objection now to us four; there are but four on us; we've sent tothers to wait without; I say you'd have no objection, I dares for to say, for my friend Trickman, who is well to do I assure you, a near kinsman of Lawyer Vampyre's, and honest Bob Perkin, and Jemmy Lambeth here, and me, to sit down with you, and have a little something to keep us alive and awake, till sich time as we can all be a-jogging in the morning?"

"No," said Marchmont, "I thank you for your civility, since I sup-pose you mean it as such; but my family would only be kept in a greater degree of suffering by such an arrangement, which would answer little purpose — so if you will tell me how I am to go, I will only stay to have a few necessaries packed up, and will be ready to go with you."

"As you choose. Muster Machmon," said the fellow in a very surly manner; "we never wants to force civility upon nobody; and as for how you be to be *conwayed,* vy the vay is to fitch a chai' from Sittingbone. Here, you — Dick Jenks," calling to one of the gang who waited without, "step and tell the chai ve ordered to be ready, to come quickly."

"You took that precaution?" said Marchmont.

"Aye, aye, Master, we thought it right," answered Trickman, "for we were pretty sure of nabbing you. No loop-holes now, Young 'Squire, to crip out on — hah! — Don't you remember the dodgings you gived us at that there hell of an ould place there doun in the west? My kinsman, Lawyer Vampyre, was plaguely out in a's reckoning, but we made surer work on't now. We took care to be upon sartin grounds."

"I fancy," said Marchmont, "it was some one of this party that passed me to-night in the lane."

"'Twas I, 'Squire," said a tall fierce figure, with a cut over his eye, and a most diabolical countenance, "I dodged you from the house into that lane. —I did not much like it; I thought you had smelt a rat, and had a mind to be off. I don't know what you took me for — but I'm sure you gave me a rare breathing."

"I do not believe I much mistook your character," said Marchmont; "but be that as it may, I suppose you all expect to drink, as I think it is always customary for you worthy operators of the law to be jolly on these occasions." He then rang the bell for Fenchurch, who entered looking more dead than alive, and bade him bring some strong beer and brandy, though the whole stock of both in the house was very inconsiderable. Fenchurch obeyed — and the fellows then demanded to eat. All that was in the larder was then set before them, on which they fell to without ceremony; while Marchmont prepared himself for parting with Althea, who now returned into the room. She was apparently calm, but her expressive countenance testified what she felt. — Marchmont eagerly enquired after his mother.

"She is better," said Althea, "and wishes to see you."

"I cannot go to her," answered Marchmont, "that is impossible. But let Lucy, if my mother can do without her, come to me; and do you, my dearest love, sit down and compose yourself. Why should I disguise the truth, when, after all, it must be known, it must be endured? I am not to be out of these men's sight till I am secured in prison. — Thither it is better immediately to go — a chaise is coming to take me thither."

"And me also," said Althea, with courage: "do not imagine, Marchmont, that any thing shall divide us. To be where you are not, while suffering under circumstances so cruel, would be to me more intolerable than a thousand prisons."

"Good God, Althea! can I bear the thoughts of taking my wife, of taking you to such a place? Impossible — Do not, pray do not distress me by the proposal."

"Marchmont," said Althea, in an earnest and determined manner, "it is the first time I have ever made a request to you — and will you refuse me? Will you mortify me by making me suspect you think so poorly of me, as that I would shrink from a few personal inconveniences? Wherever you are it is fit I should be."

"But," added Marchmont, in a lower voice, "one of these men, I am persuaded, will insist upon going in the chaise with me. Can I suffer you to be so accompanied?"

"Send then for another chaise," answered Althea, "for my resolution is fixed — nothing can change it."

Marchmont then addressed himself to the men, and enquired what accommodations he could have where he was going?

They told him he might be indulged with a room upon paying for it. He then asked if he could be allowed to go in the chaise unaccompanied by one of them, as his wife insisted upon going with him.

He was answered, "that all those things must be considered. — They had horses in waiting; and if his Honour thought proper for to make a proper present for their civility, over and above the customary see, why they'd no objection against obliging him."

Marchmont, finding Althea resolute, acceded to every thing she demanded. She then hastened to put up such necessaries as they had both immediate occasion for, and was soon ready, with a serene though wan countenance, to attend their rude conductors. To take leave of his mother was the most dreadful part of what Marchmont had to undergo: he thought indeed it was far better they should not meet; and Lucy undertook in appearance to persuade her mother not to insist upon it. She left the room, and returned in a few moments to her brother to say her mother was tolerably tranquil, and acquiesced: but the truth was, that after having been a few moments up stairs, the recollection of all she had gone through to avoid this evil, and the cruel idea of her son in perpetual imprisonment, had such an effect on her enfeebled frame, that she had fallen from one fainting fit to another, and when Marchmont and Althea departed was totally insensible.

CHAP. IX.

L'indigence va flétrir tes beaux jours; tu vas connoître les larmes cruelles qu'arrache la nécessité.

SOMETHING MORE THAN sixty pounds, part of it the last receipt of Mrs. Marchmont's annuity, and part of it a loan from Eversley, which he insisted on making, and had remitted in a letter, was the whole stock of money in possession of the Marchmont family at this period. Althea had about fifteen guineas of her own, the remains of her last dividend on her aunt's legacy. This, and ten guineas from the general stock, was all Marchmont would take. He left the rest with Lucy, entreating her to exert herself to console her mother, and support the sinking spirits of Amelia. — "Remember," said he, as he took leave of her, "remember, my dear Lucy, that by bearing evils well we deprive them of half the power of hurting us; and that there is no difference between a strong and a feeble mind, but their different powers of enduring the calamities of life. There are two ways, my sweet love, of shewing the extreme concern that I know my situation gives you; but one of these ways will mitigate, the other will increase my distress. — Which will my Lucy choose?"

The poor girl, trying to stifle the anguish she felt, promised to exert herself; but when the chaise, so guarded, left the door, all her resolution was insufficient — till the dread of aggravating the agonies of her mother again restored to her some degree of fortitude.

Althea, for whom a prison lost its horrors when to sooth and console Marchmont was in question, not only bore the first shock of entering such a dismal abode with an unchanged countenance, but assumed a degree of calm cheerfulness; which, though it cost her some effort, was beheld by Marchmont with admiration and gratitude, and it left him more at liberty, than if he had at once had to tranquillize her spirits and provide for her accommodation; while his own heart, accusing him of having brought this adored creature into a situation so unworthy of her, was oppressed with a degree of despondence, which he would never have felt had he had only his own troubles to contend with.

With so little money to command as he possessed, and not knowing where, when it was gone, he could obtain a supply, nothing was more bitter than the necessity of gratifying the demands of the vultures who had dragged him to confinement. These were exorbitant, and preferred with as much audacity as if the ruffians had conferred a favour in executing the writs against him. It was above all grating to him to be compelled the most liberally to pay the principal of them, who called himself the kinsman of Vampyre, and boasted of being employed by him at Eastwoodleigh. It is hardly necessary to say, that his name, as attorney, was to the writs for debt; and Mohun had on this occasion also employed him.

No accommodations were to be procured that night — but Marchmont, as he was now in a place of security, was allowed to be left alone with Althea; and after he had satisfied the harpies that surrounded him, and dispatched Fenchurch back to his mother, to assure her that he and Althea were well, and to bring him an account of those for whom he was so anxious at home, he sat down by Althea, who, notwithstanding her alarm and fatigue, still supported her spirits. But when Marchmont took her hand, and enquired whether she could forgive him for having brought her into such a scene, they both lost their resolution for a moment, and Marchmont wept as he pressed her to his bosom. — Althea was the first to recover from this transient weakness. She assured him, that with him all places were alike to her; that, under his protection, she feared nothing. — "My dear friend," said she, "why should we, even for a moment, yield to despondence? — Let fear and despondence be for the guilty. — *We* may be unfortunate, but we shall not be unhappy — for shall we not be together? — shall we not still enjoy the consciousness of innocence and honour? Believe me, Marchmont, I am so far from repenting the step I took when I united my destiny with yours, that, were I to-morrow at liberty, I would do the same, even though all that has happened within this last day were as certain as it now is. The only thing I apprehend in imprisonment is, your losing your health from confinement."

"And you, my angel, my Althea!" exclaimed Marchmont passionately, "do you fear nothing for yourself? Good God! — that you should be the inmate of a place like this!"

He was too much moved to proceed, but Althea continued calmly to speak. — "No, Marchmont, I do not fear illness for myself; for I have been more used to confinement, and women are constitutionally more sedentary. Give not yourself a moment's pain about me, but consider only what measures are most immediately necessary. Let us write to that dear good Eversley — Captain Forrester is probably, by this time, come to London. Two such friends will not, I am sure, leave any thing unattempted for you; and till we can hear from them, let us first endeavour to recover the fatigue of this alarming night, and then to make ourselves as easy as we can."

Marchmont, unwilling to repress those sanguine hopes which he could not imitate, now entreated her to wrap herself in her cloak, and rest her head on his shoulder, while his arm supported her, in the hope that she might take some rest, of which he could not bear she should be during the whole night deprived. — Althea, desirous of appeasing his apprehensions for her health, affected to sleep; while Marchmont, the first time the tumult of his spirits would allow him to do it, began to think over the circumstances of his situation.

Never did an unfortunate prisoner, guiltless even of imprudence as he was, look forward to a more hopeless prospect. Though he knew his friends Forrester and Eversley would give the security that the base and malignant cowardice of Mohun had insisted upon for his keeping the peace, relying on his honour that they should incur no risk, yet the debt that had so long hung over him, swelled as it now was by accumulated interest, was such as he could not dream of asking them to answer. — He knew how Eversley was circumstanced, and how much of his individual fortune had already been advanced in consequence of his generous friendship; the Earl of Stanwarden was not rich; and though Forrester was the favourite of his family, yet being only a younger brother, and one of a family of five, he had but a small allowance, and had been principally obliged, for any considerable supplies of money, to an aunt of his mother's: — she had never had a child of her own, and loved him with great affection, living very much within her jointure that she might lay by money for him. — Whatever resource such a good dowager was to Forrester himself, it did not by any means enable him to assist a friend to such an extent as was now necessary for poor Marchmont. — Other hopes he had none. He himself possessed nothing; and the fortune of Althea, if he had been capable of a wish to touch it, was not only insufficient, but so secured by his own act before his marriage, that, except the eight hundred pounds that had belonged to Mrs. Trevyllian, and which Althea had herself insisted on having left at liberty, he could not appropriate a penny of the principal to this or any other purpose.

What then was to be his destiny? — Imprisonment, perpetual and hopeless! "And is this," said he, as he looked earnestly on Althea, "is this the lot I have induced this lovely, this incomparable creature to share with me? — Is a place of confinement, tears, and lamentation — the abode of sorrow, guilt, and misery, the bridal house, whither, after three weeks marriage, I conduct my Althea?"

The fear of disturbing her transient forgetfulness, rather than any effort of fortitude, induced him to stifle the groans that swelled his bursting heart. But as before she awoke it was necessary he should determine on something that might at least look like trying to procure his emancipation, he decided to send Fenchurch, who was to return at noon, to Mr. Bargrave, and desire his advice how to act. So passed this miserable night. At an early hour in the morning Marchmont wrote his letter to Bargrave; and poor Fenchurch, returning soon after with such an account of Mrs. Marchmont as her daughters thought would give their brother as little additional uneasiness as possible (though it was far from the truth), entreated his master to let him go to London with the letter to the lawyer — though, from the excessive fatigue he had undergone, Marchmont was desirous of finding some other messenger.

Such arrangements as could be made for their accommodation were then set about. The gaoler, from the large sum for which Marchmont was in custody, supposed him to be some extravagant young man of fashion, who would spend his money freely; he therefore provided him with a small chamber well secured, and a decent woman was appointed to attend on Althea — who now found herself released from the apprehension that had been the most uneasy to her, that she should be compelled to see, if not to mingle among, unfortunate or culpable wretches; among those whose calamities she could not relieve, or whose real or imputed giult made them at once objects of abhorrence and pity. — A prison, however she had miscalculated its miseries as affecting her, was still very dreadful. The horrid countenances of the men who had charge of the keys; the expression of malignant satisfaction which they appeared to have on those countenances, when they were empowered to secure such a prisoner as Marchmont; and the precautions that were taken before Fenchurch was admitted to speak to his master, were circumstances that all served to depress the spirits of Althea. But she saw how much the fortitude of Marchmont depended on seeing her tranquil; and whatever were the pangs that assailed her heart on making observations on their present, or considering their future fortune, she assumed a steady and even a cheerful countenance, and made light of any inconveniences that Marchmont seemed to foresee and to dread for her.

The second day of their sad abode in this scene of confinement brought them a still consoling account of Mrs. Marchmont; and Lucy, who wrote to her brother, talked of visiting them on the next day but one. — Althea, however, notwithstanding the generally satisfactory purport of this letter, remarked, though she carefully concealed it from her husband, that the writing was less regular than Lucy's usually was, and the paper, in two or three places, blistered with tears. These observations impressed her with dread, lest Mrs. Marchmont was sinking under the heavy blow she had sustained; and such an apprehension, both on her own account, and because of the effect it would have on her son, was more dreadful to Althea than any other fear that she had yet been compelled silently to sustain.

Towards evening Fenchurch returned with a letter from Mr. Bargrave; in which he civilly reproached Marchmont for his imprudence in provoking Mr. Mohun, expressed himself very sorry for the general state of his affairs, spoke with a sort of horror of the serious mischief of getting into the hands of the Chief-Justice, and protested he knew not how to advise. He concluded however with saying, that the first thing Marchmont had to do, was to move himself by habeas corpus to the King's Bench prison — the necessary steps for which Bargrave said he had taken, and directed Marchmont what he was himself to do. But his whole letter was calculated to discourage and depress the hopes and spirits of his client; nor were they greatly relieved by the following letter, which Fenchurch had found at the Coffee-House in Cecil-Street. It was written in answer to Marchmont' s letter from thence on the day of his writing to Mohun.

LETTER.

"Penzance, June 27th.
Your letter, my dear Marchmont, gives me the most acute concern I am capable of feeling, and the more so because I am at this moment so circumstanced, that I cannot hasten to you as I would otherwise do;

and I am afraid you never wanted more such assistance as I can give you, though it is far, very far, from being such as my heart would offer were I otherwise situated. Nothing, my friend, can be more deplorable than *my* situation. Were it less so, I might still be tempted to envy yours; for what are pecuniary difficulties, what are all those evils of life which you have often asserted, and I am sometimes tempted to believe, arise from the abuses of our social contract, compared to the miseries that spring from the irrevocable contract of an ill-assorted marriage?

The unhappy woman, to whom, while hardly yet arrived at the period when the law allows a man a will of his own, I was tied to humour the will of others, is now in such a state, that, while humanity forbids my leaving her, my remaining with her is the most horrible punishment! You know what I suffered from the violence, the caprice, the malignity of her temper, when every reasonable person, who saw her situation in life, thought she had every reasonable means of content. But the tenderness with which I then treated her, far from engaging her gratitude or her affection, served only to accustom her to a more unlicensed indulgence of a dreadful temper, or, to speak more plainly, of a bad heart; for such surely must be possessed by a woman who, with the most decided resolution to gratify herself, is totally indifferent to the feelings of others. — Brought up to believe money the greatest good, and being heiress to the ill-acquired wealth of her father, she supposed that every creature around her was to be subservient to her. The least opposition threw her into agonies of passion, and, in proportion as these paroxysms were yielded to, their frequency and fury increased. The consciousness of her being detested then came to torment her; and though she would not correct the cause, the effect she would not endure. Indulgence in that degrading vice, that in obscuring the reason may transiently mitigate the sufferings of the miserable, next succeeded. Her temper and her blood became equally inflamed, and she lived in the wretched vicissitudes of rage or stupefaction till the state of her health alarmed her; and then, having some purpose to pursue that related solely to herself, she set forth in search of that health which, with such a disposition, it was impossible to find — and hither I accompanied her, determined to fulfil, to my utmost, the duty which, having been at first imposed upon me, has never been sweetened by affection, esteem, friendship, or gratitude. Imbecility of intellect has daily increased upon this poor unhappy being, without mitigating the violence of her disposition. She now throws herself into the most furious rage, if her maid displaces a pin, or if a word is uttered which she does not approve of, though what she likes to-day she abhors to-morrow; then feeling the impotence of her ridiculous anger, and that it hurts nobody so much as herself, she falls into tears, and bewails her hard fate, and the cruelty of those about her, in terms that would really make a stranger, for a moment, believe her the most injured and unfortunate of women. I think it is very evident that her mind becomes more and more deranged, but in her personal health I see no difference; and probably she may remain many years in this wretched state, though the physical men who attend her seem to think not. Imagine, my dear Marchmont, if you can (but indeed it is not easy to figure to yourself scenes of which you have never beheld any resemblance) — imagine what must be the state of my household! what the education, the manners of two girls who have been brought up under such a mother! what the sort of servants are, who alone will stay with her! and how much of robbery and insolence I am compelled to be blind to, lest she should be deserted even by these mercenary and dishonest creatures!

"Sometimes she declares a resolution of leaving this place, and returning home, which I most heartily wish: then she asserts her inability to go back to an estate which her money has been laid out to improve, but which she knows will be inhabited, at least for my life, by some one of the people she hates the most; for she is sure the moment she is dead I shall marry again and precisely a person who will use her poor girls very ill, and rob them of all the furniture and good things she has been collecting.

"Such is the conversation I am forced to hear — such is the faint but true sketch of my miserable condition, from which I know not how immediately to disengage myself soon enough, or long enough, to do you any effectual good by meeting you in town. Let me, however (while I try to accomplish this), let me entreat you, my dear Marchmont! to be as cool as you can in regard to Mohun; for any unguarded heat, however great the provocation, will only give him an advantage over you. Beware of Vampyre, and of the unadjusted claims of Messrs. Spriggins and Scrapepenny — I have a horror of those usurious fellows, but still more of the instrument they employ. Their answers to me were so evidently evasive, and they have both so much of Shylock about them, that my daily dread is of their enforcing their bonds. This accursed persuasion haunts me with more uneasiness, because my own

money matters (the money of my wife I make it, you know, a rule never to touch) are so circumstanced this year by the necessity I am under
of making the last payment of Linda's (I should say Mrs. Glaston's)
little fortune, and by the failure of my principal tenant, that I cannot
(as I assure you, upon my honour, I would otherwise do) come up to
the demands of these extortioners.

"Nevertheless, my dear friend, I am by no means so straightened,
but that I can give you, without the slightest inconvenience, the enclosed order on my banker for fifty pounds. The sum is small; but I
know you will be better pleased to receive such, which will not even
remotely distress me, than a larger that might just now have that consequence. My good friend, when he recollects how little I am likely to
assert the most inconsequential falsehood, will not doubt my sincerity,
when I tell him, that, robbed as I am of every domestic comfort, I can
taste no pleasure but what arises from the little power that is left me
of doing, what yet I can do, for the two people whom I most love and
esteem. Write to me immediately, Marchmont, and rest assured of the
unfailing friendship and affection of your

W. EVERSLEY."

This letter would have convinced Marchmont, if he had not been
well aware of it before, that even if he could have endured the thoughts
of owing so much to Eversley's friendship, which he had long since determined never to do, it was not in his power at this time to assist him.

Marchmont read a part of this letter to Althea, whose heart bled
to drink of the unhappy situation of Eversley, for whom she had the
most perfect esteem. — She took occasion, however; to remark to
Marchmont, how little the possession of even a great fortune secured
happiness. — "When you feel yourself disposed, my dear friend," said
she, "from your tenderness for me, to lament our present situation,
recollect how much my lot, which indeed I account a happy one, is
preferable to what I should have known if I had married the cruel,
arrogant, hateful Mohun; or, escaping him, if any of the many ob-
jectionable men I have seen or heard of had received my promise to
love, honour, and *obey.* It might have been my destiny to have met with
the counterpart of Mrs. Eversley; for such a being (I am afraid more
than one) there undoubtedly is in the world. Then, he might not only
have contrived to have rendered me wretched by the various ways in
which she torments her husband, but, privileged by his sex, he might

have dissipated my fortune and his own, and possibly have beat me, or locked me up, or sold me if he could have met with a purchaser, to give course to his brutal humour, or contribute to his selfish indulgences. Such people have existed — do probably exist now; and what would have become of me had I belonged to one? But are not *we* happy, Marchmont, whom fate cannot hurt unless it separate us? which surely can happen only from death. Yes, my dear love! believe your Althea, when she declares to you, that in this prison, and without any certainty of quitting it unless for another, she feels herself a thousand times happier than she should be in the most brilliant circle, bearing about her the value of half a county in jewels, and simpering at the sad repetition of uninteresting conversation among those who are called Great! I saw enough of the lives of people of the very first world to be thoroughly convinced I did not envy them. To live as we wish to live, we want nothing but the justice we shall surely obtain sooner or later — we shall then have a small competence; doubt not but that we shall find means to increase it. I have often known the idle make themselves miserable, merely because they had nothing to do. If, as a celebrated poet says, to be employed is to be happy, we shall have another chance of escaping from all the fancied evils of life at least — if the imaginations of those who are blest in each other can indeed be liable to ideal calamities."

Marchmont, while every word of consolation, uttered by his adored Althea, heightened the tender admiration with which he regarded her, yet could not so easily reconcile himself to see in a cheerful light events which had reduced her below her rank; and when he reflected on the machinations of the villanous agent to whom all their present misery, and that he had for so many years experienced, were owing, his heart swelled with unconquerable rage and indignation: and when he ceased to be charmed with the fortitude and soothed with the sweetness of Althea, he felt himself disposed to curse the authors of his distress — himself, the universe, and all but her and his suffering family.

He took, however, in pursuance of Mr. Bargrave's advice, measures to remove to the King's bench, and the sixth day of his imprisonment was fixed upon for his departure. Lucy, as having the most resolution and the best spirits, was on that day to come over to see her brother. She came — Marchmont was busy in another room, and Althea was alone when she entered; when, struck with her altered appearance, she eagerly enqiured, as she embraced her; whether she was well? — whether her mother and sisters were well?

"My brother is not here," answered Lucy in a faint voice; "but he is not confined separately from you, is he? — He is not shut up in the common prison?" — Althea having satisfied her that he was only accidentally absent, preparing for his removal, Lucy, fetching a deep sigh, said — "I may then tell you my dearest sister, what we must conceal from him. Ever since the fatal night when he was so cruelly torn from us, my mother has been in the most alarming state from fainting fits, so frequent and so long, that we have dreaded lest every one that has seized her should be her last. You have no notion, Althea, how sadly she is altered; Amelia and I have never been in bed for above an hour at a time since we saw you go; for we dare not leave her a moment, Mr. Wilkinson thinking her in great danger. Alas! what shall we do? — What will become of us?"

Althea, trembling at this cruel report, and dreading the effect it would have on Marchmont, was hardly able to say — "For God's sake, my Lucy, have some other advice — let something else be done; let some physician be sent for instantly!"

Lucy then told her, in a hurried way, "that Mr. Wilkinson had himself proposed it on the second day of his attendance; but that her mother had relapsed on the mention of it, and had since made them promise they would not engage any physician to come — 'They can do me no good,' said she, 'it is too late. Did you ever hear that a physician could cure a broken heart? No, my dear girls, my complaints are out of the reach of medicine: the only cordial would be the sight of your brother and Althea — your brother at liberty, and unoppressed — and that I shall never see. No; I shall never, never behold my son again!' — This (continued Lucy) is the style in which she talks. But, alas! I knew how fruitless would be my applications for my brother to go to her; and I thought it best to conceal from him intelligence that I knew he could not have supported."

Althea, whose presence of mind never forsook her in the cause of those she loved, then told Lucy, that the only thing to be done was to remove Mrs. Marchmont to London, if she were able to bear the journey — "I will secure her some lodging near the place where our poor Armyn is to be confined," said she, "and take care that advice shall be ready the moment she gets thither. Do you and Amelia in the meantime, my dear Lucy, exert yourselves to support her; assure her this arrangement is made at the express desire of her son, who can there see her —I will return to-morrow to assist in taking care of her to town the day after. My coming will convince her it is Marchmont's wish; and when she is assured she shall see him, she will acquire strength to undertake the fatigue. Settle every thing, in the mean-time, so that she may have as little trouble as possible, and expect me to-morrow night."

Lucy would have expressed her fears, lest so much fatigue and anxiety should affect Althea herself; but Marchmont at that moment coming in, Althea checked her, and the bustle of their departure prevented Marchmont's noticing, as he would otherwise have done, the ill-concealed anguish of his sister. — They parted — Lucy for her sad home, and Marchmont and Althea, guarded by several retainers of the law, for the King's Bench prison, where Fenchurch had, with great difficulty, and at a very high price, secured them a room. — Marchmont had now to undergo the disagreeable ceremony of being surrendered to the Marshal of the prison, and of seeing the precautions used to secure a person taken for such a sum. — He had besides so many fees to pay, and so many customs to satisfy, that, on examining his purse, he found it reduced within ten guineas. The disposition in which he betook himself to his bed may easily be imagined.

CHAP. X.

Sorrow seems pleased to dwell with so much sweetness!

ALTHEA, ANXIOUS FOR the sad group she had left, and not knowing how to disclose to Marchmont the truth of their situation, was unable to sleep — yet she concealed her real feelings with admirable fortitude; and Marchmont, believing her composed, and wearied as he was by the harassing events of the preceding day, sunk to repose. Such a transient relief was necessary to enable him to bear, with some degree of firmness, the communication which early the next morning Althea was compelled to make, in order to account for a journey which she knew nothing on earth but consideration for his mother would induce him to consent to. Though she softened the cruel truth as much as she could, it was impossible to prevent Marchmont from believing the worst; and as he agreed with Althea in thinking, if she was able to be removed, it would be better, both on account of advice as well as to be near them, that his mother and sisters should remove, he consented that Althea, attended by Fenchurch, should set out to assist the poor girls in their arduous task, while he endeavoured by means of one of the runners of the prison to secure them as comfortable a lodging as could be found within the rules; where he hoped he could see his mother, and alleviate some part of the anguish which his imprisonment inflicted.

Althea was to take leave of him then till the next day, which was the very earliest she could possibly return, though he entreated her most earnestly, in the pious commission she had undertaken, not to be careless of her own health, on which more than his existence depended. These charges being given, and Fenchurch strictly enjoined never to lose light of the chaise that held his mistress, Marchmont took her arm within his to conduct her to the chaise that was waiting for her. It was now that for the first time Althea formed an idea of the place, where her sinking heart told her Marchmont might too probably pass many of his days. At that early hour of the morning the most wretched and destitute inhabitants of this enclosure were just issuing from the sad places where they had passed the night. — Squalid from poverty and confinement, languid despair was in the countenances of some, while others expressed that sort of unfeeling indifference that arises from desperation worn down to apathy. The evening before, Althea, attentive only to Marchmont, and knowing that whithersoever he was going she was to remain with him, had heeded less the places she had passed through, and the people that surrounded her in them; but now the grim and fierce-looking men who filled the room called the lobby, the great keys they bore, and the precautions which were taken to let only one person at a time pass from that place to or from the prison, and the suspicion which two of them who followed close to Marchmont expressed, all served to fill her with dread. Marchmont having spoken to one of them, and given him a shilling, desired he might go to the door to see his wife into a chaise. The man was going to comply with this, when another of apparently more authority stepped forward, and, putting himself immediately before Marchmont, said, "Sir, we've pertickler orders about you — I can't allow of your going down the steps." Marchmont felt *that* to be the bitterest moment he had yet passed — but making an effort to conquer himself, that he might not alarm Althea, he replied, calmly, "Well, then, do you come with me *to* the door, that I may see the lady get in." Three or four of them immediately surrounded him as he advanced towards and stood at the prison door, while Althea, who trembled as she bade him adieu, stepped into the chaise, which was immediately driven away. The moment she was out of Marchmont's sight, all her fortitude forsook her, and she burst into an agony of tears. The exertion she had made had been long and painful, and now that the appearance of calmness was no longer necessary, she gave way to the anguish that might otherwise have had fatal consequences.

As she proceeded, however, the freshness of the air insensibly recovered her. It was now the end of June, and a summer shower that had fallen at day-break had given to every blade and leaf new verdure and sweetness. But when Althea, taking her handkerchief from her eyes, beheld the beauties which nature every where offers at this season, the image of the poor prisoner she had just left, who might never again enjoy them, arose to her; and again her heart swollen with anguish felt as if it would break, till another burst of tears relieved her.

When, however, she arrived at the first stage, the concern expressed in the countenance of poor Fenchurch, as he waited on her into the house, recalled her to some degree of resolution. She endeavoured to reason herself into more apparent composure, and, before she arrived at the place where the chaise was to be changed a second time, had in a certain degree succeeded.

Marchmont, in the mean time, who felt himself completely wretched in submitting to even this transient separation, shut himself up in his room, where he expected, in consequence of a letter he had dispatched, that Mr. Bargrave would have come to him to consult upon what should be done. But the morning passed away, and he did not appear. Marchmont sat down without appetite to his dinner; and hardly swallowing enough to satisfy nature, he felt a melancholy satisfaction in bestowing the rest on a poor man and woman, who had undertaken to do any little offices for him in the absence of his servant, necessarily shut out of a night. These unhappy people, with two children, inhabited a room in the same passage, and opposite to that where Marchmont was situated. But even this place, not above twelve feet long, and eight wide, was the bed-room of two other poor debtors, who paid so much a week for sharing it. And during the day it served as a kitchen, when its proprietors could get food; and always as a laundry, for the woman took in washing for the prisoners. Marchmont, after his dinner, entered for a moment into this abode of poverty and wretchedness, and was at once shocked and gratified at beholding the eagerness with which this half-famished group ate of what he had given them. He withdrew, however, not to interrupt them, bidding the man come to him when he had finished his meal.

"Good God!" exclaimed Marchmont, as he re-considered the scene to which he had been witness; "is it possible that for a small sum, such as it is likely such people as these can owe, their creditor has a right to shut them up from the common air, and use of their limbs, by which alone there can remain any chance of their payment? Can laws that suffer and enforce this senseless cruelty, be the very best that the wisdom and experience of mankind can devise for the government of civil society?" These reflections were resumed with yet more force when the poor man, whose name was Bensted, related his sad yet common history — "I am a Staffordshire man, Sir," said he, "and was brought up a working cutler. Since the war not having employ at Birmingham where I worked, I was advised by a relation of mine to come to London, and set up shop for myself; and though I had only been a journeyman, yet my Peggy being a pretty good manager, and our girl and boy got a little out of the way, we had scraped up a small matter to begin with; and our cousin, an old bachelor, said he would lend us thirty pound to help: so we took a house up here at London, and our cousin came to board with us. However, he paid us nothing, by reason of the money he had lent us which was to be paid him again this way, as he said, and as I thought — though there was no writing between us, except my note that I gave him for the thirty pound. Trade indeed was but dull, and I was almost sorry I had ever come to London; but, however, the thing was done, and I thought this cousin of ours, who had to be sure begun so friendly, would leave to my two young ones all he had. He had always charity and such-like in his mouth, and used to go twice a day to meeting, and made my children go along with him, and my wife too very often — indeed, oftener to my thinking than was good for our business and management at home. All of a sudden we heard out of Staffordshire that a farmering man, who was the same relation to my wife as he was to this cousin of hers, had died without a will, and left a freehold of about fifty pound a year behind him. Mr. Drape declared he was the next heir, and away he went to take possession; and I, for my part, should have let him have kept it, if a lawyer's clerk, who came just before to lodge at our house, had not, when we were talking about it one day, told me, that it was my wife and not Drape that the estate belonged to; and to be sure he made it out as plain as could be — so he got counsel's opinion upon it, and that was for us too, and to law we went. After two years and a half the cause was decided — and it was, that we were to divide the property. But the costs of the law-suit came to forty pounds more than our half sold for, and Mr. Drape arrested me for the thirty pounds he had lent me. So here I am, with expences and all, confined for above an hundred pounds, and am not worth an hundred pence in the world! But then, Sir, there's half the people here in just the same case — so it is not for me to repine! As to myself, I am used to it now and could bear it; but it is very heart-breaking to me to have my boy and girl brought up in such a place. It must be their ruin, to be sure! My girl is now almost thirteen, and what a bad thing for her to run about here! — But there's no help for it! we have no friends!"

The generous heart of Marchmont felt for this poor fellow, and the more so, as effectually to relieve him was not in his power. Having, however, assured him of such temporary assistance as he could give, he returned to the contemplation of his own sorrows — while general uneasiness was not unmixed with wonder that Mr. Bargrave never appeared. He learned, however, the next day, in conversation with one of his fellow prisoners, that solicitors of a certain degree of reputation did not often choose to visit their clients in prison; that there was some sort of discredit annexed to it; and that many persons there had been compelled to have recourse to men of the profession who practised in the neighbourhood. This conversation ended in a proposal on the part of the stranger to introduce Marchmont to one of these practitioners; but such was his dread of the fraternity, that he declined, at least for the present, any experiment of that sort; and, returning to his room, wrote again to Bargrave, though as he did it he enquired of himself *Cui bono?* too certain that, even if his solicitor entered with all possible zeal into the cause, little could be done to relieve him from his present cruel situation. But had himself alone been in question, he would have gone with tranquillity to his bed. It was the thoughts of Althea, of his mother and his sisters, that strewed his pillow with thorns, and drove all repose from him, as he sadly reflected on the justice of the Spanish proverb — *"If a man sleep too much, let him borrow the pillow of a debtor."*

The morning of the day after Althea's departure was passed, however heavily, yet without any other actual uneasiness than her absence, and the dread of what he might hear on her return, necessarily occasioned. — But the time soon came when he might expect her, and then his anxiety became almost insupportable. Eagerly watching every body that entered, he continued to walk backwards and forwards before the inner door of the prison — but the hours wore away, evening was approaching, and Althea came not. The bell rang to announce that all strangers within the walls must depart, which is always done a short time before the doors are closed for the night. Marchmont, therefore, knowing how soon that must now happen, and that Althea would be shut out, was made half frantic by the apprehension, and hastened into the lobby to gain over, if possible, one of the keepers to favour her, should she arrive too late for the regular hour of admittance: but the man to whom he had been used to speak, and whose good-will he had secured by the present of a guinea on his entrance, was not now waiting there. The place seemed to be in confusion, and Marchmont heard that a prisoner in execution for twelve hundred pounds had just before very nearly effected his escape: a circumstance which redoubled the vigilance of the keepers, who, when Marchmont succeeded in making his request known, answered him with more than usual brutality, that the thing he asked was impossible; and that they desired he would not again come into the lobby. In an agony of mind little short of desperation Marchmont then remonstrated. It was in vain, and only served to draw upon him accumulated insults, which he could neither escape from nor punish. With four or five other persons he was pushed back into the area of the prison, and, as if on purpose to distract him, the doors were instantly shut — some minutes before the usual time. The most cruel apprehensions now took possession of his mind. Either his mother was dangerously ill, perhaps dead; or Althea returning would not be admitted; and as she had not one acquaintance in London, or any place to go to, what would become of her? whither could she resort for protection? Severe as were his fears for his mother, this apprehension, which seemed the most probable, was also the most intolerable; and it is difficult to say what state of mind Marchmont might have been in before morning, if, in reconsidering every circumstance, he had not recollected that Fenchurch, who was active and intelligent, was with her; and as he knew the lodging that had been secured in the morning for Mrs. Marchmont, it was possible, and he hoped probable, that the man might have the presence of mind to conduct his mistress thither.

This supposition a little mitigated, though it could by no means appease the fears that tormented him during the night. At the break of day he was on foot, and, the instant the doors were open, sent a runner to the lodgings engaged for his mother — though without much hope, for he concluded Fenchurch would have been with him at the first moment of admittance, had they been so near. The man presently came back to say none of the family were there!

A thousand tormenting conjectures now again assailed the unhappy prisoner. His mother must, he thought, be dying; for some such urgent cause could alone have detained his wife. — Yet then surely Fenchurch would have been sent to release him from conjectures so painful, even though it were necessary to reveal some cruel truth, since the truth must at last be known.

As this second day of dreadful suspense passed away, the agitation of his mind became more and more intolerable, and he thought every distress he had yet experienced, light in comparison of the tortures he now underwent. Having no intimate friend in London to whom he could send, and as he had purposely avoided making any acquaintance where he was, he had nobody either to hear his distracting apprehensions, or to counsel him how to act. To the mercenaries of the place he applied: sent one to one place, another to another, with enquiries — all returned without any information; while Marchmont, who since the departure of Althea had taken neither food nor rest, walked about feverish from the troubled state of his mind, but giving not the least attention either to his personal feelings, or to the people round him. They of course considered him, from the agitated state he appeared in, as a poor wretch whose condition was more deplorable than their own, inasmuch as he seemed to be devoid of either the fortitude or the indifference that might have enabled him to support it as they did.

At length Marchmont beheld near the door a female figure, which he thought resembled Althea. He approached with eagerness. — It was indeed herself, but so pale, so faint, that every other fear was for a moment forgotten in the more dreadful one of trembling for her safety. She took Marchmont's arm, but appeared unequal to answering at that moment the questions he eagerly put to her. Assuring him, however, that she was not ill, she attempted to appease his terrors; but her own returned upon her with a force so irresistible, that in despite of all her efforts she burst into tears.

"Good God!" exclaimed Marchmont, "my mother is dead! I am sure of it, Althea — Do not, therefore, attempt to disguise the truth from me. Alas! it is better I should know it at once. She is dead — I shall never see her more."

Althea now found strength to speak — "No, dear Marchmont" said she, "she is not dead, and you will, I trust, see her again; but I dare not flatter you that it is likely she will long live. Since the shock she received on the night of your arrest, she has been in a most dangerous state. — If the fainting fits into which she falls, give her a transient respite, she no sooner recovers a little strength than she insists on seeing you; imagines sometimes that she is pleading to Vampyre for your release; at others, that she is herself arrested by him, and sees you in chains attempting to release her: then shrieks and convulsive groans exhaust her, till the long fits of fainting return. Notwithstanding all this, my dear friend, we have brought her to London, though not without some difficulty I own, and many terrors. I could not immediately leave her on our arrival, but the moment I could get away I hastened hither."

"And now," said Marchmont, "you are yourself ill. — I am sure of it by your countenance and manner. Wretch that I am! it is I who am destined to be the death of all I love!" He then walked about for a moment, while Althea, summoning all her fortitude, assured him that she was no otherwise ill than from fatigue and anxiety, and that a little rest, if she could once see him tolerably calm, would restore her. Marchmont then, fearing to aggravate her sufferings by yielding to his own, sent Bensted for some refreshment for her — (Fenchurch was not yet come) — and implored her before she thought of any thing else to endeavour to tranquillize her spirits and recover her strength.

Althea, who thought little of herself where the service of those she loved was in question, soon affected to overcome the accidental indisposition she had felt on her arrival, and declared herself ready and anxious to go with him to his mother, for whom, she said, the sight of him would do more than any cordial. Fenchurch, who just then arrived, spoke rather favourably of her situation; and he was now dispatched to the Marshal to ask leave for Mr. Marchmont, attended by one or two men, or under any restrictions named, to be permitted to see his mother, only for half an hour, at her abode within the rules. — All the misery and humiliation of being compelled to *ask* this per-mission struck heavily on the heart of Marchmont: his condition of mind therefore may be imagined, when Fenchurch, breathless himself with rage, returned with a positive refusal. —"Tell your master," said the Marshal, "that though I have sometimes granted this indulgence,

I cannot do it now with any regard to my own safety; and that I have besides a strict charge from Mr. Vampyre, by which I should make myself more than ordinarily liable, if any thing happened. I'm sorry it is so, but it is not my fault —I cannot help it."

It seemed as if Marchmont at this moment felt, for the first time, all the disgrace and horrors of imprisonment; his blood seemed to undergo a revulsion, and then to press back on his heart in a torrent that deprived him of breath. He felt for a moment disposed to dash himself against the wall, to tear his hair, to commit some of those wild and useless acts of desperation which intolerable and sudden anguish excites: but he cast his eyes on Althea, who, pale as ashes, sat like the figure of patient pity before him, and his fury for a moment subsided: he burst into a passion of tears, and, throwing himself into a chair, had only power to exclaim — "My mother! my poor mother! She is dying, and I am not to see her; she calls for me to close her eyes, and they hold me from her." — At that cruel image he relapsed into fury, exclaiming — "The villains! the infamous villains! the hard-hearted inexorable scoundrels! — And shall I bear it patiently, chained like a felon—like a galley-slave? Let me go," cried he to Fenchurch, who, imploring him to be patient, endeavoured to detain him. — "Unhand me, Fenchurch — dare to prevent me at your peril. No, no; follow me to the vile instrument of tyranny that has the injustice, the barbarity to confine me! I will compel his consent, or tear it from his iron heart. In this country of freedom there can be no law on his side. — Heaven, and earth, and hell shall hear me!"

Breathless and exhausted, he paused; and it was fortunate he did, for it gave Althea time to speak to him: she laid her hand gently on his shoulder, but uttered only "Marchmont!" Her voice seemed to act on his inflamed passions like a charm. He gazed at her a moment, threw his arms round her, and again fell into an agony of tears. She led him to a chair, and, bidding Fenchurch wait without the door, sat silently by him, supporting his throbbing temples on her breast; on which his scalding tears fell in showers. Then, after a moment, she said — "Marchmont, is it thus you set me an example of fortitude? Is it thus you express your tenderness for me? Ah! my dear friend, be assured, if you persist in yielding to such starts of passion, you will not regain your mother, and certainly you will destroy your wife."

"Angel of heaven!" exclaimed Marchmont, "best and loveliest of beings! forgive me — I cannot, I ought not to forgive myself, if I have caused one additional pang to this dear bosom, so consoling, so soothing to me." — A deep sigh succeeded, and for a while he seemed unable to utter more. Althea took advantage of his silence to represent to him, that true tenderness was less shewn by lamenting the sufferings of those we love, than in attempting their mitigation. — "Your mother, my dear love," said she, "is not, I trust, in so desperate a state as your fears have represented her — perhaps not so bad as my report has described her, for I am naturally a coward about sickness, and have no experience in its changes. But admitting, my beloved friend, that she is even worse than our love and our dread have made us believe — recollect a moment, how much all her sufferings would be aggravated, were it possible she could know the convulsed state of your mind, and that you endanger your personal health, and, perhaps, safety; for recollect what you told me, that a man was thrust into some dungeon for having threatened one of the keepers." — Marchmont could only sigh out that he would be more calm, and Althea proceeded:

"Though you are at this moment unhappily prevented attending the sickbed of this dear mother, I am not —I will go back and assist Amelia and Lucy in watching her. I hope to find with them the humane and excellent physician who attended my aunt, and whose goodness and skill I shall never forget. I dispatched a note to him the instant of our arrival in London, and I cannot but flatter myself that he has not forgotten me, and, however far it is from his tour of daily practice, will come as soon as he knows the circumstance, which I have briefly explained to him. Now, Marchmont, consider how I can venture to present myself before your mother; how I can answer her questions, if I leave you in this state of mind. The anguish I shall bear about me it will be impossible for me to disguise; and the consequence will be, that, believing some dreadful circumstance prevents your being with her, instead of an objection which I am sure we may find means to remove, her terrors, and, of course, her bodily sufferings, will be increased."

Marchmont, convinced of the justice of what she said, and ashamed of having added to the distress of his admirable Althea by a momentary loss of fortitude, assured her he would be calm, and soon regained as much firmness of mind as enabled him to see her depart with courage: but the instant he had again lost fight of her, he relapsed into a state of mind too terrible to be long sustained. Unfit to be seen among the motley multitude, he ran to hide himself in his own room;

but there his anxiety denied him repose, and he again descended to traverse the area, and watch the intelligence of which he dreaded the arrival.

In the mean time Althea, attended by Fenchurch, returned with trembling steps to the lodging, where she dared not appear before Mrs. Marchmont till she had concerted with Amelia and Lucy what it would be best to say to their mother to account for the non-appearance of their brother, which they had all hoped would remove the cruel apprehensions they laboured under. — Amelia, wholly depressed by this additional blow, had no advice to offer; but Lucy, more fertile in expedients, thought that it would be better to relate the truth, and say what Althea had told her was true also; that the Marshal, or some other person, his representative, to whom Fenchurch had applied, had said, on a second remonstrance from him, that if Mr. Marchmont would find any friend to be bound for his re-appearance in the full sum and penalties for which he was detained, he might then, with an attendant, be suffered to go to the place he requested. Lucy hoped, that by assuring her mother Mr. Eversley was soon expected, who in a matter where the security for his safety was Marchmont's honour, would, she knew, answer for him to any amount, she might appease her suffering mother with hope, which, perhaps, a few days might realize, and by which they might at least gain time to try what could be done.

They hastened then to adopt this plan; Althea, by an effort of exalted heroism, appearing undoubting, and even cheerful. Mrs. Marchmont, on whom her looks had a forcible effect, bore the intelligence of delay, thus softened, better than they had expected. She seemed to have suffered less than they had feared from the fatigue of her journey, and to be consoled by the idea of being within less than a quarter of a mile of Marchmont. This mitigation of actual suffering was principally the good work of Althea, and she was amply and instantly rewarded by reflecting on the comfort she should afford her husband when she returned to him.

To return she of course became impatient; but she still hoped that her medical friend, however late, would find a quarter of an hour to gratify her with his advice — and as he was a stranger to the rest of the family, she determined to wait for him till the last moment.

Having dispatched Fenchurch with a note to Marchmont, accounting for her stay, Althea sat by the bed-side of her mother, while Amelia, Lucy, and Milly busied themselves in putting their clothes into drawers, and giving what order and neatness they could to an abode which it was most likely they were long to inhabit.

It was seven o'clock before Dr. Warrington arrived. Earnestly as Althea had wished to see him, she received him with confusion; and though she had briefly stated to him in her letter for whom she wished his assistance, and the relationship in which this friend of hers stood to her, she had need of all her presence of mind to give verbally a more distinct account of her present situation, to one who had last seen her in circumstances so different.

Dr. Warrington, who to the greatest professional skill added an uncommon goodness of heart and sensibility, understood at once the cause of her embarrassment; and while he was concerned that she had made an imprudent marriage, he hastened to convince her that the regard he had conceived for her, while he saw her in attendance upon her aunt, was not to be shaken by mere change of fortune. He therefore spoke to her with the most fatherly tenderness; told her how pleased he was at her recollecting him on this occasion; and, having succeeded in re-assuring her, followed her to the chamber of the patient.

Althea, while he was making the usual enquiries of Mrs. March-mont, anxiously watched his countenance, and thought she saw in it a confirmation of all she dreaded. When his visit was over, Althea followed him into a parlour, where he desired pen and ink might be brought; but, before he began to use them, he told Althea she must sit down and compose herself — "We will have a little conversation together, my fair young friend," said he; "I am sure that with all the trembling sensibility that I see in your face, and know to be in your bosom, you have sense and fortitude above your appearance; I make, therefore, no scruple to tell you the truth. The disorder of the poor lady above stairs is beyond the reach of medical aid; she is truly and literally dying of a broken heart."

Althea's countenance expressed what she had no power to utter. — Dr. Warrington saw how much she was hurt, and hastened to say, "But I do not, however, mean decidedly to pronounce, that though a physician cannot cure her, she is past all cure: on the contrary, if the dreadful pressure could be removed from her mind, I believe she is not so far gone but that she might recover. I am now interested for her, for her own sake as well as for yours; and one cannot see without deep concern those three lovely young women, to whose defenceless state I suppose her life to be so necessary. Tell me ingenuously the condition of your husband's affairs. For what and by whom is he imprisoned? What are his hopes and his resources?"

Althea, charmed with the benevolent interest this excellent man took in their destiny, related as briefly as she could the history of her first acquaintance with Marchmont (but without naming the person on whose account she had been sent to Eastwoodleigh): on the family, and the causes of its decline, she enlarged more fully, particularly on the nature of the engagement that had caused him to be imprisoned. She spoke particularly of the refusal of Mohun and Lady Dacres to pay her fortune, and of the cruel and malignant conduct of them both, but especially of the former, who had provoked Marchmont by unworthy treatment, and then taken so base an advantage of the anger such treatment could not fail to excite. She concluded by stating the amount of the whole sums for which Marchmont was in custody, and the refusal of the keeper of the prison to let him, unless with sureties, visit his mother.

Althea, mild and calm as she was, was so certain that nobody could hear a detail of such injustice without indignation, that she wondered the Doctor listened to her with so steady a countenance; expecting that, entering into her feelings, he would have expressed his detestation of Mohun almost as warmly as she felt it. She was, therefore, half repulsed when he said, "I know Mr. Mohun very well, and have attended him. He is a violent and positive man, but I should hardly have thought him capable of acting so dishonourably. — Perhaps he has been irritated by some falsehood, or by the arts of that attorney. I think, if matters could be explained, or softened, this complaint of his would be withdrawn, and then it might be seen what could be done about the rest. I am afraid," added he, pausing, "that at this time of year Mr. Mohun is not in London. However, I will enquire at his house, and find out where he is, and you may depend upon my trying what is to be done, and that directly; for indeed the nervous cordial I am going to order for the suffering lady above will be utterly useless, unless her son's prospects clear up a little." He then sat down to write the prescription; which done, he called for his carriage: and seeing Althea about to present a fee, while she murmured something of the trouble he had taken in coming so for, he stopped, and said, "I will once for all tell you, my dear young friend, how I expect to be made amends: put your money in your pocket — I shall take none of it. The only way you can gratify me is by letting me see I do good to a person of whom I

think so well as I do of you. I had a sincere friendship for Mrs. Trevyllian — a more excellent woman never existed; her memory will always
be dear to me, and those she loved it will always be a pleasure to me
to befriend. I am not a man of many professions, you know; and very
likely in the present case very little may be in my power; but what I *can*
do, I will — Do you keep up your spirits, and consider how many miseries there are in the world, infinitely less supportable than those you
now share, bad as they are." He then promised to let her know what he
had done, if he could not see her the following day, and assured her he
would at all events visit Mrs. Marchmont again whenever she sent for
him — but that for the present nothing could be done but to follow his
prescription, and to keep her as calm and as much in hope as he could.

Dr. Warrington then departed, and Althea, with a lighter heart
than she had felt since the evening of Marchmont's arrest, went first
to his mother, whom she left considerably better in spirits from the
doctor's visit, and then hastened to her poor prisoner, who waited for
her in the severest suspense. To him she appeared indeed a guardian
angel: fraud and falsehood seemed to lose their power before the firm
purity of her character — like Ithuriel, he thought she could baffle the
fiend Vampyre himself, and at the sound of her sweet voice malignity
and rancour and avarice must, he believed, be put to flight.

Soothed by these sweet illusions, and relieved by supposing his
mother better, together with the certainty of her now having the best
medical advice that could be obtained, Marchmont tasted this night
repose to which he had long been a stranger. The next day rather
strengthened his fortitude and his hopes. He received a letter from
Eversley, who told him he had written to Mr. Bargrave, giving him
the fullest powers to make use of his credit to any amount within the
compass of his fortune; and assuring him that nothing but the situation of Mrs. Eversley, which, though not likely to take any decided
turn, rendered it impossible for him to leave her, should for a moment
prevent his hastening to London himself. So friendly a letter, and the
disposition of Dr. Warrington to assist them, offered more consoling
prospects than Marchmont had dared to look for; and as the excessive
agitation of his mind subsided, the resignation and fortitude which he
had found it easy to talk of to others, but not always possible to practise himself, was again restored.

CHAP. XI.

... Yield not thy neck
To Fortune's yoke; but let thy dauntless mind
Still ride in triumph over all mischance.

MR. BARGRAVE NOW appeared, and excused himself as well as he could
for not having attended Marchmont's first summons. He had been out
of town on indispensable business, and wished to hear from Mr. Eversley before he took any material steps. He then talked over the affairs,
but not very sanguinely. As to what Mr. Eversley had said in his letter,
to what did it amount? For, in short, what could be done unless to
give bail for the whole debt? Such was the tenor of Mr. Bargrave's
conversation: and Marchmont acknowledged, that, as far as related to
Eversley, his way of seeing the thing accorded with his own opinion;
for he would not for the world have engaged Eversley to answer for
so large a sum, which he saw no prospect of ever being able to pay
himself. So scrupulous was he of intruding too much on his generous
friendship, that he had made no use of the order on his banker which
Eversley had last sent him; though such had been the plunder he had
suffered, and such the high prices at which every thing was retailed in
the prison, that his purse was very much reduced — while that which
Lucy managed for her mother was, from having paid half a year's rent
of their cottage, and the expences of their removal, greatly lowered
also. Nothing was due to Althea of the dividend on her aunt's legacy
till October; and Marchmont, when Bargrave had left him, after giving
him so remote a prospect of being *out* of imprisonment, began to
consider how he was to live *in it.*

The speculation was melancholy enough. One only resource was
offered by what he could do for himself, and that lay in his literary talents; but if these afforded him but scanty advantages while he enjoyed
liberty and some degree of consideration in the world, what could he
hope to derive from them now that he had not opportunities to mark

the manners, or adapt his writings to the taste, of the passing day. Or, if he took any line in which that knowledge was not necessary, he knew how readily, not only booksellers, but all men in trade regulate their offers of purchase by the necessities of the sellers. There was little hope, therefore, that he should find his labour rewarded as if he had been in happier circumstances. It was besides very probable, that the principal dealers in literary traffic would hesitate at purchasing the work of a prisoner who was likely, besides the disgrace of the connection, to vent in his writing some part of the discontent that imprisonment is very apt to engender. — The passage from discontent to murmurs against the oppression, real or imaginary, is very short; and murmurs may favour of seditious notions, and seditious notions might carry a man nobody knew whither. What rich and substantial vender would hazard any thing like this in these times? Marchmont, in considering this over, was aware that purchasers might still be found; but from some his pride recoiled, and from others his prudence. He knew how much the success of a book depends on the manner in which it is ushered into public; and that the mere name of the publisher secures to some all that sort of recommendation which influences those who are to be told how to like or dislike; and in books, as in every thing else, that is at least half the world.

But though this self-held council ended in Marchmont's persuading himself that his profits in that line must be circumscribed, still those profits were an object to him. He was not now to learn how much any pursuit, and above all one in which a man engages from the influence of duty, elevates while it occupies the mind: the only difficulty was to call off his thoughts from the surrounding circumstances, and obtain command enough over his faculties to exert them; convinced that the very attempt mitigated somewhat of the evils he suffered, and that it was more like a reasonable being to struggle with than helplessly to lament them. Some days afterwards, in a letter to Eversley, to whom he had expressed himself most grateful for his unwearied friendship, and declined every assistance that might, however remotely, injure his friend, Marchmont wrote thus:

"Since I have been easier on account of my mother, and have daily hopes of seeing her, my mind has regained the force which I am willing to allow if ought never to have lost. I have even projected some literary undertakings, and am enquiring for a bookseller to whom they can be disposed of to advantage. I find that I should do well enough if I could but withdraw my thoughts altogether from two or three persons: but when I look round me, consider where I am, and by whose means — when the dark scroll of accumulated villany is unrolled by memory before me — when I consider the cold-blooded malignity with which the most worthless of the brutes that disgrace the human race triumph in my distresses, while a group of helpless and amiable women, a mother, a wife, yet indeed a bride, and three sweet sisters, are their victims — rage and indignation, not the less violent for being impotent, tear my heart to pieces; and I am forced to fly to Althea, whose presence checks these paroxysms — I hasten to hear her voice —I bid her read to me, and the monsters for a moment disappear. I dissolve into tears, and seem suddenly removed from being tormented by demons to the soothing society of an angel.

"But I have given up many hours of my wife's time to my mother, and once Lucy and Milly have come to visit me. This, however, is not a place for them even to enter, and I insisted on my patiently dejected Amelia's forbearing to make the experiment. Among so many persons of almost every rank, there must be many profligate, daring, and unprincipled. — Sustained in effrontery by numbers, and careless of consequences, because they can hardly be in a worse situation; such men are not certainly those to whose licentious eyes and remarks I would expose my sisters: yet among them daily does my Althea pass. They generally understand who she is: and as, guarded by my arm, she crosses the area in going or returning, I see them, Eversley, look upon her with awe. Lovely, uncommonly lovely as she is, their admiration seems to have so much reverence mingled with it, that I do not believe, even if she were unprotected, one of them, noisy and boisterous as they are, would offer her the slightest insult. Yet there are times when I cannot forgive myself for having been the cause of making her an inmate of such a place! and whatever fortitude I acquire for myself, I am a coward when for her I survey the present, or look forward to the future.

"Did I suffer alone, I think I should not fail in endurance; and after all, my friend, since I must accustom myself to imprisonment, I ought to consider it philosophically, as it is very likely much of my life is to pass in it, to divest it of its horrors. The greatest for me is the sight of misery it is impossible for me to relieve — to see the progress of despondence and ill example on the young, whom some folly of their own, or the villany of others, had brought hither, and the helpless and gloomy resignation of the old — to mark the palsied hands of industry, which, if not struck by the withering demon of legal oppression, might still have been busy in contributing to the public stock, and in maintaining in comfort and competence those who now linger out their lives in fordid wretchedness, and become unfit for society; which having taught them to consider themselves as outcasts, who can wonder that they learn to prey upon it? Nothing is more depressing than to pass through that part of the prison where the rooms of the poorer debtors are situated. Dirt and famine are every where visible: the observer of any feeling is shocked to see a thousand miserable contrivances to support an existence which seems so little worth having; and shudders to think that half these stratagems go to the acquisition of those coarse and destructive spirits, by which this very existence may be forgotten! What I see around me is only one great example of an evil that pervades the whole kingdom, and of which every county presents its share. I set about calculating the numbers so confined in this land of freedom! and I enquire whether no remedy can be found against a circumstance that surely is as disgraceful as pernicious. Nay, I even venture to ask whether such an attempt would not do more honour to our Legislature than their arduous undertakings to preserve hares and partridges for the pleasures of the rich. If I had enjoyed my paternal fortune, Eversley, should I have thought thus? Perhaps not. We are certainly, more than we are willing to allow, the creatures of accident; and it is very likely that if I, like many other men of my age, had from my infancy had nothing to do but to enjoy, I might have thought as little as they do of those who have nothing to do but to suffer. You, my friend, who *are,* or at least *were,* an Optimist, and have often declared for the doctrine of Leibnitz and Pope, will, perhaps, ask me — 'Of what use is all this reasoning but to make yourself more unhappy? Admitting that all is *not* right, can you make it otherwise?' — Alas! no. — But it is by reason only that abuses are gradually removed; and if we dare not use this privilege, and apply it here and there as we can, we are indeed sunk below the savage, who lives and enjoys his animal existence without it.

"The man born in a mine, accustomed to a certain manner of life, and to have his wants supplied in his gloomy souterrain, has no wish to gaze upon the sun, to inhale the fresh air, to feast his eyes on the lovely colours of nature, because he knows not what they are. But let him once ascend to the surface of the earth, let him have the privilege of breathing freely, of feeling the vivifying influence of the sun — and he must be a stupid and worthless being if he would voluntarily return to the darkness and stagnation of his former abode, although his actual subsistence, and even gross enjoyments, are there easily within his reach. Just such a being the man seems to me, who is contented to re-sign, after having once felt it, his power of investigating truth (though he cannot always find it), and content himself with systems formed for him by others who have an interest in keeping this reasoning faculty in subordination. —I mean the men who say —

> 'But they in sooth must reason! — Curses light
> On the proud talent! — 'Twill at last undo us*'

"Lawyers (you know how I love them, and with how much reason) have certainly cause enough to dread its exertion, and, while they affect to make it the rule of their own profession, absolutely deny the use of it to their clients. Indeed those who *voluntarily* have any thing to do with *them* have usually not much to lose.

My simile of a mine, and of human beings buried in it, brings me to remark on the landscape, or rather the prison-scape around me. Even in the squalid wretchedness of these miserable habitations, where, though lodgings are given in rotation, the poor sell their right of shelter to those who have still something left to purchase it, and are huddled together in caverns, where a man of only moderate fortune would not suffer his hounds to kennel; even in these nose-offending regions of poverty and punishment that instinctive love of nature pre-vails, which points out what man ought to be, and marks his place in the creation as a cultivator of the earth; for, even in the dungeon, some faint memorial of vegetable life is consoling to him — and the wretch-ed woman, who toils from the dawn till the night, and hardly earns enough to keep from perishing the meagre and ragged infants that surround her, makes even here some poor attempts at a garden. —

> '...There the pitcher stands
> A fragment; and the spoutless tea-pot there;
> Sad witnesses, how close pent man regrets
> The Country — with what ardour he contrives
> A peep at Nature, when he can no more.†'

"I too feel a sort of calenture of the mind, and languish for the wood walks and downs, which are continually present to my imagina-tion, peopled by my family and my Althea; and I tremble, as I watch

---

* Walpole, now Lord Orford

† Task, Book IV

her lovely countenance, and dread lest the unwholesome air, which must be generated in an enclosure like this, in the heats of summer too, should injure her health. I sometimes fancy that her eyes look heavy, and as if she had been weeping in secret. I persuade myself her complexion changes, and there is more of languor about her than she is willing to avow; and then, Eversley, my fortitude again fails, and the moment she leaves me, so as to be no longer affected with it, I relapse into unavailing transports of rage and despair. She returns to me — she gives me an account of my mother; holds out some new hope that she has gathered from Dr. Warrington, who seems indefatigable in our service, and the tumult of my spirits subsides, and once more I blush at my weakness.

"I believe that women, whom we have proudly called but children of a larger growth, have, when they possess good understandings, more fortitude than men. Not to recall to observation the heroines of Antiquity, I feel ashamed of my impatience, when I contemplate the most illustrious woman* of modern times sitting in her dungeon amidst the most degraded of the human species, to whose insults she was every moment liable. Torn from her only child, and uncertain of the fate of her respectable husband, while her own seemed decided, and the scaffold absolutely before her — yet such was her firmness of mind, that she could arrange her miserable apartment, and call off her attention from the present horrors that surrounded, and the future that threatened her, and apply herself to botany and to music. However the part this extraordinary woman took in the republican government of France may have raised prejudice and hatred against her, who, that is capable of feeling true greatness of mind, can contemplate without admiration and respect such sublimity of mind? Who, circumstanced as I am, whatever may be their party or their politics, can read without being sensible of this elevation the following sentence:

'...Peut-être un jour mes recits ingénus charmeront les instans de quelque infortunée captive, qui oubliers son sort en s'attendrissant sur le mien; peut-être les Philosophes, qui veulent peindre le cœur humain dans la suite d'un roman ou l'action d'un drame, trouveront-ils a l'étudiet dans mon histoire†'

---

*   This is again an anachronism, but such as may well be forgiven
†   Hereafter, perhaps my ingenuous narrative may sooth the sad moments of some unfortunate captive, who may awhile forget her own destiny in deploring mine. – Perhaps the Philosopher, who in the progress of a romance or the action of a drama would describe the human heart, may find his studies of it afflicted by my history. – Appel à l'impartiel Postérité, par la Citoyenne Roland, vol. II page 67.

While several days were, amid these thoughts and these projects, passed in a sort of fluctuating philosophy by Marchmont, Althea, appearing before him always calm and occasionally cheerful, was very far from possessing internally the composure which, by efforts of courage and virtue, she assumed. The hopes she had indulged that Dr. Warrington could find means to soften the malignant ferocity of Mohun were gradually diminished; for though he had done all, and even more than he promised, he obtained, by his first enquiry, no other information than that Mr. Mohun was gone into Lincolnshire, and his return uncertain. Dr. Warrington then procured a direction to him there; and, without mentioning his business, wrote to say he wished to know when he would be in London. The letter followed him to the houses of some of his friends in other parts of the county; it was after many days longer than the usual course of the post would have brought it, that Dr. Warrington received an answer from Mohun; who, imagining he wanted to consult him professionally, condescended to inform him, that he believed he should pass a few days at his house in London, the last week in August, on his way to his annual shooting excursion in Wales; and that then he would send to the Doctor, and be glad to see him. This put off any farther efforts for three weeks at least, and then they were so uncertain of success in removing not half the setters by which Marchmont was bound, that Althea looked forward without hope of redress; while, on the other hand, Mrs. Marchmont, without any positive accession of illness, seemed daily to decline in strength, and to be very far gone in that disease which is slowly, and almost imperceptibly, fatal,

'The pining atrophy!'

For the sake of Althea, and of her daughters, she struggled against the deep despondence that made her trying to live appear a task equally heavy and useless; and even forbore to repeat aloud the desire that preyed on her heart to see her son — internally resolved, if she could obtain strength enough, to be carried thither, to seek him in his prison, since he was not allowed to come to her.

Dr. Warrington, who continued to visit her, saw, with concern, the progress of a malady out of the reach of any skill to cure; and when he understood that the small annuity, on which she and her family now subsisted, and which had been re-purchased by Mr. Eversley, dropped with her life; that her daughters would then be entirely destitute, and without a friend or a protector on earth but their imprisoned brother, his humanity urged him to procrastinate at least, if he could not entirely avert, the hour when this unhappy mother was to be torn for ever from her helpless girls. This, he thought, might be done by procuring her an interview with her son out of his confinement, for into it he would by no means hear of her going. The Doctor, therefore, offered himself as security; but there were forms which could not be gone through on the day he took this good-natured resolution, and on the next he was under an absolute promise to visit one of his patients thirty miles from London, which would inevitably detain him the whole day: this humane prescription, therefore, was, of necessity, postponed till the next. Althea, as she took leave of Dr. Warrington, warmly expressed her gratitude. — "Alas! my dear Madam!" said he, as he held her hand, "I would to God I could do more than this, which will be, I fear me, of little final use towards the preservation of our valuable friend. I am by no means rich, notwithstanding my extensive practice. In the early part of life I had a large family of collateral relations to assist; I married a woman I loved without a fortune, and have now six children of my own — so that to pay such a sum as three thousand pounds is not in my power. But something or other must be done for the relief of all of you; I cannot bear to see so many worthy and amiable people so cruelly circumstanced."

Althea, speechless with gratitude and emotion, saw him depart; and again nourished hopes that their troubles might, by such a friend, be removed. Some ray of comfort was indeed absolutely necessary to sustain her fainting courage; for circumstances had lately occurred, which, added to her continual struggle to appear cheerful while anguish preyed on her heart, nearly overcame her.

One of these was, the impertinence with which she had frequently been spoken to by a young man of genteel though careless appearance, who was almost always in the lobby, and sometimes walking in the space she had to traverse between the prison and Mrs. Marchmont's lodgings; and though Fenchurch was with her till Marchmont himself, who always waited for her, gave her his arm, yet neither the uneasiness his addressing himself to her evidently gave her, nor the spirited remonstrances of her servant, seemed to have the least effect. His conversation consisted of the most extravagant compliments on her beauty; in declaring that a man, who had such a companion in a prison, ought to think himself in paradise, and other rhodomontade of the same nature, which, if it terrified and shocked her at first, gave her still more serious alarm when it became constantly repeated; for the moment she was out of sight of Marchmont, this persecutor suddenly appeared, and followed her with his insulting speeches till she reached the house she was going to.

To speak of this to Marchmont would be to cause a quarrel that might produce the most dreadful consequences; yet she thought that, if it ever should come to his knowledge, he would be extremely hurt at her enduring, even for one day, insolence of such a nature. She in vain expostulated with the man, and represented how cruel it was to affront a woman, who, while attending on her imprisoned husband, could not escape from him. He protested that he meant no affront; that he intended only to shew his respectful adoration, and to ask, most humbly to ask leave to wait upon her, as the most devoted of her slaves. — Althea bade Fenchurch enquire who he was, with some intention of entreating Dr. Warrington to speak to him. Fenchurch learned that he was a young man of family, who, having spent his own fortune, and as much of theirs as they would part with, was now confined for a debt of seven or eight thousand pounds; and that his family, knowing no way of keeping him from imprisonment, whither he would certainly plunge again, by his wild extravagance, as soon as he was released, had determined to let him remain there, and contributed among them, as they were all very rich, to his support: so that, making up his mind for the present, he had taken possession of the rooms called the state rooms, where he lived in a constant course of deep drinking, and such dissipation as was yet within his reach. He failed not to find companions enough, and consoled himself for the loss of better society, by being the principal person in that he now collected around him. In consequence of the money he scattered heedlessly about, all the turnkeys and runners of the prison were his most humble servants; and, security having been given to the Marshal, he had the liberty of the rules.

From the intrusion of such a man Althea was utterly at a loss how to defend herself, without involving Marchmont in a quarrel with him. He was artful enough never to attempt speaking to her when her husband was with her, but had made some civil advances towards an acquaintance with Marchmont, which Althea had discouraged, saying, that any acquaintance in their present situation would be distressing to her, and would merely break in on the time which they could either pass together quietly, or in consultations upon business; and that such a man as Mr. Carlingbury was represented to be, was not a proper person to associate with his sisters, should they ever come to their apartment. Marchmont, to whom society was not only indifferent but painful, had no will but that of Althea, and shunned any connection either with Mr. Carlingbury, or any other of his fellow-prisoners.

Within the last week it was not only the insufferable importunity of this person, but the strange manners of another, that had perplexed and alarmed Althea. She had observed a man about sixty, plainly and rather coarsely dressed, and without any thing remarkable in his appearance, whom she had several times passed near the door of the prison, and twice or three times within it. He had fixed his eyes upon her with so steady, yet so odd a look, that she shrunk from him involuntarily; but when, assailed by her daily tormentor, he had met her without the walls, his countenance had indicated something, which, though Althea did not give herself time to investigate what it meant, made her tremble. — Yet, as he had never spoken to her, she had no pretence to complain, though every time she saw him her terror increased.

The interview only for a few moments procured with difficulty between Marchmont and his mother, by the intervention of Dr. Warrington, produced a scene which only served to distress them both, while Althea thought she perceived Mrs. Marchmont grow worse afterwards; and Marchmont himself, shocked at the appearance of his mother, was, during the rest of the day, in a state of the most dreadful depression. This was, however, somewhat alleviated by a letter from Eversley, which, without mentioning particulars, gave him hopes that this steady friend would soon be with him; and he said in a postscript, "Have you heard that your wife's cousin, Mr. Trevyllian, the last male of the family of Hascombe Court, has been dead some weeks? His two sisters also are dead long since, and (which I did not know till lately) of the remaining branches of the family none survive, but Mrs. Marchmont, your wife, and a Mrs. Thoresby. I have always understood that the landed estates were so entailed, that they could not be alienated; I know them to be between five and six thousand a year, and Trevyllian, if he could, would not have impaired them. On the contrary, I always heard, and had reason to believe, he laid up money. I have written to desire Willis, my steward, would enquire whether he made a will, and who are said to be his heirs at law. On your side it might be worth while to make some enquiry. Employ Bargrave if he can be of any use to you. I, on my part, will let you know, should I hear, in the newspaper phrase, 'of something to your advantage.'"

Marchmont had thought so little of any thing but Althea herself, that any such contingencies as the present were quite new to him. Althea herself hardly knew more of them than he did. She recollected having gone into mourning for one of her cousins, but, as she had never seen any of them above once, when she was in town for a few days, *they* had made no impression on her memory at all; while all she could recall of Mr. Trevyllian himself was, that her aunt was slighted by him, and disliked him; which, together with the hurry he was in to have her remove from the house where her aunt had left her, did not make her feel at all concerned to hear he was no more; while the hope of possessing a share of such a property, and giving it to Marchmont at this period, made her for the first time in her life eager about an affair of money. Who Mrs. Thoresby was, or how much she might have the advantage of her as to nearness of kindred, Althea knew not: but the hope of eventually possessing enough to liberate and enrich Marchmont was so flattering to her imagination, that she wished to set out immediately herself on the enquiry, and proposed going the next morning to Mr. Bargrave, and giving him such information as she was able to recollect, to guide his enquiry. To this Marchmont consented, though far less sanguine as to the event than Althea. He had already experienced the difficulty of making out claims, which there was no money to support; and he had reason to remember his little success, when a lawyer told him of the usurious and dishonest proceeding of Sir Ralph Gunston, in regard to his father's mortgages, by which his adviser thought that some of them might be set aside; but who, when he found that Marchmont had no money to carry on the suit in Chancery, had declined engaging in it; talked of the uncertainty of the law, and the delays and expences of a court of equity; and concluded with saying, that the first loss was the best. This man, however, had contrived to keep his papers, and to make a heavy charge against him, which deprived him of the power of attempting to procure redress by means of any other person; while, by what he *had* done, he only irritated the malignity and alarmed the cupidity of Sir Ralph's heirs, and gave a more immediate cause of hatred to Sir Audley and Lady Dacres, besides what they naturally bore him, on account of the poverty and decay of his family, and the injuries they knew he had sustained, which, as they had the advantage of those injuries, they could not forgive. After such an experiment, Marchmont could not venture to flatter himself that fortune did not again mean to mock him; and Althea doubted while she tried to hope. There was, however, a person better informed than either of them — Lady Dacres had from her youth been accustomed to calculate on contingencies; and when both the sisters of Mr. Trevyllian died within a few months of each other, she had bent a keen eye on Althea's chance of succeeding to half his estate. So good did she believe this chance to be, that it almost influenced her to check her ill-humour and avarice, in order to keep Althea with her, and unmarried: but the perverse circumstance of her going to the Marchmont's baffled her schemes; though she persuaded herself that while she withheld, and made her present fortune doubtful, she must still remain single. Her marriage, therefore, and with Marchmont, of which she was immediately apprised, had extremely vexed and irritated her; while, as if to punish her by more immediate evils for all she had inflicted on Althea, her eldest son; who had sold out of the army, and who was not yet nineteen, had entered on such a career as threatened to dissipate, even before he came of age, the large property which he was to inherit from the usurer his grandfather, and the placeman Sir Audley. He had already taken up considerable sums of money, and, unaffected either by duty or gratitude, openly repined at the large income his mother possessed, and the fortunes secured to his brother and three sisters, which prevented his being able to anticipate to a still greater extent his future revenues. Lady Dacres, unwilling to complain of a son whom she had always supposed must be a miracle of perfection, had the daily mortification of hearing of exploits, and consequent expences, which she had no longer the power to check, or even to attempt restraining; for her son never came near her, and the intelligence she gained of him was either from the notoriety of his conduct, or from Jews and money-lenders, who applied for information whether the statement he had given of his future prospects were just. This severe mortification did not sweeten the lady's temper; but, miserable herself, she found a sad satisfaction in making every one about her as miserable as she could. The only smile that had been seen on her face for some months, was observed there when she heard that Marchmont was thrown into prison; where, from the magnitude of the debt, it was likely he would remain for life. She not only recounted this to every body who visited her at Capelstoke, with the utmost marks of satisfaction, but gave to all that would listen to her a long history of Althea's misbehaviour to herself. Then making an episode, she described the Marchmont family, who were, she said, a set of wretched paupers; and concluded with a dissertation on the challenge, which she said Marchmont had had the effrontery to send to Mr. Mohun, only for his friendly zeal in wishing to execute the will of her late dear Sir Audley, and for which she heartily hoped he might be severely punished. Yet notwithstanding all her Ladyship's sagacity and perfect information, as to Althea and the family to which she now belonged, she chose, on receiving the news of Mr. Trevyllian's death out of the west, and an enquiry what was become of her daughter-in-law, to answer very coldly, that the young lady having left her for some time she knew nothing about her, and rather believed she was gone abroad. Nobody but Eversley was interested enough about Althea to trouble themselves with her claims; and Mr. Thoresby himself brought up a lawyer, and, recollecting the good old saying, that possession is nine points of the law, was already in possession of Mr. Trevyllian's landed property, when Eversley wrote to announce to his friends that the succession was open. Althea having called on her way on Mrs. Marchmont, and communicated the cause of her present expedition, and having found her too rather better than she had expected from what she had observed the evening before, set out, with a lighter heart than she had long felt, attended by Fenchurch, to walk to Mr. Bargrave's chambers in Lincoln's-inn, which she thought she could easily accomplish; and having never seen so much of it before, she purposed going through the city: but she had not half achieved the Borough, before, disgusted by bad smells and disagreeable objects, and half stunned by noise, she was glad to follow the advice of Fenchurch, and get into a hackney coach, which soon conveyed her to Mr. Bargrave's chambers. She sent up Fenchurch to let him know she was there; but a clerk appeared, who informed her that, the summer circuit being begun, Mr. Bargrave was gone to York to be present at a cause that was to be tried there of very great importance to one of his clients; and that as he afterwards intended to make a tour among his relations, who were of that county, his stay in the whole might possibly be of six or seven weeks.

Vexed at a circumstance which must not only delay the enquiry about which she was so eager, but cruelly impede all the business so material towards Marchmont's enlargement — she was now to return disappointed. As she had yet time for a walk, she discharged the coach, meaning to proceed on foot at least some part of the way back to Marchmont's sad abode; and remembered that she could take this occasion to purchase some coloured papers, and other materials, for Amelia and Lucy; who still, as far as their attendance on their mother would allow, continued their little manufactory. Pensively meditating on what could now be done to promote an enquiry about Mr. Trevyllian's property, she heeded not the noises around her, till a voice was heard eagerly calling to her, and ordering a carriage to stop. Althea looked up and saw Dr. Warrington before her, who taking her hands in his friendly way, but with even more than his usual warmth, said, "I am glad, very glad indeed, to have met you so unexpectedly; for I should not otherwise have seen you till the evening, so indispensably is my day engaged. But we have so little time, that I am happy to save so much on your account. Mr. Mohun is in town some time sooner than he intended, but only for two days. I have seen him; and really, from the conversation I have had with him, I do believe, that if you were yourself to see him, all these disagreeable differences might be removed, and the affairs in general, at least so far as depends on him, settled to your satisfaction."

Althea blushed deeply, utterly at a loss what to reply. Dr. Warrington appeared not to have the least idea of Mohun's former pretensions to her: she had avoided mentioning it before, and now it was impossible to explain it. She remained a moment confused and hesitating. — Dr. Warrington, hurried by his own business, and eagerly anxious about hers, said, "Suppose, as we are not far from his house, and I know he is at home, I were to carry you thither? I am obliged to go directly into the City myself, from whence I must return to an appointment in Hanover Square at one o'clock; but I can set you down in Lincoln's-inn-fields, without going out of my way: and who knows, my dear Madam, but thus by one successful sally we may carry our point? Come, come," added he, "you have so much sense as well as sensibility, that from such a cause I know you will not shrink, and I am sure it is impossible for any one to resist such a pleader." As he said this, he led her towards his chariot. Fenchurch had already let down the step; and Althea, hardly knowing how she got there, was seated in it, where it was rapidly driven the little distance from Holborn to Lincoln's-inn-fields. Recovering her breath and recollection, and being well assured that Marchmont would greatly disapprove of her going to Mohun's, whatever advantage might accrue from it, she at length said, "But, dear Sir! let us consider before I decide to wait on Mr. Mohun; I am not quite sure it is proper — I am afraid that..." "Not proper?" interrupted Dr. Warrington, "my dear—

Mrs. Marchmont, why not proper? Can there be any impropriety in
your applying, on business that so nearly concerns you, to your father's
friend, to his executor, to the man to whose care he in some degree
entrusted you? I am persuaded there is not a prude in the kingdom that
would think so. I really am very solicitous for the interview, because I
know it will do a great deal of good to our poor suffering friends; and
so take courage, my fair and resistless advocate, and God speed your
endeavours!" Thus saying, the coach stopped, the door opened, and
Althea was left standing before Mr. Mohun's door — so undetermined
to go in that she meditated her escape the moment Dr. Warrington was
out of sight: but the quickness of his footman had prevented her; for,
accustomed to rapidity by attendance on his master, he had thundered
at the door before the carriage drew up: and now it was opened by Mr.
Mohun's servants, who advancing to Althea, who was, they concluded,
the person to be admitted, one of them told her that Mr. Mohun was
at home, but that moment going out. Althea, glad of an opportunity
to escape, was hastily retreating from the door, when Mohun appeared
at it hastily going out. He seemed surprised at the sight of her, and
still more when his servant said, "A lady, Sir, desires to speak to you."
Bowing, he retreated a few steps into the hall, and, throwing open the
door of a parlour, desired her to walk in. Althea still hung back, and
hesitated: "I believe, Sir," said she, "the present is no proper time —"
She was unable to finish the sentence; but already in the room, and
hardly able from confusion of mind to support herself, she sat down.
Mohun, whose eyes eagerly ran over her person, placed himself by her.

CHAP. XII.

Fà di tutto quaggia gioco insolente
La severa fortuna, e al pianto e forda.
....
....
Cosi da lieto stato a vila acerba
Ne sospinge a sua voglia; onde più fermo
Contro a cappriccj suoi non hassi schermo
Che ripensare ognor che fè non serba
E mirarla d'un votto non curante
Qual semina vagante
Di nostri voti indegna, e che tradisce
Per malvaggia natura;
Poi volubile torna, ed offerisce
Quand attri men la cura.

HAD NOT ALL these circumstances followed each other with a rapidity that gave Althea no time for recollection, the dignity of conscious
worth, and the contempt she felt towards Mohun, might have enabled
her to have gone through the scene with calmness, if not with courage;
but now too many uneasy sensations assailed her at once, and suddenly.
She apparently was come to ask a favour of a man, whom she had always
detested; and who had been the cause of the coldness and separation
between her and her father. But these injuries were light, compared to
those he had since inflicted on her by the tyrannical attempt to withhold
her fortune in conjunction with Lady Dacres, and the cowardice and
cruelty with which he had first insulted and then confined Marchmont.
Instead of addressing herself to him, she wondered how she had suffered herself, by the sudden and mistaken zeal of Dr. Warrington, to be
hurried into the presence of a man, whose very sight was odious to her:
and when (his countenance expressing at once his triumph, and all the
hateful passions he felt) he asked to be favoured with her commands,

Althea was unable to find words to answer him. Mohun, who, whatever other motives he had for distressing Marchmont, had never hoped it would throw her into his power, now began to see that it might very possibly have that effect; he therefore softened his voice, and, desiring her to recollect in what he could serve her, rang, and directed that some glasses of ice, and other refreshments, might instantly be brought. Althea found her voice to decline them, and arose to go; but Mohun was by no means disposed to let her. He thought that the confusion and distress in which he saw her were occasioned partly by her repentance of the indiscreet step she had taken in marrying, and partly by her wishing to repair it by regaining his favour. His presumption, his total want of principle and delicacy, carried him still farther; and he believed it possible, that Marchmont, weary of poverty and imprisonment, from which he had no other means of escaping, had sent his wife as an advocate by whose eloquent beauty his chains would drop off. Exulting in this idea, Mohun could hardly help saying aloud, "Marchmont, thou art a more sensible fellow than I took thee for!" But the species of satisfaction his tongue forbore to utter, was expressed by his eyes, as, directly fixed on the varying countenance of Althea, he waited for an answer to his question — "What were her commands?" "It was Dr. Warrington, Sir," said she, "I did not myself think of troubling you ... .but the Doctor ... having ... I having met the Doctor, he thought, he supposed ..."

"Whatever or whoever procured me the honour of seeing you in *my* house, Madam, has conferred on me the greatest obligation; *you* can only add to it by putting it in my power to shew you how greatly I love the memory of my dear friend, your excellent father; and how happy I should account myself, if...."

Hypocrisy was always so detestable and so contemptible in the opinion of Althea, that such an instance of it served by rousing her indignation to restore her resolution. Interrupting therefore this insulting cant, she said, "If you had any regard for my father, Sir, the only way to shew it, the only way, indeed, to acquit yourself with integrity to the world, is to act justly as his executor. If I have indeed any business with you, though I did not voluntarily come hither, it must be, you are well aware, on the subject of my fortune — which you can, I know, have no legal power to detain. He, whose right it is, you have cruelly, and I will say basely, prevented from asserting his claim. — Though I certainly did not mean to come to this house; yet, since I am here, I beg Mr. Mohun will understand, that I come to make that claim myself."

"Charming creature!" Mohun longed to say, as while she spoke he watched the play of her beautiful countenance, animated as by anger — "Charming creature! and thou art thrown away upon a beggar!" If he did not say this, there was such an expression in his eyes, that Althea turned from him with terror. He seemed meditating how to model his answer to promote the views which now arose so invitingly in his imagination; while Althea, whose swelling heart would, she thought, betray her into tears, once more rose from her seat, and, making an effort to conquer the hysteric sensation she felt, said, "I believe, Sir, the question I have to put to you is very easily answered — Will you or will you not transfer to Mr. Marchmont the two thousand pounds that become mine on my marriage?"

"The question, my dear Madam," said he, offering to take her hand, but she turned from him, "the question, I do assure you, is *not* so easily answered. There are in the simplest cases of this sort rules, forms, precautions of law, which..... It is quite impossible for me to explain them to you; but, upon my honour, it is *not* in my power to act with the precipitancy, the haste, and in the unguarded manner which seemed to be expected of me. Besides, my dear Madam, recollect that I am only *one* executor; and without the concurrence of Lady Dacres, who set her face against the measure, which (you will excuse me, I speak only after her Ladyship) she thought as ruinous to you, as contrary to the direct will of Sir Audley —I say, Lady Dacres, who in this case possesses equal power with myself — being averse, what could I do?"

"You might at least," said Althea, whose spirits and presence of mind were now much restored, "at least have treated like a gentleman the person to whom I have given a right to make the demand: you needed not, Sir, have added oppression to insult."

Mohun saw what turn he could give even to this nefarious transaction. He knew so little of the mind and heart of Althea, and was so thoroughly satisfied of his own masterly talents, that he fancied he could deceive her even in what was most evidently against him. — Affecting, therefore, to sigh deeply, he said, in an under tone — "It often happens, dear Miss Dacres —I beg your pardon — it often happens, Madam, that we are, in the course of irresistible events, dragged, compelled, driven, urged, forced to take measures to which our hearts, feelings, sentiments, and tendencies, are utterly averse. What would you say, if you were told, that the measure I adopted against the person who on your account alone could give me a second thought, was intended to prevent greater and more serious calamities?"

"I should say," replied Althea, "that of such a pretence I did not believe one word."

"And yet," said Mohun, advancing his chair a little nearer to hers, as he offered her some of the refreshments that were brought, "and yet it is possible that nothing can be more true. —" dare not, I do not wish to hint the most remotely at any faults of temper, or deficiency of prudence, in any of those *you* honour with your regard. It is too late indeed now; would to heaven it were not! — but indeed the family of the Marchmonts — why must I say it? — the misconduct of the young man has been too evident. If you had deigned to have consulted your true friends — but I see you take what I have to say amiss — yet a moment's patience, I conjure you to hear ..."

"No, Sir!" cried Althea, rising and hastening towards the door, "I have already heard too much. If your former conduct excited my indignation, is such conversation calculated to abate it? — No, Sir! it merely adds another sentiment to my abhorrence, and that is — contempt!"

The haughty soul of Mohun, instead of being repulsed and abashed by the resentment of offended innocence, rose arrogantly to contemplate the delight it would afford to humble this indignant beauty. He scorned not, therefore, to stoop to the meanest concessions to appease her — besought her to hear him; and being always of opinion that women, whatever slight difference of character may arise from understanding or education, are really alike in weakness and vanity, and to be won by the same means he ventured, after giving Althea to understand that the fate of Marchmont was entirely in his power, to hint, in terms that could not be misunderstood, that it was his unconquerable passion for *her* that had betrayed him into such harsh conduct towards the man who had supplanted him in her favour, and whom he could not bear to see happy and triumphant. He pleaded that

"The faults of love by love are justified!"

and imputing Althea's silence to the combat between vanity and interest on one side, against the dignity and reserve she thought it necessary to affect on the other, he proceeded to the most unequivocal professions of his passion for her; and at length added, in terms that could not be misinterpreted, that Marchmont's release and future prosperity depended altogether on herself; and that, on condition of her allowing him to renew his acquaintance as one of the intimate friends of her father, and looking upon him as the most devoted and attached of those friends, Marchmont should be released, and her fortune be immediately given up — himself, however, continuing her trustee; and he added, that his interest should be used to procure for Marchmont some establishment, that might put him into a rank not unworthy of that of the wife it was his supreme good fortune to possess.

If Althea remained silent while her ears were affronted by such an harangue, it was not because she suffered it patiently, but amazement and terror took from her, for a moment, the power to answer. Ill as she had ever thought of Mohun, such a daring and cruel insult exceeded all she had believed him capable of; and she was petrified with horror at the idea that she was in this man's house, and perhaps might not be allowed to escape from it. Disdaining to answer what she was shocked even to have heard, and recollecting with comfort that Fenchurch waited for her, she turned indignantly from Mohun, before he had finished the last sentence, and rang the bell with such effect that two of Mohun's footmen, accustomed to obey instantly their master's summons, appeared; and Althea, desiring one of them to send her servant up, walked directly into the hall, and from thence into the street — where, Fenchurch immediately following her; she enquired which was the way to the nearest stand of coaches. Fenchurch, alarmed by her look and manner, enquired if he should call one? — She could only answer — "No, no! — do not leave me! — but shew me the quickest way to a coach." — This he did; and Althea began to walk so fast, that when they arrived at the spot she was breathless, and with difficulty stepped into the hack which Fenchurch beckoned to — directing him to let it be driven over Blackfriars-bridge to the prison.

It had proceeded almost half way, before the stunned senses of Althea allowed her to consider steadily the scene she had just gone through: but when she became able to reflect upon it, she saw at once all the difficulties and dangers which the well-meant but ill-judged zeal of Dr. Warrington had brought her into. To perish in indigence was her fixed resolution, rather than ever again apply to Mohun, or suffer him to be applied to on her behalf as a matter of favour. But how could she venture to relate to her husband the insult she had received, when she doubted whether he would not feel himself injured and offended by her having unguardedly made the visit that had brought it on? Yet how to him, from whom she had never concealed a thought of her heart since he had been its master, how should she hide the accumulated troubles she suffered under? Still, to disclose to her husband the conversation with which Mohun had dared to entertain her, was to aggravate all his anxieties of mind by impotent anger, and perhaps give him such an impression of her imprudence as he might never forget. While this point was yet in debate, she saw herself near the end of her journey; and, stopping the coach, directed Fenchurch to order it to Mrs. Marchmont's lodgings, determined to consult Lucy before she took any resolution. It occurred to her, that she must give Fenchurch a caution not to say to his master where she had been; and even this precaution, though given with no other design than to save Marchmont from pain, was so unlike the usual tenor of her conduct, and had, she thought, so odd an appearance, that, as she spoke to him, her voice faltered, and her cheeks were dyed with blushes. Lucy flew down to her. — "Well, my dear Althea!" cried she eagerly, "you who are always the bearer of comfort and good tidings — my mother has been very impatient for your return, persuading herself that you are to be every way the guardian angel of her son: but what is the matter, my sweet sister? You look greatly fatigued!"— Althea then briefly related what had passed; which she begged Lucy not to mention to any body, and to advise her what it was best for her to do as to revealing or hiding this disagreeable encounter from Marchmont.

Lucy heard her with a degree of horror. — Having already conceived a dreadful opinion of this man, as well from his general character as from Althea's and her brother's sufferings, she now imagined that he had a motive, and certainly wanted not will, to complete their ruin. Marchmont, though one of the best-tempered men in the world, was, when roused, extremely passionate; and Lucy thought with Althea, that if to the injuries he had already received from Mohun this cruel affront were added, his just indignation, which, prisoner as he was, he could not shew to the cowardly wretch who had insulted him, would either break out in some start of violence injurious to his interest, or prey upon his temper and his health. Mohun, it was probable, would go out of town, and think no more of the calamities he had inflicted, than to triumph in their continuance. It was possible that nothing might ever be known of the visit; and then they were only where they were before, if Althea could only assume courage enough to answer any questions Marchmont might ask in a way that might give him no reason to expect any thing extraordinary had happened. Of the circumstances of her morning's walk she had only to relate, that Mr. Bargrave was not at home; and if she could not put on her usually calm and cheerful air, her dejection might easily pass for the effect of disappointment and fatigue.

This advice coinciding with Althea's own opinion, she determined to pursue it. She endeavoured to compose herself, and paid a short visit to Mrs. Marchmont; and Fenchurch being returned from his master, to whom she had sent him, she went back to the confinement where Marchmont expected her.

He had already learned from his servant, that Mr. Bargrave was not to be found; but when he had put two or three other questions to him, the poor fellow, unused to any prevarication with his master, appeared so confused, and blundered so much, that Marchmont was alarmed, though he knew not at what. — When Althea appeared, whose nerves were not steadied by having met on her way both the men whose constant notice persecuted her, Marchmont no sooner saw her, than he perceived that something unusual had occasioned her agitation; while the questions he put to her so much increased it, that she at length felt her spirits quite conquered, and burst into tears. Marchmont then reproached himself with having suffered her to go. — "I know not," said he, :by what oversight it was that I consented to your going in search of Bargrave: if he had been met with, and had set about the enquiry with more zeal than I expect, little would it indeed avail me if I were to purchase it at the expence of one hour of your health. But," added he, "what is the matter with Fenchurch? — The fellow looks as if he had seen a ghost; and, instead of answering my questions, gaped and stared as if he were struggling to hide some great secret. My mother I saw this morning while you were absent, and she is not surely fallen since into a state which you wish to conceal from me?"

Althea now assured him, though in faltering and weak accents, that nothing more than unusual fatigue had affected her — added to some degree of chagrin at the delay in all their business that Mr. Bargrave's absence must occasion.

Of this, since it seemed to hurt Althea, Marchmont made light; but his spirits never were in reality more depressed than they now were for some days. The intelligence he expected from Eversley came not; and the prospect of Trevyllian's succession seemed fading into air. Of Forrester, whom it would have given him so much pleasure to see, he heard nothing. He had once sent his servant to enquire at Lord Stanwarden's, but had very little satisfaction from the answer; and at Lord Rochdale's he was told, that Captain Forrester was in England, but very ill, and, by the advice of his physician, gone to Bath instead of coming to London. — If from distant quarters all seemed a blank, his home view was yet more gloomy. — Althea visibly lost that elasticity of mind which had hitherto been the cheerful support of them all. — Marchmont saw that she struggled against the despondence that every day became deeper. He observed something particularly apprehensive in her manner whenever she went out, and uncommon anxiety to have the servant with her; and he learned that the walks in the fields she had sometimes taken with his sisters were now entirely at an end. — The unpleasantness of such walks at this season of heat and dust, and her wish to pass every moment either with him or his mother, were assigned as her reasons for this alteration; but Marchmont still thought he saw some mystery which he did not comprehend; and, without any decided object, his restlessness increased, and his confinement became more insupportable.

Dr. Warrington too, after his accidental interview with Althea, seemed, for some days, to have forsaken them. — He persuaded himself that her seeing Mr. Mohun would do every thing that was effectual towards the accommodation of the affairs; and that such an arrangement was the only circumstance that could restore the health of Mrs. Marchmont, for whom the power of medicine could do nothing effectual: and having been extremely harassed with business, he took the opportunity of the absence from London of most of his patients, to enjoy a short interval at a house where, during the summer, his family resided in Hertfordshire. — Every one of the friends then, on whom Marchmont and Althea had depended, seemed at once to have forsaken them; and there had not yet occurred, in the life of the former, any period at which manly resolution was so necessary to enable him to rise above this accumulation of evil, and to prevent his forsaking himself, or rather those who alone were objects of his solicitude.

With what courage and tranquillity he could, he now sat down to his literary labour. He had found a purchaser who agreed to give him a liberal price for a work of imagination, if, upon perusing the first volume, he found it likely to answer his purpose; and, discouraging as this condition was, since the taste and judgment of his purchaser might be influenced by considerations that had nothing to do with literary merit, he proceeded as steadily as was possible, without access to books, or any hope but of obtaining a subsistence in a prison!

Althea was his critic and his assistant; and while she sat with him thus occupied, he observed her former cheerfulness sometimes return; but, whenever the hour came that Mrs. Marchmont expected her, she seemed distressed: yet, next to being with him, he well knew that nothing gave her so much pleasure as alleviating the sufferings of his mother.

Marchmont one morning conducted Althea to the door, and saw her proceed towards his mother's abode, attended, as usual, by the servant. He then returned to his room, and sat down to his morning's task; in which he was deeply engaged when Bensted came breathless into the room, and said — "Oh, Sir! — there's Chapman has just come in, and says that Mrs. Marchmont has fallen down in a fit under the wall just without — and Fenchurch is like a distracted man, and bid somebody, for God's sake, run to you."

Marchmont totally forgetting that he would not be permitted to go out without some ceremonies that took up time, and not remembering, at that cruel moment, any thing but Althea, he ran through the area and into the lobby, the door of which was, at that moment, open; and he was proceeding with equal velocity to go out, when he was rudely stopped by two of the turnkeys, who cried — "Why so fast, Sir?—Stay a little, if you please." — Rage and terror now combined to rob Marchmont of all prudence and presence of mind. He struggled to disengage himself from the grasp of the men who held him, now threatening, now imploring; while they, who thought him seized with phrensy, called other assistance, and forced him out of the lobby.

It is impossible to describe the agony of frantic despair he now underwent, or to say where it would have ended, if an old man of decent appearance had not come up to him; and, having obtained a hearing with some difficulty, said — "Mr. Marchmont, be calm, be pacified. Your wife is recovered — she is well; at least she is safe. I have myself seen her conveyed to her mother's; and have, as far I could, chastised the rascal who has insulted her."

This address recalled the scattered senses of Marchmont. He seized the hand of the person who had thus brought him intelligence that snatched him from the most insupportable torments, but what he said was wild and incoherent; and he entreated, in the urgent terms of this new-found friend, that he would procure him the means of seeing his wife directly, wherever she might be.

This the man, who did not seem himself to be a prisoner, promised to effect, if he would compose himself; and Marchmont, hardly knowing what he was doing, was led back to his room — where when he arrived he insisted that he would not remain, but would go, at whatever hazard, to his wife: and such were the dreadful apprehensions that now again assailed him, that he would have relapsed into the undistinguishing wildness of furious passion, in despite of his friendly counsellor, if Fenchurch had not that moment appeared. — Marchmont inarticulately demanded news of his mistress; and the man then, with evident marks of agitation, said — "Thank God, Sir! she is quite safe and recovered, and with your mother and the young ladies. They sent me off to say so to you, Sir, for I was afraid that I had sent you a message that would have made you very uneasy; and indeed, if it had not been for this gentleman, I do not know what I should have done."

Marchmont then renewed his acknowledgments for the kindness received, though of what nature it was he knew not; but his impatience to go to Althea returning, he asked his new acquaintance to accompany him when he went to procure the humiliating permission he was compelled to submit to; and bade Fenchurch, as they went, relate the circumstances that had so alarmed his mistress.

"It was owing, Sir," said he, "to that Mr. Carlingbury; who, for all my lady has kept it to herself for fear of some quarrel, has behaved extremely impertinent to her very often: — and my lady, ever since that day at Mr. Mohun's ..."

"At Mr. Mohun's!" exclaimed Marchmont. — "What do you mean? — When has your mistress seen Mr. Mohun?"

Fenchurch now appeared extremely confused; but his master eagerly, and even angrily, repeating his question, he said — "Why, Sir, my lady charged me never to speak of it, because she thought you would be displeased, so ill as he has used you, that she went to his house."

"To his house! — Althea! my wife! — go to Mohun's house? Surely the man dreams. — It is impossible! — It could never be!"

"I am sure, Sir, it is true, though," said Fenchurch with great simplicity, "but I wish I had not mentioned it, for, to be sure, it had nothing to do with what happened to-day: only I was going to say, Sir, that ever since that time mistress has been so timmersome, that every thing has frightened her a great deal more than it did before: so that just now, when that Mr. Carlingbury came up to her (though he did not, that I know of, say much more impertinent stuff than he used to say, only he seemed, to be sure, more in liquor), my lady turned so pale, that I went forward; and she said, 'Fenchurch, I must take your arm —I am afraid I shall drop.' — 'No, no,' said that rude impudent fellow, pushing me on one side — 'I will never suffer a servant to have that honour while I am here.' — So he pushed me away, Sir, and I could not bear neither that, nor to see my lady so frightened — and then I seized him by the collar, and he struck me two or three times. My poor lady shrieked out, and made back this way; and this gentleman then came up to her, and bid her not be frightened, for he would take care of her. —I gave Mr. Carlingbury, who I am sure is no gentleman, a good blow or two — and he offered to strip and fight me; for he said he had learned that sport, and would cure me of being saucy to gentlemen as long as I lived. But my business, I thought, was to take care of my lady, for there was a crowd got about her. So I left him held by some of the people that were there, swearing he would kill me, I believe — and I presently found that my lady had fallen down insensible, and this gentleman was taking care of her; and then an empty coach, that had just put some-body down here, passing, he and I lifted her into it, and carried her to Mrs. Marchmont's: and presently he came back to you, and I staid there till Miss Lucy came out, and said, my lady was come-to, and wanted to speak to me — so I went into the room. She is quite well again, Sir, I assure you; and desired me to come directly to tell you so — and hopes you won't be frightened."

Marchmont, distracted by anger at the insolent conduct of Carlingbury, and by surprise at what he had heard about Mohun, yield-ed, however, to the more immediate impression; and was flying to seek Carlingbury, whom it was fortunate he did not meet at the moment. — The remonstrances of his new acquaintance, whose name was Des-borough, restored him to a better way of thinking. — "Come, come," said the old man with an air as if he had been used to be attended to, "let us, my good Sir, have none of these rash doings. Of what *use* will it be if you meet this drunken fool, and break his head? I know that he deserves more than either I or your servant have given him, and yet I did my best — but I will tell you what *harm* it will do. If any uproar happens between you, you will both be confined; and as he has the most interest of the two in this place, because, I suppose, he is the richest, you will have the worst of it. Let the poor wretch alone, for a very contemptible wretch, believe me, he is, and think of your wife; who, I can tell you, deserves greater sacrifices than that of your anger against such a blockhead as that. Come, I will go with you to speak to the worthy gentleman who is to give you leave out; my credit with him is pretty good, I believe — and perhaps he may trust you with me without any other attendant."

"I thank you," said Marchmont; — "after all you have done, you have a right to expect I should take your advice. I am rather surprised, however, as I thought you were yourself a prisoner, because I have so often seen you."

Mr. Desborough answered drily, that he *was* there frequently; and, without any farther explanation, proceeded with Marchmont to the officer on whom his going out of the prison walls depended. This, on Mr. Desborough saying a few words, was granted; and they then went together to Mrs. Marchmont's lodgings.

Arrived at the door, the old man turned to him, and said — "You are in my custody, you know, and so you will see the reliance I have on your integrity by my leaving you: but the name of Marchmont is no stranger to me; and though chivalry exists no longer, yet, in a point of real honour, I am sure I may trust to the descendant of the old cavaliers." — Marchmont looked at him with wonder; his language and his appearance were altogether incongruous. — "Do you know me, Sir?" said he. — "Were you acquainted with my father?"

"Yes," answered the stranger, "I was once acquainted with your family; and though that has been long over, I am sorry to *see you* in such a place, and still more sorry to see your wife here. Indeed you should never have brought her to a prison." — "Pray tell me who you are," cried Marchmont eagerly; "you excite even painful curiosity."— "No," replied the stranger — "Go and look after that poor terrified young creature, and I will wait for you an hour at a coffee-house in the Borough, and then call for you again. The intelligence of who I am, will do as well another time: perhaps I may see you again in the evening."

Marchmont was then hurrying to Althea, but Fenchurch overtook him on the stairs. — "Pray, dear Sir," said he, "do not mention to my lady what I told you, in my hurry, about Mr. Mohun. I know she is so unwilling you should know it, and it would vex her so that I am sure it would just now make her quite ill" — Marchmont, relapsing into his first astonishment, hastily said — "No, no —I shall say nothing to distress her;" and then entered his sister's room, where Althea was yet unable to sit up.

The sight of Marchmont, however, seemed immediately to revive her; but, before she would relate the cause of her terror, she insisted on his promising not to resent it. This he evaded doing; yet he appeared so much calmer than Althea had expected, that she ventured to relate what indeed she guessed he knew already — the frequent impertinence of which Carlingbury had been guilty — "which," said she, "I never mentioned, because I knew it would occasion a quarrel, and I dread every thing of that sort."

"And is *that*" said Marchmont, looking at her steadily, "the reason why you should also conceal other alarms that you have had, Althea?" —— Althea blushed from consciousness; yet not suspecting that Fenchurch had been so unguarded, she only said, "I had no other alarms here but from an old gentleman who appears now to be rather likely to protect than to offend me — for it was he who saved me from the insults of the mob that surrounded me, while poor Fenchurch was scuffling with that drunken brute."

"And what alarms could he have given you?" enquired Marchmont: — "What did he do?"

"Nothing, perhaps," replied Althea, "that ought to have alarmed me: but whenever I have met him, which has been almost every day, he has fixed his eyes on me in so singular a manner, that I have fancied he knew something of farther mischief that might be intended us; for me thought he had a look of compassion — yet it was stern — and he seemed to long to speak to me, not as that insolent young man did, but with reproach."

This account increased Marchmont's curiosity, but it increased also his disquiet — "Who could this man be? and why did Althea conceal from him her having seen Mohun? Why did she seek him? How know where he was, and how determine to hold with such a man even momentary converse?" Such were the enquires he was silently making, when he was informed that two men were sent by order of the Marshal to conduct him back. He went down to speak to them, and was told that he must immediately go with them; for that a new order was come in respect to him, as they believed, or that something or other had happened, that the commander of the fortress was extremely angry at finding he had left it.

He was hardly suffered to go, in the anguish of his heart, and take leave of Althea, as he insisted upon her remaining where she was that night, and sharing Lucy's bed. It was with the utmost difficulty she was prevailed upon to consent to this; but she was still so faint and ill, that she was conscious of her unfitness even for so short a removal.

Marchmont, on her earnest entreaty, promised he would take no notice that day of Carlingbury; and then, in indescribable agony, he bade
his mother adieu! doubting if he should ever see her again, and tore
himself away.

Many very miserable hours had in the course of his short life been
passed by Marchmont but none had ever been so overwhelming as
the remainder of this day. — Why he was to be more closely confined, he could not learn; all he could hear by bribes and enquiries
was, that the swivel-eyed attorney, as the runners called Vampyre, had
been there twice that morning: and Marchmont doubted not but that
this additional cruelty was the work of that malignant demon: — and,
probably by the order of Mohun, compelled to submit to oppression,
which he more than ever despaired either of escaping from or aveng-
ing, and distracted with a thousand fears for his mother and his wife,
he sat down alone in his room, and began to consider what he had of
consolation or support. — Except Althea, whose conduct for the first
time in his life he now thought wrong, there seemed no being on earth
towards whom he might look for comfort — for of both his friends
he was deprived: — at least he began to doubt, whether even the long
confirmed friendship of Eversley was not worn out by his unceasing
distresses; for he had twice written to him — time enough had elapsed
for repeated answers, yet no letter came: and of Forrester he began to
doubt, whether, like many other young men, he did not hastily form
friendships, and as hastily forget them. Even these fears, however,
were less torturing than the rage and indignation he felt in thinking
of Mohun, and the reptile he employed. He now indeed guessed part
of the truth; that Althea (though by what means induced to take such
a step he could not imagine) had seen Mohun, who having dared to
affront her with that libertinism to which he was avowedly addicted,
he had in the meanness of revenge sent orders for the rules of the
prison to be enforced. When this idea had once taken possession of
him, it was insupportable. He walked up and down his narrow room in
the most cruel perturbation. He cursed his existence; he felt tempted
to end it, rather than endure injuries so intolerable; and he was yielding
to this phrensy, which in his moments of cooler reflection he was the
first to condemn, when his last-made acquaintance, Mr. Desborough,
entered the room.

His manners were plain, and even blunt, and he seemed to assume
privilege from his age. — "Hey-day," said he, as he entered, and saw

the disorder in which Marchmont appeared, "what is all this for? If you desire me to visit you, you must not enact Alexander or Orestes, or any of your mad heroes. — You don't want sense, I am told, and you don't drink. There are no other excuses that I know of for a man's behaving like a fool. Sit down quietly, and talk to me —I want to hear why you are in this place — for what sums — and what you intend to do? Be explicit — I am a plain man, and perhaps you may think not likely to do you any good; but when you have told me all, you shall hear what I have to say."

Marchmont then related, in as few words as would do it justice, the history of his life previous to the distressful situation in which he was left when his father died — his engagements to the two men who had employed Vampyre against him — his acquaintance and marriage with Althea; and concluded with a relation of the conduct of Mohun in the detention of Althea's fortune — and its consequences, which had placed another barrier against his freedom. — "Yes," said Mr. Desborough, when he had heard him out, "Mohun is a villain; and as to the monster he has employed, if ever he should come to the gallows (which, well as he deserves it, I am afraid he will have cunning enough to avoid), I will venture to assert, that a wretch so stained with crimes never came under the hands of the executioner in this or in any other country. I do not except the Robespierres or Dantons of France, who were, I think, though they had by a strange chance the power of doing more extensive mischief, less systematical scoundrels than either of these; but let us talk no more of them, but rather of the means of getting you out of their hands."

Marchmont answered in a tone of deep dejection, that of ever escaping from them he despaired. He then made an ingenuous display of his hopeless situation. The fortune of Althea, he said, he held sacred; nor could he, even if he would, touch it; and the debt considerably exceeded it. While he spoke of the inviolable regard he should hold it in, his auditor nodded approbation: but, when proceeding to state the chance he thought Althea had, unless there were any claimants he was unacquainted with, to succeed to a considerable property, the old man's eyes brightened with joy — and he eagerly enquired why it was not looked after, and how such a thing came to be neglected. Marchmont related what had been done, which was indeed all the time allowed; but added, that he was much afraid nothing would be effected in such a case without a suit in Chancery: "and for that you know, Sir," said he, "I have no money."

"I have," said Mr. Desborough: "I have money enough for such a thing as that, and it shall be yours. I had some doubts about you, I own; I was afraid you had not acted honourably by that charming girl; but I find you are an honest fellow, and I will be your friend."

Marchmont, amazed, and hardly knowing how to trust to professions so sudden and unexpected, thanked him, but it was with hesitation: "I see," said Mr. Desborough, "that you are surprised at these sort of offers from an acquaintance of a few hours: but I have known more of your family than you are aware of; for, though I am related to you, I question whether you remember having heard my name."

Marchmont again expressed his wonder and satisfaction : Mr. Desborough proceeded thus:

"When your grandfather lived in great splendour at Eastwoodleigh, I was the youngest son of a clothier in the West — a smart fellow for those days: and so your aunt thought. I made love to her — there was no Marriage Act then — and so we marched off together, and were married at the next town. But the old gentleman never forgave us; nor did I ever see him afterwards. His daughter had five hundred pounds of her own left her by some relation, and her father gave her nothing: indeed he had nothing to give — for his son, your father, was to have all, that he might keep up the old place. Your father, who was a good-natured man, though he had his foibles, and who is without? came to see us once or twice; but we were so opposite in our notions, that we had no great delight in one another's company. He was what I called a tory, and he called me...not a whig, but a republican. I did not much quarrel with him for ranking me with such names as Sidney and Hampden, but I hated to see him, poor man! ruining himself for his principles, as he called them, which nobody cared about, or thanked him for. For a great many years we had little or no communication; I lost my wife, who left me no children; and my father having a concern in the West Indies, it fell at his death to me. I was now an unconnected being, neither rich nor poor; and by way of having something to do, I went to look after this property — but I could not endure to be master of slaves. The whole system of a plantation was repugnant to all my feelings, and all my principles. I sold my cane lands, and the unhappy people who worked them, to whom I would have given their liberty if I had been allowed to do it. It was a blessing I could bestow only on a few. I came home, rich for a man that wanted so little; but I was soon tired of having nothing to do, and nobody to care for so I went for some time rambling about the world — not much pleased indeed with any thing I saw in it. They say I'm a misanthrope. I may be so — It is very true that I hate fools, and I am sure one meets with a vast majority of them; and more, I think, now than when I was a young man. But whether I hate or no the bulk of mankind, I try all I can to do good to individuals; and none move my compassion more than poor silly fellows, who without any fraud, or any other fault than a little thought- less extravagance, have got cooped up in this or any other such cursed place. I have got two or three of them out lately at little expence; and it was in one of my visits for that purpose that about a fortnight ago I first observed your wife. I was struck with her youth, beauty, and that air of innocence and intelligence which one so seldom sees united. It seemed to me very strange and inconsequent that you should bring her here; for I soon learned who you was, and I was afraid all was not right. I am now convinced that you deserve I should have a better opinion of you; and though I hate the nonsensical cant, that 'all is for the best,' and such stuff, when one sees every day that nothing can be much worse than things in general, yet for once good is come out of evil, perhaps; and I may find a way to get you out of the clutches of these harpies. We'll try, however, what is to be done, and set about it to-morrow: and now, my dear boy, you shall not say a word of 'thank you,' and all that. I can suppose it very well, and have no time to hear it. So God bless you! I must be gone: but to-morrow at ten o'clock I will be here again; and in the meantime keep yourself quiet, and let nothing of all this transpire, even to your pretty wife. I have a mind, perhaps, to surprise her with a present — We shall see." Mr. Desborough then, without waiting for Marchmont's answer, arose and disappeared.

Marchmont in vain attempted to compose his spirits. All that had passed appeared like a dream, from which he feared by inves- tigating it to be awakened. He sent Fenchurch very early to enquire after Althea, who wrote to him to say she found herself quite well, and would be with him at his breakfast: but as he dared not reveal the hopes he had that their troubles would be at an end by the inter- position of this unexpected friend, he wrote again, telling her that he had some people to come to him on his affairs, which he had reason to hope would turn out satisfactory; and therefore begged she would not come before one o'clock, as he thought her being present when people she did not know were discoursing on business, would be disagreeable to her.

The assurances this note contained, that the persons whom Marchmont was to see were not unfavourably disposed, were necessary to
quiet the spirits of Althea, who, tormented as she was by the fear of
his resenting the insulting rudeness of Carlingbury, had yet another
cause of apprehension. In the midst of her terror, when the impertinence of this man had so shocked and alarmed her, Vampyre, whom
she well recollected, had passed near her; and could all the scourges
deprecated in the Litany have appeared personified before her, she
would have suffered less than the view of this old hideous monster
inflicted on her. Of his machinations against Marchmont, therefore,
on whose account she supposed he visited the prison, she had the
most cruel apprehensions; and the more so, as it was too probable the
unprincipled Mohun directed this diabolical agent. It was owing to her
having seen Vampyre at the very moment that Carlingbury spoke to
her, that Althea had fainted, or very near it; for in general her resolution and reason were sufficient to secure her from such accidents.

But firmly persuaded that Marchmont would not deceive her, she
awaited as calmly as she could the hour at which she was to see him.

Marchmont was not so tranquil. Till the period when he expected
the man to whom he had within a short time been taught to look for
his deliverance, he traversed the area with restless steps. — The hour
passed, and Mr. Desborough did not appear. Fears and doubts then
arose — Perhaps he was of that description of persons who delight in
raising expectations only to disappoint them. — Perhaps he forgot in
the morning the benevolent resolutions of the preceding evening. Yet
he did not appear to be such a man, and the account he had given of
himself was certainly true; for Marchmont now recollected his name,
and alliance to his family; though, no intimacy having ever subsisted
between the brother and sister, he had never seen his aunt, and remembered her only in the catalogue of family pictures that were seized
and sold at Eastwoodleigh, all of which had been carefully marked
with names and dates by his father. Another hour passed, and still his
newfound friend came not. As he walked backwards and forwards he
entered into conversation with a clergyman, with whom he had sometimes talked before. The poor man had been two years a prisoner at
the suit of a near relation, and seemed to have little hope of ever being
released, though his original debt was but a hundred pounds. Marchmont having seen him once or twice speaking to Mr. Desborough,
now enquired what he knew of him.

"He is what is called a character," replied his companion: "but to be sure he is humane; for he has released three persons who have been confined here for debts, one of them not very small, and has compounded with the creditors of two others, and liberated four or five who lingered here merely because they were unable to pay the expences of their release. However, he is accounted a very odd eccentric character."

"And not without reason," said Marchmont; "for, unhappily, such actions are very uncommon."

"He is said also," continued the other, "to be of doubtful principles."

"Principles!" repeated Marchmont: "Of what sort?"

"Both religious and political," replied Mr. Wingrove; "and indeed I am sorry to say that he has on both subjects very heterodox notions. I have taken some pains to combat his unhappy prepossessions when we have talked together, but I grieve to think that he is most obstinately bigoted to a set of notions…"

"Which cannot, however, be very prejudicial to society," interrupted Marchmont, "since it appears that his life is passed, and his fortune expended, in doing good."

Mr. Wingrove, who had been educated in the strictest of what used to be called High-church principles (in the reign of Queen Anne), and had never ventured to entertain or listen to an idea that favoured of schism, either in church or state, would now have entered into a long discourse, to prove that it was impossible any body could have common sense who did; but in the midst of the first *head* of his argument, which he divided sermon-wise, Marchmont felt somebody touch him gently on the shoulder. He turned, and beheld in deep mourning his friend Eversley.

The pleasure which the sight of this estimable man gave him was not abated by the dress in which he saw him; since it afforded reason to hope, what he found to be true, that Eversley was delivered for ever from the wretched woman who had occasioned all the unhappiness of his life. They retired immediately to Marchmont's room; where, as soon as they were able tranquilly to discourse, Eversley related, that the miserable state (which might well be called a degree of phrensy) in which the last month of his wife's sad existence had passed, had prevented his being able to act in regard to Marchmont's affairs as he would otherwise have done. "But I believed," said he, "that it was

drawing to a crisis, and thought I should soon be in a situation effectually to assist you. Much as I had cause on every account to desire
that Heaven would rescue me from such an intolerable burden as I
had long sustained, while to herself the poor woman's existence was as
little desirable (for she was the martyr of intemperance and her own
constitutional failings); yet I could not help being affected, when the
moment came, with sensations of mingled pity and horror. A very
little reflection however, restored me to a sense of my release, and to
the power of engaging in the duties that I still had to execute. I attended the remains of Mrs. Eversley to the place where her parents were
buried; and I afterwards went with my two daughters to her aunt, with
whom she made me promise that I should place them. Having settled
all that related to them, till I can see farther what will be most likely to
counteract the unhappy education they have hitherto received, I hastened, my dear friend, to you — happy if I can now, however late, give
you proofs of the interest I feel in all that relates to you."

Marchmont now gave Eversley an account of all that had lately
happened, and ended with the odd circumstance which had occurred
the preceding day. He heard with great satisfaction that another friend
was likely to assist him in the release of Marchmont, which he meant
at all events to effect. — "Nor," said he, "in undertaking this alone,
my friend, shall I incur a greater risk than I can very safely afford, for
I suppose you cannot doubt your wife's succession to half her cousin's
estate?"

Marchmont eagerly enquired what intelligence he had gained
on that subject, and Eversley took from his pocket a letter from Mr.
Thoresby, written in the true spirit of a lawyer; for, with a great many
sentences that sounded very fairly, is really meant nothing more than
that if Mrs. Armyn Marchmont could make out her claim, of which
he knew nothing, it must be referred to the proper place, there being
doubts as to the entail and other circumstances. This proper place was
undoubtedly Chancery. But Eversley re-assured his friend by saying,
"All this is mere equivocation, to elude for the present any enquiry. He
thinks that it is no business of mine; that people are seldom very stren-
uous for others; and that, till a person more immediately concerned
appears, he can baffle enquiry. He has been told, and from Lady Dacres, that your wife is abroad, and heartily hopes chance may so far befriend him, that he may keep possession of the whole estate. However,
I think he will hardly do that: for Mrs. Thoresby is the daughter of one,

and your wife of another sister of the late Mr. Trevyllian's father; and
of their having exactly the same claim there cannot be the shadow of
doubt. I have consulted upon it an old lawyer, who knows all the circumstances of the estate of Trevyllian the grandfather perfectly: and
he assures me, that there is not a question as to your wife's right; and
that, if Mr. Thoresby means any thing but merely to equivocate from
habit, he waits only in the hope that some advantage may be maintained against people who were evidently in no condition to undertake
a Chancery suit. When he finds that only expence and disgrace follow
his resistance, I am convinced you will have no farther trouble."

Bensted now entered, to inform Marchmont a gentleman enquired
for him. He of course expected to see Mr. Desborough — instead of
whom Captain Forrester, supported by his servant, appeared.

Marchmont, though shocked to see how ill he looked, expressed
his pleasure at their meeting. "And I, my dear Marchmont," said he,
"rejoice to see you, though indeed I had rather have seen you any
where else. Don't fancy however, that I should not have found you out
in *any* place, the very moment after I could disengage myself from my
own family. But this wound of mine broke out again, and confined me
to my bed for above a month. They carried me to Bath, and I have but
just contrived to crawl about again. I came to Town yesterday; and to-
day I determined to see you, and to know what can be done to set you
at liberty. I think I need not say, that all I can do you may command;
and if that is not enough to be effectually useful to you, my family
will come forward to oblige me in the only favour I am likely to ask
of them." Marchmont warmly expressed his acknowledgements, till
Eversley, eagerly interrupting him, cried — "What then, as Captain
Forrester is so kindly disposed, what hinders us from going immediately together to give bail, since two will be required? And why should
you stay another hour in this place?" Forrester earnestly entreated that
not a moment might be lost; while Marchmont, who thought security
for so large a sum, more than either he or Eversley ought to undertake,
felt himself at once happy in having two such friends and yet recoiling
from obligations which it might never be in his power to discharge.
Their debate was suspended, and indeed concluded, by the entrance
of Mr. Desborough.

He sat down with the air of a man vexed and fatigued. "Well,"
cried he, "I suppose you had given me up? And I began to think I
should not get to you to-day. I have never undertaken such a knot of

scoundrels — they have given me a good breathing — but courage, my dear boy! you are out of their hands." He then told Marchmont he was at liberty, adding, "But you must come down to the Marshal-room. You know, or I suppose don't know, that there are personal ceremonies to go through. If you make haste, you may chance still to find honest Mr. Vampyre there, who took the trouble to come himself to object to my bail, and for other special purposes — among which, was to lodge two detainers against you; one, I think, from Lady Dacres, for your wife's board for some months, and money which it seems that worthy dame paid for her." Marchmont looked amazed. "Nay, my good friend," said Mr. Desborough, "you and these two gentlemen look as much astonished as if you had never before heard of or experienced the villany of mankind." "I hope, my dear Sir," said Marchmont, "you have not paid these sums?" "I have paid none of them," replied Desborough; "but I have given bail for them all with the assistance of a friend I brought with me. The iniquity I have discovered even in so short a time as I have employed in it this morning is really beyond the calculation that, misanthrope as they say I am, I could have made of the depravity of Vampyre himself. But come, Marchmont, I am impatient to see you at liberty, and to offer to my fair friend a present that I know she will thank me for. There is yet more to be done than will take us up an hour, before I can have that pleasure."

Eversley now offered to assist this worthy and friendly man in his benevolent work; and Forrester, overjoyed at so unexpected a change in his friend's affairs, retired — since he was not wanted — having first desired Marchmont to let him know where he could see him the next day; which he promised as soon as he knew himself. It was every way improper to suffer any sudden news even of this joyful tendency to be carried to Mrs. Marchmont and Althea. Forrester would have undertaken any commission to them, but he was quite a stranger. Fenchurch, however, reminding his master that his lady was to come at one o'clock, was dispatched with a message, which he promised to deliver with great caution, importing that Mr. Eversley was come, and with his master would be with the ladies in an hour; but he was not to reveal abruptly that the imprisonment of the latter was at an end. The poor fellow ran away giddy with transport to execute this order, and Marchmont and his two friends repaired to the Marshal-room, where the attorney employed by Mr. Desborough waited, and where Vampyre had left his clerk. Every pretence by which he had attempted to detain Marchmont being overuled, the fiend, disappointed in his infernal malice, had fled: and it was fortunate he had, as Marchmont might have been unable to check his indignation at the sight of him.

Every form being gone through, and every fee, which the sub-executors of our mild and equitable laws are suffered to extort from the unfortunate debtor, being paid, Desborough, whom Marchmont was utterly unable to thank, took his leave, appointing a place of meeting in the evening, where he said he had something to propose to Marchmont, and desired to see Mr. Eversley with him. — "Since it will not be quite wise, I believe, to execute my plan of surprising Mrs. Armyn Marchmont, you shall only carry her my love, and tell her I shall have a great deal to say to her when we meet."

It would be difficult to describe the change from extreme despondence, to hope and joy, that was diffused through Marchmont's family, when his liberation was, with precautions, made known to them. — Althea was unable to remain in the room — but retired to give course to her tears; while Marchmont went from her to his mother, soothing them alternately, and alternately embracing his three sisters.

Eversley, as soon as Mrs. Marchmont seemed composed enough to bear it, related to her what had happened to himself; and he informed her then of the probability there was of her son's immediately succeeding, in right of his wife, to so considerable a property. The half-extinguished lamp of life seemed to be renewed; but faint, and almost ready to doubt whether after so much misery a ray of sun-shine might gleam on her declining days, she could not long support the conversation. The two friends, at the hour appointed, met Mr. Desborough; who, when Marchmont would have acknowledged as warmly as it deserved his unexampled kindness and friendship, spoke thus:

"You are not at all obliged to me, for what I have done was to please myself: not exactly because you were a relation of my wife's, for that would have been no recommendation if I had found you an idle, good-for-nothing young fellow—such, for example, as that Carlingbury. They say I am a reformer. They say wrong: for I have long since given up any such chimerical idea, as that of being able to make men happier who are wicked and miserable by prescription. Withdrawing, therefore, from any such Utopian and hopeless attempt, I believed the best thing I could do was, to relieve, where I could, individual distress, and to lighten the chains that villany often imposes on simplicity under the name of law. In this I have done some good, and what else ought a man to do on this earth? It is *my religion* to believe, that I serve God best in contributing to the happiness, or rather in relieving the misery, of his creatures. In this my form of worship I have sometimes been subject to imposition; I have often been laughed at; oftener reviled — and sometimes I have met with ingratitude: but I persist, because I expected no other pleasure than that I have found; and it is not in such places that, if I any where sought gratitude, I should hope to succeed. Now then let us talk of all this no more. Let us consider how we can the soonest remove your mother, wife, and sisters, from the bad air of this Borough; and then we will bestir ourselves to find you a house of your own to put them in. I suppose you have yet fixed on no plan?"

Marchmont answered — "No." — Mr. Desborough then said — "I have a house on Clapham Common, which I call my home, though I sometimes am absent from it for three or four months at a time. I have a careful old woman there as a housekeeper, with a cook and a housemaid: there is room enough for you all: the distance is easy, and I can order the house to be ready tomorrow. What do you think of becoming visitors to me for two or three months? There is nothing that will oblige me so much."

Marchmont, forbidden to express, could only look his gratitude. This plan, with the perfect coincidence of Mrs. Marchmont, was the next day put in execution. Marchmont did not, however, take final leave of the prison, without undertaking the relief of his unfortunate neighbour, Bensted. Mr. Desborough compounded his debt — released, and sent him happy to his own country.

Althea and Marchmont now looked forward only to happiness, and saw that it was not yet too late to hope that the mother they so fondly loved would be spared to their prayers; while new prospects of additional satisfaction opened to her. Mr. Eversley, who was almost every day their visitor, was impressed by the mild merit of Amelia: to *his* merit she could not be insensible; and it was settled that, as soon as the usual forms admitted, the marriage should take place, by which Eversley hoped to forget the miseries of his first union.

Captain Forrester, whose affection for Marchmont induced him to look with partiality on all his family, needed not this bias to attach him to Lucy. Her beauty, her vivacity, and sweetness of temper, soon taught him to overlook her want of fortune; and to her family Lord Stanwarden himself could not object. Such had been the fears of his family for the life of Forrester, that they now dreamed not of opposing his inclinations. Lord Stanwarden therefore consented to this marriage, and agreed to make such a settlement on his son, as, with what his female relation engaged to do for him, would enable the young people to live in affluence.

Whatever opposition had been meditated by Mr. Thoresby to Marchmont's claim in right of Althea, he soon gave it up when he found that Mr. Desborough supported those claims. In about four months, there fore, the moiety of Mr. Trevyllian's estate was, as settled by arbitrators, relinquished to Althea. The income of it was seven-and-twenty hundred a year; and a part of it comprised the house formerly inhabited by Mrs. Trevyllian, where the happiest days of Althea's life had passed, and where she now proposed, and Marchmont readily consented, to take up their future residence.

Mr. Desborough had no sooner got that important point adjusted for them, than he began to enquire into the former circumstances of those embarrassments that had hastened the death of the elder Marchmont, and overclouded, for so many years, the life of his son. Indefatigable in his enquiries, and with money to second them, he soon traced the scheme of iniquity in which Vampyre had so deeply been engaged; and a great part of the estate, including the house at Eastwoodleigh, was recovered. Marchmont, without any design of living there, or yielding to the fatal pride that had ruined his father, visited the place as soon as it became his. Mr. and Mrs. Wansford had long since been dismissed by Lady Dacres, and lived in great poverty in a neighbouring village. Marchmont removed them to a farm near his intended residence, and placed with them the old faithful Mrs. Moseley, to end her days in comfort and repose. Phoebe Prior, to whom, as well as to Mrs. Moseley, Althea had frequently sent assistance, had been dead for some time.

Mohun, after an ineffectual struggle, by which he only shewed the daring injustice he thought himself capable of maintaining, was compelled to pay Althea's fortune; but he was too high in his profession to care what was said of him; and Marchmont, at Althea's earnest prayer, as well as in consequence of Mr. Desborough's remonstrance, forbore to seek him. — Lady Dacres, the most unhappy of mothers, learned to wish, in the bitterness of her heart, that she had never had a son.

Mr. Desborough, who became hourly more fond of Althea, lived very much with them. He still continued to expend a great part of his yearly income in charity: the whole of his fortune, after his death, he has given to Marchmont and his posterity.

The virtues that Althea so early possessed, and which adversity had served to improve and strengthen, were far from failing under the influence of prosperity; and the happiness of her husband, and of his family, which was her work (for without her they must have been lost); the blessings she diffused around her, as well by her example to the rich, as by her benevolence to the poor, were her earthly reward. — Marchmont indeed sometimes trembled as he considered his felicity; and, believing it too great to fall to the share of any human being, he, with awe and gratitude, endeavoured to deserve its continuance.

THE END.

FURTHER READING

Fletcher, Loraine. *Charlotte Smith: A Critical Biography*, St. Martin's Press, 1998.

Gamer, Michael. *Cambridge Studies in Romanticism: Romanticism and the Gothic: Genre, Reception, and Canon Formation*, Cambridge University Press, 2000.

Keane, Angela. *Revolutionary Women Writers: Charlotte Smith and Helen Maria Williams*, Writers and their Work, 2013.

Knowles, Claire. *Sensibility and Female Poetic Tradition, 1780-1860: The Legacy of Charlotte Smith*, 2009.

Labbe, Jacqueline M. *Charlotte Smith in British Romanticism*, Routledge, 2016.

Labbe, Jacqueline M. *Charlotte Smith: Romanticism, Poetry, and the Culture of Gender*, Manchester University Press, 2003.

Labbe, Jacqueline M. *Writing Romanticism: Charlotte Smith and William Wordsworth, 1784-1807*, Palgrave Macmillan, 2011.

Mellor, Anne Kostelanetz. *Romanticism and Gender*, Routledge, 1993.

Myers, Sylvia Harcstark. *The Bluestocking Circle: Women, Friendship, and the Life of the Mind in Eighteenth-Century England*, Clarendon Press, 1990.

Richter, David H. *The Progress of Romance: Literary Historiography and the Gothic Novel*, Ohio State University Press, 1996.

Smith, Charlotte. *The Collected Letters of Charlotte Smith*, Judith Phillips Stanton, Indiana University Press, 2003.

Smith, Charlotte. *The Works of Charlotte Smith*, Stuart Curran, Pickering & Chatto, 2005.

Wilson, Carol Shiner and Joel Haefner. *Re-visioning Romanticism: British Women Writers, 1776-1873*, University of Pennsylvania Press, 1994.

www.ingramcontent.com/pod-product-compliance
Lightning Source LLC
Chambersburg PA
CBHW020458260626
47156CB00006B/1776